Darren Allen is from old Whitstable, in the county of Kent. He writes outsider fiction and radical philosophy. He currently lives in a small tent in the gardens of the ruined temple.

FIRED

DARREN ALLEN

EXPRESSIVE EGG PUBLICATIONS

Published by Expressive Egg Books

First published in 2022, in England.
Darren Allen has asserted his moral rights under
the Copyright, Designs and Patents Act 1988.
Front cover illustration by Ai Higaki.
Text design by Darren Allen.
Set, rather too generously, in 10 pt Sabon Next on a 13 pt line.

ISBN: 978-1-7391294-0-8 (paperback)
ISBN: 978-1-7391294-1-5 (ePub)
Also available for Kindle.

10 9 8 7 6 5 4 3 2 1

CONTENTS

This book is dedicated to poet, flâneur and cloud,
Mr. William P. Barker, without whom Joe Geb,
Margaret Geb and Ralf Pugh, along with most
of their greatest thoughts, would not exist.

DRAMATIS PERSONAE

The Gebs

Joe Geb	*A misfit*
Neil Geb	*Joe's brother*
Ursula Geb	*Joe & Neil's sister*
Margaret Geb	*Joe, Neil and Ursula's mother*
Neville Geb	*Joe, Neil and Ursula's father*
Maria Geb (née Cruttenden)	*Joe's wife*

41 Dace Road

Lilly Pumphrey	*A young woman*
Chiyo Gehō	*A Japanese woman*
Hunter Braff	*A young man*
Tanish & Diana Hass-Nag	*Neighbours and nemeses*

The Station, The Street

Clive Marsh	*A crippled author*
Dave Davage	*A manager*
Hayley Greyling	*A receptionist*
Irving Bone	*A cleaning-services manager*
'Laughing' Ralf Pugh	*A down-and-out schadenfreudist*

Herbert and Vole Funeral Services

Nina Eedie	*A funeral-home owner*
Carl Rowden	*A handyman*
'Taul' Paul Saul	*A funeral man*
The Bhuvanagiri Brothers	*Funeral bearers (sons of Meera)*

The Thottesley Estate

Max Thottesley	*A wealthy landowner*
Joris Thottesley	*Max's twelve-year-old son*
Ian Cremwave	*Max's lawyer*
Patrick Lawless	*Max's ex-groundsman*

Supporting Characters

Victor E. Perry	*An outsider and bhagavān*
Louis Gallardo	*Margaret and Neville's servant*
Gaynor Babcock	*Senior police officer; Neil's boss*
Meera Yadadri Bhuvanagiri	*Restaurant owner & bhagavati*
Sun Wukong	*A very old Hakka businessman*
Cherry Wukong	*Mr. Wukong's granddaughter*
Gloria Boyce	*A cross-dressing hairdresser*
Tim the Vicar	*A vicar*
Sophie Wolpe	*Tim's girlfriend*
Bronya Cosslett	*Social worker; Maria's 'friend'*
Andy Dandy & Raimonda Dargis	*Social workers*
Tom & Heather Cruttenden	*Maria's professional parents*
Prince Jayamma Chukwu	*A Nigerian down-and-out*
William Fairweather	*A furious dying man*
Aaron, Moira & James Waylan	*Joe's neighbours (number 90)*
Mary Euryphaessa	*Joe's neighbour (number 86)*
Keira 'Keeks' Passmore	*A nurse and slapper*
Denise & Alice Davage	*Dave Davage's wife & daughter*
Malcolm Raggoo	*A job-centre employee*
Spence Gregory	*A sad young man; Chiyo's date*
Lee Riddley	*An unwell street cleaner*
Vikas Agghi	*A bus driver*
Sri Baba Gaurav	*An Indian Mystic*
Guanyin 'Janice' Bēiāi	*A masseuse; Ralf's girlfriend*
Brenda Gambrill	*Old woman; Ralf's landlady*
Simon Lincoln	*A cremation technician*
Old Roy Towers	*Margaret's friend & neighbour*
U.G. Somasundaram	*A Sri-Lankan Taxi Driver*
Omana	*Manageress at The Other*
West, Axton, Bryce, Bear	*Lifeline Employees*
Bracken, Noun, Pencil, Koa	
Zoltan, Denitsa, Mercy	*Duat Employees*
Nada, Jianjun & Claire Baqri	
Memphis	*A pig*

Who knows but life be that which men call death,
And death what men call life?
Euripides

Dreams are real as long as they last.
Can we say more of life?
The Upanishads

How shall we sing the Lord's song in a strange land?
Boney M.

This is a true story

PART ONE
Might as Well Live

Neville Geb is staring at the sun. He has been staring at it all day, until the foveal point of his retina burnt away, leaving a black disk in a white sky. He sits, a rangy, weathered man, in the spring of his fertile forties, naked and blind on the roof of his home-county cottage, stroking a young pig. Tears trickle over his high cheekbones as he silently mouths, through his thin parched lips, a prayer;

'Homage to thee thou who art Ra when thou risest, and Temu when thou settest. O thou divine youth, thou heir of everlastingness, worshipped be thou whom the goddess Maāt begatteth at morn and embraceth at eve. Thou dost travel across the sky, heart of sun, swelling with the ten-thousand joys, whereupon thou dost lie in nullity, in the fecund river of the night. The Apis bull hath fallen, and his two arms are cut off, and his two legs also.'

A few hours later, Neville is dead, his head shot from his shoulders by the cannon he has dragged from his workshop into the meadows behind the back garden; although the head cannot be found and so, according to the instructions left in his will, he is buried, by his wife, Margaret, and his three young children, Neil, Joe and Ursula, with a cannonball where his head once was, with two long, crude cartoon eyes painted thereon.

As Neville's head is blown away he experiences a combination of intense pain and vivid, unreal awareness. As it is for everyone, so it is for Neville, that 'this is actually happening, now,' is, in the moment of death, his last comprehensible thought. And, as it is for everyone, so it is for Neville that the surprise and sadness of this is that it has always been so.

Then a new kind of astonishment, not at what he is witnessing, but the 'I' that is witnessing it, as if his awareness had, his whole life, been viewed through a letterbox, the sides of which had created what he thought of as his self, but now there is no letterbox, no door, no house and nobody in it.

After this, nothing, not for Neville, for whom there is no 'after' no 'before,' no time at all.

For his family however, gathered round his headless corpse, there is something to be said.

The sun couldn't be bothered to rise. Neither could Joe Geb, but it happened anyway. He opened a cold blue eye onto an unfamiliar world, wondering, as he often did, what he was doing here, in this white, white suburban bedroom, white but for a floral gold wall-sticker, silk-filled jasmine duvet and two burgundy-red sari-fabric cushions bought at a delightful little roadside stall in Bali, plump now on a cornflower blue New Yorker armchair. He didn't feel at home, at home.

He sighed, a futile attempt to exhale away a weight on his chest which never left. He looked over to Maria, who seemed small and delicately beautiful from behind, and reached out, with one of his big paws, to tenderly stroke her thick auburn hair.

Her eyes flicked open. 'Get off,' she said, as if talking to a persistent dog. Joe pulled back his hand as if from a wasp.

He slumped into their clean, tidy bathroom, slumped naked because he slept naked. A few months before, there had been a street-waking argument outside; neighbours, three doors down, with overflowing bins and no net curtains, screaming at each other; 'you don't fucking understand what it's like no *you* don't fucking understand what it's like,' and Maria had said to Joe 'aren't you going to do something?' and, obeying her, which was easier than any other grief, easier even than inertia, he'd ambled out into their front garden, bollock-naked, planted himself in front of the two swaying drunks—she with a hoody-shrouded head like a big lightbulb painted white, he a kind of evil shaved cat—and had said, 'now then my mad little dragons, how about we sort this silliness out and get ourselves a good night's sleep?' Angry, confused and afraid—three emotions Joe often generated in other people—the two scrags had sheepishly returned home.

Joe stood now before his one contribution to their tasteful bathroom of turquoise and purple tiles, dreamcatchers, oyster shells and geranium nourishing cream; a signed photograph of a full English breakfast, pinned to the bathroom mirror. He was a very large, well-built man with long arms and short legs—slightly ape-like. He was in his thirties, but already touched with the exhaustion of life. He had a large head, a high brow curving under a slightly receding hairline and lazy, friendly—but ice-cold—blue eyes, under which bags were appearing. The overall effect was a disconcerting mix of affable and remote, noble and ridiculous, earthy and not-of-this-realm. He leaned into the mirror, shook his large head sadly, then nodded enthusiastically, then stretched his cheeks out, pulling at his skin, revealing his eyeballs and gums, then he picked up and delicately kissed a bottle of liquid soap standing on the sink. Finally, he said, to nobody, or perhaps to himself, 'I'm the invisible man's little, visible, friend.'

Half an hour later, Joe and Maria's bodies—not much else—were having breakfast together. Joe was sitting at the kitchen table, Maria, hand on hip, was standing next to the sink, both now dressed for work; Joe, in his blue Network Rail half-suit, Maria in a tidy management skirt, thin black leather belt, a blouse which revealed her mighty cleavage, and kitten-heel booties which were very tight on her small feet and made her calves look oddly fat and pointed, but she didn't realise that.

Joe looked up from his food and met Maria's eye. She was short, but well-proportioned. Her lips were thin, her features regular, delicate and sharp, her hazel-brown eyes, under a round doll-like brow, were either fierce and sarcastically suggestive, or, as now, wearily, cynically, lazy-lidded and bored, bored, bored.

She squinted at Joe, distastefully; 'You're not about to say something weird are you?'

Joe glanced at her with a momentary glint of pleading confusion, then returned to his food.

He ate slowly. The microwave oats had turned to a kind of grey mush which he spooned at without pleasure.

Maria's voice. 'Can you take that mug to work?'

Without looking up, he gestured towards the ordinary cream mug before him on the table, 'What, this one?'

Maria opened the cupboard drawer behind her, full of identical cream mugs, but for one shaped like a large, highly realistic and brightly coloured baboon head.

'No, this one.'

Joe turned his head up again, brow doomed, larger and heavier than it had been a few moments ago. He took a deep breath, went to speak, then, thinking better of it, sank down again.

Maria found Joe's silences maddening. Was he going to take the mug or not? Why didn't he just say so, either way? The vagueness, Jesus, the *vagueness*. Oh yes; 'Did you get that application off?' she asked.

'Application?'

'The technical author thing.'

'Oh that.'

'Joe. It's thirty-к rising to fifty. Some technical authors earn a hundred pounds an *hour*. Do you want to have to work in a ticket office your whole life?'

'I don't want to *have* to do anything.'

'You *have* to wake up, you *have* to get dressed, you *have* to eat.'

'I wouldn't do any of those things if I didn't have to.'

'That's ridiculous.'

Joe closed his eyes. He and her, the two of them, had become things again. The room had become a collection of things. The argument had, as all arguments do, shattered the world into bits. What was the point in going on, because the solution wasn't in bits, it was the whole thing.

'Also,' she said, seizing on another bit, 'when are you going to fix the chicken coop?'

'Soon, I suppose.'

'It's too small. We need a bigger one.'

'A bigger coop? Why? They're all right aren't they? Japanese people live in tiny little hutches. Surely a chicken doesn't need more space?'

'Don't be racist. Chickens are not Japanese people.'

'And I'm not a carpenter.'

'I'm sensing hostility. I'm not asking you to be a carpenter.'

'You're asking me to be a chicken person.'

Maria shifted weight, hand on the other exasperated hip, 'But why aren't you a chicken person?'

'I've just never got into the whole chicken thing. I don't connect with them. They make me feel uncomfortable with who I am.'

'Is there anything that doesn't make you uncomfortable with who you are?'

Joe gathered up his attention, which was sinking further and further into the murky pit where his breakfast was accumulating, and allowed it to wander over this interesting question, the first she had asked him for about nine months.

'Flapjacks,' he said.

∞

Edding is identical, in every important respect, to every other lower-middle-sized, lower-middle-income, lower-middle-town in lower-middle-England; the same kebab, flower and burger stalls are staffed by the same large women with cat problems; the same spindly beggars prick the guilt of the slightly better-off with chirpy friendliness; the same sad bachelors stand in the cleaning products section of the supermarket wondering which clingfilm to buy; the same John Lewis shoppers who volunteer at the church look down on the same welfare women who wear grey tracksuit bottoms and furry slippers to go shopping in; the same work-from-home, stay-at-home ghosts cower in their brick burrows or drift through town as if in a virtual dream; the same ambitious young office men in tight blue suits and fawn brogues think about cars; and the same items of food are mysteriously left on walls; whole loaves of Hovis white, miniature Melton Mowbray pork pies, coleslaw.

Joe Geb lived on the organic bacon side of town, 88 Gordon Road. Thirty minutes away, on the tinned-pie side of town, at 41 Dace Road, his younger brother, Neil Geb, was playing a Sirba 3 HR76 synthesiser in his bedroom. The large, perfectly ordered, black and grey room comprised a well-made bed, a tidy notice-board, a wide standing desk covered with high-quality stationery, a massive PC (Baltezar XR, i5, 5TB SSD) with two 30" monitors and an even bigger wall-mounted clock, the size of a Lazy Susan at the Dragon Wok. There was tech everywhere; smartphones, headphones, FLAC players, audio recorders, SD cards, every object neatly arranged in parallel with every other. On several sections of the wall straight columns of Post-it notes flapped like DayGlo mud flaps. A bullworker leant against one wall next to a 1.5 pood kettlebell and a set of resistance bands. A bookcase, with spines arranged by the shade of the cover, contained titles such as; 'How to Command a Roman Army,' 'Clausewitz vs Göring,' 'A Hoplite Colouring Book' and 'Jesus Christ; Military Genius?'

Since they had been children, people would look at Joe, and then to Neil, and then back to Joe and say to him — people only ever spoke to *him* when the two brothers were together — 'I can't believe you're brothers!' The insinuating implication was veiled but clear; Neil was the product of an illicit union between their mother, Margaret, and a runty milkman. Where Joe's imposing cranium commanded attention, Neil's head seemed to be too thin to even notice, where Joe's features seemed to be engraved in stone, Neil's facial expressions scurried over the surface of his face like ants, and where Joe's bones appeared to have been made from monumental pylons, Neil's seemed to have been assembled from the leftovers of a chicken dinner. Joe was conventionally ugly, but he communicated acceptance, ease, dignity, even nobility.

Neil's face was handsome, even pleasant, but there was a restless, self-conscious pride and fear in his eyes.

Although he had worked out continually, he was still, now in his late twenties, small and delicate. Instead of building him up, as exercise is supposed to do, it had whittled him away, exposing the ropes and pulleys of his system, operated by resentful anxiety. He drank protein shakes and creatine, he benched his bodyweight, he worked on his posture and his stance, he thrust his chest out, he projected confidence at all times, he was impeccably dressed, he was, for Christ's sake, an officer of the law! But he could not bolt on impact. He was always to others, or he always felt like, 'Neil Down,' the nickname he had been given at school, and which he still heard, whispered in dreams.

He was dressed now for work, in his police uniform, shoes cleaned, hair brushed and parted, a pair of massive headphones clamped to his ears, rippling his agile little fingers up and down the keyboard, glancing for inspiration at his framed Prince's Trust Gold Award letter signed by Prince Philip and his (as yet) unsigned photo of Jesus Christ on a donkey. He was listening to a track he'd spent two months composing for his flatmate Lilly, but which, the night before, he'd discovered she hated. He'd been too afraid to give it to her, to present it as an authentic expression of his soul's desire, so instead he'd put it on casually in the background while Lilly was making tea.

'What's this?' she had said.

'Oh I dunno, some band. A friend at work recommended it.'

'It sounds like the backing track of an airplane safety video.'

'What's wrong with that?' Neil was horrified. He *had* been inspired by the backing track of an airplane safety video he'd watched on his stone-rubbing trip last year to Ephesus (arguably, with the obvious exception of Pompeii, the best preserved Roman city in the world). He'd added, with the help of his Moog soft-synth, some quirky flair—because Lilly loved things that were out of the ordinary—but she'd just sniffed at it; 'I'm not interested in that world,' she'd said. He'd even had the lyrics, giclée printed on warm-white 310 GSM paper, and professionally mounted. He sadly scanned the ungiven gift.

> *Got the opportunity to travel to distant lands*
> *And learn all about the shifting sands—of life*
> *Where I'll end up, no-one knows!*
> *Just gotta take it as it comes and as it goes.*
> *(woh, woh, as it goes… as it goes…)*
> *Left my past behind me*
> *To see what I could find me*
> *Oh baby, baby—I hope you're just fine*
> *Did you know I think about you most of the time?*
> *I made my way to the Indian sub-continent*
> *A little trip that was heaven sent*
> *Took a trip around the Taj Mahal*
> *An architectural miracle!*
> *Across the seas, to Shanghai and Japan*
> *I felt real good, I felt like a man*
> *Went round the Magellan Strait*
> *Spun me round, that was my fate*
> *Now I'm a little closer to home*
> *I'm in Canterbury at the mome (ent)*
> *Lambeth Palace is such a beautiful place*
> *A crimson castle for the human race!*

There wasn't much point recording the vocals now was there? But nevermind, nevermind. There was still hope. Prepare for battle. He put on his instrumental synthetic-organ version of 'Bat Out of Hell', then stood up, hands on hips, legs splayed majestically, chest out, and began his power-breathing routine. This was the confidence-boosting exercise he always performed before difficult conversations with his boss and any time he was called out on an ASBO.

☙

Downstairs, in a shabby, shared kitchen—cornflake-encrusted bowls in the sink, cupboards papered with magazine cutouts (a black Arnold Schwarzenegger, Karl Marx in drag, 'I overthink therefore I am'), fridge door fluttering with pink and yellow post-it notes, dining table unwiped from last night's Vietnamese takeaway—there sat Lilly Pumphrey herself, mournfully regarding a bacon sandwich.

Lilly was twenty-two, with long, fair, chestnut hair. Her hazel eyes, wry and intelligent, passively enquired behind thick glasses. She wore comfortable, tasteful, homemade dresses, of warm, dark floral design. She feared turning into one of those big-hipped, pink-cheeked young women who dress like geriatrics and wear woollen hats and make 16mm films about women's rights in Tibet, and seem all soft and girly but are actually hard and calculating and grim.

She was soft-voiced, soft-featured and soft-hearted. People found her softness beautiful but if they told her she was beautiful, as they very occasionally did, she simultaneously felt great and wished they wouldn't because she hated the way that beautiful people acted like beautiful people, and anyway she wasn't beautiful, and anyway does it even matter, and anyway what does it even mean? That's the thing isn't it? When people told her she was beautiful she wanted to ask 'what else do you find beautiful?' because if they said Angelina Jolie, or a Maserati, oh right you're mad then, or if they didn't know, then alright, but perhaps you don't actually know what you're saying, but if they said a red squirrel or a Romanesco cauliflower or one of the Wives of the Meadow Mari, well then that meant something.

Standing next to her, as she pondered the repulsive beauty of the bacon sandwich, was a tall, smooth, chubby, sleepily-cheerful, fluffily-bearded, immaculately-clean and immaculately-scruffy young man, Hunter Braff. He was speaking into his smartphone just as he spoke into Lilly, or into anyone else who had inadvertently stepped into what they believed would be a conversation but which, actually, was a trading of impressions.

'Why? *God* knows!' he said, his plausible, nasal voice cutting through the walls to a radius of 20 metres, 'I've NO idea. I'm like "I don't need to hear this." I think Jaxon forgets that I'm not, like, a *work* person…? What?… Has he? No! Oh my God, oh my *God*. What is *wrong* with that boy? Is he *actually mental?* I thought Teagan was smarter than that, ef-ef-es. And he was going to come in with us… With LifeLine. What!? You haven't heard? Yeah! Our new app! Basically it's like, you put this little monitor under your skin, and…uh…? oh, I don't know, ask Prig, he's the boffin… anyway, it tells you literally everything about what's going on in your body. It's going to free the world from doctors. I know! Yeah, what? Oh sorry, yeah, me too! Hahaha! Okay, okay. Ciao, ciao, little cow!'

While he was speaking Lilly whispered to the bacon sandwich a tiny, quiet, 'sorry,' the sense of which was still lingering in her chest when Hunter hung up and turned to her, as if continuing the conversation he'd just finished;

'I was coming out of the shower last night and I got a message from Ollie.'

'Oh?' Lilly looked up, surprised that she was involved here.

'It just said "are you okay?"'

'Why?'

'No idea! I. Have. Got. *No* idea. I wrote back. I was like, yeah, I'm fine! *Hahahaha!*'

Lilly smiled weakly. Hunter bustled out of the room, still unable to believe the madness of it all. As he passed Neil's bedroom, the door—brass nameplate officially declaring its bearer, 'P.C.Neil Geb, B.A.Hons.'—opened and Neil, a head shorter than Hunter, emerged. *Yes*, Hunter had passed, unaware of Neil, who enjoyed a fragment of relief that there was no need for a morning acknowledgement or, worse, small talk. Neil feared small talk, particularly with people who were on the threshold of being someone you know, but not quite, like shopkeepers he'd accidentally had a conversation with and now had to avoid (thank God for supermarkets and internet shopping). He also feared saying hello, which was tremendously difficult, but not as hard as goodbye. He once climbed out of a hotel window to avoid having to say goodbye twice to a doorman.

Conversation was problematic. He wanted to get deep, but for some reason he was afraid of the shallows at the first step. It was so hard to predict where chit-chat would go and so he had developed various strategies to control it. He would direct the flow of information towards cars, tools, insulation, the new ring-road on the A654, the foolishness of fighting a European campaign on two fronts and similar such safe spaces with an 'innocent' question, such as 'had lunch yet?' or 'is W.H.Smiths open on bank holidays?' or 'I wonder if Mongolians are good at swimming?' which he would then guide towards a nice, comfortable conversation about protein, stationery or how Genghis Khan contributed to the modern world.

Neil's relief was momentary. Chiyo had silently and swiftly exited from the bathroom and was now standing, oddly tilted, wet hair hanging to her side, staring.

'Oh! Ah! Morning!' he said, unnaturally loudly.

Chiyo—inscrutable age, inscrutable face, inscrutable feelings, pale, slim, breastless and horribly beautiful—said nothing.

'Morrr-ning,' said Neil, conscious that he'd repeated himself and already given away his awkwardness, which he began every other day promising to himself not to do. He tried not to look at Chiyo, into her eyes, because there was a little ghost in them that seemed to reach into him and squeeze his prostate, and make his voice rise an octave. It was difficult though, looking away, because there was something compelling about her long, slim body, always dressed in black, and her long, slim face, also always dressed in black, just as there is something compelling about a bottomless chasm or a murdered body. Sometimes he resisted the compulsion physically, by wincing, or raising his palms and stepping backwards. But actually, now, she wasn't looking at him at all, but over and past him. He turned, following her blank gaze to the corner of the stairwell ceiling.

'What… are you doing?'

'Looking the space.'

She continued looking.

'Looking the space,' he repeated quietly.

Chiyo's head shook, almost imperceptibly, then her glance fell on Neil. 'No,' she said, fixing him with a look that felt like the opposite of a torch or candle. Just as they lighten up the night, so her eyes darkened up the day.

'Ri…' Neil swallowed reflexively, mid-utterance, as he tended to do when his anxiety-meter hit red, '…ight,' then tenderly stepped past her and down the stairs. As he rounded the newel post he spotted Lilly in the kitchen and his face—hard, focused and resisting—switched into alert, mobile and eager. A surge of fearful awareness prickled his back and a light scent of his own stress sweat reached his nostrils. No matter. The time had come, his fate would be sealed. By the time he'd finished his tea and toast and washed and wiped up and put the plates away he would know if Lilly would go on a date with him.

Neil did not have much success with the opposite sex. His last date had been in London with a woman he had met on the internet, a puffy, hungry, red-lipsticked restaurant manager called Carrie who'd described herself on her profile as 'a sassy geek who loves philosophy and accessories.' The meeting was in tube-less Tottenham, so a long train journey was followed by a two-and-a-half-hour bus journey across North London; a total of five hours to get to a bleak, windy corner on Lordship Lane, to meet a woman who, the instant she saw Neil said 'Oh. You're much shorter than I thought.' 'Yeah, erm,' he'd laughed nervously stressing his words erratically, 'I was a normal *sized* child, *as* a child, but I never really had a final, you know… *spurt*… uh… but, uh…' He'd trailed off, realising, from her lip-pursed disappointed scowl, that he wasn't able to explain his size or convince her that it was not actually undesirable. 'Shall we call it a day?' he'd said, heart shrinking, and she'd agreed and he'd travelled five hours back home.

In the films you asked a girl out, and then five minutes later you were ecstatically fornicating in a weirdly clean public toilet. In real life it was a long arduous process, requiring all kinds of devices and stratagems, success always far from certain, even at the last moment, even with her knickers in your hands there was a good chance of failure. It was like climbing Everest, requiring months of planning and training and then, all the way up, there were dead frozen bodies and litter from those who had gone before you, and even when you got to the top, right in reach of the pointy-point, it could suddenly just detach itself from the mountain and fly away.

Lilly was perfect. No, not perfect, she was quite strange, and not exactly his type, physically, and she liked completely different things and she probably didn't like him very much; but perfect. She wasn't too pretty, that was important—nice face, lovely and cute, but a bit too big to put too many fellow suitors in his way and, much more important, a bit too plain for her to consider Neil too far beneath her. Neil had imagined what it would be like going to the restaurant with her, she would look good, and he'd imagined presenting her, with pride, to his mother, and he'd imagined Lilly knitting him a tie or something, and it all just... worked.

He collected himself and walked purposefully, but not too purposefully, into the kitchen. He offered to Lilly a casual, but not too casual, 'hello', noted that her 'hello' was several degrees more casual, and then, slightly hurt by this, set about preparing his breakfast—toast cut into four exactly equal quadrants, each with a different spread (Marmite, peanut butter, jam and mar-malade; rotating from 'main course' to 'pudding'). He was trying to ignore the sick, acidy fear in the pit of his neck, but the more he tried, the more he felt like he might, at any moment, burp up a teaspoon of bile.

'If I discovered my comb was made from the bones of a dead relative, I don't think it would really bother me,' said Lilly, half to herself.

Oh Christ no, it was a 'creative' conversation, one in which you were supposed to say interesting things, but he hadn't prepared anything. Play it safe. Agree and deflect. Agree and deflect.

'Oh yes,' he said, 'first day on the job. Are you nervous?'

Hunter's squeezed-frog voice cut through the house like a boring axe dropped from the bathroom two floors above; *There's no hot water! Again!*

'Yeah, a bit,' said Lilly. 'Would it bother you though?'

'Actually, I was wondering… Would what bother me?'

Hunter appeared in the doorway, frumpy and dramatic. 'There's no hot water Neil.'

'No? Isn't there?'

'I think the thermostat's bummed.'

'If,' said Lilly, 'you found out a dead relative had been used to make your vegetable rack?'

Neil calculated his conversational priorities. Dispatch Hunter with a succinct instruction, then try again to deflect Lilly away from this mad, surreal line of questioning. 'It's not the thermostat,' he said to Hunter, 'it's the element. We'll have to drain the whole boiler.' He turned to Lilly, 'Erm, I don't know. I don't have a vegetable rack. I don't trust them.'

The toast popped up, burnt. Neil ground his teeth. 'Drat.'

Hunter slouched further, hand to temple. 'How do you do that?'

Lilly sighed, 'No, I don't know either. Nothing's really certain though is it? Not when it comes to death.'

Neil was down to the crust, he didn't want to go shopping after work for another loaf of bread, because, when twenty harried home-goers were being reminded to take their receipt or use their loyalty card by an automated-till voice, multiplied by twenty, that, like all automated voices, sounded like it was trying to get children to be more enthusiastic about playing a game they didn't want to play, and which was set at a murderous biddy-skull penetrating volume, Neil felt like he wanted to smash the place up with his Monadnock PR-24 side-handle baton. This, along with the small-talk-to-shopkeeper problem, was why he preferred to get his food delivered, and why he now accepted the burnt slice, rattling and tugging the crippled husk from the jaws of the toaster. 'You have to find the drain cock and then the inhibitor...' he said rapidly to Hunter, then turned to Lilly with sighing dismay and returned her much harder to hit conversational volley with a pathetically inadequate drop shot which he knew wouldn't even reach the net, 'erm. Isn't it?'

Hunter waved the problem away with a small hand, 'Oh I don't have time for this Neil. I've got a meeting with investors. Let's talk about it later shall we?'

He left. Neil, sweating now, collar damp, needled by Hunter's implication that he was at fault here, continued to work meticulously at his toast, but because it was burnt it broke up under the pressure of his knife. He could detect a slight 'pre-blackout' shimmering around the edge of his vision. He hardly knew what he was doing, or saying, or being, but it was now or... not 'never,' perhaps later, but that was bad enough.

'Erm,' he said, clearing his throat and sucking up the last quivering dregs of his casualness, 'I was going to say though, did you see my note?'

'Which one?' said Lilly, sipping her tea, 'There are so many.'

'Oh, right. I er...'

'Not the one about leaving the TV remote control in the remote control box?'

'No, I, actually...'

'Or the one about how much pressure to apply to footfalls when climbing the stairs?'

'No, no. It was more...'

'Or was it the one about taking the celery out of the fridge before it shrivels up and goes brown?'

'No, none of those. I... uh...'

'I think you need to date your notes Neil. Then we can keep track of them more easily.'

'That's a good idea actually. I'll do that. Erm, but, no, this one,

I decided to put on your…' He opened the fridge and gestured inside with a surprisingly elegant sideways splay of the hand, as if speaking to a crowd of connoisseurs. '…apple juice. I thought you'd… because you have apple juice every morning, you'd read it. But I notice you're not drinking apple juice this morning, sooo…' He hesitated, pulling back from the abyss, then brought a piece of toast to his lips to conceal the terror, then realised it was the wrong piece (marmalade before peanut butter), put it back on the plate and then closed the fridge, a little man in his head screaming, 'terminate, terminate!'

'Perhaps,' said Lilly, sighing, 'you could just tell me what it says now?'

'Right.' He opened the fridge again and removed the note, some kind of wind roaring in his ears. Impossible to abort. This is it, this is the moment. Say it now, before Hunter or Chiyo come back. Say it *now!* 'It says… It says "would you like a dr… (swallow) …iiinnnnnk with me this evening? From Neil."'

'Oh…' The thought had vaguely occurred to Lilly that Neil was sort of asexual, that he didn't really have romantic feelings; but apparently he did, and apparently they were directed towards her. This was unexpected. Despite her surprise though, and despite not really being in the mood for a life-critical exchange with Neil over breakfast, she immediately understood that the wrong kind of answer here could smash him into tiny little pieces. 'I don't think so,' she said hesitantly, and softly, 'I don't know Neil. I'm going to be spending all day with death. I might not be in the mood for… you know, life…' She wanted to say 'your life,' but held her tongue.

'Okay!' he said brightly, volume and confidence enhanced by a kind of relief. Strange that she'd responded to his suggestion so casually, as if he'd offered not his heart but a chip or a biscuit, but that made it better, it made it normal, and at least it was over, 'Well, if you change your mind, just, I'll leave an empty note on my door. Just take it off if you want, if, as I say, if you change your mind, that is, or you could write on the note, that you'd like to… um… change your mind? He furrowed his brow. For some reason he had pronounced the word 'mind' more like 'marrnd'.

'Or I could just tell you.'

Neil considered this. Interesting idea.

'I prefer the note system.'

৯

Joe emerged, closed the front door and held out his hand. It was raining. Not cold, might as well get wet. He took a step down the garden path, and felt his bowels shift. He stopped. Late again, he thought; but I need a poo. He turned, put his key back in the door, stopped before opening it fully and sighed, whispering to himself 'That was quick.'

'That was quick,' said Maria as Joe walked past the kitchen and into the downstairs toilet.

He sat on the toilet. No point straining, but how wrong it was to shit when you 'had to be somewhere.' Why do I 'have to be *somewhere*'? I am here. Here, out of history, out of the world, but always being always called back into it, into this 'somewhere,' which I have to get to, on time, or be punished for it.

A few days ago he had been walking through the cemetery next to St Mary's and had seen, nestled under a sodden yew, a tent. 'How good,' he'd thought, 'to live there, out of it all.' Maybe it was just a convoluted death wish, the same urge everyone has to just step forever off the merry-go-round, or to sleep and sleep and deliciously sleep forever.

Joe was, it had to be said, a lazy man, forever deferring chores, going to great lengths to avoid small distances, annoyed when things went wrong not because they had gone wrong but only ever because of the work involved in putting them right. So maybe that was it? Just plain old laziness. And yet, Joe knew. Laziness is a way to guard inner activity from actually being still, from actually stopping, before the nothingness of mere being, meat-like, without inner movement. So perhaps that was it. Death seeks out the lazy man like an excitable dog runs after someone fleeing from it. At the beginning of the year Joe had seen someone throw himself from the Cable Street bridge onto the flyover, screeching brakes and screams, horror in the air, and people rushing to catch the moment on their smartphones. On the same day, four hearses had turned up at his house; a mystery nobody could explain. And a few months ago he'd started getting emails from a woman called Elaine who'd mistaken Joe's email address for someone else's, someone whom Elaine felt she had to keep to date on the deteriorating condition of a man called William who, said Elaine, 'was leaving this world without dignity.' She explained that this William just wouldn't stop cussing, upsetting the poor hospice staff, about 'his pointless f-ing life, in this sh-ty f-ing world, full of c-s…' Joe had written back, letting Elaine know that he wasn't whom she thought he was, but the emails kept coming back anyway.

Death seemed to be everywhere these days. Perhaps, Joe wondered, his 'exit fantasies' were really down to destiny, that the abyss was whistling to him, 'come Joe, lay your big head down; call in dead.'

Joe left the house again and hummed his way into Edding, daydreaming still of easeful death rather than a life running towards ever-receding finishing lines, of full daydreams, rather than snapped-off fragments, unhurried poos rather than bowel movements squeezed out under the Clock of Damocles. It's not too much to ask. He looked at the people around him, charging forth, head down, nobody looking at anyone or anything else, everyone squeezing past each other, stepping over sleeping bags, so many obstacles to overcome, work another obstacle, relationship another one, then fun, that was an obstacle too, except there the overcoming came before the obstacle… Reality is just a boring obstacle course, so of course a nice poo is unrealistic.

A suited man rushed past him, lop sided, the line of his shoulders proclaiming the asymmetrical slope of the lifelong one-strap rucksack carrier while, waiting on street corner, checking her mobile, a young girl stood belly slouched, neck lolling, spine flopping forward like a dying daisy, essentially the posture of a broken mule. Shame really; she could've been so beautiful. Joe considered his own gait. He had immense feet, like tractor tyres, which couldn't thereby relax downwards through the stride, making him look like he was walking on unstable planks. His head had a habit of jutting out slightly, as if peering through hard rain, and, if the morning had been difficult, particularly if Maria was in the middle of laying an egg, a tightness would grip the top of his head and push him down, like the difficult-to-get-into lid of a bottle of aspirin. He couldn't be bothered to fight it, but at least there was awareness there, an awareness which itself was a kind of natural power and elegance, which splayed his feet slightly through the stride, which reduced his automatic harry to a meandering simmer, which pulled him back from the peering squint of the 'having to be somewhere', and opened the lid of his head, letting the air in.

A pregnant woman on a bicycle with a hippo backpack sailed past, smiling. Joe smiled back. He was in town now, which, at a cloud-like velocity of dawdle, had a gummy, dewy alrightness to it. It was overcast, chill, and a certain late-summer sadness was settling on the town. Vans—the only vehicle Joe had ever been proud to drive—were driving past, and commuters were on their long trek to places unnecessarily far away; but the crack addicts weren't up yet, the shoppers weren't out yet, and there was hush and space and time; until the tired man passed.

He was middle-aged, balding, below-average height, slightly pudgy and dressed well enough, in a loose worsted suit. There was nothing particularly particular about this man, except, as he passed Joe, the man had looked at him, a little longer than usual, with a tired half-smile on his face. Joe noticed him, and vaguely remembered him; he had seen this man before, but where?

The tired man was like a worry which, although forgotten, leaves a residue, something that the mind feels it should get back to, but there was no back to get to. No fixed memory.

In a state of drowsy agitation Joe floated into his current place of work, Edding train station. Gokhan, the bearded Turk who stood sentinel at the ticket barriers was answering standard passenger queries—'What platform to Birmingham?' 'Has the 9:14 gone yet?' 'My ticket won't work'—in his staccato baritone. As Joe strolled in there was a scuffle at the nearside barrier. A passenger, a beady-eyed, bread-faced businessman, had pushed another, an obese woman in a massive piss-yellow coat which looked like a rained-on haystack, out of the way. She tutted loudly; 'Why not just barge past me and push me out the way, eh? *Twat.*'

The man ignored her. The woman waddled after him so as to continue venting her spleen, but got her gigantic bulk caught between the barriers. She began heaving and straining and whining to Gokhan, 'excuse me, excuse me...' Passengers built up behind her, including a small, turtle-headed man, around 60, impeccably attired in a tweed suit and green waistcoat who started crying out, in high pitched Queen's English, 'strange! strange! strange! strange!' Gokhan caught Joe's eye, sighed, climbed through the crowd and began pushing the fat woman through barriers.

This was the second time in Joe's life he had seen someone get wedged between these automatic ticket gates. The first time, fifteen years ago, it had been Neil, then fifteen years old, with a huge rucksack full of his worldly possessions, running away from home. Joe had reluctantly tracked him down to the station just as Neil had got stuck like this fat woman, except Neil had tried to jump his way out, which had left his legs uselessly running in mid-air, like a cartoon character, as station staff and passengers all stood around laughing at him. This had been one of the final straws between Neil and Joe, one of a bale actually.

The 'ticket-office-slash-control-room' where Joe worked was that of a medium-small-sized railway station; computers, folders, CCTV screens, smell of plastic and cheap seat-coverings and, at the back, a small counter with a kettle, mugs, tea dribbles, a crusted sugar bowl and a free newspaper. Joe unlocked the door—above which, the life-shaping legend '*network rail: really going somewhere*'—and greeted Clive and Haley's backs, both seated at the ticket windows serving customers;

'Plum sandwich anyone?'

Clive Marsh ignored Joe because Clive ignored everything that he wasn't compelled, by absolute necessity, to engage with. He was a small, skinny, sandy Stoke man with a large, weary, squarish head, grey eyes set far apart, a withered right arm, which he had been born with, and a limp from a leg shattered twenty years ago, when he'd jumped out of a third-floor window 'for a laugh', a promise that had gone unfulfilled, as he hadn't laughed in the twenty-five intervening years; an almost imperceptible smile, breaking over his smooth, thin, yellowish skin, was as far as his enjoyment of life now extended.

Hayley Greyling ignored Joe because she was an Very Important Professional With a Very Important Job to Do, and because she *was* an Important Professional With a Very Important Job to Do she felt it was her duty to be always fully made-up, with total-blemish-concealing foundation, perfect eyebrows, and unrevealed roots. She looked to Joe indistinguishable from eighty-five percent of all young women, whose faces had been erased and a disturbing puffy plastic mask stencilled on instead.

Hayley also considered it her duty to be upbeat, optimistic, youthful and can-do at all times, particularly when customer-facing; but none of this extended to pandering to Joe Geb's wanton casualness, which she hated, openly. She would have liked to openly hate more people, but she couldn't let her flatmates, her friends, her family, her bosses, her customers or anyone who couldn't speak English know that she hated them too, because there would be repercussions. None such for co-workers, particularly if they were male, white, hetero and able-bodied, so Joe got the full force. Also he was happy and unusual and therefore a constant awkward reminder that she, like everyone else, was miserable and usual.

So Hayley and Clive ignored Joe and continued dealing with customers, Hayley brightly and briskly and full of front, Clive clinging to every last calorie of potential energy like a miser clings to a final sovereign.

Joe hung up his coat, put his bag down, rubbed his hands and said, 'Wadup rastas. Weh yuh ah deal wid?' Every muscle in Hayley's neck and back visibly clenched, as if her body had thrown up a spiny shell. Joe detected this, a sense that suddenly he was in a hostile environment, but why was a mystery. He had no real sense of what was considered socially acceptable and was always surprised to discover that he'd said or done something 'wrong.' Surprised and afraid; for doing something wrong inevitably meant that hatred, ostracism or a plain old sacking was just around the corner.

Clive took a moment from sales and leant back in his chair to explain the situation to Joe. 'Everything is the same. Everyone is the same,' he said, his lazy Staffordshire lilt, somewhat honeying the bark of his bitter negativity.

Hayley threw her head round with knowing drama.

'Joe, you know as well as I do that nobody can make station announcements until you get here. Two of us have to be at the counters during rush hour and that means… Good *morning!*' A customer had approached, switching Hayley back to bell-bright and accredited, 'How can I help you?' she trilled.

Joe nodded and sat down at the workstation, various windows of administration open, various cursors blinking away, all demanding *information*. He looked at the screen, thought to himself, 'I can't be bothered with *that*' and turned instead to the intercom. He bent over the mic and pressed the 'speak' button with great tenderness.

'This is a station announcement. Flawless pedestrian etiquette is the ticket to paradise.' He pressed 'off.' Hayley shot him a tight squint of disapproval. He paid no attention, instead taking in the station through the CCTV monitors; standard platform scenes of silent standing single staring people; staring into their phones.

'Paradise doesn't seem to be a very popular concept these days,' said Joe, half to himself. He thought for a moment, then pushed the speak button a second time, leaning down to the mic.

'The next train is bound to purgatory. Passengers wishing to go straight to hell should alight here and wait for the 9:13 to Bristol Temple Meads. Passengers with no sin they wish to burn off, should return home and play Twister with a loved one.'

Hayley put her hand over her client-microphone, half turning, teeth clenched, 'Joe, if Dave finds out, you'll be…' Another customer walked up to her window. She turned back. 'Good morning! What brings you to Edding railway station today?' This was the official Network Rail greeting, loved by staff and customers alike.

Joe sighed and wandered over to the ticket counters.

'You do announcements and admin if you like,' he said gently.

Hayley walked over in a stroppy huff, but from the way she smoothed her dress, sat down brushing an invisible strand of hair from her face, chirpily announced all the standard information and tip-tapped away at the open spreadsheet, it was clear that she preferred the announcing role. Like everyone destined for management she detested human beings and reality generally and was much more comfortable handling facts about them.

Joe sat down in her vacated seat and faced the waiting customer, a tall, deep-voiced, large-nosed man who, thought Joe, probably had an immense penis.

'I'd like a single to London please and a travel card,' the man's bass voice boomed through the minicom.

'Do you want the travel card starting today or tomorrow?' Joe asked.

'Today.'

'Tomorrow?'

'No,' said the customer, 'today.'

'Starting today?'

'Not *starting* today. It's a one day travelcard. *For* today.'

'Today?'

'Yes.'

Joe leant forward, adding emphasis. 'You're sure today?'

'Yes, today!'

'Okay, calm down please sir. And London? Why's that?'

'Jesus, does it matter?'

'Well, it's a bit rainy today, and I thought you might prefer, I dunno, a nice walk along the beach?'

'No thank you. I want to go to London.' The man was surprisingly patient. Joe was beginning to like him; he really did want him to have a better day than it looked like he was going to have, dressed in a cheap suit and on his way to London.

'The north Norfolk coast is lovely in the rain.'

'I'm sure it is, but I want to go to London.'

Joe threw up his hands. 'Alright, have it your way.'

He entered the data into his computer.

'That'll be £412 please.'

'What!?'

'Norwich is only,' he checked, '£180, and if you wait until off peak…'

The man interrupted him, not hearing Joe add, very quietly, '…*it's 6p.*'

'Why,' said the customer, trying to control himself, 'would I want to go to Norwich?'

Another good question! The second today. Joe looked at the question in his mind, or rather through the crack in his mind where all the interesting answers lay, waiting.

'Because it rhymes with porridge?' he suggested.

At Clive's counter, another customer, a stout, flat-headed, friendly-looking fellow with an impossibly thick bowl-head haircut—possibly a wig—was getting irate.

'Yeah, but what I'm saying is,' he said with a pleasing Manc twang, 'whenever there's a problem, it's always the system's fault. Everyone always seems to blame everything on the system, don't they? Is it the system's fault? Yes? Well then, my question is, perhaps, have you thought about this, perhaps we don't actually need the system? Maybe me and you, humans, we can work this out between us? No?'

Clive said nothing. The poor man slumped.

'Alright, give me a ticket to 1974 please. If the system will allow it.'

'I'm afraid our trains only travel through space sir.'

'Fuck it. I'll walk.'

He left. Clive turned to Joe and said, without irony, 'You really should learn to deal with customers better.'

Rush hour passed, passengers dwindled to day-trippers, relative-visitors and out-of-workers off to interviews. Hayley stood up.

'I'm going for breakfast. Joe, you're on announcements and admin.'

Joe turned to Clive, both still at their ticketing desks. 'She's been here five minutes and she's already telling us what to do.' He thought about it. 'But then, I suppose someone has to.' Every time I take control of my life, he thought, and tell myself what to do, I end up with more problems than I started with. It was unpleasant to let his drifting boat be pushed by Hayley and Maria and Dave and all the other bosses he'd had, but much more unpleasant to take the oars and start pumping up river to… to where exactly?

'She was born a manager,' said Clive, 'and you were born an employee.'

'What were you born?'

'A miserable cunt.'

'Where did it all go wrong, Clive?'

'For humanity?'

'I was thinking specifically for you.'

Clive pulled himself up and hobbled over to the intercom.

'Watch,' he said, pressed the speak button and leant over the mic. 'If you're happy and you know it, clap your hands.'

Joe rose and they both watched the CCTV monitors, at the people on the platforms. Nobody waiting made any kind of movement.

Clive turned to Joe. 'You see. Underneath the social mask…'

Clive had forgotten to turn off the microphone. His dour

drawl echoed around the quiet station over the PA, along with Joe's responses.

'...we're all miserable cunts.'

'She's not a miserable cunt.'

'Who?'

'That one there, the curvy one with long brown hair.'

Joe, focusing on Lilly in the centre of camera 4, did not realise that other people in the station, listening to their conversation, were now furtively looking around, trying to find the 'curvy one with long brown hair.'

Clive was also unaware. He was looking at a taller, one-armed woman, standing next to Lilly.

'The one with one arm?' he said to Joe, and to thirty-odd others, who had now stopped looking around, because nobody wants to stare at a woman with one arm.

'No, the one in blue.' Lilly was wearing a blue velvety dress, Dr. Martens and a choker. 'If someone told me that she was the future queen of the New Earth, or God's wife,' said Joe, 'I think I'd be instantly okay with that.'

Now it was Lilly's turn to look around. Nobody else was wearing a blue dress; it had to be at her that these words were directed, presumably from the ticket office. She took a step away from the platform, asking herself—should I?—but at that moment her train trundled round the far bend and she couldn't possibly be late on her first day at work. So she stepped back and waited for it, flushingly conscious that other people could see that this bizarre conversation was directed at her.

'It wouldn't last,' said Clive to Joe and everyone. 'Anyway, you're married, you shouldn't be ogling young women.'

'Don't you ogle?'

'No. I've given up on sex.'

The train pulled up. Most passengers were reluctant to leave this fascinating exchange, but momentum forced them onwards. Lilly was also desperate to hear how the it would end, but she too let the force of gravity push her towards the train.

'Have you?' said Joe

'Sex is okay, but you can't beat the real thing.'

Joe guffawed, a smirk that, now the train had pulled away and the platform was empty of trains and of people, echoed round the station and into the office. 'Did you know the microphone is still on?' said Joe.

There was a long silence, rich with meaning to the few people waiting on the other platforms, which was followed by Clive's voice over the intercom; 'If I didn't get off on my own and other people's humiliation, I'd have a miserable life.'

∞

Lilly stood in a small windowless room full of tasteless coffins. Half an hour before, a mysterious voice had fallen from the sky and said that she could be a future queen of the earth. It was funny, she'd thought to herself as the train had rattled away from Edding towards Nutbourne, it only takes a single ray of sunshine to forget a million years of rain. She had been on a kind of dark trudge since she had decided not to have sex with Nick again, the first man she'd almost had an orgasm with. She'd known it was supposed to be casual and he'd had other girlfriends, but he kept saying and doing hurtful things, like showing her photographs of his skinny exes or telling her to eat less, and although the sex was almost amazing at the start it was becoming hollow and numbing. Finally, six months ago, they'd gone to a travel tavern in Northampton in the middle of the day and eaten soft pasta and had detached sex, and he'd finished quickly and said 'Christ, I needed that,' and got dressed and said he had to get back home because he was expecting a delivery from Amazon. After that, although she was still attracted to him, she felt like he was a complete stranger, an alien even, something not quite human. She decided she wouldn't seem him again. Every girl, Lilly thought, had to have a Nick at some point in her life, but she did feel for women who ended up with Nicks.

He occasionally sent texts like 'you're not the prettiest girl I've met but you do have the best personality,' but she didn't reply. The feeling returned, a sense she'd long had that living was a lonely thing. It was a kind of base state, loneliness. Everyone was alone. You could temporarily forget about being on your own and being fundamentally unloved, and you could forget about it with a fling, and the excitement convinced you that you were really in love, but it soon wore off, and then the normal-ordinary returned. It was at this point that she'd decided she wanted to work in a funeral parlour and spend her life with dead people because dead people had been the only people she'd ever really felt comfortable with. When she saw her dead parents she felt a lot closer to them than she ever had when they'd been alive.

She'd started to get the irrational and therefore compelling feeling that this was her life now, but then this morning Neil had asked her out and even though it was only Neil, it was actually lovely that someone was thinking about her like that, and not just Neil apparently, but also a mysterious voice from the heavens had said that she could be God's wife. And now, standing in the tacky coffin room, she found herself feeling almost okay. She had the sense, which she sometimes got, that she'd just walked into a building which was going to be an old friend.

The coffins were decorated with setting suns, fake ivy, pink plastic knockers and what looked like massive nylon doilies. A small, twitchy, hipless, rodent-like woman, with frizzy hair and thick-lensed glasses that made her look like a nocturnal monkey, was talking very rapidly to Lilly in a feeble high-pitched querulous tone, punctuating her speech with rapid, nervy tics and pointless gestures.

'...the neighbours put fat balls in their fir tree, you know, for the birds? And the squirrels keep taking them, and so, the squirrels are getting really fat because these fat balls are enormous. And so now the squirrels look like middle-aged women that have gone to seed. I've got these squirrels, with gigantic rear-ends, waddling around my back garden. It's just disgusting...'

The woman, Nina, sighed greatly, and continued the tour. 'Anyway, this is where clients choose their caskets, we've got all kinds. Football teams are popular—this one is uh, Everton I think isn't it? I'm not interested in sports, it's just men fighting over eggs—so are cats, popular I mean, they don't eat eggs…'

She gestured towards a coffin with massive, poorly-rendered and rather creepy-looking airbrushed cat's heads. It looked to Lilly like the occupant was a cat-person destined for cat hell. As she murmured vague appreciation a rough, muffled 'you lucky git!' came from the closed plywood door next to her.

The source of the mild profanity was a squat bald man with a thickset face like a friendly fist. He was standing in the back workshop-garage of the building, in an outrageously 'quarter-to-three' posture, in front of a half-made coffin, his eyes twinkling with good-natured irony. Next to him another man, also bald, but extremely tall and thin, with a long ruined face, hollow cheeks, a massive aquiline nose and deep-set, heavy-lidded eyes, was bent over a plank of medium-density fibreboard (with 'elm' style laminate) on which they were playing 'Pass the Pigs.' The taller man, Paul Saul, had just rolled the two plastic pigs, which had both landed tilted upwards on their snouts. The body of the shorter man, Carl, tensed in frustration.

'Double leaning jowler!' Carl cried, '…ooooh you fuck bag!'

The door opened, Paul swiftly gathered up the pigs and stood upright, with his hands behind his back. Nina entered, talking to Lilly, who followed behind her.

"…and this is the workshop,' said Nina. 'This is Carl, and this is Paul.'

'Hello,' said Lilly, 'I'm Lilly.'

Carl's little eyes coldly and super-rapidly assessed Lilly's hips and buttocks—superb—then squeezed up in genuine human warmth, transforming his bored taxi-driver face into that of a friendly uncle. 'Wotcha,' he said. Paul said nothing, bowed elegantly, slowly blinked, slowly exhaled, and slowly walked from the room.

'Are you a carpenter?' asked Lilly.

'Hahaha! No! I'm a jack of all trades! Undertaking yesterday.'

'Funeral directing,' interrupted Nina.

Carl ignored her, 'Coffin-making tomorrow.'

'Caskets,' said Nina, tightly, 'they're caskets.'

'Then picking up stiffs tomorrow.'

'Cadavers Carl.' She sighed 'Please use the correct terminology, and please can you not swear so much? I have asked you. This is a place of…' she closed her eyes reverently, searching for a reverent word to describe their reverent business, but one wouldn't come.

'Yeah, sorry,' said Carl. He wasn't.

'Good, anyway,' Nina continued, opening her eyes, 'this is Carl's room really.' There were various coffins in various states of completion laying around the large L-shaped room, which, round the corner, gave onto the garage where the company hearse and a large black minivan were parked. 'But,' she said, gesturing Lilly to two doors at the back of the workshop, 'you'll be working back here.'

Nina first opened the door to the left and, without looking inside—in fact, Lilly noticed, with her eyes scrunched up—hastily nodded Lilly to look within. It was a strip-lit cold room, with rows of long racks, enough to hold thirty bodies but which now held twelve. They were either in coffins or covered in burgundy cloth with yellow tassels. Lilly was given only a moment to look before Nina pulled her out and, face screwed up, closed the door.

'Those… that's… that's… those are our clients…. And I always say,' she said distractedly, 'death, it's terrible, tragic really. Erm…' As she mumbled on, she opened the facing door, on the right, over which pvc strip curtains hung, leading Lilly into the mortuary.

It was a small room, clean but dingy and cramped, smelling of perfume-infused bleach. In the middle were two stainless steel tables, like upside-down rectangular-based pyramids with grilled tops over which operating-theatre-type spotlights hung. Around the walls were cabinets covered with hazchem safety warnings, a wash trough, a sluice and hose, a massive ledger and a wall phone. In the middle of the room was a naked dead body—a crumpled-looking old man—with a strip of what looked like waxy cheese paper covering his genitals.

Nina stood in the doorway, facing away from the body, still vaguely monologuing about tragedy and loss and it being all so terrible and awful. '…yes, erm, yes, clients, they, well, they're,' she sighed, 'they've passed away, and erm, *there!*' She flung her arm out violently, for no apparent reason, and smacked her wrist against the phone.

'Agh!'

'Are you okay?'

'Yes, yes,' she said rapidly, wincing and holding her hand, 'over there,' she stabbed her head sideways, 'you see it? on that shelf, there is the shaving kit, make-up kit—forty pounds crematorial foundation costs—soap, we get that bulk. He—who is this?' She opened the ledger, following the rows of names down to the bottom. She didn't seem to quite know what she was saying or doing. 'John Mattingly,' she said, then followed the column through sex, age, weight, height, cause of death to 'notes'. 'He needs to be shaved,' she said, 'it says here, "shave and tidy beard". And make-up. You'll need plenty of foundation, watch the collar when you put his shirt back on, and pluck the nose hairs; they grow. Weeds.' She retched. 'You know death, it's a very serious…' she was clinging to her wrist, in pain, 'always be serious, with the clients, like Paul… and, I've really…' She made to leave.

'But, erm,' said Lilly with a panicked look in her eye, 'I'm not sure, I mean I know theoretically, but…'

'I'm so sorry Lilly, I really must go. Carl will help you. Just remember,' she said as she left, 'if you cut him, he won't bleed, but he won't heal either. He'll look a state. The body I mean, not Carl. He bleeds, I've seen it. So be careful. You're shaving a balloon. And,' she nodded to the phone, 'there's a phone—I'll phone from… when I want to… Uh…'

She left Lilly alone with the dead body. Above the table, on the wall, was a poster which said 'Mission Statement. Bringing death to life, but in a nice way.' Below that, a dead man. Not nice at all. Dead.

Death again. Its aura of silence, even amidst the noise, its repulsive yet irresistible actuality, it's somethingness and nothingness, together. Even as Lilly felt acid worry bubbling up, there was something about it she liked, that steadied her and that enabled her to act. Without thinking, she took down the shaving equipment from the shelf, foamed up the shaving brush in the wash trough and turned towards the body. The dead man was thin and bony and greyish with high cheekbones, deep, dark eye sockets, a hairy, bubble-like belly, sunken greyish nipples and long skeletal fingers and toes.

'Hello John,' she said, 'I'm, erm, my name is Lilly, and I'm going to be shaving you and tarting you up. You've probably never worn make-up have you? Or maybe you have. Maybe you were a pole dancer in a gay bar? Or a dentist? Your teeth are very nice. To me… you look like Don Quijote. Perhaps you were a mad Spanish knight in a past life? Or in a future life? I think you'll come back as a Spanish Starlord. Or an elephant. I'd like to come back as an elephant. Something kind and indestructible. A hill maybe. Can you reincarnate as a hill? A nice warm hill.'

She lathered John's face, then paused. What kind of shave was it to be? She checked the ledger again; 'shave and tidy beard'. But tidy into what? She took her phone out and put 'beard styles' into the search engine. The fourth result was 'Movie Villains and their Badass Beards' and General Zod looked good, so she propped the phone up against John's dead wrist and started lathering. She pushed the jaw shut, but it slowly opened, she pushed again, brow furrowed and squinting, as if prodding a dead rat, but again it slowly, mockingly, fell agape.

'Please shut your mouth John. This isn't helping.'

She carefully lathered around the open mouth then, standing above him, holding the razor hovering above the nose, readied herself for the first stroke. She bent down and looked in his eye. It was milky and blank—and deflated.

She jerked back.

'Carl! Carl!'

Carl's voice carried through the door; 'what?'

'Can you... give me a hand please?'

The door opened and Carl pushed through the plastic curtain. He came in awkwardly, dragging a leg between his legs. 'Heh, heh,' he chuckled, swinging into view, 'how about a leg? I've got one spare.'

'Oh God what's that?'

'I know! Some one-legged fella's just come in with it. Wants to have it buried. Why? No idea! I'll leave it here.' He leant the leg up against the wall, then considered it.

'Gonna be a small, thin coffin,' he said quietly to himself.

'Erm, Carl,' said Lilly with a sigh of dismay, 'I, ugh, I'm finding all this a bit difficult to be honest.'

Carl turned and, frowning, took in the situation. 'Dressing? Can't help. Women's work.'

'Is it? I see, then, I suppose, I should wait for Nina to, er, start my training?'

'Ha! Nina!? You must be joking. She won't help. Unless she stands to be out of pocket.'

'But she's a qualified mortician.'

'And I'm a qualified ballerina.'

'But, err.'

'I'm not really. I do a bit of business around town. Trained as a printer, but it wasn't for me, fucking boring. Then I started my own business, electric roller garage doors, Openings it was called, but,' he sighed sadly, 'it closed.'

'Carl!'

'Ah, don't worry!' he said, perking up, 'You'll be fine. Just get stuck in. You got a boyfriend?'

'Er, no.'

'No!? There are loads of fellas out there who like... you know...'

'What?'

'A girl with a bit of meat on her bones.'

'Thanks, erm…' Lilly looked down at the floor.

'I mean you're not at all fat. Very nicely shaped I'd say.'

'Thanks for your help Carl. I'll be fine.'

'Yeah, you'll be fine.'

He left, leaving Lilly again alone with the dead.

8

Zinzan Street, like many in lower-middle-England, was prim, tidy-gardened and daisy-curtained at one end while, at the 'less desirable' end, air vents were stained black, upvc front doors didn't close properly, green bins without house numbers written on were stolen in the morning, mattresses were dumped in skips at night, sun-bleached crisp packets, wind-blown down front paths, joined menus for Piri-Piri chicken takeaways and 'Mad-Ladz' barbers, forming gloss-lamination snowdrifts against porch walls. On every sixth or seventh paving slab there was dog shit or, pushing through the cracked concrete, pigweed, spurweed, dandelion and thistle, nature's skirmishers, sent in advance of the grande armeé in waiting. Here, on the corner, in the midst of all this ordinary grot, was a house which stood out, which had resisted the spread of 'development'—the partitioning of ex-family homes into three or four cramped 'studio flats' occupied by Romanian carpenters, Chinese nail technicians, Moroccan students, Nigerian security guards, Brazilian whores and Polish delivery drivers—and was still a whole house. Whole but, even to the hard, sour, ratty scrags and meaty Roms, wholly troubling. The house was covered, from top to bottom, in painted ideograms and glyphs, vaguely Egyptian-looking, but eccentric, unorthodox; fish-eating fish, speaking bananas, weeping pigs, rat-headed judges, pigeon-footed armchairs, egg-headed policemen and so on. In the dirty windows were outward facing posters with sun-bleached slogans reading 'Go with the flow or sit with the shit', and 'You can't dream your day awake' and 'When in doubt, work out.'

In front of this house stood three men, Terry, Neil and Victor. Victor, the householder, was a manic-looking overweight Rasta, wearing a stretchy rubber 'helmet' type rubber dreadlock tam decorated with ostrich feathers, an 'electric guitar' T-shirt with buttons that played digital boing-boing sounds, and dirty track-suit bottoms studded with home-sewn sequins. He had a large expressive mouth, with a wide gap between the front teeth, large, dark eyes, also far apart—which gave him an alienesque look— separated by a deep, crescent-shaped scar just above the bridge of his nose. Although his expression was ordinarily sad, impish and weary, his face was now wrinkled up into a wild, dark fireball as he screamed with joy, alternating long, laughing, whooping 'wo-ho-hoooos' with high-pitched 'yeek-yeek-yeeks.'

Terry was a thin pudge-cheeked, fat-necked man in his early 20s, who looked much younger. He was holding a large box with '*whole body vibrating machine*' written across it in futuristic let-tering. The box was indeed vibrating, and, as he made his way to his van, talking to Neil—who was sniffing the air suspiciously— so was Terry himself, his voice juddering with the rattling box.

'And tha… a… at,' said Terry, with some effort, 'was whe… e … en we got a breakthrough in the case. That's when my Krav-Maga training came in ha… a… andy. Fu… u… u… uck.' The box had started vibrating more violently, causing Victor to laugh even louder. 'How d…do you sw… sw… sw… itch this fucking th… th… thing off?'

As Victor made chicken gestures, slapped his thighs and put his fingers delicately to his chest in mock overwhelmment Terry threw the box into the back of his large van, on the side of which, in sober lettering, the dread words, 'County Collections.'

Terry was a bailiff, although he liked to believe he was more of a wild-card, maverick, loose-cannon detective type just doing a bit of bailiffing on the side, or as cover.

'It's not a case,' said Neil, 'only police deal with cases. And you don't know Krav Maga.' Neil was often given these clearout cases, and often had to listen to Terry's absurd stories while they obliterated someone's life. Last week Terry had related a tale of being in a car chase in which his car had literally leapt over the top of a car coming in the opposite direction.

'With all due respect,' said Terry, with no due respect, 'you're wrong there. We have cases as well. Tough ones. Like Victor here.'

Terry had returned to the house, but Victor was playfully standing in his way. Terry sighed, 'Mr Perry. I have a right to enter your property under section 10 of the 1977 Criminal Law Act and reclaim your property for county auction. Please stand aside.'

Victor pranced out of the way and Terry walked in. Neil continued sniffing the air.

'Bullshit!' said Victor.

'Enough of the language sir,' said Neil. 'He's quite right, he can enter your...'

'He's a boy.'

'That's as may be, but he's quite right.'

'It's not *that* you're right, it's *when* you're right.'

Neil felt an upsurge of emotion. Any kind of challenge or disagreement, from anyone, even one he didn't understand, would shoot a jolt of agitated animus through his system, readying him for a fight, on any topic. He had argued about how cavemen used to cut their nails, Christ's brother's surname, the easy and hard problems of consciousness, why gravity is so weak, how the bus driver closes the door before he leaves, why there are no baby Gordons, where all the moths had gone, how embryonic cells know what to develop into, why women don't put good sound effects into their stories or quote movies, whether Hoovers work on the moon, the purpose of dreams and if baby pigeons really exist. It wasn't that he was a know-it-all—he knew he knew very little and was quite happy to let people who knew more know more, it was the challenge that rankled, a sinking feeling, with the added sense that *he* was sinking because he was being sat on. It didn't matter to Neil that he couldn't become right by making someone else wrong. They just had to be pushed off, that was all, or he'd drown.

'Actually, wrong,' he said to Victor, 'The law is always right. Law-abiders understand that.'

'Can't trust a law-abider.'

'To be a citizen, to be a party in the social contract, is to adhere to the laws of a society. Can you smell that?'

'I never signed no contract! Where is my contract?' Victor was laughing in Neil's face, making him feel quite arresty.

'It's not a literal contract,' said Neil, tight.

'Then I ain't a literal ci-ti-zen.'

Just as Neil was about to escalate, Terry emerged with a laptop. The blood drained from Victor's face.

'My music…' he whispered, his lips suddenly contorted in horror and fear.

Neil looked from Terry to Victor. 'Music?'

'Sorry sir,' said Terry marching towards the van.

Before Neil could react, Victor was hurtling towards Terry, screaming, an ear-splitting falsetto, '*noooooooooooooooo…*'

He leapt on Terry and bit into his necks. Terry cried out, and elbowed Victor in the nose. Victor staggered backwards, beating himself, slapping his head, wailing and moaning a dire, world-ending sick kind of howl. Neil froze, unsure what to do. Net curtains were quivering. He had to do something.

'Give him the laptop!' he cried.

'No! It's county property!'

'Fuck that. Give it to him!'

'No!' yelled Terry, with a bizarre note of petulance.

'Agggghhhhhhhhhh!' Victor roared and lurched once more towards Terry, who turned and ran. They made two circuits of Terry's van, Terry nimbly hopping round it, Victor lurching, yawping, dribbling until, out of breath yet completely beside himself, he screamed, leapt up into the air, arms and legs outstretched, and landed, face down, in the middle of the road throttling himself. Neil unhooked his radio. Should I call it in? he asked himself, or intervene with Victor's self-strangulation? He hesitated; surely you can't strangle yourself? He lifted the radio to his lips, then changed his mind—because; perhaps you can? He took a step towards Victor who, at that moment, choked himself out.

Silence. Victor lay in the middle of the street. Neil and Terry exchanged glances. 'Sierra One-Five, Alpha-Mike One-Zero,' said Neil into his radio, 'Code One. Please send ambulance backup immediately. Address 29 Zinzan Street.'

The radio crackled; 'Alpha-Mike One-Zero. Received. Over.'

Terry, shaken up, was standing over Victor, still cradling the laptop.

'I think I'd better take that,' said Neil distractedly, staring at Victor's left hand—which was missing two fingers, 'You take what you need from his house.'

Terry, without looking up, handed over the laptop, as if under a spell. He was looking at Victor's feet. One of his shoes had come off, exposing a sockless foot, which was green.

8

Joe had one worldly skill. He could get any low paying job, no matter how tight the job market. Fortunately, he also had several other-worldly skills which didn't just enable him to lose any low-paying job, they all but guaranteed it.

After leaving home at nineteen, he had got fired from leafletting, for binning a clump of leaflets then spending the afternoon next to the river where his manager just happened to be boating with his mistress. After this, he got fired from teleselling corporate marquees at Tring golf course after getting zero sales for days on end and deciding instead to sell his CDs to his targets (and succeeding; a secretary at Proctor and Gamble bought his Bob Dylan bootleg boxset). He got fired from working as a remedial treatment surveyor—climbing about in attics checking for woodworm, taking readings of walls in search of rising damp—for spending whole afternoons going through the porn mags, board games and photo albums that people stored up there. He got fired from a job as a turkey inseminator after having dropped a tray of semen phials that a fellow farmer had painstakingly wanked out of forty-odd male birds.

It was difficult to get fired from the turkey farm. There aren't many people who enjoy having bird jizz sprayed over their face, and so turnover was high. The few that stuck it out were psychologically deformed outcasts. There were two hermaphrodite lovers there who used to enjoy tripping up a simple-faced, brain-damaged man-boy who used to come in to the farm early, roger one of the heifers while standing on a bucket, then sit in the yard playing a handheld computer bowling game. Another guy used to rugby kick live turkeys, converting many a 'try' over one of the barn beams.

After this, there was a string of rapid-fire sackings; from thinning out woodland (bunking off for meadow reveries), cutting firewood logs for pikeys (carving into the planks words selected at random from a dictionary of historical slang), delivering blood transfusions (getting lost in Mill Hill, and then again in Maidstone, and again in Grays; he enjoyed getting lost and tried to make sure it happened often) and cracking crabs (continually getting sick from eating too much crab). Joe then decided to aim a little bit higher and trained up as a bus driver, but he got the sack after a gale blew a trampoline in front of his bus. Having helped two kids move it back into their front garden and securing it to the patio, he got on and boinged up and down for a bit, while the perplexed bus watched on.

He then decided to get a professional job, something serious, and went for a degree in journalism while working part time as a temp. He graduated and got an unpaid intern job at the local newspaper, but the only stories Joe wanted to pursue were, in the words of his stiff editor, 'evidence of mental illness'. 'Nobody is interested in photo features of people missing trains and buses,' he'd said, 'nor are they interested in the mayor's twelfth favourite colour', referring to an interview that Joe had conducted under the headline 'Mayor too fat to skydive'. In the end Joe was let go for sneaking childishly silly fake ads into the classifieds ('lost:

fly', 'hermaphrodite monoped seeks similar', 'For sale: Orange Bermuda shorts size xxxxl only worn 394 times, a little faded but still eye-catching. £3000 or in exchange for 781 packets of Buitoni Fusilli pasta', and so on).

After a few more sackings—chocolate tasting (scoffing every sample and rating them all ten), trimming cowhides at a tannery (insisting on wearing a World War One gas mask) and mucking out at a stud farm (actually no reason for that firing; Joe was simply hated by the horse people who were and are, as a group, evil)—Joe got a call from his agency asking him to go to Scotland to deliver some pheasants to an old shooting estate. He'd shared the ride with a retired old guy called Rod who was boosting his pension with a few days' driving. Joe suggested a quick coffee at a roadside garage, but this didn't go down well with Rod who already had a nicely packed lunch and a big flask of coffee and only wanted to stop exactly halfway along the journey. 'Ok', said Joe, 'I'll just get a takeaway coffee', and sauntered into the minimarket and up to the coffee counter, before realising he'd left his wallet back in the truck where Rod was bristling with impatient ill-will, drumming his fingers on the steering wheel. 'I'll be right back', said Joe, but when he returned the queue had grown and people had begun ordering complex deviations from the standard—soya milk, kid's temperature milk, vanilla syrup, and one of the baristas was new, and time was piling up, but Joe felt he'd already invested this much, and was desperate for a cuppa, so he waited it out until Rod came in fuming and started tugging Joe away from the queue. By then Joe was in second place and there was no way he was giving up his position, so close to the prize, so he resisted, and they argued, lots of built-up tension, and somehow ended up shoving one another like kids in a playground. Joe, misgauging both his strength and Rod's slight, lanky lightness, shoved him hard enough to send him flying backwards, the sliding doors behind him courteously opening, out into the rain. Joe turned back to the queue and Rod drove away, leaving Joe to hitch back to town, jobless, again.

This was the last job Joe had had before he'd gone for, and got, this railway thing, where he'd worked now for a record-breaking three months. He had guerilla gardened the out-of-reach limits of the platform, secretly growing wisteria, buddleia and aspidistra, he had emptied the snack machines of crisps and thrown them over the railings to the beggars, who would gather in the station car park like seagulls, and he had spent hours in his socks, moon-walking around the lovely smooth floors of the office during the late-night shifts, but, as yet, Dave Davage, his regional manager, had not found sufficient grounds to fire him.

Dave was on his way today, so there was a little extra brisk-ness about daily matters, but he didn't usually roll up until the end of the day, so the three of them, Joe, Clive and Hayley, were eating lunch during a slack half-hour. It was a dull room. Joe thought a sneeze would liven it up, but none would come, so he munched away in silence on his croissant. Clive was eating a bacon sandwich, and Hayley had a plate of potatoes on her blotchy, too-white knees, plastic-forking starch into her mouth with one hand, texting with the other.

Finally, Joe spoke. 'I notice you have a lot of potatoes there Hayley.'

She glanced up in fear, then looked down at her plate and then, with reflexive pep said 'Oh yes! I've got hash browns, potato scones and a deep-fried potato!'

'Are potatoes a particular thing of yours?'

'I suppose so.'

'Could it be called a fetish?'

'No,' she said suspiciously, 'potatoes are normal.'

'Yes, but are they?'

'Not as weird as train-spotting,' said Clive, heavily and sadly.

Joe gave an oily-fingered gesture of concession. 'There's a lot of fetishes connected to trains.'

'Driving them, for a start,' said Carl.

'I was thinking more of getting on the roof and dangling off the side, like James Bond.'

As Joe said this, Clive's face tic-quivered into a brief, emphatic pout, an habitual spasm which tended to unsettle other people, but which Joe was a big fan of. Hayley, meanwhile, was eating more quickly, eager to exit the interaction.

'You mean,' said Clive, 'catching trains just to dangle from them?'

'Exactly. If everyone had to have a fetish…'

'You mean by law?'

'Yeah, by law. That would be mine.'

'You'd dangle off trains.'

'Yes. I'd be a dangler.'

A customer turned up, an uptight University Challenge type. Joe pointed to the sign next to him which he'd put up at lunch hour; 'All Trains Are Cancelled Due To A Scheduling Conflict'. The last three words had been crossed out and replaced with a hasty hand-written 'The Unravelling Of Civilisation'. The customer sighed—clearly this was old information—and left.

Joe nodded at the last piece of Clive's bacon sandwich, now wrapped up in a piece of clingfilm.

'So you see,' said Joe, leaning over Clive and pointing out the various elements of his lunch in much the same way that an archaeologist might explain a dig map, 'you've basically eaten most of that bacon sandwich but you didn't fancy the last crusty corner so you've wrapped it back up in the clingfilm. Not to keep it fresh, because that's no longer necessary, but just because it feels right to seal it up… okay?'

Clive eyed Joe with a mixture of annoyance, curiosity, suspicion and ennui.

Joe looked down at his own croissant. 'I wonder if there is anything flakier than a croissant,' he said.

'Eczema?'

'A man with eczema eating a croissant.'

'In the wind.'

'In the wind. Now that's a flaky scene.'

Hayley stood up and swept out, the largeness and clunkiness

of her shoes having seemingly been chosen for their power to accentuate a good, grumpy leave-taking.

Joe watched her depart. 'Is she angry?'

'Is it not obvious?'

'No. Yes. Why is she angry?'

Clive had now finished his lunch, and was speaking from behind a newspaper outfolded in front of him; 'What I've learnt is never, ever, ask a woman why she is angry. No good can come of it.'

Joe got up, took his baboon cup out of his bag and put the kettle on. The mug chinked as he put it on the sideboard.

Clive looked over the top of his paper. 'No more porcelain cups,' he said, 'Health and safety. We have to use paper cones from now on.'

'What, for tea?'

Clive sighed, 'Ask Dave.'

Joe was ruefully inspecting a flimsy cardboard cone with 'Network Rail' stencilled on the side. 'He's not interested in reasons. He's interested in West Ham, Jaguars and Malaga.'

'Dave has an institutional pallor that no amount of Spanish sun can hide. He's the kind of man who takes out his wasted decades on those who've spent them well.'

'And anal sex. He's interested in that. He told me.'

Hayley re-entered without Clive, still behind his paper, realising. 'I've always felt that anal sex was overrated,' he said.

Hayley, with a horribly offended intake of breath, swivelled on a sixpence and bumped into Dave, a chubbish, bullish cockney with thin lips, fat neck and narrow, muscular shoulders, dressed in an oddly proportioned suit with a utility manager's accoutrements; badges, lanyards and Bics. His face displayed no signs of introspection or irony, rather a heavy, literal certainty of what was right and what was true; and there was something not right and true in this situation. There never was now that Joe was in it, although it was hard to work out why; but Dave was feeling beneficent, indulgent, practically regal. He'd just had an hour with a fabulous new pro, a high-energy Thai girl in Mary's

Mead who'd opened the door dressed in a wet-look leather one-piece, dragged him to a sink, vigorously washed his cock and balls, while squawking 'I'm raping you! I'm raping you' before piking onto her bed, upon which Dave also jumped, pulling her skirt off, crying 'now I'm raping you!' and then engaging in frantic, bedspring-destroying coitus, while, the whole time, Radio 4 played in the background a documentary about locust plagues in Kenya. It was good to smite one's sexual tension upon a woman so glad to be smitten, but to learn something new about the world at the same time was something like the full package, although she did have a huge poster of John Terry above the bed, which was offputting.

'Is Hayley upset?' Dave asked with plump bemusement.

'Upset is her default state,' said Clive, 'Everything else is a flimsy corporate mask.'

Dave peered at Clive, contemplating the odd little man that he was. 'Do you actually *like* people Clive?'

'Nobody likes *people.*'

'What's wrong with people?'

'All they have in common is their stomach and genitals. That's all they talk about. All their plans lead to their digestive and reproductive organs. The machinery. Talk to them of something you can't get from the output end and they look at you like you're a government man.'

'Oh come on, cheer up.'

'Why David? We are all monsters.'

'Jesus Christ, look, I've got to have a private chat with Joe here, could you leave us for a moment?'

Clive wearily limped out.

'You want a cup of tea Dave?' asked Joe, 'The kettle's just boiled.'

'Oh yeah, cheers sunbeam.' Dave flopped heavily into the chair that Clive had just vacated. He looked around the room with bovine self-satisfaction as Joe prepared tea in one of the paper cones.

'I wanted to talk to you,' said Dave, 'because we've had a few complaints… oh, how's things? Everything okay at home?'

'At home?'

'Yeah, yeah, everything okay is it?'

'Well, I think my wife hates me.'

'Don't they all these days? I tell you mate, the legs of the world closed in 1995. Getting mish today is like climbing Mount Sinai. Back in the 80s it was all *available*. Now, nothing. You can't do anything. When I was young, for example, you could call a Jew a Jew, a gay a gay, a woman a woman, you could smack your kids—not abuse mind you, I fucking love kids, just a little shock, enough for them to understand you've got the fucking power here—and you could let 'em run all over town, no problem. You could admire a lovely arse, *openly*—and they loved it, the birds, they honestly did, I remember 'em smiling and laughing after a little squeeze. You could joke about anything you liked, you could. Now? Fuck all. Fuck all!' He looked at Joe, waiting for a response. He even gestured a little, nodding as if to say, 'you can agree with me now,' but Joe gave him nothing. This, for Dave, was the problem with Joe, although he wasn't one of *them*, the drama queens in charge of the planet—you could say anything to Joe, anything, he never, ever judged—but still, responsewise, you never quite knew where you were with him. He didn't ever seem to react to anything in a normal way. There was, Dave had decided, something *inhuman* about Joe Geb.

'Yeah, but anyway,' Dave continued, 'I just wanted to grab you for a couple of mins, have a chat. First of all, we've had multiple complaints about your station announcements, yeah? Now, we all like a laugh and a joke. I'll hold up my hands here—I've been in trouble myself for it. But we've got a serious, dependable world to maintain Joe, a world of responsibility… and schedules… and you know… normality, yeah? When people come through those doors they don't know it, but they want to see things that make sense. Trains late and cancelled… that makes sense. It's annoying, but it makes sense. Handing out leaves instead of tickets… it doesn't make sense. It's not what the punters are paying for, yeah? You've got to turn *down* the humour,' he made a dialling down gesture, which he then reversed; 'and turn *up* the actual information. So forget the funny stuff. Don't say 'train's not coming' in a high-pitched squeal. Calmly say what's happening… and tell the passengers *why*, in ordinary language. And give details. People like details. They're reassuring, and, I know it doesn't seem like it at times, but that's what we're all here for, to reassure people, the world is as you expect it to be. You see?'

'Details. Right.' Joe was concentrating on the tea. It was difficult because the cones were hot, but there was nowhere you could put them down while the tea steeped.

'Also,' said Dave, 'We've had a few complaints from punters about the way you handle their complaints. Now. Sometimes, we come in to work, we're tired, we're stressed, yeah, but remember what we talked about at the last meeting? Empathy Joe, *empathy*—let the customers… They have to express their feelings. Remember the company vision? Remember the vision?'

Joe handed Dave his tea and sat down in front of him. The cone was very hot, so Dave held it awkwardly, clawed at the top.

'Yeah, I remember the vision,' says Joe, somewhat distracted by the fact that, on the shelf behind Dave an alarmingly beautiful naked woman has appeared. She is long; a long and pale 'Modigliani' face, long, thick, blond curly hair, long fingers, long feet. It is his sister Ursula. The last time Joe saw her he was twenty and had been riding away from home on a horse. She must be, now, what, forty? And yet she looks half that.

'Revolutioneering,' Dave Davage chugged on, 'Revolutioneering. You see what I'm saying? It's engineering, and revolution, in a revolutionary way.'

'Revolution, right,' said Joe, on autopilot now.

Dave's paper funnel was dripping tea from the base of the cone. He kept talking, all the while trying to keep himself free of drips. He couldn't put the cone down though, so he held it awkwardly out in front of his knees.

Joe looks distractedly at Dave as he speaks and then, without being too obvious, glances up at Ursula who, with each look, is covered in more and more flowers and vegetation and things of the field. Grass is growing from under her arms, tiny daisies from her ears, her hair is clogging up with twigs and spider webs, a mouse crawls over her and nibbles a cherry on her breast. A sparrow emerges from her hair and then another, and another. They hop down onto her shoulder, cheeping and peeping.

'So,' said Dave, finishing his tea and triumphantly screwing up his paper cone, 'nod your head frequently, yeah, say "I understand", maintain eye contact, say "uh-huh" from time to time; back-channelling that's called, making the person speaking to you feel like they're being listened to, even if they're not.'

'Uh-huh.'

'Good, yeah, you get the picture. Don't yawn. Don't pour the customer a glass of Ribena. Don't sing, beg, or tell long anecdotes, or pretend to walk down invisible stairs behind the counter. Yeah? Oh and, Joe… gesturing customers towards where they're already going. Don't do it. It's unnecessary.'

'Okay Dave.'

'It's all about providing a great service to our passengers, Joe. You're the face of Network Rail, an ambassador. Be bright, be optimistic. Don't be bizarre. That's the secret to life. Look at me, I'm happy, I'm normal. I'm not at all weird.'

'Right.'

'Right. And I tell you what Joe, because, I'll be honest with you, I like you. You're fucking strange, but you're alright. So, what I'm saying is, act a *bit* more normal, keep things smooth with Hayley, because she's trouble, and I'll get you a ticket for Dominus, yeah? Whadayasay?'

'Dominus?' asks Joe, distractedly. Dave's words are all reasonable, but the atmosphere of the man is dense and fatty. It is like talking to a large cube of expanding meat, suffocating, sweaty matter, squeezing your presence from the room. As Dave speaks Ursula opens her legs and a greyish snake with black diamonds on its back, slides out of her vagina, loops down onto Dave's shoulder, pulls back the flesh around its flat head and sinks its fangs into his neck.

'Mate, oh mate,' Dave blew out his cheeks, as he did when referring to good food, young, sexually active women and excellent half-volleys, 'We are talking the finest casino and strip club in the country, and I've been to a few. Skanky fucking dens the lot of 'em, but this, this is *class*.'

'Here? In Edding?' Joe wonders distantly where his voice is coming from.

'Don't be daft,' said Dave, 'It's out in the sticks.'

'Not really my thing David.'

Dave sighed. 'You get in what you put out Joe. Or, er, you get out what you put in… Whatever. Look at Clive. Look at him.'

They both regarded the CCTV screen. Clive was outside on platform one. Just standing there in what appeared to be freezing wind. Hopelessly.

'That man,' said Dave, 'is going nowhere.'

Joe looked from Clive, to the now empty shelf where, a few moments before, Ursula had transformed into the corner of a meadow, to the sign above the door, to his leg and then back again at Clive.

'I envy him,' said Joe.

∞

Lilly stood over her first prepared body. Dead John didn't look right at all. There was far too much lipstick, for a start, overall the colouration was unnatural, like his head had been cooked in brine, and there was a nasty cut across the cheek. Lilly felt sick thinking of his wife or children looking at the dead body, wondering where noble John had gone and who this pickled drag queen was.

The plastic curtains rustled and the rancid waters of Lilly's fear trickled into her gorge. Nina entered, crabwise, throwing anxious glances at Lilly. 'How did you get…' she trailed off as her eyes met the corpse. A lost customer… a bad review… sued, ridiculed… all vague fears orbiting the single unexamined dark star of money at the centre of Nina's universe. Her bottom lip started trembling, a reflexive sob bubbled up and broke into tears.

'Oh my God,' said Lilly, helpless, 'I am so sorry, I just, I didn't… I wasn't sure…'

'Did you wash him?' asked Nina, eyes clenched.

'No. Should I have?'

'Did you put the blue stuff on? The stuff in the bucket?'

'The blue stuff?'

'I told you, I *told* you. Oh my God. Again, *again*. We can't get anything right. Caaarl…'

She turned away weeping and wringing her hands. Lilly went to console her, thought twice about touching her—Nina didn't seem the touchable type—and instead pulled a tissue from her pocket.

She wanted to complain—she'd been given no training and there was no mention of the blue stuff—but Nina looked so pathetic, and she didn't really seem to be blaming anyone, so Lilly said nothing and stood helpless while Nina, with mounting theatricality, getting off somewhat on the drama, shivered and sobbed and moaned 'Caarrrllll…'

Carl entered and guffawed at the body. 'He looks like Lady Gaga's evil twin.'

'Carl ple-ase,' said Nina changing her 'please' mid-word from a 'this is no time for joking' please to more of a standard begging please, '…can you help?'

'Why? Put him in a pink leotard, he'll be ready for Eurovision.'

'Oohhhhhhh…' Nina tottered out.

'Oh for Christ's sake. Just wash it off. Start again.' Carl un-hooked the hose and blasted the body as if it were a piece of dirty machinery. Lilly stepped back and watched on, distraught, while Carl gave her a rough, pared-down caricature of the training she had been expecting.

'First hose 'em down, then slap on the blue stuff,' he nodded towards a bucket next to the sluice, 'then glue up the mouth and the cut—glue on the shelf there—then put a bit of blusher on… there, there…'

'Okay, okay.' Lilly, gratitude and relief warming her chest, hopped round to Carl's peremptory commands. He washed and scrubbed and daubed, inexpertly, but well enough. John began to look more John-like, less meat-like.

'When you get home,' said Carl, 'check YouTube. Plenty on there on making stiffs look lively. There's a guy, forget his name, Simon something, does great tutorials. Plays the guitar too, fucking amazing. Lincoln. Simon Lincoln?'

Carl chucked the hose into the sink, slapped the corpse's arse and left Lilly, once again, alone with John who now had foundation dripping off his face and, having been blasted with a hose, was laying in an odd position—bent double, mouth open, almost laughing.

∞

Joe had been held up by the scudding shoe of unwanted conversation. Going over old ground with a vaguely friendly colleague reminded him of a rust-speckled garden chair. Now though, he was once again free of work, free to do all the tiresome chores that employed confinement piled up in the background. He was tired, which always reminded him of roasted cashews (rather than alert, which was more of a metal mango), but he had a good amble ahead of him.

He had to call in to Zara on the way home to pick up a pair of trousers for Maria, but he couldn't find the street, so he asked a large, sweaty, pouty-lipped street cleaner who gave a long, overly detailed explanation, then kept calling Joe back to make sure he'd got it, adding drama to the explanation as if he were sharing prison escape plans—'opposite Costa, there's a bus stop there. It's right there. You can't miss it, it's right in front of you…' Joe, who always found it difficult to concentrate on directions any-way—after the first instruction he'd find himself caught up in the inner world of the speaker, wondering what kind of fetish they were prone to, or what they'd had for breakfast—left with the feeling that this man hadn't spoken to anyone for months and that he would soon be dead.

Joe emerged onto Edding High Street from the multinational clothing-retail company, wondering what the 'rib-knit loungers' were that he held in his hands. A pretty, perky, bony, Persian girl jumped in front of him.

'What's your name!?' she squealed.

'Joe!' said Joe, shocked into volume.

'Oh my God cool! I love your… what is it?' she pointed at Joe's Network Rail gilet.

'A gilet.'

'So amazing. Where did you get it?'

'Work.'

'Cool, cool, what do you do Joe?'

'Fart around.'

'That's so brilliant! High five!'

Joe left her hanging. 'Look,' he said, 'I don't want to give you any money.'

'Bye then!' she cried and immediately walked away.

Joe, feeling soiled, turned away from the charity whore and found himself in front of a vaguely recognisable, vaguely friendly face, possibly an ex-colleague, or school friend, or what? The face, on a middle-aged man's freckly spherical head, seemed to be looking for the same answers. It said, 'Hi, how are you?' Joe, confused, mixed up 'I'm fine' with 'hello' and said 'I'm hello,' but before he could correct himself, the face had vanished into the high street leaving Joe feeling just too big for the world.

He chose to go the wrong way home, just to see something different, and walked round the desolate out-of-the-way suburbs that crowded round Edding like clean, square warts, all nice little homes bundled together round green verges and birch trees;

newly built and yet already sad, exhausted. The houses looked like they'd been at work all day. There was rubbish everywhere. It was kind of poor, yet kind of comfortable, nice hard-working, middle-class Indian families, sleekly proud about *getting somewhere*, alongside totally aimless mind-corrupted teenagers, too boring to be dangerous. Joe remembered he was also supposed to pick up some milk and so popped into Londis which had padlocks on the cheese fridge. As he came out, a woman with a large rabbity head turned to a silver-haired man wearing a nylon suit over a rugby-shirt and said, with a resigned sigh, 'So now she just masturbates behind a glass screen.'

Joe ambled on, sensing that time was against him, but ambling anyway. The amble was a potent gesture of resistance. He would not be rushed. He would rather be hit by a bus than hurry over the road to avoid death. It was morally wrong to run, unless you had a crippled child to rescue.

He found his way into familiar streets, then into Gordon Road. He paused before the house opposite his own. They often put out plates of frozen meat on the window ledge to thaw, which Joe would spend all morning watching, hoping that a magpie would come along and steal it, which happened often, and yet they kept doing it. There was meat there now, a shoulder of lamb.

He crossed the road, slipped down the side alley next to his house into his back garden and then into his shed. Joe's approach to gardening was to buy random seeds, sow them wherever there was a space in the borders and see what happened. Around the roughly shorn lawn, between the chicken wire and slatted sides of their chicken coop, grew marigolds, cornflowers, slug-eaten cauliflowers the size of golf balls, well-tended burdock, blackfly covered nasturtium, mysterious and rather creepy star-shaped tulip-like things, two unidentified bushes that attracted bees, bright 'Bishop of Dover' dahlias that had grown deformed for some reason and were yellowing at the tips of the leaves, bent and broken geriatric gladioli, dock leaves, dandelion and massive hairy clumps of dead poppies shaking their seeds over the pebble-strewn area around the shed, from which Joe emerged wearing camouflage gear and rustling with branches. Around his neck was a pair of binoculars.

At the bottom of the garden, spreading over some garages behind the street was a large chestnut tree. Joe leapt up to the lowest, heaviest branch and pulled himself into the tree, making himself comfortable among the foliage and, while he waited, tracing the ridges and valleys of the bark with his nail. As the misty cloud-shrouded light of day dimmed, he checked his watch, and then looked through the binoculars. In the bedroom window of the house next to his, number 90, were their neighbours, Aaron and Moira, young adults—she with well-defined Greek features and thick dark eyebrows, he contained and carrying a layer of smug grazing fat from home-working. They were undressing.

Maria, a member of the informal, world-wide network of Neighbourhood Analysis and Diagnosis, spent a great deal of her home time speculating about the comings and goings of the either-sides and the over-the-roads. She could determine from daily Jollibee deliveries that the unseen teen over the road was a pale, bloated herbivore; from the fact that the man two doors down at number 92 put knee and elbow pads on to do his weeding and used a dustpan and brush on his lawn that he had been bullied as a boy; and from the muffled tone of conversation between Moira and her mother through the wall and from the way Aaron's interruptions to their daily lunch-chat were received with a kind of stiff condescension, that both women considered him a man of little consequence. Maria also noted, from the sound of their crockery being shelved, they had expensive dinner plates.

Joe wasn't interested in tittle-tattle, he preferred to secretly watch people have sex. It was more honest. And why not? It wasn't so much ogling the sex act which was enjoyable, more the combination of detachment, freedom and wrongness. It wasn't the same over the internet, you never really *saw* anything through the screen, but through the binoculars there was the fleshy vibe of it. From this tree, Joe had a good view of six neighbouring bedrooms, although only two regularly presented human beings mating; the cheerless humping of the dumpy Pakistani woman in number 84 and her bored boyfriend, and these two.

Moira turned round and leant out of the window inviting Aaron to take her from behind. Bobbing back and forth she watched, without interest, as the clouds purpled and the sparrows roosted and… what was that? She turned, vanished—Joe just saw her say something urgently to Aaron, pointing—then out went the lights. The last thing Joe saw, before dropping through the branches, fleeing through his garden, shedding his camo gear and noting that the old woman in the top floor of number 86 was nailing a plank of wood to her bedroom window, was the lean gleam of Aaron's own binoculars.

Joe had assumed that Moira and Aaron had seen him, and that they were now watching him scuttle home, but it was not a rustle in the chestnut tree that Moira had seen and that Aaron was now watching, but the telephoto lens poking out of the police car behind it, and, sat behind the camera, a police officer making notes on the spreadsheet open on his laptop.

∞

Neil was not looking at the couple, and did not know that he was now being observed. He was watching Joe, methodically making notes, and periodically swiping away at a fly which was trapped in the car with him.

Where conventional 'wrong' for Joe was a vague, abstract flicker with the same power to alter his behaviour as a mathematical formula, for Neil it was an immutable barrier as unignorable, and as impossible to step through, as a wall; unless knowing more about Joe's life, all the better to ruin it, was involved, or revenge for any of the slights that had been inflicted on him over the years. Then the door to his conscience was bordered and barriered with the psychic version of the yellow tape he so enjoyed sealing off any other crime with. For everything he did, everything, was to right wrongs. If someone, through sheer feckless incompetence gave him wrong information at a train station, making him wait at the wrong platform and miss his train, it was *justice* that compelled him to ruin their lives, ever so slightly, by getting their car impounded. And it was *justice* that was written under the no-entry sign on the door to his conscience. If he stepped too close, he felt anxious, because he knew that something unpleasant was there, behind it, but then he read the official notice—*justice*—and immediately, reflexively, stepped away; and then everything was okay again. There was no need to reason any of this out, any more than a deer has to analyse its flight from a wolf; in fact bringing anything he was doing to get his own back on those who inconvenienced him, or to disrupt the happiness of his brother, was breaking through the cordon, was opening the door to right and wrong.

This was how he could illegally access council records to see what Maria earned, or use police equipment to bug their telephone line and listen to actually quite boring day-to-day phone calls to the plumbers, or stake out their house on his off hours. It was also how he could send a fleet of hearses to Joe's house, or drop a fox from a local animal sanctuary off in their garden (didn't work that though; for some reason the fox ran away from Maria's chickens) or phone the stable that Joe worked at and tell them he was a known and convicted zoophile. It was also how he could harass queue jumpers, electric scooter users, litterers and people with loud annoying voices in restaurants by asking them for their papers, because of 'police business.'

There were two problems with all this petty espionage and sabotage and own-back getting. The first was that with the door to his conscience closed and cordoned off he didn't just have difficulty hearing the voice of morality, which whispered '*it is wrong to want to know every detail of your brother's life so you can better wreck it,*' but also to the voice of sanity, which told him that he looked and felt ridiculous spending so much time on this consuming task. The other problem was that, in Neil's case, the door to his conscience was, for some reason, never *quite* closed completely. He could still sense that something was wrong, and that something was always wrong, and the feeling made him distracted—which he dealt with by getting furiously angry with anyone or anything that got in the way of what he was doing—and nauseous—which he dealt with by ingesting quantities of Gaviscon. This was why his temper was often flickering so close to explosive, and easily touched off, and why his stomach was so bloated and farty.

Neil, like many people, believed that problems create irritation, when the reverse is true. Just as people who hate themselves find people to hate them, and people who are envious of others find people to be envious of, so Neil, forever wound up, would find things to wind him up, or they would be drawn to him. Litter thrown next to the river would seek him out, people who watched deafening television would choose to live next to him. If there was a young man on a train, listening to his tiktok hip-hop videos through the speakers of his phone, he would choose Neil's carriage. If someone with horrendous bodily odour needed a filling he would get an appointment on the same day as Neil and sit next to him in the dentist's waiting room. Neil's world wasn't just full of inconsiderate people, too insensitive to realise that the cost of their pleasure is the pain of others, the world itself, life itself, was inconsiderate. To Neil; specifically to Neil. Reality had something against him. This was why he had become a police officer, to defend himself against a careless, bastard universe.

'Fucking fly fuck off!' he screamed as he drove away, uselessly flapping his free hand around.

∞

Misery haunted Lilly on the way home. The luminous cheer she'd travelled to work with had gone. With Carl's help she had stumbled through the day, but the sickening feeling of botching such an important job, the distraught, horrified wife of John, who had been heartbroken to see the mascara her dear departed husband was wearing, the fact that two of the bodies were young suicides and the strange air of loneliness that Lilly often found she felt on the first day of work had all penetrated her innermost and now, as the grouts of Edding—the stick-thin scrags who charged along with such bizarre urgency, the single mothers heaving their children, their regrets and their shame across the Lidl car park, the nobody-fucks-with-me young black girls telling someone or other down the phone that nobody fucks with them, the squads of teenage pikeys, surrounded by a force field of invulnerability conferred by the psychotic uncles they could call on, swaggering down the road, the south Asians looking left and right for a business opportunity, all this wretchedness reflected back the hopelessness that had entered Lilly's bones, completely occupied her core, and again made the universe, from the very beginning of time, not much different from a broken bus shelter, a closed-down vape shop and a bin overflowering because the council were short staffed.

She stopped off at Tesco Extra, just off the long grotty Oxford Road and found herself arguing with a small, contained, bulldoggish woman on the customer service counter, 'Bev' proclaimed the name tag, who huffed and puffed about 'losing her break time' and tried to blame Lilly for everything that had ever gone wrong in her life. Lilly was asking for a refund for some phone credit she'd bought, but none was possible, for bizarre and complex reasons. The boss hovered over, a little Pakistani called Pahi, who explained 'the rules' which gave Lilly the feeling she was trapped in an experimental movie. All she wanted was a refund but this was impossible for reasons which led to other reasons, then other reasons, which eventually led back to the first reasons. Then Maggie turned up, another careworn working-class auntie type but, unlike Bev, with a face that bore evidence of human emotions. Maggie understood the situation immediately and started campaigning to give Lilly back her twenty quid, but Pahi wasn't budging, until Maggie, as desperate as Lilly, said, 'Look, I'm just going to give her the money.'

'Okay,' said Pahi, leaving with Bev, 'but your till will be twenty pounds down, and it will be your responsibility.'

'Fine,' said Maggie, handing over the voucher, leaving Lilly, all smiles and thanks, 'Oh you are lovely Maggie,' she said, 'Your family are lucky to have you.'

'I lost my son a few months ago,' said Maggie.

Lilly burst into tears, then Maggie started crying too, and so Lilly went behind the counter and they hugged each other and sobbed for life, the two of them, behind the Tesco Extra customer service counter.

When she got back home, Hunter was sitting at the kitchen table with a tight young man-faced woman — tight hair, tight lips, tight cheeks, tight polka-dot dress. She was talking to Hunter, or rather firing monotone, nasal word-bullets into his sleepy, pudgy face.

'I was asleep by ten,' she said, 'I was like oh my God, I can't *believe* I'm asleep.'

'*Hiiiiiii!*' cried Hunter.

Lilly wanted immediately to leave but swivelling away would be far too obvious. Unwilling to let any kind of sadness in her voice — which might invite a river of treacly insincerity (if they noticed it, which was probably impossible) — she summoned a friendly 'hello.'

'This is West,' said Hunter.

Lilly offered her hand, but West did nothing.

'West is a designer and influencer,' said Hunter.

'Half a million followers doesn't really count as an influencer in today's terms,' said West to nobody in particular.

Lilly said nothing, so West, believing Lilly to be rude, turned to Hunter, continuing where she'd left off.

'...and, anyway, there was this strange noise in my room. I was like what… is… that… noise?'

'Hahaha.'

'I kept looking around. It turned out to be the *kettle*. I was like what? I have a *kettle* in my room!?'

'Hahaha!'

Lilly had often noted that the barrier between laugh and not-laugh was, for Hunter, as it was for many of his friends, weirdly distinct. There would be laughter, sometimes very enthusiastic, and then, suddenly, there wouldn't be. Nothing of the laugh, the merriment, lingered into the next moment, each emotion in the conversation was sharply separated from all the others.

'That reminds me actually,' he said, 'I got to sleep last night and sometime later I heard voices. I was like what *are* those voices? I thought it *can't* be the neighbours, because they're all in bed. But then I thought it could be Neil's TV. I was like you shouldn't be watching TV at such a loud volume. So I thought shall I get out of bed and go and knock on his door? then I was like, no, I think I'll go back to sleep.'

'Hahahaha!'

'Hahahaha!'

Lilly left, went upstairs and knocked on Chiyo's door.

ॐ

When Chiyo Gehō was seven, her father, Tomio, found her squatting outside their house peering at a large, dead spider through his magnifying glass. The next day he returned from work with a three-dimensional detachable spider-anatomy model.

A year later, a family of seven, not too far from Chiyo's house, all starved themselves to death and Chiyo realised that it was possible not just for life to end but for people to choose to end it. She asked her mother, Junko, what other ways there were to kill yourself and the next day Junko bought her daughter *The Complete Manual of Suicide*, which had 650 five-star ratings on Japanese Amazon.

A year later, the family were watching a documentary on Beatrix Potter and learnt that the famous British illustrator had, when her pet rabbit died, boiled its flesh away in order to study its bones. Chiyo said she wanted to do the same thing when Hanako, their old cat, died and so, four years later, after Hanako had crept under the sofa to have a heart attack, that is what they did, the three of them pulling boiled flesh from the bones of the family cat.

Beatrix Potter was also, according to the same documentary, an expert in mycology, which Chiyo said she wanted to learn. From that day on she, Tomio and Junko studied field guides, went out to the woods every autumn to collect specimens and slowly amassed a working knowledge of Japan's five thousand species of mushroom.

Chiyo started a new high school and made as few friends there as she had in her junior school. It seemed to her classmates that Chiyo was on another plane, a 'deep thinker', but the truth was that she was entirely and terribly in the present moment, that she hardly ever thought, and felt more comfortable feeling her lips than letting them speak, and listening to the sound of voices rather than their content, and peering into the form of letters rather than reading what they said. If it were not for the intensity of her presence, people would have thought she was retarded, but nobody ever thought this. She was never teased at school, although this was not just because of her voidlike aura, but because the day she got a haircut with a single lock dyed white there was a thunderstorm and Mashu Higaki (who secretly fancied her) was hit by lightning and his eyebrows blown off.

Chiyo did not do well at high school, except in art class. When her kindly geography teacher, Kawabata-sensei, who knew she was smart, asked her why she didn't try harder, she said she wasn't interested. When he asked her why she didn't have any friends, she said she wasn't interested. He took it upon himself to visit her parents, expecting to find devil worshippers, but instead was welcomed by two of the warmest-hearted people he had ever met, who explained to him that they didn't care about Chiyo's school grades, didn't care whether she had any friends and didn't care about her future. They said that care was not love and Kawabata-sensei found, after talking with them for two hours, that he agreed with them on every point. From then on, he secretly helped Chiyo graduate, falsifying her grades and protecting her from the opprobrium of other teachers.

Chiyo went to art college, where she specialised in anatomically perfect drawings of animals, illustrations of mushrooms and large Francisco de Holanda-inspired paintings of the cataclysm. Her skills did not go unnoticed, and, through the connections that one of her tutors had, a path opened up to working in one of Japan's largest manga studios, but when she returned from a three-week holiday in Hokkaido, where she had gone alone one October to conduct personal research into the rare mountain mushrooms of the North, she surprised everyone by calmly informing them of her decision to go the United Kingdom. Her final words to her parents were these:

'Mother, Father, I will never return to Japan. You will never see me again, but you will know here (she pointed to their two bellies) that I am well. In fact, here (she pointed again to their two bellies), you will discover, in exactly five years' time, we were never apart, that we are fundamentally the same entity.'

A year later she was in Edding. She didn't work, nobody knew how she paid her rent—independent wealth was assumed—or even what she did all day. Most people avoided her, but Lilly found Chiyo's presence restful and her oracular comments always seemed, although they made little sense, to help; which was so much better than the usual thing of being told clearly what the problem was and how to solve it, which was of no use at all.

Chiyo didn't seem to have any friends or want to have any. Since Lilly had lived at 41 Dace Road she had heard men have sex with Chiyo, agonised croaky grunts coming through the walls, although she'd only seen one of them, a trim sixty-year-old man; gentle and mild looking, not a perv; but still, an unlikely choice.

When Lilly knocked on her door, Chiyo, in her minimal white world, of futon, wardrobe, chest of drawers, singing bowl and what appeared to be a large, original, black and red Rothko painting, or uncanny look-alike, was squatting, as if having just landed. She straightened up and walked to the door.

'Hi,' said Lilly. Chiyo nodded, returned her low kotatsu table and knelt on the floor. Lilly, a little unsure, closed the door and did the same, both facing each other across the walnut surface. Chiyo poured Lilly a glass of water.

Hunter's muffled laughter rose through the floorboards. Chiyo looked down, seemingly through the floorboards. 'I want to stab him with the eyeball,' she said, focusing, beaming her juju down there, before slowly returning her gaze to Lilly, to take her in fully, the care-strictured brow, the slump around the shoulders, the human pain of the girl.

'What happen?'

'I'm so tired Chiyo.'

'Did you touch the dead body?'

'Touched, washed, shaved, talked to.'

'It talked?'

'No, no, I did the talking.'

Chiyo nodded slowly. Lilly went to speak, but stopped. She took a sip of the water. It was hot.

'How many dead people there?' asked Chiyo.

'Thirteen? Fourteen?'

'All dead?'

'All dead. They were all alive, a few days ago, and now they're all un… alive. But I can't, couldn't, think of them as things, even though I'd never met them. The first one, John, I do think he was actually there, helping me choose his goatee, but in the end, I let him down terribly...

'What temperature was John?'

'Temperature? Cold.'

'Like turned off radiator?'

'Erm.'

'Like winter seaweed?'

'Probably more like that.'

'Or like the ray of sun, before he touch earth. The cold sun, in empty space?'

'Uhh…' Lilly turned to the painting, 'is that new?'

'Empty,' said Chiyo, although it was unclear whether she was referring to the painting, or to the sun, or to death.

'It's… er, powerful?'

'Not there.' Chiyo stood up and walked over to the painting. Her face was exactly eighteen inches away from the canvas. She gestured Japanese-style, palm-down, for Lilly to join her.

'Come, come.'

Lilly got up and joined her.

'Now,' said Chiyo, 'see.'

It was a large black rectangle, bordered by two stripes of deep, ember red. Lilly looked up at the strip at the top of the painting, then down at the bottom.

'No,' said Chiyo, 'not look at, not look at. See, see whole thing.'

Lilly's attention softened onto the picture. She let herself blend into the shapes, strangely familiar, yet strangely strange, unworldly, something you might find in a forgotten temple in a forgotten forest. The black and red of the paint became blacker and redder, until there seemed to be more black and red than paint, a purity of blackness and redness, a totality pouring into Lilly's consciousness like blooded flood waters pouring into a town; diabolic, darkening red, overwhelming and awful, super-dense, ardent black, burning light to nothing, burning red of the unseen core, bleeding through fissures in obsidian black, volcanic black and brooding red, endless red and black immeasurable, red of nightmare and black of the nothing from which nightmares come. It engulfed Lilly, filling her, with no room for her, for anything else. What little of herself that still remained wanted to pull itself away, but could not, her will had been extinguished by the vast, dreadful, stillness of the red and the black, and the dread lack of everything else. She whimpered, as she did in nightmares, when she couldn't move or cry out, panic, yet the panic too was suffocating, just a trembling horror in her throat, guttering now, nearly extinguished, nearly, nearly nothing…

…she fainted backwards, and as she did the awful void let go.

'Euuuwww!'

Chiyo stood composed next to the painting as Lilly staggered away, colliding with the back wall, legs weak she lurched out of the room onto the landing where, shaking and sweating, rising and falling within, as if stoned and drunk, as if her inner eye was on a nauseating rollercoaster, she grabbed the bannister. Breathe, she told herself, breathe, deep breaths. She sank down to her knees, gathering herself, returning to the real. The chipped paintwork on the baluster, the dank smell of the unhoovered carpet, and the corner where it was coming away from the skirting board, all this was so reassuring, as reassuring as her hands and legs and heaving chest. She inhaled and exhaled, and again, and… could hear music.

It was drifting from Neil's door, at the end of the corridor, slightly ajar. She listened, a piano, so sad, and beautiful, a tremulous synthetic organ over the top. She closed her eyes and saw a middle-aged woman, sitting on the edge of a railway bridge, the one on Haversham Road, looking sadly down at a passing train, and felt the suffocation of the suicidal, the need to escape, at all costs. She saw Tesco's Maggie in her kitchen, cooking beans, which her son always felt she didn't cook enough—the bean should dissolve at the edge, merge somewhat with the sauce—and she felt the sword of loss enter her. She saw a group of oddly pale people in a meadow, greeting a naked young woman who is stepping from a crushed microlight, and she felt the electrifying immensity of their love, not heavy, but creepily beautiful and so perfectly empty.

And all to the otherworldly music floating from Neil's door. She approached his door (ignoring the neat Post-it note, squarely in the centre with 'drink? 07:00, 12.10.18'). She could see Neil standing at his desk, listening to the music.

∞

Neil's expression, listening to the music, was a mixture of condescension, disgust and amusement. So amateurish, so cheesy, so childish; nuts! Some charm, perhaps, but oh dear oh dear, oh dear. The curiosity which had seized him at Victor's house, that had compelled him to 'borrow' the laptop and listen to the music on it, faded away. He shook his head. What was he thinking? How could this plinky-plonky nonsense help him with his musical woo? The man was obviously a fruitcake, and obviously fruitcakes don't make good music. Look at Bruce Springsteen, look at Chris Martin, look at Brandon Flowers; all sane. They were successful businessmen. Even that guy from Radiohead ran a profitable cheese farm. If Lilly didn't like 'music from the world'—whatever that meant—then she was obviously mistaken.

'That is so beautiful.'

Neil jumped, sweeping forward and stabbing the music off.

'No, no, leave it on, please,' cried Lilly, 'It's lovely.'

'Is it? Is it?' said Neil, panicking. He put the song back on and Lilly approached the laptop.

'Did you make this?' Perhaps Neil's fear was really that of exposure, that she was glimpsing a carefully guarded innerness?

'Yes I did,' he said. 'Absolutely... damn right.'

Lilly listened and Neil watched Lilly listening, a gentle smile playing around the corner of her oh God, so beautiful red lips. 'I...' she turned to him, eyes soft and bright with the loveliness of the song, 'It's wonderful. It's so... accepting. I didn't know you had it in you. I thought... I mean, no offence, but that other stuff, you know the one about structural engineering, it's, erm, you know...'

'Oh that! Oh yeah. Nonsense! I just do that for spare cash. This, um, is where my heart is.'

As he said this, an almost impossibly high falsetto wail rose over the instrumental track, a long ruptured lament, 'ooooooohhh-hhwoooooowowowowooooooo.'

Lilly's eyes widened. 'That's *you*?'

Neil forced the word 'Yep' through his squeezed neck. 'That's my heart,' he said, minimising the 'now playing' window just in case the name of the artist should be visible.

'I had no idea.'

Neil cleared his throat, 'Well, I, you know, I don't, it is very personal, I don't like to share it with many, erm, people but with you...'

The track came to an abrupt, codaless end.

'Wow,' said Lilly. 'Can you play another one?'

'Another one?'

'Yeah. What else does your heart say?'

'Erm, well, errr... another one...'

The titles of the files were not promising; *Turd Trumpet, Dinomarch 9, Royal Wedding on Galthusunian Beta, Boogie Cream in my Brain Pipe, Don't Fiddle With My Balls.* No, No, No, God, No. *The Dads of Industry, Babylon Chicken, Putting Bits of Me into Bits of You, My Simple Love Song* ...ah, yes! *My Simple Love Song.*

He double-clicked, '...this one for example.'

Synth gurgles and human wails, weird wibbly-bibbly sound effects and sampled machine-gun fire, karate-chop grunts and the dirtiest parpy-parpy trumpet blasts erupted from the speakers. With relief bordering on ecstasy Neil noted that, in the middle of this carnival of nightmares, was a sung melody that a human could appreciate, and that the voice, although black man resonant, still sounded thin, and like his own.

> *'I'm lost, I think.*
> *I made, a stink.*
> *I need, a shrink.*
> *My head, feels pink.*
> *Come back and show me where you went.*
> *My road was straight but yours was plenty bent.*
> *I know I said I knew but that's not what I meant.*
> *I meant I knew I didn't know, but now I repent.*
> *But there you are, where've you been?*
> *I doesn't matter coz I'm still keen.'*

The chorus was an octave higher and so loud the torn edges of distortion could be heard in the recording.

'The price of rice.

The squid defender.

Plentynice.

Your opposite gender.'

The finale of the song was frightening, demonic. Neil nodded along, trying to hide his wincing, his horror; surely this would appal her? But no, Lilly listened in rapt astonishment until the final, apocalyptic, power chord slammed down on all the tracks.

Silence.

'You wrote that for me, didn't you?' she said.

Neil, face strained, exhausted, nodded.

'Oh God Neil, thank you,' she burst into tears, head down. Neil, unsure, stepped towards her. Should I touch her, he thought, as she opened her arms. She's opening her arms—Jesus Christ, I'm being let in. Beside himself with delight and charged up confusion and oh my God thank you, thinking now or never, he lunged in for the kiss and Lilly, weeping, surrendered, null; let him.

It had been a long time since Neil had kissed a woman. Lilly's full lips didn't quite feel right. They were soft and receptive, but in his panic and joy they seemed to Neil inert, puffy and pillow-like, *things, there,* rather than the sensate joining point of two communicating creatures. He worked at them, pushed his tongue in, then wondered if that might be too forward at this point, and withdrew, but then thought, look, here I am kissing a girl who's letting me kiss her, so come on Neil, what would Prince Philip do? He'd get in there, he'd masterfully twirl Lilly towards his bed, so come on Geb, come on.

She seemed terribly passive, not really helping much, not throwing him around, which would have been better, but nevermind, it all seemed to be advancing, her cardigan was off, so that was a good sign, lift up the skirt or undo it?

'Neil, there's no need to rush,' whispered Lilly.

'No, no, thank you,' he said, but there was the possibility that at any moment she could change her mind, never forget that women are like that, they'll swipe back the jewels right at the last bloody minute, so it's imperative to go as fast as possible in order get as far along as possible, but oh these poxy zips, why do they make them so *small*? They should get The North Face to design zips and clasps for women's clothing, chunky, yes, but they never jam.

'Neil? Neil?'

'What? What? I'm almost there.'

'Neil really, let's...'

'Ah ha!'

The dress was unzipped, but now the bra had to be overcome, and oh God, thought Neil, why didn't I buy a bra and practice—I was going to, but... oh... oh sweet Lord...

Lilly had taken her bra off. *Finally*, thought Neil, finally, look, there they are! *The breasts!* He stared at Lilly, overcome. He had seen breasts before, live ones, but none were anything like as good as these two. He hadn't seen nicer nipples, even in porn. He wanted to tell her this was the best moment of his life, far better than becoming an officer of the law, but it might seem a bit previous, better to stick to the task at hand, all the signs were looking good.

'Neil,' said Lilly.

'What, right...' yes, thought Neil, enough gawping at the breasts, let's move on. He opened his bedside drawer, took out a condom (placed for easy access), checked the expiry date and ripped it open. As he fiddled away with his penis, working fast, concentrating hard, like changing a tyre in the rain, Victor's music played in the background. The pounding wibble of *Dinomarch 9* had segued into the colossal timpanis, exploding volcanoes and 36-piece digital horn section of *Royal Wedding on Galthusunian Beta*, unreal really, thought Neil, making love to a warped triumphalist orchestral wedding march for extraterrestrials, but there you have it, Lilly likes it.

He was inside her. He couldn't feel very much, but mission accomplished. Nothing can stop me now! He moved his attention from his own sense of victory, to Lilly's arches and curves and roundnesses, up to her face, which looked so beautiful, if sort of quiet and even rather sad. It was so good, although hard to tell how she was feeling, but nevermind, nevermind, deal with that later.

'Thank you, thank you, thank you, thank you, thank you…' he murmured.

'Stop thanking me Neil. It's not necessary.'

'Oh, uh, Lilly, Lilly… I've waited for this for fourteen… no, maybe sixteen months. Before that I was interested in a girl at work… called… erm…'

'Please be quiet,' whispered Lilly, a tear emerging from the side of her right eye and sliding into her hair.

'Okay,' said Neil, 'I'll get…' he didn't finish the sentence, as there was a lot to concentrate on. It was time to really get down to business.

Lilly turned her face away from him, as he was looking quite ugly now, sort of frog-like, but all red and furrowed up. Neil's bedside lamp caught her attention.

'Is that lampshade from Ikea?' she said quietly.

'It's a Jättendaaaaaaaaaaaaaggghh… *Neil Geb!*' He whelped, like a dog that's just been trodden on, and collapsed onto her.

Lilly burst into tears.

'What's wrong?' said Neil, pulling himself up onto his elbow. Lilly's eyes were closed, her face wrinkled up.

'What's wrong?' he said again.

'I just feel like something is utterly wrong inside of me.'

Neil disengaged. He wasn't sure what to say. What do you say to that? It wasn't very complimentary, but she'd obviously had a very hard day. 'Shall I throw the condom away?' he said.

'Do you want to keep it?'

'No. I'll throw it away.'

He sat up and dragged the duvet from Lilly, who pulled it

back to cover herself. She was still sobbing, quietly.

'It's okay,' said Neil, 'I don't mind what you look like.'

'Thanks.'

He found his mint green underpants and put them on, feeling a kind of relief as he did so, then stood up, hesitating, condom in hand, not sure what to do.

'Shall I put the television on?'

'If you want.'

'Deal or no Deal is on.'

'Oh well in that case, yes, put it on.'

Neil loped over to his massive television, picked up the remote and brought Deal or No Deal, in all its gameshow glory, into the room. He carried the condom over to his voice-activated 'induction trash can' and said 'open.' Nothing happened.

'Open,' said Neil, 'Open. Open. O. Pen.' He turned to Lilly, 'this has never happened before.' Then back to the bin, *'open, open!'*

'Leave it Neil.'

He wrapped the condom in a tissue, gently placed it on the bin-lid, which then opened, sliding the tissue towards the floor, which he neatly caught and popped into the bin before it closed again. Nice! He came back over to the bed victorious, and as the commercial break came on, and an advertisement for a sit-in bath for the elderly started, he felt quite ready to explain to Lilly how this was a stupid investment as the rubber seal around the door would be sure to perish and by the time it did the company would be bust and there'd be nowhere to get a new one. You'd have to have one specially made in China.

∞

Maria, glass of wine in her hand, scrolling through the website of the local French baker, sat in her front room of Peruvian rugs, eco-friendly cotton throws, little blobby ceramic sculptures and distressed wooden picture frames. Either side of the blocked-up open fire hung stained glass mobiles and a Swedish diffuser blew sandalwood-scented water vapour over the exposed floorboards. Maria felt that the limited palette of whites and greys created a cohesive balance.

She selected, from the site, two salted caramel eclairs and a kouignette for evening delivery tomorrow then reopened the application form she was working on to move up to level 4, grade 9 Advanced Practitioner, and a salary of £48,000. She was working on the second part of the 'suitability for the job' section; 'what personal qualities can you bring to this role?'

'I am mature, professional and serious.' she wrote. 'I can handle just about anything life throws at me. I am a skilled multi-tasker and communicator, able to tease out and respond to the deepest needs of my clients. I understand and respect client confidentiality and never overstep the boundaries they set, unless I am instructed to by a grade 10 or above. I am patient under pressure and fiercely accepting of diversity.'

She read it over. Needs work, she thought, frustrated by her inability to really get herself across in these things. No one believes you if you tell people you've been through hell and back to become the woman you are, that you understand life in ways that other people just don't, that you're patient and perceptive and understand others as unique, three-dimensional individuals. She sighed and took another sip of the Chablis. I need to go to an antique market, she thought.

'What shall we do this weekend?' she called out.

'What?' Joe's voice came back from the kitchen.

'I said what are we going to do this weekend?'

'I dunno. Maybe something outside?'

Maria sighed. 'Could you be a bit more precise?'

There was a long pause, then Joe's response floated through. 'Dunno. Ask me in January.'

'Why? Why?'

'I've noticed I'm more specific in the depths of winter. In autumn everything still seems a bit hazy and unreal. A hangover from summer I suppose.'

She sighed again. 'For fuck's sake,' she said to herself.
'What's this?'
'What!?'
In the kitchen Joe, munching a large flapjack, catching the crumbs in an under-cupped paw, was standing in front of a fridge-poster, newly pinned. It looked like the kind of thing you'd see in a doctor's waiting room. The headline read 'Stop! Think! Word!' Underneath that; 'Words are literally real: they can KILL PEOPLE.' Then, underneath that, a list of words. Those at the top of the list were in a 'red zone', those in the middle, 'amber', and those at the bottom, 'green', graded by 'safety'.
'It's a new thing,' Maria shouted, guessing correctly, 'for work.'
'But I don't understand. What is it?'
'It's a racism league-table. It reminds us who is the most offendable.'
At the top of the list were Jews, Muslims, Trans-people and People of Colour. Joe followed the list down, past Irish, Gypsies, Chinese and Indians, past Americans, Chavs and Germans to the bottom of the list, where it said 'Joe.'
'Why is my name here?'
'What?'
'It says here...'
He looked again. It didn't say Joe. It said 'Gingers/French.'
'...oh. Nothing.'
He tipped the last of the flapjack crumbs into his mouth and sighed. He'd felt out of sorts since getting home. The fridge was reassuring though, in its mute thing-ness. Joe liked things. They might not work, but you know where you are with things, they're always there for you, always here and now for you. He patted his mmmming friend, then returned to the living room.
'Do we really need that poster?' he asked. He stood in the middle of the lounge, edging sideways.
'Only a white man would ask such a stupid question. You don't know what it's like doing something important. These poor people, they get *so* much abuse, they're *so* fucking scared Joe.'

Joe didn't really like the way Maria said 'fucking'. Not that he minded swearing, but, he couldn't quite explain it to himself, but it was as if she didn't deserve swear words. 'I'm pretty worried myself,' he said.

'It's not the *same* Joe. I deal with children, every day, who will never make anything of themselves.'

'Even more tragically,' said Joe, brightly, 'they might not make nothing of themselves either.'

'What does that mean?'

He had reached the edge of the room, just next to the edge of the sofa, but tilted away from it, towards a blank space of wall. He opened his mouth to speak, but said nothing.

Maria, tight, returned to her phone. Joe remained in the same place, looking at the fire, but not directly, sideways, with his head twisted far to the side. Maria glanced up, looked back down at her phone, and then looked up again, irritated.

'What are you standing there for?'

'I don't think I've ever stood here before, not like this.'

She tried to return to her phone, but could not settle within. As usual Joe was hovering, like a groggy bee, in her mind, and had to be let out before she could settle down.

'I was just wondering if the smoke,' he said, 'rising out of the chimney here, has something to do with us, whether it expresses, you know, "our thing".'

'I don't want "our thing" floating across Edding.'

'Oh you wouldn't have to worry about that. You'd need to be a smoke expert to know what we mean, we as smoke.'

But what smoke? The chimney was bricked up. Maria sighed a relationship-weary sigh and put her phone down.

'Why must you spend your life fannying around?'

'I've spent forty years fannying around. I'm not going to stop now. I'm almost there.'

'Where Joe? *Where?*'

Joe met her cold, hard, blank eyes. He felt skewered, pinned, that feeling of all feelings that he hated most. He would do anything to escape the skewer of definiteness. 'Nowhere,' he said, quietly.

'What *is* your problem?'

'My head keeps falling off.'

'I'm serious, what is your problem?'

'I am a fridge.'

'For Christ's sake Joe. I'm asking you seriously. Please tell me, what is your problem?'

'My leg really annoys me.'

'This again!'

'I can't help it. I just,' he looked down at his leg in despair, 'it wants me to fail.'

Maria held her head in her hands, wondering what she had done to deserve this. 'Oh God, must we?' she muffled into her palms, 'I've had an awful day Joe.'

A heavy metallic 'rolling' sound. Joe looks up. A cannonball is rolling along the corridor. He jumps, and turns to Maria—whose head is also a cannonball.

'Aggh!'

Maria jumped up. ''What!? What!?' Like many women entering their forties she had started to add 20% to any expressions of surprise.

Her head, her real head, had returned. Joe, spluttering, sat down on the sofa…'eugh… errrr…'

'Oh God Joe, what's wrong? What is it?' There was concern in Maria's voice, although most of it was for herself, how she would deal with a psychotic episode.

'Nothing.'

Maria peered piteously at Joe. He needs help, she thought, he needs a professional. Not me though, another one.

∞

The next morning, Joe, wearing his work uniform, took a taxi out to the outskirts of Nutbourne, where his mother, Margaret, lived. The car was a massive BMW, which made the bird-boned Sri Lankan driver, with a blanket over his legs, look like Mother Teresa in a space station. Joe often took a taxi to see Margaret, and every time it was a different, very expensive car driven by a different but very knackered-looking South Asian. Few seemed to enjoy talking, but when Joe asked this little man what the gurgling, foreign voice on the radio was on about, he immediately leapt into an enthusiastic, high-pitched monologue.

'That one pawnshop Wembley he give money for story, that one story India, India London he meet, he come London, very famous, he meet and he say he in big fight, so he in big fight, that one story, he give money, he *hundred pound* and that one he say have party and *big* man he come he find woman and he say, give fire, he come fire next house, he next next house, tree inside he…' On and on he went, in a dry, squeaky voice, swerving all over the road as he got more and more into the incomprehensible tale. Joe managed to work out that 'he' stood in for every English object and subject pronoun, but it didn't make the monologue any clearer. The man's voice was musical though, as rural-seeming as his driving, so Joe just let it wash through him, until it seemed to take on an entirely new meaning and the man was actually telling him an ancient Hindu myth about an unhappy demon gatecrashing a lesbian-only party, stealing a hundred pounds, then tumbling out of the window to find himself surrounded by fire engines because the tree's neighbour was stuck in the cat… The two stories ran parallel for the whole journey until the taxi driver slammed the brakes because he'd missed the turning into the road that led to Margaret's and now had to reverse, but was blocked by another car behind. Joe turned to see a bald head in the car behind.

'Okay, he okay,' the Sri Lankan chirpily warbled, checking the bald man in his rear-view mirror, 'he no angry, he okay, no problem, no problem because he have *big knife*.'

'*You* have a big knife?' said Joe.

'Big knife.'

'Can I see it?'

'Secret,' whispered the little man, 'secret.'

Joe paid and got out. Margaret's detached brick house was set back from the nestled and anaesthetised suburbia of Nutbourne. After Neville had died and Ursula had left home, the farmhouse and workshop that Joe had grown up in had been repossessed and they had moved into council property, a remarkably well situated ex-gatehouse, which would now sell for three quarters of a million, and which the council—the housing company, that is—had been trying to get its hands on ever since.

He knocked at the door, above which a wooden sign read 'Kom Ombo,' and waited until, as usual, it opened a crack and a well-built, but hunched over—and hunchbacked—Filipino man wearing ragged shorts, a Hawaiian sunset shirt and flip-flops opened it. His dark impassive face instantly lit up when he saw Joe.

'Oh, ah, ooh, hello sir!'

Louis, Margaret's manservant, was in a permanent state of high-energy, super-attentive, glee. He never stopped giggling, or jerking, or shuffling from one foot to the other, or nervously cleaning. He spasmed and bowed as Joe entered an expensive and tasteful front room of worn green Aubusson furniture, Arts and Crafts ebonised oak screens, a small dining table covered with a silk Lyonnaise brocade tablecloth, a dark red, lacquered, Chinese armoire, a sphinx dedicated to Sesostris, six silver candlestick holders, a television from the 1970s, an ancient Egyptian headrest and resplendent sun mask and, in the corner, a triangular cabinet full of pale blue and green Iznik ware. Around the room were several blue and white Chinese flower vases in which blushing anemones, spidery nigella, powdery gypsophila and various other ragged, velvety flowers dangled. On the walls hung, in tarnished gilt frames, Pre-Raphaelite-style paintings, but of scenes from Egyptian mythology. The muted haze of a nearly sunny morning spread a lazy light through the dust of the room, covering all this faded phantasmagoria in a kind of blessing.

They walked through the house, talking, Louis' speech continually punctuated by sniggers and giggles.

'How have you been sir? Oooh hoo, ha ha.'

'Please call me Joe, Louis.'

'Yes, sir. Your mother is wellll… but, ah? sirr?'

'Yes?'

'She burnt her head on the toaster, so I nailed it on the wall.'

'Her head?'

'Ooh! Hahaha! Noooo sir,' he lightly slapped Joe's elbow in a 'silly billy' gesture, 'the toaster!'

Louis indicated the toaster. It was, indeed, now eight feet off the ground, nailed to the lower landing.

'Nice solution.'

'You think so sir? Phew! I am very glad. But, uh, sir? I think we need a better solution. She is very dangerous now.' He clenched his hands and pouted with a pre-impact wince.

'Okay, leave it with me.'

'She loves fire!'

'Does she?'

'Yes,' said Louis, whispering now as they had reached Margaret's bedroom door, but still ooh-ooh-ah-ah giggling, 'I am afraid she is going to blow up!'

'Okay, okay, Louis. I'll think of something.' He knocked on the door. 'Mum?'

A cracked, well-to-do voice came from the other side 'Is that you Joe?'

'Can I come in?'

'Yes, come in.'

Margaret was old, with long white hair piled up on her head, strands hanging round her ears, her strong face, with its wide cheekbones, fine arched eyebrows and large dark eyes, was still beautiful and dignified, commanding respect from people who dealt with her; but there was now a vagueness to her gaze, and a delicate elusiveness, as if she were retreating from the world, into a comfortable but darkening chamber.

She sat bolt upright in a double bed, the walnut headboard of which was a large masonic pyramid, with a carved eye of providence floating above the apex. The room continued the theme of the rest of the house, except here it was both worn and better cared for; William Morris wallpaper, a vase of roses and mandrakes on a Sheraton cabinet, finely embroidered shawls hanging over high-backed Charles Rennie Mackintosh chairs, a curious medieval painting of St. Christopher with a dog's head carrying what looked like two Christs, and, leaning against a mahogany wardrobe, a stack of classical music albums (Richter's Bach, Furtwängler's Beethoven, Böhm's Mozart and other German conductors conducting German composers).

Louis closed the door, backing away, bowing and giggling, before, in the last microscopic moment before the door shut, his mien of frolicking servility dropped into stony seriousness.

Joe sat on a wicker chair stuffed with ostrich feathers. His mother threw him a tremendous glance, like an exultant nabob.

'You alright then Goosey?'

'*This* place today is very pleasant,' said Margaret pointing to a small pine desk, 'but *that* one *there*,' she pointed to an oak dresser in the corner of the room, 'yesterday that was an awful place.'

'Oh? What happened?'

'Well, it was not right.'

'You mean it was untidy?'

'Yes, well, no,' she shook her head, 'It was absolutely tiny.'

'Tiny? You mean it was smaller?'

'Yes,' said Margaret, quite put out, 'it was awful yesterday because it came up tiny. Absolutely tiny.'

Joe sized up the desk. 'It looks okay now. I think it's definitely bigger than yesterday.'

'Mmm... well yesterday it was an awful place. You know, it was so, so,' she hunched forward dramatically whispering, '*tiny.*'

'It certainly looks bigger today.'

'Well, I'm not so sure.'

'Let's leave it for now, see how big it is by the time I leave.'

'Okay then,' said Margaret, clearly full of doubt.

'I saw Ursula yesterday.'

Margaret threw her hands up. 'So did I!'

'Did you? What was she wearing?'

'A pilot's outfit.'

'She had clothes on then?'

'Oh yes. I didn't think of that. Yes. And she hadn't aged a day.'

They sat in silence for a while. In some way, thought Joe, Margaret, in her confusion, was becoming not less dignified, but more. It was as if, surrounded now by a world that was coming away at the hinges, haunted by ghosts and fragments of ghosts, she had said to herself, somewhere in her marshlit soul, 'well, if magpies and gardeners are to be interchangeable, and numbers are to take physical form, and little square-limbed Aztec men are to crawl over the walls, and Shirley Bassey is to get in bed with me, all of this is very difficult to understand, in fact it's sometimes quite appalling and nightmarish, but if that's the way it's to be, then I'm going to deal with that, I'm going to do my best and let's not see if I can't enjoy myself at the same time.' Her eyes sometimes darted left and right, anxiously, or they screwed up in disgust or incomprehension for no apparent reason, but for the most part she smiled gently and nodded gently and accepted a world now upside down and inside out.

Joe remembered the last words his father had said to him; 'When I met your mother I was high on mushrooms.' Neville had always wanted to be a smith, but he started off building marquees for rock festivals, and one year he worked at the Isle of Wight music festival on Ashworth Farm, owned and run by Margaret's father who, self-described 'disciplinarian' as he was, had forbidden his sixteen-year-old daughter from visiting the festival or even leaving the house. With the help of a friend, she had escaped one night, climbing down from her bedroom window and, using pilfered red-pass 'hospitality' tickets, gained access to heroes of the sixties independent music scene; Sly Stone, Miles Davis, David Gilmour and Tiny Tim, all of whom were, while Hendrix played a twenty-minute improvisation of *Nine to the Universe* on the main stage, in the middle of a table-tennis tournament in the green room of the VIP area, settling their pop rivalries over the ping-pong table. As Miles Davis delivered a rattling smash to Tiny Tim, who returned it with foppish elan, Neville had approached Margaret, mesmerised by the scene, and said, 'fancy a game after these guys have finished?' And that, at least as Neville told the story, was how the Geb family had begun. They had eloped, Margaret's father had died of a massive stroke, leaving her brother his estate on the Isle of Wight and Margaret enough money for her and Neville to set up as gunsmiths in Nutbourne.

Margaret was an aristocrat, with the lack of pretension of people who don't need to pretend, and the taste of those who have been raised before walls covered in centuries of judicious theft. She was open-minded, because she could afford to be, a tolerance of difference founded upon sexual disinhibition. These qualities formed, as they sometimes do, a link between her heart and that of her working-class husband. Their marriage foundered not on the free and easy atmosphere of her attractive house, but the cold, hard heartless ground upon which it was built.

'Mother?'

'Yes?'

'Would it be okay if I tied you to a piece of rope?'

'Well I don't know dear. How long?'

'Long enough.'

'Would I be able to sit in the garden?'

'Yeah, you could go into the garden, and the bathroom, and, erm, half of the living room, but you couldn't reach the kitchen.'

'Would it reach the canal?'

'Probably not.'

'What if I needed a snack?'

'Erm. We'd put a little fridge in the living room.'

Margaret considered the idea. 'That would be okay, yes dear, if you want.'

'Alright,' said Joe 'I'll come back after I finish work.' He nodded towards the pine table. 'How's…?'

'Oh it's almost come up normal now.'

'That's good. You give me a call if it comes up tiny again.'

Margaret smoothed down her shawl, then looked out the window.

'I wonder why Ursula was wearing a pilot's outfit?'

'She must be a pilot.'

'Yes, that's probably it.'

'I wonder if Neil saw her?'

'Who's Neil?'

'Patricia.'

'Oh, Patricia, she doesn't see anything.'

∞

Neil sat in his squad car, iPad on his knees with a well-formatted spreadsheet open. The title was 'Justice,' with columns such as 'Person,' 'Crime,' 'Time/Place,' 'Impact/10' and 'Retribution.'

Anyone who had ever harmed or insulted or hurt Neil, in any way, was listed with the relevant details. Joe's name featured heavily, with a list of high scoring 'crimes' from their youth, such as ruining his chances of becoming an Olympic walker, deliberately shrinking his favourite jumper, the 'wolf moon' one, and humiliating him in front of his first girlfriend, Amanda Jeffries, who had come round to visit Neil and found Joe and Margaret eating bowls of soup with no utensils, just plunging their faces into the bowls, then coming up for air and, lips smeared in Tesco's own-brand pea and ham, singing *Greensleeves*. Amanda was alarmed at first, then disgusted, then she made her excuses and ran off to tell all her friends, leaving Neil with one of the greatest pains a self-conscious young man can feel, shame at his own family in his own home.

Various other co-workers were listed too, old schoolmates, flatmates, clerks and shop assistants, and random people in the street, each one followed by a few suggestions for revenge. Even Lilly was there, twice, for offhand comments she'd made which had touched off his hair-trigger self-esteem, although the retribution sections said, beneficently, 'forgive (until further notice)'.

It helped being a police officer; there was a lot of power that came with the job, access to information and useful technology, but none of it was of any use if the 'criminal' in question was a fellow officer, particularly if it was his boss, D.C.I. Gaynor Babcock, the massive headed, grim-lipped, hulk of a woman whose long shadow cast itself over Neil's working world. He had just finished having an humiliating interview with her, and now was diligently putting her down in the column of wrongs, but what retribution was possible against such a powerful woman? His fingers quivered over the keyboard.

'You are a police constable Geb,' she'd said in her broad Welsh accent, arms folded across her desk, 'You see that number on your epaulette? You see that's all there is? A number. No chevrons, no pips, no crowns. *Nothing*. That means you are at the bottom of the cabinet. One little flick, and you'll fall out; off the big boys' shelf, and back into the toy box where you came from.'

Neil had murmured that he understood, although he could barely concentrate. He could hardly focus on anything. His eyes floated all over the shop, skidding over noticeboards plastered with pictures of wanted people, maps outlining the extent of criminal organisations, pushed-out chairs and paperwork. He felt there might be a text for him, he thought about Lilly, he realised he should be paying attention, he wondered whether the next Spiderman film would reintroduce Sandman—yet none of this came to full awareness. All his thoughts, feelings and impressions were just a fragments, as if his will were a tissue in the wind, twitching this way and that, without any intelligent momentum of its own, following restless gusts in a supermarket car park.

'I wonder if you do understand Geb. Because this morning I received a complaint that you'd been watching a couple engaged in sexual intercourse, from your patrol car, through binoculars.'

Neil had fuffed and blustered and, outraged, totally denied the charge. 'I was watching my brother up a tree,' he'd said.

'Why?'

'I'm staking him out ma'am.'

'Why?'

'I'm afraid… I can't… I mean… I think… that is, I have reason to believe… that he is a grave threat…'

'To…?'

'To civilisation.'

'I see. Listen very carefully Geb. You are not to use police equipment for personal use. And you are not to confiscate the property of vulnerable members of the community either. You know what I am talking about. And you are not—and this is the last time I tell you—to fall asleep in a lay-by while on operational duty. You are not to lie about your rank, bully new recruits and tell them to pick up your dry cleaning, tell sloppily dressed school children they risk a jail sentence, order baristas to smile more authentically, alienate the Zoroastrian community or swagger.'

'Swagger?'

'Yes, swagger Neil. Why can't you walk like a normal person?'

'I am like a normal person ma'am.'

'That is exactly what I'm afraid of.'

She had told Neil that this was his final warning. He had wanted to explain to her his concept of *total justice*, but he could read her body language, her massy slab-like shoulders weren't open to reason, so he'd moped out and consoled himself with the spreadsheet.

I'll finish it later, he thought, wrinkling his nose at a whiff of excrement.

∞

The large old woman laid out on the anatomy table, Gail Dillon, had drowned in a puddle. She'd keeled over in Lawrence Street after a heart attack and landed face down in the gutter as people had stepped over and around her. Eventually, someone had stopped, but it was too late. Now she was dead. Lilly had cleaned her up, made her up to look reasonably undeathlike and stitched up the area around her left collar bone—poorly, but well enough. Next to the body was a bloody pacemaker in a kidney dish.

'Look,' said Lilly, 'I did it. It's not easy cutting machines out of people's bodies I can tell you, but apparently they blow up. Did you know that? I didn't.'

She held a hand mirror over the woman's face. 'Do you like it? I spent all night researching what morticians actually do. I suppose I thought… I don't know what I thought. I suppose I didn't realise you'd all come in so very… dead.'

She put the mirror down. Gail looked like a nice person. You could tell, even with dead people, although the individuality of their faces was, in death, blended with something… what was it? Something that seemed common to all people, something oddly reassuring, as if, in the return to matter, to the mud we come from, *everyone* was in some way there, on the slab.

'I actually,' said Lilly, distractedly wiping up, 'I slept with Neil last night. He's my flatmate. I don't really fancy him, but I think I misunderstood him. He might actually be some kind of genius. And, well, he was, he was there for me. But… but then we had sex, and, it wasn't enjoyable at all. It was… I just looked at the ceiling and wondered how I'd ended up in Neil's bed. Then he came, and shouted his own name, and I burst into tears. Then we watched Deal or No Deal.'

Lilly gently touched Gail's cold fingers.

'What do you think? Did I make a terrible mistake?'

Carl came in, plastic strips dramatically jangling behind him. He stood, bandy legged, palms out, excited, like he was announcing a special guest; 'We've got a pickup at the railway. A jumper!' then he left.

Lilly looked at the dead woman.

'Thanks for listening.'

8

Dave Davage drove down the M16. He'd had a bollocks morning. First off his wife, Denise, had lost his lucky pair of pants and he'd had to give her a telling off, then Alice, his daughter, had been in a fucking strop because he'd missed some stupid school thing. It was the fucking derby, but he didn't tell her that as she wouldn't have understood. Then he'd tried out a new 'pump and dump' that he'd seen recommended on 'punterpal', the prossie rating-and-review site he used. The girl, this 'Dani69', had a long horsey face with grey teeth and acne, nothing like her photo-shopped pictures. She gave him a borderline friendly welcome, made him have a shower, and gurgle some mouthwash, then she did a close-up inspection of his flaccid penis in a brightly lit room, spraying alcohol all round the bell, then she hugged him without much enthusiasm, told him French kissing was thirty quid extra—thirty!—and at this point Dave was ready to walk, because for this price point he could go into London and do any number of top-notch service-providers, but he had the horn, so he went through with it, and, to be fair, she did have an impressive rack—bubble butt, bolt-ons (but tasteful) and nips like Scammel wheel nuts—but it was like having sex with your sister, no passion whatsoever. He got the impression that she didn't want to be in this game at all, which is not just unprofessional, it's probably unethical. Anyway, she took a load, without flinching, so it ended up okay, but it left him with a bad feeling. He'd popped into the Rising Sun for a swift one before work, but even that had been sour because he'd bumped into fucking Hayley who was having a day off and he had to have a conversation with her, which was boring because, like so many women, she wasn't interested in a) sports b) horses c) crime d) politics, and when he told one of his fascinating stories about the years he'd worked on the tracks she just looked at him with a gormless smile on her face, so he thought fuck that and downed his pint and headed off to Edding station, where he was supposed

99

to finish the review he'd actually already finished yesterday but those bitches in head office expected him to be there for two days, so even though it meant another depressing conversation with Marsh and Geb, he'd have to show his face.

'Cunt! You *cunt!*' he screamed as some moron cut him up on the slip road north to Edding. Why was the world *full* of cunts?

∞

Passengers shuffled past the window. Clive at the ticket counter wearily watched them come and go, with an absolute lack of interest. The drear rut of his life had scarred deeper and deeper into the sterile clag of the world. He woke, every day, and let himself roll, painfully, with spastic efforts, down the same ruined channel, to the same little plastic stairway that took him, via troubled dreams of being lost in foreign cities, back up to the top of the machine, and down again. He felt like the Playful Penguin slide he'd had as a kid, what a thing to give to a child, but then realistic, because that's your life, isn't it, to lurch up the same stairway, then down the same nauseating slide, then back up the same stairway, forever and again, until you died. At the start it was bearable, because the runners were smooth and there was a nice pair of tits at the top, and a line of Charlie perhaps, but over time it all rusted and perished and before you knew it the playful penguins had nothing to play for, and just rattled painfully all over the shop, with a weird, anguished fixed grin on their little penguin faces, because if you stopped smiling, a big fat fist would come down and batter you, but then the machine just stopped working anyway. Fucking game. Not a game at all. Just a lump of plastic that tricked you into smiling at it like a loon for a few years before you realised you'd done, and could have done, nothing.

Joe at the admin desk watched the closed-circuit television screens. A train had arrived and one man was pushing his way past people getting off. Joe spoke into the microphone.

'You! Man pushing to get on before everyone else has got off. I can see you! I know you really need to get on. Everyone really needs to get on. Just be patient.'

He clicked off and stood up, still watching the screen. The man looked around, perplexed, then resumed his struggle.

'I can't help thinking that guy's got it coming,' said Joe.

Clive pulled a very rapid, almost subliminally quick, pouty face to a customer just leaving. 'We've all got it coming,' he said.

'I think,' said Joe, 'I might go out and embrace some passengers, weep cleansing tears of sorrow with them.'

'Why don't you do some actual work?' said Clive, sharply. He meant it.

'Work?'

'Yes, work. Like everyone else. Like normal people who live in this world, the one we actually live in.'

Joe deflated. 'Okay,' he said, sitting down.

He turned on the microphone. 'This is a station announcement,' he said, 'There has been a platform change. The 2:19 to London Paddington will now arrive on platform four. Passengers waiting for the 2:19 to London Paddington please go to platform *four.*'

Everyone on the platform three screen started heading up the stairs to change platforms. Joe clicked 'off.'

'I'm doing it Clive. I'm working.'

'Good.'

Aaron and Moira approached Clive's ticket counter. Their son James, a handsome six-year-old boy with large glasses, stood behind them as they spoke. Joe, seeing them before they saw him, shrank behind a computer monitor.

'Two tickets to London' said Aaron.

'I don't see why it's all down to me,' said Moira. They were clearly mid-row.

'I just…' said Aaron out of the side of his mouth, 'God, we have to make a decision and I'm asking your opinion, that's all; why does everything always have to be this big drama?'

Moira stepped back, hands on hips. 'Me? Me? I'm the dramatic one? Are you joking? I can't believe it.' She turned to Clive. 'Who, here, is being unreasonable?'

'I don't have enough evidence to make an informed judgement,' Clive drawled. 'but chances are it's you now, but ultimately the cause is his bullshit.'

The couple were silent.

'Single or return?'

'Return,' said Aaron, chastened.

Meanwhile, Joe had turned his attention back to the CCTV. A train was approaching. He had plugged the desktop, along with an experimental music site which he'd opened up, into the intercom. A fierce synth version of Ride of the Valkyries rose up over the PA.

Clive sighed, a heavy, final sigh, and turned round. Joe's eyes were glued to the CCTV. People on platform four were looking around, listening to the music, smiling at each other. The train behind them, over the tracks, glided into platform one and the doors slid open. Joe, waiting for just the right moment, hit the 'on' switch. 'Hello again everyone,' he said, 'It's me. You know I said the Paddington train was coming in to platform four? You're never going to believe this, but that's it there! On platform one!'

Everyone tensed in a moment of unbelieving.

'Better run,' said Joe.

The passengers belted towards the stairs. Aaron and Moira also flew through the ticket barriers, dragging little James.

'I'm guessing about twenty of you will make it. Because the driver will close the doors in, ooh… thirty seconds?'

A pulsing swarm of people flowed along the causeway, trying to make their train as Joe stood, intercom in hand, taking in his 'work'; commuters, scuttling like ants in an exposed nest, across the screens. He clicked 'speak' again. 'I am the sun. I am the stars. I am the universe. I am the one who made himself into millions…'

The train doors closed on the suspended pain of the crowd, held up by the effort of getting to a train now, as it pulled away, never to be got, and fell—upon Joe. They ran into the station, leaping over the barriers to get to the ticket windows.

'… I am very, very lonely.' He put the intercom down, just as the first fists of furious passengers struck the control room glass.

Clive turned away from the wall of glass-pressed passenger flesh. Something seemed to have softened in him. 'I've got some very powerful downers in my coat pocket,' he said.

'Go on then.'

Clive rocked serenely over to his coat while Joe checked the door to make sure it was locked, then picked up a ringing phone.

'Yes… Okay… Really…? I see… Okay… Could you be a little less specific? No, no, less, *less* specific… Right… Yes, thank you… Thanks… Bye bye…'

He put the phone down. Clive handed him a pill and a cup of water in the baboon-head mug, which Joe took, lifting the intercom mic to his lips.

'I'm afraid all trains have been cancelled until further notice,' he said. 'Also I've taken some rather strong tranquillisers so the office is going to close as well, as will my mind I think, and that's fair enough isn't it? Clive, could you close the windows…?' Clive pulled down the Network Rail blinds, screening the people out from the room, so that only their shadows, horde-like, quasi-demonic, could be seen at the counters. It was strangely beautiful.

'Someone somewhere has died, is dead,' said Joe, 'although you probably want a bit more than that, do you? Well, there's been a death on the tracks.' The two of them were seated on the floor, leaning against the back monitors, sipping whiskey from Clive's hip flask. Joe, mic in hand, expressed his thoughts to the station. 'A suicide it was,' he said, 'The body was torn in half by 185 tonnes of steel. I mean it—torn in two. Three, actually; the foot flew off and got lodged in the exhaust pipe. Chunks of the ex-person are now being gathered up by the authorities.' He paused, 'A classic dangler's death,' he said to himself, 'not so bad really, although hemlock is preferable.' Then; 'sorry did I say that out loud?'

He turned to Clive, 'these are pretty pokey.' The chemical fudge was warming his abdomen, spreading painless muffle-ment into his chest and neck and face. Clive nodded, a mixture of conspiratorial comradeship, forgiving cynicism and gentle, anxiety-suppressed mellowness on his pressed, pale face. Joe went on speaking. 'Hemlock,' he said, 'is actually a very good option if you ever fancy offing yourself, much better than us-ing a train to smash yourself in three pieces. Hemlock is easy to find, it looks like cow parsley, but it has little red spots on the bottom. It looks deadly, you get a deadly vibe from it, and um, Socrates, he had it, remember? It's a nice way to go, painless, you just get more and more numb until you're just… nothing. Although, um, come to think of it, that's what the world does to us… doesn't it? Hemlock life, spreading through the bodies, deadening it out, doing away with us until we're all just… sitting here… Clive… you okay? Clive's okay, don't worry about him. Um, yes… suicide. One of my best friends committed suicide, about a year ago… or two now… He'd had enough. That's what his suicide note said. "I've had enough." Just that. To be fair, he *was* a temp. Temping's enough to finish anyone. I dreamt about him actually, not long ago, I dreamt he was being prepared for embalming and burial. Two other friends were getting ready for the embalming when, this, figure came in, uh, a woman, and, uh, she was carrying the body over her shoulder and, little thing she was, and she dropped it. The body rolled out of the canvas shroud and looked up at me, smiling. I let out a big gasp then I burst out laughing. "Edward, you're alive!" I said. Right before my eyes he transformed into a newt, or amphibian-like creature, and scuttled off into a wall. Not sure what that means. Umm. But I woke up feeling very positive about the day… Ikea are selling bowls called 'Enthusiasm,' apparently, Maria told me that this morning… although they've sold out… I'm not inter-ested either… she complains to me, Maria, really getting into the complaining, like she's been building up a good complaint all day to unleash on me. Well, I'm not… I just can't get into that with her, so what I do is… I offer something general, a general comment like, um… are you interested in this? Okay, well… she's complaining about a colleague who won't listen to her and I'll say, I'll say… "yeah, people know just where not to look…" and then she'll look at me, eyes kind of glassy, and say, "yeah, yeah, yeah," but there's no connection there at all, no, she's just cueing up the next volley… Do you have that kind of thing happen to you…? Because it happens a lot, I find, everyone's just in their own little world, nobody is communicating at all, there's just… conversations are just… sort of, tiptoeing around inner landmines, trying not to blow your legs off because you've brought up a subject they can't deal with or because you've said something ever so slightly out of the ordinary, even a little bit… people get so angered by strangeness. Just sitting in a different way enrages them… Just complete mutual misunderstanding… it's no wonder we're all killing ourselves… Although God knows I'm just as guilty as anyone else… I'm difficult, I know I am. Maria told me I can't be trusted… I think my relationships tend to be deep and lasting because they've all had to overcome the fact that I've been in them… I find, to get through the day with Maria, I have to either pretend to love her, which works surprisingly well, or, I tell myself that I'm going to split up with her tomorrow, or she's only got a few days to live, and then I enjoy the whole day with her and love her completely, then… that way… I find undiscovered upswells of love that not only get me through the whole problem, but make it so pleasant again that I don't want to split up anymore, so I suppose… you guys should try that… I think… if you assume that you are going to split up soon, with life… and we've only got a few years left, then, you know, we can love the world, even this shithole, love it… love it… uh… I'm not talking about joy, or pleasure, that's an easy peach, I mean… wholeness… a much rarer fruit… I worship Ogma… my eyes hurt… Do you ever get the feeling you've been looking at too many things? I think things are overrated, they're all a mess, I know that, the world is a mess, but… I can't be bothered, I just can't… It's just, mmm… easier to drift…… oh, hello Dave… Dave's here… not sure why he's dressed as a Roman… he's… Dave's my boss, he's here for my monthly review I think… Might as well live…'

Joe's voice is getting quieter and quieter and drearier and slurrier. It is now a distant, faraway thing, coming from some other place. The people too have stopped hammering on the windows, their faceless faces, pressed against the glass, are melting away, becoming nothings. The world itself is passing away, at the edges. Joe murmurs two words, very quietly, 'imbecile gods.'

Clive was gently snoring, having also melted away and only Dave, hard, real, practical, slightly maroon David Davage was standing. His rough voice, blending with the barbiturate-infused fog that the large armchair of Joe's mind was gliding through, reached him as if from a dream.

'You're fired.'

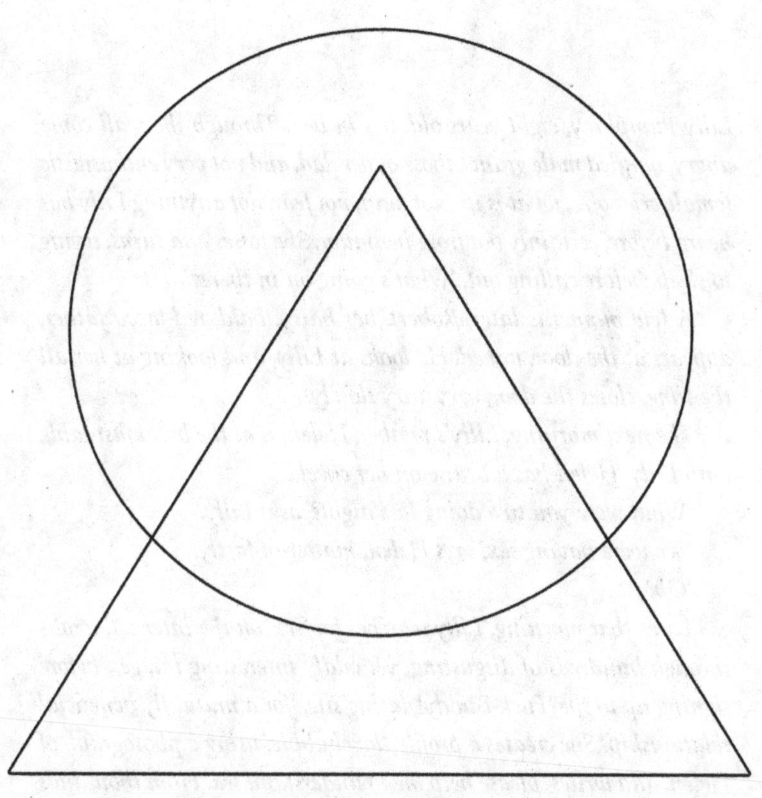

PART TWO
A World of Frozen Curry

Lilly Pumphrey, eight years old, lies in bed. Through the wall come angry, muffled male grunts, those of her dad, and not very enthusiastic female cries of… what is it? Not pain, not fear, not anything Lilly has heard before, certainly not from her mum. She tosses and turns, trying to sleep, before calling out, 'What's going on in there?'

A few moments later, Robert, her hairy, bald, red-faced father, appears at the door, naked. He looks at Lilly, and looking at her all the time, closes the door, very, very slowly.

The next morning, Lilly's mother, Helen, is at the breakfast table with Lilly. Helen has a bruise on her cheek.

'What were you two doing last night?' asks Lilly.

'We were having sex,' says Helen, matter-of-factly.

'Oh.'

Later that morning, Lilly searches for 'sex' on the internet, scrolls through hundreds of disgusting, yet oddly interesting images, before signing up to the 'Fuck-Buddy' dating site, 'for a mutually beneficial relationship.' She creates a profile, 'lovebubble,' using a photograph of Helen, and writes 'please help me to understand sex.' From thousands of responses, which appear almost instantly, she chooses that of a handsome-looking man called 'Max' who explains to her that 'sex feels like your whole body is in the centre of an exploding sun' and then says they should meet to explore the matter further. Lilly agrees, realises she is supposed to be going for a swimming lesson and instantly forgets about the whole thing.

Later that day, Helen comes home and finds the computer still on, 'Fuck Buddy' still open, along with Max and Lilly's conversation, which she reads—the expression on her face turning from confusion, to astonishment, to horror—and dashes out of the house to intercept Max.

They collide at the clock tower, Helen, angry, afraid, confused, Max, tall, angular, utterly assured. They talk, they get to the bottom of what has happened, Max, gently smiling, speaking with languid assurance, says that he has fallen in love with her, Helen, with her image. He tells her that she is beautiful, assured, complete, an absurd daytime soap opera seduction, yet almost impossibly compelling. He asks her to dine with him, just a glass of wine and by the end of the afternoon Helen is putty in his hands, under his spell, giggling, demure, loose.

They drive, in Max's Jag, to his massive Regency estate. Helen laughing, at one with life, Max brilliant, beautiful, enigmatic, yet reassuring. They wander around the geometric garden, designed in imitation of Versailles, and Max asks her if she would like an hour-long orgasm. Helen says yes, and he leads her to a tall mahogany box, 'based,' he says, 'on Reich's orgone accumulator, but with modifications.'

She steps in, the box glows a rich gold, she begins murmuring and moaning, then laughing, then crying out, rampant, wanton screams of unbridled sexual joy. The box glows brighter until, as she climaxes within, a blinding flash of light erupts from the box, blowing Max off his feet, leaving a curled, charred, exploded wooden husk; and no Helen.

A wind had picked up. Joe, working the central pedestrian area of Edding, was sweeping fallen leaves, mixed with carrier bags, cigarette papers, sycamore seeds, chocolate-bar wrappers, betting slips, and nitrous oxide cannisters, which were hurtling around the shops in blustery arcs. Every motion of Joe's broom pushed the leaves into the maelstrom, or out of it; it didn't matter.

He ambled along the streets, pulling his cleaner's cart, picking up the odd banana peel or tissue or condom (which never seemed to be used; a mystery, why do people just pull condoms out of packets and throw them in the street? If they were used, that would be weird too though; why would two people in love joyfully rub their bacon together on the one-way system that led to the trading estate? Unless… they *weren't* in love?). He had switched to the witch's broom that he'd made a few days before, working away in the backyard, tying birch twigs together, while Maria, succumbing to despair, had watched him from the kitchen window, watched him work so hard at being nobody. And indeed this was, Joe had found, one of the great perks of being an urban hygienist; you *were* a nobody, so nobody looked at you, nobody cared. His dark blue overalls and high-viz gilet, with 'Hale Valley Cleaning' written across the back, were more effective than an invisibility cloak, enhancing his powers of detached voyeurism.

He approached a car at the end of street, gently rocking back and forth in time to the groans and ecstatic sighs of a couple, dimly perceived, in the steamed-up interior. Joe pattered around the car, sweeping and brushing, bobbing up and down, mat-ter-of-factly going about his business, while the couple within, unconcerned, continued humping. So perhaps this was where the condoms were coming from, slung from windows during a post-coital drive off?

Joe took out his notebook and wrote down; 'Everyone ignores idiots and geniuses, everyone is annoyed by idiots and geniuses, everyone laughs at idiots at geniuses. Are idiots geniuses, or is it that people just can't tell the difference?' He paused, aggressive-ly chewed the end of his pencil, and then wrote down, 'I am an idiot.' His handwriting was appalling, unreadable, a mix of cap-itals and lower-case letters, all over the lines, all over his child-ish drawings. The page he had just written on had a sketch of an old man he had seen that morning; impossibly broad head, close-cut crew cut, deep lines across the brow, thick angry eye-brows, grey flannel tracksuit bottoms pulled up almost to his nipples and a T-shirt displaying a massive cat's head which, due to Joe's inexpert sketch-work, looked like it was emerging from his trousers. Underneath this, five sentences;

- There's a fine line between subtlety and imaginary subtlety and that line is both subtle and imaginary.

- Both subtle paranoia and mild starvation can produce the notion that onions are ever so slightly watchful, ever so slightly "on to you".

- This tangerine and tinned asparagus salad has something of the flat-footed bench salesman's chortle about it.

- At first I thought it was a magpie but when I looked again I could see clearly that it was a tiny flying killer whale.

- Exposure to rapid-fire superficiality can leave victims with a per-forated, weeping soul.

Joe vaguely considered himself to be a writer. As a young man he had fallen in love with Jack Kerouac and Charles Bukowski, with their flowing evocations of spiritual freedom and exultant loneliness, and he had embarked on something of a cultural quest, reading any books which might help him feel the same fiery urges that the Beats had had. He'd read Miller and Ginsberg and Burrows, Lawrence also, and he'd tried to write like they did; but nothing had come of it. He'd looked into ascended masters, off-world entities channelled by human hosts and the Galactic Council of Thoth, but that didn't seem to lead anywhere either. He felt he had something inside to release and express, but he also felt he had been born crippled in some way, with an atrophied will, a very basic 'can't-be-botheredness.' Writing anything other than a few ludicrous notes was as much an effort as anything else was. Meditation and mindfulness were a grind too, and didn't help with management, or with Maria's moods. In the end it was easier and more enjoyable to watch the boxing or take his gun—he'd saved a long slide Glock 24 from Neville's workshop just before it was sold off—and go out shooting pigeons.

He wandered on, until he reached the pedestrian walkway under the B259, where he pulled out the rolled-up AI self-adhesive vinyl posters he'd had made, and, leaving his cart back at the town side of the flyover, strolled under the roaring motorway, all the while peeling off the backing of a poster which he then placed on the mottled, greyish, graffiti-addled abutment at the piss-reeking far end where pedestrians took short cuts to the council offices and job centre. The posters read 'Free Concert: The Absentees!!! Electro-funk disco sensation. Edding Town Centre. Sat. 14th.'

Joe had, after getting fired from Network Rail, looked around for work in the usual places. He'd had one mysterious interview in a large empty shell of a building with a hyperactive shiny-suited man with a sculpted 'high fade' haircut and restless beady demeanour, called 'Clin,' who, while being suspiciously vague about what Joe would actually be doing, told him that he'd be doing it all the time. The 'interview' had been conducted, standing up, on the doorless, windowless, walless top floor of the newly-built block, which was intensely cheap-carpet-smelling and stiflingly hot, as there was no air conditioning and no way to open any of the floor-to-ceiling windows.

'We've all got lives to live outside of work,' said Clin, sweating, 'whether it's looking after your kids, playing the cello or sailing. That's why we've implemented a flexible 24/7 shift pattern, so that *you're* available when *we* need you and *we're...*' he trailed off.

'You're right,' said Joe, 'regular hours are so restricting aren't they? I didn't realise how liberating 24/7 availability could be.'

'Yes, we're all 24/7 entrepreneurs now, that's just how it is. I'm always on duty whether I'm in the car, by the pool or at the tailor's. I've never taken a day off in my life so why should my employe... partners, my partners? I mean, think about it, the whole country would grind to a halt!'

'Hahaha, yeah. Next they won't want to work at all!'

On it had gone, with both of them getting hotter and hotter until they'd almost passed out. Clin had shaken Joe's hand as he got back into his air-conditioned Audi sports car, told Joe the job was his, and driven off. Joe had come back the next day—and nobody was there except a street cleaner, the one who had so enthusiastically given him directions to Zara. This man, whose name was Lee Riddley, was slumped on the floor, passed out and breathing with difficulty, so Joe had called an ambulance and gone with him to the hospital where he'd discovered that Lee's only 'friend' in the world was his boss, Irving Bone, who'd turned up at the hospital shortly after Joe and offered him Lee's job. Joe had taken it, temporarily, assuming that Lee would get better, but a week later Lee died.

Joe was the only person at the funeral, although Irving turned up later, while 'Wings of a Dove' was playing, and whispered to Joe that he could go permanent if he wanted, and Joe had accepted because it seemed that's what Lee would have wanted.

Irving Bone was a small, neat, middle-aged man. He wore a carefully tended beard through which poked two suspicious, small, but somewhat bulging, red eyes. He carried a plastic holdall and wore deck shoes, because 'they are non-leather, cheap and comfortable.' He 'expected more of this job,' although he'd been doing it for eighteen years, since leaving his previous job in water treatment, 'because water people are dark.' Irving didn't smoke, didn't drink, didn't eat meat, had no family and didn't trust barbers, because they 'are all incapable of paying attention.'

'What are you doing?' he asked, in an oddly gentle and high-pitched voice. He had, as Joe had been putting up his poster, quietly padded up behind him. His gait was surprisingly graceful, like a fastidious panther.

Joe, startled, turned round. 'Oh, hello. I was just… wondering if spiders yawn.'

'No you weren't. I was watching you. You were putting up posters. On company time,' said Irving, hands clasped in front of him.

'Technically I'm having a break.'

'Do you want to take that up with management?'

'You are management.'

'I mean the next level.'

'Not more than the average amount… of wanting… to take it up with the next level, which, on a world scale, is probably very small.'

Irving's feelings towards Joe were complex and contradictory. On the one hand he pitied the poor man, who was so sanguine about his ignorance and lack of focus. Irving had several times tried to engage Joe on topics of import, such as Brexit and re-incarnation, but talking with Joe Geb was like trying to find your soap in the bath. Nothing ever seemed to quite get fixed, including Joe himself, who was just drifting down and down, into a world where pigeons ate puke.

Pity alternated with annoyance, but there was a point in between this oscillation when Irving felt something else, something which he interpreted as a kind of amazement but which was actually a form of envy that he could never admit.

'You're not paid to think about the world, Joe,' he said, 'you're paid to clean it. And when I say clean it, I don't mean spending half an hour scrubbing a single slab of pavement with a wire brush. I mean picking up litter. Just that.'

Joe nodded in a 'quite right' way, bent down, picked up a tiny piece of fluff, and carried it off towards his cart.

8

Neil was tired. He had spent all night hiding microphones in trees around Edding, and then had got home to listen to his neighbour's baby saw through his brain. A lanky, tired-looking Indian programmer had bought the whole four-bedroom house next door and moved in with his pregnant German wife. She had given birth and they were using the room next to Neil's as a nursery, so Neil spent all night every night listening to the screams of a baby who has landed in a home that is happy and cheerful on the surface but underneath all is bleak and mechanical.

After another night of enduring someone else's problems, Neil didn't need his own; an argument with Lilly which was now being conducted, gripped and tense, in the kitchen, underneath Hunter's telephone call.

'As soon as he said he had arranged a zero's-themed party,' said Hunter, 'I knew he'd gel with my friends… Hahahaha! Every word of that sentence is sort of slightly disgusting! …Seriously, you know what, putting this project together, I've really grown as a person…Yeah, yeah, yeah, yeah, *yeahhhhh!* …No, not yet, but it will soon, I can just feel it!'

Chiyo stood, long and black, with her slim, well-postured back to the room, at the frosted-up kitchen window. Lilly, in a tealy-green pinafore dress and hoopy stockings, and Neil in his police uniform, were seated at the table facing another kind of frost. The two of them ate heads down, talking into their toast.

'I just don't know where the inspiration has gone,' said Neil, 'That's the thing about creativity, you have to understand, it comes and goes. Look at Elton John. His 2008 collaboration with Bernie Taupin, "The Captain and the Kid", was his last critical and commercial success. The soundtrack to Gnomeo and Juliet just wasn't in the same league.'

Lilly sighed, and looked up. 'I'm just saying it's strange. You wrote twelve amazing songs and then, since you've been with me, nothing. Nothing at all.'

Neil looked up, then away, the old, awful sensation of exposure trembling in his jugular notch. He often had the feeling, rarely examined or acknowledged, that other people could see straight through him. This in itself was painful, even without the further fear that they could see things he himself could not. This was why he found it almost impossible to make a move on women, because first of all, they would *know* he was making a move on them, everyone would, and second of all, they would, as he showed his hand, see… see… but see what? Neil never got this far, because that would mean looking at his own cards, but the fear was on him, Lilly was not looking at him, but *into* him. He clamped down on his feelings, unconsciously folding one arm across his chest, to deflect her psychic laser beams.

'No, no, no, don't worry about that…' Hunter went on, his one-note voice cling-clanging round the room, '…money is no problem, no problem. No, no, I'm not a businessman, I'm a culture-maker.'

Seven years before, 'culture-maker' Hunter Braff had left his five-bedroom home in Canterbury, bought by his mother, a television producer, and his father, an ethical equity fund manager, and had gone to Oxford University through which, and with a little help from his mother, he'd got a job at the BBC, where he'd worked for five years, until he'd started to feel constrained by the stuffy institutionalism, and so, as he explained in an interview with The Guardian, he'd decided to 'explore the ground floor of the British economy, taking temp jobs in warehouses and call centres.' A delicious feeling of having no real responsibility was 'a Petri dish for ideas' from which grew his plan for a completely new 'culture of health,' based around a completely new concept for LifeLine, a smartphone app that would supplant the 'hegemony of the medical profession' forever. Hunter had done next to nothing to develop the tech; his job was running the business. His partner, 'programmer and anarchist', Prig Raschke, had been the 'boffin'. The question was how to get the funding to turn the dream to reality? 'Somehow', he told the Guardian, 'we came through the year of living on air and secured £500,000 of start-up investment.'

Chiyo, still drawing on the window, glanced back at Hunter as he prattled on, her eyes deserted and dark, then she turned to Lilly and Neil, who were now wordlessly washing up.

'Don't wash the glasses last', whispered Neil, 'or they'll get greasy. Wash them first, when the water is clean. Didn't you read the Post-it note? I err…' He looked around. 'Where is it?'

'I took it down', said Lilly.

'Why?'

'I've taken them all down.'

'But why?'

'Because we don't need them. Either we already want to do these things and don't need notes to tell us, or we don't want to do them and notes won't make us.'

Neil looked around again. They *had* all gone. He couldn't believe he hadn't noticed.

'Where are they?'

'They're in the bin.'

Neil pulled out a clump of Post-it notes, pasted together with potato juice and butter drips.

Lilly, a wave of hopelessness overcoming her, whispered, 'Jesus, Neil', and left the room, while Neil sat at the table untangling the bright yellow squares. He read through them.

- This fridge seems to have a funny noise. Anyone else noticed?
- The bathroom smells of sex.
- Someone is overfilling the bins. The plastic bag then splits when you take it out, or it cannot be tied properly and the overfill has to go into a second bag.
- Everyone okay with yellow Post-its? Other options: pink, green and orange.

- Not sure why someone has watered the cactus?
- Problem? Tea drips. Solution? Cupped hand; thus. (with a well drawn icon of a hand; Neil had a talent for finely realised diagrams)
- Have you seen any strange shadows on the lawn?
- My pocket SAS survival guide has been repositioned next to Rosemary Conley's Hip and Thigh Diet. Why?
- Radiator 4a (see map) now gurgles slightly. Please don't use until I've drained it.

This last one was so useful. Very unfair to have taken it down. Who else is going to drain it? Who else can *do* something in this house? Nobody. Nobody.

Neil looked up. He was alone. Dirty light dribbled in through the steamy window, on which, he could now see, Chiyo had drawn a little old woman and a Japanese symbol (他界). Neil stood up to inspect it, attracted by its elegance and order, but as he approached, and their scrubby, unkempt, blackberry and dockleaf-choked garden came into focus, so did Chiyo, now walking around outside, barefoot, hair wet. That's not right, he thought, fascinated and repulsed by her slight figure picking its way through the freezing weeds. He went through the utility room, a corrugated plastic annex that the psychotic pixie who owned the property had more or less glued on last summer, picked up his Wellington boots, and went outside to give them to Chiyo, who looked blankly at them, as if he were proffering a used water filter or a pair of onyx wedding rings.

'I thought you could use these,' said Neil, feeling foolish.

Chiyo took the boots and looked at him, and kept looking.

Neil looked away—it was unbearable—mumbled 'anyway, I'd better get back to…' took a deep breath, held it, realised he hadn't finished his sentence, realised he wasn't breathing, exploded the words 'DOING SOMETHING,' and went back inside, feeling ashamed for no reason at all.

He went upstairs and made his final preparations for work. He checked his 'what to wear app' which had solved a problem that had plagued Neil his whole life, of never going out with an optimum quantity of layers, always too cold or, once he'd loaded up with shopping, far too hot, sweating from the inside like a Beef Wellington. None of that now though, check the app; wear three layers, base-layer thermal. What did we used to do without apps? It seemed impossible to imagine how anyone ever managed to get all the various bar charts of the self down into the green. He then filled his backpack with tiny microphones and surveillance cameras, stroking each one as they went in. Neil loved technology almost as much as he loved stationery, and could cheer himself up by thinking about either, particularly his godmighty synth, but it brought him no pleasure now. It represented something unpleasant. Mournful and tight-lipped, he sat down in front of the keys, touching them lightly. What was wrong? Was it the sex? Is that why Lilly was going off him? The problem was that he couldn't get certain unwanted thoughts out of his head during coitus. He would think of the pope, not this one, the one before, or he would think of Japanese knives (the JKC range), or he would think of oh God, all kinds of nonsense. It made it very hard to get the job done, but he did, he did get through it, so what was the problem? It was the songs, that's what she kept bringing up. Something would have to be done there, but what? What? How could he get more?

Next to him, in a kind of alcove in the corner of his room, was a side window, through which Neil had a sudden, urgent sense, there might be an answer. He moved the chair towards the sill and looked out into the garden. Chiyo, below him, had the wellies he had given her on her hands and was walking around the garden on all fours.

∞

In a small, plush and comfortable, burgundy and baize lounge, tastefully but sombrely decorated with Tiffany lamps, vintage spectacles and framed hygiene certificates, Paul Saul, poised and hushed, fingers gently steepling under his nose, was sombrely advising Aaron and Moira on what would happen now. He spoke very slowly and very deeply, with long pauses, during which, due to smoking close to forty Gauloises a day, which the Murray Mints he continually sucked could never even slightly conceal, he breathed noisily.

'At least you have your memories,' he said, reverently bowing his bald, pitted, deep-templed head.

'Yes…' said Moira, not listening, 'Yes…' They sat together on the sofa in front of Paul, their hands clasped, faces exhausted and punished with grief. Moira's mother had thrown herself in front of a train; she it was who had been divided in three by the 2:23 to Bristol Temple Meads.

'She's in a better place now,' said Paul.

'I just… I've never…' Moira whispered.

'We just don't really know what to do,' said Aaron.

'Of course, when a loved one passes,' Paul closed his eyes reverently, almost ecstatically, 'the last thing you want to be thinking about is this kind of thing. But that's where we come in, to lighten the burden…'

'Oh God… I… I…' Moira began to cry. Aaron squeezed her hand and took over. 'The thing is,' he said 'we don't have… a lot of… *money*… I mean, we do want to do the right thing. But how much…? Erm…?' Aaron whispered the word 'money.' He felt ashamed to be talking about worldly matters.

Paul, infinitely pained, held his massive hands outward in a gesture of spiritual giving. 'What price family?' he said, 'what price love?'

There was a long pause. From long experience Paul knew that it did not matter what you said to a grieving couple. You could read a takeaway menu, or talk about the hard skin on your feet, it didn't matter, as long as you did it slowly, reverently and, ideally, in a voice two octaves lower than normal.

'Our services begin at one-nine-nine-five,' he said, 'That's our simple funeral, which includes bringing your loved one into our care, dressing her…'

As Paul delivered his solemn sales pitch, in the bare office down the hall, Nina Eedie was staring, rapt, at her computer monitor, which displayed a live video feed of the mourning salon. Paul's voice was coming through the two little speakers, the bass rattling their cones; '...in a suitable gown and providing continuous care while she is in our protection, a casket of your choosing, with all the appropriate linings and fittings...'

Lilly also overheard Paul. She had just got to work and, as she walked through the empty reception and passed the frosted-glass door at the far end, heard his muffled but still clear voice, which carried as far as that of the sperm whale he resembled, '...we provide a private chapel of rest and prepare, collect and distribute the required documentation and payments which are legally required for your funeral to proceed...'

She walked on into the workshop. Carl, smoking a chubby little rollie, was inspecting a wooden clothes hanger.

'Morning!' said Lilly, brightly.

'I bought this for my wife,' said Carl.

'Why?'

'Why? As a present.'

'A present?'

'Yeah, what do you think?'

'I dunno. I think she might find it a bit... conventional?'

'Useful though. That's the point.'

'Is it though? Is it the point Carl? I don't think it is the point.'

She walked into the mortuary. Carl, nettled, upped and followed her. 'What *is* the point then?' he asked.

A large, late-middle-aged woman with a purple rinse, was laid out on one of the anatomy tables; Susan Dodsworth. Lilly looked around the room. 'God it's so dingy in here.' She inspected a corner of one of the tiles, laced with bacterial green, 'Isn't there anything we can do about this mould? Surely it's unsanitary?'

'There's nothing you can do about mould on grouting. Besides, who gives a monkey's? It's not as if a corpse going to get infected.'

'I suppose not.' Lilly began preparing her day.

'So what do you think I should get her?' There was a note of aggression in Carl's voice and—legs splayed, chubby fingers gripping the hanger—his posture too.

'I don't know Carl, what does she like?'

'Like? How should I know?'

Lilly, pulling on her rubber gloves, stopped. 'You don't know what your wife likes?'

Carl sighed, exasperated. 'The same things that all women like,' he said in a tone of 'it's completely obvious.'

'Well…' said Lilly, getting back to work, 'I like sewing, and collecting pinkish stones and antique toys from Czechoslovakia, and making woollen birds. And I play the oboe.'

'My wife isn't a freak. No offence.'

Lilly sighed. 'Get her a curry then.'

'Are you… is that a serious suggestion, because… I'm not being funny…' He stepped fully into the mortuary, one hairy forearm on the nearer empty anatomy table. '…because, don't tell Nina, but I've been using the hearse for a bit of moonlighting, delivering for the Yamaraja curry house. I could easily get a deal on a mixed grill.'

'Why don't you give her the clothes hanger *and* the mixed grill?'

Carl made a single laughing snort. 'Nice one,' he said, impressed, even a little moved. 'Nice one,' he whispered a second time, more to himself.

Meanwhile Nina, peering at her screen, hands gripping the desk, listening to and watching Paul on the screen, was approaching the moment of do or die. 'So you see,' said Paul, 'the full service, for three-four-nine-five, gives you the kind of caskets your dear departed would be proud to be seen in and a funeral that your friends and family will feel is worthy of her, your dear mother. She will be given that special, extra, final, touch, of, love.'

Moira's voice. 'Yes, yes, I see… well… oh dear…'

'…it's a bit steep…' said Aaron.

'Just think of your dear, dear mother,' said Paul, 'That's why we're here. For her.'

Nina's eyes narrowed. The sale… the *sale*.

'Yes,' said Moira, 'No, yeah, it's what she would've wanted. We can, course we can. Can't we?'

'I'll get the money, somehow,' said Aaron, 'Yes, the full service. Definitely.'

Nina relaxed, overcome, limp but for her clenched fists and her gritted teeth, through which she hissed '*Yes*,' falling back into her chair with the relief of victory.

∞

Joe was rummaging through a litter bin outside the Aldi supermarket on the edge of the ring road. He picked out a coin and inspected it; one side was completely smooth. An overweight woman passed and threw in a screwed-up receipt. Joe picked it out and unfurled it. As he was reading, Clive emerged from the supermarket carrying a bag of shopping. He hobbled up to Joe.

Clive was born in Stoke where he dealt drugs until he was eighteen and went to university, where he dealt drugs. He studied English literature, until he was kicked out for dealing drugs, although this was no great loss as the course was taught by two women who were less well read than he was, and his tutorials were on the Terminator films or Julian fucking Barnes or some other bobbins. After this, Clive moved to Manchester, where he learnt how to manufacture Ecstasy, a complicated process which involves a long list of hard-to-find chemicals, including concentrated hydrochloric acid which, while tripping nuts on the Golden Teacher mushrooms he was growing in his shoe cupboard, Clive spilt over his bathroom floor. The acid burnt through to the bathroom below, Clive's flat was engulfed in suffocating sulphur fumes, his consciousness plummeted down to hell where, believing he was dead and screaming in infernal pain, he was found by the police some thirty minutes later with acid burns over his withered arm. Clive spent three years in prison, then moved down to Edding where, with the money he'd earned fuelling most of the Manchester raves of the 90s, he put a deposit on a flat and started work on a series of novels which he couldn't get published and nobody had read. He was starting to slow down, lifewise, although he still had enough energy to pop back up to Manchester one weekend, get wasted and throw himself out of a window, shattering his leg.

The only thing Clive had loved, in the past ten years, apart from his books, had been his three-legged dog, Mark, a half-spaniel, half-Barbet mongrel. Clive considered animals to be superior to people in every way. When Mark died, Clive took two weeks off work and sat in his garden high on Ecstasy, weeping like a child.

After this, Clive devoted himself full-time to his first love, complaining. He complained about the fact that young people think they can save the world by meditating and using computers ('They don't want to work though do they? They just want to *do* things—that's not fucking work'), about rock musicians who are more interested in their investments than in producing music you can listen to ('I met Jimmy Page once; he mistook me for an accountant and told me about his fucking assets'), about baseball caps ('make men look like village idiots') and modern fashion generally ('swamp-wear'), about washing up complicated objects ('French presses, garlic crushers, flasks'), about cowardice ('God hates a coward, and so do I'), about remastered albums ('take a work of art, mixed to perfection, give it to a fucking graduate to brickwall it and digitally strip it of character'), about shoddy workmanship ('people who don't really care about what they are doing, or who haven't learnt to do it well; scum of the earth'), about the sale of Britain's infrastructure to the Chinese ('Chum-chows' he called them; 'talk too loud, never say anything interesting and treat you like money-shitting cattle', he also claimed that ninety-five percent of men from the Indian subcontinent were con men), about inherited wealth ('money-grubbing, third-generation mediocrities'), about socialism ('basically capitalism for people who listen to Belle and Sebastian'), about telling people about your problems ('young people are not depressed, they've just got too much time on their hands'), about democracy ('bullshit; we could do with three to five years of benevolent dictatorship') and about modern literature, which was one of the few subjects he could talk about with Joe, although Joe had erratic tastes in books, and seemed to place Ian Fleming on the same level as James Joyce.

Clive had in fact just been looking through the book section of the supermarket and picked up a Booker Prize winner, by Poppy-Eleanor Anderson called 'The Cold Heart of Tomorrow'. The first page read:

…it was forbidden, a secret, the melancholy voice of the earth,
plunged, long fingered into the grass, feel its truth, eternal message
her arms, slashed with shards of grass, body crisscross-crissed-and-
crossed with broken worlds, broken promises, broken body, body, my
body, blood's body, life's body; yet whose body? whose?

Brittle fury rose in Clive's craw. These fucking people are in control of culture, producing this drivel, and nobody can see it… there's just nothing there! What about the world? What about that? What about other people? In modern books other people don't fucking exist. They aren't described, they don't have names, they hardly speak, and when they do, they all sound like an intellectual homosexual sitting in a coffee shop listening to music produced for fucking coffee shops.

'What are you doing?' he said to Joe, charred and deadening with rage and hatred.

Joe looked up from the bin. 'I'm adapting to changes operationally on a daily basis.'

'It looks like you're reading receipts.'

'Yeah, I don't know why she's getting all that Ryvita when she's already got two packets of rice cakes.'

Clive's head didn't like Joe too much, he was barmy on the crumpet, workshy, he had appalling taste in everything and he was uninterested in… anything, really; just floating over life like a pondering puff of thought. And yet it was restful, being in Joe's company. Nothing Clive said ever annoyed Joe, no matter how brutal. Joe accepted it all, like the ocean accepts everything thrown into it, children, rocks, chips, nuclear waste. Anything. On one occasion, while they were ordering at a greasy spoon, Clive, just to test how accepting Joe was, had asked him whether he, Joe, would rather go down on his mum or his dad, and Joe had said, 'my mum, obviously, fancy sharing an extra plate of toast?'

'Fat bird was she?' said Clive, nodding at the receipt, choler cooling somewhat in Joe's still waters.

'Erm, a little bit perhaps. Yes, no, yes she was.'

Clive craned his neck to inspect the crumpled receipt. 'Discounted cheesecake. Chocolate hobnob family pack. She's compensating for all that stodge.'

'Oh yes. I didn't think of that.'

They lurched together down towards the high street—Clive limping, Joe, a head taller, tugging his heavy cleaner's cart. The path was dotted as ever with man-shaped sleeping bags, stepped-on beer cans and sallow fag butts. There seemed to be construction everywhere, men at work, road works, work in progress, sorry for the inconvenience. Sausages-and-bacon-stuffed bald men conglomerated in fat DayGlo huddles contemplating wet ashphalt, thinking about tea and the transfer market.

'How are you then?' said Joe.

'What kind of a stupid question is that? Any day I don't have to phone a call centre is a good day, although I say 'good', but what I really mean is that the pain, the emptiness, the pointlessness are slightly more bearable.'

'I know what you mean. Modern life is such…a waste of time.'

'The only thing that brings me any pleasure,' said Clive, 'is creosote. And russet emulsion.'

'Maybe you need a break?'

'Why? People are always saying that. Take a break, go on a holiday, go out. Why? What's the point? We only end up back here.'

'Are you sure? You know what they say, "you can't step in the same river twice."'

'Yes you can, and it's not a river, it's a big dog turd, which you can step in over and over again. In fact you must. You must spend your life trudging through dog shit.'

'Have you tried roller blading?'

They passed a huge advert on the side of the brick, window-less walls of 'The Range' shopping centre. It displayed a motley assortment of oddbods; a man dressed as an octopus, a woman on a skateboard playing a trumpet, Queen Victoria on a space-hopper, an Italian revolutionary of the unification era, and so on. The slogan read: 'Have you spotted your unique delusion yet? Just thought you should know: we have!'

Clive's face jerked reflexively, almost a pout. 'These new fonts haven't made us any happier,' he said.

'They're all cute and chatty adverts are now,' said Joe, '"Ooops! We boobed!" or "Need an extra colostomy bag? We thought so!" I wonder who writes them?'

'I do.'

'Do you really?'

'Yeah, in my spare time I pretend to be a wanker.'

A young man in carpet-like tracksuit sprinted past and hurled a Scotch egg at Joe. It bounced off the side of his head and landed on the ground.

Joe looked at the egg. 'If I had a pound for every time some-one threw a Scotch egg at me, I'd be a rich man.'

Clive too, with his vacant greyish gleam, regarded the de-structed egg, crumbs rolling down the drain. 'You enjoying it then? Cleaning Scotch egg shrapnel off the streets?'

'Scotch eggs are fine, crumbly you see, dry. It's frozen curry that gets me down.'

'I do not want to live in a world of frozen curry.'

'It's alright though. When I do what I want, pretty much anything is okay. But then the boss shows up.'

'Oh, Dave says hello.'

They continued walking, turning off the dual carriageway and into the suburban outskirts of town, where the fancier shops were located.

'Does he?'

'Does he fuck.'

Dave Davage assumed, as all people of low sense do, that everyone had the same crude, primary-colour outlook on life as he did, at least everyone male (women had 'morals' and had to be dealt with accordingly). It wasn't a lack of imagination or intelligence—Dave, in his own way, did have these overrated abilities—rather an absence of sensitivity. He was encased in himself. This is why he shared his stories and his opinions with anyone who would listen, even Clive, who, only a few days ago, Dave had shown his 'punting diary', a small black book which listed all the pros and dodgy massage parlours he'd visited, each one marked with a brief review and a mark out of ten.

'I see him around town sometimes,' said Joe.

'Do you?'

'Yeah, look.'

Joe stopped and pulled from his pocket a bunch of photographs and handed them to Clive. There was a photo of Dave at the supermarket, Dave at the bus stop, Dave in the pub, Dave getting into his car, Dave slyly checking to see if anyone could see him enter 'Asian Haven Massage'... As Clive looked through the images, Joe absent-mindedly chewed the top of his broom.

'This is not right Joseph,' said Clive, handing back the photos. On they walked.

'It's not illegal though.'

'Illegal and wrong are not the same thing.'

'I saw Hayley the other day too. We passed each other on the towpath and both of us had the same thought, "I don't want to stop and have a conversation, but I might have to if the other one stops," but neither of us did, we both gave a big cheery "hello" and then walked past each other, which... it exposed all our friendliness at work for the complete lie it all really was.'

'Between us all is a calm hatred,' said Clive, and then screamed 'ARSEHOLES!'

'What are you doing?'

'When I walk past Planet Organic, I always make sure I shout some abuse.'

They were indeed outside Planet Organic from where, at just that moment, Maria was emerging, fear on her face, which, when she spotted Joe, turned to her habitual irritation.

'Are you joking? Because it's not funny.' She looked him up and down; disgusting, she thought, disgusting job, disgusting. Necessary of course, the world needs cleaners and bin-persons, probably, but really Joe, really…

'That wasn't me! It was him!' said Joe, pointing at Clive.

Maria's sluggishly cynical eyes swung over to Clive who reflexively stepped back, his crippled leg swivelling unnaturally. On seeing this, Maria's eyes lit up. 'Oh, hello!' she said, brightly.

'Hello.'

'This is Clive.'

Maria turned to Joe, impressed, 'You never told me you had any differently-abled friends Joe.' She turned back to Clive, bending down slightly, 'How are you today? I see you've got some shopping there. Are you going to cook yourself something nice for dinner? Did you remember to get some vegetables?'

Clive peered at Maria, then at Joe, then back at Maria. 'I don't think we live on the same planet do we?' he said.

'We first met here, didn't we Joe?' said Maria, straightening up, eyes all fiery with gladness.

'That we did,' said Joe, marvelling at the transformation that had overtaken Maria on encountering a raspberry ripple. Maybe she's some kind of paraphilic, turned on by amputations and prostheses and that? Perhaps, he thought, I should go and get my leg trapped in a tractor PTO shaft? Or maybe she just loves people who can't get away from her?

The two of them had indeed met at Planet Organic, during one of Joe's temping phases, when he had been assigned to the

Eco Supermarket, from which he had eventually been fired for flouting their system of emotional management. He hadn't accrued a smile bonus ('we call it 'smile or die' a co-worker had told him during his first coffee break), or any wisdom perks (extra hummus if you shared a motivational quote because, as the company brochure had it, 'you change the physical world with your thoughts'), his Wow card remained uncharged (fellow employees, and mystery shoppers hadn't tagged him on social media) and he found it very difficult to strictly adhere to the company policy of mandatory optimism. Maria had walked in on his second day, while he was standing with a frozen smile on his face in front of the shrink-wrapped corn snacks, and asked him where the capers were.

'Capers?' said Joe.

'Yes, the capers.'

'I don't know, sorry.'

'Why not?'

'I have never worked here before and I don't know where anything is.'

'But you've got a badge.'

'Yes, but look; do you see that my uniform is slightly different to the other ones here? Same colours, but not actually a uniform. These are my own clothes coordinated to fit in with Planet Organic. It's because I'm a temp, which means I'm being temporarily held hostage by the happy police. Actually I work for an agency contracted to the supermarket. In *fact*, contracted to an agency that's contracted to the supermarket. I've never been in here before.'

'But you're holding a packet of quinoa!' She was astonished, outraged even, but the novelty of the exchange, the serene undercurrent to Joe's apparent lack of self-consciousness and his imposing physicality softened her, raised an inner eyebrow.

'Yes,' said Joe, 'I have no idea what it is.'

'Quinoa?'

'Yeah, what is it?'

'It's a kind of grain, actually a seed, very high in fibre but with a low glycemic index.'

'There you go. You know more about it than I do. In fact...' he assessed her basket, overflowing with marinaded Norwegian tofu steaks, crystal-encrusted seaweed Pringles and Kale, Pear and Banana ice-cream, 'do you shop here often?'

'I do, yes.'

'Well... perhaps you can tell me where the quinoa goes?'

'Aisle four, next to the spelt.'

'Thanks.'

And so it had begun, in sweet ignorance of the fact that years later they would be pretending to be a happy couple outside the same shop.

∞

Lilly was setting the features of Susan Dodsworth. She had rinsed out the innards and bundled them back in the cavity with absorbent packing fabric, which she had then sewn up. She was now stuffing cotton wool into the neck, suturing the mouth shut and inserting eye caps under the lids. As she worked, she chatted away.

'Neil is intolerable. It just doesn't work. The other day he seemed very snappy and aggressive, and I tried to get him to open up and tell me what was wrong... what am I doing? but he just claimed no, no, there's no problem. I said there *is* a problem and it just went nowhere, until finally he said he was very upset about us, about *us*, and that's why he he's been spiky and irritable, and I said what about us? and he said I wouldn't really commit to anything or be definite about the future, and oh, alright, but the thing is, he's always that way. Whenever we're together he's always, like ten times a day, no exaggeration, asking me what the plan is, what are we going to do, which gets on my tits. It's my responsibility? Can't we just see, go with the flow? No, no. He's closed to the random factor, chance encounters. It has to be in *the plan*. Always the plan, although actually, he doesn't really know what he wants, which is the real problem.'

Lilly stopped for a moment. Susan seemed the understanding type, a woman who had learnt a thing or two. She had a powerful, beautiful nose. Lilly thought of what her grandfather had once said to her, with odd passion, 'give me a man with a nose.' Then she thought of Neil's nose, which was, well it was alright, but not a lot of character in it, a fairly policemany nose.

Lilly sighed. 'He's just so fidgety. It works okay when I get drunk with him, he relaxes a bit more. But mostly he just seems so irritable, and he's like that a lot with me. I must really annoy him. I really don't want to, but I don't know what it is I do. I just can't seem to get a straight answer out of him either, so how can I change or improve?'

Susan said nothing, laying there, all peaceful. Neck a bit inflated, which made her look a little like she didn't quite believe what she was hearing, but at least she *was* hearing. The dead were such good listeners. Their eyes were all glazed over, just like living people, but at least they didn't pretend to be interested, or say something in a nice friendly voice that was actually incredibly mean, or generally have no real curiosity about life and so just with nothing to say and instead, oh God the inanity, the food conversations, the fake laughter. None of that with the dead.

Lilly went on. 'And he has what he calls his "strong moral code", all forms of theft, even downloading films, or doing a runner from a restaurant that has just served us overpriced and horrible food. I wanted to run. I got up, but he sat still, and paid. Even crossing the road, I'll say, right, it's okay now, go. Loads of space there is, but no, wait for the little green man. I don't know. Maybe I am immoral? But I just think my moral code is bendier, and involves some other concept of what is just.'

'I probably shouldn't shoplift. I admit that. I told Neil about it and he just said 'I don't want to know! I don't want to know!' And I felt terribly guilty, which Neil seemed to enjoy, but then I thought about it and it doesn't hurt anyone does it? Those supermarkets are horrible, evil, and anyway, that's beside the point, I just don't feel all that comfortable in Neil's company. It pains me to admit it, but I just feel a crushing sort of rigidity about him, that I just can't deal with. I find myself saying incredibly stupid things when I'm with him. Childish, sexual talk, let's go gang rape someone. I just want to shock him out of his… what is it? Inflexibility. *Neilness*.' Lilly paused, thinking to herself, then said; 'I think he might have single-personality disorder.'

She was applying blusher from her now lovely, well-stocked kit. It was a nice job this, although sometimes the relatives complained that there wasn't enough make-up, as if these people went around in their living lives caked in foundation. But she did a good job, she knew it, delicately rouging up the cheeks, putting just the right amount of lipstick on.

'Oh yeah, I was flicking through the TV channels at the hotel we stayed at in Oxford, and I came across gay porn, and it was on, oooh, 2 seconds, and he was shouting, *get it off!!! Now!!! Get it off!!!* and I know he was *this* close,' she held up her finger and thumb, three millimetres apart, 'from getting up and ripping the plug out of the wall, or pulling my arm off. What's the big deal? Is he homophobic? But then sometimes he plays at being camp, and he knows some bona-fide gaymen and he likes them, I know he does, so I don't see what's so shocking.

'He told me the other day that he wants to buy a house in Edding. That's his ambition. He's… I mean, okay, you want a house, lots of people do, I'd like one, but for him it's a way to wall himself up. I understand he doesn't like sharing a flat and paying rent to Jason. I don't. But he says its degrading. It's not *degrading* though is it?

'Also,' she went on, 'this week he brought four books, a factual one about a battle in World War Two, a 'Warhammer' novel, which, well, it's more war obviously, a biography of Nelson, more war, but he's also a big fan of Lord of the Rings, so he bought The Hobbit, which is a sorta quest stroke battle, but he found that dated and childish.'

She finished up and admired her work. Susan was looking okay now. A little less dead.

'What a strange bundle is Neil. I guess, the bit I like or, love, is that he cares, he really cares about the world, in his weird angry way, and I think I can see in him a silly, playful side. When we're alone he pretends to be a pigeon or does a robot dance, and… And, he's clean, also, always smells good, and he can *do* things, I like that too. I like to see him take apart door locks that aren't working and work out why the shower head won't stop dripping. Oh I dunno, he's good, or he could be. But you can't just pick the bits you like about people, can you? And in the end, it doesn't matter that someone is good on paper, it's a physical thing, a material thing, and that's where the problems are, because, well, every time we have sex with each other, I just cry afterwards. Obviously that's not very nice for him. But then he starts crying too. We finish and then both burst into tears. In the end it all just became too sad, and so I just stopped being interested which, well, he gets annoyed that we don't have sex now. He gets really angry and frustrated.'

She sighed. 'Every conversation leads to an argument and every argument ends up with him saying "we haven't had sex in a week Lilly. I just want some blow jobs or something. I give it to you." But my argument is, "I'm not asking for this—you just do it." He has a lot of rage, during sex I mean. He's trying his best, but I tell him, "I just can't feel anything", and then he gets more angry and of course I'm not in the mood at all then, so, I just don't bother.'

The last job was to dress Susan, put her in her Sunday best for the viewing. Lilly worked away, huffing and puffing, pulling her bra on, hoisting up the legs for the dress, all the time talking away.

'All his anger is behind this massive wall of "nobody puts me down, nobody messes with me. I've got a reputation at work that if you mess with me, I'll fuck you up." You know, we're talking about Edding police station. He thinks he's at the battle of Troy. You don't have to be like that!

'So, I try to end it. I say to him "maybe we're not, you know, right for each other," and then this wave of guilt flows over me. And I think, oh what am I going to do, because I see him all the time, and when I see him upset I think, "have I made a mistake?"

'Then yesterday we had another one of these conversations, "I dunno if we're meant to be together", and this whoosh of guilt came over me again, and he gets really upset then, you know, and he threatens to kill himself, and I think, for fuck's sake, and, he'll get up and he'll say, "I'm just going to go and *hang* myself," or, what he prefers to do is, he leaves his Post-it notes around the house. "Lilly, I am going to kill myself, 1600 hours approx." And I think, well, "we all say that though don't we, every now and again?" and I don't think about it, but then, I go and knock on his door, and he's just weeping, on the floor, weeping. He gets *so* emotional. And it's weird, you don't see men like that, to see someone, a man, utterly break down, knowing you've caused it, and, I think, I don't know what to do. What shall I do?'

Susan lay in silence. Nina, who had been listening to the entire conversation through her speakers, was also silent. Lilly too was silent.

Finally Lilly spoke, 'I actually think the world is ending.'

∞

Chiyo, carrying a large rucksack, left the house towards midnight. She was wearing a fur-lined parka and chunky walking boots, which made her intervening legging-clad calves look like black saplings. The full moon, the harvest moon, was low and large in the pink, towny sky. People say the moon reflects the sun, but Chiyo knew that the moon's light, in truth the glowing opposite of light, was its own.

She followed the canal, beyond the bright macadamised outskirts of Edding, then left the tow-path and headed through the back roads of South Haleshire, through small, dark, villages—great wealth here, great silence, great fear—past the wastelands called 'farms', along moon-dark country lanes—the unnatural pinkish skies now simmering behind her—reaching Chitham Forest in the dead of the night. A few streetlamps threw scoops of yellow light, but this only made the dark behind them more imposing and complete, as if all the night were there. Eventually, she left the long one-lane, ditch-lined road, carefully climbed over a low barbed wire fence, and stepped into the black-gleamed forest.

Ribbons of pale moonlit mist drifted between shadowlike trees. It was silent, except for the occasional snuffling of foxes and badgers. Chiyo squatted down in a patch of ferns, pulled down her leggings and knickers and pissed. Her urine contained information for the forest. It would know she was here now, and what kind of creature she was, and what she needed too.

She stood, pulled up her leggings and crackled off into the woods, criss-crossing through it, apparently at random, over paths or parallel to them, or deep into nowhere, guided by that most dangerous of instincts, whim. It was so quiet she could hear moths cleaning their furry wings. The roots underfoot glowed dark to her, leading her on as the channels of a river guide an experienced helmsman, taking her to a patch of fly agaric. She squatted, reaching out reverently, stroking the night-licked blood-red hoods, their white spots glistening like little stars.

She walked on a short distance, then crouched again on her haunches, inspecting a bristling city of honey mushroom, growing around the base of a beech tree, killing it; the invisible filaments eating through the root. Using her mushroom knife, she sliced them away from the ground, then ate them, cool, mucal, sweet umami, mingled with the scent of rich earthy mulch.

The moon now was high and far away, and yet, at the same time, its hushed unlight was intense, flowing through her like a kind of radiation, melting the barriers and walls that she used in the world, that were the world. Her teeth were charged, her eyes too, her nervous system glowing with the same neural moonlight. Her moon body underneath was emerging, and rising to meet the falling spiderlight, falling through the skies, cobwebbing towards her, to merge with her, to merge with all moon bodies emerging from the world; a world which, like a discarded snake skin, must fall away, *its* barriers and walls sloughed off, leaving the earth naked in the lightless light of the moon.

She stopped. She was in a dried up, but still moist river bed, ringed with alder, ash and colossal sweet chestnut trees, their moonlit forms electric and flowing. She threw her rucksack to the ground and pulled off her parka, her dress and her thermal slip, then her leggings, knickers and shoes. It was freezing, but the cold didn't touch her, she was one with it. She fell to the ground, face down, pushing her face and fingers into the moist, mossy mud, into the world of root, filling her senses with it. Everyone wants the fruit, of love and production—and they always want it overripe—but that's all they want, so they cut it off from the root and the vine withers in their hands, and they're left with a rotten husk and they don't know why. Chiyo's slim, damp fingers pushed into the wet earth, her slender white arms and legs embraced the fungal underworld, feeling out its electric filaments, feeling through to the mycelial strands, the roots of the roots, the wet mould of the world through which the trees of the forest speak to each other, speak to her also.

The ground opens up and red light rises from the core. It catches the edge of the world, and the fire tears across its surface, engulfing trees, houses, oceans, everything. Everyone on earth is trapped in their homes, unable to get out, but afraid to try, to even look out of their windows. They sit, choking, until the walls are eaten away by the fire, the walls of their homes, the walls of their bodies and the walls of their selves, yet still they do not move, even though they burn. And how they burn.

Osiris is in a stone, cold coffin, quite calm. Then she, Chiyo, is in the coffin. Then there is just the coffin, gutted. Then the coffin is a room, a large room, a theatre, with a huge triangular proscenium, and Neil Geb is there, on the stage, also on fire, also terrified and Enma-sama, the king of the underworld, is laughing at Neil. Then Enma-sama is laughing at the denizens of hell, running through forests of swords and drowning in oceans of freezing blood, and pus, and being eaten by Enma-sama, who is laughing, but the laughter is her own.

Chiyo doesn't see any of this. It doesn't happen in her, to her. It happens. It is not a hallucination, it is not feeling. In her body, the all-too-actual, pregnant flesh of it, there is a white hot plummeting into hell, there is the appalling, endless, hopeless squandered misery of the eternally damned, there is the ruptured sorrow, at all this dream suffering, and there is the mania of joy at being awake, but *she* does not see it, *she* does not feel it, because *she* is not here, and that shelessness, as her she-self coalesces again, gives her self perfect confidence. She is held up by an ocean of death, terrifying and perfect.

The sky in the west was staining blue. Her mind was settling back to the shared and ordinary world. She realised she was clothed, although unsure how—had she dressed herself? She was filthy, but intact, and very hungry. She opened her bag and took out her breakfast; miso soup in a flask and rice-bran pickles. She ate, perched on a fallen log, as tiny mulch-green frogs crawled and hopped through the rotting leaves at her feet. Dog walkers and joggers were out now. She couldn't see them, only hear their wealthy, throat-squeezed 'good-mornings' to each other.

It was time to finish her work. She set off again. Streams of gold-white light sharpened her daytime senses, although she wasn't focused; a totality of vision is necessary for mushroom work, an ability to see the panorama, which was why men, with their little targeting lasers, were so poor at it.

The fungal network guided her towards their fruiting bodies, towards the mushrooms, which spoke to her as one of their own. Like them, she had parachuted down from the moon at night. Like them, she brought life and death to the woods. Like them, she shattered time and space. She filled her sack with horns of plenty, grey spotted amanitas, peppery bolettes, safron milkcaps, a morel (strange it should be out so late), a few small puffballs, a wolfhorn and a handful of soothheads, then, as the morning lightened to waxy day, she trudged uphill to the farmland on the edge of the woods, until she found herself walking through grass, intertwined with the distinctive, straggly, nipple-topped heads of liberty caps.

She ended her morning under a sweet chestnut tree, gathering its scattered, ignored harvest. When her bag was full, and heavy, she crossed the meadow back to the main road, having walked an eight mile crescent parallel to where she had started. Her feet were sore, her legs were aching, but she knew, raising her thumb, that someone would stop soon, a lonely young man, fair faced but tired, who feared life and wanted to escape from it. He would be here soon.

∞

Joe and Clive sat on a low wall, the former eating a flapjack, the latter smoking a dishevelled rollie and sipping from a hip flask of whiskey lightly spiked with temazepam. Next to Joe on the right side sat a tall, flat-faced, emaciated and androgynous-looking man of indeterminate age, possibly middle aged, possibly older. He was dirty, deteriorating—clearly homeless—and constantly laughing, a quiet, trembling background chuckle, which, at the slightest provocation, such as a louder-than-normal passing lorry, exploded into joyous, raucous laughter. This was the man known by many in Edding as 'Laughing Ralf.' Opposite the trio, across a quiet road, a young couple were passionately kissing on a park bench, and next to these two was a postbox with something made of paper or white card balancing on it.

Ralf spoke in a broad Welsh accent. 'I won't lie to you Joe, I've got a small penis. Hahahaha!'

'Does that affect your confidence?'

'Well, it did, but at my age, I'm practically impotent anyway, hahahaha! And, I ask you, what woman would go near a total failure! Hahahaha! I've got nothing!! Hahahaha!! I'm so lonely!!! HAHAHAHA!!!!'

Clive looked at Ralf, infinitely pained. 'You must have someone? Somewhere you can go?'

'I was in love with a Chinese girl, see, but she was deported! Hahahaha!' Ralf sat with his legs splayed and his large, elegant hands on his knees. A ladybird crawled up his trouser leg.

'But why is it so funny?'

'It's not! It's fucking tragic! Hahahaha!'

'But why are you laughing?'

'It's a trapped nerve. It started when I had a fight with my landlady… Just over there actually, on the high street.' He nodded towards the corner of the road.

'What do you make of this Joseph?' asked Clive. Were it not for the benzodiazepines now in his bloodstream he'd be suffocating with dyspeptic wrath. As it was, the darkness had receded to a faraway place.

Joe is looking at the couple over the road. It is his missing sister and his dead father, both naked, all over each other.

'Uh?' he said, turning to Clive.

'What do you make of Ralf's story?'

'He's suicidal. Most people are.' He turned back, but the vision had vanished. The young couple had returned.

'Are you suicidal?' Clive asked Ralf, face reflexively pouting.

'Yes!!! Hahahahahaha!'

'Me too.'

'Hahahahaha!'

'What *is* that?' said Joe, looking now at the letterbox. He got to his feet, walked over to it and picked up the paper object; a plate of food.

'It's a toad in the hole!' he called back to Clive and Ralf. He touched the pastry, 'It's still warm!'

Ralf got up and joined Joe, the couple next to them snogging away. He picked up the sausage and bit into it, then turned to Joe, making an 'mmm, not bad' face.

Clive held his head in his hands.

∞

Bronya Coslett's bucktoothed, freckly, shallow-chinned face was permanently contorted into a semi-scowl, emphasised, or advertised, by too-red lipstick. Her hair was scraped back into a ponytail so tight her roots were raw. She had a very prominent rear end, the result of much cycling, but her sides and hips were loose, so she bounced along like a willow branch dangling over a slow river, a juddery gummy chin-driven walk.

Bronya had studied Italian at university, after which she went to live in Italy, where she taught English—learning to believe that helping people get the present perfect right was a kind of religious duty—and conducted a shoddy relationship with an Italian man called Pietro who 'spent more time looking in the mirror than I did', who considered himself the next David Lynch because he'd once got a film review published in Time Out Rome, and who dumped her with the same casual boredom with which he'd got rid of his previous girlfriend, a Korean girl who was still living with him when Bronya had moved in and who ended up returning to Korea addicted to antidepressants and forever convinced that life was naught but a lonely drift to extinction. During all this time Bronya slowly built up a hatred of Italy, which she refused to admit to herself because the country represented, to her forward mind, culture, honesty and freedom. She would spend the rest of her life praising the light of Sicily, the energy of Naples and the wild, free warmth of the Italian people; slowly forgetting that all the time she had actually lived amongst these people she had constantly complained to herself about the heat, which brought her out in disfiguring rashes, about the brutal insensitivity of the Italians, their revolting conformity, their 'stupidity' (by which she meant their inability to detect irony), the fact that the men were smug, insensitive mummy's boys and the women were bone-hard, in-your-face viragos, and that really the country was just as boring and stressful as any other. Bronya herself was an insensitive, irony-immune, slouching conformist but this wasn't important, nor was her Italian, which was as clumsy and laboured as her body.

After being dumped by Pietro, Bronya told herself that she felt rotten not because of broken pride, but because forcing bored Italian teenagers to correctly pronounce unstressed vowels was not really contributing enough to the welfare of the world, and that she should return to England and become a social worker, a very cultured and well-travelled one actually, in which capacity she had worked under Maria's tutelary management for two years now.

Every Wednesday the two of them took a light, healthy, lunch at the 'Coffee Manifesto' cafe in Shenleybury Park, where they now sat, sipping white wine at a picnic table, surrounded by young mothers who had brought their children to the nearby 'adventure playpark' over which they could keep a distant eye as their toddlers, too young for the flying foxes, ran around the cafe garden, whooping and shrieking.

'I think I could have a lesbian relationship, I mean I just *get* it,' said Maria, looking at her nails.

'Oh me too.' Bronya fiddled with her digital lanyard.

'Women are superior to men in every way.'

'I know, I know,' Bronya leant forwards, conspiratorially, 'Is he still exhibiting challenging behaviour?'

Maria sighed a full-life sigh, 'Yes,' she said, 'He's passive-aggressive about it though. He just doesn't understand how his,' she made a 'scare quotes' gesture in the air, '"humour" conceals misogynous and, frankly, highly offensive ableist attitudes. Not that I'm surprised...'

'You expected it of him.'

'Yes. I expect it of men generally. They always let you down. Always. That's just how they are.'

'Yeahhh,' Bronya screwed up her face, thinking of Pietro.

At the table next to them, sat Aaron and a mournful Moira, back from the Chapel of Rest and now eating with their son, James. Aaron, face frozen in a mask of forced mad gaiety, had his smartphone camera pushed into young James' face. 'Pull a funny face! Pull a funny face for Daddy! Come on! Come on!' he cried.

James looked at his father with a pained, confused expression as Aaron took the photograph. 'Good, now I want you to list for me all the animals you've seen today.'

'We haven't seen any animals Daddy,' said James quietly.

'Okay,' said Aaron, irritated, 'I want you to list for me all the *colours* we've seen today.'

James turned to Moira, seeking aid, but Moira took this as a cue to give him the bad news. 'James darling,' she said, 'Grandma, yesterday…. we wanted to say… she…'

'She's gone to Russia in a hot-air balloon,' said Aaron quickly, as if diving to save a dropped plate.

James looked at him, then at Moira, and shrugged. 'Okay,' he said, and the two of them crumpled in relief; problem solved. Moira's mother had died, but there was no need for James to know this, not at his age. What did eight year olds need to know of death? Nothing.

'Can I go and play now?' James asked.

'Yes!' cried his parents together, almost joyously.

Maria took a bite of her salad. 'God I adore butter-beans,' she said, which reminded her; 'I'm thinking of starting a supper club.'

'Why?'

'For Syrian refugees.'

'Do refugees eat supper? Ooh, I must tell you about this new olive oil I got,' Bronya leant into her bag, 'it's…'

Her lanyard beeped and a red LED light began flashing. She checked her phone. At the same time, a four-year-old child started trying to climb over the low fence around the terrace. His mother rushed over, almost in tears, 'That's not allowed Sammy! That's not allowed! You can't go there!'

'Another time I suppose,' said Maria, shrugging.

'Oh, that's weird…'

'What is?'

Bronya was looking at her phone. 'It's from the inspectorate. I'm to go to Thottesley Hall.'

The general child commotion moved up to a higher pitch.

The boy at the fence was clinging to it, screaming, while his mother tried to prise him away. Another boy was thrashing a kid three or four years younger with a stick. James stood against a wall, his little fingers knitted together behind him, watching the scene with fearful fascination.

Maria glanced around. 'Fucking children, screaming like *turds*.' She turned to Bronya. 'That *is* a bit odd. Probably a formality.'

'It's just…' Bronya regarded her half-eaten lunch, 'I hadn't finished.' She spoke with a moany cockney accent which became more nasal in times of stress and doubt.

'Well, you know as well as I do how small client contact is these days Bronya; we have to keep to the schedule or vulnerable people could—*will*—end up suffering.'

As Bronya, mourning her peach and nutmeg salad, threaded her way to the exit, another child threw his tiny self into the hellish melee, running out from the cafe into the garden with an iPad in his hands, screaming and screaming, then smashing the mobile computing device down on a picnic table, repeatedly, over and over again, screaming and screaming and screaming.

∞

Neil had been to the gym, and worked out with psychotic intensity on his favourite piece of equipment, the cross trainer; he had read through his 'revenge spreadsheet' and added, next to 'Lilly doubts' a new solution, *need songs now*; he had eaten two Gregg's sausage rolls in his squad car, but forgot to put the handbrake on and rolled back into another car getting oily bits of pastry over his trousers; he had listened to his various concealed mics, trying to pick up Joe, and had some success—recording his conversation with Ralf and Clive—and he had got into an argument with an aggressive albino.

The main problem today was a strange twitching pain in his lower back. When anything out of the ordinary happened in Neil's body he would first focus intently on it, imagine some dark, evil matter throbbing in his chest or head or wherever, then he'd investigate the problem on 'HomeGP.com' and refine his increasingly anguished mental picture of what was going on; his insides being eaten away by a bacteria, or a diaphragm rupturing and bits of the stomach wall poking through the hole, or a stone, an actual *stone* travelling down his urethra. God it was horrible what could happen to the body. He'd checked out the most recent problem and decided it was either a kidney infection or cancer. It was probably not the time to go nuclear, so he'd ruled out cancer for now—everything was potentially cancer according to HomeGP.com—and researched E.coli infections which 'can travel from the anus to the genitals during sex, crawl up the urinary tract and then start multiplying in the kidneys.' You know you're infected if you have blood in your urine, which—even the thought made Neil feel cold and sweaty as the blood drained from his face (he often got close to passing out while researching medical problems on the internet). He'd booked up to see his doctor—a condescending old Jew who had long given up pretending not to be exasperated by Neil—but until then he was treating himself with gallons of water and obsessively washing his penis and testicles with hot water.

He was now waiting in Margaret's eclectic drawing room, sniffing the air because his old enemy, 'a vaguely shitty smell' had returned, as it periodically did throughout the day. He had tried everything to get rid of this dungy odour, including powerful-smelling salts, concealed nose bungs and even therapy, but nothing had worked. The therapy in fact had made things worse as he'd enrolled on a week-long 'Hoffman Technique' programme in a 'secluded farmhouse' on the Isle of Wight, which involved punching huge pillows that represented one's parents, and hurling abuse at them, but, strange to say, the therapy room looked out, over rolling hills, directly onto the house that Margaret had grown up in. He felt the rage but it got all twisted up with guilt, so now, whenever he smelt something shitty he felt bad about the past, as if he'd said something stupid recently to someone but couldn't quite remember what.

Louis appeared, shuffling and giggling and ducking and camply ooh-hoo-hooing.

'She will see you now sir!' he said.

Margaret was in her old leathern armchair, her hands encircling an invisible globe, which seemed to be expanding and shrinking, like a spherical heart. As Neil entered, Margaret put the 'globe' down.

'Oh hello Patricia,' she said drily.

'Can't you call me Neil?'

'Why would I do that?'

'I… Oh it doesn't matter.' He sat down bollock-tender on one of the Mackintosh chairs, 'How are you?'

She shook her head, lips pursed. 'Every time I sit in this chair I can hear a strange noise,' she said.

'What sort of noise?'

'I don't know. It's just a strange noise.'

'Does it sound like a buzzing noise?'

'No, I wouldn't call it a buzzing noise.'

'Screeching?'

'No, I wouldn't call it that either.'

'What would you call it then?' asked Neil, getting a bit fed up now.

'I don't know.'

'Well you must have some idea!'

'I just haven't cared to think about it Patricia. It's not that important! All I'm saying is that every time I sit here I hear a strange noise.'

'Well don't sit there then!' cried Neil.

'There's no need to get angry.'

'But…' Neil took a big therapeutic sigh, trying to calm down, 'Look, why don't you sit here, and I'll sit there?'

'Why?'

'Well then you won't hear the noise will you?'

'But I might hear another noise.'

'Shall we see? Shall we?' asked Neil, leaping to his feet and gesturing towards his seat with an angry flourish.

'Okay.' Margaret stood up, the thick, cream-coloured rope around her waist revealing itself.

'What's that?'

'What?' She was busy shuffling over to Neil's seat.

Neil gave a little tug of the rope as she passed. 'This. This rope.'

'It's a rope. It was Joe's idea because... I... erm...'

She sat down.

'Yes?' said Neil, lowering himself into Margaret's chair, 'what?'

'You're right. I can't hear anything here.'

'Mother. Why has my brother, your son, tied you to a rope?' He suddenly looked around, alarmed.

'Now you can hear it too, can't you?'

'No!'

'*Why* must you lie Patricia?'

Neil jumped up and ran to the door.

'Louis! Louis!' he called, stepping out into the hall. Louis came jiggling along.

'Yes sir?'

'Was that you?'

'What sir?'

'Nothing, forget it. Did you tie her up?'

'Errrm... Whooops! Hahahaha!'

Neil stormed off. Louis followed him to the front door, his face—indeed his entire tense jerky body—dropped, stony-cold, into watchfulness as Neil waddled away, rapidly, like the Olympic speed walker he had once yearned to be.

∞

Joe spent the morning trundling around Edding, listening to people's conversations, looking at them, generally taking it in. There really was a lot to see. A small broken man in an invalid buggy furiously rubbing lottery scratch cards. Two women, one said, in a seductive voice 'I buy some funny things, I bought some chilli sausages once!' A crumbling, greyish, middle-aged man in checked shirt and tight shorts, carrying an eco 'jute bag,' bent over, shaking, stumbling around, pissed out of his mind, trying to roll a cigarette. A very unhappy-looking girl handing out flyers for a gym; Joe had taken one and said 'miserable task,' and the girl had said 'thank you' in a tone of sorrowful gratitude. A couple, mid bicker; every time Joe passed a couple, one of them seemed to be boring or annoying the other. A beatific, moon-faced Asian man in a purple tracksuit hovered past on an e-scooter. An old boy, red face, probably five or six union jacks at home, was shouting 'YOO WOT?' into his phone, over and over again. YOO WOT? YOU WOT?' There was a lot going on, in people. Most of it was hideous.

Along Stray Street and down Cambridge Hill and through the Charles Avenue Arcade, people everywhere, modern people. They seemed to Joe to nearly always be built on a limited kind of animal template. The kind of people that deal well with a world of trash are the same as the kind of animals that do; pigeons and crows, rats and raccoons, foxes, cockroaches and termites; hardy vermin. Farm, zoo and domestic animals do alright too. Where the upper-middle spods of North Edding reminded him of the latter; bored cats, overfed dogs, mindless, dopey rabbits and, occasionally, a soul-dead lemur in a cage chewing its tail off, those of South Edding resembled the former; haunted pigeons, hungry rats and scheming foxes. No surprise. Townie animals, townie people. 'The townie shall inherit the earth,' thought Joe. There will surely be, statistically speaking, some meek amongst them, but I really don't fancy their chances.

He passed several rows of tower blocks, newly built but already looking crummy and scorched. A dog started barking from a seventh or eighth floor balcony, and a hipster type passing Joe tutted and said to his companion, 'it's wrong to keep animals in those high rise places.' Fine to raise children in them apparently, thought Joe. Three hundred caged human animals squashed together in little cupboards, going out of their minds, that's okay, but it's wrong to put a dog up there.

He passed a row of Edwardian brick houses converted into flats. Because the lower, single-room basement 'studios' were windowless many within had, despite the cold, their front doors wide open into which passers-by could look upon all manner of degradation and squalor. Most rooms were covered in litter, not much different to the street, with a few fatties sat on their envelope-and-biscuit-box-covered beds, staring at their phones.

Joe turned into 'Willow Way'. No willows. Like 'The Oaks', 'The Meadows', and 'Badgerset Avenue'. No oaks, no meadows, no badgers. Edding had a White Claw Festival, to celebrate the gathering of the native crayfish from the River Hale, but the river was dead now, poisoned from the raw sewage dumped into it by Valley Water. In fact there were no more White Claws in England, so the invasive American species, the Signal—larger, more aggressive but without flavour, even when wild—was farmed in vats on the Isle of Dogs and brought in for the festival, and people ate it, deep fried, in pop-up stalls next to the shopping centre.

A homeless man who looked completely normal, unhomeless, neat, was sitting casually in the doorway of a barber's. Joe gave him a fiver and asked him what he was doing on the streets, because he didn't seem the sort, and the man said he'd come home one day to find his girlfriend having sex with his best mate.

'It was her house, so I just walked out,' he said.

'Didn't you get angry?'

'I tried, but I had a funny feeling I deserved it, do you know what I mean?'

'Yes I do. It's not very considerate though is it?'

'No, I deserved it,' the man insisted.

'You deserved it?'

'I didn't love her.'

'Oh I see.'

'Still tragic though,' said the man shrugging.

'Yeah,' said Joe. The man seemed quite philosophical about

it all. Joe wondered if he'd be so forgiving if he had been kicked into the streets by Maria. If I was homeless, he thought, maybe I wouldn't be nice to people with houses. 'Haven't you been back?' he asked.

'Nah, that was two months ago. 'waiting for me crane license.'

'Can't you get another job?'

'Where?'

'I dunno. In that barber's?'

The man turned round. 'Nah,' he said, 'fucking hate heads.'

As they spoke, at the bus stop opposite, a very old Indian woman was ripping up chips and throwing them on the floor for pigeons, which had surrounded her, gulls too, guzzling up the white chunks of starch. Joe wondered if pigeons got a post-chip mood slump and sat around at 4PM feeling like they were wasting their lives. The general public waiting for the bus were not impressed with the columbid feeding frenzy, looking at the old woman with disgust bordering on horror, and shooting each other 'can you fucking believe it?' looks. She looked to Joe as if she just wanted to take care of the animals, but it reminded him of his insane grandmother, Neville's mum, who would just stuff sugar into the mouths of any creature who would take it. Somehow it was all about her.

Finally, the old woman screwed up the bag, threw it onto the pavement and got on a bus. Joe wondered if he should go and pick it up, but he couldn't be bothered. So what? More litter. He couldn't see the fuss about littering. Irving got so angry about it, like Neil used to; lots of people did. But why? It was wrong in nature, but here? That's what this town is, a huge pile of refuse.

The only thing he'd picked up in the last half hour was a burst balloon. He stood now next to his cart, on a small piece of grass on the corner of a suburban street, holding it, inspecting it. One side was silver and the other green. He bent down and matched it against the grass. Squatting, he moved around the grass, until he found a piece of moss on the side of a piece of stone wall, the same colour as the balloon. He checked, pleased. It was exactly the same colour. He stood up (wondering what colour this was; probably somewhere between decadent chestnut and German bread mould), to find himself looking at a woman, a young brunette in a dressing gown, very good looking, but with a rough, rubbery, stung hunger to her face. She was hurrying over the road towards him, hugging the lapels of her dressing gown.

'Excuse me! Excuse me!'

Realising he was still holding the balloon, Joe squatted down, carefully placed it on the stone he had matched it against, and then stood up again as she reached him.

'Can you help me?' she said, out of breath; evidently not having run further than ten yards since she was twelve.

'It's so hard to tell.'

'I need a cleaner... I mean I need someone to help me clean... my boyfriend...' she took a deep breath, gathering herself, 'I need someone to help me clean my flat. It's a total mess, and my boyfriend, he gets so angry, and he said, he said,' she was getting tearful, 'if I didn't have it tidy before he got home... he'd... he'd...' she was sobbing, 'oh God, please help me...'

'Okay,' said Joe, 'come on.'

'Really?' Her eyes were teary and joyous, 'Oh thank you.'

Joe crossed over, following her, and entered her house, one of a row of newbuild council houses, made of powdery breeze blocks and drywall, and covered in a uniform, featureless, smooth veneer of wire-cut red brick. A few incredibly small, square, black PVC windows squinted suspiciously at the street. These houses didn't look like places where human beings were welcome.

The front door opened directly onto a low-ceilinged front room into which Joe stepped and surveyed—with a one-notch increase of awareness, as always happens entering a house for the first time—foetid chaos; overflowing ashtrays, filthy plates and cups (also used as ashtrays), magazines (OK! Heat, and Christianity Today), clothes everywhere, unopened letters, wine bottles, all simmering in a slightly fatty, slightly sweaty background smell. It wasn't entirely disgusting, not a crack den or anything, rather clogged and forgotten and slatternly. The only really clean area was a small tray on the front room coffee table with a crumb of dope and a pouch of tobacco.

Sophie looked helplessly at Joe. 'He'll be back in three hours. I keep trying to start, but I don't know where to start; and then I just think about him getting back and I'm… paralysed… do you know what I mean?'

'Yes,' said Joe earnestly, 'it's best not to think.'

'Why not?'

'If thought worked, it would have worked by now.'

∞

Neil rang Victor's bell. Inside he could hear the chime sound — the theme to Call My Bluff — but no answer. He was tempted to walk away but the little rucksack with Victor's laptop inside, knocking on his shoulder, and his tensed desire to keep hold of Lilly, knocking on his heart, pushed him on, and so he rang again. Still nothing. He stepped back and looked up the bizarre house, tattooed from top to bottom in unfathomable glyphs and ideograms, to a first-floor window, behind which a curtain twitched. Victor's voice, muffled but triumphant, echoed from within, 'I will not submit to the Zone of Evil!'

'I've got your laptop,' Neil shouted up, 'Don't you want it?'

Heavy thumping could be heard from within; Victor rushing across the hallway and down the stairs. The front door opened a crack, on the latch, and Victor's weathered, gap-toothy face appeared. 'Give it to me,' he said.

'I will, of course, I mean I want to give it to you, but, erm… can I come in please?'

'Why?'

'I… Look, I'm not from the Zone of Evil, I'm here as a… person… can't I come in?'

The door closed. Neil, perplexed and anxious, sick as ever with the perpetual sense of being watched and of being found out, waited, inventing as he did so excuses, lines of attack, ways to make it all look innocent. The white of Victor's eyes, stark against the blackness withal, flashed in the door crack.

'If you wear this,' said Victor, and, removing the latch and opening the door a little wider, offered what appeared to be a fantastic tribal headdress, covered in bits of moss and glued wood with a mighty papier mâché mushroom, with two long cartoon eyes, like a number '11,' rising out of the centre.

'Oh come on Victor. Don't be...'

The headdress withdrew and door began to close.

'Okay! okay!'

Neil took the magnificent hat, looked around furtively, then put it on.

'Open up then,' he said, 'come on.'

The door opened and Neil stepped into a pandemonium of haemorrhaging, high-density polyethylene, havoc. Within the ordinary suburban house with its large living room, its kitchen on the garden side, its stairs leading up to a master bedroom and two smaller bedrooms, in every room, there were piles upon piles of cheap, pointless, cardboard, carton and plastic tat. There were pet umbrellas and hamster wigs, beehive cake moulds, a full-body lobster costume, an ABBA monopoly set, unicorn hats for cats, a life-sized eagle-head pencil, an enema simulator, hand-held EMF readers, a malachite stela, a hair-growth helmet, latex shower titties, a box of edible tarantulas, Strong Dick Liquid, a cube of cubes of cubes, a shark-repelling wristband, condiment pistols, sushi bazookas, a big bottle of matches... on and on it went... every available space was packed, including the spaces within the spaces, creating in some areas solid blocks of monstrous dross. The walls were also plastered with the mad, the cheesy, the obscure, the obscene ('Advice from a Wolf' inspirational poster, 'cardboard kill' animal heads, 'Beethoven vs. Dracula' film print, photos of tribesmen in the one-leg resting position, childish drawings of cricketer Geoff Boycott) as were several bookshelves ('My Dildo is Haunted,' 'Web Design for Babies,' 'The History and Romance of Elastic Webbing', 'Cooking with Poo', 'Hip-Hop For Dogs'). Through all this, valleys had been hollowed out, or perhaps designed, tunnels also, and covering everything, all of it, black and yellow paint, a mind-blowing organic-symbolic lattice of hieroglyphs, body parts and cartoon eyes, similar to that on the outside of the house but finer, more carefully arranged. Somehow, thought Neil, as he gently prodded a fried-chicken phone case, and discovered that it had been glued on, that it was *all* glued together, somehow there was care here, and cleanliness, and perhaps even beauty, some mad supernatural, artistic order at work, but it was appalling, wrong, so far out of the ordinary that its owner and designer could only possibly be a threat to humanity; and yet here I am, Neil said to himself, cap in hand. It's wrong, I should leave, I should get out of here, report this lunatic to the proper people. He paused, even turned an atom to leave, but Lilly hovered before him, Lilly's respect, Lilly's love, which he must, at all costs cling to. That, after all, is what love is; desperate, fearful clinging.

Eyes wide, scared for his life, grasping his bizarre hat, which barely fitted through the columns of nonsense, he followed Victor's immense, dark frame upstairs, along the hallway and into a kind of nest hollowed out in the middle of the main bedroom where, on one side, arranged in a semicircle on the floor, was an 11lb jar of Nutella, an 8lb bag of marshmallows, a box of chocolate-covered pork rinds and a survival pallet of edible glitter; and on the other, a microphone, a guitar, a MIDI keyboard, a preamp, a small mixing desk, a trumpet, various percussion instruments, a kazoo and a small electronic drum kit.

Victor waddled in, flopped backwards, and four carbon legs fell out of the wearable chair he had strapped to his large frame, supporting him like a tripod stand holds a ceramic mortar.

'Songs, pig,' he said, without emotion.

'Now look Mr. Perry, insulting a police officer…'

Victor put his hands on his knees, as if to stand, 'Okay, goodbye,' he said.

'Okay okay, here…'

Neil took the laptop from his bag and handed it over. Victor opened it, checked the files, and then plugged in his speakers, mic and keyboards.

'You see…' Neil began an explanation, but was cut short by Victor's radiant smile, revealing the enormous gap in his front teeth. His glaucous eyes wrinkled up in a kind of sweetness. 'Here it comes,' he said.

Neil quietly, tentatively, took a seat. The outer edge of the igloo he was sitting in was made up of a thousand Sip-N-Spoons, a bev tie ('the tie that holds beverages'), a face that eats coins, a horrible pizza bed, a Star Wars immersion blender, various baby bibs stencilled with anti-suicide inspirational quotes, thirty mini horse lamps and what appeared to be hundreds of inordinately lifelike latex human fingers.

'What exactly are you doing?' asked Neil, almost to himself.

'I'm destroying the world.'

'What do you mean?'

'I'm killing the world.'

'How?'

'By injecting pharmakon into it.'

'What's that?'

'Poison and cure, life and death.'

'Oh,' said Neil, thinking 'I see; he's demented.' Nevertheless, he couldn't resist a challenge, even from a fruitcake. 'But we need the world,' he said.

'The world needs us,' said Victor, whose eyes, deep in his head, seemed to Neil to be mocking, pitying, but also far, far away.

'Yes,' said Neil, feeling anger rise, 'but how would we feed ourselves without it? How would we clothe ourselves? We're helpless. If the world goes down, we'd all die. Imagine the chaos. Do you want to murder millions of people? No. No. What we need to do is make the world better, so it takes care of us better, that's the moral thing to do.'

Victor chuckled. 'A pig talking of morals.'

Neil saw his soul leap out of his chest, throw Victor's soul to the floor, cuff it, and drag it off to the nick. But his body remained still. He clenched down on his fury. He had to get Lilly, and nothing was going to stop him. His head fell forward, his eyes screwed up tight, breathing heavily.

After a while he opened his eyes. Victor was tapping away at his laptop, checking something apparently, or setting something up. Rammed into the dome next to him were cupboards lined with c90 tapes. These were also covered with yellow and black symbols. Neil, to calm himself, noted the names on the spines, Wesley Willis, Daniel Johnston, Omar Shooli, Robert Wyatt, Pinduca, M.Ashraf, King Somalie, Shooby Taylor The Human Horn, Herbert Butros Khaury, Joe Meek, Sri Darwin Gross, Vivian Stanshall, Gökçen Kaynatan, Moondog… who were these people? Were they musicians? Neil couldn't understand why he hadn't heard of any of them. Losers, no doubt.

'So, anyway, I was wondering…' he said, trying to seem casual and off-the-cuff, 'because… *ever* so good your songs… really… I thought they were, erm…'

Victor looked up. 'The fat is bubbling, skim from the stock.'

'Sorry?'

'What do you want, piglet?'

'I was wondering if you had any others? Other songs? I wanted to…' He trailed off.

Victor stared at Neil again. It was so unsettling; the look of a madman, or drug addict, horrible, intense, cold, penetrating and yet unseeing, or seeing something else. Not distracted, quite the reverse.

'Something fishy here little piggy,' said Victor quietly.

Neil turned away. 'P.C.… Neil. You can call me Neil.'

Victor smiled again, but without humour. 'Something don't smell right, Police Constable Bacon Sandwich.'

'I just…' Neil reflexively swallowed, 'I like your songs, that's all. Honest.'

'And you want to hear some more?'

'Yes, no, I was hoping I could take them home and listen to them there, at ho—o—ome, seriously, on my own, and, uh, there, or there*by*, gain, a deeper, broader view of the, uh, the meaning, the musical meaning of what it is, you are…' Victor was staring at Neil's forehead, which was making it spew up all kinds of nonsense through his mouth, '…you are, you know, saying, saying to the world, um, to, well, not "to" anything I suppose, it's just artistic expression isn't it? I suppose, and I, too, am an artist,' he finished, rather magnificently, he thought, but the whole speech was delivered into his own chest.

'You want to take some more?' asked Victor, 'You took the others?'

'No, I *listened* to them. I didn't, I don't… I don't steal. I am of the police.'

'No, police don't steal. How can *law*man steal?'

'Well exactly.' Neil looked up, a little hopefully, as this seemed to be some kind of agreement.

'What music you like?' asked Victor.

'Uh…' Neil, as ever when holding a losing hand, looked down at his feet for another card to play, one that might have earlier fallen from the heavens, but Victor stopped him.

'Tell me the truth,' he said, 'don't lie. I'll know.'

'Alright.' Why should I lie, thought Neil. 'Elvis,' he said, 'Falco, late Vangelis, Esquivel, Pérez Prado, Foreigner, Neil Diamond obviously, The Moody Blues, again, obviously, uh, Jennifer Warnes… uh… Lots more, but not much after 1989, except for Coldplay. Music died the day The Bangles split.'

'And you want my music?'

'Yes, I want to broaden… and deepen… a—ahnd…'

Victor's face was immobile, inscrutable, although there might have been a touch of pity in there. 'What do you have to give?'

'Fort… Fifty pounds?'

Victor rummaged behind him and pulled out a pen drive from his alien nest, handing it over to Neil with his three-fingered left hand. Neil whispered a quick prayer to Jesus.

'Five hundred songs here Police Constable, Unstable, Pork Jelly in a stable. And what I want from you, what I want, peee seeeee, is... your bellyfat.'

Neil was aware that a proposition was on the table, a deal, but, although he didn't understand it, it didn't sound like a very good one. 'Uh, a hundred pounds?' he suggested weakly.

Victor handed over a can of spray-on bacon.

'Spray on some pig, pig.'

'You don't want money? Why?'

'I don't work for money.'

'You don't?' said Neil quietly, 'neither do I.'

Victor leaned forward and set a drum beat going on his computer. It sounded like a Binatone theme. 'Sing for your supper. You sing, you get the songs.' He reached to his side and picked up a bass guitar, thwacking a stuttering brain-damaged bass line. Over the top he began singing a tribal chanting recital, apparently ad hoc.

'Into the empty world... I threw the fullness of my mind... into the arms of the all-destroyer... I threw my the vitality of heart... into the mud of desire... I threw the purity of my blood... and into the cunt of the void... I threw the *enormity* of my balls...' He threw his arms wide and cried '...I boiled away in Baba Gee's cauldron, boiled and burnt myself clean away... and there, from the ashes of my self, grew... MUSHROOMS!!!'

The word 'mushrooms' was screamed, a ragged falsetto that made Neil's eardrums throb and his anus contract.

On a tiny keyboard on his knees Victor's chubby fingers began dancing, a screwy, farty, parpy, arped synth part over the top of a thumping bass growl, looped and playing by itself.

'The body is the door... set fire to the law... grow... PO-LICE-CONSTABLE!... Death has left the bed... dancing in the street instead... with a snake egg... POLICE-CONSTABLE!'

His screaming voice was horribly discordant, animal, not music at all. 'POLICE THE EGG!' he roared, 'POLICE THE EGGY EGGY... POLICE THE EGGY EGGY!'

The bleepy-bloopy music continued, louder now, filling the demonic igloo, filling Neil's mind, until man and matter became one. It was ghastly, but not, oddly, without…*something*. Somehow, brutal and weird as it was, there was some easy-listening soul here, a real melody, but horribly violated.

'Now *you!* Sing it! *Sing it!*' rasped Victor.

The bass line and synth continued autonomously; was he just miming? No, because now a deranged rumpy-pumpy out-of-tune upright piano part had joined the mix, and Neil could see and hear him hit 'wrong' notes.

'You better start squealing if you want those songs!' bellowed Victor over the music.

'Police constable mushroom,' sang Neil, without enthusiasm, let's get this over with. No different to lying to D.C.I. Gaynor, just with a stupid backing track. Also he needed a piss and his balls hurt.

'More! More! No heart, no songs!'

Neil shouted a bit louder, 'Police constable mushroom.'

'Not *effort* piggy-piggy, *heart-heart*.'

'Police the egg!' Neil yelled, following the chords with a basic, sung arpeggio.

'Mooorrre! Yaaaggghhhhh! From the behhhhhhlllllllleeeeee...'

Neil could feel the old bilious uprush; anger, or frustration, or fear… they were the same thing.

'Police the eggy egg! Police the eggy egg! Police the eggy eggy eggy eggy egg!' he sang, and shouted. Victor too, who was roaring, voice box ripping like a slashed amp, 'BELLY MIND POLICE CONSTABLE, NOT HEART. GIVE THE BELLYMIND EGG! EGG! BACON! ONION! MUSHROOM! NOTHING AT ALLLLLLL! AIIIIIEEEEEEEEEE!'

And, at this point, the relentless electronic drum track beating in Neil's skull like a loon with a soft-faced hammer, the synth track like baby snakes on amphetamine worming into his brain, the piano chords jangling through his bones like pachinko balls, the thundering brown-note bass-cannon loosening his bowels, and all the time overheating, enveloped in Victor's sweat and his own, hundreds of tiny horse-shaped lamps flaring, dazzling, pink, yellow and orange… at this point something ruptured in Neil, something clinging inside slipped, slipped, and let go, and he started yelling, barking, bawling. 'POLICE CONSTABLE EGG GLORY! POLICE OF THE SPORE! OFFICER OF THE OVUM! FLESHY FLESHY EGGY EGGY PLOD PLOD NOW!' A piston in Neil's psyche that held him together, or that concentrated his energy down the channel his life had engineered for it, tore free from the pin and the mechanism just began flying around, clattering, smashing the sides of the engine; but in bent rhythm. He broke into a piercing falsetto, like a castrato, eyeballs swelled in wonderment, 'I AM THE PIG OF CHRIST!'

'The kazoo! The kazoo!' cried Victor.

Neil, unthinking, picked up the kazoo and enthusiastically—if still aggressively—fuzzed away to the song, while Victor continued singing; 'Fertile egg-flesh… onion fecundity… mycelium love-nest… fungal profundity!… HAM AND EGGS! HAM AND EGGS!' Neil was lost, kazoo-lunatic.

Victor nodded to himself. 'Very great. Very great.'

∞

Joe finished hoovering the landing and stepped into a bedroom shambles. Clothes, booze and fags were everywhere, sexy underwear, T-shirts, frocks and the like dribbled over the bed, bedside tables and a bean bag. On the wall, looming over the bed, a large painting of Moses standing before the burning bush. Next to a chest of open drawers, which had regurgitated its load of socks and pants onto the floor, stood a coat rack upon which hung a series of multicoloured dog-collars.

'Honestly,' said Sophie, standing behind him, 'I'm so sorry. I'll pay you.'

'It's fine, really,' said Joe distracted, looking at the dog collars. 'What does your boyfriend do?'

'He's a priest.'

'Is he? A priest?'

'Yeah. He's obsessed with Moses.'

'And he's given to spleen?'

'He's got a terrible temper. He's always smashing and punching things. He says I'm like a vegetable, although he's right there, I am like a vegetable. I feel like one, most of the time.'

'If you don't feel like a vegetable, you haven't lived.'

'But I should do more work.'

Joe picked up his bin bag, getting to work. '"Should" is the devil's favourite modal verb,' he said, 'your boyfriend could tell you that.' He inspected the wainscotting, upon which a few photographs were balanced. He picked up a family photograph—a group of Australians it looked like, or possibly South Africans, somewhere hot and white—and as he did Sophie grabbed his elbow, turning him round.

'Look,' she said, gazing into his eyes. 'please, let me give you something for your trouble.'

Joe looked at her pretty, cat-like face, her dark, moist, slightly drunk or slightly hung-over eyes, her red, perhaps too red lips, parted, selling eagerness. He carefully put the photograph, held behind her back, into his pocket and said, 'sorry, I can't.'

'Why?' she said, searchingly.

'It's my leg.'

'What's wrong with it?'

'It doesn't let me do certain things.'

'Oh,' she slumped, 'Okay.'

'But, err, I wouldn't mind one of your boyfriend's dog collars.'

Sophie was quite sunk now. She waded over to the coat rack.

'Which colour do you want?'

'White's fine.'

She handed it to him. 'Here.'

'Thanks.'

'What do you want a dog-collar for?'

'My wife is giving me grief about our chickens.'

8

The family of Maximilian Lord Thottesley—the man known as Max Thot—stretched back to the Norman invasion of England. He was a direct descendent of Hugh de Thottesley, Lord of Conches, and companion of William the Conqueror, with a confirmed pedigree stretching back to the Father of Europe himself, Charlemagne. His ancestral home, Thottesley Hall, built in the 12th century, had a private chapel (even older), the remains of a prehistoric stone circle (older than the pyramids), an underground swimming pool, and a walled garden in the Italianate style on a rising slope providing good views of two immense woodlands and their herds of fallow deer. He had successfully reintroduced the Eurasian lynx to his estate, as well as beavers and a herd of European bison, which occasionally wandered into the perfectly ordered emerald gardens, landscaped, in the style of classic French formalism, by André Le Nôtre himself, and decorated with cloud busters, sealed gazebos and various pseudo-scientific contraptions; a 'hobby', he said. The ensemble, one of the oldest continually inhabited homes on the British Isles, loomed before Bronya as she stepped out of her Nissan Micra, which looked out of place next to the fleet of Bentleys, Jaguars and Aston Martins (including an enormously valuable DBRI, the pinnacle in classic automotive machinery). She was carrying a clipboard, an old flapover briefcase with a broken latch and a few loose papers which, flustered, she continually struggled with.

She approached the huge oak front door then paused. From deep within she could hear two voices, one stentorian, aged, another youthful, pubescent.

'Louder!' cried the older man's voice.

'Milky lemon glow!' came the boy's voice.

'Stuttering!' barked the man.

'M… m… m… milky… l… l… l… emon… g… gl… glo… glow!' came the staggered response.

'Backwards!'

'Wolg nomel iklim.'

'Bored housewife!'

'Milky lemon glow,' cried the boy, this time in a feminine register, complainy and indolent.

'Sandpapery and camp!'

'Milky yellow glow!' This time throaty, harsh, yet also a bit queeny.

'Retarded, bearded!'

'Milky yellow glow!' Drooling, deep and self-satisfied.

The weird Q-and-A went on, uninterrupted by Bronya's banging and calling, which she eventually abandoned to wander round the estate. Her trudgy body language, like the tone of her voice, bespoke engrained annoyance with all that occurred or ever could. She was born moaning and spent her life looking for a good reason to justify her base-state.

'Sore-throated weariness of a lower-middle-class jeweller who has spent the night snoring!' cried the man.

'Milky lemon glow!' cried the boy, with rough lassitude.

'Plum-quartz-quince-whicker-firecrest salmagundi!'

'Milky lemon glow!' Phazed now and sprinkled with tremelo.

'Hello!? Hello!?' shouted Bronya, walking round the back of the house. 'Anyone here!?' She looked through a window, down a long corridor. She could see the boy, around nine he looked, semi-naked, wrists and ankles bound with some kind of bright cord, jumping down the hallway with a huge fat boxer who was blindfold, wielding colossal boxing gloves and randomly taking swings at the boy. An older man, regal in his fez and house-suit, smoking a beautiful Russian cigarette, calmly walked behind them both. All three disappeared from view, but the otherworldly interrogation continued.

'Scatter!' cried the man.

'Milky lemon glow!' Staccato and broken, as if sent through a bitcrusher.

Bronya rapped hard on the window. Sudden silence. She waited. No answer. She knocked again, then stepped back, looking up, eyes shaded, at the dark-curtained windows. Was someone up there? In the darkness? She had a shivery feeling there was, a sense of being scrutinised, assessed, not just her outer form, but her inner being.

She turned away and jumped. A stocky, craggy old fellow, with a closely shaved crew cut, browny orangy tracksuit bottoms hauled up to his armpits and a big-monkey head T-shirt was watching Bronya with steely hard, needle-blue eyes, while slowly polishing one of the priapic mechanisms on the lawn, which gently hummed.

'Oh,' said Bronya, putting her face on, 'Excuse me?'

The man stopped polishing but continued to grip her with his ball-bearing eyes. She approached and started speaking. 'Sorry to bother you, but I was wondering… my name is Bronya Cosslett… um, you are…?'

'Patrick,' he said.

'Patrick…?'

He was silent, no surname forthcoming. 'Well,' she went on, 'I'm from social services and I'm here to see, um,' she checked her clipboard, 'Joris-Karl Thottesley, and, um, I need to know what is going on here. We've had reports… I mean they don't have to let me in, but I have a job to do you know. I know it's not your fault, but we think, I think, there might be an at-risk youth here… erm…' As she spoke he either bored her with his unpleasantly intense gaze or he glanced behind her towards the house, warily; in both cases not listening to a word she said.

When she ran out of steam he screwed up his eyes, locked onto her, and let fly, in an intense and gravelly Glaswegian Scots, a bitter tirade. As he talked he got more and more worked up until, by the end of this speech it felt like he could do anything, pull his clothes off, grab her by the neck, run his rake through her, anything. Bronya stepped backwards by degrees so that, by the time he had finished she was at a somewhat impolite distance.

'Nae idea… ah've goat *nae* fuckin idea whit's gaun oan roon here. But there will be a reckonin, right enough. Aw sorts ae dodgy shite gaun oan in that hoose. Men, grown fuckin men, dressed up like weans… man, that poor wee yin, the things they dae tae him. Aw sorts ae animals, aw sorts ae boxes, his weazen face aw screwed up like a ghoul; an d'ye ken how it's possible? How he made his fuckin money, Mr Mucky-Muck? Aff the backs ae workin folk. *Oor* money, *oor* land, *oor* labour… aw just *gone*, poof, lifted by that cunt an his cunty lot before him. He ca's himsel a Catholic. A Catholic! Whit kinda fuckin Catholic's that wi aw that diabolic shite? He says… ah've heard him masel… he says he's aw fur the betterment ae mankind, the brotherhood ae man, an that's why he's stickin money intae aw they green companies. It's pish. Total fuckin *pish*. He's a devil… a fuckin *devil*. Ah'm tellin ye, ye've goat utter gobshites like him in there, gluin jewels tae tortoises an aw that carry-on, an who's fuckin payin fur it? Us. The workin man. The labourer, the joiner, the nurse, folk that actually *graft*. We get shat oan, day in, day oot, while they're arsin aboot wi headsets an drones an smart water But he'll pay. They aw will. Ye cannae keep a lid oan things forever. Ye can only crush freedom fur so fuckin lang. Freedom's like a wumman, ye cannae keep her under yer thumb forever. Mind ma words: the day'll come when the common folk rise up, like a fuckin ocean, an these bastards'll *droon*…'

'Right, thank you. That's great. Bye then. Bye! Bye!'

8

Lilly was on Nina's screen, and Joe was on Neil's. Joe was pulling his cleaning cart up the road to the funeral home, and Lilly was cleaning up an old woman's arsehole, the former watched by his spying brother, the latter by her spying boss.

'I saw your children this morning,' said Lilly to the dead woman, 'Paul was stealing their money, basically, so that I, me, a stranger, could handle your body and so Nina could buy herself a new… actually what does she spend her money on? To be honest with you Wendy I'm starting to wonder if this is entirely right. I mean we're friends, you and me; I like you, I do, but paying other people to handle the people you love, like this… I'm starting to think…'

Looking after the dead had brought Lilly to life, releasing the weight that school, university and the various jobs she'd had until now had pressed down upon her. One of her first jobs, while she was trying to pay her way through university, was temping for a market research company collecting and collating 'profiling data' on the customers of this or that business, at least customers mad enough to fill in survey forms in the hope of winning a voucher. Occasionally, someone submitted some kind of honest comment, or they wrote something unexpected, and instead of 'I really wish someone would produce orange-flavoured instant coffee' a response would come through pointing out that the CEO of the company she was researching for was a kiddy fiddler, or asking at what point a bowl becomes a basin, or declaring that 'the internet is death', or 'triangles feel pain', all of which injected a little reliefy darkness into the over-lit, strip-lit, savagely plastic office. But any such moments soon got swallowed by the atmosphere of… what was it? Not sadness, not loneliness, not boredom, not anything. A notmosphere.

She worked then with twelve other graduates, also temps, and a few other older permanent staff, all hunched over their workstations, and in the corner was a landline which often rang, but which none of the young temps would ever answer. When she asked one of them, a bleakly pretty ginger girl called Aloe with eyebrows that looked like they'd been threaded by a robot, she said that she, Aloe, was anxious about the ringing phone, because 'it might not be for me'. This, for Lilly, said it all. Aloe's phone only rang for her. Always for *her*. They did speak to each other, in the 'real world', but their speech was so peculiar. Lilly had *had* conversations, she remembered them, at least she thought she did, with her grandmother for example, and she remembered, when actually speaking, contributing to a strange, lovely, flowing, living thing between us, growing, by itself, its own thing, and yet also ours. This hadn't happened at university, where people didn't talk, they exchanged memories and opinions. They only knew memories and opinions. Something was only true if you could have an opinion about it, and opinions were the only truth. If Aloe's opinion was that she could levitate, or that she had ankles that bend both ways, or that chorizo was a pathogen, then that was real and to even raise an eyebrow was not much different to giving a Nazi salute and goose stepping round the office. None of them seemed to know anything beyond their opinions, or the opinions of their opinion-machines. Everything that had happened before they were born was an illusion. When Lilly said that Paul McCartney now looked like a budgerigar they all said 'who?' They hadn't heard of Morrissey or Nick Drake or Louis Armstrong or Rachmaninov; nobody before they were born. Not just musicians, nobody. It was as if in the year 2000 a knife had come down upon the endless, billowing tapestry of culture and sliced off a piece of fabric the size of a sticking plaster.

Her course was music, which was alright, at least they forced her to work harder than she would have otherwise, but the whole cost was going to be something like seventy thousand pounds. Why not instead go and live in Finland and hire a good piano teacher there, or two, one to teach and the other to do an interpretative dance? And it was all so suffocating, so dreary, like a long church sermon. She felt like she was adrift on a dull grey ocean. The bastard Nick situation hadn't helped, but that was a symptom not a cause, and the cause was still mysterious. A sense of not fitting in anywhere started seeping into her life. She had become aware that everyone was thinking the same, that *they* were the misfits here, too beautiful for this world, radical outsiders; and yet they all basically accepted the path they were on, they basically accepted that it had to be this way, or that there was no point in changing. They all knew that they were destined to graduate, and get some kind of professional job, and have kids, and vote, and see their parents every few months, and get old, and fat, and angry, and die. They all knew it, and they said they hated it, and they complained about it, or joked about it, or listened to rebellious music, or read edgy books, or went off to teach Nepalese orphans how to use Excel, or sat at home smoking genetically engineered brain-melting skunk and playing video games, or wrote novels about transsexual novelists, or marched in the streets for the bees, or for the poor, helpless black people, or whatever, it didn't matter, because they all basically accepted it, the whole thing, the big, boring picture, the general down slope which, whatever grooves we choose to roll in, is only ever going down and down and down.

An all-pervading sickness had settled on Lilly. The nice ordinary world of university, with nice ordinary lectures, and nice ordinary people, doing nice ordinary things, suddenly this had become a plaster cast world, a ghastly, dreamy, hollow shell of things. So she'd left.

This bold act didn't lift the weight at all though. If anything, it got heavier after she signed on, and looked for a job, and found a job, and lost a job, and found another one, and all the time a dry, excruciating, spine-draining sense of total futility was making her shoulders ache and her stomach sick and she had to do these big sighs all the time to try to be rid of all her feelings. Until the dead came into her life. Then, something peculiar happened. A new kind of alrightness appeared. She'd never really worried about 'mortality'—that seemed to be something men did—but still, some underlying worry about *getting* somewhere, *achieving* something, seemed to dissipate in the company of the no longer living.

The worst thing was the families. God. Death really brings out the worst in people. Totally and utterly broken, completely bewildered or absolutely cold were the three basic modes, and they all seemed false, or unnatural. Lots of people were dreadful hypocrites, really; all solemn and sad, but thinking of themselves, what this will mean to *me*. How much *I* can get out of it. Every week she'd hear of a family at each other's throats over an inheritance, it was all so ugly. Ugly! The poor families were okay.

More likely you'd find they actually cared about losing someone, sometimes with a kind of softness which actually meant something. Most people just seemed secretly glad it wasn't them.

'Hello? Anyone here?' Joe's voice floated in from the garage.

'Carl!' Lilly shouted. No answer. She poked her head through the PVC strip curtains. 'Hello! …oh!' She wasn't expecting a priest. 'Hold on a mo!' she said.

'Okay,' said Joe, fiddling with his dog-collar, which was too small and was making his voice a little strangled and awky.

As Lilly passed the phone on the wall, it rang. She took a deep, tense, breath and picked it up. 'Hi Nina,' she said.

'Lilly, I've just been to the supermarket…' said Nina, twittery and tremulous. '… and I don't understand why they don't put the celery in with rest of the vegetables.'

'Where is it then?'

'It's in with the salad foods.'

'But it is a salad food.'

'I just don't *see* it as a salad food, and I know I'm not alone.'

'I think most people see it as a salad food.'

'What about the carrots? They're not a salad food, not mainly, you fry with them.'

'God alright, but why is this a problem?'

'I just waste far too much of my life looking for things in supermarkets.'

'Don't we all…?' Lilly wasn't confident enough to cut short conversations that were going nowhere, but she could feel the pressure of the man waiting outside. Fortunately, Nina, whose only significant relationship was with her father, a man who boiled over with rage whenever she rambled on, was overly sensitive to any hints that she was talking too much.

'Oh yes, yes, yes… have you, um, finished Mrs. Watts?'

'Not yet, no.'

'Only we've got three more to fit in today. We *have* to get them done Lilly.'

'I know, I'm going as fast as I can.'

'Erm, okay, okay, but as long as you do finish. Sorry, but, *will* you finish?'

'Yes, I will.' She went to hang up before the irritation rising in her chest could reach her mouth and emerge as some unpleasantness, but Nina caught her, 'And, I was going to say, sorry Lilly, I'm sorry, but could you… do you think you could *not* wear dresses at work?'

'Why? Nobody can see me. Nobody alive at least.'

'Oh, but that's not the point. It's just not professional. I'm sorry Lilly, I'm just saying, um, perhaps you should dress more like a mortician?'

'Perhaps you should pay me more like a mortician?' Lilly replied, under her breath.

'Sorry? I'm sorry? What?'

'Perhaps I *should* dress more like a mortician. You're absolutely right.'

Nina hung up. Lilly slumped, then straightened up.

'Just washing my hands!' she called out.

She emerged, shaking her hands dry. Joe, in the workshop, was measuring his eye-width with a sliding T-bevel, which he put down when Lilly appeared.

'Not that it matters,' she continued, 'those strips of plastic must be, can you *imagine* what's on them? I don't like to think about it. Life's a lot easier if you don't think about death isn't it?'

'I find the opposite is true.'

'So do I! I suppose that's what *you're* employed for though, to think about death for everyone else. You're employed to think about it and I'm employed to tart it up with Maybelline Buff Beige foundation. Sorry, I'm rambling, I hate long hellos don't you? I'm just a bit stressed. You probably don't have boss problems?' She looked at Joe, and was struck with a sense of recognition, an oh, you, yes, I knew that you existed. There was something familiar about his soft voice too.

'I do.' Joe looked upwards, significantly.

'Yes, but He doesn't give you grief does He?'

'Oh He does, continually. He finds failure far more entertaining than success.'

'What about your colleagues? You know, church people, do you get on with them?'

'I don't really talk to them. I've got selective mutism.'

'What's that?'

'It's where you're totally fine and talkative in one situation and then, when you're at work, you're completely unable to say anything.'

'Oh yes. I have that. Actually, not so much here. I do work with a bit of a pig, but I actually quite like him, although I don't want him to know that. And Paul, he's an odd fish, but I think he might have a child mind. It's… I just wish my boss would apologise once in a while… do you know what I mean? She's always saying sorry, but she never really *apologises*.'

'No chance of that. Downward-apologisers don't rise.'

'Maybe God will apologise, you know, when I die. He doesn't seem the apologising sort though.'

'God? No, no. He has issues around the idea of admitting he was wrong.'

'I think, I just want no bullshit. A world that is the opposite of bullshit.' She peered up into Joe's eyes. 'What is the opposite of bullshit?'

'Cow's milk?'

Lilly smiled. She could feel herself relaxing. There was an unmoving expanse in the middle of this conversation, a relief, like getting into fresh air after being stuck in a hole with someone you don't like, which was more or less what the world was.

'Sorry,' she said, 'you've probably got things to do, erm, you know, Goddish things. What can I do for you?'

'I'm here to pick up the coffins.'

'Oh that's Carl's business, he's not here right now.'

'Right… Carl…' Joe said to himself, thinking back to the hearses that had turned up at his house for no reason. 'I think I've met him. Tall man? Looks like Lurch from the Addams family?'

'That's Paul. Carl's short, shorter than me. He doesn't have any hair.'

'I don't remember his hair,' said Joe.

'That's because he doesn't have any.'

Lilly burst into laughter. Joe laughed also, and Lilly suddenly felt an overwhelming desire to confide something to this man, anything, it didn't matter what; as much to give him the gift of a confidence than to get anything off her chest.

'I'm just not designed to be happy,' she said, surprising herself. More surprising was how this departure from the unspoken rules of conversation was taken, by this strange, large godman, in his stride.

'Perhaps the world isn't designed to make you happy?'

'So what do I do? Leave the world?'

'I don't know about that. I try to ignore it, but it won't leave me alone. It's a real attention seeker, the world.'

'I think,' said Lilly, 'that the world used to be a simple thing, like this...' she picked up a plastic fork which Carl had left in a can of baked beans, 'like this fork, which you could use, or which would, erm, fork you. Now it's not a thing, it's a person, the world is a person, and *as* a person it's... it's erm...'

'A bell-end.'

'Right,' said Lilly, frowning, 'a bell-end.'

'The world is a bell-end,' Joe repeated the judgement with religious seriousness.

'It's just so hard to get along with, isn't it, the world? It won't let you... You know, I used to think I could do anything, go anywhere, be anyone. I mean, that's what they teach you isn't it. Be your best self. What's to stop me being a carpet-weaver or a train driver...?'

'Oh, don't. They're all wankers.'

'Are they?'

'You know they're on fifty thousand a year?'

'*Are* they?'

'It's very boring as well, driving a train. Just one track.'

'All jobs end up boring though don't they?'

'They do.'

'But why? I sort of feel they shouldn't.'

'It's because we're living in the end times.'

'Oh yes! I was *just* thinking that today.'

'That's not a bad thing though,' said Joe.

'It's not is it?'

'Sometimes I lay awake at night, in a cold sweat, afraid that civilisation *won't* collapse.'

She smiled. Joe smiled. He felt like she was looking through him, or perhaps like she wanted to look through him, all the way through. 'There's always so much admin too,' she said, 'Is that connected with the end times?'

'Yes, many people are surprised by the amount of paperwork involved in the apocalypse.'

'And there's no getting away from it, the world I mean.'

'No. It's everywhere. It even follows me into dreams. I had one last night where I was in a Chinese supermarket, I was shopping there, and a customer came up to me and said "where's the soya sauce?" and I said "I don't work here," and they said "I want the low sodium kind," and I said to them, "but I don't work here," and then another one came up to me and said "where's the black vinegar," and again I said, "I don't work here," and they kept on coming, asking me for chilli oil, dumpling dough, oolong tea and dried shrimp paste, hundreds of them and I just went down, submerged under them, shouting "I don't work here! I don't work here!"'

'*Do* you work here?' Lilly asked.

'If there's one thing I can say about myself it's that I do not work here.'

She nodded. She felt much better. Kind of sadder, but it was a good kind; definitely much better.

'Anyway, you know which coffins are yours?' she asked, and then immediately regretted it because this question would draw the conversation to an end.

'Errm, yes, those two.' He pointed to two coffins.

'Okay, well, do you want some help loading them?'

'No it's okay, I'm on foot.'

'You're going to *carry* two coffins down the road?'

'Oh it's fine, people think I'm in fancy dress anyway.'

'Maybe you are?'

'Maybe I am.'

∞

Maria wanted normality and stability; and—the source of both for her, although she was not aware of it—power. Power meant control over the threateningly strange, it was a guarantor of stability and a stand-in for genuine joy, a state she was unfamiliar with. Her power drive manifested as professional 'caring,' as an ambitious scrabble up the ranks of social services and as a kind of vaguely promised, vaguely threatened sexuality, a well-advertised implicit suggestion that if you give me what I want I'll tear my bra off and moo. Not a suggestion which she made good on, nor one that worked on any but weak men, but most men were weak and some of the people she had to climb over to get to where she wanted to get to were men, so she wore tight blouses, tight skirts, and liberally applied arch, knowing smiles when she needed a man to give her something, none of which was conscious, nor was her spontaneous decision to prude up her wardrobe when she had to have a meeting with a powerful woman.

She had now reached management level three on the caring ladder, and had adapted her personality to fit someone who has their own office. She was, or she endeavoured to be, serious, professional, multi-skilled, understanding and worldly-wise. She had seen it all; you couldn't possibly imagine the horrors she had heroically battled through working with the human refuse of Edding, all of whom she hated, unless they were 'nice'—which meant needy and submissive. She liked the 'nice' ones, the ones with the imploring look in their eyes, the ones you sort of felt like slapping. Everyone else was a scumbag. Arseless drug addicts mostly, or hard-faced, high-cheekboned Rom pimps without a word of English, or twenty-stone slobs who spend all day watching Phil and Holly and stuffing their faces with Toffee Yum-Yums, or poxy old men with medieval diseases who just sit in their own piss, or ratty jobless psychos who play their hardcore one-note dance music so loud that neighbours four doors down complain and some absolute cock-end emerges and says 'I'll ring the police and have you done for harassment,' which does happen. The funny thing though, Maria had often noticed, was how all these people, no matter how scummy or selfish or stupid, they all demanded respect! What for? What is there to respect about *you*? Fuck all!

Over the years she had grown in confidence and had become more and more outspoken, obstinately identifying problems and their solutions, which she fired through the people beneath her like cannonballs. They didn't like it. They said 'I don't know what to do,' and Maria would tell them what to do and they'd get angry, or fall apart. She had to keep them in line though, or they'd screw up the paperwork or offend someone, the two greatest social-working sins. It was Maria's job, if anyone ever criticised Muslims, or women, or transsexuals, to remind them not to be racist, sexist or transphobic, and then, if they persisted, to discipline them. Again, not popular policies, but this is the world we live in now, one where all minorities must be respected, even if they can't do their jobs for toffee, or own half the town and screw their tenants for every penny they have, or are serial killers, or set up child prostitution rings. None of that matters if you're a disabled, black, Peruvian transsexual, and that's as it should be—I mean, just think of the Holocaust—but it was very stressful because people were such bloody bigots and just didn't understand what all these poor people went through.

Fortunately, today's problem involved a white, heterosexual man with no religious affiliations—an unoffendable sitting duck—and so Maria was happy to listen to Bronya's buck-toothed whining. She, Bronya, stood in the doorway of Maria's standard, tatty, cheap, government office giving her account of her visit to Thottesley Hall.

'…so I *really* think something suspicious is going on there,' said Bronya, 'I mean, it was just weird. Not right at all. Definite *issues*.'

'Okay, so write it up.'

'I'm not sure how to, I mean…'

'It's in the procedures manual.'

Bronya took a deep, strained breath. Her fear of paperwork was making her nauseous, and this was a perilous one. These princely types could flick you off the surface of her majesty's payroll if you wrote the wrong thing. 'I'm just wondering about the "factors affecting potential litigation",' she said, referring to one of the entries in Max's casework file, the most important one as far as higher-ups were concerned because it alerted them to legal problems, bad press and negative Facebook posts, 'because' she said, 'the referral…'

'Bronya, please, I've got so much to do here…'

'I, it, I mean it was a very nice looking house, and, I'm worried about the son, but… I just want to make sure, you know, we're, *covered*.' She whispered the word 'covered,' 'I'm worried it will come back on us.'

'We've talked about this. If it's not written down, it didn't happen. *Nothing* that's not written down or recorded ever comes back on anybody. Okay?'

Bronya's face, screwed up, slowly disappeared behind the door and Maria returned to the lifestyle section of the Guardian and the article she was reading by a writer who, every week, wandered around her three-bedroom North London flat, picking things up and asking herself if she could get a column out of it. This week was about dry cleaning duvets, a subject of no great interest to Maria, but a demonic force within her, which could not be ignored, was soothed by it.

Bronya returned to the main office. A combination of central heating turned up too high, fleshy bureaucratic stress and cheap furniture filled the small room with a kind of gluey haze. Five sunken social workers sat at their computers. There was overweight Chris who never washed and played World of Warcraft for days on end—he could easily have been a client, but was difficult to fire, as he wasn't agency. Opposite Chris was Sammy, a sweet, camp Nigerian who went home crying every night. He *was* agency and his contract was hanging by a thread. Next to Sammy sat a fat, restless half-Saudi, half-American girl called Aisha who spoke and thought like a seven year old, but was surprisingly aggressive, even abusive to her clients, treating them all like babies, which they all enjoyed—Aisha always got the highest approval ratings—and finally, at the back of the room, sat Raimonda and Andy, a slick double act—he, tall, handsome, ginger, going places; she an asexual half-Brazilian, half-Lithuanian, born with a clipboard in her hand. Both Andy and Raimonda had books balanced on their heads, for reasons that Bronya didn't want to know. She didn't really like talking to anyone in the office. Chris smelt of death, Aisha never listened, Sammy made her feel guilty and Andy and Raimonda made her feel second-rate.

Bronya stared at her computer screen, frantically chewing a pencil while she fretted over her paperwork. Her c14b assessment form was partly filled in, but she could go no further. She gripped her head, pouted, made a micro-gesture towards Raimonda, to ask her what she thought she should do, stopped herself... and then the phone rang.

'Hello, Bronya Cosslett.'

'Hello, is this social services?'

'Yes.'

'This is P.C. Neil Geb, I've just visited an elderly lady in a cottage just north of the b434 who is, in effect being restrained by her primary carers. I'm extremely concerned about this, can you arrange a visit to assess the situation?'

Bronya gave a big theatrical sigh. 'Well, I'll see what I can do... We're run off our feet here.'

'Deprivation of liberty safeguards Ms Cosslett,' said Neil, 'Adult safeguards. Am I clear? It's quite urgent.'

'Oh God alright, alright. What's the address?'

8

Joe, concealed behind the six-foot-tall fence of a dentist's car park, changed out of his priest's uniform. His two coffins were balanced either side of his cleaner's cart forming a large wooden 'X'. As he was changing he could hear a conversation from the other side of the fence, two women.

'I thought you two broke up?'

'I tried to, but he's so nice to me—so now I just cheat on him discreetly.'

'He's *too* nice, I find. Being nice wears you down.'

'Yeah. He's also stiff.'

'What do you mean, uptight? I never got that impression.'

'No, physically stiff. When he walks he looks really stiff. He looks like he's got a gun muzzle pressed into his back, so I… I find I can't walk next to him. I have to walk out in front of him. He doesn't like it, but what am I to do?'

Poor fool, thought Joe, but then Maria probably thinks something similar about me. She might even be having an affair. Maybe I should? It would at least liven things up a bit. The only thing I've got to look forward to at home is the next episode of Captain Unemployment.

How, he wondered, have we managed to stay together? Both of us are waiting for a better day. Our dreams are so different, she wants to go up and up and up and I want to go down and down and down. We're both deluding ourselves that there's a middle ground, when there's not. There's just a superficially satisfactory ledge.

What does she see in me? Joe wondered. It's like she considers it her duty to be with me. Does she see me as some kind of child? Maybe that's it. She doesn't want kids, she hates them, but she's always dreaming of them. Maybe I'm just a big helpless child to her? Something safely pathetic? Someone who won't get in her way, or challenge her eruptions. But I can't be bothered. The problems between us always seem to come down to whose fault it is that *she* is in a bad mood. Well, either it's her fault or it's my fault, but what I don't understand is why we can't deal with the problem like a couple of chaps. Put it behind us. Okay, it's my fault, fine, how about a game of Yahtzee?

This approach, which seemed to Joe the only one worth taking, infuriated Maria for reasons he could not fathom. They would be late for a lunch date at a fancy restaurant because he had been so slapdash and floppy and yeah, yeah, yeah about ordering a taxi and she'd spent all morning getting prepared and looking forward to it and Joe *knew* she was looking forward to it, and here they were Saturday morning, all the taxis busy of course, sure to be late, sure to lose their table, and Joe, happy as a retarded baby with an ice cream, would be saying, 'yeah, I can see why you're annoyed, you're quite right, I should have booked the taxi earlier.'

Sometimes, Joe felt he wanted to leave her. He thought about it, but then it seemed to him like walking up to your mother and punching her. While she's just sitting there reading a newspaper. It was senseless. Sometimes he defined this as weakness, but that didn't seem to inspire him to act. People, thought Joe, can just be okay with being cowards. He then turned this round in his mind; could sadists find the same thing, that defining their cruelty as a weakness didn't help, that 'people could just be okay with being a bastard?' Would that be okay? Joe decided that it would be. It was all okay; but did that make it okay?

After he'd changed back into his cleaner's overalls, he started wheeling his unsteady load down the road, the two coffins now lengthways on the cart, strapped on with pink and lime-green bungee cords. He turned the corner of Palmerstone Avenue to find Irving, bitterly neat, scornfully compact, stretched and drawn, seemingly waiting for him.

'Oh, hello!' said Joe cheerfully.

'What are you doing?'

'Funny what people throw away isn't it?'

'Where did you find these?' Irving stepped to inspect the caskets.

'Greggs.'

'Greggs?'

'Budget bakery chain. Famous for its sausage rolls, although I don't know why, they're…'

'I know what Greggs is,' Irving interrupted, 'What are they doing with coffins?'

'Greggs is the devil's work.'

'I'm serious,' said Irving, needled, grieved, 'who threw away two brand new coffins?'

'Who would have old coffins?'

'You know what I mean.'

'I just found them, here on the street.'

'Really? Did you?' Irving seemed impressed, 'Well, no point hauling them yourself; if I were you I'd call the mobile team.'

'But what would you do if *you* were you?'

'I *am* me Joe. I *am* me.' There was a long pause between them. Neither man wanted to say anything. Finally, Irving broke the silence; 'Who are you?' he asked, but not to Joe. He faced sideways so that he seemed to be asking a young pink-faced man on the other side of the road.

'Who am I?' said Joe. He thought for a moment, then said, vaguely; 'I'd be lying if I said anything.'

Irving fixed his red little eyes suspiciously on Joe. 'Where do you see yourself in five years' time?'

'I see myself a field.'

'In a field? What field?'

'Not *in* a field; *a* field. I want to be a field.'

Irving sighed heavily. 'Why are you doing this job Joe?'

'I have a passion for cleanliness.'

'But you never clean anything.'

'I picked up a paper cup earlier. Two.'

'We're swimming in filth.'

'Well exactly. And how many urban custodians is the council employing?'

'It's just you and me.'

'You see? How am I supposed to keep a town of 100,000 people clean? Hang on, your *whole* job is managing me?'

Irving took another immense sigh, picked up a match and surreptitiously put it in his satchel. 'Yes,' he said, 'someone has to.'

∞

'There's a completely dreadful man in the kitchen.'

'Always dreadful man in kitchen,' said Chiyo.

They were in Lilly's room, a warm assemblage of homemade birds, Eastern European wooden toys, Moomin prints, woodcuts (Dürer, Holbein, Gill), handmade clothes, a hurricane lamp, a bass oboe, a bass guitar… Lilly sat on her bed and Chiyo stood at the window, looking out at the cloud-muted sunset.

Lilly had got home to find Hunter, West and an American man, one of Hunter's many contacts, filling the kitchen, the house, the universe, with their enormous, hollow beings. The American, an ordinary-looking, big-lipped, neat toothed, pudgy man in a Tesco T-shirt, had immediately walked up to Lilly, stood too close to her and said 'are you okay?' then immediately said, even more intensely, 'no, really?' and then, before Lilly could reply, he'd stepped back and airily announced that he was 'thinking that languaging is not necessarily the proper route to sensemaking' and 'if we are to have a dialogue we need to transcend…' he'd then whistled, long and low. Lilly later discovered that this was his modus operandi, to amaze the room with his depth and originality which just annoyed everyone in it. When they reacted with confusion and irritation, or as Lilly did by walking out, he felt hurt and alone. Neil was the same, in his way, just without the intellectual pretensions.

'An American man,' said Lilly to Chiyo, and went on to explain what had happened.

'Americans,' said Chiyo, which seemed to sum it all up entirely.

'Don't you like them then?'

'They tell me about their lives. I don't ask, they just tell me.'

'I don't know any,' said Lilly, 'Only on the internet.'

'If they grow up next to water, okay.'

'Americans you mean? If they grew up near to the ocean?'

'Or lake, or river.'

'Hmm. West grew up next to water. She comes from Brighton, and she's dreadful as well.'

Chiyo said nothing. Perhaps this rule had a few exceptions.

'She says she's bisexual,' said Lilly, 'but she's just being trendy.'

'Everyone is lesbian in England.'

'Girls *are* pretty though aren't they? I almost never see a man I think is fit, but I always see beautiful women.'

Chiyo turned away from the window and sat in Lilly's armchair, posture immaculate. She never slouched, although there was nothing studied or forced about her bearing. 'Yes, all men ugly,' she said. Her lips hardly moved when she spoke, her face was almost completely calm; but there was movement, and it conveyed just as much power as Lilly's more florid gestures.

'Are they?' said Lilly.

'Yes, but that is good. I love ugly men.'

'I know what you mean. I sometimes think I want a handsome man who fell from the third, no second, floor. Third,' she corrected herself, 'Third. A bit damaged.'

'How strong?'

'How strong?'

'Yes, how strong?'

'How strong do I want a man to be?'

'Yes.'

'Oh, I dunno. Strong enough to protect me from himself I suppose. Why, how strong do you want a man to be?'

'Strong enough to dive into a volcano for truth.'

'That strong? That's very strong.'

'With strong man I am strong. With weak man I am evil.'

'Actually I did meet an interesting man today. And he was handsome and ugly, or ugly in a handsome way' said Lilly. 'He had a big head, I mean the thing was big.'

'Like famous man?'

'Do they have big heads, famous people?'

'Most.'

'You're very observant. Well this man said he was a priest, but he wasn't like any priest I've ever met.'

'What are priests like?'

'Oh, they're all history teachers. That's what God likes, apparently, really boring little old men with round heads who love France and rubbings.'

Chiyo again said nothing. She picked up a Michael Nyman score on the table next to her and leafed through it.

'Haven't you met anyone? Anyone interesting?' asked Lilly, 'Since you've been here?'

'I am interested in all men.'

'What I mean is, uh, I saw a man go into your room, last week.'

'His name was Grant.'

'He was very old.'

'Sixty-five.' Chiyo put the score down and looked past Lilly, five degrees to her left, like a cat would.

Lilly had no idea how Chiyo was taking this conversation. Did she mind talking about her love life? It was almost impossible to read her. Lilly decided she would press on until she got a definite signal. 'Is that… you like older men?'

'All age okay. I like men about to die.'

'Oh. Erm.' Lilly had no idea what to say. She wanted to ask why Chiyo liked men who were about to die, where she found them, why they never seemed to spend more than a night here… Finally Chiyo spoke;

'I am looking for someone I can die with.'

'But don't you die alone?'

Chiyo turned her head slightly towards Lilly. 'When the time is right a man will come who I can die with.'

'Isn't that… magical thinking?'

'I am magical,' she said, her dark eyes burning.

'God, I wish I was.'

'What do you wish for?'

'Oh I don't know. To be happy I suppose. Isn't that what everyone wishes for? I suppose I should think of something specific.' Lilly rolled onto her back, pondering. 'A wild, drug-fuelled orgy and ramen-eating competition. On a space-station.' She sighed, 'I… It's hard because… Neil sort of gets in the way…'

'There is problem?'

'Well… I mean I like him… I don't want to wish him out of the picture or anything… He just gets so angry… and then so sad. I don't think he realises he's making such a fuss. He thinks he's the normal one.'

'He is.'

Lilly turned on her side, facing Chiyo. 'He *is*, isn't he?' Then, to herself, wonderingly '*He's* the normal one.'

There was a knock on the door. Chiyo immediately stood up, bowed slightly and moved to leave.

'No, no, you don't have to go,' said Lilly, but Chiyo ignored her. She opened the door and slipped past Neil, standing there with his hands behind his back. As Chiyo passed him she pulled a brief, absolutely incongruous, disconcerting face, eyes wide, nostrils flared, which only Neil could see. He whimpered, and then corrected himself with a manly grunt, slipping into Lilly's room and closing the door behind him with a shuddering 'euurghh!'

'What?' said Lilly, sitting up.

'I…' Neil reflexively swallowed, 'erm, can I come in?'

'You're in aren't you?'

'Yeah, I suppose so.'

'And anyway of course you can. You're my boyfriend.'

Neil blinked, surprised. He stood by the door, hesitating, he wanted to say something.

'And no,' said Lilly, reading his thoughts, 'you can't have that in writing.'

Neil sat down in the chair Chiyo had left and gathered himself. He looked very serious.

'She's so… flipping… strange.'

'But nice though. There is something restful about her.'

'Nothing… demonic in there?'

Lilly thought about it. 'No,' she said, 'No more than anyone else. Less, if anything.' She folded her legs and smoothed her skirt down. 'I do think her wardrobe is full of dead husbands.'

Neil looked confused and alarmed.

'It's a joke Neil, a joke.'

He began picking at a fragment of worn wool on the arm of the chair, both distracted yet hyper-focused on the fabric. Lilly waited, clearly something was on his mind, let him bring it out.

'When I was twenty,' he said very quietly, almost mumbling, 'before I entered the police force, I went for a job as a "Beverage Executive", and I bought some new shoes, last few quid, but they were a size too small, so by the time I got there, four miles out of town, up towards Culver, my feet were sausage meat. Anyway, the place was closed—I'd got the wrong day I think, or they just couldn't be bothered to meet me, so I had to walk back, except I couldn't walk, it was too painful. I had limp along the side of the road and of course I didn't want anyone to see me like that, so whenever a lorry or whatever passed, I stopped and put my hands on my hips and looked around casually at the farmland.'

Lilly listened intently. It was interesting, but why? Where was this going?

He took a deep breath and forced a mouth-only smile. 'Nothing's wrong,' he said.

'I didn't say it was,' she said tenderly.

There was a strange long pause. Eventually Lilly stepped in; 'You do seem… tight… again.'

'I'm fine!' he said, rather too loudly, as if sensing that more volume would mean more fine.

'Don't you ever have fun?' Lilly asked, 'At work I mean? Have a laugh? Chill out.'

Neil's face darkened further and his chin sunk into his chest. 'We don't joke at work. We're very, very serious.' He thought of the time at the last Christmas party when he'd passed out on a desk and his colleagues had put burlesque make-up on him and tarted him up in a feather boa and left him outside the station where he'd woken to find someone had urinated on him. He pushed the ghastly thought of 'office fun' from his mind. 'Anyway,' he said petulantly, 'I came home today and made you a new song.'

'Oh, did you?'

'Well, do you want to hear it or not?'

'Yes please?' she said.

Neil pulled out Victor's pen drive and squatted down in front of Lilly's laptop. He plugged the drive in and found the track he was looking for; 'Garden in the City.' An echoey, melancholy tune emerged, tinny, low-fi but sweet.

On high heeled mountains
Under skies silked and pearled
Climb soft necked trees
Around cool brown branches curled
In soft limbed valley
From meadow's heart to dive
Into dancing streams,
Warm and alive.
There's a garden in the city.

While it played, Neil fiddled distractedly with the beak of a woollen crow.

While it played, Clive, after accidentally dropping a toilet brush in the toilet, handle-down, sat on the bathroom floor and stared at a line of mould around the base of the sink.

While it played, Bronya, drunk, talked angrily to her bathroom mirror, covering it in spittle which she wiped off with the first thing that came to hand, an unused sanitary towel.

While it played, Nina brushed her teeth, then stopped and looked in the mirror. Her gums were bleeding.

While it played, Dave Davage stared at a photo of himself outside a shop window, stuck on the same shop window, then looked around in the direction of where both photos had been taken from.

While it played, Irving added a match to a replica of a middle-aged woman, made entirely of matches, he was building in his dining room; a model of his wife, who had committed suicide a month ago.

While it played, Chiyo danced a slow, gloomy dance of odd, ancient, poised and posed gestures.

While it played, Maria sadly looked at a photo of George and Amal Clooney in their house in Sonning, just down the road from the guy out of Led Zeppelin.

While it played, Aaron and Moira sat silently in their living room both looking stressed and unhappy while little James, at their feet, drew a woman with white hair in a hot air balloon.

While it played, Paul painted the black railings outside the funeral home blacker.

While it played, Joe worked at the chicken coop in his garden, extending it with the coffins which he had sawed little windows in and was now asphalting. As he worked away, bald chickens in little cardigans picked and pecked. In front of him, to his left, at number 86, an old woman was boarding up a fourth window to her house; only two windows remaining clear now. And across all the visible windows of the street reflected the glorious gold-red clouds.

The song finished. 'Don't you like it?' said Neil unhappily.

Lilly, hands resting in her lap, head down, spoke; 'Yes. It's amazing Neil.'

'So what's the problem?' he looked up, angrily, his face contorted, pleading.

She raised her head. 'What do you mean what's the problem? It's lovely.'

'You've got no idea what it takes to get… write a song like that.' He picked away at the crow's beak, loosening one of the threads. Lilly let him. She was too sad to be annoyed that he was ruining her crow.

'Can you just tell me why you're angry or is that cheating?'

'I don't cheat,' he said, 'I don't lie. I don't get angry.'

'What? I don't… who… what kind of person do you think you are, exactly?'

Neil smiled inside, grimly; this was an easy one. 'I'm creative. I'm interesting. I'm smart. I'm driven. I'm a visionary. And, I have a well-established proven track record.'

'And… nothing negative?'

'I… I love you Lilly,' he said glumly.

'Do you? Really?'

'Yes! Of course I do.'

His elbows jerked outwards, a little flapping movement.

'What are you doing?'

'What? Nothing!'

Lilly's face dropped. Neil shook his head slightly but rapidly. Silence. He clutched his head. It was all wrong, it was all going wrong. Why? Everything is okay on paper, but it's all going wrong? Why? It's so *unfair!*

'You spend all day at work,' he said, looking up, desperately, 'with your dead bodies and I'm out there, with the living Lilly, keeping the *living* alive, and it's not fair, he's not even a real priest.'

'Who isn't?' asked Lilly.

'What?'

'*Who* isn't a real priest?' Lilly repeated. She could feel a kind of distant rumbling in her heart, like a far off herd of bulls were on their way. Neil looked panicked. He could hear them too.

'Nobody!' He smiled weakly—as Lilly looked on, suspiciously, darkly—and then he said, in a little voice, 'Can we have *seeeeeex…?*'

Lilly shook her head, very, very slowly.

∞

Joe and Maria's sex life had been alright. He wasn't keen on the way she talked to his penis, saying 'Who's a good boy? Who's a good boy? You're my one true love—Joe? No, he's useless.' Nor, if he was to be honest with himself, did he very much like the way that her reasonably sweet, feminine voice transformed into that of a squat-thrusting gorilla when she was turned on. But it was alright.

Over time, however, the passion, such as it was, had petered out—Joe became aroused, but as Maria hungrily approached, he wilted, which made her feel disgusted and unwanted. Both were now sexually frustrated, but a psychic curtain had been drawn between them, which neither could open, or look through, certainly not pass through. They were the kind of couple who never discussed sex, which, for couples with unfulfilling love-lives, is a sentence of sadness neverending

Maria had showered and was in her pyjamas, getting ready for bed, gently exfoliating with a frankincense and orange scrub. It had been another non-day, nothing had happened, nothing was going to happen. She had replaced all their lightbulbs with the brightest ones Sainsbury's sold in order to torment Joe, who was hypersensitive to light, but as usual he hadn't complained, just winced and frowned. She had an uninspected instinct to annoy Joe. She didn't think about it, it was just there. She had to do it, but nothing came back from him, no human reaction, which made her more annoyed, which made her more determined to get a rise out of him.

'Say something interesting,' she called out.

'Err…' Joe's voice came through from the bedroom. 'I don't like to be put on the spot.'

Typical, she thought. 'You were *born* on the spot,' she said.

'Well, alright,' he said, 'Someone on Island Road had thrown away five Breville toasters.'

'That's not interesting.'

'But who would *have* five Breville toasters? It doesn't make any sense.'

'It's not interesting Joe.'

'I suppose you had to be there.'

She'd finished and was splashing up. 'It's *all* "you had to be there." *Life* is "you had to be there",' she said, re-entering the bedroom. Joe was delicately kissing the wardrobe.

'What are you doing?' she said with unconcealed revulsion.

'Isn't it obvious?'

She looked at him, into him. There's just nothing there, she thought, but this stupid random shit. 'So that's it then,' she said, her mind jumping to the real problem, 'You've completely given up on any kind of career?' She turned on the top light.

Joe turned towards her, his eyes screwed up against the 5,000 lumen brightness. 'Why would I want a career? Why would anyone? It just doesn't make sense to me.'

'You wanted to be someone Joe. You wanted… Don't you want to be a journalist still? Or do copywriting? Surely… something more creative than sweeping the streets?'

'You'd be surprised. You can get a lot out of a street.'

Maria, who had been standing, hand on hip, looking full on at Joe, raised her jaw slightly in a nod of inner understanding. The relationship was reaching a new stage, slowly tipping beyond even dismay.

'It really makes no difference to me whether you speak or not,' she said, getting into bed and picking up her phone.

'I'm going to take that as a compliment,' he said, standing at her side, absorbing her pain, which revealed its meaning to him. He nodded with understanding. 'You're still annoyed about the chicken coop aren't you?' he said.

'No Joe,' she said, not looking up, 'I love having two coffins in my backyard.'

'I could only get two. That was difficult enough.'

'Very funny.'

Joe got down to his knees and looked under the bed. His head poked up over the side of the bed. 'Shall we make love under here? What do you think?'

'No.'

'Why? I'm sure there's enough room.'

She threw the phone down and glared at him, skewering him. 'Because it's *weird*, it's weird, don't you understand? I want normal. I like normal. Normal is… normal. Can't you just be *normal?*'

Joe picked up a hairbrush next to the bed. He looked in the mirror and brushed his hair, very neatly, into a side-parting. It was conventional, but also not at all right. He turned to Maria with a fresh, honest 'how's that?'

She peered at him, steadily, 'I had a dream about you last night,' she said, 'I dreamt that I put my hand against your crotch and couldn't feel anything. The thought occurred to me that I'd been mistaken about you, that you had a pussy, which was fine, we'll have some nice pussy-fucking, so I unzipped your trousers, but there was nothing there, no cunt, no cock, *nothing*. Because *you* are nothing. You see? You're nothing, and so you are nothing to me. You might as well be a window or an onion.'

'An onion is something,' said Joe, sadly getting into bed.

Maria turned off the light. The blackness was stark, humming. 'You peel onions,' she said quietly, 'and you keep peeling them until, finally, you get to the last little bit, and then inside that, what do you find?'

'Tears,' said Joe, cheeks wet.

∞

The next day Joe put up more posters. These ones read 'Tonight! The Absentees! Concert of a Lifetime! Edding Pedestrian Precinct!' He'd started off up towards the posh, park-end of town and was now making his lazy way along one of the main roads into the centre. A chubby, rosy-cheeked man passed, wearing a trilby, a bright blue turtleneck, white flannel suit jacket, badly fitting nylon trousers and enormous white trainers. Joe caught one sentence, which the man delivered ostentatiously into his mobile phone; '*Manning will bring peaches.*' Angry-looking bald middle-aged men wearing pink stripy shirts drove past in expensive-looking cars; there were a lot of them up this way. Also, a lot of women who were pouring their whole unloved hearts out into their dogs, who would have been just as happy with half as much.

Joe didn't want to be here, in Edding. He wanted to be on the side of a Welsh mountain performing ecstatic moonlit ceremonies. But he also felt that it didn't really matter where you were and this shabby untown was darkly fascinating, like the insect room of a zoo. Or perhaps like the end of the world. If it was the end of the world, and all the signs seemed to point that way, then, thought Joe, I'd like to stick around, to see it. Just sitting, watching the horror and the chaos, eating a boiled egg, over there…

He stopped. Over there, in a car park in front of a few shops, was that man again, the tired balding man, sitting in a black Hyundai. He was looking at Joe. Their eyes met, then the car pulled away, revealing a vet's and three girls, sitting on a wall in front of an oak tree, very bored looking, tooting a horn on a guy's bike. The oak tree had shed, over the car park, thousands of acorns which popped under the wheels of the Hyundai as it pulled out.

Joe walked on, smiling. Is that little man following me, or is he getting his cat spayed? Who cares? Nothing really matters that much, nothing that happens at least. We too, we human acorns, were produced in our millions, just to fall on a car park and get crushed by a Korean car. Just mulch. His cleaning cart now had a squeaky wheel, but he didn't care about that either. 'So-whatism will set you free,' he thought, and the thought made him feel warm and invincible. Futile job; so what? Wife doesn't love me; so what? Impotent, penniless, going nowhere in a world of mulch; so what? So what?

He stopped on a corner opposite a coffee booth, at a wall of plywood hoarding ranged around a renovation project which had been ongoing for years, now apparently abandoned. He started putting up his posters, which flapped around in the depressing wind. After a few had gone up he began to get a sense of being seen. He turned to find a little boy, James from next door, calmly watching him.

'What are you doing?' the boy asked.

'I'm putting up posters for a concert.'

'What does 'absentee' mean?'

'I means not present. Not here. Somewhere else.'

'Does that mean they won't be here?'

'Yep. Nobody will be here.'

'So... *why* are you putting up the posters?'

'I want everyone to get together and wonder what they're doing here.'

'But why?'

'Don't you ever wonder what you're doing here?'

'No.'

'Okay then. Come along, you can see what it's like.'

'Bye.'

The little boy returned to the coffee booth where Moira and Aaron were waiting for their lattes. Behind it, next to a boarded-up pub, was the old man in the checked shirt Joe had passed yesterday, still blind drunk, still struggling to roll his cigarette, the wind blowing the dust of his old dry tobacco into the road. Joe walked up to him, took his tobacco pouch and rolled the cigarette for him. The man watched Joe, head jerking and shuddering, took the fag, put it in his mouth, mumbled thanks and staggered off tapping his pockets.

Suppose I'd better do a bit of work, thought Joe and bent down to pick up a sweet wrapper, which the wind lifted from his reach and gusted along the pavement. Still bent over, he followed it, but again it blew away.

Neil, watching Joe from his squad car at the very end of the road, put his binoculars down. He had long given up trying to work his brother out. The man was mad, it was as simple as that, but there was a mystery to Joe which continually stung Neil, a 'why?' a *why?* which was always there in his mind. While Joe was completely unmoved by any attempt to arouse his inquisitiveness, Neil went into paroxysms of curiosity at the suggestion of a secret. To start to speak to him and then say 'oh nevermind' was to drive a skewer into his neck; which was what his brother was to him, a skewer in his neck.

A hearse drove past Neil's car. In it Carl was listening to *Always the Sun* by The Stranglers, singing along, as he did to The Stranglers, The Jam, Ian Dury, Squeeze, and Wire. He didn't know all the words, so he filled in the gaps with la-la-las, da-da-das and whatever came into his mind.

> *'How many times have you been told*
> *If you don't ask you don't get?*
> *How many da-da-da-da...*
> *And who has the fun?*
> *Is it always a man with a gun?*
> *Someone must have told you,*
> *If you work too hard you can sweat.*
> *There's always her bum. Mm-hmm,*
> *There's always her arse.*
> *She always takes it up the shitter.'*

He chuckled to himself. Then, a few 'la-la-las' later, and half a mile down Joy Lane, he started speaking to himself in a naff American accent. 'Are you crazy? Are you outta yer god-damned *mind?* I don't need this shit!' Then, in his own voice, 'Me? I could have any woman in this town. Any. Damned. One. So what if I'm a carrion snatcher, a cold cook. Someone has to handle the dead, and if I didn't...' he had one hand on the wheel, the other hand panned out questioningly, '...who would?'

A Citroen pulled out in front of him. He slammed his brakes down. *'Fuck my arse!'* he cried, then bellowed through the open window, 'WANKER!'

Clive Marsh, standing in front of his front-garden fence, heard this 'wanker' waft down from the end of his road. He looked up, but couldn't see what had happened, and so returned to the fence, which he had come out to paint. He was wearing a thin, worn Stone Roses T-shirt tugged by flaws of wind, now spitted with rain, cold, but 'the work will warm me up'. He bent down to open one of a few cans of 'russet outdoor emulsion', fiddling a butter knife under the crack, squeezing down until it pupped open. The colour of the paint, however, was not a deep rich brown but a kind of pinky-greyish brown.

Clive pulled himself to his feet, regarding the paint pot with dismay. 'Puce', he said to himself in queer dismay, 'fucking *puce*'. The colour of John Lewis and dinnerware decisions, the colour of fringed slips and cloth napkins, the colour of blood-engorged fleas and scrofula. Puce of reasonable discussions, moral sepsis and rotting popcorn. Why bother? thought Clive, what's the bloody point? He dropped the paint brush in his hand onto the ground and hobbled back into his house, leaving the pots where they were.

Fifteen minutes later, Carl pulled up outside Clive's house. He, Carl, had just had a street-side argument with the Citroen driver, a batty woman who'd pulled out in front of him and couldn't do a three-point turn to get out of the way. He was furious with her to start with but had ended up feeling sorry for her and finally had actually got in her car and performed the manoeuvre himself, which meant the curries he was carrying were all a bit cold, but not to worry. He swaggered up Clive's front path, noted the open paint (it'll dry out; can be saved though; add more carrier and squeeze out the lumps), and knocked on the door, which, after a long wait, opened with the same reluctance as Clive's thin, grim mouth.

This was not a well man. Even Carl could see that something was up.

'Here!' he said triumphantly, 'This'll put a smile on your face!' He pushed the stack of takeaway boxes into Clive's one good hand, 'Best fucking curry in the county. It's gone a bit cold, but bung it in the microwave you'll be right.'

Clive, wan, red-eyed, tearless, lifeless, the horror of the world etched into his gaunt face, didn't move, didn't speak. He stood cradling his curries, looking into the far distance, a broken man.

'You alright mate? Whassup?' said Carl.

'I can't finish the fence,' said Clive.

'What, that fence?' said Carl, turning back to the discarded decorating equipment, 'Forget it! Ain't worth it.'

'No, not worth it,' repeated Clive.

Carl went to speak, but something in Clive's manner stopped him. 'Alright, well… uh… you heat those curries up. They'll sort you out,' he said, and gently retreated to his hearse, unsettled by the deathly look of the man. It was one thing to haul stiffs around all day, but… Carl pushed it from his mind and turned the music up; *What a Way to End it All,* by Deaf School. What are the chances? thought Carl, listening to the jaunty suicide song. I'll be seeing that fella on the slab soon, he thought, one of the 'three-a-day,' which was how he, Paul and Lilly referred to the many suicides who came in. Lilly was always upset by them, but Carl was philosophical. 'If you can't leave the game it's not a game is it? It's work.'

In fact this observation, thrown out the side of his mouth as casually as a comment on the weather, had hit Lilly with force. Is that what work is, she'd thought to herself, a game you can't stop playing? It seemed to make sense. She loved listening to Rachmaninov and she loved studying, but as soon as she *had* to study Rachmaninov it had become an almighty chore, a grind, which she couldn't get out of, and once she had decided that she could, that she was free to walk off this stupid campus at any moment or tear up this stupid assignment; that was probably one of the loveliest feelings she'd had as an adult. Maybe there was such a thing as a good suicide, or maybe there wasn't, but it was reassuring that you *could* walk out at any moment.

Lilly wasn't at that moment at work though, thinking of killing herself, she was at home, thinking of killing Neil. She was looking around his room, determined to find the answers to a few questions. She opened a drawer in the chest under the window. His socks were folded and placed with all the care of a sock boutique in Primrose Hill. She opened another drawer; it was full of knitting needles, wool, knitting patterns, and folded crochet work. She picked up the front panel of a cardigan. It was good work, complex stitching, not just knit and purl, but Kitchener stitches, double moss; complex stuff.

She moved over to his desk and picked up a police notebook. It was full of little drawings of them both, Neil and Lilly, with love hearts floating over their heads. Next to these were various notes for what looked like song lyrics, fragments along the lines of 'I'd plaster a ceiling for you (actually a complex job) / I'd returf a large garden for you (up to two acres)' and 'You're deeper than the ocean / You're smoother than moisturising lotion / You're more use than a Leatherman multi-tool.' She put the notebook down and hit the spacebar on his computer. An image appeared of Richard Branson and a padlock-icon window with a 'password' dialogue box. She thought for a moment, then typed PRINCEPHILLIP. Branson vanished and the desktop appeared.

∞

As Lilly started looking through Neil's files, Neil, still in his car, was being blasted with Ralf's mad laughter. Ralf, who'd spent the morning, as all mornings, aimlessly wandering around Edding, chuckling to himself, had noticed a microphone dangling from the branch of a lime tree. He had climbed up, picked up the microphone and almost killed himself laughing.

Neil pulled away—past Joe, who, until that moment, had been pursuing the sweet wrapper, but, out of breath, had stopped and waved his hand in a 'forget it' gesture—and, sirens blazing, headed towards the location of the mic. He hurtled down Marescroft Road, past the Cash and Carry and the trading estate to the Raspberry Hill park—a desolate triangle of grass with a lonely broken set of swings in the middle. He got out of his car, and, teevee cop style, leapt over the shin-high railings and ran over to the lime tree where Ralf was dangling, laughing like a maniac. 'Get down!' Neil cried, 'Get *down!*' but Ralf just kept laughing and dangling, so Neil had to jump up and grab Ralf's ankle, which was beyond Neil's five-foot-five reach, so, beside himself, he cried 'look! I'm going to fucking pepper spray you if you don't get down now!' He jumped up and down, swiping away, until Ralf, out of pity, dropped down to the grass.

Neil, when his anger reached a certain pitch, would fling abuse and, if he met with no resistance, would throw an unrestrained tantrum, very bright but actually without heat and so of no real consequence to anyone, least of all Ralf who just continued laughing as Neil arrested him.

They drove back to the station, Neil grimly, hotly silent while Ralf, from the back seat, sprinkled laughter over him.

'What's so funny?' Neil asked, through his teeth, 'I'm arresting you. You're going to prison.'

'Hahahaha! I'm at rock bottom!'

'But there's nothing funny about that. What's funny about that?'

'Shall I tell you?'

'Tell me what?'

'About the life of a schadenfreudist?'

'You find other people's pain funny?'

'Yes, but not as funny as my own! Hahahaha'

Neil said nothing. He'd had enough of fruitcakes.

Forty-five minutes later, crestfallen, he stood before the desk of D.C.I. Babcock, her chunky arms folded across her vast chest.

'Why?' she said, 'Just tell me why.'

'National security,' whispered Neil, taking out a pair of swimming goggles from his pocket (he had planned to go swimming later) and pulling back the rubber to stretch them over his head.

'What are you doing?'

'Sorry ma'am, I'm nervous,' he said, returning the goggles to his pocket.

'You're not right in the head Geb. There's no point even explaining to you what the problem is with bugging the entire town, is there?'

He hung his head lower. 'I'd rather you…ou…' he gulped a reflex swallow '…didn't.'

'*I'd* rather I didn't. Collect your things. We'll be in touch about legal proceedings.'

'You can't…' His whole body was folded in on itself, even his toes, like a six-year-old being scolded.

'…No? I can't? I can, and I have. Go home Geb, and never come back.'

Neil dared look up. 'It's because I'm short isn't it?'

'No Neil, it's because you're a twat.' Her Welsh accent gave the 'twat' a most resonant emphasis.

'Please ma'am. I'm begging you.'

As with all life-or-death moments—or, in this case, those which seem it—Neil had become hyper-aware of the situation, of the frizziness of Babcock's hair and the smallness of her ears, of the smell of the overripe banana that she had eaten twenty minutes before he came into the office, of the quantity of paperwork she hadn't got done yet, of the fact that one of the little plastic legs which propped up her keyboard had snapped and it was lopsided.

'Oh. Interesting,' she leaned forward, 'You're begging are you? Good. Good. Beg. Get on your knees and beg to me.'

'Really?'

'Yes, really.'

Neil thought about it. What could be lost here? Nothing. He got down on his knees.

'Ple…'

'With your hands together Neil. Like a beggar. Get a good beg-on.' She demonstrated an urgent supplicatory clasp, which Neil copied.

'Please ma'am,' he said, fingers gripping each other so tightly they were white at the knuckles, 'I am begging you. Please do not do this. I love being a police officer. I was born police. Please. Please? Pleeeeaaaase…

A look of pain and distaste squeezed Babcock's brow. 'Have you no self-respect?'

He thought about it. 'I don't know,' he said.

Babcock said nothing, just looked at the small begging man.

'I don't know!' he cried.

Babcock's face suddenly twisted up in pain. She grabbed her heart.

'What?' said Neil, 'What?'

'Something has broken,' she said, not listening, not looking, rising and running through the police station to the toilets, where she threw up her toasted cheese sandwich.

∞

It was the thread that held Clive's little life to the earth that had snapped. He had walked into his large, cold, untidy garage, sat down, eaten his now cold curry, drunk half a bottle of whiskey and then opened all the cans of paint he owned, twelve of them, all of which contained puce. The unlikely, frustrating, nonsense of the situation had at once fused all the pain of his entire life into a single, unignorable entity. It wasn't the puce, it was everything. It was all unending pointless misery. It was his fucked-up social-climbing mum and his poor dad broken on the wheel of her hollow ambitions. It was the sanitised do-nothing society ruled over by smug know-it-all middle-class technicians. It was the rats scuttling over the unemptied bins and the fact that all our best plums were exported. It was the hysterical Salem witches that ruled swooning over university arts departments. It was the maroon balloons begging the government to buy more nuclear weapons. It was the death of music, the death of literature, the death of culture. It was literary agents. It was the reserve army of labour brought in by their half-millions every fucking year to drive wages down and rents up. It was the whole Godless universe, the pointless accident of existence, which winks man into being, gives him a few years of fucking, if he's lucky, then slowly takes everything away from him, his health, his creativity, his dignity, everything but whatever crumbs of credit-power he can grub together, leaving him, at best, the richest cunt on a mountain of gash. What is the point, he asked himself, of hauling my broken body through the wreckage of another day? I have no family, no friends, no ambition, and no pleasures but out-of-date dance music and home improvement. But why dance? Why improve? Why not put my head into that one-gallon can of paint?

His face pulsated and spasmed.

∽

While Clive was considering extinguishing himself, the people of Edding, cold in the damp autumn half-light, were building up for the non-concert. Joe was wandering around the pedestrian centre of town, broom in hand, benign half-smile on face. He looked in a bin and, pleasantly surprised, pulled out his baboon mug. Surely a good sign? Couples and small groups stood around chatting, waiting for the great band to appear, amongst them Chiyo. Irving was there also, at the other end of the street, suspiciously picking at one of the Absentee posters. This has gone too far, he thought.

The initial mood of the crowd had been easy and warm, but as the afternoon had passed into early evening it chilled. A dog was barking manically. People were looking around wondering where the band was. Chiyo seemed to have seen something, or someone, she'd been looking for; young James. She edged towards him. Joe was chewing his broom with more intensity now, disconcerted at the dog's barking.

Neil, broken-hearted, was also there, wandering through the crowd on his way home, but hearing and seeing nothing. He had lost his entire life. They had taken his body armour, his name badge, his collapsible baton, his personal radio and his cs

201

incapacitant spray. If they had removed his arms they couldn't have deprived him of more of his essential self.

He got home with one thought on his mind. He ran straight up to Lilly's room and, without knocking, opened the door. Lilly was at her desk, but looking at the door, apparently expecting him.

'Lilly?' he said.

'I've had an interesting day.'

'Lilly… There's something I have to tell you…'

'No Neil, there's something I have to tell you…'

'…but…'

'Neil! Be quiet. I've got to get this out now or it will never come out.' He looked strange, wearing only a shirt, his face crooked, but nevermind that.

'But, but,' he said, and lifted his shirt up, to show his belly button. There was nothing there, but Neil, in moments of perfect fear, or need, had a teenage-boy instinct to do something bizarre in an attempt to appear interesting or important, or to arrest the terrible flow of the moment.

'*Agggggggggggh!*' Lilly screamed.

'Sorry, sorry, sorry, I, just, it's just…' Neil began, instinctively, to furiously apologise while, at the same time, feeling like it was all her fault, because it had to be.

'Listen,' she said, cutting through his randomised faff, 'I know you didn't write any of those songs, I know you've been watching me, spying on me, and that man, who is not a priest at all, who is he?'

'He's my brother.' Neil felt he wanted to put his fingers in his ears, it took all his will not to.

'Oh right. He's your brother is he? Well, that's bizarre,' said Lilly, a strange and to Neil, hauntingly neutral confusion hushing her disgust.

'Can I explain?' said Neil, screwed up, lips contorted, eyes wincing as if looking into a pot of boiling vinegar.

'No Neil,' she said quietly, wearily, 'you can't explain, because the problem is not what you do, it *is* you. You can't explain you, because… because you *are* you. Do you see?'

Neil began sobbing, 'Oh God Lilly, if you only knew, please, please… uh… please don't fire me.'

'I'm not firing you, I'm dumping you.'

'It's the same thing!'

'No, it's *not*. You're not my employee. It's over.'

'Oh no, oh God, please, please.' Sobbing and whimpering, slumped, he looked like he was sort of hanging from his own shoulders, like wet laundry. 'I need you…' he whispered.

'Why though?'

'I just, to be my best me I need support and, uh, oh,' he looked up, 'you're *so* beautiful.'

Her eyes narrowed. 'Beautiful like what?'

'Like what?' Neil's wet face was wrinkled up in confusion.

'Yes, what else do you find beautiful?'

'Erm. Er… er… Okada 125 chisels?'

Lilly said nothing for a moment, and then, with a kind of benign not-botheredness that was so much worse than anger, or emotion, or anything, she said; 'Neil. I like you, I do, but… It's over, it is.'

'I'll kill myself. I'm going to kill myself!' he shouted.

'No, you're not.'

'I am, I fucking AM!' and he charged out.

Lilly was left looking at her open door. She was breathing hard from the emotion.

And then, suddenly, a memory popped into her mind. She had been with Nick in London. They had been to see a film at the BFI, Ikiru, which she had enjoyed but he had hated. He had been irritable all day though. Everything she did annoyed him, and he had picked at it all. He was annoyed that she wanted him to choose where to sit in the restaurant they'd eaten at, he was annoyed that her swallow was strangely loud, he was annoyed that she wasn't interested in a story of his, about some stupid tart. And then, as they were walking down to Westminster station she had said to him that he was in a bad mood, and he had hit her, slapped her hard across her face with the back of his hand.

She had stared at him, holding her cheek, blinking, eyes welling up. Then a few people had appeared from the tube exit, so nothing else happened, but amazing things were going on in Lilly. Firstly, as they descended into the station, she was *turned on*. Secondly, she hated herself for being turned on. Thirdly, she had the utterly incredible thought that 'this is what utterly degraded people must feel,' the kind of doormats she hated. Nick was a bastard, and she wasn't going to put up with it. She didn't care about him, not the least bit. But what was this? She was *enjoying* how disgusting she was, and she was suddenly sure that many, many people must know the same sickening thrill.

Like Neil. Somewhere in him he wanted to be humiliated and hurt. Enjoyed it. Why?

∞

Agitation was spreading in town. Some people were trickling away, when a large white van appeared. On the side was written the words 'the ever absent one.' A ripple of interest and relief rolled over the crowd. Joe stopped gnawing at his broom, watching, as everyone was, the van make its way through the crowd; everyone except Chiyo who was behind James, reaching out… carefully taking hold of a single golden hair… and tugging it.

'Aghhh!' cried the boy, looking round and up into Chiyo's unreadable face, which then vanished into the crowd.

The van crept to a halt, the doors opened, the crowd craned forward to see what was inside. Parrots flew out. Two extremely pale people, dressed in keffiyehs and clip-on glasses, emerged and pulled out rails. As they did, a squirrel leapt from the van, hopping away, and then a rabbit.

Joe was properly gnawing at the end of his broom, it was fairly splintered up now. He was tense with expectation. He wanted to see, and yet, at the same time, not to see. A curious thought touched upon him. Something extraordinary was going to happen, but to *see* it—what good would that be?

He closed his eyes.

∞

Clive stared at the paint. Stared into the paint. Everything that was wrong with his life, and everything that was wrong with the world had merged into one single can of Pantone 13-1518 paint.

After all, why not? What is the bloody point?

He plunged his head into the can which wedged over his ears as suffocating, caustic paint filled his nose, eyes and throat.

∞

Lilly listened. The house was quiet. Neil wouldn't really kill himself, would he? She crept out onto the corridor, nothing, then inched her way towards Neil's ominously silent room.

She slowly opened the door.

∞

Two assistants are pulling something from the van, something large, requiring more and more people to take its weight. Whatever it is, is covered with flowers. People are straining to see; they are pulling themselves past each other, to see, to see, to see.

At *this* moment, an enormous bier rolls into the street. It is covered in flowers, small animals, living plants, crottle lichen and, in the centre, magnificent, and naked, and dead; Ursula's corpse.

Joe's eyes are still closed. He can hear the commotion, he can hear distant sirens, but he doesn't want to see. Why this mania always to *see*, to gluttonously stuff one's eyes full of some big, looked-at wow?

Joe wants to feel what was happening in his bowels, in his thighs and in his balls. There is a pounding in his face and a kind of leaping lightness beneath it, flickering up his spine. It is the feeling that Ursula's company used to give him, her magnificent beauty and poise, which he loved so much. Ursula is *here*, and she is *dead*.

A bark. He opened his eyes. A black dog black was bounding towards him. Fear surged and he turned and ran, head-first into a lamppost.

∞

Although Clive's final thought was, as is usually the case when someone commits suicide, '*I want to live*,' the tin of paint couldn't be pulled off. He thrashed around the shed, tugging furiously at the deadly helmet, an emulsion-saturated, frog-mouthed jousting helm. He smashed into his tool shelves, picking up, by chance, a tin opener which he tried to prise off the smothering tin of paint with, but it was no use. He suffocated, keeled over and floats down through the pale purply-brown liquid, down into darker, bluer waters, and down into darkness itself, which washes him up on Fraisthorpe beach, where Lou Reed, Albert Finney, Frederich Nietzsche and a thousand friendly penguins are waiting for him.

∞

Lilly opened the door. Neil was curled up on the floor foetus-like with a plastic bag over his head. Lilly, nonplussed, crouched down beside him. She plucked off a Post-it note on the bag and read it; 'I've put my head in a bag. Neil.'

'Well done. Take your head out now.'

He slowly took the bag off his head.

∞

Bedlam in Edding. People were swooning, crying, appalled, outraged, running this way and that. Babies were crying, children wailing in dreadhorror. The van was driving away, south, with flashing lights and sirens at the north end of the high street.

Joe opened his eyes. He was crumpled against the lamppost. His mouth was full of splinters. In front of him stood Young James, quite calm.

'Oh, hello,' said Joe.

'Hello.'

'You see. This is what it is like to wonder what you're doing here.'

'Joe,' a familiar voice. Joe looked up.

Irving's screwed-up bloodshot eyes squinted out through his black beard, which shuffled left and right as he spoke; 'I think it's fair to say, you're fired.'

PART THREE
The Schadenfreudist

As the flaming microlight collides with the earth, the mind of Ursula Geb dies. This mind has been creating a consistent and persistent experience of time, a journey along thirty-three years of being Ursula, from birth to death, that she has experienced piecemeal, bit-by-bit, moment-by-moment, in the ordinary way. And just as the Roman Road which led from Edding to Glower appeared, to someone walking along it, piecemeal, revealed bit-by-bit, moment-by-moment, in the ordinary way, just as it appeared to Ursula, high above, as a whole; so her life now, as her brain is crushed by the fuselage sidewall of the lightweight aircraft, becomes, to the high-up, microlight of her mind, a whole, a single timeless entity.

There is no thought in this, no mental recognition, because there is no brain to think. Nor does she become anything, nor does anything change, because time, the appearance of change and becoming, dies with the mind which produced it for her. There is no time, there is another dimension of space, one which had appeared as change and becoming, living and dying, coming into being and passing away, coming together and coming apart; but which in truth, does nothing, goes nowhere. As Ursula's brain and body die, so do all her beliefs, all her hopes, all her opinions, all her possessions, all her perceptions, all her desires and all her memories; revealing nothing, because there is nothing here for anything to be revealed to. There is just her life and every other life it has been one with.

There is Neville teaching Ursula, a little girl, how to identify the calls of her favourite bird, the long-tailed tit, 'it's a high and thin "seeeee?" but sometimes it's followed by a little chattering rattle.'

And there is the life of the long-tailed tit itself.

There is Ursula, eighteen, arguing with her mother. Ursula is naked and Margaret is saying 'Aren't you ashamed of being naked?' and Ursula is saying 'Aren't you ashamed of being clothed!'

And there is the life of Margaret herself.

There is Ursula on a horse approaching Joe, sixteen years old, who is standing in a field shooting with a handgun at a squirrel in a sycamore tree as Ursula rides up next to him and says 'That squirrel, is you.' and Joe says 'I am not a squirrel,' and Ursula rides away, and just as she passes out of sight she calls back, 'Yet.'

And there is the life of Joe himself.

There is Ursula, walking through the desolate and scoured rocky grasslands of the Brecon Beacons, wondering where all the forests have gone.

And there is the life of Wales itself.

There is Ursula at the Milford Fish Docks. She is pouring gin into a hip flask while Jonathan, a beefy, bearded, long-haired Welshman, dressed in fisherman's oilskins (with a death-metal skull sewn into his jacket) is weeping on the dock, empty nets piled up around him.

And there is the life of Milford itself.

There is Ursula and there is Jonathan, naked in a lighthouse playing knucklebones on the buttocks of another huge bearded Taff, spread out on the fireside rug. Ursula is screaming, joyously, dancing round the room.

And there is the life of Jonathan himself.

There is Ursula standing on the stern of a fishing boat, waving goodbye to a tearful Jonathan who is standing on the dock next to bulging fishing nets.

And there is the life of the ocean itself.

There is Ursula in Białowieża forest, scrummaging around under a bush, pulling out a magnificent penny bun and taking an inelegantly big, wide-eyed bite from it.

And there is the life of the Polish forest itself.

There is Ursula alone in a sparse forest cabin. Survival implements, stove, a few books (The Canterbury Tales, Tom Jones, The Rainbow) lie scattered around. She is reading aloud from The Tempest.

And there is the life of English culture itself.

There is Ursula outdoors in the snow, sombrely dancing the waltz in Saariselkä, northern Finland, with twenty or thirty very old Finns.

And there is the life of Finland itself.

There is Ursula, naked in a Helsinki studio, being painted by a nut-brown Finnish woman with laughter lines striating her face like fossilised fern filaments.

And there is the life of Finnish culture itself.

There is Ursula, dressed as Little My, sprinting through Paisley, Glasgow, pursued by children with swords.

And there is the life of Glasgow itself.

There is Ursula smashed out of her mind at a nightclub in Manchester, crying with laughter with Genevieve, a tall black woman with long dreads; both of them are looking at plain wallpaper.

And there is the life of Genevieve herself.

There is Ursula, naked, walking up a long driveway towards a woodland speckled with habitations, at her side is a large black dog.

And there is the life of the black dog itself.

There is Ursula gently embracing Neville outside his huge house. There is Ursula, Neville and several others, standing at midnight in a spinney, facing each other round a fire. There is the same group, now naked, all dressed in animal headgear, waltzing by candlelight.

All these moments, and every moment in between, form a single decades-long entity, a tree of human being, unmoving and ever moving, Ursula and every person and creature and place and culture she had *ever come into contact with. It all came from nowhere, it is all going nowhere; the only thing that comes and goes, can't even be called dead, because it never really lived.*

Neil's dreams were troubled. He was helpless before immense, inhuman forces, fleeing from them, trying to get to safety. Or he was beating someone up, and it was strangely enjoyable, a relief, but he didn't know why he was doing it, or he was being beaten, again without apparent reason. Nothing made sense, except the need to get out, but there was no out to get to, the dreams were eternal, and that was what was so disturbing about them. When he woke up, although he felt relief that the events were over, there was a sense, that he carried with him all day, that, actually, the terror that they conveyed was a primal truth which his waking world was thinly concealing from him.

Since he had split up with his job and been fired from his relationship, the pain and confusion of his night visions had acquired a new freakish dimension. They weren't just horrible, but were also cruelly bizarre.

He had dreamt of being just a head, sitting on a small toy car operated by the direction and feeling of his eyes; a sly glance to the left drove seductively leftward, a lazy-lidded wry grin crept forward in second, shocked eyebrows raised straight up braked sharply, and so on. The dream involved his toy-car head whizzing around the first floor of the British Museum, terrified before clashing Greek hoplites, writhing Mayan stelae and moai.

He had dreamt he was made of some kind of glass material and had to get home from work while cannonballs rained from the sky. Everyone else was wearing medieval armour, and strolled down the high street quite unconcerned by the massive iron spheres, which bounced off them like tennis balls, while Neil anxiously skipped and scooted from doorway to doorway.

He had dreamt of being in the top floor of a tall skyscraper, opposite many other such buildings. He had been enjoying a pleasant chat with Billy Joel about songwriting when an horrific wail rose from the window, like the world screaming. He looked out the window and the buildings outside were all falling over, all at once. Then he realised he was sliding across the floor, and it was *his* building falling, and *he* was the one screaming.

He had dreamt he was in a vast stately home, a place of calm, fragrant poise, magical, but deeply unsettling, because there was nobody there, and the intensity of the emptiness was dreadful. One room after another, some with covered furniture but increasingly empty of objects also, each containing no one. But why; why was it so awful? And then, just before waking up in horror, Neil realised what was so unbearable about the desolate, deserted mansion. Nobody was there; and he, Neil, *he* wasn't there either.

He had dreamt of being a tiny oiled homunculus sliding over and under and round and round the warm gelatinous folds of a massive naked, fat woman, who was laughing madly. Over her rippling shoulders he slid, between her huge wrecking-ball breasts, into the soft mountains of her buttocks and the alien world pudendum, back up into the gelatinous folds of her titanic belly, faster and faster, sliding, hurtling over the disgusting monster.

He had dreamt of sitting in his bath as mushrooms sprouted over his naked body, thousands of tiny enoki-like stems flourishing over his chest and stomach and legs, which he wiped off, long fungal sheets, but which kept growing, and growing… It was grotesque, sickening, slicing away at himself, reducing his self…

He had dreamt of daytime television presenter, fishing aficionado and celebrity omelette-man, Jeremy Radley, demonstrating a one-man trampoline on his mid-morning chat show—on a weird triangular stage—but for some reason Jeremy was wearing a poorly fitting pair of underpants which only with difficulty concealed his erect penis. Jeremy was trying to read from an

Autocue, bounce up and down on the trampoline and pull the skimpy fabric of the pant, practically a G-string, over his cock, and was getting more and more stressed doing so, until something seemed to snap inside him and he just gave up reading and fiddling and let his erection wang about while crying 'weee! weee! weeeeee!' as Neil, in the audience, looked on in horror.

Those were the dreams he had had recently, remembered in every detail. They didn't seem like dreams; they were so real, so sharp. Waking seemed dreamlike in comparison.

Now he is in a dream cricket pavilion surrounded by people, all naked. Ursula is here, as is Neville — in fact everyone he knows is here, including Jesus. The only person wearing any clothes is Neil. He is in his police uniform, and they are all nude. And *they* are laughing at *him*. They are in hysterics. Neil, anguished, is going from one to the other, 'What? What? What?' as the merriment increases. He feels shame, but he has no idea why, and so, in his agitation and confusion it converts to rage, which only seems to amuse them all more. '*You're* the weird ones!' he cries, '*You're* the weird ones! Look! Look at you. I'm not weird. I'm normal…' He is whimpering now, his voice hoarse, 'I'm normal. I'm normal…' until Joe, holding a small hammer, walks up to him and strikes him squarely in the middle of the forehead, painless but shockingly loud, and he woke, still whimpering, 'I'm normal', to the wall-vibrating sound of blows from next door.

The neighbours had decided to convert their nursery to an office and so Neil had woken every morning to sawing, scraping, smashing, screwing and hammering. He had gone next door to ask the gangly husband, Tanish, to please start work later in the morning, and the mild sleepy man had said, in a pacifying tone, 'I'll see what I can do, I'll see what I can do', a phrase he had learnt at work which essentially meant, 'I'll do nothing, and if that's not good enough it's because you are callously blind to my heroic desire to do something.'

Neil ground his teeth, anger coiling in his chest, an anger that never left him now. All the injustices he had worked so hard to wipe away from his life, all the inconsiderate acts of others, all their noise and smell and ugliness, it was all now, without the protective cloak of The Law, rubbing against raw civilian flesh.

He sat up. His room was now even more ordered. Where previously everything was neat, now it was abnormally measured; the distances between things precisely balanced, the right angles aligned, not a single microscopic mote of dust lay on any surface, each of which gave off the faint alcoholic whiff of the antiseptic wipes he was now buying in bulk from Costco. But the order was being dirtied and disrupted by the chaos of next door's sound, of furniture being dragged across the floor, of shelving being drilled into place, of clonking workmen and their local radio playing Lewis Capaldi, Ariana Grande and ruddy Drake.

Powered by irritation, he leapt out of bed, straight into the power stance. He looked at himself in his full-length mirror, combed his hair rapidly but perfectly, and then lay back down in bed, smoothing his duvet either side of him.

'I'm normal,' he whispered, face contracted.

✤

Max Thottesley's rational lawn, machine-gunning with steel raindrops, looked like a vast rectangular rice paddy in a tropical storm. Next to a molehill, Joe Geb, spade in foot, rain dripping from his every waterproofed joint, spanked himself with the blade, then turned on the shaft and throttled the handle, then squatted down and made a sweeping kung fu-like thrust with it, as if wielding a trident-halberd. Max himself, in a waxed raincoat, under a huge black golfing umbrella, had appeared on the far side of the papping lawn with his gun dog, a brown and white English pointer, but Joe was facing away from him, from the house and from the lawn, dotted with collapsed molehills, which, smeared by the heavy rain, looked like melanomas. By the time Max was twenty-five yards away, Joe and the spade were on the ground, getting off with each other.

The dog leapt on Joe and humped him. Max barked 'Samael! Samael!' Joe, shocked and afraid, turned to fend the whelping dog off but Max had already pulled 'Samael' from him.

'What are you doing here Joseph?'

Max's face, leathered by many months spent on his Adriatic yacht, was webbed with fine but deep wrinkles. His lips, thin anyway, were the same orangey-brown as his face, making his mouth look more like a slit. His eyes too, tight from squinting into the sun, were slit-like, two hard, dark glassy glints occasionally skewering whoever was before him, as Joe was now.

'Er, oh, eurgh, wrestling. Always worth practicing. I'm getting a bit rusty—like this spade,' he said, tapping the blade.

'Yes, but, what are you doing *here*?'

'Here?'

'Yes, here, why are you here?'

'For me it's not so much why I'm here as why everyone else is.'

Max's face betrayed no irritation, no confusion, no humour, nothing. 'I mean, on this part of the lawn,' he said.

'Oh! Oh, oh oh… I'm about to start digging. For the mole,' said Joe, heart stiffening under Max's cold peer.

'I asked you to dig over there. I made myself quite clear. The spot is even marked with an X. It couldn't possibly be clearer. So, I'll ask you again, what, are, you, doing, here?'

'The thing is, there's only one mole. I know it looks like there's loads, but I kicked over the hills yesterday, and this one appeared overnight. So the mole has to be here. It's silly to dig anywhere else.'

'I don't care where you *think* it is. You're not paid to *think*.'

'You're paying my mind to be empty?'

'Just dig where I ask you to dig, and have some respect.'

'Okay Mr. Thottesley. I'll get to work, but I'm not sure moles have respect. I don't think I've ever met a respectful wild animal.'

Max's black eyes twinkled. 'I've already removed one wild animal from this estate, it won't be difficult culling another.'

'Okay sir,' said Joe quietly.

'Good', Max turned to leave. Joe, not wanting to speak, but having to, said; 'Once I've done that, do you think I could leave early today? Only it's my sister's funeral tomorrow.'

'So why do you need to leave today?' asked Max, looking at Joe from the corner of his eye.

'Just… I was just…' Joe, head down, looked disconsolately at the carnation border he'd planted the week before.

Max continued staring sideways at him.

'…thinking,' said Joe, 'that most men get their first bunch of flowers at their own funeral.'

'When you've finished the hole, I want you to clean the south chimney. Don't talk to anyone.' He turned away again, 'Come along Samael.'

Joe thought Max was about to leave, but he didn't move. He spoke, facing away from Joe; 'Do you believe in God Geb?'

'No.'

'You're an atheist?'

'I don't believe in God and I don't not believe in God.'

'You're an agnostic then.'

'I'm not that either. I just don't do any believing.'

The rain fired down like it was being shot from heaven. Thunder cracked in the distance. Joe gazed vaguely at the uncanny back of Max's head.

'What do you think though Geb? You're an imaginative fellow, you must have some idea of what lies on the other side of the sun? Of where the boat of a million years will dock?'

'You're mistaken Mr Thottesley. I'm not in the least imaginative. Imagination makes me unhappy. I'd be better off without it.'

'Your sister's funeral is tomorrow?'

'Yes.'

'Does that make you unhappy?'

'No.'

Thottesley again rotated sidewards, his black slits now scrutinising Joe at the very slenderest of angles. 'I've got a proposition for you Geb. First dig the hole and clean the chimney. The kitchen door is unlocked. I'll be back presently and then we'll communicate.' And away he went. Joe took a small flapjack out of his pocket and had a munch as Max walked away. A handsome man, thought Joe, even if he is inhuman and has a duck-arse.

The rain heaved down in tipping sheets, but there was unseasonable warmth in the air and here, at the edge of the cruel geometry of Max's gardens the wild was allowed to poke in. Joe sauntered alongside the wood, thinking vaguely of Max Thot, thinking vaguely of Ursula, but vaguely not thinking, because the woods didn't give him anything to think about, which is why he liked and had kept this job. He had initially believed that the appearance of Ursula's corpse in the centre of Edding had been an hallucination. It had not appeared in the news, and, initially, reports of what had happened hadn't reached him, so he had continued his absurd sauntering life as before and got another job, here at Thottesley Hall as a groundsman. Soon after this the police had contacted him, and it had all come out; Mysterious Body Left in Central Edding. He'd been interviewed, he'd identified the body and signed it over to the police for an autopsy, his mind had presented him with an emotionless grief, and he'd told Margaret. She had been sitting up in bed, Joe next to her, and he had been just about to give her the bad news when she'd said,

'Have you seen Ursula?'

'Ursula?'

'Yes! I saw her last night. She's *this* big now,' and she'd opened one hand, palm up with the second cupped over it, as if holding a just-hatched chick.

'The thing is mother… I was going to say… Ursula is dead.'

'Of course she's dead.'

'Oh. Did you know?'

'She's always been dead.'

'I'm pretty sure she *has* been alive.'

'Well we've all been *alive* dear,' Margaret had said, as if reminding him of something all adults know, and then leant over towards Joe and said, 'What's that?'

'What's what?'

'That.' She had reached forward and was pointing at a birthmark on Joe's forearm.

'That's a birthmark.'

'What's it for?'

'What's it for? Nothing. I've just got it.'

'But what did you want it for?'

'I didn't want it. I just got it. In fact, you gave it to me.'

'Did I? Didn't you want it then?'

'I… I don't remember. I'm not sure. Maybe I did?'

'I'm sorry if I gave it to you.'

'It's fine,' he'd said, 'I'm happy to have it. It just happened. You've got blue eyes. You've just got them.'

'But I *wanted* blue eyes,' she said, offended. 'I'm glad I've got them. And I'm glad I gave you that birthmark too.'

And then Joe had noticed that Margaret was crying, and he'd started crying too. For some reason it was unbearably sad, but they had continued the conversation.

'Well,' he'd said, through his tears, 'is there anything you've got that you didn't want?'

'No.'

'You wanted to be a mad old woman?'

'Of course I bloody well did!' she'd said, indignant, sniffing, cheering up in her affront.

'Nothing at all you didn't want?'

And Margaret had looked at Joe for a long time, before sighing and saying, 'I didn't want to drop my breakfast this morning.'

As usual, it had all made good intuitive sense. Visiting his mother was like talking through a wormhole to someone in a, parallel mirror dimension, where all our real selves are, and receiving garbled backwards information which, once it had been put this-dimension-way-round, made better sense than anything on the radio.

He'd felt the dropped breakfast thing though. You really see who someone is when they drop their food. Margaret's wistful acceptance at the cracked eggs, splattered bacon and carpet-matted bacon and onions spoke for her nobility.

The next day, Joe had come to work, intending to resign, but while walking through the woods on the walk up to the main house he had encountered a bison. Its head had poked out of a bush and had looked at Joe, and Joe had looked at it, and it was as if, after speaking through to Margaret's counterclock dimension he could now feel it, in his bison heart; a bison world, in which there are no words to speak, no things to see, no opinions to defend, no movement towards or any away, just a blank animal sensing, like the sun feels on the inside, like the moon does. The world just had so much on top of that sensing, so much extra to make you look and think and choose, that Joe had choicelessly stayed on here, in the simple world of bisonvibe, where he could feel through to the longed-for other place, where his real life was going on.

He approached the 'X' that Max had drawn into the far edge of the lawn with a grass-marking paint roller. It was in the dead centre of the stone circle; not a very likely spot for moles, indeed the fallen heel stones and cracked lintels, covered now with moss and lichen, almost black in the pelting rain, had something about them that repelled life itself. Joe found he had no desire to enter the strange monument, much less start digging it up. Nevertheless, this was the spot.

He worked away for half an hour, making a narrow crater, about two arm's lengths deep. With each thrust of his spade he felt a kind of shaking in his stomach, a terrible wrongness, which he tried to justify as being the usual moral nausea of having to do, at work, not just what you don't want to do, but what you know is at best pointless, and at worst plain wrong. But there was *something else* here, *something else* telling him to stop; so he did. He took a break, 'have another little tickle at it later' and, leaving his spade, he headed up to the little caretaker's lodge at the back of the kitchen. He changed into overalls, located the chimney-cleaning equipment—pipes, rods and brushes folded up into a large shoulder-bag—and then, passing through the immense basement kitchen, made his way up into the mansion proper.

The house had a Regency flair, but was largely made up of arcane, grotesque, morbid, erotic and absurd esoterica. Across the wall of the estate room, for example, spread Kuniyoshi Utagawa's massive haunting triptych, 'Takiyasha the Witch and the Skeleton Spectre.' Elsewhere, there were peculiar inquisition torture instruments, a Mancala board, a priest's ciborium, mummified foxes, stained-glass 'danse macabre' illuminations, double-sized nudes in wax, a false teeth collection, Marilyn Monroe's excrement in a little display cabinet, chrome lasers, light fittings from the Moscow underground, various video games from the 1980s, David Bowie's Ziggy Stardust outfits and several portraits of French aldermen. And yet, despite the seeming randomness of it all, there was a theme, or an atmosphere. Greek vases, Roman statues and neoclassical art predominated, fixing the ephemera in a recognisable milieu, making it all seem reasonable.

Joe wafted around the empty house, inspecting or sometimes playing with the items. He picked up a squidgy rubber tit, kicked a 1938 FIFA 'Allen' football down a long corridor, admired a Greek statue of Laocoön and his sons struggling with serpents, rapidly rotated on a huge 3-axle astronaut training strap-in gyroscope, played a bespoke whack-a-mole machine in which all the 'moles' were little grey bums, had a play with a miniature model of the countryside around Edding (a country house with tiny models of naked people surrounded by tanks, model policemen and a couple of army platoons) and had a go riding a 'Rodeo Noel,' a fairground ride in which one sat on the back on a big plastic man called Noel in his underwear which flew around like a 'buckin' bronko,' finally throwing Joe onto a crash mat.

He wandered through a lavishly-equipped library of first editions, thousands of ancient books, mostly works of Enlightenment philosophy—Descartes, Diderot and Voltaire—but a significant collection of necromancy and the black arts; The Book of Raziel the Angel, The Sworn Book of Honorius, The Picatrix and The Pseudomonarchia Daemonum. From here, Joe strolled on into a salon in which family photographs were arranged on various marquetry tables. All the men had the same inexpressive leathery, hawkish faces as Max and all the women had heads like parrot skulls. Joe took one of the assembled group photos, which looked like a circus freakshow dressed up in posh clothes, and replaced it with his photograph of Sophie's family.

He rolled on through several other rooms, before arriving at the master bedroom, which contained the same mixture of torture instruments, random items from every conceivable culture on earth and furious decadent finery; a huge felt cat's head, a prehistoric lionman figurine, a red-and-white skull cap, a harpischord, a small stone oriental head with a broken nose and a triumphant smile, a wild ass' skin, a Republican sword on a medieval hackbutt, an ivory ship in full sail on the back of an immense tortoise, a large pair of porcelain breast nipple taps from A Clockwork Orange, a large glass apothecary jar labelled 'Pantoil', and a 1930s street sign, 'Wabznasm.'

Joe opened a wardrobe and looked through some of Max's clothes. He took out some ruffled shirts and impossibly elegant waistcoats and frock coats of vicuña, guanaco, cervelt, shahtoosh and similar ultra-fine fabrics, placing them against himself in the mirror. Some looked quite good, and seemed to be a decent fit, so he bundled them into his bag and continued his drifting bimble.

The mood and feel of this enormous house was, on the outermost edge as it were, fascinating, beautiful, a place to spend days wandering and wandering, but as Joe floated further and further along its stately corridors, he began to feel an under-oppression, something like, oddly enough, the anguish that large supermarkets induced. The anxious, fragmented feeling wasn't soothed by the fact that, as he meandered through the house, he could now hear, muffled through the walls, the slap of human flesh against flesh, each hard spank followed by an owl's hoot. Slap slap, hoot, slap, hoot…

Time to get done. He hurried along to the rear drawing room and unpacked his equipment, covering the furniture in sheets, so that he could work away at the massive hearth, attaching pole into pole and feeding the brush up the chimney. He pushed and pulled, cleaning the highest part of the stack, fountains of soot falling down into his sack; when the brush stuck. He pulled. Nothing. He pulled harder; still nothing. He tugged and tugged until, in an extinction burst of aggression he aggressively yanked the brush, his full weight behind the tug, and pulled down a cascade of masonry, smashing down the chimney, cracking the hearth and filling the room with soot and brick dust.

He leapt away from the clouds of smoke, which slowly settled, leaving the room covered in a layer of black felt. The slapping-hooting stopped. Someone had heard. Joe began hurriedly packing the wreckage into two large masonry bags.

When he had finished, he tested a bag. It was extremely heavy, perhaps twice his body-weight, both full bags would be a trembling stress to heave. He put it down, stood up straight and jerked in shock. In the doorway stood a boy of around twelve, dressed in an immaculately fitting cream suit. Apart from the slickness of his attire, there was something unnerving about him—something in his unchildlike posture, his confident but tremulous tone and the inhuman smoothness of his face, combined with a supercilious, hateful glare to his eye, that was deeply unnerving. Joe knew this was Joris, Max's son—they had quietly passed each other on a couple of occasions—but he had the impression now that he was speaking to a creature not quite human.

'What are you doing?' asked Joris.

'I was cleaning the chimney.'

'You're supposed to be digging. I know.'

'I did a bit but it was raining, so I thought I'd do this first.'

'You're not paid to think are you?'

'Quite right young master, quite right,' said Joe in an obsequious cod West Country accent.

'Are you mocking me?'

'No, not really… and… anyway,' said Joe, 'it's cleared up a bit, so I'll get on back to the mole hole.'

'What was the noise?' Joris looked around at the dust as if so many dead enemies lay at his feet.

'What noise?'

'The noise I *heard*. Like a wall falling over.'

'Nothing.'

Joris walked slowly around the room. Everything was filthy, but standing. 'It don't feel like nothing. What's in those bags?' he asked, pointing at the bulky masonry bags.

'Just coal dust.'

'It's very dusty in here,' said Joris retreating, brushing his arms, apparently now concerned for his suit.

'Yes, dusty old job,' Joe raised his eyebrows, half-apologetically, 'Dusty old world.'

'I don't like you,' said Joris. His total confidence was horrible. Joe could feel a coldness settle in his pit. 'Oh?' he said, 'erm, I suppose…'

Joris, now standing again at the doorway, interrupted, '…I didn't like the last man either, but he was translucent. Saturday morning. You are opaque. Muddy. Thursday afternoon.'

'You think? I, uh… I always fancied myself as a mid-Friday morning umber, or…' he trailed off under Joris' blank regard. Then said, quietly and in quite a high register, '…mauve.'

The two stood looking at each other. Joris' eyes like dry black stones, Joe's like reflections of Uranus.

'Well…' said Joe taking an intake of breath and holding it in, as if to say 'I must get on.' Joris, unmoving gave a small 'go ahead, I'm not stopping you' head nod.

Joe picked up the bags, with outward calm. The muscles under his overalls bulged, the tendons in his neck went piano-string taut, his back tensed and his whole body strained to make the load, which weighed as much as two sofas, look like it was a bag of ash. His face twitched, but Joris, apparently looking for something else, missed it.

'I'm watching you,' said the boy, stepping aside to let Joe out.

'Okee-doke!' Joe croaked, concealing, as best he could, the immense strain in his voice.

❧

The rain banged on the slanting reinforced windows of the mortuary like a thousand little fists. Lilly was working on a young man, Paisley, who had collapsed in his tiny bedroom and had had a cardiac arrest after spraying himself, for the third time in one day, from head to foot, in deodorant. Paisley didn't look like an especially interesting or understanding lad, with the same tense, nondescript, pudgy and narrow-jawed face as the male half of Edding, or at least the young ones—some old men came in with jaws like a JCB bucket—but he was dead now, so none of that mattered and Lilly could suppose he was interested in shoegaze and tassel-making and woodland creatures.

'I fell in love with animals, I think… I was ten or eleven?' Last night had been Diwali and she had gone out in the garden with Chiyo to watch the fireworks, only to be reduced to tears by the terror of the birds shooting past in all directions. Chiyo had put a light arm round Lilly and said 'I'll make humanity pay for their fun,' which wasn't very consoling, but it had made Lilly think. The suffering of animals had been on her mind all morning. 'We were visiting a farm,' she said to Paisley, 'me and my mum, you know, one of those petting farms, and I was looking at the pigs, and they had *eyelashes*, so that was it. I gave up eating meat, or at least anything which once had eyelashes, because I felt so bad. Cows have eyelashes. I don't trust animals without eyelashes. Or people for that matter. I don't mind people without eyebrows, although they always look slightly surprised, but no eyelashes is creepy, lizardlike.'

She added a little blusher around Paisley's nose.

'Your eyebrows are okay I suppose, although they don't look like they've moved very much. Some people go through their whole lives without moving their eyebrows at all.'

Carl entered, lugging a very heavy-looking, thick plastic sack. With effort he placed it down on the floor.

'Fifty heads,' he said with breathless triumph, 'Twenty five in this one. Surprisingly heavy, heads. Amazing that necks can hold them up.'

'Why?'

'Nina has a deal with the hospital. After the trainee doctors have finished with them, we take 'em down the crem.'

'They're going to set fire to fifty heads tomorrow?'

'Yep. Twenty five tomorrow. They do 'em in batches.'

'I'd like to see that.'

'We're down there anyway. The police are dropping a body off in a few minutes, that bird they dumped in the town centre.'

'Ursula?' said Lilly, catching her breath. She put her brush down. Since the visit from the police, Neil hadn't been the same. She'd try to comfort him, to talk to him; she'd felt the guilt of the damned, but he just tried to twist every offer of consolation into some kind of invitation to get back together, or have some 'sympathy sex,' and she couldn't allow herself to guilt-tripped into intimacy, even if Neil was destroyed, although, at the same time, it was so hard to tell, because, at the same time, he seemed to be not affected by it all, just as 'Neil' as ever, if anything more so.

'Is that her name?' asked Carl, 'She flew into a windmill.'

'She what?'

Carl shrugged, 'I dunno. Shame really. Well fit. A nine, easy.'

'Nine what?'

'Nine out of ten. I'd say ten, but I like…' he made a hand-cupped 'big tit' gesture… 'you know what I mean?'

Lilly nodded, sadly.

Carl nodded at the bag, 'Shall we have a look at some of these heads then?'

'Later Carl. I've got to get on.'

'Alright,' he looked at Lilly, who had returned to work. 'You're an eight, if you were wondering,' he said.

'Thanks. I wasn't, but thanks.'

'Some would say less, but it's a subjective thing…'

'Hello? Anyone there?' A voice called from the workshop and Carl left.

Lilly returned to Paisley. She'd gone to pick him up with Carl; bare house, cheap grey carpets, humongous flat-screen television. Paisley had a kind of shrine to Tottenham Hotspur in the corner of his room, and a large brown lizard in a large glass cage, sitting on a rock looking dispassionately at Paisley's dead body. The broken mother had come in and asked if Lilly and Carl wanted a cup of tea and, trying not to look at the corpse, had turned towards the lizard and addressed it, saying 'I suppose you'll miss Paisley now too?' Then she'd burst into tears and left.

It was horrible, it was always horrible, but it was real. It was all so *actual*, death. No matter how appallingly sad, even when the family didn't really care and were just pretending to mourn, even then there was something impossible to ignore about it all, something that made the rest of the world seem fake; fake because it *could* be ignored. So Lilly went, and she kept going.

This week alone she had picked up an old man who had died in his chair in front of the television. Next to him was a biscuit tin which he had been using as a toilet. The whole house was filthy and untidy and smelt of concentrated old-age flesh mixed with piss. He had no family and died alone.

She had picked up the body of an obese old woman which needed five people to carry down the stairs of a nursing home. The woman had decided to lose weight, bought a bag of carrots and choked on the first one.

She had picked up an old Syrian man who'd had a heart attack. He had, his completely unconcerned son had told Lilly, just found out that the money he'd hidden in his shed, about thirty thousand pounds, had been chewed to shreds by rats.

She had gone out to Clockel Wood to pick up a man who had committed suicide by handcuffing himself to a tree and throwing the key into the bushes. The police had pointed out that the position of the handcuffs and the marks found on the tree, indicated that the man had probably changed his mind.

And she had picked up two suicides. One, a man who'd overdosed on Xanax, after losing his job as a school year-head after having been accused of sexual misconduct, and another, the worst of the lot, a girl of thirteen who had slit her wrists, leaving a suicide note that just said 'I was already dead.'

Lilly had come to realise that it was possible, in grief, to commune with the bereaved. The ones closest to the deceased were often at their most exposed, their most sensitive, their most honest. She could help them, in a way, not by doing much, but by already being in that same state, or kind of. Carl's brutal matter-of-factness was surprisingly comforting too; she was astonished at how well people took to him, the way he'd nod up the stairs and say 'he's up there is he?' like a plumber asking where a burst pipe was. It brought some weird kind of relief to people, but still, the really broken ones liked being with her most, and she liked being with them. She had to be with them, for her own sake as much as anyone else's. She had to talk to people who were raw. In fact, she had to admit to herself, that grieving people were often far better company than anyone else.

Carl called back from the workshop 'Lilly! She's here now! Ursula!' Lilly went out and ten minutes later both of them were standing in front of Ursula's dead body, laid out on Lilly's second anatomy table.

'I don't understand,' said Lilly, 'She's been dead for, what, two months?'

'Something like that.'

'And look at her.'

'I know,' said Carl quietly, with deep, dirty, awe.

'She's beautiful.'

'I know.'

'How old is she supposed to be?'

'Late thirties?'

'She looks the same age as me,' said Lilly.

'I know.'

The way Carl was looking at Ursula made Lilly's stomach churn a bit. 'Shouldn't you be somewhere?'

'I know.'

'Go on then, off you go.'

Carl snapped out of it. 'Why are we whispering?' he said chucklingly, his normal cheerful aspect returning.

'Reverence I suppose,' said Lilly.

'Yeah… Sorry, I just go into the fuckstare, you know what I mean? I can't help it. It's like when you go round a mate's house, and you're all pissed up, playing Axis and Allies and it's all cheers and vomit, and then someone gets the bright idea of putting some hardcore porn on and one by one everyone just goes silent and hypnotised, staring at a pair of black lesbians.'

'I hate it when that happens.'

'So, I'll be back this arvo,' he said, then whispered, 'Yamaraja are doing a lunch special this week.' He waited for a reaction, but none came. 'Right,' he threw a last grasping look at Ursula, then left.

∞

Maria stared into space, a look of blank, bored, annoyance frozen onto her features. Life was alright, kind of; the problem was that all human beings were basically, essentially, total cretins, every last one of them. Being a manager would be okay if you didn't have to rely on the flakes beneath you, but even overseeing an army of mentally defective subnormals would be bearable if you didn't have to go home to one. It was starting to become clear to Maria that she had to get out of this absurd charade, but every time she seriously considered leaving Joe she would feel a pain in her chest. It wasn't just a case of pulling out a thorn; the thorn was part of her, it was her. It had grown into her body. He was one thing, she was another, but there was this part where they overlapped, where it was hard to say who was who.

She had, a few days before, gone to see a fortune teller, a skinny man with a stupid wide-brimmed hat and the kind of 'yeah-yeah-yeah' intense 'lovey-starey' eyes of an ex-Ecstasy addict who she didn't trust one bit, but who had been glowingly recommended to her by the women at her weekly Kundalini Yoga. They had said that 'Matt' was the best palm reader they'd ever been to, so she'd met him in a café in Nutbourne and he'd glanced at her palm and said that she'd never get a promotion, nor get a better job, that if she left the man she was with at the moment she would never find anyone else and would die alone and that she was in the early stages of glaucoma and would be blind within fifteen years unless she got steroid eye-drops.

Maria had stood up and left without paying him; that's not what you go to a fortune teller for. They were supposed to tell you that you were having problems with your family or your partner or your finances, but it would all be sorted out if you stayed firm, respected yourself and made peace with your past. And yet, she couldn't shake the feeling, irrational but deep, that although the known was the clown she was living with, the unknown was a kind of emptiness, an endless salt desert, hot, dry, lonely, white and interminable.

A knock on the door shook her. 'Come in,' she said mechanically. Bronya's head slid from behind the quarter-opened door like a character in a cautiously opened pop-up book.

'Er, someone wants to see you.'

'Who?'

Bronya, pointing behind her and with much eyeball-wide exaggeration, half-mouthed, half-whispered; 'It's *him!*'

'It's who?'

'Max Thottesley.'

'What does *he* want?'

Bronya shrugged, tense, anguished even.

Maria sighed. 'Can't you deal with him?'

'He insists on speaking to you.'

Maria thought about it. She wouldn't normally handle a

complaint—that's what the cannon fodder were for—particularly not from one of the propertied reptiles out in the sticks, but Thottesley was far, *far* above the bitter Cotswolders who very occasionally came in moaning about a schizophrenic neighbour's son rolling around naked on their front lawns. In fact there was a kind of force field, erected around houses with more than eight bedrooms, that repelled social services. Their problems did not get out, and Maria's heroic problem-solvers didn't get in. That Bronya had been told to visit was strange enough, but that a multi-millionaire would float down from the celestial realm to visit her, Maria; that was unheard of.

'Alright,' she said, 'show him in.'

Bronya disappeared. Maria heard her nasally, muffled whine, then a deeper, loud and lazily confident voice, then, without knocking, Max himself strode in. With his golden-orange tan, Shetland tweed, pale blue turtleneck and unhesitating gestures, he looked completely out of place in the office, like George the fourth at McDonald's, like a lion in the pigeon shed. He sat down as if the chair, the room, the town were his, which they probably were.

'Good morning Maria; can I call you Maria?'

'Yes, erm… sorry…?' She pretended not to know his name.

'Max,' he smiled, teeth unnaturally regular and white.

'Max, yes, what is it talk you wanted to about?'

While she was speaking Max, legs elegantly crossed in front of him, had removed a cigarette from a silver cigarette case, tapped it, and put it in his mouth.

'I'm afraid there's no smoking in here,' said Maria, surprised at the note of apology that had crept into her voice.

'Not even a little opium?' he asked, archly.

'Oh no! Hahahaha!'

He put the cigarette away. 'Your husband is working for me now. Interesting creature.'

'Yes, I know. I mean I didn't know,' she said, wondering why she was so confused.

'Yes, and your… that girl there, what's her name? The one with a face like a slapped arse?'

Maria smiled guiltily. 'Bronya,' she said.

'Yes, Bronya is paying me courtesy calls.'

'Well, we've had reports…'

'From whom?'

'I honestly don't know. Higher up.'

'Mm. Well I thought it was about time I met the mastermind behind these little sorties, find out what she was after.'

'I'm not after anything!' cried Maria, and did a little fart; just a single, non-resonating 'brub.' She blushed to her ears, but Max gave no sign he had heard, and it was a very quiet one.

He pulled out an absurdly large handkerchief. 'I know you're not, I know that' he said tenderly dabbing the corner of his lip. 'Look, Maria, I won't lie to you. I could cause you and your department all kinds of problems, you understand…'

'…yes, I suppose you could.'

'But,' he said, with an airy wave of the hand, 'that's the last thing on my mind. In fact, it's right at the back of the queue.'

There was a significant pause. Maria felt herself getting hot under her collar. A heaving, prickly kind of flush, a heavy kind of ecstasy, spread across her chest, making her breath more deeply. Looking into Max's hard, dark eyes, she felt pinned, speared, wanting to get away, but not wanting. It was dreadful and marvellous. 'What's… I see… What's at the front of the queue?' she asked.

'Butter beans,' he purred.

'Oh! Really?'

'Would you like to dine with me?'

'Oh… Um… Well it's… *when?*'

'Today. Lunch.'

'Um…' she made as if to look like she was thinking, when all she could actually think was that she couldn't think of what to say because she was thinking that she couldn't think of what to say.

'I know,' said Max, smiling slightly, 'it's not very professional. I have a regular table booked at my favourite restaurant. I'll send a car to pick you up in… forty-five minutes, is that okay?'

'I'll think about it…'

Max stood up. 'You do that. It's been a pleasure to meet you Maria.' He held out his hand.

Maria stood up too and shook his hand, looking up into him, her eyes burning with wasting fire, giving him license, to burn there too—I don't care, she thought, I don't care, yes.

'Come as you are,' he said.

ॐ

Lilly was looking at Ursula's body. It was long and slim, slightly full at the hips, and thighs, strong, like it had carried her through a life that uses a body, fully, but yet also delicate, slender. Her long, thick, blonde hair, her long fingers, her fine, graceful neck, her long, slightly bent nose, her full lower lip and faint overbite reminded Lilly of a painting she had once seen of a muse, or a dryad, or something like that.

'You really are lovely,' she whispered, 'It's hard to believe you're dead.' Ursula's pale skin looked deathlike, but it was immaculate, unlike any corpse Lilly had yet seen, even of children. There was no swelling anywhere, no mottled blistering, not even the rigidity they all had. She looked like she was languidly resting. Her lips were as red as rowan berries.

'It's hard to believe you're Neil's sister,' she added. Two people more unalike-looking could hardly be imagined.

'He's all over the shop,' she said, 'He's trying to guilt me into getting back together with him. He's quite good at it, although I already felt bad.'

She took a deep breath then exhaled heavily, puffing out her cheeks, trying to rid herself of the Neilish unpleasantness. 'I think it's much worse being the break up-er than having someone break up with you. I mean, it's horrible someone dumping you, but you kind of think, "well, if they don't want to be with me, there's nothing I can do about it." Whereas I feel when you break up with someone, there's always, you know, regret, doubt, guilt. You have all that, don't you?'

Ursula looked like a vestal virgin, lying on a sacrificial slab, ready for a cult priest with a big silvery sun crest to plunge a flint knife into her sternum.

'Actually I bet you never had that. I bet you had a wonderful life. I get this South American vibe. Llamas, rickety bus trips over the Andes, jaguar rescue centre, Mexican artist town, volcanoes, lizards, cactus, or cacti is it? Sorry I do ramble on.'

She sighed again. 'God you're lovely.'

Nina, at her computer, was, as ever, watching Lilly. Not so much out of suspicious anxiety now. Lilly was safe, but she was certainly interesting. Munching away at a bag of monkey nuts, Nina watched Lilly leave the room, and return with an instrument case, put it down on the floor and take out her bass oboe, which she started playing, a chillingly beautiful requiem.

As Lilly played the bass oboe Victor, in his Nutella and camel-ball-gobstopper womb, added synth sounds (a squelchy bass, a theremin style whine, etc.), a far-distant otherwordly element to the infinite longing of the tune.

As she played, Joe dug at the big X, the same spot where Lilly's mother had gone up in a phosphorus flash. He stopped, looking at the hole, troubled.

As she played, Aaron and Moira were buying their week's food at a supermarket, bitterly arguing in undertones.

As she played, on a lovely secluded wildflower speckled hill, D.C.I. Gaynor Babcock, dressed in full mourning attire, face wet with tears, was unscrewing an urn and, as she scattered the ashes therein, whispered, devotedly, 'Gaynor Babcock and Clive Marsh. On a hill.'

As she played, Maria's stolid, pastel parents, Heather, who had been watching 'Antiques Road Trip' on television, and Tom, who had been reading 'Civilisation: A History of Ideas', were, as the TV snowed up with interference, looking at each other, confused, as if they'd both forgotten what they were doing.

As she played, Irving ate his lonely dinner of lentil dhal next to his Matchstick Mary.

As she played, Chiyo was standing eighteen inches in front of her Rothko.

As she played, Paul was playing Mario Golf Super Rush on his Nintendo Switch.

As she played, Neil was obsessively cleaning his room, although he had noticed something.

As she played, Dave Davage was waiting for a train. Peering at the fence behind him, he had also noticed something.

As she played, Hunter was looking at his phone, brow furrowed over a page which said 'A roundtable conversation with six artists and radicals.'

As she played, Patrick—Thottesley's ex-gardener—sat in the Jobcentre Plus, his hard square face set in stone.

As she played, the old woman who lived next door to Joe and Maria, was standing at her bedroom window—all the other windows of her house now boarded up.

As she played, Joe, now about three feet down, struck the earth and the spade vanished, swallowed up into small hole.

As she played, Mario, golf club raised high, froze. Paul tried to get him to move, stabbing away at his game console, but Mario just slowly turned his head towards Paul.

As she played, Aaron and Moira, who had stopped arguing, were looking at each other in horror and confusion. Aaron with a one-litre carton of Sunny D California Orange Drink in his hand, Moira, with a bottle of Johnson and Johnson intimate wash, were looking at each other as if they had entirely forgotten who or what they were. Little James was tugging at Moira's dress.

As she played, Heather was frantically stabbing at the buttons on the remote control, but all the television channels were showing Joris in an empty room, dressed as a black crow with a white diamond on his forehead jumping up and down shouting 'NO! NO! NO! NO! NO!' Tom's book was filled with the word 'no' over and over again, a thousand pages of 'no.'

As Lilly played, Victor's accompanying tracks were diverging into a discordant and disturbing—even nauseating—chaos. He sang; 'The heart of the world is breaking.'

As she played, Chiyo was still standing eighteen inches in front of the black and red painting; a gentle smile now on her damp, purplish lips.

As she played, Mario's face was sliding off, revealing, to the horror of Paul, Paul's face.

As she played, Gaynor Babcock was on her knees, heaving grief into her palms, sobbing and moaning, clutching at the grass beneath her.

As she played, Hunter, in horror, stared at a mountain of dead bodies on his phone, trying to turn the phone off, swipe away; nothing doing.

As she played, Neil, pulling a flaky piece of Gregg's sausage roll from under his bed, was gagging and shuddering.

As she played, Dave was staring horrified at a photograph on the wall of the station platform. It showed Dave looking at the same photograph. He looked around, wildly, eyes tense in fear.

As she played, Irving sat staring at his empty plate. His face was white, drawn, like he hadn't slept for weeks, the face of a cracked mind. 'Keep busy, that's the main thing,' he whispered.

As she played, Joe, who had fallen against the hole, was looking into its blackness, a cold wind dimly roaring from the void.

Lilly finished playing, the discordant elements of the song faded away, leaving the lovely melody. Then she very gently, very tenderly, kissed Ursula.

∞

Max Thottesley attracted people with the same kind of crude, calculating, power-hungry look as he had; sycophants, debauchees, gamblers, gourmands and mergers-and-acquisitions analysts; but unlike those who served him, Max's glance was not hesitant, not blinking, but dry, fixed, calm, glistening and openly devouring.

He moved slowly, and powerfully, he ate slowly and powerfully.

'I love this place,' he said.

'Yes…' Maria was somewhat awakened from the spell he had put her under by the ordinariness of the scene; the large feature wall, the African-inspired upholstery, the bored irritability of the Polish waitress and the garlic and herb sauce. 'Do you?'

'Corny Browns,' he said, taking a forkful of stodge, 'Normally only available at Gatwick Airport.'

'I didn't think a man like you would eat at Nando's.'

Max said nothing, chewed, swallowed, took a sip of Gingerally, and then spoke, very slowly and carefully, staring at Maria, once more pinning her consciousness, butterfly-like, to the back wall of her mind. 'In the coarseness of the world,' he purred, 'there are ecstasies beyond the bounds of time, that the wise shudder at.'

'Oh my God,' she breathed, 'that's beautiful.'

'The pursuit of pleasure must be the goal of every rational person. There is only life, so of course every moment of it must be lived to the absolute limit.'

'I couldn't agree more.'

He smiled and nodded, as if to say, of course you couldn't. 'So what are we going to do about Joe and Bronya?' he asked.

'I don't know. What do you think?'

'Well, Joe's quite happy where he is. Bronya, I think, otherwise.'

Max regarded Maria calmly, his shapely hands, almost sinister, resting on the table; some kind of appalling, disintegrating electricity seemed to be passing from his body to hers, and she was receiving it, a sullen, unconscious film seemed to cover her eyes as she looked at him, all the sardonic bitterness of her previous life gone, leaving this strange new compelling, slave-like, sickening emptiness which she wanted nothing more than to completely surrender to, that it might be filled.

'Do you follow me?' said Max.

'Yes, I follow you.'

'It is better to follow a lion, much stronger than oneself, than live with ten thousand rats of your own species.'

'That's not a fashionable idea,' she said, 'People don't like the idea of superiority these days.'

'No of course not. That's why they need democracy, equality, rational order and useful machines. They should all be equal. I'm all for socialism for people who want it. They deserve it. It's the same with people as with books, very few play a great part. Let the others have their fifteen minutes of fame, a few upvotes and good ratings; then tidily arrange them on their desktops.'

Maria had the feeling she was talking to a great emperor. Max seemed to radiate nobility. It was true what he said; we do need great people. Where would we be without someone to admire?

'You're right,' she said, although she wasn't really paying attention what he was saying, the tone was so completely absorbing.

'It has always been this way,' he went on, 'In ancient Greece there were the people, bound by the law, equal before it, and then there was Zeus and Ares and Apollo rampaging around the world doing whatever they pleased. Same in Judea.'

'Yes,' Maria whispered, 'yes.'

'Bronya isn't cut out for social work,' he said, 'She'd be much happier testing stair lifts.'

'Yes. Yes. I'll see to it.'

Max took a big ugly mouthful of chicken thigh. 'Good,' he said, 'What are you doing tonight?'

Something spoke from inside Maria's chest. It was her voice, her body, but where it came from she had no idea. 'Everything,' said the voice.

Max nodded slowly, like a connoisseur. 'Tell me,' he said, 'What do you want?'

'I want a powerful man,' said Maria, without hesitating, 'I want to give myself to a man strong enough to take me. I don't care if he is the devil, just as long as he isn't *weak*. I detest weakness in men, and they're *all* weak.'

'You're right. They are. Man submits to woman, to her heart and to her cunt. Her emotions control him and they both hate him for it. She begs to be free, for man to submit to her flesh and to master her. Tell me a memorable dream,' he said.

'When I was young I dreamt of pirates, of being raped by a boat full of pirates. One after the other.'

'Filthy.' He smiled, revealing lines in his face that were appallingly coarse.

'Do you live alone?'

'I have a son.'

'Who's the mother?'

'He has no mother.'

Maria laughed, 'Where did he come from then?'

'I have no need of woman to spawn. I can reproduce through intelligence and the spoken word.'

'So you're bringing him up alone? A one-parent family?'

'Yes.'

'You're a good man.'

'I'm wealthy enough to afford morals.'

This touched something in Maria. She felt, without examining the feeling, that the rich and famous were intrinsically good; but it didn't actually matter, because once you were elevated to status your sins fell away like dried-up rose petals.

'The only thing that matters, on top of the world mountain,' said Max, seeming to read her mind, 'is power. Money power, property power, fame power, industrial power, processing power, cunt power, cock power... It doesn't matter what kind, or how you acquire it, or what you do to maintain it, you must have it, and you must keep it.'

'It's so... pure,' she whispered.

'More or less. If you spend any time with the great and the good, you'll soon see, dripping through the seams of the mechanism, the oil that keeps it all going, is fear. They are all afraid of losing their power. That's how they can be kept in place.'

'Who is keeping them in place? You?'

'Me? No, no, the system itself does. Once you're in it you have to conform, to stay in it. There's really very little work for me to do... What's that?'

'What's what?'

Max tilted his head. 'Can you hear that?'

Maria listened. 'No. What is it?'

'It's a bass oboe.'

On the next table to Max and Maria, two large women with painted-on eyebrows and thick, hairy designer eyelashes that looked like they were made of spider's legs, were talking about clothing. The girl with her back to the grey window, Gem, was wearing fishnet tights and a garter over her enormous pink pegs, making them look like ham hocks in meat netting. The other girl, Keira ('Keeks' to her friends) was wearing a loose T-shirt which said 'It's all your fault.'

'They're "Inspire" by New Look,' said Gem, 'That means that they're fat girl's trousers.'

'They're not trousers,' said Keeks, 'They're *jeggings*,' she said.

'Whatever. Fat girls wear 'em.'

'Hayley Mellish wears 'em.'

'Exactly. She thinks she's sizzling, but she's a fucking dog.'

'She's not a fat fucking dog though.'

'She's got a fat fucking neck.'

'But her jeggings ain't on her fat fucking neck,' said Keeks.

Gem blew out her cheeks. 'Fat ankles too.'

'Whas the connection?'

'What, between your ankles and your neck?'

'Yeah.'

'It's your body, innit?'

They both burst into rough, cackling laughter, then stopped suddenly, glancing uneasily around. Keeks looked anxiously at Gem, 'can you hear that?'

'I'll pick you up at around nine outside here, and then take you to my club,' said Max, distracted now, and with it somewhat diminished, but Maria still hung suspended.

'You have a club?'

'Mm hm. It's called Dominus.'

'Oh. My. God. That's *yours*?'

Max gave a suggestive nod.

'Doesn't… Isn't,' she dropped her voice to a whisper, 'I've heard things… Isn't it, they say it's… *things* happen in there…'

'Disgusting bliss.'

'Oh.' Maria felt another surge of strange, dark energy overwhelm her.

'Does that bother you?'

'No.'

'Do you have an open mind?' he asked quietly.

'Yes,' said Maria, at the same volume.

'You are the future Maria.'

'What do you mean?' They were almost whispering now.

'When all barriers have been broken down, and all can enjoy and be enjoyed with total, boundaryless freedom, then the human race will be perfected. But it takes power to break such boundaries, it takes power to become something new…'

Max suddenly stopped eating, listening carefully. The bass oboe music had morphed into a jaunty, but equally creepy polka. A kind of drone, as if from a hurdy-gurdy, ground out a brain frying monotone dirge throughout.

'Can you hear that?' he asked Maria.

'Where's it coming from?'

'It's coming from The Other,' he said, eyes clouding over.

'What's The Other?'

Max appeared to be possessed, eerily absent. 'From your perspective it's both heaven and hell,' he said, as if under hypnosis, 'A state totally beyond the boundaries of good and evil, life and death, here and there.'

'Sounds like my kind of place.'

Max watched her, unseeing yet seeing, a gleam of recognition now in his blank face. 'Does it?' he asked.

'Yes,' she said, grasping his hand, '*yes.*'

The lights go out. A powercut? There is blackness, absolute and pure and forever. Nothingness, but full of fear, which seeps through the curtain of darkness, a red light which casts the room in hazy, demonic shadows. Max leaps to his feet, throws his arms open, and breaks into song; a magnificent, charging music-hall number of dirty trumpets and rancid accordions;

> *'Te verberare volo, lividum te caedere volo.*
>
> *Mordere te volo, spinas tuas frangere volo.*
>
> *Occidere te volo, cadaver tuum lacerare volo.*
>
> *Secare te volo, equo meo te pascere volo!'*

Maria stands up too, singing the chorus in a husky, full-throated contralto. Again, her voice seems to be someone else's, and seems to come from somewhere in her chest, bypassing her larynx. It is the voice of an elemental woman, a proto-woman, the proto-woman that all women are connected to, singing for her life, with the man of her dreams.

> *'Tota vita expectavi,*
>
> *Deum ut signum mitteret,*
>
> *Virum qui intellegeret*
>
> *Flumen sanguinis quod per manus meas torrens fluit.'*

Max takes up the verse, hopping round Nando's like Gene Kelly, a muscular manly dance with a very low centre of gravity, his large rear-end, all muscle, springing him from table to table like a lorry shock spring.

> *'Ustulare te volo, tortos clamores ligare volo.*
>
> *Frigere te volo, cum fabis te vorare volo.*
>
> *Saxis te gravare volo, arte constringere volo.*
>
> *In stagnum te iacere volo, mature dormire volo!'*

Maria stands on her chair, blood red light spilling over her, seemingly *out* of her, as she sings the chorus, a demonic backing choir harmonising from fathomless depths:

> *'Tota vita expectavi,*
>
> *Deum ut signum mitteret,*
>
> *Virum qui intellegeret*
>
> *Flumen sanguinis quod per manus meas torrens fluit.'*

As she sings, the music becomes nightmarish, discordant, out of time and space. Joe's spade has slipped into the belly of the earth. A wave of intense, devilish wrongness passes over the chain restaurant. Diners look at each other in naked horror, stripped for a moment of the filter of normality that they have been dining through, seeing now the truth of the peri peri chicken, its putrid otherness, its fleshly proximity. They jump to their feet, wailing, many hysterical, over-the-top revulsion and disarray.

'I have to leave,' says Max.

'Where!?' cries Maria, 'Where are you going!?'

'Home.'

8

The acidic grievance that was always smouldering away in Neil's thorax made it difficult to finish a full meal, so he was just pushing his fried egg and mashed potato around with the back of his spoon. Chiyo, sitting opposite him at the kitchen table, was eating a bowl of shelled edamame beans, precisely lifting one after another, with chopsticks, carefully watching Neil. Some of her beans went in her small mouth, some were neatly placed on a side plate. Neil occasionally glanced up at her, nervously.

Hunter was standing next to them, texting. 'It's tragic Neil,' he said, not looking up, 'It *really* is. You must be in bits.'

'What is?' even Neil, who performed so much of his life, found Hunter's hollow emphasis—the sense that everything that came from his mouth was being recited, was part of a script— annoying. It was the completeness of the adopted role that was so unsettling. There was nothing else in there.

'What's what?'

'What's tragic? Losing my job, my girlfriend or my sister?' Neil put all his bitterness and scorn into the question, but Hunter, unnoticing, chattered on, although he did look up to consider this puzzle.

'All three I suppose, job… girl,…sister…' he said, 'In that order.' He made a 'stepping up' gesture with flattened fingers.

'I'm not "in bits",' said Neil, 'I'm completely together, in one piece. And I'm going to get her back.'

'But she's dead.'

'Not Ursula, Lilly,' he said tightly.

It was strange, *strange*. Why had Lilly left him? He had done everything by the book. He had engineered romantic accidents to give her the impression that it was 'meant to be,' he had projected a stable and sincere ideal image of a provider, the kind that all women desire, he had used the chancellor's power stance, often, and had gripped her hand with manliness; and yet, somehow it had all ended up as an emotion-fuelled own-goal cruise-missile counter-strike custard-in-face wipe out.

'What should I do?' he said unintentionally aloud and then wondered if he had said this or just thought it.

'Sorry?' said Hunter, torn between Neil and his phone.

'Nothing,' said Neil staring at his pap of eggy glute.

'Just be yourself,' said Hunter, mechanically, which was his solution to all of life's problems.

Chiyo sucked the air, wincing, head-tilted, expressing intense scepticism in the Japanese style. 'Be yourself?' she said quietly, then shook her head and, after a long pause, said; 'this; suicide.'

'Who else can I be?' said Neil, looking up. He had a blob of mashed potato on his bottom lip.

'Nobody.'

Silence.

The long unsettling moment was broken by a burst of shallow outrage from Hunter; 'Bum! *Seriously?* Bangladeshi people are the sloppiest coders in the whole world. I respect their socio-economic mitigations, but they're worse than the Vietnamese…' He looked up, expecting understanding comradeship, 'I want a clean front end, clean and pure, like a mountain stream, and look!'

He showed them his phone screen. The landing page for his app, 'LifeLine,' was a chaotic mess. The logo and tagline ('heal thyself') were visible, but underneath was a hellish, broiling mayhem of unrelated pixels.

Chiyo and Neil paid him no attention, so he frumped out of the room. Neil looked down at his plate. The skin of the yolk was breached, warm yellow liquid spread over the peaks of scraped potato like orange sunrise light dripping through the valleys of a mountain range—spreading over a cold land. Had his own egg been pierced? If so, by what…?

Chiyo was staring at Neil. 'Something on face,' she said and reached forward, scooping the piece of potato from Neil's lip with her clammy index finger, and then, slowly, slowly, she put her finger in her mouth. She swallowed and spoke, very quietly; 'Nobody. Turns. Me. On.' There was nothing seductive in this motion. It was matter-of-fact, blank, which made it all the more disturbing; although not as disturbing as the glimpse Neil has of her tongue. For a moment, he is sure he has seen a thin split down the middle of it, that her tongue is forked.

Shuddering inside, he pushed the image away. An hallucination, he told himself, a stress-induced mirage. He closed his eyes, took a deep breath and opened them again. Chiyo sat unmoving; it was as if her soul didn't move. She had made a perfect 'chan,' a circle of beans with, in the centre, two long cartoony eyes. Neil had sculpted his potato into a crude stick man, splattered with destroyed egg.

Neil looked from his plate, to hers, and then back to his own. 'Mine's be—e—etter,' he said.

૪

Nina, like Neil, was also ceaselessly afraid. Where his fear alternated with irritation—the two were one—hers translated into a permanent, twitching hunger for that which promised relief, but never gave it; money. She never stopped thinking about how much she had, how much was going in, how much was coming out, what things were worth, what they could be worth, how much everyone was earning and why. Most of her internal dialogue, walking around Edding, was made of up guesses as to how much each house she passed was worth—when she checked, she found she was only ever wrong by about ten percent. If someone mentioned they were going to a concert, Nina would ask 'how much were the tickets?' then multiply the figure by the estimated capacity of the venue, subtract their take, agents' fees and so on, and then say, impressed, 'not bad.'

She had room in her soul for another worry, although this one took up only about a quarter of her anxiety space; her 'disgusting father,' the nominal owner of the business who, fortunately, was too lazy to visit it and too drunk to understand what was happening in it, but who occasionally sobered up long enough to work out a way to burn up five hundred bloody pounds on the horses, which he spent all day watching, stewing in his sweat, burping, farting, scratching his fat, hairy belly and telling Nina to bring him another packet of nuts.

Nina's life had been, for the most part, a battle against the irresponsible profligacy, debauched slovenliness and precarious disorder that her father represented. She had picked up a visceral aversion to disease, uncertainty, risk and death. She was uncomfortable around any kind of novelty, or anyone unusual; all of which she designated as 'fringe.' 'Fringe foods,' such as aubergine, or okra, or fruit served with meat and saveloys; 'fringe people,' such as well-read plumbers, teetotal Paddies and rock stars in stable marriages; and 'fringe things,' such as sporks, swingball and comedy-horror. All these things served the same function for her as the various categories of 'unclean' do for Jews and Muslims, as a means to keep her neatly ordered world together, to protect it from the abyss which surrounded her, and which she hid from, all day, in her carefully-ordered (yet, curiously, quite dirty) office, cracking monkey nuts and watching eighties pop videos, rugby highlights and amusing cat videos. Sentimentality is the consolation of the cynical. Like many people who always expect the worst of others—who assume everyone is secretly as petty as they are—Nina was given to teared-up mawkishness, in her case over the music of her youth, the courage of sportsmen and kittens.

The phone was ringing. She picked up the receiver, adopting her best 'solemn and respectful' tone.

'Nina Eedie, Herbert and Vole Funeral Services… Yes…Well, it's best if you speak to Paul, our…. No, I mean he's… *Who*…?' She straightened up, eyes widened, at once fascinated 'Oh…! Oh…! Oh…! *How* much!? Er, er, errrr…' She remembered herself, lowering her temperature back to a cool, solemn modesty '…yes, yes, of course. Yes, we'll be right there… Okay! Bye! Bye!'

She hung up, made a grimace of pleasure and then called out, almost shrieked, '*Paaaaauul!*'

Paul was in the middle of talking to a distraught old lady when Nina burst in, flush with pleasure.

'Paul, you'll never guess…' She noticed the old woman and was sombre again, but still quivering with delight, 'Oh, God, sorry… Paul, we have to…' She turned again to the woman, again 'respectful,' 'I'm sorry about this, but something has come up…' Then back to Paul, excited again, 'Paul you have to go somewhere… *very* important!' Then back to the woman, 'I'm afraid we'll have to reschedule this. I'm really sorry for your loss. Bye!'

She left, her molten form sliding through the frosted window, to give the good news to Lilly and Carl who she pulled together in the workshop and explained that they were to arrange the burial for *the richest man in the county*. For some reason, unclear to Nina, they did not receive the news with hysterical delight, merely shrugged and prepared the pick-up van. She twittered round them, sprinkling fussy instructions like confetti, and they 'yessed' and 'of coursed,' without reassuring conviction, but what could she do? She had to work with the tools she had. She did her best, made sure they were looking presentable—Paul too, who had joined them—and watched them pull out of the garage as a mother watches a train carrying her emigrating children to the Antipodes.

Carl drove, as usual, Lilly in the central passenger seat and Paul on the left. Lilly liked being between them. Freaks that the three of them were, it worked. The sun was almost shining. It was cold and damp outside, but the cab was warm. Chris Knox sang 'When I've Left this Mortal Coil.'

'Open the glove compartment,' said Carl. Lilly did so. 'Yep… that tin,' he said, 'There. Open it.'

Inside a worn tobacco tin were five long, thin, joints, neatly constructed, perfectly regular, lying in a neat little row.

'Spark one up,' he said. Lilly pushed in the cigarette lighter then, when it popped out, pressed the red filament against the twirled tip of the cannabis cigarette. Sweet resinous fumes filled the cab.

'Okay so,' she said, sour faced as her inflamed lungs tried to reject the unfamiliar weed, 'what other…' she broke into a cough, then continued, '…what other weird deaths have there been?'

They were continuing a conversation which had begun earlier, inspired by the poor lad who'd deodoranted himself to death.

'Fuck, loads,' said Carl, 'One guy got stuck inside the lightning wound of a walnut tree. Another lost control of a Segway while being attacked by a magpie and drove into a bus. There was a guy who killed himself because he was cheerful and was afraid of becoming unhappy—left a suicide note that said 'I am perfectly happy.' What else? Another one…'

'…were they all men?' She passed the joint to Paul.

'Yeah, usually men it is who die stupidly. Another one fell to his death while lawnmowing weed tufts on his roof. Erm. There was a guy that got killed by a leg of lamb when an oven in a Greek restaurant exploded. Another was on a horse that tripped over a pig that unexpectedly ran out from a dung heap. Woman that was.'

'I think I heard about that.'

'Then there was that guy who ate his beard.'

There was a long, quiet pause, broken by Paul's high pitched giggle.

As the conversation cheerfully circled, as it usually did, around decay, sickness, mortality, misery and loss, Carl motored through the shires. They got caught in a long queue on the slip road onto the A423, stopped for a roadside burger next to HomeBase, turned off towards West Woodford, passed through smaller and smaller villages, each lane thinner and woodier than the last, each one lined with larger and larger houses set further and further back. Occasionally an expensive car passed, or a family of five or six dressed in stretch-cotton khakis and padded green sportcoats. They passed the three-star Michelin 'Nono Cerchio,' they passed a long, white mansion that looked like it housed weekly orgies and they passed Tom Cruise's house, or one of them, which was surrounded by ten-foot tall brick walls, security cameras and what looked like laser guns. Many rulers of the world lived out here, in the rolling hills, far away from the scum who nevertheless occasionally drove up here to fly-tip renovation waste, left over from a new extension or a bashed-in garden fence, onto a deserted country bend.

They trundled up to a high iron gate which, after a brief intercom exchange, opened automatically, allowing them to pass up to the house. Lilly caught her breath, which had been sucked back inside her chest, a cold sense of devastating wrongness seizing her bellymind. She looked around; why? What is this place?

A small, round, nondescript man in a grey suit stopped them and directed them to the stone circle where, he said, they would find the body. They rattled and jerked over the uneven lawn, pulling up next to Joe, who stood next to one of the standing stones. A police car was approaching.

Lilly tenderly got out of the van, nodded a distracted, half-recognising, half-unseeing, greeting to Joe, and the three of them, Lilly, Paul and Carl, inspected the body of Max Thottesley whose naked buttocks and legs were sticking out of the ground, having apparently dived head-first into the hole that Joe had dug out that morning.

'Never seen that one,' said Carl.

'Hello again,' said Joe. Lilly smiled, still unsettled but pulling things together. Carl, included in the greeting, looked confused. 'Have we met?' he asked.

'Yes,' said Joe, 'you came to my house on a prank call.'

'Oh yeah!' said Carl, 'What are you doing here? I thought you were a professional queuer?'

'I was. That was a nice job actually.'

'…huh?' Carl turned to Paul. A squat, bearded policeman with large bulging eyes who had been bent over talking to a second policeman inside a now parked-up squad car, had stood up and looked over at the group, pointing. Paul, noticing, had nudged Carl and the two of them left to deal with the authorities, the two policemen and the round man in the suit who had by now joined them.

'Queuing doesn't sound like much fun,' said Lilly, turning back to Joe. He was leaning against a heel stone, hands behind his back, facing the naked legs. The sky had clouded over and spits of rain were darkening the menhirs.

'You say that,' he said, 'but when you get into it, it's surprisingly pleasant. Life is a queue. You join it, you slowly creep forward, and then, after being in line for seventy or eighty years, you get to the counter and die.'

'That's horrible!'

'Only if you think of it as *waiting*. If you're merely *standing*, it's quite nice.'

Lilly pondered, but larger, massier questions had more gravity and pulled her mind towards them. 'You're not a priest then?'

'Not particularly.'

'And you're Neil's brother.'

'Not particularly.'

'Do you want some of this?'

'Mm, alright,' Joe took the joint from Lilly, keeping half an eye on the police.

'I had to force that out of him,' she said, 'He didn't want to admit it.'

'No, he's disowned me. We had a falling out.'

'I'm not surprised. You two are matter and anti-matter.'

'How do you know him?'

'Uh, he was… we were… What happened exactly?' she asked.

'With me and Neil? It's a long story.'

'Oh, no,' she said, clearing her throat and indicating the hole, 'I meant here.'

'Him? He headbutted a hole.'

'But why?'

Joe shrugged. 'Why does anyone?'

'I'd like to headbutt a hole sometimes.'

'Is that how you'd like to go?'

Lilly thought about it. 'No,' she said, 'I… Uh… I don't know really. Everyone says, when I ask them, "how would you like to die?" they all say, you know, just as I'm at the point of orgasm, then I suddenly die.'

'Does everyone say that?'

'Don't you?'

'No.'

'How would you like to die then?' she asked.

'In a baling machine. Converted into a bale, and then buried very deep in the earth. Team of contractors digging for about three or four days.'

Lilly smirked. 'Oh well, the common answer is, erm, to…'

'…to go when you come.'

'Yeah, and maybe, I mean, as you have to die in some way, that wouldn't actually be a bad way to go? Maybe, actually— just a theory—the point in your life when you have the most intense and best orgasm ever, not just physically, but, with the person you're with, you know people are always I think, asking themselves, "is this what sex is? is this, is *this* good? is this good *now*? yeah, I *think* that was good." Well maybe the point where you've actually found it, you know *this is it*. Maybe then you die? Maybe that is the meaning of life?'

'The final level.'

'Yeah, that's, that's the whole point, to get that one orgasm, the one. And then, "game over. You won."'

Carl and Paul walked back over, both the policemen and

suited man heading in the opposite direction, back up to the house.

Carl approached. Lilly stepped towards him and said, under her breath, 'aren't you stoned?'

'I am *totally* shot away,' he said, unconcerned.

She turned back to Joe. 'This whole place is familiar,' she said, wonderingly, half to herself.

'What did he say?' Joe asked Carl.

'He said they want the body burnt tomorrow.'

'Tomorrow?' said Lilly, 'What's the rush?'

'Who's "they?"' asked Joe.

'I dunno,' said Carl, hands on hips, assessing the legs. 'Plod, and that little lawyer fella. Ian his name is.'

'Who?'

'That guy, over there.'

'Who, the policeman?'

'No, the little bloke next to him.'

'What little bloke?' Joe squinted up at the car. There were two policemen there. No 'little bloke' at all.

'Arrangements have been made,' said Paul in a tone even deeper and more bass-resonant than normal. Joe and Carl turned to him. He was standing in the middle of the circle, looking into the woods, apparently paying no attention to anyone.

Carl turned to Lilly, 'We're to take him back now,' he said and returned to the van.

'Now now?'

'Yep!' he called from inside the van.

'What, pull him out now?'

'Yep. Giz a hand.'

Lilly helped him lift the stretcher from the van.

'Don't the police want to look into it?' asked Joe.

'They're not going to,' said Carl, putting the stretcher down, 'Or they can't. We're to wrap him up, do nothing to the body, discuss nothing we've seen here, and burn him up tomorrow.'

'Arrangements have been made,' said Paul again.

'Right then,' said Carl, 'Grab a leg.'

As Lilly stepped forward, Joe did the same, placing his hand on her elbow. 'It's alright,' he said, 'I'll do it.'

Lilly stopped. 'I'd normally say no,' she said, 'But go on. I'm feeling a bit funny.'

Joe took hold of one leg and Carl the other.

'You ready then?' asked Carl.

'Yep.'

'On the count of three.'

'I can see two bison copulating,' said Paul. Carl and Joe stood up and the three of them followed his gaze. A little way into the woods there was indeed a pair of massy, shaggy bison, the male, about the size of a small car, shuddering an orgasm into the half-tonne female beneath him. They finished, the male disengaged his monstrous loins and then they both ambled away into the sodden green.

After a pause Carl turned again to Joe, 'Ready then?'

'Yep,' said Joe, taking a deep breath.

'On three.'

'Right.'

'One…'

Lilly and Paul were now watching Carl and Joe, each of whom had a naked ankle in his hand, the ankle attached to hairless calves, hairy thighs and two large, round, bizarrely muscular, rugby-player buttocks. Lilly felt sick, she didn't want to watch, but she had to watch.

'Two…'

Paul shrunk his towering form backwards, raising his hands as if in protection. One against his eyes, the other against his crotch.

'Three!'

They heaved backwards. The body came free of the earth easily, like a carrot. Carl and Joe, both expecting more resistance, staggered back, dragging Max's body over the turf. Lilly gasped, her face white. Carl retched, turning away. Paul's eyes silently closed and Joe stepped forward to see better.

The top half of Max's body, lying on the ground, is facing upwards, and the bottom half is facing downwards. His legs, buttocks and genitals, everything from the waist down, are back to front. In addition, his head is bright red and he has a pig's nose.

Joe looked down, where there had been an ominous black hole, but now there was nothing. Just a divot.

He turned back to Lilly. Her face was completely drained of colour. 'I know that creature,' she said.

∞

Maria was wearing a tight black dress with a plunging neckline, her hair piled up and carefully arranged, sexy stockings and her pointiest of pointy black shoes. She had gone home and changed, then returned to work, picking up a few gratifying glances as she swept through to her office. She felt ready to give her entire self to Max, and although she could say why, or thought she could, for he was handsome, rich, well-educated and powerful, it was all for reasons which lay underneath reasons, some hurtling thrill, like driving too fast, that he offered; some terrible but absolutely hypnotic contact that glowed darkly in her womb, that smouldered in her innermost, ready to catch. This hiddenness made the entire pleasure of her reckless need for him almost infinitely greater. The fast-tumbling, falling feeling that he had created in her, by pushing her off the top floor of herself, this mysterious sensation was worth sacrificing everything for *because* it was mysterious. She must have him, and be had by him, she must embrace the emptiness. There was now nothing else in heaven or on earth.

She had become that most powerful of human-beings; the single-minded.

She sat down and picked up the phone.

'Bronya? Could you come into my office please?'

She waited, tidying her desk, a little restless, but her nerves were irrelevant moths, fluttering round a white-hot blow torch.

There was a feeble knock on the door and Bronya entered, screwed up and scowling as usual.

'Take a seat,' said Maria.

'What is it?' asked Bronya, lowering herself onto the chair as if she had haemorrhoids. She could detect that 'something was up'.

'How are you getting on?' asked Maria, and Bronya, like all people who love to complain, launched straight into a tirade that had been lying, as it were, just under her tongue;

'Well, I hate going to smelly houses. One house right, it just, the guy had puked everywhere and hadn't even cleared it up, and I'll be honest with you, it's bad enough, I don't need that kind of shit. That isn't my job, yeah? To come out of a house stinking of someone's insides. And the abuse we get from people; you'd think they'd be glad to see us; the only thing between them and total social collapse, is us. I mean, I do get it, because we do get a lot of dodgy tip-offs and a filthy front room or, or, or, a few pictures of someone clubbing on social media doesn't necessarily mean we should take their children away, but still, there's no need to treat us like shit. But even the clients and the abuse aren't as bad as the admin. Basically, this new system, it's a whole lot of forms, to do, a lot of paperwork, mostly relating to people I've never met before. It's really boring and really stressful because writing the wrong thing can like blow up in your face. I'm serious. Admin is *literally* warfare. And I'm trying to get through all these forms, which, actually, I can never keep up with anyway, because it's just infinite isn't it? There's no end to spreadsheets, they just go on forever, down and down they go and, and, sometimes I wonder what social work is. What is it? Apart from getting covered in piss and puke and being told you're a Nazi all I do is type on a computer. There's so much recording and so many people you have to tell different things to; finances, forms, identifications, authorisations, contracts, and then fill in forms to say that you've done all these forms, and if I don't, it all comes down on *me*… and it's not as if there's even a promotion in sight… it's dangled before you for… ever… while, and then, and then, out there, with people, it's… it's all cracking up out there Maria, everyone… It's like there's this underground river, no *ocean*, of pain and sadness and anger, and I have to go round, all day, and, and, watch it explode out of people, and… wipe it up… but it's not water, it's magma and you can't wipe up magma Maria, you can't… It's just… I don't know what to do… it's… the horror… it's erupting everywhere… oohhhh…'

Bronya, head hung, was crying now, her mascara clogged and dribbling like wet charcoal ash, sobbing nostrils, twisted lips and pale blue eyes swimming in the misery of the world.

'I see,' said Maria clearing her throat, 'Well… how can I put this? We've got to let you go.'

Bronya looked up, her eyes red now, bobbling in suffering confusion. 'What?' she said.

'Yes, it seems that, actually, the department, I mean the local authority, is making some key adjustments…'

'…But what have I done?' said Bronya, very quietly.

'Nothing!' Maria cried with exaggerated reassurance, glad that she could turn this on Bronya's lack of self-worth, 'You've been *great*. I mean it, one of the best little workers I've ever known.'

'What are you talking about? You're *firing* me? Why?' Bronya's misery was drying up surprisingly quickly.

'I'm not *firing* you Bronya! It's… It's just… I *have* to.'

Bronya was hardening now. 'Oh, do you? You have to fire me, do you? You have to?'

'Yes,' said Maria, 'what can I do?' written all over her face, even her arms flopped outwards helplessly.

There was a long silence. Then Bronya spoke, low and hard; 'You giant cunt.'

Maria switched instantly to battle mode. 'I'm sorry Bronya, but I'm not going to tolerate that kind of language. You know as well as I do…'

Bronya, emptied of emotion, stood up. All the moan had dropped from her face, which had phase-transitioned from liquid misery to solid hatred. 'I do know as well as you. In fact, you know as well as I do, that I know a lot better than you do.'

There was, Maria distantly intuited, the remote possibility that Bronya could weakspot her. 'Look, don't be like that. Let's… we can still be friends, we can still have our nice lunches… I mean, I *get* it…'

'You get what you are.'

'Now come on. What does that mean?'

Bronya turned and walked out, her last words delivered, without turning, as the door closed behind her. 'You'll see.'

ဢ

After they had pulled Max Thottesley out of his hole and zipped up his body and put it in the van, Joe had tried to console Lilly, but she insisted she was fine and that she had to get back and work. Joe declined their offer of a ride home because he needed to 'get a bit of woodland in him,' but this too had been a haunting, darkening experience. The sense of being at home that Joe always felt in the wildness had not been there. It was dark, ferny and rancid, no birds were singing, no sense of life at all, and, by the time he'd tumbled out onto the road, he felt he was being pressed, on all sides, by an epochal immensity and loneliness.

He'd walked down the lane to the bus stop and, to his relief, the driver of the 292, which had rumbled over the hill twenty minutes later, was Vikas, an old friend with whom he had, when he'd worked on the buses, often finished the day smoking hookah behind the deserted bus station.

They rumbled around the country lanes and filled each other in on the intervening years, Joe standing in the 'do not stand forward of this point' area, swinging around on the front hold-pole, Vikas, an almost impossibly elegant Indian man with a waxed moustache and pony-tail, swerving down the lanes—rather too fast as usual, still with an Indian bus-drivers' sensibility, which essentially viewed the management of public transport as an opportunity to get as close to Krishna's true form as possible.

Joe had once said to Vikas, during a hookah session, 'Aren't you afraid of dying, driving like that?' and Vikas had picked up a dry leaf which had floated onto the bench they were sitting on, 'I cannot even lift this *leaf* without Krishna's approval.'

As they roller-coastered along the country lanes, Vikas explained that he had almost been fired for hitting an old Dutch guy on a bike who had turned out to be one of the leading mathematicians in Europe. Vikas had leapt out of the bus and called an ambulance, but the guy was dying. 'He spent his last moments on this earth gripping my lapels and trying to explain to me the solution to the Riemann hypothesis.'

'What's that?'

'It's one of the great unsolved mysteries of mathematics,' said Vikas, 'I didn't understand of course, but I understood the urgency. This was a dying man's wish; so I ran into my bus to get a pen, but I didn't have any paper, so the old gentlemen wrote on my arm, not much, not even a small piece of the solution, before he passed away. Here.'

He showed Joe his arm, blue with inked equations;

$$\xi(s) = s/2\,(s-1)\,\zeta(s)\,\Gamma(s/2)\,\pi{-}s/2\,\xi(\tfrac{1}{2}+it) = \xi(\tfrac{1}{2})\,det\,(I{-}A^{*}At^{2})$$

'You had them tattooed on?'

'Yes,' said Vikas, 'it was the right thing to do. To honour this great man. His name was Professor Hilberdink. Maths professors give classes on my arm now.'

Joe filled Vikas in on some of the highlights of his own life, and the two of them reminisced about their bussing days; the time one of the drivers, Pornsak Glory (real name Pornsak Rueng, 'Rueng' meaning 'glory' in Thai) had lost control, driven into a beer garden, and ploughed through a stag party, scattering them like bowling pins, and they'd all got up, cheered, and continued drinking, buying a pale ale for Pornsak. They talked about another driver, Lionel Gregory, who had got reprimanded for continually pushing the brake and accelerator at the same time, making the whole bus shake in order to watch, in the rearview mirror, the jiggling breasts of well-endowed women standing up front;

although never sacked for some reason. Joe reminded Vikas of the time a girl had thrown up in his bus and vomit had sloshed up and down the aisle making a couple of other people puke up too, which set off even more, until Joe stopped at a corner shop, bought a bucket and mops and everyone had helped clean it up together, which they'd all quite enjoyed.

'Good times,' said Joe. It was funny, he thought, looking at Vikas' noble profile as he steered the large wheel clock, all the noble people seem to be at the bottom while all the commoners are at the top.

'You know Joseph,' said Vikas, 'I miss your spirit in the office, but I am the only one who does. Most people there hated you, you know this?'

'I had an inkling.'

'It's because you bamboozle them. You are a terrible bamboozler. But where, I might ask, would we be without fireworks thrown into toilet cubicles? Where?'

'We'd be in a boring toilet.'

'This is why I have to return to mother India. Things still go haywire there.'

More people got on as they approached the outskirts of Edding, so Joe went back to take a seat. Next to him a woman was on the phone, talking to her partner and furiously lying about where she was, 'I'm in Piccadilly, darling,' she was saying, 'I won't be home for three hours.' Everyone was listening. The lower deck was now full. A minuscule bow-legged Nepali woman who looked about 120 was eating some kind of bun and bits of masticated white flour were dribbling down her tunic. Behind her was a vast black man with immense cans wrapped round his head and behind him a nice looking young woman wearing a black cardigan, black hair band and black skirt. Opposite Joe a pale moon-faced young girl was standing with a little girl slung over her back. The little girl intermittently rolled back and looked at Joe, her little upside-down face peering madly up at his. Every time she did this Joe burst into laughter, and so did she. This went on for three or four stops. Then Joe realised that black-cardie was crying. She was listening to something on her phone. Music? Someone talking? She looked so very sad, wiping tears from her collapsed red face. Perhaps she was in mourning? The lying woman had finished her call—'I love you darling, yes, I'll be home before dark'—and was looking around sheepishly. Joe's stop was coming up, so he took out his notepad, wrote, 'It's all going to be okay' on one page and 'He deserves it' on the other, ripped them both out, folded them up, gave one to one girl and one to the other, ran through the bus to the doors, just as they closed, saluting Vikas as he pulled away and checking the reactions of the two women, who were looking confused, making Joe wonder if he'd given the open-handed encouragement to the adulteress and a rather harsh condemnatory epitaph to the woman in black. On the one hand, a terrible mistake, but on the other probably also a kind of truth.

He ambled down towards his pocket of suburbia, the mechanical mannequins of Edding—home-coming and shop-going commuters—slid past him, heading for their allotted slots. A squashed handlebar-moustached man with a spotty face was arguing with an old woman whose bowling-ball breasts were banging against her thighs as she walked, 'he didn't have to set fire to the fucking *bathroom*', a squirrel-faced half-Persian woman sucked a cigarette and thought of worse times, an eight-stone townie was explaining martial arts to a blubbery friend, 'In Shaolin temples they train your tendons. Not muscles. *Tendons*. Because they're five times stronger. They don't want the bulk of muscle.' Adverts for bubble tea, and online betting, and fixed-rate mortgages, diesel and dog shit and desperation in the air.

For the first time in his life, Joe had wanted to get *out* of nature. Normally he could not make it through the day without seeing a tree, or contemplating a potato, or staring into space like a dondon. To make it across temporal deserts one must daily drink from the fountain of eternity. But from the moment Max had thrown himself into a hole Joe had had the feeling not so much of swimming in mysterious seas, but of drowning in them. The essential deadness of the woodland had surprised and appalled him, as had the farm fields a little further on. It was all dead. He needed to get back, but 'back' was really this dreary cage, just greener. But what else? Where else? I have to get out of here, he thought, but there is no *there* to get to.

Over the road was another bus. On the side was an advert. A mummified skull, the grin of death, with a speech bubble which read; 'If the world doesn't work for you, try switching it off then on again.' No clue what the product was, although this didn't seem to matter. A lot of adverts these days seemed to be speaking directly to Joe Geb; which was madness, wasn't it? That's what nutters think, that the radio is talking to them, that strangers are all secretly plotting to brainwash them, that printers have it in for them. It was all about them. Joe had felt this, that there was something me-me-me about the insane, or a lot of them, but then he'd also met a fair number of lunatics who had just had the sanity ground out of them by the remorseless mill of living.

Maybe I *am* losing my marbles, Joe said to himself, but as he was having this thought a dishevelled, desperate-eyed man passed with straggly long curly hair, a large bulbous nose and a prehistoric moustache. He was hitting himself angrily on the shoulder saying '*I can't…I can't…*' with intense, wincing emphasis. He was followed by a skinny white girl with blonde hair, about seventeen with a long face, small features, beady eyes and a cutting nasal voice telling her friend 'I was like I didn't want to go on this stupid holiday, it was *your* idea, and now you're putting all this shit on me; so I just stayed in my room, but that made them more annoyed…' And then, after her, an older woman talking into her mobile phone saying, 'No I can't come out this Saturday, I need to check all the use-by dates of things in the fridge. Then I'm going to try out a new dehumidifier.'

Everyone had lost their marbles, evidently.

'Alright or what?' He turned towards a familiar Welsh voice.

'Ah, Ralf…'

Laughing Ralf was folded up in the doorway of a closed-down fancy-dress shop. His tired face was still trembling with laughter. 'Take a seat,' he said to Joe, gesturing down to his cardboard.

Joe squatted down and then, realising that it was clean and dry, he fully slid down, legs running parallel with Ralf's, who sat, bundled up as usual, in several layers of linens. When Joe stretched out his limbs Ralf tugged a warm blanket from behind him and threw it over Joe's legs. He then offered Joe a cushion.

'You don't look too good!' Ralf observed, laughing.

'No, my sister is dead,' said Joe, 'and my boss, as a matter of fact, although that doesn't matter.'

'Hahahaha!'

Joe smiled. 'But it's not even that. I'm fine actually, I just keep having waves of terrible hopelessness today, like, you know, like the feeling sometimes you get when winter first hits, or the light of the day is going out, about five o'clock, and all you've done all day is watch porn, and you feel like everything is wasted and dying, that but more intense, a feeling of forever descending into a darkness eternal, a buried world of total comatose abandonment, like you're slipping down into a hole where what was a minute up here, is a hundred thousand years of black, paralysed deathly nothingness. Frozen in a black ocean, not cold, not warm, just dead, dead, dead.'

Ralf, who, as Joe was speaking, could feel himself drawn down into this comatose underworld, his head getting heavier and heavier, suddenly jerked his head up and cried out 'Wonderful!' making two pretty young Chinese girls jump and hurry past.

'*Is* it?' asked Joe.

'You're talking like someone who is merely falling. You just haven't hit rock bottom.'

'You're right. I haven't hit rock bottom.'

'You will! Hahahaha! Everyone will! HAHAHAHAHA!'

Ralf laughed for a long time, a laugh that ended in a cough which was mixed with the laughing, which was mixed with a joyous gasping for breath, and then more coughing-laughing. It was infectious and Joe, despite himself, was feeling a little better.

'So what's down there?' he asked, 'Down on the rocks?'

'Me and you Joe! Look at us! Look at us down here! On the rocks!'

'It is quite comfortable down here. How do you keep it all so clean?'

'Got to be honest with you, I go to the dry cleaners, see.'

'Dry cleaners?'

'Yes, or I spend a night in a hotel and have a bath. There's a nice B-and-B on Leaming Road.'

'Isn't that expensive?'

'Yeah, but I can afford it!' He was chuckling again.

'Oh. I thought...'

'I'm doing fine for money, aren't I? I just prefer living on the street. I don't like houses, never have, never will.'

'But why? How? What happened to you?'

'Would you like a glass of wine?'

'Alright.'

'Cigar?'

'Yeah okay.'

Ralf pulled out a bottle of good wine, two plastic cups and two Montecristo cigars, and then told his story, rolled out in his beguiling hills-and-valleys accent, the whole thing punctuated with constant titters, smirks, guffaws, chuckles, roars and helpless, almost desperate, convulsions of laughter.

☙

What it is, see, is that I am a schadenfreudist. I enjoy the pain of other people. I think it was probably always there, in the background, as it is with many people. You know as well as I do that if you want to get the attention of the people around you, all you have to do is begin a story with 'let me tell you about the most embarrassing thing that ever happened to me.' Happiness is the other man getting the arrow.

Anyway, it all began long ago, while I was idling on my balcony in a Sardinian hotel. I was there with my girlfriend at the time, and I was looking at the swimming pool beneath me, when a couple walked out, all ready to enjoy a nice bit of sunbathing, a little splashing around, when a waiter came up to them and said the pool area was closed today, for a little building work. And I saw their faces so clearly; slight confusion, slight freeze around the corners of the mouth, the enquiring head tilt, butting up against a future that wasn't supposed to be there, that was turning them away.

This was the first entry in my personal catalogue of schadenfreudic delicacies. *The Turn Away*. The locked door, the hand trying to turn it three, four times with 'this isn't right' written all over the posture of the guy trying to open-and-walk-in-one-gesture through it, as he is used to doing. 'This isn't right,' he thinks; but it is right. It's exactly right.

After my Sardinian moment of truth I slowly added to my catalogue of 'SF' pleasures. There was *The Body Rebellion*, when some part of the physical apparatus takes arms against your own actions. A friend of mine, for example, Ben, got a mysterious neck complaint—he couldn't turn his head to the left—when he started a job he hated. The doctors offered all kinds of suggestions, but his woman was much closer to the truth than Western medicine, 'your neck hates work and you hate your neck,' that's what she said. Another friend became physically sick every time his ex-girlfriend was mentioned: marvellous to watch. And a third got a nosebleed whenever he was put on hold. Breaking wind during a tense moment at the theatre would fall into the category of Body Rebellion too, as would literally shitting yourself in a job interview. I savoured the involuntary gulp of anxiety that beautiful women created in the petrified throats of mini-men, or the unconscious tics and squirts of evasive faces in the spotlight of truth. Any moment when the body's laws break through and interrupt the laws of man.

Brother to the Body Rebellion was what I called *The Rising of the Void*, that moment when the internal saboteur smashes through the privet hedge of one's tidy world, when the secret chaos of the heart erupts into the order of the situation, and sweeps the porcelain horses from the sideboard. I'm no fan of the mob, or of drunken destruction, but there is something to be said for a husband—crushed by his life, his family, his work, his world—getting off his face, setting fire to the family estate and sheepishly smoking a cigarette in the cinders when his horror-struck family return.

Relationships were a positive gold mine of schadenfreudic delights. I used to love watching couples, waiting for *The Love-Spurned Wince* of the rejected chatter-upper, *The Break-Up Hunch* of the sop trailing behind his too-beautiful now-ex girlfriend, *The Repressed-Hate Lip-Screw* of the scornful wife and, my hands-down favourite, *The Sotto Voce Slanging Match*, a what-would-have-been window-smashing ding-dong conducted in rushed, hateful whispers in order to preserve dignity.

I loved to watch couples instantly 'sober up' after an argument to give a big wave to the neighbours. I loved watching men in clothes shops. I loved watching tired people. I loved watching people miss their trains. I loved any kind of hold-up or frustrated disappointment—I 'shadowed' traffic wardens for miles, glorying in the SF carnage they left behind. I loved failure—I used to hang around outside the driving test centre to watch people get the bad news. Drink spillages, small-talk failure, frozen grins, awkward eye-darts, repeating a stupid gesture to make it look intentional the first time, the old hug-kiss dilemmas… on and on and on it went. I gorged on the heartless horror of the world, diving deeper and deeper into the river of suffering that ran under the city, the tidal wave of sorrow that flowed beneath the broken world.

But my favourite SF pleasure, I think, was the *Revenge of the Past;* that devastating calamity, glorious to behold, when your past wrongs—a shameful lie, a nasty bit of thievery, some kind of depravity which doesn't fit with one's public image, an embarrassing parent slobbering their unwelcome way into polite society: the possibilities are limitless—but the moment when they pop back into the light from whatever under-sink cupboard of the mind they had been hastily stuffed into. Fab-lous!

The problem was that I was a bit of a sadist about it all, see. I was laughing at *them*, to relieve myself of *my* life, and that's not, I came to understand, the schadenfreudic way. But it was a hard travelling to get to that realisation, a terrible hard travelling.

It started with an interview with my bank manager. I sat in her little office and she said to me, 'Let me tell you what's going to happen Ralf. The bank is going to recover its money. That means we'll take ownership of your house, farming equipment and land. We expect you to vacate them in the next thirty days. If you can't pay, we'll sue. We'll go to court and get you evicted. In any case, you'll be bankrupt by the end of the year. If you're looking for sympathy,' she said, 'you came to the wrong person. It was an idiotic risk, you risked everything on an ostrich farm, and you lost, so now you don't have anything. No house, no business, no money. That's it. It's… You're finished.' Then she gathered up my papers, shuffled them on her desk, stood up, said, 'and there's something else. I'm leaving you,' and walked out.

I'd lost everything, see, in one smash of God's big fist; my business, my house, my money and my girlfriend, all gone. But that wasn't all. I'd been suffering for several weeks from constipation and back pain, and I walked out of the bank, and lifted my bike off of the railings I'd hooked it onto to lock it up, and put my back out, properly put it out. I was lying there on the pavement for about an hour before someone stopped to help me.

I slowly recovered and somehow scraped together a shoddy kind of half-life at the bottom of the social barrel. I got a job in Poundland, moved in with a repulsive old, crippled woman who was letting her spare room and there I stewed, fermented in my new 'life.'

This woman, Brenda, was a horrible old witch. She was a lymphatic dwarf, always pissed up. She used to be a compliance and professional standards officer, but when I knew her she was living on a disability pension, spending all day in front of the television drinking Aldi sherry. She loved the news above all else, she loved the wars and the murders and the kiddy-fiddling. The more barbaric the better. 'Oh my heart goes out to them,' she'd say about the poor, poor children. She had become a pity-monster, you know? never really happy amongst the happy. She'd be in the caff, looking around for someone to sympathise with, until she saw a woman with a retarded son, 'oh my god that poor woman,' she'd say, with relief.

Not that she went out much. She only got off her collapsed sofa to bake cakes—she made fake homemade sponges with a LIDL cake mix, which she sold at the Bring'n'Buy sales in the local churches, passing them off as her own. Or she'd occasionally drive down town in her disabled buggy to pick up her pension or buy lottery tickets, rolling through people like a crippled bowling ball—or she'd go out into her garden and inject weedkiller under her fence to destroy the beloved flowers of her hated neighbour, a stiff Iranian woman who never put her bins out.

I'm not going to lie, I was down Joe. I'd sit on my bed, in my empty room, wallpaper peeling, condensation on the windows, suffering fluttering round inside my heart, laying eggs in my soul as the tiny white case bearing moths fluttering round my bedside light were laying eggs in my cardigans. I thought about killing myself—every day I went over how I might do it, but God knows how, I dragged myself into work and back home again. I was fuelled by hatred; hatred for Brenda's hot clothy intimacy, for my ex-girlfriend's pointless cruelty, for the plebs in Poundland, for humanity, for this stinking mass of block-solid ignorance that a perverse god had set me among.

My commitment to the schadenfreudic way only increased. I watched for it everywhere, but like every drug, I needed harder and harder hits. Before I knew it, I was smoking pure, uncut sadism. I paid for things in pennies, just to annoy cashiers. I superglued wheelie bins shut. I started watching true crime documentaries, reading about murderers and rapists. I even started watching the news, which I'd always thought I was watching for information but now revelled in its true purpose, pure sadistic pleasure at other people's suffering. And I began torturing poor Brenda, who was afraid of foreigners, down and outs and all young people, by paying such people to approach her when she went out shopping, spook her by escorting her out of Costco with a creepily solicitous 'afternoon Brenda, how are you doing then?' Terrified her, that did. I also let her church know that she was a cake-faking fraud.

Most of all I hated professionals, do-gooders, the tidy people, whose life's mission it is to make everything perfect, who won't touch reality unless they're wearing the rubber gloves of morality; you know the teachers, the protesters, the politicians, the artists, the luvvies and especially the doctors—scum of the earth—those good people, working for the good of us all, working for Universal Basic Income, and Green Energy, and Veganism, and Ethical Trading, and Clean Cities, and Public Health and *Life*. My God, I hated them, I hated their cleanliness and perfection. I hated it like a tiger hates a dinner party, I hated it like a child hates 'going for a nice walk', I hated it like a madman with diarrhoea hates crown green bowls. I just wanted to shit everywhere. I'd rather be free in shit than happy and organised and perfectly healthy.

So I did everything I could to upset them—still do actually. I smoked, I ate badly, I was a first-class malingerer and set up a popular website to teach people how to pretend to be ill, I set off fire alarms in every institution I ever went in, I sent butchers' vans to vegan protests, I paid street cleaners to avoid wealthy streets, I sent bomb threats to schools and blew the tyres of headteacher's cars. I did everything I possibly could to frustrate professionals. I got caught, was in and out of custody, but I didn't stop. All of this was keeping me alive.

Until the day I died.

I was lonely, and was getting the horn, regular like, so I started going every few weeks to a Chinese massage parlour to get a hand-job. It was always the same routine, with a chubby little bumless housewife in a sweaty room that they did their laundry in, always a washing machine going. She would start off giving a normal massage, and then she'd 'accidentally' brush my testicles, bring me to attention and then, when I turned over with a semi, she'd nod to the old pidÿn and say 'you wan' happy handy?' and I'd say, 'yes please' and she'd mechanically toss me off.

Then, one day, as she was working away, she suddenly started singing Happy Birthday, out of the blue. I asked her what she was doing and she said, 'today my birthday', and I said, tears in my eyes, 'surely I should be singing you happy birthday then?' and she said, 'okay you sing'.

So there I was singing Happy Birthday to this woman, until I ejaculated. As she wiped me up I asked her how old she was and she said 'forty', and I thought this is how you're spending it, your fortieth birthday, tossing off a weeping stranger in a utility room. I was overwhelmed, suddenly, like a colossal wave of *something* passed over me, see, or through me, *something* was happening, *something… else*. And suddenly my tears, which had, until that moment, been completely self-pity, suddenly they became oth-er-pity or all-of-us pity. Actually Joe, I'm still not sure what hap-pened, but it was as if I was weeping for existence… You couldn't even call it sadness, which is far too personal and small. It was the world weeping through *me*, while *I* was unmoved.

Needless to say, I lost my erection. The woman, Janice she called herself, although her real Chinese name was Guanyin, she was also by this time crying. I sat up and I said to her, 'I don't want to pay for any more happy handies. If you ever give me another happy handy, I want it to be an actually happy handy, not a totally tragic handy. So, what I'm saying is, Janice, I'm asking you if you'll marry me?'

She laughed at me. I was being a bit previous, getting over-excited, which I'm prone to, but we started going out with each other and we fell in love. She was a simple thing was Guanyin, a country girl, a peasant you might say, but it turned out that she had more love in her than I could believe anyone could have and, for some reason I still don't quite understand, she poured it all into me. She just continued loving me, worshipping me even. I'd never known anything like it.

She didn't give up the wanking though, in fact she raised her prices and ferreted even more cash away. I also took on another job, doing nights at a Tesco warehouse, saving up money until we could move in together. I'd got a surprisingly large sum together in the end, aided by a spot of luck one night in a casino, but that's another story. Point is, it was all going okay, when the massage shop was raided and Guanyin was deported. She was sent back to China where, it turned out, she was already married. I couldn't follow her because by then I had a criminal record as long as a table, and they don't like that in China, so we made secret plans to meet in Mexico, where people like us can disappear. I continued saving money, continued working, when the radio went dead; Guanyin stopped writing to me. I couldn't contact her, I had no idea where she even lived, let alone the faintest idea how to track her down, so that was that. That was that was that was that was that was that.

I was heartbroken. Devastated, like I'd been raised out of the mud only to be plunged ten times deeper into it. I'd also just been in for a hip operation and was on strong painkillers, which didn't do much but constipate me again. I sat at the end of my bed, in emotional and physical agony. I felt I had reached the end of the end. And yet, it wasn't the same. I sat in the same scummy den of grief I'd spent so many hours of misery in, staring at the wall, with the same feeling of drowning, suffocating despair and dread. And yet, something had changed. I was richer, but that certainly wasn't it, because in every other respect I was just as badly off and, in losing the love of my life, far, far worse. So, what was it?

I got up to go for a walk. Children were giving their parents hell, boyfriends were reeling under the tempests of their girlfriends' moods, old people were tripping up and looking back with scornful hatred at the exposed bit of pavement which had been responsible, beggars begged for pennies, buskers begged for fame, Jesus people begged for Jesus; everything was as it was, and I loved the pain as ever I did, but something was different, in fact two things were, and these were, I'll tell you; discernment and empathy. Firstly, I found I could only now laugh at people who clearly deserved it, and secondly I felt for those who didn't. But what was that based on? What had changed in me, I wondered; and just as I did wonder, Brenda threw herself on me.

She had found out that I had ruined her, that I had revealed her fraudulent cake-making ways and that I'd been paying people to terrorise her. So enraged was she, she ran down the high street looking for me—her disability had been a painstakingly maintained illusion—and then, when she found me, she leapt on me like a massively overweight cat. We fought there and then in the street, her accusing me of every moral crime under the sun, and me agreeing with her. 'You're a selfish bastard!' she cried, 'I know!' I yelled as we wrestled. 'You're a fiend! A fiend!' she gasped. 'I am! I am!' I said. 'I ratted on Janice!' she screamed, and I knew that too.

Just at that moment, just as a small crowd had gathered round us, filming us, a bird shat on us. Not a little stream of watery white over my shoulder, but a gargantuan turd-pie, splattered over my hair, nose and across my lapel. Two boys, around twelve, saw it and, with typical city-child aggression, fire flashing from their eyes, barked AAH-HA-HA-HAs, really lording it over us, fumbling for their phones to broadcast the event to the world.

Brenda rolled off me gagging and, as the sticky white excrement, which also smelt vile—like cat-shit vile—crept down my face, it happened. That's when I realised the truth of my life. I felt something crack, at the base of my spine, near to where I'd had the operation, but it was a spiritual crack, just as much as a physical one. I metaphorically and literally cracked up. I started laughing, and I didn't stop. I couldn't stop. I could see, right there, a new world opening up, split open in front of me; a richer, realer thing, a sense that the superb spectacle of horror, and I, were changing places, or melding, or becoming one. I stood, shitty as hell, as the laughing sun-gods burst from behind the clouds of my mind, and the glorious truth that I had been feeling for these past years exploded. It was the laughing version of my tears for the world, a divine laughter, a laughter to shake the universe to its cold black roots.

I checked a German dictionary to coin the right word for my new state, but 'selbstschadenfreude' didn't quite cut it—bit of a mouthful I thought—so I settled on *euphiasco*—perhaps the greatest art of them all—of deriving pleasure from your own delectaflops. I was to be a *euphiasker*, a *risablist*, a grand cham in the timeless dance of self-mockery.

I saw straight away that, just as the greatest schadenfreudists are not in the least bit sadistic, so this new practice must have nothing of masochism, self-pity or passivity about it. No, no, no; euphiasco cannot come from a fear of responsibility, a need to assuage guilt, or a pathological confusion of feeling alive with the raw sensation of self-mutilation. It was far higher than human emotion; something mysterious, you see, something beyond was at play here.

I disentangled myself from Brenda, apologised to her, gave her a grand—didn't know much else I could do, but she sloped away—while I hit the streets, where you find me today. The best place for a euphiasker, I find. Here I can laugh at everyone, because I laugh at myself, and I can laugh at myself, because I can laugh at everyone. I'm beyond sadism and masochism, beyond pity for myself or for anyone else. I don't care about your feelings or for mine. Innocent children, lovely women and animals; and the innocent, feminine, wild inside us all, I weep for that, but for your stinking self and mine, only laughter remains Joe. Only laughter.

'And now,' Ralf concluded, 'you knows it all.'

∞

Joe crossed over the road, pulling his cheap, padded raincoat tight against the now cold rain and, to warm up a little, jogged home. The house was empty—unusual—so he made his own dinner; a tin of chickpeas, a tomato, a red onion, a peach, cured ham, a glug of Maria's exotic olive oil and a random sprinkling from her spice shelf. You could probably call it a salad.

He finished, put the plate in the dishwasher, made a cup of tea and went upstairs to the walk-in wardrobe at the end of the corridor. He sat down, baboon mug at his side, and pulled out a box which he hadn't seen before; full of tiny cardigans. He pulled out another, also loaded with miniature cardigans. They looked like they were for doll babies, but what kind of doll was shaped like a large turnip? Chickens. These were the chicken jumpers that Maria was so cagey about.

He reached further back and found another box, this one full of his old notebooks. One was titled 'Plans for Internal Revolution'—a guide he had written when working at a sugar beet factory in Suffolk. The owner had decided, because Joe was the only staff member without webbed feet, that he should 'take the reins'. He'd been asked to present a twenty-point plan for leading the company into the future, which he had done, scribbling out, in a secondary-school exercise book, the following;

1. Leave a King Edward potato by the main gate every Thursday morning.
2. When talking about yourself to colleagues don't point to your chest area. Point to your elbow. If referring to others, point to their elbow. Discreetly ask senior management to do the same.
3. Inform all staff by email that a health inspector is coming to inspect the building and the staff. Tell them that their hair will be inspected for nits and lice and that they should all wear a flat side-parting that day to facilitate the process.
4. Arrange a meeting with a key worker and tell them their walk perfectly matches the company ethos. Tell them they have been selected to represent the company to train new recruits how to

walk the right way. Tell them to produce a PowerPoint presentation to be included in the training sessions. Be most insistent and encouraging.

5. Promote the use of 'constrained writing' in order to make emails more creative. Send a circular banning the use of all words with the letter 'n' along with all regular past tenses, in emails or in conversations that take place inside the building.

6. Every month change every object (all furniture, stationery, IT, plants, etc) in the main office for a precise replica that is 5% smaller. A few weekends later do the same, but 7% larger. Keep making 'subtle yet massive' changes like this—repaint the whole place one microscopic shade darker, replace lights five watts brighter, etc.—always just below the threshold of awareness.

7. At exactly 3:30pm on the 2nd Tuesday of each month, pretend to be in a highly elastic bubble, floating through space. Encourage employees to do the same.

8. Build a company sauna, hire Turks to run it.

9. Also, build lots of secret passages in the building. Start leaving clues around that guide your workers to them. Aim to create a network of secret rooms containing special gifts. Make sure this is never explicitly spoken of.

10. [Related to 9] Build a flying fox from the top floor (only accessible from a secret passage), across the ring road, over the railway tracks and down to the turf section of the garden centre.

11. When a colleague gives you a specific piece of information ask them to be a little more vague. When they do so, ask them to be vaguer still. Keep going. They will be forced to convert 'red' into a 'colour'; 'socks' into 'item of clothing'; 'one' into 'under 30' then into 'under 1000'; 'husband' into 'a relative' then into 'a person' then into 'a living thing' and so on. What you're looking for is sentences like 'I'm going to buy under a thousand items of clothing for a carbon-based life form.'

12. Train wild birds of prey to occasionally enter the workspace. Eagles, Kestrels, Buzzards, Owls.

13. All meetings to be conducted via puppets. Buy high-quality hand puppets for staff and get some puppet artists in for training.

14. Order a Toggenberg goat for the sales director.

15. Play the Gifford Lectures over the P.A.

16. Replace 'Dress Down Friday' with 'Quote Milton Thursday'—all employees must slip quotes from the devil's speeches from Paradise Lost into their chat, or face disciplinary proceedings. Cash bonuses for epic (but not overly demonstrative) delivery.

17. Then, a bit later, replace 'Quote Milton Thursday' with 'Hunter-Gatherer Wednesday.' All staff to wear loincloths, ingest peyote, worship the great Cham, dance ecstatically until 5:30 then clock out and go home as normal.

18. Begin firing people who are frightened and confused. Begin hiring people with elaborate tests of their improvisational skills and/or based on eye-warmth, speed of smile fade and ease of gait.

19. Tell everyone that exactly one year from now you will hand the entire company over to the staff and give them collective power over the allocation of surplus—but only as long as, by that time, they've all learnt to play an instrument and can perform six classic ska tracks together to a high standard. Give staff two days off a week, paid, with free lessons. Construct a huge stage in readiness for the concert, build the event up (start giving staff more paid days off to practice), invite friends, etc. Fit everyone out in spangly seventies costumes. More buildup. Then, on the evening of the concert, just before they are about to play, tell them that you're going to give the company to them anyway, no matter how well they play.

20. Kick it!

He rifled through previous notebooks, old school reports, British Falconer's Club newsletters, Black Ark albums, fezzes, FX pedals, a cup painted with rampant uraei wearing sun-disk crowns, resin food models for display in oriental restaurants and similar such items—the only things in the house which, apart from a few items of clothing, belonged to him—until his fingers found the laminate edges of what he was looking for, a photo album.

Cross-legged on the floor, Joe leafed through the collection of Polaroids. Joe and Ursula, as children, sleeping naked on the roof of their house. Joe and Ursula, again children, giving each other haircuts. Neville, wide smile on his young face, firing two antique pistols, mid blast, into the air. Ursula, Neville, Joe and an uncomfortable looking Neil holding hands in a ring in the middle of which an old woman, dressed in hooped woollen stockings, white muslin, bright red seventeenth-century make-up and a braid wig, was in a mid-spin blur. Young Neil unpicking a pair of trousers. Younger Neil Olympic-walking along a canal, young Margaret next to him holding a stopwatch. Joe and Ursula building, from tree trunks and twigs, a giant man with a formidable erection (which they later set fire to). Neil, Ursula and Margaret playing Abba monopoly. Teenage Joe up a tree looking for kestrel eggs.

⚏

As Joe looked through his photographs Neil was reviewing his video footage of Joe. He had thousands of hours of material, which he was cutting down into usable chunks. He watched Joe in Sainsbury's, juggling soup cans; in a pear orchard, doing a kind of ballet; in a churchyard, painting headstones bright pink—with the word 'me' on each one; on an archery range, shooting flaming arrows into a wicker reindeer and in the post office, spinning round like Zangief. He watched Joe polishing a shop doorknob with Brasso, slapping a cliff, pooing in a snowy field and sending a four-wheel suitcase trolley hurtling along an airport concourse, chasing after it and passing it so it looked like the bags were chasing him, running and shouting for help. In all these scenes, and many like them, Joe was surrounded by panicked and angry folk. Only a few smiled or laughed. Children watched, gawping.

Neil, bolt upright at his standing desk, clenched and unclenched his fists. His brother was a menace, an existential threat to the order of things. Everywhere he went, he caused disruption, disorder. He *must* be dealt with. It would clear the air.

As he put together his plan, a fierce wall-juddering *thump, thump, thump* started up next door. They too must be dealt with. Neil had decided to give his neighbours a week more. If they hadn't finished redecorating he would deal with the matter. He sighed. There was so much to *deal with.*

Chiyo, down the corridor, was also *dealing with*. She was pouring fine black powder, which she had spent an hour pestle-grinding, into a tiny glass phial. She unlocked a small wooden apothecary's drawer in her dresser and gently placed the phial within, inspecting the contents with silent pleasure. She had collected a stoat's tooth, a virgin's hair, a strawberry Opal Fruit, a very small window, a charred Death tarot card from the Visconti-Sforza deck, bone marrow serum from a cow, a handful of dried psilocybe azurescens, the tears of a pig, a crumb of asbestos and a copy of the 1974 Whizzer and Chips annual. Only a little more was required.

She closed the drawer and finished getting ready for her date, piling up her long, black, damp hair and holding it in place with a fox-mask clip. Two hours later, wearing black silk gloves, long black boots and a black, sleeveless dress with white lace collars and cuffs, she was sitting down in Nono Cerchio—a typical wealthy eating place in which highly skilled artisans make exceptionally good food for people who pay it no attention—opposite a pale, skinny young spectacled man, clearly uncomfortable in a badly fitting cheap suit. They had arranged to meet the week before, after a brief meeting in Costa Coffee. Chiyo had been passing the large windows, walked inside and sat down in front of him, saying nothing. He had made a squirming, gulping attempt at the conventional and she had said to him, 'you are not like other people.' They had spoken for half an hour, the young man, Spence Gregory, had shown her his book, *Dvoretsky's Endgame Manual*, then he had told her that he wanted to go for a walk, but he didn't like walking in the country because laws for pedestrians in the UK were illogical, then he had tried to explain to her the difference between the East and West Roman Empire after 476.

Chiyo had listened to all this, said to him, 'You dress like tramp. Buy suit and take me nice restaurant, and I solve your problem,' then left, leaving him with her phone number.

'I didn't think you would come,' he said now, his small square mouth mumbling into his cuffs. He didn't look at her. He didn't seem to look at anything, his thick glasses distorting his grey eyeballs, fusing them to the glass, which reflected the subtle lights of the swanky restaurant.

'I come,' said Chiyo, watching him calmly. Her face, to Spence, was unfathomably still.

He expected her to say something, but she didn't. Her silence was awful, her beauty appalling. He didn't know what to say. He felt as if she was judging him, he was probably a pathetic kind of thing to her, why else would she say nothing? Did she want a conventional conversation then? Was that it? Was she a normie? A thirst-trap? Just another NPC? With a heavy, heavy heart he began the stupid performance of small-talk, chit-chat, exchanging dead nothings with yet another sadistic woman who was just stringing him along for the lolz.

'What do you do in your free time?' he asked, without interest.

'I'm observing mushroom…'

'Why?'

'They are huge.'

'Huge?' he didn't care. Mushrooms.

'Huge entity… the most mysterious thing…'

Spence was becoming more and more annoyed. He felt sure she was mocking him somehow. 'Mushrooms are normal,' he said sulkily.

'If you see the mushroom as sitting on the Aldi shelf, you just see the surface of mushroom, it's very simple, but mushroom is universe, it controls universe, it controls animal… there is mushroom, Cordyceps, they spore, their spore land on insect body, they slowly, slowly start… nani, not absorbing, gee-waa… growing, yes, growing inside insect body, reach on their brain and then insect become part of the mushroom. Mushroom make insect body go to damp place, wet part of forest, then insect bite ground and die, and mushroom grow, gee waa…'. Chiyo spoke in a low voice, it was impossible not to listen. Spence felt like his attention was a cork, rolling down a river of quiet magnetic speech. 'Can you imagine', she said, 'if mushroom decide parasite human, then whole Edding like that, like wasp corpse, all dead body, people go the most suitable environment, kowakunai? Human is parasited by mushroom and then go to the dark part of park, in the corners, and bite ground and die, and then lots of human mushrooms in park, dead, with mushroom coming from them…'. She was now smiling, delicately, 'is that nice way to die, do you think Spence-chan?'

Spence felt as if he had fallen into strange, dangerous world. He wasn't sure what the rules were here. He took a bite of the beef-flavoured jelly-like substance on his plate, the starter. 'What do you do?' he asked, helplessly, still with some bitterness.

'I sometimes work in cafe and if customer ask, I do Tarot.'

'Why would they ask?'

'I've got reputation. Tarot.'

'What do you charge?'

'That depends on customer. Customer can decide.'

'I don't believe in all that', he said, his lips twisted in a sour refusal of all forms of superstition.

'Me neither.'

'So why do you do it?'

'It doesn't really matter if you believe or not, people just want be told what already know.'

Spence put his fork down. 'I believe…'

And then he explained everything he believed. He was an anti-natalist, neo-monarchist, eco-dharmic anarcho-capitalist accelerationist and he was obsessed with a peculiar psychological theory he had come up with himself that there were seven types of people, which corresponded to the colours of the rainbow, and that red people don't understand green people, and yellow people are attracted to orange people, and so on. He held the strangest and most contradictory opinions on all kinds of other subjects. He described himself as a 'Muslim,' but only because he believed Islam, being a 'scorecard religion' was the most market-friendly ideology, but then he also believed women should run the world as they did in the good old days, but then he also loved Trump and Putin and 'strong moral leaders,' and he had a thing about efficient buses and trams, and civic duty, and 9-11, and he believed that we would all soon become transsexual vegan typists and he detested all of humanity. He wished a mighty sword would burst what he called 'The Bubble,' which seemed to mean the world or the system or something of that nature.

All of this emerged in a tight, nerdy soliloquy which Chiyo listened to without comment, without reaction of any kind, just watching him speak, often with his mouth full (a piece of barley fell from it, without him realising; Chiyo watched, fascinated) until finally she said, interrupting him as he was explaining why starting a family was as good a decision as breaking a leg in that it immediately made people respect you more; 'Can you stop it,' she said quietly, 'I'm not interested in.'

He stopped, the surprise on his face turning to anger, which then turned, as soon as he fully absorbed the death-look in her eyes, to confusion and fear.

'Shall we change the subject or you can leave,' she said.

He said nothing, churning over inside.

'That is all about not you, it's just about the thing,' she said, munching on a piece of wild asparagus. 'Nobody really interested in the thing. You pretend you are intellectual cool thing, but I know what is true.'

'What is true?' he asked, morosely.

'Your life is true.'

'I am talking about my life.'

'You're not… you're talking about life as thing. Opinion.'

'Well what do you want to know then?'

'Oh no, the question. Conversation doesn't work like that.'

'How does it work?'

There was a long pause. Chiyo watched him as he mechanically shovelled food into his little rectangular mouth. He looked like he was about to cry. Or perhaps he would get up and sweep everything off the table, like they do in American films. She was very interested in what would happen next.

'These things all surface,' she said, 'so you are hiding something, you really want to talk about…'

Again there were no words between them. Conversations from nearby tables floated over and through them. People were discussing celebrities, politics, their relatives' work problems, the marvellous concert they went to, their children's schools. Extremely tasteful piano music played. Waiters slid back and forth like elegant automatons.

Chiyo and Spence sat in silence, for one, two, three minutes, five… Chiyo watched Spence, an almost microscopically slight smile around her lips and the corner of her eyes. Spence looked at his hands, loose in his lap. He sighed deeply then, still looking down, he said, in an altered voice, less throaty, 'I'm so miserable.'

He glanced up at her, then looked down again and started speaking. All the anger had drained out of his tone, leaving something softer, but deflated, cracked but yet eloquent. He said he had frequent attacks of what he called 'The Terror,' in which an intense dread and horror gripped him and split him into two, with one part, the upper part in his chest and arms, absolutely and completely alone and sure it was going to die, and the other part, which was underneath that, in the belly and the legs, sort of looking on confused and depressed. He said he came from a very wealthy family, with six sisters, who either hated him, pitied him or ignored him, that he usually felt 'The Terror' was worst of all in their company and the worst day of the year was Christmas Day, when they were all together. Last year he had left during the agonising Christmas dinner, unable to take his mother's shrivelled insinuations and tart put downs ('don't give it to Spence, he'll just drop it', 'oh don't ask Spence about the real world, he doesn't live there or know where it is...'), or the way his sisters would, their faces stiff and abstract, pretend they cared about each other, or about anything. He had to get out, away from the airless room, away from the words which came out of their mouths like large hollow plastic things, crushing...

It was cold and dead and bleak and the branch-dead country roads were as empty of life as he was. The corner shop was closed, the curtains in the houses were all drawn, there were no birds or animals. Just nothing. He kept on walking, through the little village of Glower and out towards the new bypass being built through the countryside. Nobody was working, Christmas Day off, so he wandered around the work site, looking at the machinery and gravel and bollards, not really seeing them, not really seeing anything, just tight and disgusted.

He came to a knee-high tunnel under part of the road— perhaps for wildlife, or for drainage. He bent down—a minute circle of light visible at the far end, under the silent, unfinished four-lane road above. And then something unusual happened to him. He felt a sudden, overwhelming, gripping need to crawl through the tunnel. He felt sure that, stupid as it seemed, this was a purpose, an adventure that he could actually make from the cold, hollow, unadventurous day, perhaps even his life. Without inspecting the feeling he got to his knees and crawled into the cold, wet confined passage, pulling himself along with his elbows.

It was difficult. He could feel himself get hot in his thermal underwear and quilted jacket, and frustrated, and then he wanted to go back, but pushing himself backwards was far more diffi-cult, so he kept on, legs now wet and cold. Then, about halfway along the tunnel it had narrowed and his bunched-up jacket had lodged against the sides. He panicked and tried to move, but it was impossible. He then thought that perhaps his struggling would bring down the mass of earth above him, crushing and suffocating him, so he stopped moving. He felt he was going to die here, and wept. Stuck in a tunnel, lost and broken.

After he had cried himself out he tried to move and, strange to say, it was now easier. He hurried his way to the end of the tunnel, scraping away, tearing his trousers and jacket, but freeing, freeing; and then free. He emerged from the side of the scraggy cutting and stood up, dirty, dehydrated and completely miserable. He had done something absolutely pointless. Nothing could be said of it. It was nothing, nothing, nothing, *nothing*.

Since then, he had thought about killing himself every day. The only thing that had stopped him was the possibility that if he worked hard enough to learn computer programming he could develop a virus that would burst The Bubble which, he explained to Chiyo, was actually the real cause of his misery and everyone else's, but it was a huge job, learning code, and although he'd come up with something, he wasn't sure whether to test it out and anyway all he really wanted to do was fly around all night with the magical moth girl and then burn up together in the sun.

By this time they were at the end of their meal, on the coffee. Chiyo removed a small pink plastic box, decorated in cute Miffy skulls and, opening the top, let a packet of cards slide into her white hands. The backs of the cards displayed childish gummy bear illustrations.

'Here,' she said, offering the pack, 'take. Which you choose?'

Spence stared, lost, at the pack. His eyes were moist, something basic in him had dissolved at the edges. He chose a card: two crudely drawn, but cute gummy bears were tumbling from the window of a tower on fire which was being struck by a jagged yellow arrow.

It seemed very terrible. 'What does it mean?' he asked, with a falling heart feeling.

She said nothing.

'What does it mean?' he repeated. He felt dizzy.

Chiyo stood up and gestured, palm up, for him to do the same. He was a hand shorter than her. She put her moist arms around him. A few diners snapped polite glances at them.

This was the last time anyone ever saw Spence Gregory.

∞

Joe held a photograph of Ursula in his hand. She was standing in her work pinny in an aisle of Poundland, her expression, as ever, sleepily wry. She had worked at the cheap variety store, but not for very long because, a week or so after this photograph had been taken she had been fired for unprofessional acts of radical generosity; allowing anyone who looked like they had a hard life, which was pretty much everyone who shopped in Poundland, to take their shopping home without ringing any of it up. She'd turn off the scanner or reset the till or just wave harried housewives through. When her manager, a razor-faced woman, had told her that her till was 'down about £3,500' Ursula had shrugged and said that the sales-assistant-customer relationship was 'an unhealthy sub-dom, master-slave thing' and she was doing her bit to release us all from its shackles. After this — Poundland PLC didn't press charges, they couldn't — Ursula had started campaigning for 'the end of people', walking around Edding with a crudely drawn sign calling for human beings to simply cease existing. This period of surreal misanthropy (combined with a period of, in her words 'rather repulsive promiscuity') had not lasted very long, but as she had ridden away shortly after, Joe's enduring memory of her was from this period, from the time he'd popped into Poundland with a Polaroid and snapped her, giving him, and humanity, a two-fingered salute.

He looks at her, so full of defiance and sweetness she is, so heartrendingly beautiful, and she looks back at him, and then speaks. 'Is it you there, am I?' she asks, leaning casually on the Toblerone special offer shelf.

'I'm me here, aren't you?'

'What are you doing Joe?'

'I'm talking to a photograph.'

'What are you doing in your life?'

'Eugh… my best?'

'Nobody is interested in your best.'

'I've noticed this.'

'So come here.'

'To Poundland?'

The front door slammed. Joe turned, hearing Maria's keys jingle. He turned back. The photo was, once again, a photo.

He could hear from Maria's hatey footsteps that she was angry, brittle, armoured. When she appeared at the top of the stairs — still wearing her black dress, but her hair was loose and wet and her face flushed and rain smudged — hatred was glittering in her eyes, scorn wafting off her hard red cheeks, steam from a disgusting, disgusted cry.

'Who are you talking to?' she asked.

'Marlon Brando,' he answered, gently putting the photos back and swivelling around on the carpet to face her.

She gave him a bitter look.

'You look nice,' he said.

'I'm not in the mood.'

'For what?'

'For your smart comments and put-downs.'

'Alright. Fancy a game of 52 Bunker?'

'No. I do not fancy a game of "52 Bunker". I'm going to bed.'

'Okay,' said Joe, sadness creeping into his voice, fracturing it with hairline cracks, 'I'll be at my mum's all tomorrow. I'll see you there.'

'I can't go,' said Maria, raising herself slightly, defiant.

'To my mum's?'

'No, to the funeral. I'm working.'

'At the weekend?'

'I'm afraid so.'

'But… it's my sister's funeral.'

'I can't help that Joe!' she cried, as if he had asked her to wash a shirt stained with turmeric. She turned into the bedroom, kicking off her heels.

'You can't help that,' Joe whispered to himself.

He can't even be angry at me, like a man, she thought. All couples comprise one half who wants to make a fuss and one who doesn't; one bastard and one coward. Maria wanted Joe to be a bastard, and he wanted her to be a coward, but this was not possible, so they sought their own kind. Can that work?

She had waited for Max, outside of Nando's, in the dark, driving rain, for twenty minutes and then had phoned him. There had been no answer, so she had waited ten more minutes, argued with herself about whether to call again, thought 'fuck this' and dialled again.

Joris had fished his phone from a feathery pocket. Dressed still as a crow, he was standing at the head of a long dining table, surrounded by chief executive officers, hedge-fund managers, special envoys, property tycoons and actors. With their hard faces, predatory eyes and cruel lips, they all looked like gangsters. A massive shark sprawled across the table, which they repeatedly stabbed chunks of flesh from.

'Hello?' said Maria, 'Who is this?'

'Joris-Karl Thottesley, son of Maximilian Carmody. You are,' he looked at the phone screen, 'Maria Geb,' said Joris, his face and tone, as ever, utterly without expression.

'Yes, is Max there?'

'He is no longer with us.'

There was a pause. 'Oh, well, where is he?' asked Maria.

'He is in The Other.'

'I'm sorry?'

'He is, according to your limited understanding of space and time, dead, although he was never really what you could call alive.'

'*What* are you talking about?'

'Dead, Maria Geb. Dead. Dead. Dead. Dead. Dead.'

'But I was just with him!' She stepped back into the doorway of the 101 club, out of the way of the Friday evening flids in their best jeans.

'Were you?' said Joris, sipping a glass of wine, 'Why?'

Maria thought quick. 'Business.'

'His business is in the seventh realm.'

'But he can't be dead. How can he?'

'He can be, we all can be.'

'I just don't believe you.'

'Belief has nothing to do with it.'

'Who is this?'

'Goodbye Maria Geb. Don't call again or I'll make your life unliveable.' He had hung up, sent a photograph of Max's corpse to Maria, then returned to his meal, leaving her to trudge home back to the Man of Failure, cross-legged in the hallway playing with his finger puppets or whatever childish fartplay he was engaged in today.

She lay on the bed, fully clothed, damp, every molecule of her body hating.

∞

Box in hand, Bronya, hungover, eyes red, face blurred but determined, appeared at the door of the empty office. She considered options for revenge; stealing sensitive documents, urinating in everyone's desk drawer, good old-fashioned arson; but it all seemed like too much bother, so she slumped over to her desk and was just about to start throwing things into the box when it occurred to her that the muffled voice she could hear was Maria's, and it was coming through her half-open door. Bronya approached.

'I'm telling you, mum, it's all been a nightmare. A. Night. Mare. Joe's slipping away. He just gets vaguer and vaguer. The other night I caught him sleeping in the chicken coop… Yes, those coops…. Thing is, everything just slips off him, he's like soap, nothing to grip onto, and, you know, I try to explain, I *try* to get through to him, but he just retreats further and further into himself, until, I just don't know *where* he is, do you know what I mean…? He's… yes, that's right, it's selfish, that's what it is, but it's all wrapped up in this wacky 'originality' of his, like let's not have a normal bowl of soup, let's eat it like dogs on the floor, or let's not talk about our day at work, let's talk about *owls*… exactly… and he won't binge watch *anything* with me… hm…? I don't know, something with a strong female lead, or something about the black experience, I don't mind, anything, but he's not interested in *any* television. He just wants to stand in unusual ways, or see how many grapes he can fit into his mouth before one pops… honestly Mum it gets so exhausting, I've had enough, I really have… And he won't buy boring things at the supermarket either… aluminium foil, napkins… It's so tiring… God no, work's shit too. That's the thing, if one part of your life is awful, you should be able to escape into the others, but you can never get it all *nice*, do you know what I mean? Like, alright, your relationship is okay, but you've got money problems, or the money is fine but you can't find a reliable plumber, or you *can* get a reliable plumber but your kids have got cancer… No, I know I don't have kids… No, let's not get into that again Mum… Can you imagine? With *Joe?* Exactly! It would be like raising children with Paddington Bear. The point is, it's a mess with him, but then I get out of the house and come *here* and it's… well, not worse, no, but oh God, it just goes on and on and on. *None* of my staff here get the picture. They're so cliquey… Bronya!? She's not nice at all! She's a total bitch. In fact I had to fire her… Yep. She *repeatedly* betrayed client confidentiality, she's *always* banging on about Italian food, which, I don't see what the fuss is about, it's all just dough isn't it?… and, she, oh my God, she *loves* moaning. You say, how are you Bronya? and she says "oh fine" and then ten seconds later she's living all over you… Oh yes, she'd bitch about that. Mmm… *And* she smells funny… eh? Like a damp bra… oh, for fuck's sake…'

Bronya had pushed the door open with her foot, standing arms folded, to make it clear that she had heard the whole thing.

'Hello,' said Maria

'You're dead meat.'

Maria spat a 'phone you later' into the phone and followed Bronya out of the room—'Bronya, really, there's no need for this…'—as Bronya picked up her box and, without speaking, left Maria standing in the empty, quiet office.

No biggie. Maria went back to her office and considered the situation. What could Bronya do after all? Bugger all. She turned on her computer, brought up Bronya's caseload, and rifled through her files. She actually did have quite a lot on—but nothing a good delegational spree couldn't handle.

Something caught Maria's eye; 'Kom Ombo Cottage, Nutbourne' This was Margaret's address. She read the notes; 'Old woman. Margaret Geb. Possibly under restraint. Low priority.'

That was strange. She sat back in her chair, vaguely but disdainfully looking at the collapsed building where her life should be. Offloading to her mother hadn't helped, because she couldn't bring herself to explain the principal issue here, that the man she had fallen completely in love with, and would happily have plunged a sacrificial sword into her belly for, had inexplicably committed suicide by throwing himself into a hole. The argy-bargey with Bronya hadn't been anywhere near satisfying enough either. What was it? What did she need to do?

With this question came the answer, as clear as a drop of mountain water onto a parched tongue; be with Max and break Joe. But neither was possible, the former was dead, the latter immortal, but, but, but, but, *but*… There *must* be a way.

She picked up the phone and dialled her contact at head office, a cardiganed little cube-headed man who she had tied to the end of a piece of string she dandled from a bored paw.

'Hi Glen, it's me, Maria… How are you…? Reaalllly?' she purred, 'Look we *must* get together soon, but I'm ringing right now because I need you to look into something for me… We had a call-out to Thottesley Hall last month, ongoing case, and this morning Thottesley killed himself. Can you dig up any details for me…? Hm? Oh anything, how it happened, where he's going to be buried, anything you can.'

She hung up and waited. Thirty minutes later Glen called to tell her, in his eager little voice, that he knew nothing whatsoever about Thottesley, all the files had mysteriously disappeared, but that a contact at the police station had told him he was going to be cremated at Chilham Hatch that very afternoon.

She picked up the phone again, dialling Joe.

'It's me. Yes, I'll come. Yes, yes, be quiet, I'm coming to the funeral. I'll be there in half an hour.'

∞

Lilly, dressed formally in a dark skirt and blouse, stood next to Max's body, scalpel in hand. Things had got very strange after Joe had left the estate. First of all Ian, the little lawyer, had taken Carl, Paul and Lilly aside, told them that this was a very sensitive case, that nobody must know that Thottesley was dead, that his body was to be sent immediately to the crematorium, that all they had to do was their jobs and that if they didn't, his organisation, which had the police, the government, the whole world in its pocket, would see to it that Carl's children, Paul's Norwegian half-brother and Lilly's grandmother would wake up tomorrow in the same kind of body bag Max was sealed up in.

Then, when Lilly had got back to the mortuary to Max and unzipped him, he was just a normal old geezer, a skinny silver fox with a normal nose, normal skin colour and rear-end entirely the right way around. She had wondered if the whole thing had been a dope-induced 'episode.' It seemed likely, because even Carl had become confused, but here was Max, the same Max she had accidentally seduced when she was eight years old and who had very much unaccidentally seduced her mother. Here was Max, and something had to be done; so she got sewing.

Max's face, although weathered and finely lined, still looked young, or, it seemed to Lilly, ageless. His face, with its prominent cheekbones and angular jaw, had the bony deformity of the 'handsome, wealthy man,' as if the skin had been shrink-wrapped round a lumpy skull.

'I know you did it,' she said, 'I just… Don't know what you did.'

Max had claimed, during the police enquiry which followed the disappearance of Lilly's mother, to have taken her, Helen, for a drink, heard her complain about her husband—a common problem—suggested to her that she leave him and start a new life abroad, and then left her in town. This was the last anyone had heard of her. Lilly had also spoken to the police, as had her dad, the police had interviewed Max a second time, a third time, conducted a thorough search of his property, or so they said, found nothing and finally dropped all charges against him. If there's no body, there's no crime. Eventually the drama had settled down, people stopped talking about what had happened and the search for Helen Pumphrey was abandoned. But Lilly knew.

Max seemed to wear a slight supercilious smile, as if he knew too. Or as if he had achieved his death, on merit.

'I'm going to fix you up,' Lilly said, 'and then, this afternoon, I'm going to watch you burn.'

∞

Joe and Neil sat either side of their mother, the three of them together under the same roof for the first time in nearly two decades. They were comfortably planted in Margaret's gorgeous drawing room. Joe was dressed in high Regency style, wearing clothes pilfered from Max's wardrobe, with the addition of Tim's dog collar. Neil was dressed in a black suit, Margaret in an elegant lavender and cream lace dress, her rope still tied around her waist. Louis, looking like he was falling apart with grief, stood in the corner staring at the floor. He was wearing black shorts, a black Lacoste T-shirt and black sandals. Margaret's friend and neighbour, a skeletal, liver-spotted ninety-year-old heronlike man called Roy Towers sat at the back of the room silently staring straight ahead through two sunken, rheumy eyes, his spindly hands, knotted with thick blue veins, gripping the ivory moon-head handle of a walking stick. Next to him sat Laughing Ralf, who Joe, after listening to his moving story the night before, and discovering that Ralf's path had crossed with Ursula's at Poundland, had invited to the funeral.

Neil turned up and saw Ralf, who he had tried to arrest and lost his job over, quietly chuckling in the corner. Neil had spent much of the previous night planning exactly how he was going to be during this afternoon, how he would be languid, and pen-etrating, and sardonic, and respectful, and subtle, and completely ice-calm, amazing everyone and making them wonder what was really going on in his deep mind; so he made a special effort to look casual, but it was extremely unsettling to see Ralf there, grinning and giggling like a moron.

'What's he doing here?' he asked, bottom lip tight.

Joe shrugged.

'He's a friend of Ursula's,' Margaret said.

'Him? *Him!?*' said Neil, stabbing the air not just with his sharply pointing finger, but with his entire triangular body. He remembered Ralf's mocking recommendation, to find pain fun-ny, to be a 'schadenfreudist'. That man is laughing at… me… at… He's laughing at all of us.

'Yes, he's a *very* nice man,' said Margaret.

'I'm not… with him… going to my sister's…' Neil sat down and closed his eyes, held his breath and counted to ten. He had read this was an effective anger-management technique, although it did tend to mean that the next thing to come out of his mouth was blasted out like a tennis ball from a practice machine …'funeral!'

Nobody said anything. Silence reigned for a full ten minutes, Ralf's contented, almost babyish gurgle, the only sound, pleasing to Margaret and Joe, maddening to Neil.

Finally, Neil spoke. He nodded to the rope that had also been playing on his nerves and that he'd saved up another ten seconds of held air to overcome his anger about, and burst out with; 'Can you untie her please Louis?'

'No Patricia,' said Margaret, firmly, 'I want to stay tied up.'

'Mother, you can't go to your daughter's funeral on a rope!'

'Whose funeral? Who are you talking about Patricia?'

'Ursula's,' said Neil with hopeless dismay.

'Don't be silly.'

'She's your daughter!'

'I know who she is!'

'The point is,' he said, 'the point is… we have to untie you. Otherwise how will you actually leave?'

'Yes, that's right. Louis?'

Louis untied the far end which had been clove hitched to the radiator and handed it to Joe.

'Where are we going anyway?' asked Margaret.

'To the funeral!'

'Oh, but I can't go!'

'Why?' said Neil, feeling the old anguish overcome him, the old shame.

'Because I'll have to go *there*.' She pointed to an area of the room in front of the hallway. 'They made it very clear that I was not allowed over there.'

'Who? Who did?' said Neil.

'They did.'

'Alright, why?'

'Well, because you have to pay, and I haven't paid,' said Margaret with a touch of sad fatalism. That's just how it was.

'Look,' said Neil, 'you can go there. It's fine. There's nothing there, nobody there. Look. Look.' He opened his hands, palm outwards, at the perfectly ordinary area of floor. His plan to remain composed was already in shreds.

Margaret was unmoved. 'Not without paying I can't. I'm not to go there.'

'Don't worry Mum', said Joe, 'I paid for you. I made a special payment yesterday. I suppose they just haven't updated their records yet.'

'Oh *did* you!? That's marvellous. Thank you so much… because it's been such a *nuisance* not being able to go there.'

'But he didn't Mother', said Neil, clenched up against rising violence, 'He didn't pay anyone anything.'

Margaret turned, worried, to Joe. 'Didn't you?'

'Yes, I did.'

'You see,' she said, turning back to Neil with a pleasant smile. Neil sank back into his chair. The room was quiet again. Joe glanced at Neil, but said nothing. Yes, thought Neil, I can see what you're thinking, you smug bastard. They were all in on it though, the old conspiracy, against me—they probably decided before I got here to humiliate me. He sat silently, eyes darting from mother, to brother, face screwed up.

Neil was about to speak when the doorbell rang. Louis, sobbing, walked down the hall and opened the door to Maria. 'Oh,' she said, surprised to see Louis, 'you.'

Louis gained instant and complete control of his grief. He regarded her quietly.

'Where are they?' she asked, endeavouring to cover awkwardness with a display of mourning.

'Inside,' he said.

Maria returned behind Louis, cautiously entered the drawing room and stood 'there,' just where Margaret hadn't been allowed to go.

'Oh,' said Margaret, turning to Neil, 'You didn't tell me Boris Becker was coming!'

Maria, without annoyance—for she had heard it many times before, said 'I'm not Boris Becker,' then turned to greet Neil who sighed with relief; finally, he thought, someone who was not off their rocker.

'I see you're allowed there Boris,' said Margaret.

'Don't worry, I'm allowed everywhere,' said Maria, forgetting her performance of grief, smiling, and indicating her social services lanyard. A look of panic crossed Margaret's face. Louis shot Maria a look and Maria lowered her head again.

'Sit down,' said Joe, 'They'll be here soon.'

'I'm so sorry for your loss,' said Maria with heavy seriousness, sitting down on a wobbly stool with one leg shorter than the others. 'I didn't know her, Ursula,' she said, trying to maintain tragic composure while, at the same time, arranging the stool so that it wouldn't tilt, 'but it's just awful what happened… damn thing…' she said, tightly, standing up and sitting down again, 'erm, anyway, *how* have you been Margaret?' she asked, as if she were the only person to have considered Margaret's feelings.

'Oh, I'll be dead soon. We all will be.'

The doorbell rang again. Louis, wiping his wet face, flip-flopped again down to the front door, then returned to announce that the funeral cortège was outside. The 'family,' such as it was, rose and joined Nina and Carl outside, which took a long time as Roy Towers took a full ten minutes to dodder out, carrying his rattling body as five-year-olds carry cups of tea.

Carl, in top hat and black herringbone frock coat, stood in front of the hearse as Neil, Joe and Margaret took their seats in the first car, Joe holding the loops of Margaret's rope and Neil swatting away a fly which continually landed on his forehead.

'Shall we play a game?' said Margaret as they pulled away, following the hearse, which was being driven by Nina, peering short-sightedly over the large steering wheel at Carl who was walking slowly and seriously ahead of the cortége.

'Mother. *Please*,' Neil moaned, under his breath.

'Come on Joe,' she said, 'ask one of your funny questions.'

'No, no, don't.'

Joe thought to himself. 'Alright. Is it better to be a goose in an oven, or an oven in a goose?'

'This is sick,' said Neil, 'How can you…?'

'An oven in a goose,' Margaret interrupted, folding her hands across her lap contentedly.

Ahead of them Carl had got back in the hearse, Nina taking the passenger seat, a thick plastic bag of twenty-five heads nestled between her legs. 'There's a funny smell in here,' she said.

Carl shrugged, 'air freshener.'

'It smells like curry.'

'Curry-scented air freshener.'

Neil in the car behind was feeling physically ill. He desperately wanted to get out and walk, but, despite himself, he was drawn in, unable to face down Joe's chaotic mind-bomb.

'Ovens don't have feelings,' Neil said quietly, looking out the window.

'Come along, you've never been an oven Patricia,' said Margaret reproachfully.

'Yeah,' said Joe, 'how would you know?'

'No, you know what, yes, it's true, you're right, you're absolutely right, I've never been an oven, but they don't have a nervous system, do they? And if they don't have a nervous system, they do not and they can not have feelings, can they?' said Neil, glaring now at both of them.

'To be fair,' said Margaret gently, 'I don't think many people have considered the question.'

'They don't have to!' He swatted again at the fly, 'Sod *off*,' he hissed.

There was a moment's thoughtful silence. 'How do we know that geese do have nervous systems?' asked Joe carefully.

'Look! It's obvious! It's all obvious. To everyone. There's just no point to all these stupid debates. Accept the fucking worl…' The fly flew into his mouth, making him cough and retch.

'Everything has feelings,' said Margaret quietly and tenderly.

Meanwhile, in the second car, Maria, Louis, Ralf and Roy sat in laughter-punctuated silence. Louis' grief had abated and he now looked red-eyed at Maria who, trying to look casual and calm, stared out the window. Roy, who had taken out a small leather-bound book and glasses, read quietly from it, although evidently with some strain.

Maria felt the weight of unspokenness press upon her like a slab of concrete on her chest. She hated death, it was just so bloody awkward.

'What are you reading?' she said to Roy.

'Sorry?' said the old man, looking up in surprise.

'I said what are you reading?'

The old man lowered his gaze to his book and started reading in a quaking but clear, sandy voice.

'Nut is woman, celestial sow and the galaxy in which our earth sits. She arches her long, beautiful, milky back above the land, touching it at one end with her feet and hands, thus forming the firmament that separates the world from the waters of chaos and the darkness of the undefined place. In the evening she swallows the sun, which sails along her watery body during the night hours, fertilising her, glowing in her belly, until it is reborn at dawn, with the red staining of the morning sky bearing witness to her labour. As a long-horned cow, Nut suckles the king of the world and, after death, raises him into the sky, where she protects him.'

'I see,' she said. Another headcase. Was anyone on this planet even halfway sane? 'And, um, sorry, but we haven't been introduced,' she said, holding out her hand to Ralf, who, eyes merry and twinkling, told her his name.

'What's your relationship to... um... the departed?' she asked.

'I taught her Poundland's fire safety regulations! Hahahaha!'

'Riiiight.'

Louis spoke. 'How is *your* work madam?' All his huffing and hooing was absent. He spoke with quiet authority.

Maria shot him an anxious glance and said nothing.

'Are you having problems madam?' asked Louis.

'What are you talking about?' said Maria quietly, an old fear hovering in her craw, trembling her voice.

'You know what I'm talking about.'

'Look,' said Maria, exhaling heavily and smiling, 'We got off on the wrong foot you and I... I don't know why, but it's... it's

Ursula's funeral, let's… Shall we just let bygones be bygones? Shall we?'

'You don't care about Ursula,' said Louis. 'You don't care about anyone but yourself.'

'Look…' said Maria severely, calling, by habit, on her Voice of Professional Authority, but Louis cut her off; '…I hold all the cards' he said, with a malicious smile, 'as you know.'

Ralf, who had been following the conversation, burst into joyous laughter.

Roy began speaking again, Ralf laughing away the whole time; 'Oh Nut, You have united the earth in every place. O mistress over the earth, you are above your father Shu, You have the mastery over him. He has loved you so much that he set himself under you in everything. You have taken possession of every god for yourself with his boat. You have made them shine like lamps, Assuredly they shall not cease from you like the stars. They will make your darkness bright for the world…'

Ralf laughed and laughed and laughed.

∞

Paul Saul, dressed in full formal funeral director attire, sat in the second company hearse, Lilly by his side, Max Thottesley's body laid out behind them. They pulled out of the garage and drove through Edding, on their way north to Thottesley.

'How much are these people paying us for this?' Lilly asked.

'I don't know.'

'Yes you do.'

Paul gave her a blank look. 'When we get to the house, stay in the car. They've got their own cortège and their own bearers. They'll follow us to the crematorium, take the coffin in, and then that's it. Don't talk to anyone.'

'Okay, okay.'

'After they've finished, Nina and Carl will turn up with the Gebs. I'll come back with Nina, and Carl will wait for you in the car park. Just stay in the background, the whole time. Look like death.'

'What does death look like?'

'Serious, respectful, nice.'

'Not ludicrous, disrespectful and sadistically grotesque?'

They stopped at traffic lights. Paul checked his tie in the mirror.

'No, none of those things,' he said.

'Can we put the radio on?' asked Lilly.

Paul turned it on. A BBC reporter was saying that a new strain of terrorism had been discovered in Korkınıştan possibly necessitating a new inoculating, emergency-response procedure. Lilly twiddled with the knob, until Elliott Smith came on. Ah, Elliott, she thought. Elliott Smith and Nick Drake and Ian Curtis; their sadness was true, not like the theatrical despair of... oh, who was it? She could never remember names. She liked to listen to broken-hearted boys with exquisite voices, but hardly any of them really meant it, none of them were actually exposed, like Elliott was. They played at being 'too beautiful for this world,' they played off their ordinary sadness, but it was hollow.

She looked over at Paul, who hummed pleasantly along to Miss Misery. He was a funny onion, Paul. Lilly had the feeling that, for all his professional seriousness, he'd be quite happy sitting in a shallow rock pool inspecting crabs.

They drew into Thottesley, and the same chill wind rustled through Lilly's heart as the last time she'd driven through those immense iron gates. They headed up the gravel driveway, parked in front of the Audis, BMWS and Mercedes, and Paul led them out as Carl had done for the Gebs, Lilly driving behind him, impressed at his magnificent gravitas, although he was probably thinking about mini Babybels or James Bond's grappling hook.

She stopped the car and shifted over for Paul who drove away, all the other cars following. They drove through the frosty countryside towards Chilham Hatch crematorium and cemetery, forty minutes eastbound down the A741. The sky overhead was dark but darkly gleaming, like wet iron, from the low muted sun shining underneath. A few indecisive washes of rain swept over the hearse. Elliott Smith had stopped singing and now Yamasuki was playing, ridiculous fake Japanese children chanting to seventies proto-dance music, but Paul hummed along and Lilly didn't mind. Her thoughts were elsewhere.

They pulled into the crematory grounds and everyone got out of their cars—Joris and the wealthy set he'd dined with the day before—and strolled up to the chapel. Those within earshot of Joris were quietly and respectfully solemn and silent, while those at the back of the sauntering line of people were quietly and respectfully chatting.

'Did you see Nigella last night?' asked one corpulent woman to another, quietly and respectfully, 'She had some *amazing* ideas for pheasant. And I just love her chilli shelf.'

'Oh, I *adore* Nigella,' said the second, quietly and respectfully, 'but she's a dreadful cunt for the butter.'

Another woman, with a face like a man but an immaculate haircut like a TV chatshow hostess, was quietly and respectfully reprimanding her stunted reptilian husband, who owned most of East London. 'Don't snigger like that darling, you look positively demonic.'

Two beady-eyed celebrities, one so featureless he looked like he had a stocking over his face, the other a straggly grey-haired ex-rockstar, barge-owning type who considered himself a rebel because he smoked dope and had played with Pink Floyd, were quietly and respectfully talking about types of yoghurt.

Two old women, multi-millionaires, one of whom a regular on Dragon's Den, both with long flappy faces and overly-styled yellowish hair, were talking in quietly and respectfully conspiratorial undertones, their cold, hard eyes glinting like broken razor blades; 'He was *poisoned*,' said one, 'Tom told me, but nothing could be done because, apparently...' her voice dropped to an intense whisper, 'all his blood had turned to *milk!*'

'Good God!'

Joris at the head of the line, dressed in an Anderson and Sheppard mourning suit, looked pinched and angry. His eerily smooth face unnaturally crumpled around the eyes, which stared malevolently ahead.

Inside the chapel, the respectable assembled were waiting. All exhibited reverential sadness, while looking around to see who else was there and thinking about food, money, adding value, developing systems and golden-egg laying geese. Only Joris looked even slightly touched by grief.

The coffin—now open—was brought down and laid at the altar. Max, even more handsome in death, immaculately presented by Lilly, lay with his beautiful brown carefully manicured hands folded across his chest.

Tim the vicar, wearing a blood-red dog collar, took to the altar. He was thin, bald, beaky and had a flushed, angry-looking face. He looked as if he were always thinking of some furious wrong—possibly the slovenly housekeeping of Sophie, his slatternly girlfriend, or possibly the ridiculous, slapdash defending of Arsenal whenever they play a top-six side, or possibly the disgusting atheism of the modern world.

When everyone was assembled, the doors were locked and Tim gave his angry eulogy which he more or less spat at the crowd.

'We are gathered here today,' he said, 'to pay homage to Maximilian Hugh Lancelot Cassius d'Auffay Thottesley 14th Baronet, 6th Baron Thottesley. Father, brother, friend, colleague, benefactor and lo…' The mic cut out for a moment then back in, 'Maximilian was the foundation to the life and work of so many instit…ions.' Tim, irritated, patted the mic head. 'Patron of the arts, inventor, pioneer, researcher, educator. He was a tra… nsformative force in our community, a real one-off, an eccentric, unforgettable to those whose lives he touched so very deeply…' Again the mic cut out, this time for longer. Tim, close to boiling over, worked away at the connecting cable, until it came on again, and, gathering himself, he resumed speaking, 'I don't need to tell you what Max

Thottesley brought to each of our individual li…, we all ow…
him and his foundat… a massive debt of tha… for God's *sake…!'*
The slender thread keeping his anger from tearing loose, snapped,
'It's not too… uch to ask to… ave a microp… that… *Simon! Si…'*
bald head as red as his dog collar he began shouting off stage. A
man appeared—with a soft, friendly face, red cheeks, beautiful
little red lips and huge, intelligent eyes, made even larger by
his immense '80s snooker player' glasses—and inspected the
microphone. As he did so a pounding smash rattled the doors
at the far end of the chapel.

Outside, Max's anarchist former groundsman, Patrick, had
managed to evade security and, sprinting up the gravel thor-
oughfare to the crematorium chapel doors, had leapt, full force,
shoulder first into them. They had buckled but remained closed,
so he threw himself at them again, and again, until they burst
open, the congregation swivelling round.

A couple of people recognised him from his 'whole head'
animal T-shirt; today a massive squirrel's head was tucked into
his jogging trousers. He ran, stumbling, down the central aisle,
a team of massive hired muscle bringing up the rear. Everyone
watched, frozen, as he leapt onto the coffin, which fell to the
floor, releasing Max's body.

'What is *this!?'* screamed Tim.

There was ungodly commotion in the aisles. Joris jumped
from his seat, screaming, and grabbed at Patrick, but his childish
strength was no match for the older man's density. 'Die!' cried
Patrick, *'die!'* Security rushed forward, piling on. Chaos; only
Simon was calm, cheerfully watching the scene from the stage.

Patrick now had his hands round Max's head, several body-
guards pulling in several directions. Then silence, an eternally
still moment of horror.

The head had come off in Patrick's hand, easily.

Joris, eyes like boiled eggs, screamed. And *screamed.*

∞

Meanwhile the Geb cortège had just passed a large sign that read 'Chilham Hatch Crematorium.' Margaret, looking out of the window, up the hill to the crematorium, smiled. 'Oh,' she said, 'We're going shopping! Why didn't you tell me?'

'It was a surprise,' said Joe.

'We're not going shopping,' said Neil in quiet, condensed fury.

Neil had treated Ursula's death casually. He had felt that they had never been close, he had never really known her, and although he 'should' be upset about it, he just wasn't. He had performed grief for the benefit of everyone else, to look correct and fit the situation, but had felt nothing. The reason he felt nothing however, quite unknown to Neil, was that he had an almost hysterical, but entirely unconscious, fear of death. He could not bear to think of losing anyone or anything, and so pushed all such thoughts utterly and completely from his mind, into the same all-purpose junk room as he stored his conscience.

Now, however, looking up at the last place on earth that Ursula would ever be, death crawled into his awareness and nothing he could do could push it out. An all-absorbing horror opened up in the hollow chest, as if he held a chasm in his stomach, a black pit that led straight down to hell, and his tiny little head was toddling on the edge of it and he had to keep himself rigidly still, for fear of tumbling in.

'Then why are we at the supermarket?' asked Margaret, turning to Neil as the car crunched slowly up the approach road.

'It's not a supermarket. It's a crematorium. They burn co...' Neil reflexively swallowed, '...orpses here.'

Margaret looked again out of the window. There appeared to be a great deal of commotion up there. Joe and Neil also squinted at the chapel. Neil recognised two of his ex-colleagues, thick-lipped Gordon and frog-eyed Michael, arresting an ox-like man wearing a squirrel T-shirt. Joe recognised Joris, restrained by someone familiar, but pulling himself free and running off, howling.

'Must be the sales,' said Margaret. 'Is it the sales?'

'Yeah. New Year sales,' said Joe.

'Oh good!'

Tim approached their hearse. His jutting jaw and balled up shoulders expressed tense wrath. Carl and Joe wound their windows down.

'As you can see,' said the vicar talking to the hearse and the front car, 'We've got a complete mess here. A disgruntled former employee apparently, whining about injustice and evil and Tories and Christ in Heaven knows what else. *Ridiculous.* But what do I care? I don't care. I really don't. I've had enough. Bollocks to it all.'

'What, shall we do then?' Carl called back from the hearse.

'Just go straight in,' said Tim, 'Walk around. They'll be cleared soon. I'm off. I'm done. Fuck 'em.'

'Do you still sell rabbit slippers?' asked Margaret.

Tim ignored her. He was walking off over the Garden of Rest, throwing his dog collar into the calendulas. He would vicar no more. Why bother? Nobody believes in mystery any more. There are no more sins, just illnesses. There's no more culture, just fun. People celebrate at weddings and mourn at funerals; they have it all the wrong way round. Well… sod 'em!

'They used to sell fuzzy rabbit slippers,' said Margaret withdrawing her head back into the car and addressing Joe and Neil, 'They were ever so cute, but very well made too. Very warm.'

Margaret leaned out the window again and called to Carl in the hearse. 'Come along driver! We'll miss the best deals!'

The cars drew up alongside the chapel, and the family got out. Carl slid the coffin from the hearse and Joe, Neil, Roy and Louis lifted it up onto their shoulders and walked around the foaming crowd towards the entrance. Just as they were about to enter, Joe noticed Lilly and a tall man with huge glasses and a mullet enter a side door. Neil noticed Joe notice Lilly and, in his confusion and annoyance he dragged at his corner of the coffin which made Joe, at the front strike the door.

'Pay attention,' hissed Neil.

Meanwhile Maria had slipped away.

Lilly was surprised by how very noisy and industrial-looking the crematory actually was. The 'transfer room' was clean but imposing, like an army barrack kitchen. There were three huge cremators set into a green tiled wall; each oven had a square iron-framed glass door and, next to it, a panel of large red and green mushroom buttons. One of the cremators was quiet and dark, the other two were roaring away, throwing vivid red light over the far side wall. Lilly was bent over, looking in one of the live ovens. The twenty-five heads that Carl had dropped off—before taking the remaining hearse to the back of the car park, skinning up and listening to The Fall—were now down to the black charred bone. It was, as granny would have put it, a 'mad old moment,' like a few weeks back when she had, at one in the morning, gone outside to free a rat from the recycling wheel-ie bin. It had been frantically jumping up the inner walls and leaping its head against the lid for four hours and, when she lowered the heavy thing down and lifted the lid, it had bolted off down the empty orange-lit street bouncing off the cars and curbs. There weren't enough 'mad old moments' in life.

The double doors at the end of the room opened and the rosy-cheeked man Joe had seen Lilly with, Simon Lincoln, pushed through a trolley, laid out on which was Max's body and head; the latter lying next to but not connected, to the former. Lilly stood up straight.

'This who you were looking for?' Lilly wondered how old Simon was. It was impossible to tell his age; he could have been in his twenties or his forties.

'Yep,' she answered.

Lilly had recognised Simon. It was from his YouTube videos that she had learnt basic corpse prep. He had explained to her, as he'd shown her around the crematorium, that he used to do her job, but he'd fancied a change, so had moved into ovens and YouTube.

'Someone had tampered with the head,' said Lilly, 'but the police aren't interested. They told me to finish him.'

'All very irregular this,' said Simon. 'There should have been an autopsy.'

'He was very rich.'

'I know. So why are they using this place? Cramming him in between the proles? People with his money can afford absolute privacy. The best of the best.'

'I don't know,' said Lilly, 'but his lawyer was most insistent.'

Simon shrugged. he walked round the trolley and set the controls on the empty oven. 'Well anyway. Gas mark 145, 900 degrees, roast for ninety minutes,' he said. His voice was pleasant, caressing, but also twangy and nerdy.

'An hour and a half? That seems quite a lot. He's pretty trim.'

'The fat ones go much faster,' he said.

Lilly nodded. 'I suppose that makes sense,' she said.

Simon opened the door of the empty oven. A light puff of powdery ash drifted out. Lilly blinked.

'Yeah, it's quite unpleasant,' said Simon, noticing her grimace, 'the ash gets everywhere, in your ears, in your nostrils. Sometimes I finish work looking like an semi-corporeal ash ghoul.'

Lilly nodded; seriously, but not overly disgusted. As Simon slid the body into the oven she briefly congratulated herself. The idea that she'd be spending the afternoon inhaling the dead would have, only a year ago, freaked her out, but now it was no more unpleasant than cleaning the toilet; even, with the nobility she now recognised in the profession, less so.

'How strong are these doors?' she asked, tapping one with a fingernail.

'These? Military grade. You won't feel a thing.'

'Good. Could they withstand an explosion?'

'Well, good question. It depends on the brisance of the explosive material, but it could absorb a hand grenade, probably a light mortar shell. Sixty mill, say.'

'Oh, sixty mill. That's reassuring.'

Simon stood back, hands on hips and nodded at the control panel with paternal encouragement. 'You want to fire her up?'

'Can I?'

He gestured towards the panel. Lilly held her hand over the largest red 'ignite' button. 'Should we say something?' she asked.

'Well I have a little thing I say,' said Simon, a little sheepishly, 'but, erm, I usually just say it to myself.'

'Okay, say that.'

'Can I?'

'Yeah, go on.'

Simon knitted his brow. 'I feel a bit silly,' he said. 'It' erm, it's, I mean I got it from D&D.'

'I don't mind, say it,' said Lilly, charmed at his bashfulness.

'Alright then.' He cleared his throat and drew himself up to his full height; well over six foot. 'Stop the planets in their orbits,' he said, 'obstruct the course of the moon, smash the mountain peaks, dry up the lakes, uproot the trees, stir up the waters of the oceans and atomise them in the sun. Melt the flesh of the city, crumble the bones of the world and let the dust of humanity blow away in the rude winds of eternity!'

Lilly smiled. 'Bitching,' she said and hit ignite.

∞

Joe, Neil, Louis and Roy carried the coffin through the chapel which was filling up with people. Neil was behind Joe, looking at the back of his brother's head which, for some reason, was even more hateful than the front of it.

As they entered, Neil looked around at the assembled mourners. They moved quite strangely. It was hard to say how, just not quite with fluid naturalness. Many appeared to be wearing a great deal of make-up. A folkish, droning Celtic-drum and hurdy-gurdy cover of the Velvet Underground's 'Ride into Sun' played over the speakers.

'Who are they?' said Neil, as they put the coffin down.

'They're friends of Ursula,' said Louis, smiling and bobbing again.

Margaret—still attached to Joe by a long rope—wandered around the outside of the room. 'I can't get over just how much this place has changed,' she said, 'They used to have the tinned fish over there...'

Joe gently pulled her over to him. 'Come on Mum. Let's sit down for a bit.'

'It's very thoughtful to have so many seats isn't it?'

Neil approached one of the mysterious mourners, a young woman. 'Excuse me,' he said, 'erm, who invited you?'

'Ursula,' said the girl.

'How can someone who is dead invite someone to their own funeral?'

'We are friends of hers,' said a man leaning across. 'You can ask Louis. He knows us.'

'Look.' Neil, pulled within three different directions at once—one way towards propriety and order, one way away from the void, and a third direction towards frustration at the mad stupidity of the situation—decided to put this interaction on pause. 'Can I speak to you afterwards please?'

'Yes, of course,' said the man decorously.

Neil returned to his seat, next to Margaret who was looking around in mild confusion. 'What's happening now?' she asked.

'Bingo,' said Joe, 'It's a special bingo afternoon.'

'What, in a supermarket? But where are our cards?'

'Here.' He passed her a Bible and took a pen out of his pocket, handing that to her too. She opened the Bible and prepared for the call out.

Neil was squirming around on his pew, his bloodless face violently distorted. It wasn't just that they had no shame, his abnormal family, but that they were determined to bring everyone and everything down into their maniac underworld. Look at him, thought Neil, staring at his brother, he doesn't care, he just doesn't *care*.

Behind Joe, one of the shady folk leant forwards and whispered in his ear. She had a Spanish accent, and a extremely sweet, girly voice.

'Joe,' she said.

'Yes?' said Joe, turning back.

'Are you having your thoughts, or are your thoughts having you?'

'Six of one half a dozen of the other.'

'You do not belong to you,' whispered the girl, intense urgency in her voice.

'Who do I belong to then?' whispered Joe.

'It's not who you belong to, it's when you belong to them.'

'When do I belong to them then?'

The music finished. The Spanish girl gestured towards the empty pulpit. Joe looked at it, then to her, then to his mother, and then around the chapel. All this strangeness felt inevitable, like he was watching a film that had already been written.

He stood up and walked to the lectern. He had told the authorities that he would give the eulogy and lead the service, although he had no idea what he was going to say, being unable at the best of times to prepare anything and, in the heightened state he had been in over the past few weeks, barely able think, much less write a speech. He now stood, shoulders limp, looking at the silent assembly. He could feel layers of himself peel away, leaving a troubling nothingness, or thisness. How funny to be here, in this cold, pinewood room, how funny that the last place on earth Ursula would want to be is the last place on earth she actually is.

He had his eyes closed, but was aware, in his solar plexus, that eyes were on him, expectant. He opened his mouth, hoping that words would come out, and, eventually, they did.

'One thing I...' he tried to clear his throat, which had dried up, then took a sip of water. 'Erm, one thing I can certainly say about Ursula... Is that she was my sister. To be honest, everything else about her is a bit of a mystery. She got around, I suppose.

Travelled a lot, mainly on a horse I think. I hope that a celestial flock… Or herd… Or shoal of horses are galloping… No trotting, or perhaps simply walking… Yes, walking over the fields of… erm… her heart?'

Lilly, having watched Max's head and body burn for a few minutes—a peculiarly dark shade of red—was now standing at the door of the chapel, watching and listening to Joe, entranced. Margaret listened also, benignly wondering why Joe was reading this nice poem. Ralf, sitting next to her, occasionally whispered a number into her ear, 'Garden gate, eight, Turn the Screw, sixty-two, staying alive, eighty-five…' which Margaret dutifully ticked off from her imaginary bingo grid. On the other side of Margaret sat Neil, whose anxious hatred of Joe, of his family and of his life, which at the start of his speech had been hovering around the red zone was now threatening to burst the apparatus. He was gripping the pew, eyes tired, burning and feverish. Old man Roy, next to Neil, simply sat hushed, fervent in prayer.

Joe had stopped speaking. He wasn't making much sense to himself, let alone to anyone else. Not that it mattered. You could armpit fart your way through a eulogy and people would 'get it', but still, here I am, he thought, I might as well say what is on my mind. 'What I've realised,' he continued, fully entering the neutral state of awareness, 'over the past few weeks, is that, when someone you love dies, someone inside of you dies too, a copy of them, a double that… You've made with your… It's here,' he pointed to his chest, 'and I think the double has to die. It is dying, which is very strange to me. I feel, I've been feeling that I'm not really here any more. There's what's happening, what's going on—here is my body and here are my thoughts—but I can't actually locate myself in it. It's as if Ursula has taken me with her. Does that make sense? Probably not. What I mean is, if you think about Ursula, you're actually just thinking about the double, not her, and that's painful, because the double is dead. But the double always has been dead, because it's a thing. The person is,' he pointed to his belly, 'here. She's here now, like

I'm here, now, like we all are, and we're not things. As soon as you think of people, they become things which are either living things or dead things, and when they're living things you worry about them becoming dead things and when they're dead things you get upset because they're not living things any more, but they were never things in the first place, they only seem like things if you think so. I've been wrong for weeks now, since I heard the thing of Ursula had gone, but I've also, at the same time, been not wrong, because Ursula the not-thing never went, how could she have? It's the same when something wonderful happens, when I fall in love, I am alright, because a loved thing has come, but I'm also not right, because of course it was always here. And what is true for me is this, that in the world, there are thing people, who live their lives trying to get what they can never get their hands on, and there are not-thing people who live their lives letting go of what was never theirs in the first place, and the thing people have to suffer until they become the not-thing people, like I had to, like you had to, like Ursula had to.'

Music begins, a grim-reaping, grand-weeping creeping celesta and vibraphone number with a low, slow, drumming bass-line. Joe worldlessly howls a weird lament as Ursula, naked as always, climbs out of the coffin and joins him, the two of them waltzing around the chapel.

∞

Joe stood in front of the congregation clutching his dead sister. Margaret was staring at her Bible, 'Bingo!' she cried.

'*You mad bastard!!!!*' screamed Neil, sprinting forward and leaping on Joe. The two of them tumbled to the floor, Neil, yellow with rage, bawling, 'you fucking stain, you cloud, you nothing man, you ruined me, you *ruined* me, you… you…'

Joe elbowed Neil in the belly, winding him. It was the old situation; little Neil has worked himself up into a paroxysm. He can't handle anything out of the ordinary and it is again up to

Joe to restrain him. Margaret paid them no attention, she was focused on her 'bingo card'. Louis watched, waiting to intervene. The assembled watched passively on as the brothers fought.

Suddenly, the back doors burst open. All turned as police flooded in. At this point it was hard to tell quite what was going on. Joe had Neil in a headgrip. Neil punched Joe repeatedly in the leg until he let go. Ralf was crying with laughter. Lilly, having rushed onto the stage, and caught Ursula, was tenderly back in her coffin.

'Neil! Please! Chill out!' cried Joe, stumbling back into the 'cult wall' behind him; the mysterious funeral-goers had risen to their feet and were pressing into the police.

Neil, having squirmed his body round, had Joe in a headgrip. '*Chill out!?* You destroy all my relationships, with my mother, with my partner, with the Olympic committee...'

With extraordinary effort, Joe turned his crimson-suffocating head round so it was facing Neil. 'What partner?' he croaks.

'*Her!*' Neil, screeched Neil.

'What!? Who?' Joe's locked head could not see whom his brother was speaking of

'Bingo! Bingo!' Margaret held up her Bible and realised that her two sons were just in front of her, grappling on the floor.

'Patricia!' she cried, 'Let him go!'

'Why? Why? He's a... Fool! A psycho! A... A... *Failure.*'

Margaret got up, dropping her 'bingo card' and pen. Joe and Neil, chastised by their mother, had sort of forgotten about their fight, but they remained in the same position; Joe on his knees in Neil's headlock.

'A failure?' yelled Margaret, over the commotion behind and around her. She stood over them both with her hands on her hips. 'Joe's the most successful person I've ever met.'

'What? What? *Successful!? Him?* You're out of your mind. He's never... He hasn't achieved anything! He's a total and utter loser! He's... He doesn't even *try* to succeed! You used to understand this!'

'He's got a point,' croaked Joe, then turned to Louis. 'Louis old scout, could you give me a bit of hand?'

Louis, who has been standing poised, ready for action, effortlessly pulled Neil from Joe, the latter limping to a pew to steady himself. 'Get Margaret,' Joe said to Louis, 'Take her out. Ralf, help.'

Louis wound Margaret's rope around his fat fist, then, with cold, powerful efficiency, picked up a massive candlestick, and began swiping it left and right, scything his way through the crowd in order to bust out of the Chapel of Rest, through the back door. Ralf, still joyously tittering, pushed away at the backs of the police, angling a pew away from Margaret and Louis to aid their escape and beetling out after them. As Margaret left she said, 'I know these people; that's Auntie May… May…' But Louis dragged her out; 'Later,' he said.

Neil turned again to Joe, but was knocked to his knees by Gordon, an ex-colleague of Neil's, quite happy to give the latter a good drubbing, just for the hell of it. Joe fell on Gordon, but another policeman pulled him off and threw him across one of the pews, prayer books clattering over his head.

Lilly, having dealt with Ursula, rushed forward to help Joe. The whole chapel was now a seething mass of grappling, brawling, people.

'Ah! There you are!' said Joe as she pulled the books from him.

'What's going on?' she cried, kneeling next to him.

'Erm, well, there's a lot going on actually. Neil's being beaten up. I'm going to give him a hand, but,' he ripped a page from a prayer book and handed it to Lilly with the pen now rolling at his feet, 'Give me your number first, before my leg wakes up,' he said. Lilly took the pen and wrote her phone number down, just as a series of explosions begins pounding through the back wall of the chapel.

'Shit, I have to go,' said Lilly, 'I've just blown someone up.'

'Okay, bye!'

'Agggghhh!' cried Neil as he was pulled into the tumult. He could see them talking, Joe and Lilly. He cried out 'Lilly!

Lilly! *Please* come back to me… *Please* help me… *Please, I need someone, anyone…*' But she had gone, skirting back through the rear entrance as Joe took the page, pushed it into his pocket and threw himself into the mad hive, not really sure why, but sure that the stranger people, Ursula's guests after all, needed his help.

Roy Towers, still seated in the same pew, opened his eyes, which had been closed in solemn worshipfulness, slowly straightened his long bony body and, unnoticed, or at least untouched, hobbled past the bundle of bodies and out of the chapel.

∞

Lilly ran down the corridor. She was quite surprised to find she was the kind of person who would sew explosives into a corpse out of pure malevolent instinct. But you never really know until you're standing, with a scalpel and a bag of explosive pacemakers, in front of the body of the man who killed your parents, quite what you'll do.

Meanwhile Maria, mascara running down her tear-streamed face like rivers in hell, was standing at the oven in which Max's body was exploding. She had found her way into the crematorium, through a rear entrance, to watch the one great love of her life explode. The pacemakers that Lilly had sewn into his head and chest had detonated and bits of him were now ricocheting around the oven, his flaming skull bouncing off the observation panel. The head, which had whipped around the inside of the oven and shattered across the jaw, looked back at her, the skin tightening and charring across the bones, the eyeballs melting in the sockets, the cartilage of the nose poking through, gelatinously trembling, then falling away.

She left the room through the back door and wandered off towards the car park. A few moments after this, Lilly entered and took the same position as Maria had, silently before the oven, watching Max burn. She could feel something burning away in her own belly, some kind of weight, which she had been carrying for a long time. She smiled, and as she did so Neil lurched through the doors.

'Lilly,' he said, breathless, floundering against the far wall. She didn't turn, but continued looking into the fire. 'Lilly,' he said, 'Lilly, I've been thinking, you really have to take me back because I am the most person, who, more than anything in the world, anything.' He took a deep shaky breath, aware that his words were tripping over themselves in their rush to get out, 'I'd do anything for you,' he said, 'There is nobody, *ever*, you will never, ever find anyone who is as… *desperate* as me. I know desperation is not a very attractive quality, but… desperation can *help* you. You'll have a slave, a complete slave, who will give you anything you want. You want to be protected? You want money? Stuff? Fun? Lovers? I don't care! I just don't care at *all*, as long as you'll be my girlfriend and let me be your… What are you doing?' Suddenly he stopped. She was turning round, slowly, and something about her, as she faced him, caught him mid-flow. He became afraid. There was some kind of appalling, cold triumph in her eyes. 'Say something,' he squeaked, but she said nothing. 'Please,' he whispered, so quietly that he couldn't hear the word himself.

'You are an empty balloon Neil,' she said quietly. He could feel himself about to faint, the edge of his vision was glowing white. 'I'm going to throw up,' he said, and ran out of the back door.

He staggered towards the Garden of Rest, fell to his knees and vomited next to a patch of Sweet Williams. He then fell forwards, over the bush, clutching flowerless shrubs and grasses, pulling them towards him, scratching at the cold earth. His mouth was open, jaw locked, and he was moaning, a kind of choked-out squinting growl, his face clenched up, an occasional sob, but no tears, no thought either, just a cold, wretched, spasming that seemed to last forever. He wanted to enter the earth, melt into it, the agony was that this was impossible. He could never get *in* to anything, he was always on the surface, the outermost edge of everything, including himself.

As he lay, body pressed into the mud, seemingly random images flashed into his mind; the time his drama teacher *forced* him to play Dorothy in the third-year Wizard of Oz production; a rancid bulb of garlic he'd argued about in the Iranian corner shop; the time he had shit himself in a police department hockey match and waddled off the pitch buttocks clenched; the cardioid microphone he had returned to the shop because of audible hiss; the vegan woman who died in his car…

'You alright son?' Roy Towers was standing over Neil.

Neil didn't move, didn't speak.

'I'm off,' said Roy, 'I'm going to Mexico.'

Still Neil said nothing. He wasn't sure if the voice was coming from inside his body or out of it.

'You should move as well,' said Roy, 'change your environment. You'd be amazed what it can do, if you're stuck, like.'

'I can't move,' said Neil, still face down, talking into the freezing mud.

'Come on son, don't be silly.'

'Leave me alone.'

'One day you'll be glad of all this,' said Roy, quietly, 'one day you'll look back on your whole life, and it will all just… fit. Every time I've been where you are, I've ended up being grateful for it.'

'Leave me alone.'

'Alright son, alright,' Roy patted Neil's shoulder, lightly, shyly, distractedly, and then, still partly hunched over, the old man walked away, never to be seen again.

∞

Joe felt himself fighting an avalanche, and losing, he was slowly submerged by police. Sometimes a hand found him, one of the stranger people, and lifted him up again, or protected him from a blow. Sometimes he was surging forward with them, sometimes falling back. His consciousness, riding on the raft of his mind, swelling on waves of fear and desire, was madly entertained.

More police arrived, kettling the funeral-goers against a side alcove. Just at that moment, Joris burst in to the chapel, his face red and sodden with tears, the only ones he had ever shed or ever would again.

'You! You! Geb! *You!*' he shrieked, his childish voice cutting through the melee like an icy knife. He was standing on a pew, his eyes burning with hatred, stabbing his pale finger at Joe.

Joe, fighting his way through the chaos, looked up. 'Oh, hello again,' he said.

'You! *You!*' screamed Joris, his high-pitched, prepubescent voice skull-piercingly sharp, 'You're dead! You're damned! You're *fiiiiirrrred.*'

PART FOUR
Dreaming Clods

Joe, fourteen, wanders around his dead father's store room. He picks up a primitive sculpture from Oceania, a Man Ray print, a trompe l'oeil etching, a tiny Egyptian sarcophagus, a papyrus scroll and a female mannequin head, made from porcelain. This last object he considers for a moment, then places upon it a three-handed wig from an Inuit totem. It looks ridiculous, the hair is wild and knotted with dried flowers, birds' nests and pine cones, and yet it is also kind of sexy, in a voodoo kind of way.

He goes upstairs to his bedroom, places the mad primitive head at the top of his bed with two pillows underneath. Beneath that he carefully arranges two more pillows, end to end. He then lies on the 'body' and starts humping it, kissing the china head and, hand in trousers, pleasuring himself.

The rocking of the headboard, knocking against the wall, is heard by Neil, getting ready to go on a 10km race walk—he's been training for weeks and today is the regional finals. Neil bursts in on Joe and screams, pointing with triumphant laughter. Joe jumps to his feet and runs after Neil, rugby tackling him in their parent's bathroom, easily overpowering his younger brother. Neil struggles as Joe reaches out, grabbing the first thing to hand—Remington clippers—and shaving Neil, screaming in horror, half bald. Neil tears himself free. 'I hate you,' Neil shrieks, 'I fucking hate you. And mother hates you. And now that father is dead, that means I'm winning!'

Thus half-shaved and apoplectic, Neil runs down into Neville's now empty workshop, grabs one of the guns that Joe spends days at a time murdering birds with, and then runs down to the woods to where Ursula spends most afternoons, swimming in a large woodland pond. Neil gets to the water just as she is emerging, naked, covered in pond-weed, lichen and black mud. He leaps out from the undergrowth and points the gun at her.

Ursula calmly asks Neil what he thinks he is doing and he tells her he is kidnapping her, so she shrugs and says 'alright then,' and follows him to his 'base'—an abandoned pillbox—where she sits, still naked, her pond-shroud now dried and green, but quite relaxed, while Neil paces up and down anxiously.

She asks him why he is kidnapping her. He tells her to shut up. He doesn't know what he is doing. He has a vague idea he will hold Ursula for ransom, but he hasn't got further with this and thinking about it just makes him angry, so he paces up and down the pillbox until late-afternoon shadows have filled the surrounding area and Ursula is starting to shiver. Neil gives up, defeated, and says 'alright, alright, come on, come on, let's go.' Ursula gets up and elegantly walks out. Neil follows, but, as he emerges, a spurt of blood blooms over his trouser leg, just above the knee. He looks down, surprised, and realises he has been shot, pain following on shock.

Joe gets up from his hiding place and waves to Ursula, but she doesn't wave back. She has turned to Neil who has dropped to the floor screaming, 'my leg! my leg! my leg! aaaagghhhhhhhh!'

Joe was dreaming. His dreams had always been intense, surreal, but they were becoming more like science fiction movies written by lunatics on acid; alien lunatics.

He dreamt he was eating a town—half Edding and half some other place nearby—first the sticks, and wildflowers, and stones, and soil on the rural outskirts, then the red, uniform, newbuilds on the greenbelt, then the grotty service stations, builders' yards, desolate roundabouts and squalid, exhaust-stained, suburban sprawl clustered round the megamarts, and finally the offices, smart flats and chain shops of the town centre. Joe ate and ate and ate his way through the whole town. He wasn't massive, munching on whole buildings like croutons, nor was he eating in some sped-up blur; he was just eating one piece of brick at a time, but dream time had concertina'd the monolithic meal into one, leaving him finally, in the middle of nowhere, feeling rather full.

He dreamt he was a gigantic '360° vision' eyeball, set slack in the dead centre of the universe, his 'limbs' a translucent ganglia of light-years long ribbons fluttering away into the furthest reaches of space, getting tangled up in black holes and white giants. He felt like a god, like the one true God, but it was so lonely being God, there was nobody here, so he decided to split himself into two and pretend to himself the other half was the unknown, but when he had done this, and was facing another golden-glowing suneye floating in space, a foreign entity, he became sore afraid.

He dreamt of being his true dinosaur self, romping and flopping on the moons of Jupiter, with the multicoloured mastodons and pterodactyls and stegosauruses of all the other lovers and dreamers and misfits whose worldly existence was partial at best. As they rolled around and lazily fought and made mountain-crushing love and luxuriated in lava pools, an alien tribe of peanut people worshipped them as gods, building obscene shrines to them, towering amphitheatres, bedecked in carved trees, which the dinosaur folk honoured by sleeping in.

He dreamt he was walking around town and could see people in their timeless forms; apparently blending back into all the food, light and experience they 'have had' and apparently flowing out into the infinite events which they think they are 'going to have' but, actually, electromagnetic fractal vibe-ribbons cobwebbing the arboreal multiverse in superluminous strings, tree people whose roots and branches spread into the past and future but which Joe could see out of time; whole, unmoving. Sadly, nobody else could see this, which was why they clung, grimly, to themselves, only Joe, transdimensionally free behind his time-body, could play with his mask, but play with whom?

These epic visions increasingly blended into more troubling dreams. In one, he dreamt of finding his house so funny that he could no longer live in it. He began by chuckling at his plug-in Morphy Richards kettle, smirking at his Ikea place mats and guffawing at the cheap Persian rug in the hallway, went on to full-blown cracked-up laughter at his Beko fridge-freezer, the 'bag of bags' hanging behind the kitchen door and shoe tree in the hall. Everything in his house made him laugh but the laughter was hollow, empty of delight, like sneezing with broken ribs, which got worse and worse until he threw himself from his ground floor window, repelled from his house by the agonising hilarity of it and afraid to return, because it was just too funny.

In another, he dreamt an ancient civilisation had made him from cheese, then stored him deep underground for many thousands of years, where he could ferment and mature, until he was ready to be brought up to the world, and everyone could eat his delicious 'cheese body.' They, the cultish celebrants, were joyous, but 'cheese Joe' was horrified, watching them slice bits of him off, spread him on toasted thins and eat him with figs and quince jam.

Perhaps the most horrible dream of all involved getting home from work with a netted bag of onions, opening up his food cupboard and realising that he already had a full bag of onions. He looked from the bag of onions in his hand to the bag of onions in the cupboard and then back again, and thought to himself, 'we've just got too many onions.' He'd woken up in a cold sweat after that one.

Now he is dreaming that he is sitting in an empty room on a rocking chair. The house, which both belongs to him and doesn't belong to him, is empty, as if it is brand new; except for one large, new, cheap pine wardrobe and a row of many-paned casement windows, one of which breaks, smashed by a stone which lands on the floor. Joe gets up and, ignoring the stone, opens the wardrobe which is full of overcoats, takes one, puts it on and sits down again. Then another pane breaks; another stone bouncing off the floor, wind rattling through the cracked pane. Again, Joe gets up and puts on an overcoat, and again another stone shatters another pane, then another, then another, until Joe, who has stood up after each one to put on another layer, is crammed into his rocking chair, wearing fifteen? twenty? thirty? overcoats. Wind rips through the house. More stones fly into the room, bouncing off the woollen pupa he has become.

Finally, a stone hit him in the head.

Joe's sleeping brow had banged against the railing of the bus seat he was sitting in. He woke, surrounded by deflated shadows, workers, all on their way to Duat, the multinational online e-commerce company, one of whose warehouses, or 'satisfaction centres', had just been built outside Edding and which had only the day before reached the strange and troubling conclusion that they should hire Joe Geb who was now, at eleven at night, on the company bus to start his first shift.

The comfortless people-carrier rumbled through the dark countryside, westwards towards the dead sun. Joe took a deep, deep breath and held it… and held it… until a creaky, strained whine came from the back of his throat. An Arab wearing a baseball cap, sitting on the other side of the aisle with a book on his knees, was looking up at Joe, annoyance wrinkling his features.

'Why are you doing that?' he asked, more of an accusation than a question.

Joe let the air out in a noisy gush. 'Why not?'

'Because it is not normal.'

'You're happy with normal?'

The man sighed and held up the book he had been reading. 'Have you ever read the holy Koran?'

'Have you?'

'Yes,' said the man, piqued.

'Have you *heard* of it?'

Joe could barely make out the man's dark head in the night. It bobbed around in the thin overhead coach light. The shadows across his face looked tired and angry. 'What?' said the man 'What are you talking about? I'm trying to give you some advice, for your life.'

'But why?'

'Look, you are sad…'

'I'm not.'

'Yes, yes you are.' The man was trying to be patient.

'No, I'm not. I'm not sad, I'm not angry, I'm not even bored. I'm just a bit disappointed,' said Joe, drily.

'But this is only your first day.'

'Not with the job, with reality. It's just not good enough. It doesn't meet my standards.'

The man jerked his chin upwards, triumphantly, 'Then you should lower your standards.'

'I prefer to raise reality.'

Joe's smartphone beeped. He took it out, the screen brightly proclaimed, 'Gypster! Are you available to degrade yourself? Yes

/ No.' He selected 'no' and returned to the conversation, but the Arab's soul was again buried, in The Book.

The bus pulled up to a colossal unmarked warehouse, the size of a small town, surrounded by high fencing which was topped with coils of razor wire. It was pouring, puddles everywhere shuddering under shining sheets of rain, bright yellow, like showers of sparks in the deathless LED spotlights. A sodden queue of hunched forms waited before the cramped, humid gatehouse where guards pushed them through a metal detector, patted them down, searched them, and stood them on scales which displayed their precise weight.

Aggressive dogs were everywhere, dark-snouted Alsatians barking and snarling in the gatehouse, and in the 'forbidden zone' between the gatehouse and the building proper, which was an almost unimaginably large, white, oblong of fibreglass, steel and corrugated plastic. It was so smooth, so rectilinear, so monumentally ordered that Joe, who occasionally felt ill standing next to large, modern buildings, was overcome with a nauseating feeling of oppressive heaviness, a kind of 'ground-floor vertigo,' as if the featureless, monochrome cliff were not just pressing down on him, but filling him, making him dense, and grotesquely real.

He waited in the queue before the gatehouse, rivulets of rain trickling from every fold of his coat. A long, thin, emaciated man shuffled out, after having been weighed and searched, and passed Joe. His face was devoid of both life and death; he looked like he didn't exist. Joe turned to watch him slosh over to the car park where a car was waiting, an extremely old Ford. An old woman got out, weeping, and cradled the man, wiping his brow.

The queue got shorter. As Joe neared the gatehouse a taxi arrived and a man, covered in blood, stumbled out. He half-ran, limping, splashing, up to one of the guards, a small ginger man with face that looked like it had been stretched at the ears into a pale, rubbery mask of smugness.

'What happened to you?' said the guard without interest.

'I've been involved in a road-accident,' the man wheezed.

'Go home.'

'I can't. I'll be pointed.'

'Your shift started four hours ago. You'll be pointed anyway.'

'Please let me in. *Please.*'

The guard shrugged and let the man through to the metal detectors. Joe turned back to look at the Ford. The old woman was feeding Pepsi-Cola to the tall man by filling up the bottle top and pouring it into his mouth, like he was some kind of lanky baby bird.

Each person, as they entered the gatehouse, showed a pass badge, which was scanned by one of the guards. They were then weighed and given a thin silver neck band with a little light on the pendant side. Joe had no badge, and so was taken aside, where his name was checked off a visitor's book. He was then weighed and patted down, given a blue square badge to pin to his sweatshirt, and allowed to pass over the no-man's-land to the entrance of the warehouse, over which a sign, in large friendly yellow and black letters, read 'Work Makes Play.'

Joe pushed through doors and portals until he reached the inside of the warehouse proper, an unimaginably large, cavernous space, bleak and poorly lit, the only natural light coming from slit-like windows high, high up in the vast open spaces, at least by day. Everywhere else, at all hours, was bathed in a yellowish glow from grey steel lamps which hung from the ceilings.

Joe caught a glimpse of the principal work bay, in which colossal towers of *stuff* stretched away into a black vanishing point, seemingly miles away. The massive scale of the chamber, the minuteness of the people scurrying around the towers, was overwhelming, terrifying. It was a place, Joe felt, which not only should not, but *did* not, belong in this universe.

A thimble-headed man, looking anxiously around, as if scanning the warehouse for a wild animal, wearing a luminous red triangular badge and, like everyone else, carrying a glowing tablet, stopped Joe with a peremptory-yet-distracted 'no badge; in there, second door on the right,' directing him towards a heavy pair of doors which opened onto a more brightly lit yellow corridor, the yellow and black walls and carpet of which were 'branded' with diagonal lines and blurred triangles, which, Joe found, was extremely disorienting, not to mention creepy, as if it had all been designed deliberately to mess with his depth of field. He half closed his eyes and let himself be led by instinct.

Through 'the second door on the right' Joe found himself in a standard, bland, corporate training room, large, hot, airless and smelling of antibacterial surface spray. Around the edge of the yellow and black walls, which were covered with various colourful motivational posters ('Fun will set you free!' 'Physically many, emotionally one!' 'Sublimate anxiety!'), were chairs and tables, pushed away from a centre, in which a semicircle of twenty-five trainees—twelve men and thirteen women; a motley crew of immigrants and ne'er-do-wells—were standing around awkwardly. A small, dark-eyed, woman, neat-featured and every bit the manageress, stood in front of the group, nervously tapping her fingers on her folded forearms. When Joe drifted in, she said, with some annoyance, 'okay, good that's everyone,' and then started her speech, many times recited but breathless and tremulous, like a too-confident thirteen-year-old girl whose imitation of bright surety masks existential darkness.

'Good evening associates! Welcome to the Duat satisfaction centre. I'm Claire Baqri and I worship the customer.' Her voice was squeaky, chipper, condescending, awkward and, at the same time, wilfully cold. 'Now I know what you're probably thinking,' she went on, '"woah! Where *am* I?" It's all new and exciting, I know, I know, believe me *I know;* I've been there, a blue badge, just like you gu… people.'

We people. Yes, the other trainees were all wearing the same glowing blue badges. Only Claire had a red star pinned to her blouse.

'But um, listen,' she said, 'we don't have much time, so let's crack on shall we! Huddle up, huddle up!'

She bent forward and arced her hands, gesturing everyone to hunch down together with her. Most of the trainees reluctantly linked arms. A few just vaguely squatted down.

'Come on! Come on!' She broke off and stepped back. 'Right,' she said, tight-lipped, insinuating that we must 'get something straight from the start'.

'Now,' she said with world-weary patience, 'the first thing we *all* have to learn is participation and teamwork. Anyone who… If you don't… If you're not team-playing—we call this "solo-boating"—then you lose a point. Lose ten points and we don't renew your contract… *for tomorrow*.' She whispered the last two words, then spoke 'confidently' again. 'So let's… Come on… Let's work together here…'

She bent over again, and again everyone huddled down, this time with a little more enthusiasm.

'Now,' she said, 'after me, "we are not one of them!"'

The group repeated the slogan mechanically; 'We are not one of them.'

'Points people, points,' she said, face now reddening with enthusiasm, 'With spirit. All together. "We are not one of them!"'

'We are not one of them,' said the group, with, in lieu of enthusiasm, volume.

'We are us.' Claire said.

'We are us.'

'We are us!' she cried.

'We are us!' everyone said loudly; while Joe, at a volume which didn't quite fully make it into anyone's awareness, said; 'I am a porcupine.'

Claire's brows wrinkled. Something wasn't right. Someone had said something non-standard, although who or what was not clear. 'Okay,' she said, 'One more time, and this time break and group hug! Ready… We are us! Yay!'

'We are us!' they all put their arms around each other.

'I am a lasagne,' said Joe and stuck his hand out for a formal greeting.

Claire stood back, not impressed. She tapped away at her tablet. 'I'm afraid that's one point deducted already Joe Geb. There's humour, and there's cynicism. Do you know the difference?'

'Is it the same difference as between the kiss you plant on your grandmother's cheek and the pillage of India by the British Raj?'

Claire sighed. 'Humour is "we are us", cynicism is "I am them". Do you see?'

'Yes, I think so.'

'Good, okay, now, points. You're probably all wondering how you can lose points, and how you can gain them. As I say, you can lose *ten* points before we release you. You lose points for not hitting your productivity rates, which we call 'prods', for uncouth behaviour, for taking extended breaks, for cynical attitudes and solo-boating,' she gave Joe a significant look, 'for arriving late and leaving early, for gaining weight, for transphobia, anti-Semitism, rape, disagreeing with management, cultural appropriation, sexualised staring, irony, excessive use of metaphor and not wearing a funny T-shirt on Fridays...'

She raised her eyebrows to Joe. He looked around. Everyone was indeed wearing an 'amusing' T-shirt.

'Perhaps I didn't get that memo,' he said, pronouncing 'memo' 'mee-mo.'

'It's okay Joseph, there are some spares over there.' Joe turned round, hesitating. 'Go on,' said Claire.

He walked over to a shelf with piles of T-shirts on. He looked through them and chose one with a pair of hairy ape breasts across the front, pulling it over his sweatshirt and reattaching his badge. He then returned to the group, conscious of the fact that Claire had had to stop for *him* and everyone was waiting for *him*.

'Anyway, the full list is in the staff room. Also, don't get ill. Ever. If you're going to be ill you need to phone in two weeks in advance to let us know. You still lose points though.'

She looked around again, mustering up confidence and defiance, but there was a gleam of fear in her eyes. Fortunately, nobody expressed dissent, even subtly.

'Probably the most important thing though,' she said, 'is not hitting your prod rates. You *must* find and fulfil the requisite number of orders or, at the end of the hour, your prod collar will deliver a mild electric *reminder*. Just a prod—just to remind you.'

She walked over to the side of the room and returned with a canvas bag, full of see-through plastic pouches containing a digital tablet and one of the slender silver collars that Joe had seen everyone—everyone with a blue badge—wearing. She handed them around.

'The collars are paired up with your tablets, which tell you where to pick up your orders, what your prod rate is, how many points you have, when your next toilet break is and how much you weigh. Remember everything that goes into and out of your body is weighed, and if there's any discrepancy when you leave, you'll be pointed. The reason for this is that Duat cares about you, which is why we've teamed up with LifeLine to monitor your health, on an ongoing basis. Your tablets will let you know your energy levels, your emotional state, where you are on your cycle and which muscles need stretching. You can take the tablets home, although they remain company property and if they get lost or damaged you'll be pointed or arrested. Now, collar-up.'

Everyone put their collars on. A glum, three-chinned woman with thin blond hair held her collar limply in her hand. She was tremendously overweight, but the fat was distributed strangely over her body, like she'd stuffed newspaper into her leggings. 'I have a heart condition,' she said.

'Sorry, but you did sign a waiver when you accepted the job. You can leave now, or, at your own risk, continue working.'

'I'll… It's okay… I'll…,' she said, and awkwardly put the collar on. It bit into the wet, doughy flesh of her neck.

'Don't worry,' said Claire, 'you only get *reminded* if you do something wrong. People who are innocent have nothing to fear.'

Joe too hesitated, but he too clicked the collar around his neck. Can't be all that bad, be thought, a little electric shock now and then. Might even liven up proceedings.

'Sorry,' said Claire, 'but we've got a lot to get through.' She checked her watch. 'It's already eleven forty-five and I want you on the floor by one.'

She had the habit, common amongst managerly managers and teacherly teachers, of assuming that those she had been charged to lead were motivated by a desire to please either her — 'you've really impressed me', 'you've really disappointed me' — or their own hidden 'higher self' — 'you've really let yourself down', 'you should be proud of yourselves'. That both were of zero interest to most of the trainees didn't occur to her, so she automatically and, given her base assumptions, quite logically assumed that they had 'no respect', either for 'her' or for 'themselves'. Fortunately though, Claire had all the power, which is absolutely necessary to deal with 'people with no respect', and could guide them through the extensive training, out into the big, wide world of 'history-making wish fulfilment on a global scale' and up to a condition of maturity, in which the proper degree of respect comes naturally, as it does for all decent people.

෫

Work began. People were sprinting around the immense space, pushing large trolleys, each one overloaded with tottering boxes, or 'totes'. The harried workers would glance from their tablets to one of the towers of consumer goods, check the name of the aisle, and then disappear into one of the interminable trenches that ran the length of the warehouse. When they had found the precise location of the item they required — aisle R4, column 122, shelf 44 — the wall and the shelf, reading their presence, would automatically slide forwards and down so they could scan the object, place it in their totes and run on to the next order.

This was the noble task of the blue-badged 'pick monkey.' When the tote was filled it would be loaded onto one of the conveyor belts which snaked through the factory, where it would trundle down to the loading bay and the items passed on to the 'pack monkeys,' wearing green badges, some of whom boxed up goods to send out to the customers, others unpacked products that came in from manufacturers. Packing was considered preferable to picking as there was somewhat less time-pressure and most of the task—labelling, boxing and unboxing—took place in one location, not running around at a murderous pace like the blue boys.

Joe, a blue boy, wasn't running around. He was strolling, taking in the novel experience of more literally living inside a machine than he had imagined was possible, and inspecting with interest the various items his tablet had told him to pick up. His boxes included such things as: a Nick Cage pillowcase, a rubber horse lamp, a BDSM colouring book, a Victorian doghouse, a portable pizza case, a can of spray-on stripclub, whatever that was, and a disposable pet-grooming fork. All of these wondrous objects were destined to be delivered to one 'Victor Perry.'

Joe picked up a 'Bag of Knuckles,' a plastic blister pack of realistic latex finger joints. On the back was written, in crude letters, 'MAD MAD 狂,' apparently with a Sharpie. What did it mean? I am mad? This object is mad? This factory is mad? This world is mad? Probably all four. I too am mad, thought Joe; but then I'm glad with it. Perhaps that's the difference. The half-dead slave who made this is not glad. If the world could be joyous in its madness, it would be sane. A wave of misery passed through him as he held the box, united in grief with the poor creature who made the bag of knuckles.

Suddenly he winced with pain; a *'pvoum'* and a shock-giving bright yellow glow had pulsed from his collar.

'Agh. *Twat!*'

☙

Victor, wearing nothing but a pair of Vladimir-Putin-embroidered underpants, was laid out in his inner sanctum, patiently attaching himself to a fungal bush of electrodes. He now had the solution; a digital virus which would sufficiently destabilise The Bubble, stun it. It would still float around, but it would be decaying from within, like a peccary shot with a poison-tipped arrow, only a matter of time before it dropped, or popped. Victor was ready to launch the virus, but, just to be sure, he had spent three days and nights charging himself up with divine energy, beamed down from the planet Arcturus. He would send the virus out into the World Brain and, at the same time, he would channel unimaginably powerful torrents of pure spiritual power into the machine-body.

∾

Joe pulled at his collar. The tablet beeped loudly: 'Warning,' said the large friendly letters, 'Removal of productivity collar will result in three points deduction!' A cute little teddy bear underneath the words had its paw over its mouth, with a little speech bubble which said 'oopsy doopsy!'

A squat, fat, balding, large-mouthed, large-eared, large-nosed manager, not unlike a goblin, walked past the end of Joe's aisle, tenderly and jealously stroking his red badge. He also wore a gay-pride rainbow badge and an anti-fascist arm-band. On hearing the beep from Joe's collar he snapped out of his reverie and growled to no one in particular 'Come on guys! Move it! Move it! Let's go! We are us! We're all in it together!'

At the other end of Joe's aisle, a woman collapsed. The red-badge ignored her. Joe started trotting down to help her, but another electric shock and another warning from the cute bear, 'don't leave your route Joey-bones!' stopped him. As he considered tearing the necklace off to help the crumpled woman, a buggy drew up alongside her and two men in white hazmat suits lifted her onto the back of it. It was hard to believe all this was actually happening, that it was real, but if this wasn't real, what was? It's easy to answer that question when you're outside the machine, but when you're inside, it's *all* inside.

By the end of his first shift, Joe was three more points down for dawdling. The prospects didn't look good, but perhaps, he thought, as his tablet buzzed him with a 'decreased blood glucose' warning, a little food would perk him up, so, as his fellow workers shuttled past him, he strolled down to the work canteen, another massive room of inhuman proportions, organised with factory precision to process the operatives as quickly as possible. A series of hollow, rapid, thumping, beat-heavy pop songs played, presumably to hurry along the input of energy, 'cheerfully' encourage everyone to eat a bit more quickly.

Blue and green badges—'people', as were—were eating at a furious rate, stuffing stodge into their mouths and swallowing it, half chewed, grimacing with indigestion, burping, nobody caring, rushing over to towering trolleys on which trays were deposited, and sprinting away. Joe took a plate of beans, a mound of mash and a couple of pale sausages from the frosty-looking tank-like women serving, and seated himself at a table of people furiously shovelling chips and breaded chicken wings down their throats. Joe, eating at a normal pace, turned to a swarthy, hungry-eyed Hungarian man, who was sitting next to him slurping away at his weak coffee.

'I wonder what this is', said Joe, spearing his half-eaten sausage which appeared to be made of some kind of playdough.

Nobody spoke. He put the sausagething down. Try another approach or give up?

'Have you ever been slightly tired?' he asked the man.

'Uh?' said the Hungarian, Zoltan, not looking up.

'I was just wondering if you've ever been a bit tired?'

The man looked up, then back down at his food, brows knitted in what could be anger, confusion or dyspepsia.

A moony Bulgarian girl, Denitsa, turned to Joe. Her smooth skin was pinched in confusion at his improbable presence. 'Why are you working here?' she asked, speaking, like everyone else, between hurriedly-chewed mouthfuls.

'My chickens don't want me in the house during the day.'

'But you are English. You could be weather man or own carpet shop or do media-studies degree.'

'I don't think there's much difference,' said Joe.

She seemed to understand. 'All jobs hell,' she said, 'even good one.'

'I wonder why. Strange isn't it? Nobody wants this world, and yet here we all are taking care of it.'

A limp Chinese man, Jianjun, joined in.

'Money,' he said sourly, 'everything *money*.'

A Serbian woman, Nada, said the problem was greed, and then a beautiful Congolese woman, Mercy, disagreed and said that the real problem was the immigrants.

Zoltan looked up, his wasted eyes hot dark holes, 'No,' he said, trembling with emotion, 'the problem is the machine. It is the machine which turns the whole world into a boring prison. It is the machine which breaks up families and forces them to emigrate. It is the machine which gives billions to a fragment of a brain-stem and takes everything away from the whole body. It is the machine which drives us out of our minds, or into our minds, because we must become machines to fit into it. Politicians serve the machine, nature serves the machine, money serves the machine, children serve the machine, everyone, we all serve the machine. Nobody can go against the machine. Nobody. Look at us, just look, we have become machine monkeys, ingesting our fuel, pressing our buttons, watching the screen.' His face seemed to be on fire with a passion that was eating him away. All around the table had stopped eating while he spoke, but they started up again as soon as he released them from his quiet grip.

Everyone's collars buzzed at once and they yelped in fear and pain. Their tablets began flashing at the same time. Joe's said 'This is not a positive topic of conversation. Please change it. Here are some suggestions: the US election, the sweets you used to eat when you were young, the match last night...'

Denitsa turned to Nada and said, voice laden with sarcasm and misery, 'did you see the match last night?'

Joe had read that Duat were developing some kind of brain implant that could interrupt 'negative thoughts', such as 'I hate working here and I wish I could die', and replace them with 'positive thoughts', such as 'I've heard the next Snow White will be a man'. Until then they'd have to use these crude collars.

'What are you doing here?' Joe asked Zoltan tentatively, 'you sound like you should be leading a cult or writing your erotic memoires.'

'I came to England seven years ago and worked at this place when they were just starting out. Then I went to college, then to university, I got a degree in philosophy, then a Ph.D., then I wrote a thousand-page metaphysics of existence, and then I came back here.'

'That's interesting.'

'Only when it's over,' said Zoltan. 'All pain is pleasure to look back on, all pleasure is pain.'

They all hurriedly shared their stories, as they hoovered down their food. Denitsa was a concert violinist who, poor and unable to support her family, had been lured over to wealthy England by posters of Prince William and Harry Potter. Nada, although Serbian, had grown up in Romania under Ceauşescu which she had escaped from, with her family, crossing the Danube in the middle of the night while being shot at by the Romanian secret police, then from Serbia they had come to England, for a 'better life'. Mercy had escaped a civil war, in which half of her family had been killed, worked for two years in London as a prostitute, then came to work at Duat, although she wasn't sure if whoring wasn't better. Jianjun had left China out of sheer boredom and didn't mind it at all because he said it was all like this everywhere. He seemed to be half-dead.

The conversation turned to the cupboards they stored their bodies in when their shifts were over, or 'home' as it was once called; how nobody had one, and how this, combined with the Duat shift schedule made everyone act with a kind of desperate lack of interest when work was over. Zoltan said that he'd had a

Bird's Eye Roast Chicken Dinner for breakfast, Jianjun said he no longer washed his socks because after two weeks they went solid, then they softened again and the smell went away, and Nada said that her kids no longer recognised her.

A raw digital siren tore through the canteen. It sounded like nothing on earth, and yet also, at least to Joe, as if Duat itself was speaking, a bit-crushed scream of absolute, terror-inducing, hatred for humanity; except it wasn't 'hatred', because it was without feeling. A computer had determined that such a sound was the most useful, it produced the desired effect, and so that was the sound that had been used. It was painful, but it was far more painful for thousands of customers not to get their stuff on time, so the agonising siren was 'better', or 'fairer', which were euphemisms for absolute ruthlessness. Perhaps Zoltan was right. People sometimes said that 'technology is neutral', but the world as a whole is absolutely ruthless, and that's because it is, as a whole, a kind of machine, which is probably why only ruthlessness ever succeeds in it. You can do what you like with individual machines, but you have to be ruthless to fit into *the* machine, or you have to submit to its ruthlessness, which everyone does, until being ruthless begins to seem natural.

Everyone leapt to their feet and rushed towards the swing-doors for another session of frantic, thing-harvesting, hurtling horror; managers barking upbeat slogans, pick monkeys rushing around, harried faces occasionally sweeping past each other on their way to the next shelf, clanking machinery, forklift trucks and conveyor belts chugging an endless stream of yellow plastic totes and boxes through the warehouse, overhead and then outside to the lorries.

By five in the morning Joe had given up and was wandering around the satisfaction centre quietly and tunelessly humming to himself. The collar occasionally shocked him and he winced, but it was only once an hour and wasn't so bad. He had already resigned himself to getting the sack, so why not enjoy the rest of the time?

Trolley half-full, he sauntered up to his next pickup on a lower shelf. It was a tent in the shape of a baboon's arse. He picked it up and, just as he did, a bizarre feeling shot through his chest, as if he had been hit from within by lightning.

∞

Juice was humming through the mind-knotting system Victor had rigged up, flowing outwards through the fractal mass of his plastic packed house, the inside of which now felt like it was being lifted, hovering on a bone-glowing field of geomantic energy. The virus had been released, the channel opened to Arcturus, the heavenly host summoned. It was now time to strike. He was lying flat on his back, hands crossed across his chest, clutching a hook and flail, eyes closed, chanting in Coptic Greek, body burning from the inside with superintense energy, a divine fire, an ekpyrotic charge which built up and up, more and more intense—yet contained, bounded by the bodily form of Victor Perry—until, bursting its limit, it detonated, a cascading air-igniting blast firing a root-like web of white light outwards, spidering through the gryphon nest of fangled trumperies he had built around him, and out into the grand panjandrum which it modelled and masked.

∞

The lights went out in Duat. All electricity down. Confusion at first, followed by shouts and screams. Silence, then more cries; names, questions. Zahra? Mario? What's going on? Managers started barking orders but doing nothing because the unexpected was someone else's job. Joe groped his way to the end of the alley he was in towards a cluster of lights which had appeared. Someone had found a box of battery-powered fairy lights and had handed them out. Dark forms in the distance, now wrapped in pink, yellow and green flashing wires, stood around talking

337

quietly, waiting for the event to pass. People from ex-communist countries were least concerned, at least outwardly They knew that it was vain to struggle, but Joe could feel the inner mood in the darkness was on edge, as if everyone were collectively tensing up for a blow, and the blow was not long in coming. The lights flicked on, then off, then a weird high-pitched whine drilled through the skull. It sounded as if all the energy which fed the building was being fed back into itself. The lights sizzled on and off once more, the pick monkeys looked around at each other questioningly, the whine became more and more intense; and then, at once, everything exploded everywhere.

The lights burst in a shower of splintered fluorescent tubes as a series of fires flared into smoky being at the endpoints of the aisles. Screams were heard, torchlight cut the blackness and fairy-light-shrouded ghosts flew past Joe. A wave of knowledge and opportunity had passed though the floor-walkers, the un-spoken criminal instinct of slaves everywhere realising, as one, that the masters have failed, fallen or fled. Get out, and take what you can as you go.

Joe grabbed the tent along with a furry top hat and a few other items nearby, and ran into the diabolic labyrinth of shad-ows. Clouds of black smoke, blacker than blackness, were rolling down the firelit aisles now. He turned into the main central section of the warehouse and headed alongside the dull gleam of the main conveyor-belt complex, towards the east bay doors, flame-light dancing off the steel shelves and barriers. Howls and bellows echoed around the hellish cavern, torchlight, firelight and fairy-light made it possible to see one's way out, but a fierce, infernal panic had gripped everyone, disorienting them. The machine had stopped.

Joe, wearing the top hat now, looked north and south up and down the aisles. It didn't look like anyone was being left behind. A few had fallen, but they were being helped down towards the loading bay and the way out, but here too, the forbidden zone in which the lorries came and went, all was chaos. It was still dark and pouring with rain. Prod collars and tablets lay in the rain-gunned mud, uselessly buzzing alerts. People were climbing over the compound gates, rushing through the guardhouse, all carrying boxes. A few security guards were trying to stop them, and the goblin-like red-badge manager, stuck in the mass, was squealing like a pig, with his fat fingers in some poor Bangla's eye sockets, but, as Joe approached, a plastic shoe-expander flew out of nowhere and smacked the manager on the side of the head. Most of the guards had joined the free-for-all and were either pulling their colleagues away from the blue-badges or charging towards the car park.

In the middle of all this, under the slanting rain, stood tiny Claire, wet hair straggling round her distorted face.

'All of you!' she screamed, 'Back inside at once! You're all pointed. You—*you*—pointed. Dentista! Three points for you… no, four…! Everyone… Ungrateful *fuckbags*…! We *will* deal with you! The system don't forget!'

Joe ran through the storms and madness. Passing a lorry he turned to face a dog, growling for the pounce. He edged back and nudged an abandoned box of swingball poles. By the time he'd bent down to arm himself with one the dog had leapt. Crying out in shock and fear, Joe stabbed the pole at the dog, striking its neck. The dog, landing oddly, whelped and ran away.

Joe, tent under one arm, swingball pole in the other, moved on warily, gladiatorially. The throng at the gatehouse, loaded down with water filters, digital cameras, laptops and expensive moisturisers, had broken down the doors and pushed aside the full-body scanners, clearing a path to freedom. Joe, just before he was absorbed into the mass, saw Zoltan pulling an industrial pressure washer. Then Jianjun briefly rose above the mass, cheerfully waving a box of Ferrari socks. Before Joe could call to them, he was carried out into the car park.

He ran. The hills called.

Joe walked for nearly an hour. The sun was still below the horizon, stifled winter light greyed the green of the sodden fields he trudged across. Carrying his boxes and bags, he climbed over a stile and into a cow field. The cows watched him slash aimlessly through the long grass, then one of them mooed and Joe had the sense that it was an approving moo. He climbed over another stile and into another field, this one full of sheep which trotted away from him, baaing, although not approving these, sarcastic baas, either aimed at him, of perhaps in derisive imitation of each other.

Through a third and fourth field, and then an empty meadow until he came to a low, long hill, unnaturally regular, nestled on the edge of a woodland spinney; probably an old burial mound. He crossed a little stream and climbed the slope—it was just over a storey high. Plumes of smoke were rising in the west from beyond the horizon as a tabletop mountain of tools and games and clothes and trinkets went up in flames. Joe could feel a split, somewhere in the diaphragm of the world, a crack, through which something horrible poked, something which shouldn't be there. Reality had just had a hiatus hernia.

Joe erected the baboon's arse tent and unwrapped the sleeping bag he had stolen, but it was far too small—a child's bag. He crawled into the tent, pulled the little bag up as far as he could, up to about his ribs, and fell asleep immediately.

∞

Dressed in a leather belt and triangular loincloth Joe stands on the prow of an Egyptian longboat, a solar barque, looking out over a desolate, watery vista of islands, pools and reeds. From this bleak landscape an island-sized lotus bud emerges whose petals open to reveal a huge blazing cow, which rises up to the heavens, a fiery human eye between its horns. The cowgod's head fills the heavens, weeping, from its third eye, flaming people, which rain down to the earth, fire-bright godlings which, as they reach the waters, set it too aflame. The fire-people melt joyously into the now blazing waters, forming a roaring choir of angels, singing an ecstatic choral hymn of praise, a language which Joe does not know, but yet understands, he knows the joy and the all-rupturing choral gratitude, as if he too had once sung it, or written it. Yes, it is his own song…

But then he realises that something is wrong, a note of sorrow has entered the melody. He senses the weeping cow eye above is strained, in pain, and its tears are no longer of joy but of sorrow and then of misery. The immense eye is burning itself out, the fires guttering and going out, until it is dark and carbonised, husk-like, exhausted and the tears are also burnt out, charred human forms, dust, barely held together, drifting down not to a fiery ocean of heavenliness, but a smoking, choking hill of ashes, broken forms, like burnt matches, crawling over each other, snapping off powdery limbs and eating them. A cinder heap of tomb-people, wept from eye of death.

'Haven't you had enough yet?' Joe turns to a familiar voice behind him. Ursula, naked in a deck-chair, looks up at him. It is dark now, just the vaguest ember-gleam illuminates her beautiful pale face and large, clear blue eyes.

'I think I have, yes.'

'Then why don't you come home?'

'Isn't this home?'

'What do you think?'

Her blue eyes seem to glow under her blonde brows, like the distant skies of dawn.

'Where is home then?' asks Joe.

'The Fields of Aaru. In the East. I am there. We are all already there.'

'What do you do there?'

'Ecstatic groupmind-dissolving chanting rituals, improvised theatre, electro-funk jams, epic fooling around and ten-thousand god-years of divine fucking. Mostly we devote the day to doing whatever we want, taking care of ourselves, our friends, building, hunting, and playing on the great stage of life; but all this blends into neverending worship of the unnameable.'

'Do you have Netflix?'

'I think someone's got a Nintendo.'

'It sounds great.'

'We live reborn,' she says, with quiet seriousness. 'The body of man is sick and ruined, choking on the poison of his own world, reduced to a kind of savagery, living under the ruins of a dead planet. But the past has been blasted from us, the filter over our senses has been torn away. To the people of this world, how we live would seem to be worse than medieval, but, actually, we live in paradise. We have our pain and suffering, but we love them, because they no longer control us. Nothing controls us, and so we can make use of everything. We are free.'

Joe sighs. 'It sounds great. It does. The problem is… my leg. It just won't let me.'

'Your leg won't let you because your mind won't let you.'

'My mind lets me do anything.'

'But it won't let you *be* anything. It drifts over the flesh of life like a shadow without a body.' Ursula's beautiful form is becoming clearer. Joe can feel a new light glimmering on his back.

'But it's always thinking new things,' he protests.

'It's not *what* it's thinking,' says Ursula, wrapping her long legs under her, 'it's *that* it's thinking.'

'Mmm. Ahh.'

'How can you be open to real possibilities you've not thought about, if you're thinking?' she asks.

'I never thought I'd be talking to my dead sister in a buried solar barque.'

Joe feels sweat prickling at his neck. His back is hot. Ursula now is fringed with pink light; perhaps the sun has risen again. He turns. The sun is there, but it appears to be behind a bright pink plastic sheath which is letting in heat but not air, suffocating the world. Joe suddenly feels a desperate need to get out, to rip away this unnatural pink sky and let the air in. He goes to turn back to Ursula, but can't move, the plastic sky has shrunk around his wet, sweaty, desperate body. He is engulfed in a hot, smothering film. He tries to call out, but can't. Fear grips him, he will die, a pink, plastic mummy. One last push, he thinks, one last, total burst of energy…

…and he awoke, cocooned in a sweaty child's sleeping bag, inserted into a cramped baboon's arse. He sat up, tore open the tent door and sucked in lung-filling chugs of cool morning air. The sun had risen, behind thin smoky-grey clouds, which lay in the cups of the undulating land like evaporating rose milk. The hazy tree-fringed hills, rising from the mist, looked like shadow-puppet backdrops.

Joe was mortally thirsty, so he staggered down to the stream at the base of the hill and drank greedily, splashing his face and neck cool, then went back up to the tent which, he could now see in the light, was surrounded with flowers, strewn over the hill: lilies, white roses, showy peony, cosmos, chrysanthemum and a choir of Star of Bethlehem. An oak, which had managed to root itself on the mound, threw its branch-shadows over the entrance to the tent where he now sat on his rolled-up sleeping bag and, rummaging around in his pockets, pulled out a Brazil nut, his notebook, a bookie's pencil, a Hello Kitty pencil sharpener, a Vitamin D tablet and his phone, before finding what he was looking for, a scrap of paper ripped from the Bible. He wrote down 'Fields of Aaru.' Then he turned the paper round. On the back was Lilly's phone number that he had written down at Ursula's funeral.

Oh yes, Ursula's funeral. He should have brought that up with her. In fact there were a few questions he now remembered he wanted to ask his dead sister, but dreams have their own demands. He wanted to know, practically, what he could do to get back to the unreflective immersion he had, until Ursula's death, freely enjoyed. A distance, between himself and what was happening had, like the clingfilm he had just dreamt of, pulled itself down over his experience, separating him from the quality of the world. Perhaps that was the 'filter' she had spoken of? He still enjoyed lifting up paving stones and watching cheeselogs, he still enjoyed dripping cream into his tomato soup to the rhythm of Curtis Mayfield's Superfly, he still extracted satisfaction from seeing how loud an interrogative 'mmm?' could be—and he had also added some Ralfic 'SF' to his daily pleasures, getting pleasure from reading zero-star reviews of woked-up movies and watching people navigate bizarrely shaped stairs—but somehow he was no longer part of all this, he had become slightly detached, slightly knowing, slightly professional, slightly smirkful, as if the freer movements of his life were not experiences to be, but things to have, and name, and know. He even found himself thinking as boring people do, the kind who package up interesting experiences into a label; 'that's so funny,' 'that's so strange,' 'that's so witty,' and so on, unable to respond to his life by living it, only by approving or disapproving of the bits of it. The worst of it though was that things were starting to become more themselves and less anything else; they didn't remind him of other things so much, because they had been cut off from a quality which they shared with other things. The ladybird on the anglepoise lamp, the way people found it hard to say 'pardon?' a third time, the smell of a cow flank, all these things were just what they were, and nothing else, and this made them less than they were.

He dialled. Lilly answered, sleep sludging her pretty voice, 'Yes?' she answered.

'Hello. It's you. Is this me?'

'Yes,' she said, pleasant recognition lilting her sweet voice, 'that is you.'

'Would I like to speak to you?'

'Yes, I think so. Probably.'

'Are you in bed?'

'Yes.'

'Only I was wondering,' said Joe, lying down now, looking up at the too-blue, blue winter sky, 'if you'd like to spend the day with me on a Saxon burial mound?'

'You don't take a girl up a Saxon burial mound unless you're up to no good,' said Lilly.

'I am up to no good.'

'Well… "Saxon burial mound" is my middle name…'

'Bring flapjacks.'

As Lilly was leaving her room, very quietly closing the door, Neil's door flew open and he emerged with a dramatic flourish, dressed in his police uniform.

'Don't meet him,' he said, holding up his hand in an oddly polished manner, as if he had practiced the move many times.

'Meet who?'

'Meet whom.'

'Alright, meet whom?'

'You know whom.'

Lilly leant on the banister in an exasperated slouch. 'Must we have this? Every morning?'

'I *know* you're meeting him.'

'Neil, I told you, if you're still following or watching me, I'll call the police.'

'I *am* the police.' His features were set hard, a super-ordered effort that, in the effort, expressed its opposite; turmoil and chaos. His eyes had become unpleasantly fixed and starey. Lilly had the feeling that his face could, at any moment, *actually* crack; and then what would come out?

'No Neil, you're not the police,' she said quietly, 'You're just a person now.'

'I'm *not* a person.'

'You don't se… oh, you've got some marmalade on your lapel.'

Neil looked down, panicked, and Lilly walked past him. Once again he had been tricked, fooled, into revealing himself, into showing Lilly that the cleanliness of his lapel was more important to him than the unsullied glory of her heart. Drat!

He went back to his room, which was now almost entirely monochrome (he had almost finished his project of replacing every coloured object he owned with a black and white version), turned on his treadmill and began walking off his rage and disappointment, staring at the big clock on his wall, watching the ticking second hand shudder from moment to moment, but it was impossible to concentrate. Through the wall came the voice of Tanish, a wall-penetrating, back-of-the-throat, in-to-a-computer-screen, mindless, mind-boring voice, which was always there now, as Tanish was always in his office, always talking to his digital underlings, the junior programmers he managed.

Why, why, why, why, *why*…? There was, for Neil, no end to the 'why', it just went round and round and round. Why had Lilly left him? Why was she attracted to Joe? Why did Joe pull Ursula from her coffin and dance with the corpse round a packed church? Why did Joe shoot him, Neil, and why had he never apologised? Why did Chiyo, whenever she saw that only he was looking at her, drag three fingers across her face, in an opaque, creepy gesture? Why wouldn't the police accept him back? It would have helped, perhaps, if he were an atheist, reconciled to a 'just because' universe, but there was purpose to the universe, things happened for a reason. But what reason? Why was he in this shitty house, listening to an Indian android spurt his verbal static? Why was he surrounded by hateful, hurtful people? Why was he implanted with doomed dreams? Why did he spill marmalade on his lapel this morning? Why did he have a headache? These smaller 'whys' were always the worst of all. It was easier to understand why 5 million kulaks had been exterminated than it was to understand why his laces had snapped yesterday morning while he was in a hurry to get to the dentist's. Also, why did the dentist insist on explaining to him how to grow potatoes?

Not that Neil understood this gardening lecture. He now found it almost impossible to pay attention to anyone and so never quite understood what they were saying to him. He would smile, nod and 'yeah' his way through the interaction, in the hope that he would get the point in the end, which turned out to be mistaken as he found in fact that he didn't understand, but couldn't now say he didn't understand because that would mean confessing that all his understanding sounds were actually tiny little lies; forcing him to press on, not really understanding, but tense, tortured and snared in a desperate, cringing, hell.

He was walking faster and faster, treadmill responding automatically to his anguish-fuelled sprint-walk, the pain in his shot knee increasing, the rage in his chest flaring, the anguish, at knowing that she was going off to meet *him*, rising in his gorge like bilious sewage in a flooding storm drain. Again, the neighbour's deep, cutting, kicking squawk came through the wall *'For God's sake, it's not about the encodings! Please try to understand — it's about sending the data along with the operations that can be performed on it together. You can create an object and define its set of operations permanently, but you can only perform string operations on a string and list operations on a list. Don't you get it?'* A ceaseless, colourless, digital tone, middle-class, urbane, Indian, boring through the wall of Neil's bedroom and through the wall of his skull, neverending… *'Functionally, the object types are more general… it's not a bug, it's a display issue… object-oriented design … multi-threading … socket-based applications… real-time systems…'*

The weak barrier holding in Neil's swelling rage snapped and he flew out of the room, downstairs, out into the winter sunshine ('strangely warm for this time of year' said a voice in Neil's mind) and, almost blind with rage — his vision was shivering, the world was vibrating — thumped on the neighbour's door.

Tanish opened the door, tired and sleepy looking, as ever.

'Stop making a noise!' screamed Neil.

'What? What?' Tanish pouted and knitted his brows.

'Keep your bloody voice *down!* Go into another room! I've had enough!'

Tanish shrugged. 'I said I'd do what I could.'

'But I can hear your every word!' Neal squealed.

'We can't help having a baby. Please be more considerate.'

'Not the baby! Not the baby! You! You!'

Tanish shook his head sadly, 'Oh dear. Look at you! Look at yourself man. You are pointing, aggressive, right in my face.'

Neil was indeed prodding the air with his finger, which he now clenched into a fist. 'It's *your* fault. You're *making* me angry. You and your inconsiderate… insensitive…'

'No, no, no. That's not my responsibility.' Tanish was perfectly calm, smiling slightly, comfortable with the upper hand.

'Yes, it is! Whose is it then?'

'I'm sorry, I won't talk to you like this. You have issues man.'

'I'm just telling you to stop boring through my brain with your brain-drilling voice. Go into another room.'

'Ah. Now you are threatening me.'

'What? When did I threaten you?'

'Sorry, I'm not talking to you. I don't talk to people in such a state. You've lost it man. I said I'd try… I'd do my best…'

'I'm *telling* you to shut up. These walls are paper thin. I live with your moronic voice in my brain. I've had enough. Go into another room.'

'I bought my house. You are just renting a room.'

'What!? What!? What's that got to do with anything!?'

Tanish realised he had made a wrong move, and so retreated to a safer bunker. 'I'm not going to talk to someone who is so obviously out of control.'

'You think *this* is out of control?'

'You really should go on an anger management course mate.'

'You smug, condescending *bastard*.'

'Oh dear, oh dear. He's lost it, he's lost it!' He had now turned to his wife, Diana, who had appeared behind him.

'What's happening?' she asked. She was heavy-bodied, heavy-faced, heavy-eyed, heavy-minded, heavy-lifed.

'He came round, intolerant, violent, his eyes all crazy and wild. He's threatening me, using the 'F' word.'

'Okay, go away please,' she said to Neil, 'If you come round here we're calling the police,' she said, 'Goodbye.'

'I am the police! I *am* the police!'

'No you're not. You were fired. You're nobody now,' said Tanish, with a slight smug smile on his face, and closed the door.

While Neil was arguing with Tanish, Chiyo was wandering around his immaculate room. She ran her finger along the back of a hard-to-reach table ledge and inspected it; clean. She opened a drawer. It was full of neatly folded black trousers. She removed from her dress pocket a small bird skull and slipped it into one of the pockets. She then bent down, sniffed the floor, and continued sniffing. Just behind a bed leg was half a toenail. She put this into a clear plastic sample bag and left, slipping back into her room just before Neil, still simmering with ire, passed her, unseeing.

'This small Geb man is crazy—it is very sad really.' Such was the judgement of Tanish and Diana who were standing now in their newly fitted kitchen, discussing the encounter. Neil 'needed help.' But 'this is what you can expect from people like that.' They sighed together with sadness and regret, but they were, for a moment, happy, because complaining about other people was one of the few topics of conversation they actually enjoyed together, the other being the future of their baby son. There was an atmosphere of dullness in their house, of low-lying irritation with each other, the captious ordinariness of parents who don't really love or understand each other, or life. Their new-born son picked up on this and was 'difficult', a screamer, which they could only deal with by exciting him into a different, 'up' kind of scream, all of which put more pressure on the house…

But it all melted away when, together, they complained about the world, or when their son was asleep and they held each other's hands and Tanish whispered, 'one day he'll be a *cricketer*' and Diana whispered 'or a *doctor*' and Tanish whispered 'or a successful *businessman*' and Diana whispered, 'or a famous *professor*'. They were not happy, because they were successful professionals—practical, wealthy and emotionally barren—but their son, who was to be more professional, more practical, more wealthy and therefore more barren, *he* would be really alive.

As they stood shaking their sorrowing heads in the kitchen, this baby, who had been asleep upstairs, woke, screaming. Diana rushed away, unaware, as she would be in the weeks which followed, that Neil had gone back to his bedroom, recorded a high-pitch square-wave synth tone, lifted it six octaves into a register only babies can hear and was playing it at maximum volume through the walls.

Joe was asleep again; his big, restful head poking out of the tent. He had lain down, looking up into the blue, blue, blue, feeling, for the first time in years, a sense of *enoughness*. He had thought of the town people, the desert people, hard faces, hard hearts, hard lives. 'Coffin dwellers' Clive used to call them; 'stiffs' in ordinary speech. Stiff backs, stiff necks, stiff smiles, hardening at every step they take from the meadow.

Here though, this, it was not just enough, he thought, just lying, but the peace, the green glancing peace, was more than enough; it was the *something else*. It had returned. The oak branches above, so oaky, so branchy were tenderly exploring the sky, while the flashing gaps between them were sparkling electric blue blossoms. The ceaseless distant swish of the leaves were big Hessian bags of sawdust slowly tumbling down cathedral stairs. The perished nettle greenness of the scrubby undergrowth smelt of youthful freedom and intensity, living on a planet in which each moment was almost painfully, adventurously itself and, at the same time, the *something else*. Reconciled, and glad again to be immersed in qualities which bubbled up as the thing in front of him and something else entire, Joe had fallen into a deep, sumptuous sleep.

Wearing a dark blue woollen dress and thick woollen cardigan, and carrying a large leather rucksack, Lilly was standing over him. She bent down and whispered into his dreaming head, 'You're beautiful. I think you're a king. Not everyone would.

I think you're a king.' She then stuffed the pine cone she was carrying into his mouth.

Joe woke, coughing, pulling the cone from his mouth. He sat up.

'Thanks,' he said.

'I think you were dreaming,' she said.

Joe took bits of leaf and pine cone out of his mouth as Lilly removed a red checked picnic blanket from her bag, spread it before the tent and sat down.

'I was. I had a dream about magical acorns that grew into castles, one of which I swallowed.'

'I'm scared of castles. Not scared, disturbed. They're so massive; I mean they have such mass. They're just too permanent. I like temporary things.'

'Like mud huts?' Joe sat up and Lilly's beauty struck him like a physical thing. The slight plumpness of her pale arms, the soft fullness of her red lips, the clarity of her large green-blue eyes; her body seemed hardly to contain vast, dazzling vitality, an intensity of life that made Joe feel a bit unsteady, like he was cycling on a tightrope.

'Yeah,' she said, unpacking her bag, taking out food, but aware of Joe's ursine warmth. 'I think we took a terrible wrong turn, as a species, when we stopped building in mud. I feel a lot more mud-like than I do brick-like.'

'We're just walking, talking clods.'

'And dreaming. Dreaming clods.'

'Earlier on I was chatting with my dead sister in a dream,' said Joe.

'Were you!?'

'Yes, I often see her. Visions and shit.'

Lilly paused in her preparations, paper cup in hand. 'Do you ever worry you might be mad? I do, all the time.'

'Oh everyone's mad. The only question is, are you happy and mad, or are you like everyone, miserably mad.'

'I suppose I'm reasonably discontent and mad.'

They were quiet for a few moments. Lilly wanted to ask him about Ursula, but she didn't quite know what to say. Joe had much to say, but as always when people with a lot to say to each other meet, too many choices makes it hard for the mind not to skid around and settle on none. In the end, he took the safe option and directed his attention to the actual, looking at the food which Lilly had assembled on paper plates. 'You've got a nice selection there,' he said.

'Yes, flapjacks, homemade sourdough bread, two kinds of sauerkraut, boiled eggs, pickle, smoked cheese, beer, and that...' she pointed to a pretty kiln jar, 'that's vegan borscht...'

'I'm beginning to see a theme.'

'No meat? I'm trying so hard not to eat it. I just, it actually makes me cry, eating flesh, so I've given up. I do think it's wrong, and erm...' She suddenly blushed.

'I meant the spread looks Scandinavian.'

'Oh! Yes, I love Finland. I'd like to live there, in a small clean shack, next to a crystal clear Arctic stream, surrounded by shimmering birch trees. And their ghosts. I'm quite happy with the company of the dead. Here...' she offered Joe some butter as they began eating.

'What's it like, working with the dead?' he asked.

'It's good. I mean, I just know it's a necessary thing. In the end, if nobody died, the world would be full up, wouldn't it? Crammed full of bacteria, and insects, and dinosaurs and stuff. Mammals wouldn't have had any legroom to evolve. Also, I find it fascinating—and even though, it's quite morbid, you're with dead people aren't you—but they are dead *people*, with stories and lives, and kind of, why I really like it, and why it doesn't get me down, because, I dunno, it seems to me like there's more life there, than anywhere else.'

'But...' she went on, 'well, one thing is, I don't really like the smell of death. You know, it's like the old person ready-to-die smell, but much much worse, like the evil essence of charity shop. Death. It just smells like death. It's... it puts me off my food. It's just, I can't, something is impossibly horrible about it… And then, the other thing, I find this very strange, grotesque actually, that it's *me* doing it, I mean that the whole world of death is locked up in *my* dingy little room, with just little me. Where's everyone else? Where's the family? Where's everyone else? It just feels so wrong. It's like… It's like, we're sweeping something under the carpet, some dirty secret, something shameful, but, the thing is, I don't know what it is, what we're ashamed of… do you?'

'Erm, no,' said Joe, munchingly. It had been so long since he had had a conversation like this with a woman, a meandering, organic thing, with its own life. And here too, in this place. It was bizarrely warm, in the middle of winter, which probably meant the world was ending, but perhaps, thought Joe, we're supposed to enjoy the world ending, not as an interesting thing, but as something that two friends can share, in their bellies, over a glass of wine.

'And then,' said Lilly, 'also, actually, sometimes I just want to get off my face and dance in a fabulous gay club. My life… it… it also seems dead sometimes. I don't enjoy myself half as much as I should. I have a hobby actually. I enjoy shoplifting. I wanted to give up, but then I thought, "well, it's getting near Christmas, so I might as well get the Christmas dinner," so I filled up two bags in Waitrose and walked out. I just couldn't see an end to it, but then not long after that Neil came up to me one morning, while I was eating a scone, and he said—he was whispering—he said 'I just want you to know Lilly, I've thought about it, and I think you'll be alright if you get caught. You'll just be banned from the store.' So, that helped actually but, oh God I'm sorry, am I talking too much?'

'No, no.'

'Some people talk and talk, and they have no idea that everyone else is stuck, trapped in this cell they've put them in, just waiting to get out. I really don't want to be one of those people.'

'What do you think I'm thinking now?' Joe asked.

'Are you wondering if dogs understand "maybe"?'

'I was thinking…'

'…I wonder that…'

'…I was wondering why you do it?'

'Shoplifting? I just want the danger.'

Joe laughed.

'Do you think it's alright?' said Lilly, smiling.

'I just think it's hilarious.'

'So you don't think I'm a bad person?'

'I don't even know what that means.'

'It means,' said Lilly, 'someone who is alive but who is really already dead. Everything is working, they're saying things, thinking things, feeling things, but really, they're just, very, dead.'

'Then no, I don't think you're a bad person,' said Joe. 'I think you're the most alive person I've ever met.'

Lilly looked at him with love in her eyes. She didn't want to, expose herself like that, but she couldn't help it. Then she blushed again, 'I just, I worry about being too nice,' she said, 'You know, bland—I hate bland people, but then I *am* nice. I think. I like people, I love them, I want to love them. Actually I hate a lot of them, and when I think of all the people I hate, they're nice too. Maybe I should do something completely evil one day, get it out of my system.'

'You don't need to do something evil, you need to do something vivid. It's the vivid who get to heaven, not the good.'

'Hmm.' This was a new idea.

They ate the food. It tasted good. As they ate, Joe told Lilly about Duat, what had happened there.

'So you could have taken anything,' said Lilly, 'and you took a baboon's bottom tent and a child's sleeping bag?'

'It was all I needed. Why, what would you have had?'

'Erm. Probably a nice Fender bass.'

'Sorry I didn't pick one up for you.'

'What music do you listen to?' A worry flashed over Lilly's mind that this was a terribly conventional question, and this man would surely be down on it; but he accepted it.

'Black music,' he said.

'Like hip-hop?'

'God no. Classic funk, roots reggae, Mavin Gaye, Al Green, ancient blues...'

'I don't really know any of that. Maybe I should. I think the songs I listen to are the least black ever written. Do The Beatles have any black in them?'

'Of course they do. There were covered by Al Green, Fats Domino, Ray Charles, Stevie Wonder...'

'Oh that's good. When someone tells me they don't like the Beatles, it's like, to me, it's like they've just said they enjoy torturing children.'

'Black music is dead now though, like black hearts are.'

'All hearts are dead.'

'I know. It just seems all the more tragic though, with black people. I don't know why.'

They had finished eating and were both leaning back against the oak. It was quiet and still; as it often seems after the munching and slurping and swallowing of eating finishes. Joe, who was now wearing his furry top hat, fidgeted the edge of Lilly's peculiar cardigan, which was cream, unbleached, and patterned with Aztec-style geometric forms which circled her neck like a ruby gorget.

'I like this,' he said.

'Do you? I made it. People say my stuff is weird, but I like it. That's my other hobby, along with shoplifting. I'm into sewing and fashion and stuff. Very superficial, I know, I know. Fashion is all bullshit...'

'Well fashion might be, but... it's very magical making your own clothes.'

'Yes it is!'

'Could you make me something?'

'What would you like?'

'A fisherman's jumper that still smells like a sheep, but with a big sunflower design over the front.'

'Okay. Yes.' She picked up a little burgundy sorrel flower, which looked like a tiny lacquered lamp shade. 'Where did these flowers came from?'

'I don't know. They were here when I got here.'

'I think I might live here.'

'Mmm. Me too.'

'Yes,' she said, stretching her limbs decadently, 'we should live amongst the flowers.'

'Love lives in shouldlessness.'

'So we *will* live amongst the flowers.'

'Yes,' said Joe, 'live among the flowers. Until we… blow up. A long, meadow-scented, slow-motion, flowery explosion.' He picked a flower—a black iris—and handed it to Lilly.

'Don't say that,' she said, and looked at the flower, doubtfully.

'What?' Joe could detect a frosting over. What had he said?

'Both of my parents blew up. The man who did it, he blew up too. Everyone in my life I care for blows up. And now you're talking about blowing up.'

'Sorry. I just mean, that, erm… alright, we'll just roll around in the flowers.'

Lilly could feel tightness.

'I have been having some good thoughts here and it's probably because of *here*,' said Joe, attempting to smooth the mood, 'I've noticed that conversations change according to environment.'

'So this is a hill-type conversation?'

'Exactly.'

'Well, I do like hill-type conversations. Not so keen on, erm, bus-station type conversations.'

'Or farm-shop type conversations.'

'Oh no. Or coffee-shop-just-round-the-corner-from-the-office type conversations,' said Lilly.

'I'm done with all that,' said Joe, happy that the atmosphere was warming again so quickly. With Maria any problem would be held onto. He smiled. 'It's gone now,' he said.

'What has?'

'The weight on my chest.'

Lilly looked around. Down in the meadow, a fox was sloping along the side of a bush. Crows hopped around tufts of grass. A cow lifted its tail and shit. 'That's because nothing really matters here,' she said.

'Yes, nothing really matters here. If I found out the world was going to end in fifteen minutes, I'd be fine with it.'

'Thirty would be better.'

'Alright, thirty minutes.'

'Assuming it doesn't end in thirty minutes, what are you going to do?' she asked.

'Do?'

'I mean, don't you need a job?'

'I would rather sit here with you, eat some flapjacks, fool about in that stream down there and call it a day.'

Lilly smiled, 'That's all well and good.'

'Why do I have to pay for my existence on the planet with the activity called work?'

'I dunno. To contribute to society?'

'Consider the bees.'

'I do, often, but what about them?'

'They fly around all day sniffing vaginas then go home and dance.'

'We're not bees though are we?'

'Aren't we though? *Aren't* we?'

There was something so appallingly odd about this man. He was funny and expansive and harmless and so still, like the furthest bit of the atmosphere, just before it becomes space. He expressed high blue gladness with the finest, subtlest shifts of deadpan tone. It was such a relief, so easy and drifty, although she sensed something deadly there too, not in a threat-to-body way, but some other kind of danger, like something her heart needed could just drift away in his company. 'Why do you fart around so much?' she asked. 'I mean I get it, but don't you ever think you should *get* somewhere?'

'All the time. But it always seems to come down to the fact that I'm not somewhere, I'm here, so what can I do to make here into somewhere. Somewhere for me. And. That seems very important. It seems like a question of life or death…'

'Maybe,' said Lilly, 'you need to just, you know, arrange your life so that you can have both; both life and death?'

'Work-life balance,' said Joe, drily.

Lilly smiled. 'That's a horrible expression isn't it?'

'You need to balance your existence between "life", what you do when you're not at work, and "work", what you do when you're not alive.'

'I once knew someone at work,' she said, 'an awful e-marketing job I had when I was at university, there was this boy who used to be a girl, he'd transitioned, and he had what he called "time dyslexia", so he couldn't meet any deadlines or get to work on time or ever be reliable.'

'Really?'

'Yeah. I thought it was a bit shady. I mean if he can claim time-dyslexia why can't I call in sensitive?'

'You shouldn't go anywhere near work if you've come down with a bout of sensitivity.'

Lilly felt oddly conflicted. On the one hand she wanted everyone to be as aimless as Joe; on the other, she felt a compulsion to fix him to… to what she wasn't sure. But to *something*. He needed to get somewhere, didn't he? 'What did you want to do when you were a little boy?' she asked.

'I wanted to dance on the surface of the sun.'

Lilly went to speak. Then stopped. Then sighed again. Then laughed. 'I mean… What I mean is, if you could give your younger self some advice, what would it be?'

'My younger self would want to know if he's going in the right direction.'

'Is he? Was he?'

'No. I'd have to say that. For the next twenty years you'll be going in the wrong direction.'

Lilly laughed again. 'Haven't you ever enjoyed yourself in a job?'

'But that's the problem. That's all I do.'

'Oh, I see. But isn't there one that you can enjoy and not get fired from?'

'I don't think so. For me, getting fired is part of the job, like death is part of life.'

'It's not pleasant though, is it?' said Lilly.

'What getting fired, or dying?'

'Both of them.'

'But I think they could be. With work, for example, what I am looking for in my dismissals is a kind of civility and mutuality, one that elegantly sugar-coats my disengaged incompetence, where we can both leave the scene with a sense of old-fashioned dignity. That doesn't happen, but it could.'

'Can't you just do what everyone else does?'

'Bitch, moan, ironically distance myself from the inherent stupidity of the work-act?'

Lilly sighed again. She had gathered up a few roses and was now distractedly sniffing them. 'I don't understand. Nobody is happy, anywhere, and yet nobody can change anything.'

Joe shrugged. 'It's the world.'

'What should we do about the world then?'

'I really don't care. The world has nothing to do with me. It's not my business. It's their problem.'

'Don't you think we're all responsible for the world?'

'I met someone in Duat, a wizard called Zoltan, who said it was all the machine.'

'Shouldn't we do something about the machine then?'

'Zoltan thought so. Maybe it's impossible though.'

'It's not *impossible* is it?'

'No, not impossible. I just think it'll fall under its own weight.'

'I think I should throw away my smartphone.'

'Oh no. Don't do that. You only live once—you should spend as much of it on social media as possible.'

Lilly laughed. 'That's true. You wouldn't want to die with regrets.'

'It doesn't matter though,' said Joe, 'If you throw away your phone you're still left with the thinker. That's what's addicted to the phone. That's what made the phone in the first place. That's what made the world. If you take away the phone, the TV, the whole machine, the thinker will just make mischief elsewhere.'

'I'm always thinking. I just can't stop. It's a kind of mania, but,' she said, having considered this before, 'I don't think it's the problem, because the thinking is motivated by something, do you know what I mean? It must be.'

'Emotion?'

'*Yesss*,' she hissed, 'emotion.'

'Horrible substance.'

'Do you think so?'

'I won't have anything to do with it.'

'But doesn't that make you into a robot?'

'I still feel things…' said Joe, quietly.

Lilly wasn't quite listening, she was pursuing another thought. 'Sometimes I feel possessed by emotion,' she said, 'and it's like a sort of mimic of love. I tell myself I'm angry or upset or whatever, but I'm in love with the emotion, which is so close to me, like a lover, and so, and which, when a man comes along, it gets jealous and spiteful. How can you turn emotion off though?'

'Do you feel emotional now?'

'No.'

'No, me either.'

'Why's that then?'

'Because there's nothing here to get emotional about.'

'Then how do we carry this back into the world?'

Joe thought about it. 'I don't have the answers. What I do know is that I want to. I want to carry this back into the world.'

'Me too.'

'That's a start isn't it? Most people don't even want to get out, let alone bring the out back in.'

'I feel hopeful about myself, like I'm going to get out one day and stay out, but I don't feel that about other people.'

Joe picked up a soft acorn, almost rotted away. 'They're like all the acorns this tree produced in the autumn. How many will become oaks? A tree like this—this is a Holm oak, or evergreen oak—produces something like ten thousand acorns in a good year, very likely none of them becoming trees. They're all eaten by squirrels and badgers or they rot, like this one.'

'You know a lot about trees.'

'I love trees. We're the same shape.'

Lilly looked from the tree to Joe.

'So you see? Most people are like this rotten acorn,' he said, 'they're just decomposing. They don't even have souls. You have to grow a soul, and most people don't, so their pointless bodies just sink back into the mud…'

'…and feed living trees?'

'Yeah, feed them with their misery, and their sorrow, as they moulder.'

Lilly knitted her brows. 'That doesn't sound right. You're saying humanity is soulless fertiliser.'

'Yeah. Yep. Dead skin. Toenails.'

'I can imagine a Tory politician saying the same thing. Or Genghis Khan.'

'Genghis Khan was fertiliser too.'

Lilly shuddered inside. What a cold philosophy.

'Someone's coming,' she said.

A figure had appeared in the distance, a few minutes away.

'I wonder who it is,' she said.

'Probably Neil.'

'Oh God no. No it can't be. No, it's a woman. A big one.'

'Neil dressed as a big woman?'

'I wouldn't put it past him. He's out of his mind you know.'

'I know.'

'I can't believe you're brothers.'

'We were raised in separate camps. It was my mum vs my dad.'

'He's chronically paranoid, when I see anyone else. Anyone, men of course, but also women, work colleagues, anyone. I think, in fact I know he would think I was having it off if I went out with a cousin, or a brother. I can just imagine saying to him "yeah, I'm off to sleep with my brother."'

'And are you?' asked Joe, munching now on a flapjack.

'What?'

'Sleeping with your brother?'

'Well, I don't have a brother, but, you know, I don't have a problem with incest. Or with a huge age difference. Where's the problem? Nobody is getting hurt. I don't mean start a family, long-term stuff, big-faced kids, all of that; but you might really love your brother, or your cousin, so what's the big deal…?'

'With having a nice friendly shag?'

'Yeah,' said Lilly, smiling, 'a nice family shag.'

The figure had now materialised into Neil's old boss, Gaynor Babcock, who was pulling herself up the hill. She was dressed in black and carrying a large bunch of flowers in one hand and a rolled-up scroll of papers in the other.

'Morning,' she said cheerfully. Joe and Lilly both said hello, Joe trying to place where he'd seen her before. 'Sorry to bother you both,' Gaynor said, now standing before them both, slightly out of breath, 'but you're sitting on my one true love.'

'Are we?' Joe looked around.

'Sorry!' said Lilly standing up.

Gaynor gestured her back down. 'No, no, it's fine. I just, I come here regular, to lay flowers. He's a hill now.'

'Who is?' asked Lilly.

Gaynor's face quivered, 'my Clive,' she said.

'Clive?' asked Joe.

'Yes, he died recently.'

'Clive Marsh? Small fella, disabled?'

'Yes, did you know him?'

'Yes,' said Joe, 'terrible what happened.' In his mind he added 'kind of fitting also,' but he didn't let this reach his lips.

'What happened?' asked Lilly.

'He threw himself into a can of paint,' said Joe.

'Oh *that* Clive.'

'You knew him too?'

'Yes, I prepared the body.'

Joe now remembered where he had seen Gaynor before, at Clive's funeral, which had been a bizarrely un-Clive-like event, organised by his religious family and very Jesusy, and Joe was sure he remembered Clive saying that if Jesus existed they'd written all his jokes out.

'He was my… lord,' said Gaynor.

'Was he?' said Joe, now wondering if they were talking about Jesus or Clive Marsh.

'Your what?' asked Lilly.

'My lord.'

'Clive?' said Joe. 'Are we talking about the same person? Small negative Staff?'

'I worshipped him, until I broke him. He… It just went too far, see. We fought… and… He got hurt…' she waved her hand, waving away the memories, of when Clive had been her 'daddy dom' and she his 'ponygirl painslut,' of when he had gone into 'a dark place' and attacked her with a saguaro cactus, of when she had body-slammed him, breaking his good leg, all memories she refused now to let back into the light.

'We didn't see each other much after that,' said Gaynor, her voice broken, 'but I never stopped loving him.'

All three of them, Joe, Lilly and Gaynor, were silent, grimacing convulsively, their faces ticcing and spasming.

✤

Carl Rowden left school at fourteen, spent four years getting drunk, shooting rabbits and fighting anyone who came from somewhere else—blacks, Pakis, kids who came from different schools, lads from neighbouring towns; he wasn't fussy. Then, on one of the random whims that had shaped his life, he signed up for the Merchant Navy, and left Edding for five years. He trained to get his able seafarer certificate in Portsmouth and a year later he was impregnating large numbers of Chilean women while stoned on the hashish he had, six months earlier, smuggled out of Afghanistan. It was a kind of paradise; three years of punishing work, irresponsible sex and hallucinogenic drugs. It was also morally instructive, as he learnt to depend on and enjoy the company of dark-skinned seamen and to copulate with dark-skinned women from Nigeria, South Africa, the Philippines, Indonesia and most of South and Central America, which more or less rid him of the racism he had been born and bred into.

The reason these first three and a half years of sea life had been so good that he would look back on them with romantic longing for the next twenty-five was that, by chance, he had found himself part of a series of quite spectacularly lax and casual crews; but his luck could not hold out and, after a stopover in India, where he'd picked up five kilos of ganja and a dose of the clap, the entire crew of the ship he was on was replaced with career men, company men and, that most treacherous category of human being, 'nice people.' He had spent the next year more or less alone in his cabin, eating ganja, descending into a state of paranoid loneliness and pissing razor blades. His only friend, on the entire voyage, had been a lizard which he'd called Nigel. Nigel was kind-hearted, but he was given to hectoring lectures, regularly reprimanding Carl for murdering rabbits for fun, and for taking advantage of poor women, and for wanking too much, and for not adequately hydrating. Taking Nigel's advice was also a learning experience for Carl.

He got back to England, found his mother had died while he had been away, resigned from the 'merch', got work as a window fitter, married a highly-strung, emotionally needy woman called Becky, had three children, borrowed eighty grand from Becky's rich father to start his own garage-door business, which had spectacularly failed, leaving him permanently in debt, dependent on his father-in-law's benevolence, married to a woman he didn't particularly care for and raising three kids who, for the most part, annoyed or depressed him. He had a little girl of eight, Shelley, who was withdrawn, awkward and always sad—and became sadder whenever Carl tried to cheer her up—an overweight boy of fourteen, Alfie, who played video games from morning to night and never left his bedroom, and Sam, a peculiar lad of eighteen—peculiar to Carl, although all young people were—who spent his life scowling over his phone. Sam responded to anything his dad ever said with a kind of bitter, mocking sarcasm, which was painful to Carl, and it provoked him to anger, but he bit his tongue—better to avoid a scene with Becky who would go totally over the top with second-hand outrage if he criticised any of the children, even slightly, or expressed frustration that the friendly relationship he had once imagined he might have with his children, seemed to be completely impossible with any of them.

Carl was rude, racist, sexist, careless, tactless, negligent towards his family, he had a short temper and, feeling trapped by the life decisions his younger self had made, he occasionally went on the piss, went missing for days, spent the occasional evening with a cheap prostitute (he liked Northern girls, particularly from Blackpool) and gambled away his meagre earnings on the dogs. 'I'm a simple man,' he had once said, 'all I want from life is food, clothing, shelter, a doobie, the occasional bet on the dogs and to have sex with a different woman every morning.' He was irresponsible, he was a soft-drug addict—always smoking dope (although he never seemed stoned)—and, despite working in a funeral home, he had no respect for the dead, none. On paper, Carl Rowden was an unpleasant being; and yet, despite squat, ugly, abusive appearances, he was, strange to say, widely liked, by men and women, even loved. There was some kind of honesty about him, totally lacking in more ethical people, something direct and cheerful that passed from his eyes into yours, that made you feel like you were with a fellow human being, that made the insulting surface of him not matter. Just words. At least for people who could see through appearances; others, who lived in a world of words, detested Carl.

And there was also a certain hard-boiled authority to Carl, and even a kind of grandness. He was insanely generous, a quality which inspires respect even in those who take advantage of it and mock it.

He was now on his little throne, driving through town in the company hearse, listening to *'Cool for Cats'*, timelessly tapping away on the steering wheel and, as usual, interspersing tuneless singing with a theatrical monologue.

'The cowboys take position in the bushes and the grass... Why did I leave the taxis? Why do birds fly high? Why is grass green? *It's funny how their missus always look so bleeding same...* Some things just happen. Do I have to know why? No. Life is one big taxi ride and sometimes you don't know where you're going, so you tell the driver, "just drive!"'

He accelerated, out of pure enthusiasm, and caused a 1.2 litre red Fiat to swerve, horns blaring. Carl held his hands up 'bang to rights', and calmed down a bit. He almost said sorry, but that was unnecessary now.

'...but all I get is bitter and a nasty little rash...'

He pulled into the back of the Yamaraja and knocked on the green kitchen door. A large radiant Indian woman dressed in a dark red, green and gold sari opened the door. 'Good morning Carl!' she cried, arms open in motherly appreciation.

'Morning Meera,' he said, standing two steps below her and sheepishly shifting his weight from one foot to another. Meera treated Carl like one of her boys and he was happy to be treated that way. 'Smells amazing, as always, as always,' he said.

'That is the smell of my eternal love,' she said and disappeared back into the kitchen.

'Don't I know it!' he called after her. 'I tell you, I must have had a million chicken biryanis in my time. No joke. A *million*. And I have never, ever had one like yours. You... won my heart with that biryani. I'd do anything for you. I'd pull someone's head off for you...'

'Sorry Carl?' Meera emerged from the kitchen pushing a trolley full of foil containers and takeaway bags which Carl, stepping over to the ramp, took hold of.

'Nothing.'

'Carl,' she said, 'if I may say so, you are looking a little bit tired. Are you getting enough rest?'

'Yeah,' he said awkwardly, 'I bin, erm, pushing the boat out a bit... Few late nights...'

'Are you giving your wife adequate attention?' she asked, following him to the hearse as he loaded it with the curries.

'Oh you know, standard, I suppose,' he said.

'If you stop watering the tree it will die. And the tree will blame you too.'

Carl, whose tone had now dropped to a taut, awkward, sideways mumble, was no longer looking Meera in the eye, just loading his car.

'Yeah, yeah,' he said to himself.

'Oh come come Carl, don't be a sourpuss. Here, have a gulab jamun.' She offered him the oil-stained paper bag she was holding. Carl reached in and took a moist ball of milky dough.

'Good?' said Meera, enjoying the pleasure on Carl's face as he chewed.

'Yeah,' he said, mouth full, 'amazing. Why don't you have one?'

'Oh no!' she cried cheerfully, 'I am not eating for forty years!'

'Er. Riiiight. I'll be back in a couple of hours then.' He got into his car. Meera knocked the driver's side window, which he wound down.

'There is a prince inside of you Carl,' she said, 'Do not be a sheep man. You are a *ram* man.'

'Right oh!' he said, smiling and backing out of the drive.

Meera called after him. '*You are a fire-breathing ram!*'

Victor Perry had been a delicate and sensitive youth. He grew up in London, the son of a militant Jamaican backing singer mother with Tourette's syndrome and an exceedingly gentle, almost feminine Indian father who had quietly worked away his whole life as a gas fitter, bought a house in Edding, raised his children and supported his wife's extravagant left-wing activism, although she never thanked him for it and even seemed to resent his generosity. One day, he returned to Chhattisgarh for his mother's, Victor's grandmother's, funeral, had a spiritual experience he refused to talk about, came back to England a changed man, gave up meat, sex, all forms of over-stimulation and, for many days at a time, even food, before declaring he was going to devote his life to Krishna and moving to Wales where, halfway up Mount Tryfan, he died of a heart attack.

Victor, then seventeen, and prey to schizoid attacks of haunting paranoia, frequently convinced that 'ascended masters' were speaking to him through objects, set out on a life which swung between two motivating extremes, the radical mission of his mother to change the outer world through political agitation and the equally radical, yet diametrically opposed instinct of his father to change the inner world through mortification of the flesh. Victor left music school, where he was studying classical composition, and travelled through India in search of himself, but was only able to discover that his self went wherever he did and that it was riddled with a misery which motivated him to ever more extreme acts of rebellion, political and personal. He threw all his possessions in the Ganges because he didn't want to be tied to the world by any objects, he moved to Utter Pradesh and practiced extreme Yogic devotion to various gurus and masters, all of whom, Victor soon realised, were frauds, full of fancy mystical tricks and magical ideas, but empty, vain; appalling hypocrites. They taught abstention but carried on with women, or they railed against materialism, but liked driving nice cars, or they meditated for eight hours a day and got irritated with their ex-wives, or they were just boring, nothing people. Disillusion set in, so he moved south and joined an underground Maoist cell and helped to attack Indian security forces in Dantewada, accidentally blowing off two of his fingers while delivering a letter-bomb. Then he travelled through Burma and Thailand, living and working with locals, frequently turning down offers of sex and marriage, then to Indonesia where, at a tourist party on a beach in Sulawesi, he consumed vast quantities of a hallucinogenic mushroom, had sex with an Irish woman called Betty who turned into an female octopus, passed out, was carried back to his hut, died three times in quick succession and was resurrected by multi-dimensional elves. This didn't really seem to change anything though. The eyes saw visions, the mind died a death, but everything seemed to stay the same. He still carried fear with him, and quenchless sexual desire, and a sucking ennui for the world.

He made his way to Australia, where he had another schizoid attack and was nearly sectioned in Darwin for feeling up a woman bus-driver and inconsolably weeping in a toy shop; then to Jamaica, where he got knifed by a cousin for giving away his grandmother's Farsifa organ; and then finally back to England, where he faced the end of his self, the state he had so longed for, but which turned out to be nothing like he had supposed.

He was always searching, always working to transform himself and the world, but never knowing what to do. Every path he went down seemed to be a dead end, never delivering the peace or enlightenment he searched for. Sometimes he felt he was 'getting somewhere,' he felt that he 'realisations' and 'breakthroughs' were bringing him closer to the mystic marvellousness he yearned for, but then, almost as quickly as such optimistic moments came, they went, leaving him mired in degrading illusion than ever.

The end came when Sri Baba Gaurav came to stay. 'Baba-Gee' was a mystic (an incarnation of Parashurama) who travelled the world living with devotees and making their lives a misery, by insulting them non-stop, by putting unbearable pressure on their weak-points and, more generally, by causing chaos and upset and unpleasant discomfort wherever he went. Victor heard about Baba-Gee and invited him, by email, to stay in the squalid Kentish Town flat he was living in, shared with three other people. A few weeks later a minute Indian man with an expressive face and theatrical bodily gestures, and with a peculiar intense emptiness about his large, deep eyes, turned up, installed himself on Victor's bed, and began speaking, loudly and harshly, a grating and very unspiritual-sounding monologue which began at five in the afternoon and went on forever. Baba Gee stopped only for a few hours sleep and a few burgers. He didn't go to the toilet, but relieved himself on Victor's bed which Victor complained about but the angry guru said 'then throw me out, just try it bitch', and so Victor pulled the sheets off and went down to the kitchen while the monkeyish Indian continued disclaiming in his rasping voice. Victor's flatmates complained of the smell and the noise and the fact that Baba Gee insisted on having the heating on full blast in the middle of summer. Victor, who was particularly sensitive to loud noise and strong smells, was physically needled, but this was nothing to the emotional pain, the feeling of being stabbed, over and over again, by an ice-storm of wild meanings. He was irritated, then angered, then bored, then confused, then disgusted, then he fell into a strange kind of trance, then he was furious again; but Baba Gee didn't let up. He just barked away, in his hostile, guttural tone, haranguing Victor, railing at him, sometimes frothing at the mouth, eyes wild, throwing his skinny arms around. Yet Victor found he couldn't stop listening. Was it besides the pain? Or because of it? There was something alluring, soothing even, somewhere beneath the tirade, something hypnotic and needful:

'The self creates identity. *Bullshit identity*. All *bullshit*. You're black, you're an artist, you're *borrrred*, you're the big penis, you're nothing, oh you're this, you're that… *allllll bullshit*. You want something, or you think something, or you feel something, and then *pop!* there it is, this *bullshit identity* of yours. The bullshit identity thinks it is something, it feels it is something; but it is *not!* It is a petrified nothing, a bastard non-thing, it is a *dead dog my man*, but the dead dog still *mooooves*, like a zombie, because it is fear. The zombie dog, yes, it's allllll *fearrrr*. It fears life, *but!* There's also tension, because it wants to know about life, about truth, about love; it wants to get away from all these things, but it also wants to get them too, hoover them all up like a greedy guts. Eat, eat, eat, eat, eat, know, know, know, know, know. *Know!* Ha! *You might as well ask a bicycle what it knows about the bitch riding it!* All this wanting to know, wanting to get, wanting to not get, *that* my friend, is *suffering*, which feels *baaaaaad*, which makes the identity want *not* suffering, which it locates in more *knowledge*, and more *power*, especially *money*, and more *stimulation*, especially *sex*, and more holy holy holy, especially this fucking stupid bullshit called *enlightenment*. Oh my word, *enlightenment!* The lottery of the holy man! All *bullshit! Bullshit* I tell you! You cannot *locate* non-suffering. *You cannot!* You cannot *reach* a state of non-reaching. How can you!? Not by any means at all, certainly not by spiritual practice, meditation, self-sacrifice, fucking *yoga* and all that *ordure*. Look at all those meditating *idiots*, are they *one* step closer? They think they are, but they are *not*. They are *idiots!* They all flock to the wise ones and the wise ones sell them their books and videos and special spiritual days on the special spiritual cushion. *Toilets!* You think anyone can *give* you your own nature? You think I can *give* you what you are looking for? You are an *idiot*, sir! A grinning *idiot*, an *idiot* who just wants his *daddy* to give him an easy life, who runs away from hard work into whoopy-kooky ideas and *mischief. That* is what you want! You want *mischief* and you want *gratification*. You want a *big spiritual tit* in your mouth! Always the *final page* with you, always the ending *there*, never *here*, on *this* page. The real and actual end is not nice! It is *agony, agony, agony*. It is horrible, boring, stupid, useless—it is *useless!* It is of no use to the world, to you, to anyone—enlightenment is useless agony and then you wither up and die, *ooooooh!* and then, if your body survives, *if* you make it, then you have the tiny penis of a child. Is that what you want? The tiny enlightened penis of a small *boy*? No. You *say* you want *big dick* enlightenment or holiness or some other *bullshit* thing. They *alllllll* say they do, like they say they don't care about money, or about *fucking*, but how about I take you through *hell* my man? How about I pull away your *peeeel*? How about I eat your rotten *brain*? How about I take your *moneeeey*? How about I shrink your *balls*? *No, no, no, no, no sir!* Turn on the flesh box! Climb back in your helicopter to the stars, sir, pray to your bastard tribal cock God, chant away like a drooling *moron*, prowl around like the mad *animal* you are, all that's better for you, yes, yes sir, look after *number one* and pretend *alllllll* the while you're a big cheese, a big mystic cheese on your enlightened Zen cloud mountain; that's better for *you*, run along, leave me alone, *kick me out of your house*, am I *annoying* you, huh? Is it *getting* to you yet, well kick me *out* then you bollock! You don't need this, do you? *Do* you? Shut *up!* Shut *up!* You don't want to burn all your stupid money, and burn all your stupid books, and scream in endless agony as you are shit into the void, you don't want to be naked and nothing and nobody, cracked open and smashed; you don't want *that*, you want what all those fucking vegan *bitches* want, all those up-tight smiley-smiley meditating *bastards*, a nice little *high*, a nice little bit of *identity*, and then back to your fucking *toys*, and your fucking *ashrams*, and your fucking *ethics*, and your fucking *celery!* Fucking *bullshit!* None of you have got the fucking *balls!* You can't take me, you can't take me I say. *I will rob you! I will strip you naked! I will leave you naked in the street and shit on your head!*… Can I have some soup?'

And so it went on, and on, and on. Days was it? Weeks? It was a bulldozer, an all-destroying road roller, crushing everything Victor had held to, either consciously or unconsciously. Baba Gee brought it all up, all of Victor's fears and desires, and vomited them out over his shoes. Victor wailed, he moaned, the doors and walls of the building shook with the rage of his flatmates, the doors and walls of the mind shook with the pounding of his self, with nowhere to go… until it did go. The lot of it.

All at once, after who knows how long, Sri Baba Gaurav stood up, smiled sweetly, patted Victor on the shoulder and spoke with an unexpectedly soothing, loving voice—how he hadn't ripped his voicebox to shreds is anybody's guess. He spoke gently, completely unlike the rusty saw that had been working away at Victor's mind. He said 'now I'm going my friend. You should go too. You are done here,' and off he went, forever, leaving Victor in a state of total and absolute aloneness. Maybe he had friends, family, possessions, tradition, art, thought, hope, fear, feelings. Maybe, maybe not, but it no longer mattered, not one bit, and so he walked out on it all.

For another man it may have taken years of Baba-Gee, but Victor was already on the precipice, and all it took was one little prod with the shitty stick, and in he fell. But into what? And who was falling? Words cannot directly state what remained, suffice it to say that, over the six weeks which followed, the self known as 'Victor Perry' went through a spiritual death, which he described as like 'having the pain of the world squeezed out of me by an enormous fist.' He was 'puréed and fried away,' until there was simply nothing left. Just a pea of identity, falling forever in the roaring void, and a series of impressions and thoughts and actions, with nothing whatsoever to hold them all together.

He walked out of his house, leaving it all behind, everything, and straight into Boots the Chemist where he met Meera, who was working there. She had looked deep into his eyes, fallen to her knees in 'Travel Miniatures' and said, 'teach me, I will do whatever you tell me to do.'

Victor and Meera then spent the next six months alternating between the streets of London, poor, hungry, cold, or staying at her friends' houses. Victor lived absolutely in the moment, without preparing or planning even a moment in advance. He said that *things* told him what to do, and he taught Meera how to listen to the truth of things, to the voice of them, so that she would also know what to do. She obeyed him completely, without hesitation. She knew, she absolutely knew, that he was guru, that he was God in human form and, although they did nothing but walk the streets of London and sit on benches she was happy beyond happiness. Sometimes Victor talked to doormen, binmen, beggars, and other people of the street, teaching them 'the way of the thingless thing,' which meant living with a self-thing—the ordinary mind and emotions he had himself spent so long running from—being a person-thing—even being a totally normal person—and experiencing pain-thing—sometimes tremendous pain, sometimes agony—but not being a thing 'behind' all that, not 'owning' it with liking and disliking. Nobody understood any of this, or they thought they did, but in any case they liked to listen to this handsome, crazed young black man and his serene, giving voice.

Mostly though, Victor and Meera were alone, merely existing. They walked round and round the dead places of London; Moorgate, Elephant and Castle and Vauxhall, glorying in the life of their bodies, just walking. They danced in the snow on an empty Clapham Common, they sang to the birds in St. James' Park and they climbed the trees in Lincoln's Inn, where they were told to leave because it was a private garden and they could be arrested.

As they were being escorted out, the security guard had said to Meera, 'why don't you get a job?'—which was something that people were always saying to them—and she had said, 'because I am unconditionally free,' and when she said those words, she realised that, in reality, she *was* free without condition, and in that moment, just as dawn was breaking, the world became bathed in a golden light which never really left her again, which softened everything harsh for her—flavours, sounds, colours—enabling her to live in the midst of the horror of the world without ever again being lacerated by it.

One evening, they came across a carpet in Hyde Park which told Victor he had to leave. He turned to Meera and said to her that, by the end of the day, his spirit would be dead forever, where none can follow. 'You will then receive the truth and it will teach through you.'

'What will happen to you?' Meera said, shivering in the dark, trying not to let fear take her.

'The body of Victor Perry will be here, but the God will have departed.'

The next morning they were sitting in Soho Square watching a few drunkards play table tennis. Victor and Meera had been there for three hours, vibrating with unimaginable pleasure. To anyone who had passed them, arm in arm on the bench, they would have seemed a rather squalid couple of headcases, perhaps on Ecstasy or even heroin, but in truth they were both in mere heaven. Meera often remembered the light of that evening; she really could not tell if it was coming from the sun, or from Victor. He was so unbelievably bright.

Suddenly Victor stood up. 'I want to play ping-pong,' he cried. He walked over to the table, said to one of the drunk kids, 'I will play *one* game against any of you blindfolded. If you win, you can make love to my wife all night. If I win, you will escort her home, like gentleman, and *never* drink another drop of alcohol in your lives.' The boys were not nasty, but they were young, stupid and excitable. They looked at Meera, beautiful Meera, who beamed at them, then at skinny Victor, who appeared to be insane, and laughed. Even stupid young men are afraid of real madness; they hesitated, but then he tied a scarf round his head, which made them laugh again and agree to the challenge.

Victor then played a game of ping-pong that nobody who saw it would ever forget, winning every point. With each decisive blow, each point won, Victor would shriek, 'I hear!' each time louder, until, at the twenty-first point, he turned to Meera and said 'it is over!' and, with his final, full-body smash, his voice broke, his heart broke, and he slumped forward onto the ping-pong table.

He was taken to a hospital and given medication. When he recovered he had almost no memory of the previous six months. He was vague and addled. The pre-Baba-Gee, pre-fist Victor had returned, given to strange outbursts but with almost nothing of the insane wisdom which had set Meera on fire. They both went back to Edding, where they lived with his now old and ailing mother, who died not long after. All the spirit had fallen out of Victor, and out their love, until, finally, he hardly recognised her. Meera, heartbroken, yet also, in some deeper place, confident of the rightness of the situation, told him that she was leaving and he had nodded and said, 'send me curries.'

Victor began what he called 'the work,' of building a temple of unloved junk in which he would write songs of perfect beauty, broadcasting these songs through the bones of a plastic world destined to burn up in his divine fire. He put on a lot of weight and alternated between lucid confusion, catatonic inwardness and wild bursts of spasmodic inspiration.

Meera got together with the friendly owner of a local Indian restaurant, taught him to 'tread the noble path' by raising his consciousness to a level that was worthy of her, and took care of Victor from afar, sending him curries twice weekly via Carl's hearse-delivery service.

☙

Carl, after leaving Meera, drove back through Edding. He felt both needled and chastened, conscience-stricken and inspired. On the one hand, it was true what Meera had said, he wasn't giving his wife, Sue, the right kind of attention. Half the time it was impossible though, because *she* was impossible, but then again, maybe she had just cause. If you don't water the tree, it produces sour berries. I'll pop into John Lewis on the way home, he thought, get her a new chopping board.

He pulled up to Victor's house and got out of the car, two extremely large sweaty, curry-saturated paper bags swinging from his fat fingers, and knocked. The curtains twitched.

'Oy! It's me! Carl!' he shouted up. The curtains settled, footsteps were heard and the door opened. Victor, looking feverish, also looking slightly green, smiled.

'There you go,' said Carl. 'Twelve chicken tikka masalas, four whole lettuces and a bag of chips.'

Victor took the bag.

'You're looking a tad green mate,' said Carl.

'I am a god of sprouting vegetation,' he said.

'That's funny. I'm a fire breathing ram.'

'Yes,' said Victor standing at his door with the bag of curry hanging from his finger-mutilated hand, half-forgotten, 'but it is buried under many layers of mechanical activity. Looking into your hard eyes Carl I'm not sure if you'll be able to get down under them and pull the fire-breathing ram out. Your heart needs one destructing blow from the heel of God. You might be lucky enough to lose everything, but I doubt it.'

Carl, as Victor was speaking, went into the kind of trance state that teachers put him in. When the voice stopped he snapped out of it, slapped Victor's shoulder and said, 'right you are matey. See you on Thursday yeah?'

❧

Sparrows and bramblings swooped and fluttered through the leafy yew trees and hawthorn bushes below, dunnock and thrush bobbed and snuffled through the tussocky grass and dead thistles. Hoverflies darted through tiny little wormholes and Lilly was lying in Joe's arms. Gaynor had read poetry to them both, written by Clive while they were together and which she'd come here to read to herself. After she'd left, Joe and Lilly's talk had turned to intimate subjects and intimate subjects had led to an intimate entwine. A red kite carrying a frozen shoulder of lamb flew overhead.

'I become like the people I'm with,' said Lilly, more to herself than to Joe, 'sometimes it's new and interesting, but mostly it's a terrible shrinking feeling. With you though,' now she turned to him, 'I just feel more like myself; it's really lovely, but it's like you're not really here.'

'Oh I am here, but I'm not in the way of anything.'

'What does that mean?'

'Do you know Horus?' Joe asked, opening Lilly's fingers, interested in the upside-down invisible mountain between them.

'Horus?' she said, 'No, I don't think so.'

'He was an Egyptian falcon deity, a sky god, who later became reborn as the sun god, Ra. Horus chopped his mother's head off, by accident—he… well, he'd just been tricked into the underworld, by Seth, his brother, and, although he'd escaped, he wasn't feeling very well, not thinking straight, and when he saw his mother he thought she was Anubis, the lord of the dead, so he, er, he cut her head off.'

'Bummer.'

'When Horus came to his senses, he was distraught and wandered off into the mountains, and that's where Seth found him. They fought and Seth pulled out his eyes.'

'Pulled out his eyes?' asked Lilly, twisting round again to look up at Joe, his big head totemic against the sun. 'How?'

'With his fingers. I don't blame him though.'

'Who, Seth?'

'No. It's fair enough I think. Also Seth was the god of thunderstorms and earthquakes, so he had a bit of a temper. Also, Horus had pulled Seth's nob off.'

'Oh well, that explains it then.'

'Yeah.'

'What happened to Horus?'

'He lay there, bleeding to death, when Hathor stumbled upon him, she was the goddess of love, beauty, music, fertility, pleasure, cows and the moon.'

'I like all those things,' said Lilly.

'Well, she found Horus, saw what a state he was in, took her breasts out and dribbled milk into his eye sockets and he was made whole again.'

'I see. I suppose they married? Happy ever after?'

'Kind of. He still had to return to the underworld, give Seth's nob back to him, and then be reborn as the ever-quenchless god of light, and, erm, Hathor, she ended up dying too, and so did Horus, in fact everyone died, but they still ended up happy ever after.'

'Just dead?'

'Yeah,' said Joe, 'happily ever dead. They all became the stars and the air and the rivers and things like that. I like it, I mean I like those myths where characters become animals and trees and things. It's where I see myself in five years' time.'

A small bird landed in front of them, grey and softly orange.

'Oh!' gasped Lilly with reverent hush.

The bird hopped over to one of the plates, looked enquiringly at Lilly—'of course you can,' she said. It looked at the crumb, looked again at Lilly, stabbed a bit of broken walnut into its beak and flitted away.

'Wow,' said Lilly,

'A nuthatch.'

'I've never seen one of those.'

They were quiet for a moment.

'It's unreal,' said Lilly, 'Sitting here now, it just seems unreal.'

'The realest times do.'

'Do they?' she looked up at Joe again, 'I suppose they do. Why's that? Because reality isn't real I suppose,' she said, answering her own question, 'which must mean... when it seems real...'

'When it only *seems* real something is very wrong.'

Lilly said nothing. She was thinking on her all-too-real-seeming life.

'You're beautiful,' said Joe. It just slipped out.

'Really?'

'Yes.'

'Beautiful like what?' she asked wryly.

'Like this meadow.'

She laughed, 'haha! Now that's too much.'

'You talk as if you've never been compared to a field before.'

Many women, at the height of their youthful beauty, never

really feel beautiful. They confuse the feeling beauty for the pleasure of attention. Lilly, with the warmth of the hazy sun on her shoulders, and the warmth of Joe's hazy attention on the space between her fingers, did feel beautiful; she felt full of the beauty around her. She was that I am that.

'People don't say things like that now,' she said, 'They think it's sexist. They say "you wouldn't say that to a man", but I think "well, of course I wouldn't!".'

'People don't really say anything now,' said Joe. 'Talking with people is like playing Top Trumps.'

'Yes, or even if they do say something, they don't mean it. What upsets me...'

'And it seems to be getting worse,' said Joe, following his own thought.

'It is. People don't have feelings any more,' said Lilly sadly. 'They just... I don't know, they just don't. It's like a nightmare. And men, they don't approach women any more, so of course women don't go to him. Why should I? It's the minimum, I think, that you like me enough to come over and talk to me. But no, everyone meets up on apps. Meet up, have sex, split up, then go onto another one. That's it now, but they're not having more sex, they're having less sex. Much, much less. Maybe once a month. It's a sexual wasteland.'

'Covered in erotic adverts.'

Lilly was distracted, a little on edge; but it was excitement, at finally, *finally*, having someone to talk to. She phoned her Scottish Gran every now and then, but it wasn't the same. Granny Mags was lovely, and she understood things, but also she didn't; she got 'a bit funny' with some subjects, like sex, drugs and rock and roll. Here was someone who Lilly could completely say anything to and not have to worry that she might touch a sore spot which, it sometimes seemed, was all there was to people, just giant sore spots walking around trying not to get touched.

'But what I was going to say,' she said, 'is that, what upsets me about the way people speak, is how they say "bye". Nobody seems to be able to say it very well at all. Do you know what I mean?'

'They have problems with hello too.'

'Yeah, that too. But "bye", you know, it could be the last word you ever hear from someone, the last pebble in the pond, and most people, they seem to just want to get it out of the way. Sometimes it really ruins things, like we've just had this nice long conversation and then you just get this rushed, angry "bye". It's just not, erm…'

'…honest.'

'Yes, it's a dishonest "bye". But then I suppose a lot of things are.'

'What, dishonest?'

'Yeah, dishonest bread, dishonest coughs, dishonest curtains, dishonest power chords, dishonest haircuts.'

'Your haircut is very honest,' said Joe, lightly rubbing her cool brown hair.

'Do you think so?'

'I like it,' said Joe, forming its shape in the air, 'I could build a shed with it.'

'Really? Actually, underneath, my head is a funny shape.'

Joe felt it. It was indeed slightly unusual, a little wide at the back.

'Oh yes,' he said, 'It's alright though. I like women with deformed heads.'

'Do you? That's good. I also have very big knees.'

'Lift up your skirt,' said Joe. She did so. Her legs were shapely, strong, her knees also.

'Mmm. Great,' said Joe, 'I love big knees on a woman. The bigger the better. Ideally they'd be like big shiny boulders or like those spherical street lights.'

'Glowing in the dark.'

'Vast, vast, luminescent knees.'

'I also get severe, crippling attacks of anxiety and self-doubt. What about that? Do you find that attractive?'

'No, but that's because you've never really been loved.'

'That's true.' Lilly considered. 'Is there a connection then?'

'Between big knees and emotional neglect?'

'I mean, are you saying I need a man to be happy?'

'No, I'm saying you need me, now, to show you that you were always already happy.'

She looked up at him. It was useless looking, she could feel it was okay, that she was safe with Joe, but force of habit told her to look for evidence. It should be there.

'All right,' she said, 'Show me then.'

'Lie down,' he said.

She stretched forward onto the blanket and then turned onto her side. Joe lay down next to her.

'Now,' he said, 'I'm going to hug you, and love, and you're going to love as well.'

'But what if I don't love you? I don't think I do. I mean I'm not sure. I don't know.'

'Don't worry about loving *me*. Just feel the love. It's already there. If any thoughts pop up, just come back to the body.'

'Alright then, I'll give it a go.'

They embraced, softly but completely. But for the soft distant trilling of birds and the constant hushed rush of the warm air through the branches.

'Mmm,' said Lilly, letting herself go.

'Don't get excited,' said Joe, 'just breathe with me.'

The feeling of really hugging someone, after not having really hugged someone for a long time, is so similar to melting into a larger thing, that it's almost impossible to feel as if that is not happening, that the borders aren't collapsing and soon there will just be an undifferentiated pool of what was two. Usually a thing intervenes, to keep 'it together,' a thought, or some kind of restlessness, or boredom, or excitement, but something about Joe, and something about Lilly, and something about the moment, prevented that. Nothing got in the way. She flowed into him, soft water, seeking to merge at every point with his body. Maria yanked and slammed, there was distance, delay, something unphysical about her, some willing *thing*; but Lilly no. She was so physical there was no Lilly at all, just the need of her body to realise itself through living, flowing contact with a selfless other.

'Oh… oh… it's *very* nice,' she whispered.

'Do you feel that?' Joe could feel something happening, something he had never heard of or imagined.

'It's lovely!'

'I want to make love with your dinosaur self,' said Joe, gently into Lilly's ear.

'Okay then.'

But he didn't move. They lay together, embracing, occasionally looking at each other, then embracing again. There was no dry humping or grinding, no kissing; nothing was happening. They were both fully clothed and completely still, and yet both of them were overcome with a pleasure so intense that Lilly thought she might slip out of the world completely.

'I want…' said Joe, mind-addled, burning, 'I want you to play your trumpet…'

'I can't… can't play the trumpet,' said Lilly, breathless, 'will the oboe do?'

'Fine.'

'I want you to bobsleigh down my mountain…' she said.

Yes, mountain. Joe had the tremendous sensation that both of their bodies were colossal, that they could roll over and crush Edding and most of the municipality. 'We're enormous. We're enormous,' he murmured, a strange distant tickling sensation on his right buttock.

'I've never been bigger. I… ugh… ugh… *eeghuuoooh!*'

Lilly orgasmed, a long cascading climax. Joe also, although for him the physical ejaculation was like a snowflake dissolving, barely anything. It wasn't the shuddering carnality he was used to, nor the obliterating black hole of the mind he had fallen into orgasms past, but an almost horrific clarity, as if he had been launched into the air, reached the blue-brilliant apex, and for a moment time had stopped and a perfectly still alpine-clear totality was there, here, everywhere. It was eternity; not time going on forever, but time stopping revealing everything at once.

'Aggghhh… uhhh… *who's that…*' whispers Lilly with reckless urgency, flushing from her heart, all doors open.

'*Uhhhh… It's Jesus.*

Jesus Christ is sitting next to them, leaning against the tree chewing a stalk of wheat, which he's been tickling Joe's buttock with.

Lilly looks at Jesus and then at Joe. 'What's *he* doing here?'

'He's present for most sublime orgasms.'

Jesus stretches and yawns with comfortable pleasure. A girlish scream echoes across the meadow. Jesus, Lilly and Joe look up.

✿

Neil, in military gear, had been kneeling amongst the distant reeds with a telephoto camera set up in front of him. He had watched Joe and Lilly, attention squeezed and focused, for three hours. He had seen Gaynor come and go, and he had seen Joe and Lilly lie down and get fruity. He had taken photographs of them entwined in each other, but his memory card had run out, so he had put his hand into his pocket to pull out a replacement, and instead had pulled out the bird skull which Chiyo had put there earlier. This had made him squeal in alarm. A quick glance in the camera confirmed that Joe and Lilly had heard him, so he had slowly backed away, down a distant incline and away.

He walked along a country lane back to his car—he had bought a second-hand Volvo—thinking of nothing, seeing nothing. All he was now interested in was life, and everything he now did was to that end. The forces of life must prevail and the forces of death and destruction must be overcome. This is what the Bible had said, this is what Jesus had come into the world for, or at least that's what Robert Powell had said. Neil hadn't read much of the Bible, just a few bits, because it was rather heavy, but he had watched the 1977 television version of Jesus of Nazareth several times, and Jesus had confirmed to him there what the horrors of the recent past had taught him; that the world was essentially made up of whitewashed tombs, all fair and clean and interesting and edgy and entertaining and well-qualified and respectable on the outside, but inside full of inconsiderate dead men's bones. Tanish was a whitewashed tomb, Joe was, Gaynor was, Lilly was, kind of, although she only had a few dead men's bones inside, mostly her tomb was full of comfortable cushions and nice-smelling shampoos.

Jesus, Neil had decided, was essentially God's policeman, sent to uphold His laws—particularly the ones about making sure that 'every person be subject to the governing authorities'—were to punish lawbreakers—such as people who lent money at unsustainable interest rates—and to issue warnings for minor transgressions—like accidentally crucifying Jesus, as Pontius Pilate had done. Neil really felt for Pilate. The Pharisees had handed Jesus over to Pilate, and the poor man, out of the kindness of his heart, had let the *crowd* decide who to kill. *They* chose to let Barabbas free and nail Jesus to a cross; so what was Pilate to do? It was a *democratic* decision! How was it the procurator's fault that the people were imbeciles and had killed the man sent to whip them into shape? It was all a giant cock-up.

There were a few things that Jesus said which Neil wasn't fully behind. The thing about 'lifting up a stone and I'll be there'—what was that supposed to mean? Did Jesus hide a series of duplicate Jesus-midgets around the garden?—and the comment about the Kingdom being spread out before us but we can't see it—erm, I don't *think* so—and the story about the prodigal son being welcomed—how was *that* fair? But Neil had read that the New Testament was written a hundred years after Jesus had died, so of course the writers would add their own barmy stuff. Writers were always doing that.

He got in his car and massaged his painful cheek. Last night there had been a blackout. According to the BBC Radio 4 (still the world's finest news service) terrorists were more than likely involved. Neil had listened to it over his usual breakfast of dry toast and vitamin pills. He'd been so involved in the story, and so worked up about evildoers, that he had bitten hard into his cheek, something he did about once a week. He'd swilled his mouth out with warm salt water, but the terror of infection was again on him, and the thought that bacteria were, right now, colonising the wound, multiplying in his mouth, pus, from dead tissue, oozing over his gums. He hastily swilled a mouthful of Listerine, spat it out the window and checked LifeLine; alerts appeared for elevated cortisol, as usual, reduced white cell count (further risk of infection) and possible zinc deficiency.

When, wondered Neil, were they going to perfect vr? Once I've uploaded my mind into the omni-cloud, and merged with the diamond body, I won't have these problems. He sometimes read science fiction stories in which people become fused with an artificial intelligence. They were supposed to be 'dystopian' but what's dystopian about living forever, knowing everything and being able to do whatever you want? If that's not the 'Kingdom of Heaven', then what is?

Neil picked up forty kilos of ice cubes, a bag of jumbo prawns and his selective serotonin reuptake inhibitor prescription on the way back home to his bedroom — a.k.a.'mission control' — where he continued his project of upholding eternal life and taking the Satanic forces of chaos into custody. He first took a shower of piping-hot water, scrubbed his skinny white body vigorously with Lifebuoy carbolic soap, then lowered himself into a bath full of ice for two minutes. As often happened, he nearly passed out from hyperventilating (it was okay because, as the Ice Man Hof had said, with no water in the tub, drowning was impossible) and so, by the time he had pulled himself out, he was half dead; but he was also, at the same time, half-immortal. After he had recovered, he got changed into his home wear, a white tracksuit with black epaulettes, had a quick snack of disinfected prawns then opened his wide desk drawer, removing The Project, which he had been working on since Ursula's funeral.

The Project was a dossier, an A4 Stalogy folder with 'The True Joe' written on the cover in letraset Helvetica. He placed this on his desk, surrounded by high-quality Japanese stationery (electronic letter opener, Midori compact correction tape, Raymay portable scissors, Mitsubishi pencils) and continued his concentrated work, carefully placing photos and writing neat captions. The page he was working on was titled 'Animals that Joe has Killed', with a long list, including Bechstein's bat, capercaillie, Scottish wildcat and beaver. A column titled 'has eyelashes?' had a series of red ticks alongside the animals.

Other chapters had titles such as 'People Joe has Hurt', 'Lives Joe has Ruined', 'Frighteningly Weird Things Joe has Done', 'Lies that Joe has Told', 'Things that Joe has Blown Up', 'Cold Psychotic Aspects to Joe's Character', 'Relationships Made Nightmarish by Joe's Presence' and so on. It was put together with perfectionist care, backed up with photographs, references, internet links and suggestions for further reading.

Doubt prickled him, the faraway thought that it *might* not be right to go to all this trouble, but of course everyone has doubts before they do something bold and courageous. And this was justice. To present Joe truthfully, as he really was, as Neil really knew him, behind the affable loon. This was the right thing to do. Neil was sure of it, and he was sure that right behind him, nodding him on with fatherly approval, was D.C.I. Christ.

Margaret and Louis had spent an agreeable afternoon sitting on the rear patio of Margaret's house blasting away at bric-a-brac with two old shotguns. Margaret, with her waist-tied rope leading inside through her bedroom window, held her weapon like a professional, although she aimed and fired more casually than Louis, who was perfectly serious. They were shooting at teddy bears, old lamps, plates, various antiques, packets of Ritz crackers, anything she'd 'had enough of,' lined up on a bench at the bottom of the garden. After a particularly fevered round of blasting, shattered wood, plastic and glass littering the tulip patch, clouds of bitter cordite drifting across the lawn and over the canal, Louis had burst into giggly laughter and Margaret, flushed, joyous, had said, 'There are so many things to *shoot* these days.'

It was now afternoon and both, tired after the shooting and a heavy meal of roast duck, were dozing in their rooms, when the doorbell rang. Louis loosened himself from the massive Mexican hammock he had slung across his bedroom and flip-flopped down the corridor.

A chipper young ginger and inexpressive long-faced woman, both dressed in cheap nylon suits stood in the doorway.

'You are Louis Gallardo?' asked the long-faced woman.

'Ooh! Yes,' he smirked.

'My name is Raimonda, this is Andy. We're from Social Services. We would like to come in and have a chat with Mrs. Geb if we may?'

'Ah, oh, um... What about?'

'We've had someone contact us who is concerned about Mrs. Geb's wellbeing and we're here to assess her.'

'Who?'

'Well,' said Raimonda, 'several people have contacted us. I'm not at liberty to say who, but they believe that she may need extra support.'

'Louis,' said Andy, with the shallow confidence of well-educated young people, 'can I call you Louis? We really don't want to get the police involved here, but we do need access to Mrs. Geb. Do you see? It would be better if we came in, rather than involve the police.'

Louis sighed, let them in and led them through. He knocked on Margaret's door, alert for anything unusual. Her 'come in!' sounded effortful and out of breath, so he said to Andy and Raimonda, 'please wait here' and endeavoured to slip in to make sure everything was okay, possibly to warn Margaret, but before he could get in, Raimonda had said, loudly, 'Mrs. Geb I'm from Social Services, do you mind if we come in for a little chat?' and Margaret had said 'yes, yes, yes, if you must, if you must' and Raimonda, with supernatural speed, had inserted her foot into the open door and seen enough of the room to make concealing it futile.

Margaret was kneeling in her chair. She was surrounded by guns and her rope, tied as ever to her waist, was tangled up all round the room like Incan trip wires. She had clearly been contorting herself trying to get at something, but had given up, returning to her rocking chair but, bound by the now taut rope, was unable to sit comfortably in it. She nodded a distracted greeting to her visitors and then went back to absently looking around the chaos of her belongings, occasionally looking up at Andy and Raimonda to reply to them.

The two social workers gave each other a sideways glance. Louis stood behind them, his face icily impassive—unless either of the social workers turned to address him, then it would dissolve into his habitual bubbling glee.

'Hello Mrs. Geb,' said Andy, 'I'm Andy Dandy. We've come to just see how you are, and if you need any help?'

'Have you seen my new skin? I've been told I need it.'

'No, I haven't seen that,' said Andy, unfazed, 'Not today. Would you like us to untie you?'

'I had some, but it's fallen off. It does when it gets old you know,' said Margaret, 'it leaves you quite at the mercy…'

'And how's your health Mrs. Geb?' Raimonda interrupted with condescending clarity, 'Are you feeling okay?'

'Well, I think I might need the light one.'

'The light one?' Andy turned to Louis, 'The light one?'

'Oh, ah, ah, water. Water is the light one and tea is the dark one!'

'Okay, we'll get you the light one.'

'What other things do you eat and drink?' asked Raimonda.

'Other things? No other things. Just the light one and the dark one.'

Raimonda realised there was a full bowl of pea soup on her side table. 'What about that?' she asked.

'What about it?' said Margaret, irritated and still distractedly looking around her room.

'What about this soup?'

'No, I don't eat the green one.'

'Why not?' asked Andy.

'Because it's *too* green,' said Margaret, as if this were obvious.

'Would you eat it if we could get it less green?'

'Yes, but I only *eat* the brown one and the green one; but only if they're not too brown, or too green.'

'Is this true?' Raimonda asked Louis.

'Ugh! Oh! Yes! I suppose!' he said, squirming and grimacing.

'What's the brown one?' asked Andy.

'Potatoes in their skins.'

'So she is only consuming tea, water, peas and jacket potatoes?' Louis smiled pleasantly.

'She needs other… colours,' said Raimonda.

'Yes, yes. I'll make sure she has some other colours.'

'Ah! There it is!' said Margaret, beaming and pointing to the top of the wardrobe. 'Give it to me Louis.'

He stepped over the ropes to get to the wardrobe. 'Is it this ma'am?' he said, pointing at a 1,000 piece gasworks puzzle.

'No,' said Margaret.

'This? This?' he pointed to various other items on the wardrobe, a wide-brimmed felt hat, a lapis lazuli paperweight, a jewellery box, a netsuke display case—each met with an impatient 'no'—until he pointed at medieval helmet.

'Yes, that's it!' said Margaret. Louis brought down the iron helmet, a German Pickelhaube, the spiked eagle-embossed helmet of the Prussian army—and handed it to Margaret, who put it on and smiled at the social workers, evidently more comfortable about talking to them now.

∞

Joe sat at the dining table idly leafing through a scrapbook. The sound of the front door opening and closing was followed by Maria, flustered and driven, standing in the doorway, a four-litre bottle of milk hanging from her fingers.

'What's that?' she asked without greeting. She was now constantly nakedly hostile and to the point.

'It's my sacking log.'

'You've lost another one, have you?'

'Yep.'

'So you've actually reached the bottom.'

'No, no. Not quite yet.'

'Aren't you ashamed?'

'Of what?'

'Of being unemployed!'

'Ashamed? I feel less ashamed saying that I am unemployed than saying just about anything I can say about myself.'

Maria, one hand on the door frame the other on her hip, gave a long exasperated floor-staring sigh, 'You're actually happy about getting the sack… about not fitting!'

'Yes.'

She looked at him, as if realising something for the first time. 'You don't fit,' she said quietly.

'You're right there.'

'Don't you have any self-respect? Look at you.'

'What about me?'

'Look at how you're dressed!'

Joe looked down. He was still wearing his ape-breasted T-shirt and now dirty jeans.

'What's wrong with this?'

'It's a question of dignity. You have none. No dignity, no strength, no ambition.'

'I sent my book away…?'

He was referring to his notebook, which he had copied out by hand and sent away to literary agents and publishing companies, ignoring all their requirements (double-spaced sample and synopsis, brief bio., etc., etc.). They hadn't bothered to respond, and neither did Maria, who just asked him, with weary finality, 'Where are you going Joe? Where?'

'To the grave.'

'Can't you at least put up a fight?' she asked with querulous disgust.

'What? With who? With the world?'

'With me!'

'You? Why?'

'Why!?'

'Yes, why? What's the point? When I talk to you, all you can hear are words.'

Something essential snapped in Maria. 'I see, so I've got no empathy! Is that it? Me! I don't believe I'm hearing this. You couldn't give a *shit* about me. You have no *idea* what I go through, every day, the suffering I have to deal with, the world. How… Let me ask you this… How would *you* like it if you had to flee your home because your dad, who turns out to be your uncle, is beating you black and blue and your boyfriend is addicted to board-marker fumes and has also turned violent and you have to sleep in a builder's skip? Where's the justice then, eh? Where's your five-a-day, then? Where's your 'empathy' then!'

Her chest was heaving, heart at the end of its tether. 'You know,' she said, bitterly, 'I've got the world to deal with. The *world*. What have *you* got to deal with Joe?'

'Nothing.'

She gave him a final significant look, turned away, went into the kitchen, put the milk in the fridge, took out a bottle of wine, and then went up to their bedroom. After she had changed into her loungewear she got into bed and poured herself a glass of wine. A new will had settled on her. There was pain coming, walking out on Joe, but iron-cold determination had settled, the kind she knew, from experience, was absolutely invincible. This power came from being unquestionably right about what had to be done. It was here when she had to defend those who really did need to be defended, it was here when she had to attack those who really did need to be attacked, and it was here when she really could take no more. It was here now.

Joe was without feeling, without nobility, without any manly quality she could respect. He was like some kind of dark, mysterious charm, a jewel picked up in a fairy tale, which promised magic and mysterious adventures but was actually just a shiny rock, and very heavy. And somehow, *somehow*, he had something to do with her losing Max. She didn't know how, she barely reasoned any of this out; her thinking was disorganised, fragmentary, her thoughts dark sparks being thrown from the power burning in her spine, a dark fire horrible yet compelling, urging her on. She could easily go downstairs now and coolly smack Joe over the head with the geode next to the fire place.

She took another sip of wine, then picked up the book she was half reading, *The Other Me is Opening and Closing* by Sally Costello. It wasn't quite as good as *Bones in the Whisper* by Manx Shta; but what was? Thank God for books, she thought, if it weren't for the lovely feeling of recognition these great writers offered, *artists*, who really understood the human condition, she'd be in danger of thinking that *she* was going mad, that *Joe* was the sane one.

She chuckled and read on, the darkness of Joe forgotten; but a storm was about to break.

∞

The next day, grim, bleak winter returned. Joe, hailstones melting on his broad shoulders, walked through Edding. He'd aimlessly circuited the town, having forgotten what he'd left the house for. He passed the back of the cinema on Godwin Avenue, part of the new 'entertainment' complex of chain restaurants and bars. There was an art gallery there too. Clive would have loved all this. He was always complaining about the death of culture, but Joe found it strangely reassuring. So culture is dead, he thought, nobody had any use for it any more. It was a dead weight anyway, only kept alive by a few people who clung to it like barnacles. It's supposed to be for everyone, not just a handful of connoisseurs. Once all this has been cleared away, it will grow again, as it is supposed to, like the ever-growing, ever-dying grass. The world is just a crumbling, gutted, pigeon-shit-covered monument, waiting for a gust of wind to topple it, or for some secret group to pull the plug on the implacable mechanical monolith the mind has made of the world.

He found himself again interested in the distorted faces of his fellow humans, screwing themselves up against the foul weather, against their foul lives, against foul Edding, trying to resist it all away. They walked through these places of entertainment all balled up, as if expecting a blow.

But then Joe found something quite different. In the middle of Edding high street there was an old man with a P.A. singing to a karaoke backing track. He was small, unshaven, somewhat rubbery-looking and dressed in a patchy sweatshirt, dirty grey trousers, socks, sandals and a khaki-green woollen hat. His voice, rolling down the iron-wet high street, was intensely strained and totally out of tune, but his whole body was given to the performance, either hunched over or, hand on chest, delivered to the heavens, with all the passion of a celebrated opera singer. Sometimes he forgot words, or just missed a few out, but the moment's pause did not go to waste, he would use it to summon even more desperate effort, almost screaming the next toneless, tuneless syllable. The song he had chosen was Madonna's 'Like a Virgin', 'TOUCHED… for the very first time, li-i-i-i-ke a vir… SAVING it all for *you*… hold me and LOVE meeeeeee…'

Joe stopped to watch the entertainer. Everyone passing was reacting in the same way; disdain melting into disbelieving laughter. A man totally without talent was producing a more direct and honest response in his audience than anyone Joe had seen perform live, at least for many years. His concert-going days were long gone though. In fact he felt that culture generally seemed to be slipping from his shoulders.

He ambled into the Cathedral of Work and Pensions—the 'Jobcentre' as it was popularly named—and took in the standard tableau of quiet desperation; the leg-jiggling anxiety, the faces etched with profound care, the simmering, palpable hatred (although the room, like the last train home after the pubs had closed, was deliberately suffocatingly hot, to stifle violence).

He sat down on the hard, armless, knife-proof, fire-resistant settee, which was strangely close to the floor, next to two women, one staring straight ahead with a frozen, fearful look in her eyes—this was Bronya—the other with her head in her hands—Sophie. On the wall behind Sophie a poster read; 'Workfare: you've only got yourself to blame!' Another said 'Atomised? You bet!' Another one said, 'Don't have a steady job? You might be mentally ill; call this number now...'

Sophie sat up. She was dressed in a puffer jacket and ugly wasp-yellow leggings.

'Oh, hello,' said Joe.

'Hello.' She recognised him and a flicker of a smile creased her eyes.

'Are you loving Workfare?'

'Oh yeah,' she said, 'Loving it. The employability seminars are the absolute best. How to never ever sleep, or rest, or be sick.'

'It's hard work being unemployed.'

'I've never worked so hard. Filling in forms, waiting in queues, searching on the internet, filling in more forms, answering questions, getting certificates, waiting on the phone, it's just fucking endless. And then, if I do actually get work, I lose my benefits and it takes months to get them back, so when the work ends, which it does, I starve to death.'

'What about your boyfriend, the priest? Erm, can't remember his name.'

'Tim.'

'Tim works, workn't he?'

'Tim's on a zero hours contract too.'

'Is he really?'

'Yeah, he's on 24/7, like the rest of us. He's furious about it. Says he's going to give it up. But he's always angry.'

'Is he still getting angry about the flat?'

'No, I got that under control,' she said, her face brightening.

'You should smile more,' said Joe.

Her face soured again. 'I wish I had a reason.'

Bronya said nothing, just continued staring.

An advisor in front of them, 'Malcolm' read his name-badge, a small, drained beady man in his fifties, of Mauritian descent, called out, 'Joseph Geb.'

Joe got up and sat down opposite the little dark man with tired eyes, tediously surveying behind thick, square glasses.

'Have you worked since you last signed?' asked Malcolm, mechanically.

'Not really.'

'Not really?'

'Well, I haven't earned anything. I've done some temping.'

'Well, you have to declare. I mean you're supposed to. Zero hours is it?'

'Yeah, that kind of thing. I'm signed up for Gyp.'

'What's that?'

'I get pinged to go and do little jobs for people.'

'Are you looking for anything else?'

'Kind of.'

'I've got your personality profile here.'

Malcolm took a printout.

'It says here that you are lazy, unable to take responsibility, a poor team player, inflexible, recalcitrant, without any skills demanded by modern employers and quite possibly suffering from a mental illness.'

'That sounds about right.' Joe leant over to look at the paper in Malcolm's bony hand, 'is there not anything negative though?'

'You're down for a course in empowerment training.' He picked up a brochure.

'That sounds like fun.'

Malcolm read from the pamphlet. 'This course is for can-do, get-up-and-go, nothing-is-impossible, work-seeking super heroes. You'll listen to cheers of encouragement from specially record-ed crowds of enthusiasts, be whipped into shape by a godlike "empowerment coach" who will help mould a "hireable you" from the wet clay of your joblessness, through intense "positive thinking" and, finally, you'll be given tips by celebrity chef Jamie Oliver on how to make nutritious "austerity pilaf" from grains of carefully saved up rice.'

Malcolm put the brochure down. 'Bullshit yeah?'

Joe sighed the sigh of love; Malcolm was a fellow. 'I'm going to go with "yes",' he said.

'It's all bullshit. All of it! My head goes round and round like Worzel Gummidge. Do you watch Worzel?' Malcolm spoke in a high croaky outraged tone.

'No,' said Joe.

'All I want to do is sit in my back yard with a coffee and cigarette—I don't drink—and be allowed to die.'

'You're not alone there.'

'I've got—sign there—I've got cancer you see. *Claw*—see?' He pointed to his wrist, which was bent oddly. 'Going up my arm. Blocked arteries. I could be dead any second. But I'll do your claim first.'

He typed away. As he spoke—an unusual mixture of tension, desperation, anger, compassion and even cheer—he worked mechanically at the claim.

'I'll put down no work then, shall I? Just do your interviews, sign the forms, you'll be alright. You'll be alright. Bullshit though. *Bullshit*. You see. You see? We're in the same situation as you. In fact you're better off! At least you can watch Hogan's Heroes. Sometimes I start watching it—*please*, just let me watch one fucking episode of Hogan's Heroes. Do you watch it? Big one? I love the big one. Brilliant. I think I'm going mad.' He sighed, 'there,' he said. He had finished the claim.

'Thank you.'

'I say "live and let live". Do you know that? Just let people do what they want.'

'What if they want to hurt you?'

'Then batter them.'

'Batter them?'

'They've got dirty blood.'

'You're probably right.'

'In their brains. You must batter them, to get the dirty blood out.' He looked Joe in the eye. It was unclear to Joe whether he was being assessed for understanding, for fellow feeling or for the dirty blood.

Malcolm nodded, assessment complete. 'They murdered my mother,' he said, 'Sixty fucking years she worked for them. *Sixty* years and they wouldn't give her a fucking pension. Dead now. They killed her. They've killed me.'

'They're killing us all. Or something is.'

'If I saw an MP, any one, I'd kill him with my own fucking hands. *Bastards.* The *lot* of them. I'd like to take them out.'

'I'm not sure MPs have much power. It's bankers and investment people who make the big decisions.'

'I don't care. If I could get my hands around the necks of *any* of them I'd die a happy man.'

'If you really wanted to hurt them, you could delete everyone's records. Tax, police and health.'

'I've thought about that. Impossible, or it is for me.'

Joe nodded. Malcolm nodded. They shook hands.

'Just play the game,' said Malcolm, 'Put the face on and play the fucking game. Just don't get caught working.'

Joe stood up. Above Malcolm was a poster with a big smiley emoticon which read 'Don't shoot the messenger!'

♋

All morning Maria had had an odd feeling havering through her. The confidence of the evening before was still there, but a strange feary tension now also. She'd tried buying some stuff—a hand-woven wicker bliss basket, a tempered-glass gravity water filter, a jar of locally-sourced lavender honey—but that hadn't helped. When she walked through the main office, firing off her usual round of sharp hellos, and nobody replied, everyone looking at her strangely, sullenly, the feeling grew sharper, almost physically painful, and when she opened her office door and saw her boss in her chair, no-nonsense, big hitter Harriet Cousins, she knew a wall was about to fall.

'Oh! Harriet! Nice seeing you… here…' she said, trying to be breezy, but stumbling over Harriet's hard, empty face.

'Best skip the pleasantries Maria,' said Harriet.

'Oh?'

'Yes, it would appear that you were instrumental in putting Bronya Cosslett on suspension for…' she read from the screen, 'molesting geriatrics. And then you told her that she was actually fired? Without due process?'

'I can explain that…'

'Really? That's interesting. Can you explain the network of old ladies you have knitting cardigans for chickens, believing they are engaged in occupational therapy? I'd like to hear that explanation too.'

'That's all in a good cause Harriet.'

'Is it? Is it really? What about getting your staff to carry books on their heads?'

'I was doing that for their posture!'

'It's abuse.'

'How can doing something to help people be abuse? I'm sorry Harriet, that's just illogical.'

'I think you better take your things and leave. I'm going to deal with all this nonsense later,' she gestured vaguely at Maria's desk and computer.

'Bronya told you all this didn't she?'

'You know as well as I do that I can't divul…'

But she didn't finish the sentence. Maria had left. She walked as nobly as possible through the office, out into the cold car park and got in her car; but it wouldn't start. She turned it over and over again, the tension, hatred and misery were all flooding into her, building up and up, sloshing against the concrete dam she kept the world away with. She waited, trying to get hold of herself, waited, to get control, waited, and then turned the key again, and again the impotent, grinding, going-nowhere barren cranking.

'*Aggghhhhhhhhhhhhhh!*' She screamed, hammering at the horn, thumping the dashboard, 'fucking *life!*'

She stopped, feeling no better, still bunched up inside, but at least it was out. She gathered up her stuff and left the car.

Fifteen minutes later, she was at a filthy bus stop, driving rain sweeping down the office-building-lined dual carriageway. A few motley characters shivered under the shelter, readying themselves for an approaching single-decker bus. Maria, whose agitation had converted the bus timetable into a byzantine table of logarithms, turned to the nearest human, a tall, young man, and asked him aggressively, 'is this the 134?'

The young man turned to face her. His bony face was covered with acne. 'The 134? Yeah, yeah, it'll be here in a minute.'

'To the bus station?' she asked accusingly, as if he were some-how responsible for how she felt.

'Yep,' said the man, 'Can't go wrong with the 134. I'd avoid the 28 if I were you.'

The bus arrived and everyone got on. The man stood behind Maria in the queue.

'You going to the bus station then?' he asked.

'Yes.'

'Yeah,' he said, unable to read that Maria, curt and sharp, considered the conversation closed, 'they've changed it a bit recently. Much better now.'

'Uh huh.'

'My name's Gary,' he said. Maria didn't answer.

Gary sat down in the middle of the bus. Maria sat as far from him as she could, at the back. There was a scattering of passengers, among them a large man with a huge head, a tiny Chinese woman, a sleepy-looking young man with a bum-fluff beard and two old women. Gary turned back to Maria and, almost shouting said; 'Yeah, it's got air-conditioning now.'

Maria said nothing.

'What?' asked Gary.

'I didn't say anything,' she said.

'Do you have a boyfriend?' he asked.

'No, yes…'

'Problems there are there?'

Maria looked out of the window. Her phone rang.

'Maria?'

'Yes, who is this?' she asked.

'P.C. Neil Eastwood.'

'Neil?'

'Yes. Neil.'

'What do *you* want?'

'I um. I uh… Erm, do you know where Joe was yesterday?'

'No.'

'He was on a girl, with a young hill… a young girl, on a hill. They were naked and rolling around. I have photos, which I will now proceed to send to…'

'What? What? What? What are you talking about?'

'Your husband is a *deceiver*,' hissed Neil, 'Have you seen the things he does, when he's on his own?'

'How could I see him if he's on his own?'

'Er…'

'Are you a cretin?'

'I might be a cretin, but I'm a very well-informed one.'

'Alright, alright. Send me what you've got.'

'Okay, great, I was wonde…'

Maria hung up.

The bus stopped. A twitchy man with thick glasses and long, lank straggly blonde hair got on.

'A single to Edding please,' he said.

A podgy man two seats down from Maria, called out in an extraordinarily gay lisp; 'Hello Lester!'

Gary again shouted back to Maria; 'When we get to the bus station you can come round to mine if you like. I've got my own house.' Again, she ignored him.

'A single to Edding please,' said the man at the front with long hair.

'I've just given it to you,' said the bus driver, whose name tag read 'Lionel Gregory.'

'Lester! Lester!' cried the camp man, waving his hand around, 'Coo-eeee!'

Maria's phone buzzed. She looked at the photographs of Joe and Lilly enjoying themselves on the hill. The girl in question wasn't naked nor was it, annoyingly, possible to see her face. It was perfectly clear what was happening though.

'A single to Edding please,' said long-haired Lester, for the third time.

'It's there!' cried the bus driver, pointing at the ticket in front of him, 'It's *there!*'

'Lester! It's me! It's Frankie!'

One of the old women at the front tutted. 'Can we get a move on please?' she said.

'Come and sit down here,' said Gary to Maria.

'Fuck *off.*'

'Have it your way,' he said, turning back round.

Meanwhile, the bus driver was trying to poke a ticket into Lester's pocket, while he, Lester, kept stepping out the way. As this dance went on, Bronya appeared behind Lester. She too skipped left and right, trying to get round the young man, then, flashing her bus pass, pushed her way past onto the bus.

'*You!*' hissed Maria.

Bronya stood in the aisle, hands on hips. The two women looked at each other. A kind of dramatic freeze descended on the bus. Everyone suddenly had the feeling something was very importantly *up.*

'Having fun are ya?' said Bronya.

'You fucking *bitch*. After everything I've done for you!'

'Everything? Like *what*? Like work me to death? Like block my promotion? Like get me fired?'

'I'll… I'll… I'll…' Maria was now beside herself. All eyes had turned to her.

'What? What?' said Bronya, '*What* are you going to do?'

'You want to know?'

'Perhaps you've forgotten that I don't work for you any more? I don't give a *fuck* what you do.'

'You don't know what I'm capable of.'

'Do your worst. Cunt.'

Maria rushed at Bronya. The old women gasped. Bronya bent forward and raised her arms defensively. Maria too raised her hands, and closed her eyes, colliding oddly and blindly with Bronya, both clattering clumsily to the floor. Everyone stood up or leant forward to watch as the two women engaged in a weird, long and undignified, eyes-closed, scrabbling, grunting, elbowing fight, in which neither of them could land a punch. Just lots of groaning and growling and breathless swear words.

The bus driver turned off his engine and came to watch also. Even a couple of people outside the bus, faces pressed against the windows, were watching; quietly, but evidently with mild pleasure, until Maria, right arm round Bronya's waist, lashed out with her left hand, catching Bronya's face with her nails and drawing blood. The shock and pain gave Bronya a burst of energetic fury and, with a subhuman grunt, she twisted round, swiped at Maria's blouse and ripped it, along with the right strap of her bra, away from her body, exposing a large, beautiful breast, which sent a ripple of astonished awe through the audience and seemed to break up the momentum of the battle. Maria, knackered, chest heaving, completely undone, pulled herself to her feet, her naked breast, smeared with Bronya's blood, hanging savagely from her torn clothes. Bronya lay on the floor, looking up, warily, ready for more…

But neither of them moved. The battle was over. The two women got their breath back, sat down, smoothed down their hair and arranged their ripped clothes. Maria, without embarrassment, pulled her bra and blouse across her chest.

One of the old women at the front turned to the other and asked 'who won?'

The second turned to the first and said 'I think we all won today.'

Bronya, face scratched, hair like a goth wrestler, buttons torn from her now filthy coat, lurched off the bus, leaving Maria legs splayed and heaving on the back seat, and walked into town. Since losing her job she had spent every day in bed, eating Jaffa cakes and watching Celebrity Welding. Occasionally she got tired of eating and staring at her screen and would lie in bed in a kind of frantic sadness, thoughts zipping across her mind like bats in a sandstorm, yet paralysed, as if a steel padlocked band lay across her chest. She had a desperate need to move, to get somewhere and do something, yet an equally urgent fear and apathy about leaving the bed, a horrified feeling that time was pouring away, like sand from a smashed hourglass, while, at the same time, that nothing was really happening or ever would or ever could, the falling sand grains suspended in frozen time. Then, at four thirty or five o'clock, the sun would go down, and all of this would evaporate completely. She would feel liberated, freed, able to stroll around town, talk to friends—even give them advice about their lives. She wasn't sure how, but being fired had left her with a pathological fear of the day.

Only one thing could get her out of bed, and that was money. She had very little of it, and had to sign on, which is where she had been before wrestling with her former manager on the 134. Now, forced into the cold, windy, aimless outside, she could feel the futility of life like a physical presence, and not merely a temporary one, like a passing cloud, but as a fundamental primitive fact of the universe, stretching backwards and forwards to the limits of time itself. Matter itself seemed to be made of hopeless sadness. For the first time she could see, on the faces of people passing her, the reality of this squalid demoralising shadow life, in which nothing good or useful or real could *ever* be achieved. She had tried to teach people, she had tried to help people; but why? Why? It made no difference at all. Nothing made any difference, and if you ever did do something which made a difference, you'd get in trouble for it. She thought of the few times she'd 'gone the extra mile' for a client, spending longer with someone than she should, giving them advice on where to buy good, real cheese online, pulling bobbles off their jumpers; and how that 'extra mile' had actually been off the map, dangerous, unprofessional.

Futile, futile, futile. All the pointlessness of living was reflected back to her now on the futile faces of the futile people who passed. There were two kinds of face; one that expressed knowledge of the fundamental misery of existence—these were the faces that looked like collapsed soufflés—and denial of the same—faces that looked like boarded-up windows.

She sat down on a low concrete wall, not caring that it was wet. The local council had decorated it with inspiring quotes from a moderately famous writer who had drowned nearby after writing a poem about how an alien invasion would be a good thing for Edding. A down-and-out had left his wet sleeping bag and unfolded cardboard box, presumably off to work himself. Horrible weather to be out begging, but she knew that they got more money in the cold and wet. If it snowed a beggar could make as much as a crippled strawberry picker.

Suddenly the bag moved. Someone was in it. Bronya, startled, moved away, ready to leave, when a small black head popped out of the bag and harmlessly, mournfully smiled at her.

'Afternoon,' he said.

'Hello.'

'Can I use your phone?'

Bronya, suspicious, assessed him. Like all people who are poor at reading others, she was instantly suspicious.

'Why?'

'I need to call my mother,' said the man. His tremulous, slightly camp accent was broad, West African.

'Where?'

'In Nigeria. I.., I..' He fished in his pocket and pulled out a filthy tenner. His dark eyes were wrinkled up in misery. He looked like he was about to cry.

'This is all I have. Please I must talk to my dear mother.'

'Okay,' said Bronya, taking the money, hesitantly.

'Thank you madam. Thank you.'

Bronya handed over her phone and the man dialled.

He cleared his throat, composed himself, then started speaking, with startling, upbeat clarity. 'Mama? Mama. Is Jayamma. Yes o, I'm calling from London. Uh huh. Yes. Yes. London, England. Yes...! Oh too good, too good. I have my own house now, in Chelsea... yes, yes, Celestine Babayaro, Victor Moses... and... I have a fiiiiine girlfriend. She too..' he looked up at Bronya, '... she tooo fine. Her heart so, *so* beautiful. Sometimes she too sad, but I love heart, I love heart, I tell her, wounded heart bleeds ugly thoughts. I love heart, then she healed and the heart rise in eyes like morning sun in east. Wait first, I go send her picture.'

He mouthed 'please?' Bronya, unexpectedly moved, nodded, then shook her head quickly, 'wait,' she whispered, smoothed her hair down and removed her now shabby coat, then nodded again.

The man took the photograph and continued talking;

'I know. She just dey like mammy water...' he looked again at Bronya, '*the queen of the forest.*' Bronya smiled, 'Work? My work na to sell property around one river Thames. Na very big river o. The work dey pay well but I no dey get time. I go send money soon sha. Very soon Mama, soon. I have to... No, no, I have to go now. My people here dey wait me. Bye. Bye. You be my every-every. I will... I will *always* love you Mumma.'

He gave the phone back to Bronya with a timid 'thank you

ma'am.' Bronya looked at the photo he had taken; flushed from battle, moved by compassion, she looked more beautiful than she had since she was seven.

She gave back the tenner.

8

Not far away, Joe was standing in the doorway of a supermarket looking at his phone. His 'Gyp app' had pinged him a message: 'Are you ready to serve? Yes/No' He selected 'Yes' as two young mothers emerged, one saying to the other 'A frying pan for 99p? There *has* to be something wrong with it.'

A loading icon span, followed by text; 'there is a Gyp client seven metres north of you. Please confirm your degradation settings.' Initially Joe had placed these parameters at a respectable level, that of mere service, which he had long felt—waiting tables, cleaning clothes, driving taxis and so on—was a worthy, even honourable, activity. There was something of service about all the best things people did. Unfortunately, at this setting the competition was fierce. Japanese people cleaned up of course, and lower-caste Indians did as well, as did Poles and some Brits too, but the only way to guarantee work was to 'freely' accept lower and lower levels of degradation until, like Joe, you were down in the shadowy realms of 'open abuse.'

He hurried into the supermarket, towards the automatic checkout, where a harried woman was attempting to scan a tin of beans. The checkout was having none of it:

'There is an unexpected item in the packing area Amīr al-Mu'minīn,' said the machine, which had been programmed to refer to all customers as 'Serene Commander of the Faithful,' the traditional style of office for Caliphs and other independent sovereign Muslim rulers.

'Fuck right off, dick,' said the woman, removing items.

'I do not have the pleasure of understanding you your eminence. Please wait and a checkout monkey will attend you.'

One of the employees, dressed as a monkey, waddled over, grunting and 'ooh-ooh-oohing'.

'Hold on,' said the monkey, scanning his card and tapping on the screen, 'alright, you're good now.'

The woman tried again to scan her beans.

'Sorry your most holy eminence,' said the machine, 'those beans do not appear to exist in this realm.'

'Jesus fucking *Christ!*' cried the woman, just as Joe appeared. 'Ah,' she said, 'you're here. Lie down.'

Joe did so and the woman gave him a good kicking, screaming all the time, really letting it out. Other customers, too polite to look, hurried through their own scanning, as Beth let loose on the large curled-up form beneath her. Finally, out of breath, she stopped, picked up the tin of beans and scanned it. The machine bleeped and, satisfied, she dropped it into her shopping bag.

꙰

Lilly was working on an old Scot with two large buck teeth which she was cleaning with a cotton bud. His name was, appropriately enough, Rab.

'Do you know,' she said to the man, 'I think I might have been wrong about getting somewhere, about having a mission. I think my mission might be to burn with gladness. To not go anywhere, but sort of go supernova, right where I am.'

She paused, looking into the past. 'Something very strange happened to me yesterday,' she said, 'I wouldn't tell a living soul, but you'll probably get it. I had a kind of, I suppose it was a spiritual experience, with a man, and it was absolutely tremendous. It was like dissolving into this massive, huge watery world of… I want to call it love, but it wasn't that, it was nothing, but it was everything… uh, it sounds silly when I put it into words, and actually, when I got up this morning I thought I'd dreamt it, or Joe had spiked my tea, or, or… uh, it's just that I can remember what happened, like a description, but there's nothing there behind it, so all day I've been thinking I must have just temporarily gone mad, because Joe, he's, he's funny, and charming and interesting and I feel I can completely and totally be myself with him, and he's got beautiful hands, but there's also something so creepy there, he's got a look in his eye, it's like a distant star, looking down on earth, with all the misery here, and all the death and war and rape and torture and suffering and just that, the eye is just looking, just not caring at all. But then I don't think I've ever felt… I mean he was so completely into it, like he was completely into me, I've never felt so…intoed.'

She stopped for a moment and thought to herself. Yesterday was like paradise, so why did she feel such foreboding? Like she was being led into a trap, some kind of cult? Joe was almost miraculously unassuming. She couldn't imagine him telling a dog what to do, much less a human being, and yet… and yet…

It was time to stuff Rab's throat with cotton wool, which was a fiddly job. As she was finishing off the tricky final stitch the door opened and the plastic curtains rustled. Carl came in and casually leant against the back wall, admiring Lilly's arse. Something, since yesterday's delivery to Victor, had unsettled his heart. The buttocks in front of him, normally so mesmerising in their orb-like perfection, had something troubling about them, menacing even. Sometimes arses were like that, you pulled off a pair of knickers, expecting to see something raw and beast-like, and instead you got a really weird thing, not of this world.

'I've signed up for medical trials,' he said.

Lilly, finished stuffing Rab's throat, turned round, detecting the unusual discomposure on Carl's face. She assumed it was connected to what he'd just said. 'What's that?'

'Basically, you stay in a hospital for a month. They feed you a new drug and monitor your reaction. Three weeks I'll be there, so Paul will help you with removals for a bit.'

'I don't get it though. Why?'

'Just to get away from the wife and kids really.'

'You don't like them?'

'"Like" doesn't really come into it. We just don't get on.'

'You don't get on with your wife and kids?'

'No,' he said, needled, 'I don't see why I should. I don't get on with Jürgan Klopp.'

'Who's Jürgan Klopp?'

'You don't know? He's the Liverpool manager. Great manager, revolutionised the modern game, dunno where we'd be without him, but… I used to clean his swimming pool. He's just not nice to be around, do you know what I mean? There's just something…we just don't click, that's all,' he finished, getting annoyed.

'But he's the Liverpool manager.'

'Yeah, I know. I just told you that.'

'And your kids are your own children.'

'The point is, Jürgan Klopp won us the premier league *and* the champion's league, and I don't get on with him.'

'But he's not your family.'

'Did you get on with your parents?'

'No, but that's different.'

'How is it different?'

'It was their fault. Not mine.'

'But it's *not* my fault. All my kids are weird and, and… they're *fucked up!* They're like alien beings. I can't have a conversation with them about anything. I probably most like Shelley, me girl, but we don't have anything to talk about either. I mean she's an eight-year-old girl. She has no interest in Liverpool at all.'

'What is she interested in?'

'Ballet. She's mad on it.'

'Why don't you talk to her about that?'

'Ballet?' Carl winced with the ridiculousness of it, 'You're having a giraffe!'

'Carl, how do you expect to have a relationship with your children if you don't even try to understand them, to get in with them. You could, you could…' Lilly was getting heated now, '… you could learn about ballet, take her to the ballet, teach her moves. There's loads and loads you could do. Honestly, you're so…'

The phone on the wall rang. Carl, whose face was curled

up in confusion, had backed out of the room. Lilly sighed and picked up the receiver.

'Hello Nina.'

'Lilly, sorry, but, uh, could you hurry up a bit? We've got three to fit in before c.o.b.' said Nina, jittery and twitchy as ever.

'I'm going as fast as I can.'

'Erm, sorry, but… I don't *think* so.'

'I am!'

'You should easily be able to fit them in. We don't have any viewings today.'

'Okay, okay, okay.'

In the reception area, while Nina and Lilly were speaking, Paul, standing at the small front desk, was bowing to an extremely old Chinese man, whose liver-spotted skin looked like it had been smoked over his bones. He was assisted by a pretty, stocky, cheerful-looking teenage Asian girl carrying a briefcase.

'How can we help you sir?' asked Paul.

The old man looked Paul up and down, and then spoke, or rather croaked, in Hakka Chinese. He said *'The trustworthy; I trust them. The not trustworthy; I also trust them. This is the trust of nature.'*

Paul turned to the young girl, the vaguest and most respectful wrinkle of confusion on his towering brow.

'My grandfather,' said the girl in a thick Brummie accent, 'Mr. Sun Wukong, he says we would like to see Ms. Nina Eedie.'

Paul sadly shook his head. 'I'm afraid she's busy,' he said.

'In engaging in warfare it is said: I dare not be the host but be the guest, I dare not advance an inch but retreat a foot,' said Mr. Wukong, again in Chinese.

'She won't be busy for us,' said Cherry, placing the briefcase on the reception desk and opening it. Paul's eyes opened wide, shamefully wide; the briefcase was full of clean fifty pound notes.

'One moment please,' he whispered, and vanished through the frosted glass doors behind him.

Five minutes later Nina, sweat trickling down the back of her scrawny neck, trying to remain composed, was in the middle of negotiations with Mr. Wukong and his granddaughter, Cherry. All three of them were in Nina's office, all seated around her desk.

'Well,' said Nina, 'it certainly sounds feasible. Obviously I'll have to have the details looked at.'

'One who is courageous out of daring is killed. One who is courageous out of not daring lives,' said Mr. Wukong, in his own language, Cherry again translating, 'My grandfather says the feasibility study will take four weeks. If everything is in order, we will buy your business for 2.5 million pounds sterling.'

Nina's jaw worked away silently, but nothing came out. Eventually she spat out some word-like blurtings.

'...Chat with ...My lawyer ...Of course ...In touch ...Soon.' She sounded like she was chewing a rubber band.

Mr. Wukong looked at Cherry. Cherry addressed him, in Chinese. *'Without being beckoned, the way of heaven yet comes of its own accord, unhurried, it is yet good at planning.'*

Mr. Wukong nodded and slowly pulled himself to his feet. To Nina he concluded; *'What is high up is pressed down, What is low down is lifted up; What has surplus is reduced, What is deficient is supplemented.'*

'My grandfather says,' said Cherry, 'that he is convinced that everyone will conclude this arrangement to the eternal pleasure of heaven.'

Nina nodded enthusiastically, 'I think so too,' she said, 'heaven *loves* success.'

જી

The day was now bloodless and spittle-flecked; the great god of the skies a bilious vagrant, angrily shouting at no one. Joe was lying down on his side at the far north end of Shenleybury Park, blowing a raspberry at a daffodil and waving his right arm around. He stopped and thought to himself, then leant back, took his phone out and texted Lilly: 'Seeing you yesterday was like conducting an invisible orchestra while savagely licking a daffodil.'

On the other side of the park, outside the Coffee Manifesto cafe, Chiyo was sitting at a sheltered park bench in the gobbing rain. She was working away at a napkin, folding and folding it. On the table next to her, in a rain coat which had lost its waterproofing, looking extremely bedraggled, was Irving. He was staring hopelessly at the menu, despair scorched into his little red eyes, like cigarette burns in a pair of pudgy, hairy little cheeks.

'This is so wanky,' he said to himself.

Chiyo continued her napkin origami.

'Don't you think?' said Irving.

'What?' said Chiyo, still focusing on her napkin.

'Don't you think this place is wanky?'

'What is wanky?'

'This place. Look. It has a 'philosophy,' it serves food on a board, its beans are 'lovingly selected,' it 'reaches out to' customers. Do you see?'

'Wakatta, I see,' she said, now looking up at Irving, '"Passionate about socks", is wanky?'

'Yes! Exactly!' he said.

'So you are not wanky?'

'I am many things, but I am not wanky.'

'What are you eating?'

'It's some kind of falafel I think,' he said, gloomily prodding the brown mush.

'Are you vegetarian?'

'Yes,' he said, 'but that doesn't mean I like animals.'

'What is in your bag?'

'A magnifying glass, a torch and a pencil.'

'No,' concluded Chiyo, 'you are not wanky.'

'It's not much, but it's something.'

Chiyo handed him her wet napkin, from which she had created a perfect, paper baby.

'Thanks,' said Irving.

Joe walked past the cafe, passing both Chiyo and Irving, not seeing either. He was wandering aimlessly, puffed by the lightest, vaguest gusts of desire. He sauntered out of the park. As he passed through the park gates an old woman approached. He made an excessively welcoming flourish towards where she was already going.

'Just down there madam,' he said. She glanced nervously at him and hurried through.

He smiled benignly at other passers by. Nobody looked back, all were strangers. It was a world of strangers. Edding was a scummy bucket, the weather was anti-human, home was a pressure cooker of emotional pain and work was a pointless, degrading nothing, but Lilly had illuminated this moment, once again protected it from the menacing ghost of the next moment, bridging the microscopic immensity between me here and that there, spanning the distance that had opened up between Joe's consciousness and the things of life, starting with the not-thing called Lilly. For as long as he could recall, sexual activity was a curiously distanced event, something that the body got pleasure from, as it got pleasure from a hot bath, but which the mind seemed more *interested* in than anything else. Kiss the neck, stroke the thigh, suck the nipple... It was a long, long way from the delirious and immersed intoxication of youth; the feeling of naked leg on naked leg, or of reaching into a bra, was almost impossibly *close*, and in the proximity there was magic. Joe could remember feeling, as a girl's nipple first brushed against his knuckle, as if he had gained access to a fairy kingdom, as if an alien, from a transcendently other dimension had visited him and was teaching him the secrets of the seventh level—by inserting her tongue in his ear.

Then the mystery had slipped away, and although it had reached blinding heights—the first few months of sex with Maria was like taking poppers on a galloping horse—it was still *of this world*, the same world as bra advertising, agony aunt radio call-ins, sensual costume dramas and *Sluts with Nuts*. Better, realer, but part of *that*, part of everything, one among many of the things of a world that seesawed between work and fun, things made by work which become things enjoyed in fun. All just *things*. Maria was a thing-self, no matter how much he tried to get past that.

Lilly, no. They had embraced and they had not been separate bits, and so, as a result, there had been no words either. After Jesus had appeared they had been wordlessly one. Joe had wondered if words had to return at all, if it *were* actually possible to reach the silent state, speechless, yet constantly communicating, merged in a swirling pool of atmospheres and qualities, nodding, meeting each other's eyes, suddenly bursting into laughter, or dance, or wrestling, but with no need to degrade the strange knowing with mere language. It seemed unlikely that one could wordlessly beam 'don't forget to get some Greek yoghurt on your way home because we need it for the pancakes,' but maybe those kinds of things also.

But why hadn't she rung?

His phone vibrated in his pocket. The feeling of *her*, the buzz represented *she*. There was a little envelope icon on the screen, and that also represented *she*. The whole universe in a little 'you have mail' icon. He opened his email app, but it was an alert from Gyp, asking him if he wanted any work. He was now leaning against the park railings. Ursula, naked as always, is reclining in a flowerbed in the park behind him.

'Leave the script Joe,' she says through the iron bars.

He turns round, unsurprised to see her.

'But how? Even no script is a script.'

'That's just the kind of thing the script would say,' she says, dingling a wet tulip leaf against her lips.

'I don't get it. I'm sure my life used to be easier than this.'

'But was it Joe? Was it?'

'I think it was.'

'Time covers the flowing sheets of memory with flecks of believable bullshit.'

'What are you saying? That I shouldn't accept this job?'

She leans back, the alabaster whiteness of her skin almost glowing against the blackness of the soil, which doesn't cling to her. She looks like a priceless porcelain sculpture thrown onto a compost heap. 'If I told you what to do,' she says, 'I'd be giving you a reason to be irresponsible.'

'I'm not sure about that. I mean I'm not sure I'd feel good about myself accepting the advice of my dead sister.'

He thought about it. He needed the money. That was always the bottom line wasn't it? Why was dying at work any worse than dying in Disneyland? They were the same thing; if anything work was even more fake.

An enormous treble-chinned woman waddled past talking into an earpiece. 'Fucking love time and space' she said.

Joe looked back down at his phone, accepted the Gyp offer and then turned to Ursula to explain his decision, but she had vanished.

∞

'Go away Neil.'

Neil's muffled voice came through the door, almost from under the door. 'I just want to give you something, it's very important and it will change your life for the better.'

Lilly stopped playing (she had been working on the bass part for *Stand on the Word* by the Joubert Singers, a first step into the black). 'Please go away,' she said.

'I'll come in, very quickly, and then I'll leave very quickly. You'll hardly notice me.'

'God, alright then, hurry up.'

The door opened a little, Lilly caught a glimpse of Neil's terrified drawn face, there was a hand and something slid across her carpet. 'It's all in there,' he said with pursed lips through the slender door crack, 'everything you need to know. I'm just…It's you I'm thinking of Lilly.'

She put her guitar down. 'No, it's *you* you're thinking of.'

His final words, 'just look,' were whispered, ghostlike, as the door gently gently closed.

On the floor was a tidy dossier. She picked it up and opened it. The first page was titled 'Joe Geb's History Of Murdering And Torturing Animals.' There was a photograph of Joe, with a gun in one hand and a huge dead lynx in the other.

∞

Maria's parents, Dr. Tom and Ms. Heather Cruttenden, hated each other. They had met at a church do—both were enthusiastic volunteers at the local parish hall and sometimes formed a bridge rubber with Colin the vicar, who was interested in naval battles, and his wife, Penny, who made excellent chutneys. Over the decades, however, they had come to realise that they detested each other, a hatred which was only exacerbated by their mutual dependency. Rather than split up they had chosen to refine the techniques by which they tortured each other while, at the same time, sinking further and further into a flaccid, porridgy stodge of stagnant familiarity and froideur papered over with an extremely convincing display of harmless togetherness, which, to some extent at least, numbed them to each other's barbs and the corrosive tomorrow that lay before them like a lake in hell.

Because Tom was continually annoyed and because Heather was the nearest human to him, he was continually annoyed by her; the fact that she distractedly scratched the arm of the sofa when watching the television, the loudness of her sneeze, the fatness of her wrists, the tissues she left lying around, the way she pronounced the word 'their' as 'thar' along with a litany of sins against grammar, the wet *tic* sound she made at the back of her throat when she slept, the fact that she never closed the front gate… the list was long and was continually being added to. She knew he hated all these things and yet she did them anyway. In fact she made sure to do them. This forced him to get his revenge on her, which he did by attacking what he called her 'intelligence'—her 'pathetically shallow' understanding of science, history and politics—her 'neediness'—that she was terrified of being alone and clung to the people in her life like grim death—and her maniacal gluttony—she simply could not stop packing food into her obese body. She, in return, made constant snidey allusions to his cowardliness—he never stood up for himself and always followed orders—and his hypocrisy—he made much of being a pacifistic, altruistic healer, but bubbling under his bland, inoffensive doctorly personality was permanent rage at the world, and shockingly insensitive selfishness. His life amounted to what he called 'treats', moments of sensory pleasure; eating meals, unpacking history books, going to the theatre, reading the news and, while his body engaged in the mechanical business of living—washing, getting dressed, driving to work, diagnosing patients, writing prescriptions and so forth—he was always thinking of the next treat, looking forward to something. This 'looking forward to' was, actually, his entire being. If it was ever threatened, in any way, if the wi-fi went down or if there was any kind of delay to his plans, he became murderous towards whoever was nearest, which was usually Heather.

Tom hated his wife, and Heather hated her husband and they taught Maria to hate both of them, although all this nastiness and bitterness was concealed under a veneer of worldly knowledge, and quiet boredom, and public niceness, and vaguely solicitous care. Tom treated his wife and daughter like his patients and they both hated him for it.

The two of them were watching television when the doorbell dinged. Heather's fat ankles were immersed in a foot bath. She was wearing the uniform of the late-seventies Chipping Norton set; baggy sky-blue A-line skirt and fragile gold necklace. Tom, wearing comfortable flannel slacks, got up and padded softly-softly out to the hallway. He opened the heavy front door. A bedraggled Joe was standing there.

'Ah', said Tom in a tone of pleasant surprise, 'Come in Joe, come in.' Joe slopped in, removing his wet shoes. The house, which Maria had grown up in, was silent, soft and creamy. Thick expensive carpets in complacent pastels covered a hallway of oak bannisters and tasteless watercolours.

Tom never liked Joe. He always felt that Maria deserved better, someone with a carefully organised future. When they had first met—Joe had come over for dinner—Tom had casually asked him 'so, what do you do?' 'Oh,' said Joe, panicking, 'nothing at the moment, but I'm thinking about…' and had expressed a few vague desires on how to better himself. When Tom scrutinised Joe about the specifics of his plans however, it became all too obvious he didn't really have any, certainly none that revolved around making his daughter more comfortable. Joe felt paranoid, under pressure and so he had retreated into himself for the entire polite conversation and indeed, for the rest of his relationship with Tom, acutely aware that his silence was even weirder, but the very possibility of speaking was now making him feel sick. In short, Tom's first impression of Joe was that he was a useless, brain-damaged drifter who had no chance whatsoever of providing Maria with the kind of life that Tom wanted for her, and so he treated his prospective son-in-law ever after with condescending scorn, 'mounting' him whenever the two of them were in the company of others. This helped alleviate Tom's disgust, but never quite, for there was something about Joe which, even when he did nothing but squirm with fear, seemed to penetrate Tom, prick him, as if he were being reminded of a guilty secret; although quite what the secret was, he did not know.

Joe took in the suffocating room. Tom's shrivelled face wrinkling into reflexive pleasantness, Heather's heavy, round-shouldered form straining to focus her mind on Home, Kitchen and Garden thoughts, Gainsborough-style paintings of horses and hayricks, Gardener's World on the television, Staffordshire plates on the wall, a signed photograph of June Whitfield; all of it, in its comfortable, frozen exactness, said: nothing.

'How's Maria?' said Tom.

'Oh, okay.'

'We haven't seen you both for *ages*,' said Heather, not taking her eyes away from Monty Don's clematis.

'Oh, you know, we've been busy.'

'Don't be silly Joe, you're unemployed.'

'Well this app keeps me busy.'

'Oh *yes*,' said Heather, turning round and peering over her reading glasses, 'the app! Of course. It's *very* good isn't it?'

Tom, standing in the next room at a dining table, patted a black box. 'We'd better get started, don't you think?' he said.

'Sure,' said Joe. He walked over and lifted the lid of the box, but Tom stayed his hand with; 'Take the box and get changed upstairs.'

⁂

Victor had installed a huge and extremely ornate chest freezer, gold curlicues and fleurons flourishing around its corners like a Georgian coffin. It was connected via innumerable wires, to the rest of his ersatz menagerie. He was sitting inside it playing a player piano, singing a heartbreaking song with total surrender, as if the song itself could break his heart, as if that's what he wanted, more than anything:

> *'Night falls on Moorgate, pink sky illuminate*
> *No hope, no surprise, when nothing lives, nothing dies*
> *In the half light it's perfectly clear,*
> *I'm done, I'm out of here. No time to stop, no time at all,*
> *But there's time enough for a curtain call*

As he sang the second verse the fridge door slowly closed.

> *Nothing grows in Vauxhall*
> *It doesn't rain there anymore*
> *Every year the desert spreads,*
> *From my dreams into my bed.*

His muffled voice lifted to a sublime falsetto:

> *In the half light it's perfectly clear,*
> *I'm done, I'm out of here.*

No time to stop, no time at all,
But there's time enough for a curtain call

As Victor sang, Dave Davage walked down Edding high street. He was drunk, muttering to himself. He spotted a photo stuck to a lamppost, and approached.

As Victor sang, Joe, remote control in his mouth, crawled on his knees from Tom to Heather, who took the remote and patted his head.

As Victor sang, Lilly leafed through her dossier. Images of Joe riding a sheep, wearing a squirrel-head necklace, gutting a badger, stealing candy from a baby, setting fire to a football stadium, scaring people with masks, drawing a spaceman on the Uffington chalk horse…

As Victor sang, Dave was looking at a photo of he, Dave, looking at a photo of he, Dave, looking at a photo of he, Dave next to the lamppost he was standing at; just behind him, folded on the floor, was Laughing Ralf, laughing.

As Victor sang, Aaron and Moira were having an outrageously violent, unrestrained argument, screaming at each other, screaming into each other.

As Victor sang, Joris, on a magnificent throne, and wearing a mandarin-collar dress, was talking with a group of people, those who had attended Max's funeral.

In the half light it's perfectly clear,
I'm done, I'm out of here.
No time to stop, no time at all
But there's time enough for a curtain call.

As Victor sang, Dave was kicking Laughing Ralf's head in, shouting, 'Be normal, cunt! Be normal!' Ralf, laughing, coughing, spluttering, 'You are doing this! You are doing this!'

As Victor sang, Lilly was looking at a neatly-arranged page, covered with documentary evidence (hospital reports, photographs of Margaret in hospital with her head bandaged up), which declared, in neat bold writing, 'Joe shot his own mother in the head.'

As Victor sang, Aaron was slapping Moira and Moira, horrified, was walking out.

As Victor sang, Tim the vicar and Sophie were in their dirty flat, sobbing together.

As Victor sang, Tom was placing their television on the broad back of Joe, who was on all fours in the middle of the lounge.

As Victor sang, the 'hole into the void' that Max had made was opening again and Joris was smiling.

Victor sang the coda, his suffocated voice just audible from within the fridge.

> *You've been wonderful my friends*
> *But all good things must come to an end*
> *Show's over, but there's nothing to fear*
> *The lights come up when we get out of here*

Frozen in the solid darkness, he stops singing. A crocodile, curled over the freezer, has him in its jaws. Victor's last words, so quiet as to be inaudible, are; 'Set, take me.' After he utters them, the crocodile closes its jaws and cuts Victor in two.

⁂

Joe, ragged overcoat flapping uselessly, walked home, heavily, heavily. All the lights were out in his house, and the houses either side. Number eighty six was now completely boarded up, from within.

He opened his front door.

'Maria?'

Something was wrong. It didn't look right, feel right. He turned on the light, stumbling back from the light. Wincingly, eyes shielded, he saw. The hallway, blindingly bright, was empty—completely empty; no coats, no shoes, no coat hanger, no Camillia portrait mirror, no sepia photograph of an Afghan child holding a dog murdered by the Russians. It smelt strange, the cold smell of just house. He turned on the light in the front room. Also empty; just floorboards and walls.

He walked around the house, blinking under the supernovae where the bulbs used to be. Every room was empty. All the furniture, everything, had gone; except, in the bedroom, also bare, but for a few lonely, scattered objects, Joe's baboon mug, his Glock, his Francis Bebey, William Onyeabor and Funkadelic albums, his notebook, his F.O. Morris goose egg painting and his photograph of a full English breakfast. These were, apart from a few items of clothing, the sum total of his possessions.

His phone buzzed. He took it out of his pocket. Five messages appeared, one after the other. The Jobcentre: you have failed your psychological test. You have been sanctioned. Gyp: This is your third two-star review; you have not sufficiently debased yourself. You have been released. Lilly: I'm sorry Joe, I can't see you tomorrow. I just can't. Goodbye. Mental Health Services: you have been referred for an assessment. Meanwhile, if you are experiencing mental health problems, download this app and go for a jog. Duat: You're fired.

PART FIVE
Stand Up Tragedy

D.C. Gaynor Babcock speaks to Lilly's father, Robert, young Lilly watching through the curtains. She can see her daddy clenching and unclenching his white fists, which means that he is very angry.

'Maximilian Thottesley is no longer a suspect,' says Gaynor, 'He didn't kill your wife. There is no motive, no body, no weapon, nothing. He met her, they had a date, she said she wanted to leave you, and she left. It's a missing person case, and until we have some more leads, I'm afraid you're just going to have to get used to that Mr. Pumphrey.'

Robert turns, head down, charges back inside, picks up the family dog, a soppy collie called Sasha, and throws it out the kitchen window. He then falls to his knees and bites the dining table.

Later that day, Robert drives in the freezing, sheeting rain to Max's estate, parks a discreet distance from the gateway and then, when Max's fine Bentley emerges, follows it into town; to Nando's. Max is calmly eating his peri peri chicken when Robert strides in, shouting and screaming. Max looks up, snaps his fingers, and continues eating. Robert, still overflowing with fury, becomes confused, frightened, wildly looking around for Max, who watches him with easy amusement.

Meanwhile, little Lilly is investigating her parents' bedroom. She picks up a photo of her mum, then she opens her mum's wardrobe and feelingly strokes a red polka-dot dress hanging there. She takes it out and puts it on—it drapes over her feet—then shuffles through to her own bedroom and picks up the giant teddy bear her mother had bought her two years ago after a trip to Thorpe Park.

Robert, who has spent much of the journey back home punching himself, walks in to Lilly humping the teddy bear, making the same noises as Helen used to make. She has sellotaped Max's face, printed from the internet, onto the face of the bear.

Robert, with over-the-top volcanic rage exploding from every cell, grabs Lilly and pulls her from the room. He has lost his mind, but his mind is not quite his own. Max Thottesley, seated comfortably in his study, open fire cheering at his feet, holds a voodoo doll of Robert in his smooth elegant fingers, toying with it, tossing it from one hand to another.

Robert drags Lilly out the back door, lifts her up and forces her into the bough of the silver poplar at the bottom of their garden. He then starts throwing random items from the freezer at her, home-made beans, pork chops, potato waffles, all the time roaring and howling incoherently, Lilly wailing, terrified, appalled, neighbours watching.

This goes on and on. A police siren is heard, but before the police can even consider forcing their way in, Max has casually tossed the voodoo doll into the fire and Robert has spontaneously combusted. First his head blows off, then his body spins round like a hand blender, then that explodes also.

Did this happen? Not literally, no, but it happened.

You are reading a true story.

Lilly's dreams had for many years been troubled, usually involving a danger that only she was aware of, and which nobody else could see, despite it being so obvious, right there. She had animal-themed dreams, involving some new relationship with nature which had become inexplicably menacing. Or she dreamt of some completely ordinary *thing* which was horrendously out of place, a menacing object, like an Italian shoe on the bus, or a silver lemon squeezer on the beach. In her dreams, things became far more intensely themselves than in her waking life. She loved objects, she thought that it was good to be attached to them, to their specialness, but in dreams they became mysterious, usually in a threatening way, or difficult to handle, or haunted, with an unbearably menacing suchness.

She dreamt a green floral-patterned dress that she had found in a charity shop, an exquisite item that nobody alive would have willingly given up, was lying on her bed, and, as she approached it, she became fascinated and terrified by the thought that 'something was on the other side of it'. She picked it up, anxiously, and regarded the fabric and the green and purple printed blooms and was afraid; something was 'on the other side' of the dress.

She dreamt she was at university, but it wasn't university, it was in a big market for some reason, like Billingsgate, and she was living in a shared house which was haunted with an invisible gas-like presence which she was fighting against, while all her flatmates, who thought she was weird, ignored her and watched television while she 'pushed' the evil into the corner of the room, but she couldn't get it out of the house because suddenly she was too fat to fit into the corner of the room, so she called for help, but everyone was watching Britain's Got Talent.

She dreamt of a large capybara-type animal, but furrier. It was parthenogenetically giving birth to miniature versions of itself, but the young were refusing to emerge from what, Lilly could feelingly-see, was shyness. They didn't want to come out, and then Lilly suddenly felt awfully sad, because she too had 'come out' and wanted to go back, reabsorb herself back into something bigger, a furry mother-self like the capybara.

She dreamt that she was at home, the house where she had grown up, but all the rooms were sort of pink and stiff and posh, and she was a helium balloon and had floated up to the high ceiling, and she was calling down to her mum, who was jumping up, trying to catch her, but she couldn't, and it was all, for some reason, so unbearably sad.

She dreamt she was at work and hundreds of people had died in an explosion which had neatly dismembered and decapitated them all, and she had to match up the various limbs, and she knew that outside hundreds of family members were impatiently waiting for their reassembled loved ones, but it was an impossible task because there were just so many legs and arms and heads and torsos, and they too were things bits.

She dreamt she was in an antiques shop, one of her favourite places to be, and it was full of beautiful old objects, candlesticks and scales and bookshelves and lampshades; but all these things were looking at her, mutely gazing at her; she felt it fearfully, yet when she looked at a thing, it became a thing again. The watchfulness of the world hovered at the periphery, but she feared stepping back to see it, so she fixed things into place with her stare, to stop the cartoony nightmare of living things from crowding into her. But then she asked, why are they freezing when I look at them? And the horrible answer came to her; they were afraid. For the things of the world her look was petrifying death.

Now she is dreaming she is in an old foreign city, similar to Bruges, which she visited with her parents when she was a child. She is walking through an open square, where tourists are eating mussels and chips, and a penguin has leapt onto one of the tables and is attacking a plate of leftovers. The manager of the restaurant emerges with a huge shotgun and Lilly leaps onto the table to protect the penguin. The manager shouts to get out of the way, because he is going to blow the penguin away, and then the penguin starts aggressively pecking at her head and she realises that it wants to die, it *wants* to be shot, and then everyone starts shouting to her to get out of the way, that she is being selfish, until eventually, crying now, she does and the manager blasts the penguin into the next life.

The blast was from Neil's room, a screeching wailing smashing terror shuddering through her, the kind felt on the borders of dream; but she was awake, and she understood the sound had come from next door. She knew better than to check on Neil though. No good would come of that, so in the awful echoing silence which follows violent noise, she lay in bed looking into the waxy pre-dawn gloom, funereal rain lashing the dark window.

She had a mania for going through the day before it happened, going over her work for the day, or drafting conversations and what she would say and what they would say, and then of course nothing happened that way and she would end up in bed in the evening thinking about how everything had gone wrong. She had no idea why she did this, and she wanted to stop. It wasn't that she really even particularly cared what happened, but she planned it all out anyway. It was all motivated by a feeling of malaise, of aimless, formless anxiety, a wispy funk that always seemed to hang around. She feared becoming like Nina, a fretting, felty, puddle-mouthed old maid, unloved and obsessed with otters or some other stupid surrogate. But what to do?

Breakfast was fruit salad, croissant and a good coffee. She made sure to eat well, because she loved food, but now it all seemed to pass her by, the experience of eating, so that very often she found herself getting to the very end of the meal and realising that she hadn't been enjoying the food at all, and so all her attention went on the last mouthful which always tasted a little bit of tragedy, like she was saying goodbye to someone whom she only realised she loved at the very last minute.

She did the dishes and got ready for work. On her way out she passed Neil on the stairs. He was dressed in dark blue, sharply creased trousers, a navy jumper with elbow-pads and epaulettes and, slung over the top, a high-viz vest which read 'Life Marshal'. He turned the now terrifying mask of his face towards her. It was set in a permanent painting of pleading stress. She hurriedly slipped past him and out of the house into the bitter rain.

The world outside was one of smudged forms, scurrying to work through a grey miasma saturated with sadness. There were more homeless sacks, more suicides, more police sirens from nearby streets, more arguments in the street and more rubbish, always more waste. It seemed the world was reaching a point of combustion, and only the constant rain, battering everyone down, soaking their fuses, kept it from exploding.

She got to work and got straight into work, laying out an old man, Ken, who had died of liver failure after accidentally eating a death cap mushroom. While she was working on the preliminaries, Nina did her frail moonwalk into the mortuary and began complaining that Lilly was using too much colour correction cream. Lilly had come to the opinion that it was bizarre wanting a body to look like it was shining with dewy life, but that's what all the families wanted, so that's what she did.

'Sorry Lilly, but I… It's just that I don't care about that. The clients only get to see the bodies in a dark room anyway.' In this respect corpses were like prostitutes.

Nina was standing in the doorway, facing away from the dead body and from Lilly, which suited Lilly as she was starting to hate Nina's face, particularly the way her eyebrows were always pushed upwards into a pleady, 'please believe me, I'm the casualty here' expression. She was a spiritual panhandler.

'You know as well as I do,' said Lilly, 'that the clients will complain if the body looks like it's dead.'

'Just use less cream,' said Nina, 'that's all I'm saying.'

'It's five quid for a huge pot of the stuff.'

'Well, perhaps... maybe *you* can pay for it?'

'I don't even think we should be putting this stuff on. They're dead, he's dead, the cockatoo is dead, why must we hide it?'

She was referring to a stuffed cockatoo rigidly leaning up against the draining board. Ken's dying wish was for the bird—'my best friend in this life'—to be buried in his arms. His wife—not, apparently, his best friend—wasn't impressed, but she'd been overruled by two of her three children, which had split the family into two.

'I'm sorry Lilly,' said Nina, 'I *really* am, and, yes, yes, you *are* one of the best morticians I've had, but you don't seem to understand what people expect, what they need.'

'Eh?' What was she getting at?

'There are plenty of people who need a job. It's not... I mean, what I mean is, I'm sorry, but it's not the kind of economy for complaining, if you see what I mean?'

Lilly grasped the point. In the end everyone is dispensable. 'Yes,' she said sourly, 'I see what you mean.'

'Good. So a little less lipstick, and a little less hot water too. And don't spend quite so much time on the hair styles. A simple side-parting is enough for any man.'

'Okay, okay.'

'And could you come out with me tomorrow evening to an elite strip club?'

'What?' Lilly's arms fell to her side.

'Yes, I know,' said Nina, now in a distracted tone of apologetic self-consciousness, '...it's just that, erm, I have to go to Dominus, it's an exclusive club, and I thought...'

'Dominus?'

'Yes, I know, I know.'

'But why do you want to go *there*?'

'I don't want to, I have to, it's… Look, erm…' she sighed and half turned to Lilly, 'I should have told you before but it looks like I'm going to be handing the parlour over to another owner.'

'Oh.'

'But don't worry! They don't want to change a thing. You'll all be kept on.'

'I see.'

'Yes, and, actually, I think you'll really get on with him, and his granddaughter, they're lovely, *lovely* people. She's a Brummie too.'

'Right. I've got it.'

'They might even give you a raise. In fact, I'm going to discuss that tomorrow.' This last thought had just occurred to Nina. Like many misers Nina was generous with other people's money and worked hard to get them to spend it on each other so that she could bathe in the background glow of their generosity.

'And you're going to do the deal at an infamous elite strip club?'

'Haha, yes, it's a bit peculiar, but Mr. Wukong—that's his—erm, he absolutely insists on going there, before we sign the contract.'

'Isn't that suspicious? Or weird?'

'Not at all, no. He's a party animal, that's all.'

'A party animal in charge of a funeral home?'

'Oh. No, no, no…' Nina turned a bit too far and glimpsed a dead toe. She turned back. 'You see… it's different in China—that's where he comes from—there they have a very strict work-life separation. At work, you're one thing, and in your life, erm… I mean, when you're not at work… you're something else.'

'You watch women take their clothes off and hump poles?'

'Yes, yes, but look, don't worry. When you meet him you'll see. The point is…'

'I'll do it if you buy my drinks all night.'

Nina sucked the air, as if winded, and then chewed her lip. The drinks were likely to be expensive. It could add as much as, what, fifty pounds to her expenses? But she needed Lilly to be there. She couldn't admit it to herself, but she found Lilly's company calming.

'Okay,' she said quietly, and left. Lilly turned back to Ken and began work on him, shaking off Nina, shaking off the world, by returning to death.

'I understand,' she said to the corpse, 'people want to be reminded of life, but my point is, it's a funeral. It's the one time in life when you *should* be reminded of death. You probably don't agree, I mean you had your cockatoo done up nice, but then that was for your home wasn't it? This is a funeral...'

She worked away, poking, cutting, sewing, painting.

'Paul always says "at least you have your memories", but who wants memories? Do they help? Maybe I'm saying that because most of my memories are horrible. Or maybe I want to live, not remember, *live*. Do you know what I mean?'

She was suturing the mouth closed, which involved pushing a sharp needle through the teeth. It was a hard job, but Lilly kept talking.

'I met your family Ken. Your wife said to me she wanted you buried, to give life to a tree. "That's lovely," I said and she said "He was useless while alive, so he might as well have some use dead." And my first thought was she's some kind of witch, which she probably is, but it is all about use isn't it? If you don't do something useful, you're nobody, but I think, useful to what? Where are we all going? Nowhere. Even that wouldn't be so bad, but we have to travel at maximum speed, so if you slow down, even for a second, you're dead weight.' She cut off the stitches and began tidying up. 'It's not very pleasurable life is it?' she said, 'Some of the most pleasurable experiences I have had, are when I am lying in bed, thinking about someone I really like and imagining what it would be like to be with them. Not just sexually, but emotionally. I feel... it comforts me, but also... well, there's a lot of sadness, because in reality, I know that person is a psychopath and a freak and it was all an illusion and the earth is actually dying and so am I.'

She had finished Ken. The last thing to do was to place the cockatoo into his arms and sew them together. Having finished she climbed onto the table beside him.

'I don't know,' she said, 'I'm always tired these days Ken. Kind of… sort of a metal snow, in my head… I don't really have many thoughts now, so I'm kind of enlightened, but there's just this heaviness all the time, a kind of heavy, metallic fog deep in me, like it's in my womb. I don't know what it is.'

The two of them lay in silence for a while, then she said 'If you're unhappy, you can either kill yourself, I think, or you can pretend to be dead… Nothing else seems to work.'

The plastic curtains rustled. Carl entered, admired Lilly's shapely legs, and then walked over to her, still staring at them.

'Buckle your gunge and get your booty on the road, we've got a collection.'

Lilly turned, surprised, and sat up. Carl stood before her, and laid his hand on her upper thigh. 'Come on,' he said softly.

'Get your fucking hands off me Carl!'

He withdrew his arm as if he'd touched an oven tray. '*Don't* move me out of the way with my hips,' she said, with uncommon bile, '*don't* ask me where your hug is, *don't* ask if I'm on my period, *don't* bang on about what I'm wearing and *don't stare at my fucking tits!*'

Carl, staring at her tits, looked up at her face.

'I wasn't… What?'

Lilly hopped off the table and walked past him through the curtained door. She pulled her coat from the peg in the workshop. As she did so, an Indian man walked past her, carrying a potted plant.

'Good afternoon!' he said courteously.

'Hello,' said Lilly, automatically.

The man opened a slender door round the L-bend of the workshop and disappeared inside.

Carl, following Lilly, emerged from the mortuary. He looked unsettled.

'Who was that?' asked Lilly.

'Who?' said Carl, a little sulk in his voice.

'A man just went in there. An Indian.'

'In there?'

'Yes, in there. I thought it was a tool cupboard.'

'That? Through here?' said Carl, approaching the door.

'Yes!'

Carl opened the door for Lilly to look in. The room was very narrow, with two thin benches either side. Six beefy Indian men were sitting, crammed in but apparently quite comfortable. At the far end was a tea station (saucepan, grated ginger, mint plant and some spices) where the man who had just passed Lilly was finishing off some first-class chai. Everyone warmly greeted her with 'hello ma'am.'

'May I offer you some chai?' said the chai-wallah, '*Totally* authentic.'

'Nah,' said Carl, 'we gotta scoot pal. Back in thirty.' He closed the door. 'Bearers,' he said '"Mutes," we call 'em. They do a bit of voluntary work for paupers' funerals.'

'Oh.'

'Come on then darlin',' said Carl, letting go of his discomfort with the same ease he let go of every emotion. He went to touch Lilly's hips, then stopped, 'oops, err…ack…' Mumbling, he moved his hand up towards her shoulder, but didn't touch that either, instead he made an unnatural gesture sweeping past her, onto a work desk, which he absurdly patted. Then he patted himself.

They drove through Edding, the van cab largely silent but for the rain pelting the windows. Carl put some music on, *Love Will Tear Us Apart*. It irritated Lilly, but she was happy not to have to make conversation. She felt no desire to engage with the world at all, her psyche had contracted in a hurt, suspicious centre of dark gravity which she knew she had to wait out. Until then, best avoid everyone, particularly men. The song irritated Carl too, but he too, distracted, didn't want to talk. His general cheer was practically indestructible, but his children weighed ever heavier on his thoughts. Recently, he had been redecorating the front room—no carpets, floorboards up, generally a mess—and a friend of Alfie, his heavy fourteen-year-old son, had come round, but Alfie had kept the friend talking at the front door for half an hour until he'd left. 'Alfie,' Carl had said, summoning up all his fatherly concern, 'I know the house looks a state, but… just forget it. Your mate has come to see you, not all this shit.'

After some thought Alfie had replied, 'It's not the house I'm ashamed of. It's you.'

Carl and Lilly reached the house of the pick-up, which was clearly the home of a lunatic, covered as it was with crudely painted hieroglyphics, newspaper in the windows and hammered-on plastic ankh amulets, beckoning cats and ketchup guns.

Carl knew where he was. 'This is Vic's place,' he said.

'Who's Vic?'

They got out of the van. Two policemen were standing outside the house, cradling their nipples in the traditional manner of the winter constable. Dr. Tom emerged from the house.

'He's up there,' said Tom and gestured them in.

'Who's Vic?' asked Lilly again, now concerned for Carl, whose face had fallen, in a most unCarl-like way.

'He was… a friend…' he said. Lilly followed him, now suffering in sympathy, into the cathedral of junk. Ghostly music drifted down the stairs.

'What is this place?' she said, but Carl wasn't listening. He had vanished into one of the jumbled plastic mole-tunnels. Lilly followed, upstairs, along the yodelling pickle, bread pillow and handerpants-encrusted landing, and through to the inner sanctum. Light filtered red from ketchup-stained windows, and a sulphurous smell, made the place seem somewhat devilish.

The wistful music got louder as Lilly reached the heart of the plastic cathedral. 'I know this song,' she said to herself.

They reached the chest freezer and looked in. Music played from hidden speakers. It was the song that Victor had died to, the same song that Neil had played to Lilly when they had first slept together. Carl stood over the quartered body, tears running over his round cheeks.

And Lilly sang;

> *Under Wolverhampton skies*
> *Nothing lives, nothing dies.*
> *The paving stones conceal,*
> *A ghostly replica of the real.*

Her sweet voice lifted an octave for the chorus.

> *In the half light it's perfectly clear,*
> *I'm done, I'm out of here.*
> *No time to stop, no time at all,*
> *But there's time enough for a curtain call*
> *Scratch beneath Aston town,*
> *It's Solihull all the way down.*
> *When intensity causes shame,*
> *Everything becomes the same.*

She sang the chorus again, and then throws herself into the coda, with all her heart;

> *I can't lie, I can't pretend,*
> *I can't take it anymore*
> *I know what happens in the end.*
> *I've seen this film before.*
> *Bored to death, bored to tears.*
> *The movie runs for ninety years…*

While Lilly sang, Louis spoke rapidly into the telephone, worry rippling over his brow.

While Lilly sang, Maria bleakly watched the Great British Bake-Off with Heather, volume turned up to drown out the sound of distant rioting.

While Lilly sang, Paul was playing with little plastic soldiers, putting them in hollowed-out bread coffins.

While Lilly sang, Dave Davage wandered around Edding, lost, desperate, searching, searching…

electricity still ran, the ghost of Joe. There was still a kind of self, but all the 'me' had gone from it. There was no centre of gravity holding it all together—the thing that wants and doesn't want, likes and doesn't like—and, without that, thoughts just kind of floated off into space, like the contents of a spaceman's desk drawer, upturned and emptied of paper-clips and photographs and batteries and utility bills, drifting through the universe.

Without the me-thing behind thoughts, the identity, it was hard to believe that there was a head that all this used to happen in. Joe had the feeling that there was a kind of hole on his neck through which the world was flowing. When things approached, they poured into him, when he moved away, they poured out. Occasionally there was the thought, 'I am mad,' but this was no different to 'it is dark' in sunlight; just as unreal, just as unmad-like, just as undarklike.

Joe had gone properly mad once before. One summer, while he'd been between jobs, Maria had gone away for a couple of months and he'd spent the whole time in the flat. He'd felt pos-sessed with a vertiginous sense of impending loss, like he was standing on the edge of the cliff of himself and could, at any moment, just fall off. It was as if the landmarks on his map had just all at once dissolved. He panicked that he would get *absolutely lost*, and that he wouldn't be able to get back. He realised later, thinking about it, that the event had tapped into his both his deepest fear—of not trusting who he is without landmarks, of fearing that really he might be *something else*—and, at the same time, his deepest desire, which is to not really be here at all, to be a gas, to be a passive, drifting, cloud-like nothing.

And now he was just nothing.

There was no emotion and no will. There were sensations, coming and going, and there was a sense of Joeness 'behind' these, the Joe-flavour he had always had—perhaps it was his character?—but that was it. His inner life had become as light as a feather, lighter, blown around by the smokiest of whiffs. He went to stand on one side of the room, he went to stand on the other, he stared at the skirting board for a long, lonnnnnng time, and he wondered what it was. What *is* that? he asked himself. What is it, and what is it doing *there*? He bent down and touched the skirting board, and laughed. But seriously, what is it? Not that this was a real question-question. People only seek what they already have. They ask questions, but they only really want to hear answers they've already found. Joe's questions now were open invitations to the absolute. They were impossible questions, a constant speechless unable to know.

He wanted someone to help him. Sometimes he asked people in the street to tell him what things were and they looked at him with fear or pity—although most people did tell him—'that's a capping brick,' 'that's a packet of Monster Munch.' He felt it was lovely that they told him, the eyes of the Joe-body even teared up a bit, but a moment later he would be perplexed again at the capping brick and the packet of Monster Munch and would ask someone else the same question.

Once, a long time ago, he had been interested in being without suffering, in being free, in being happy, the thing sometimes called 'enlightenment,' but all these interests had gone, leaving confusion, and pain. He felt that he had reached the point he had always wanted to reach, but it was lonely, unsettling and full of pain. Perhaps it was emotional, or perhaps it was physical. It was difficult to say, but Joe felt like he was being slowly pulverised by life, like existence was a vice that pressed on every cell, squashing him from within; and yet he didn't care. Even when he felt he couldn't breathe, even when he distantly wondered if he might die in the next moment or two, there was nothing inside to care. There was just the pain. Sometimes the body moaned, sometimes it didn't.

Other times, it seemed like the layers of his self were being peeled away one by one, leaving a headless nothing. One morning he stood in his front garden and his neighbour, Aaron, emerged. Joe tried to recall a long-sunk memory, a far-away particle of knowledge; did he know this man? Did he like him?

Aaron, hesitant to cross the 'neighbour-small-talk barrier,' gave a standard morning greeting but, met with Joe's lost, utterly bewildered peer, couldn't help asking Joe if he was okay, and Joe had replied; 'My head seems to have disappeared. It was there earlier, now there's nothing, just a kind of hole, with nobody looking out. Things seem to be happening… That's about all I can say…' Aaron decided not to talk to Joe any more.

After his breakfast of cauliflower shrapnel, Joe sat in his kitchen looking at his hand for about half an hour. 'Is this mine?' he wondered 'what is it? It's certainly quite beautiful.' Then he went outside in the damp back garden and contemplated the chickens, the six remaining. He sat on a wet wrought-iron garden chair as they pecked around their coops made of coffins, chicken-wire, breeze blocks and whatever else. *What are these things?* He didn't know. Each chicken-event seemed to belong to a super-chicken which, being frozen in his awareness, was refracted, shattered into all the individual chicken-forms of the world. The super-personality of the chicken was less personal than that of the human, although most humans were also down at chicken-level. All of this Joe realised as pure information. He didn't have to reflect on it, he saw straight into it.

His body stood up, went into the shed, gathered a bucket of chicken feed, returned to the coop-complex, sprinkled cereal grains over two of the coffins and waited until the chickens had all hopped inside. When they were pecking away he slammed down the lids, nailed them shut, banged through a few air holes, lashed them together with rope and lifted them onto his back. He didn't know why.

Fifteen minutes later he was walking up Ember Hill towards town. Chicken clucks and caws emerged from the rain-slick, unwieldy caskets. People passed, shooting fearful glances his way, but he struggled on until, just as he reached the roundabout over the ring road, he stopped, then slowly sank to his knees. He put the coffins down and started massaging his leg; 'come on,' he groaned, 'come *on*…'

A loping man, boss-eyed, slack-limbed, approached Joe, con-fusion and fear in his eyes, and took a wide detour into the busy road to avoid him.

'It's alright!' cried Joe, 'My leg's broken down. Again!' He smacked it with mock reprimand, 'Bloody leg! Hahahaha!'

The pain was immense, a convulsing, cramping, alkali burn shivering his thigh and calf muscles. He half lay, half squatted in the rain-running street, furiously slapping and rubbing his soaking leg, until, eventually, it moved again and, tentatively, he could return to his Calvary. Not far now though. Destination: The Jobcentre of Golgotha, on the other side of the roundabout.

Ten minutes later, Joe was escaping. The night before he had carried four coffins of chickens down to the Jobcentre and now, before it could open, he had deposited the last of them. He had climbed into the sealed social area of the Department of Work and Pensions, opened all the coffins and let the chickens out onto the grass. The six coffins were now leaning against the fence. He took one of them, threw it over into the rear service alley and climbed over after it, limping away, dragging the casket.

He passed some graffiti on a fence which reads; 'For whom is there death?'

'Are you asking me?' says Joe, to himself. A few yards further down, on another fence, is the word 'yes'.

8

Neil was knitting, eyes and cheeks quivering with tension which he pressed desperately down upon, trying to keep it all under control. He had had 'some work done' on his face, to get it to look as orderly as possible, an effect enhanced by make-up and a morning ritual of such obsessive orderliness that he had to get up at four in the morning to fit everything into; to wash every single body part in the correct order, to record exactly how long each wash took, to count his teeth, to part his hair with a set square, to clean every last molecule of dirt from under his fingernails, to carefully wrap his thighs in cellophane, to apply make-up, then to run eight miles in the winter darkness, return, and go through the cleaning ritual a second time, but now in deadly earnest.

His room too was now at the most extreme limit of orderliness. He'd pulled up the carpet, removed it and had the floor tiled, replaced every object in the room with a waterproof equivalent or covered it in plastic sheeting, then scrubbed every perfectly square surface daily with disinfectant. But still he couldn't keep the fly out. It was indefatigable, unbeatable, immortal. It came in somehow, it buzzed, it tormented him. He got up to kill it, get rid of it, but it vanished, and then reappeared. It had been sent by God to persecute him, or by Satan to tempt him, but he did not give up; he would never give up. But again it came in—from nowhere! *nowhere!* It was there now, buzzing round in loose spiralling squares. He tried to ignore it, for three seconds, before leaping to his feet, grabbing a microphone (plugged in) and frantically, savagely and with deafening feedback, psychotically bashing the fly to paste with it. He then broke down in tears.

This ruined his make-up. He had to start his morning routine again, so he headed out to the bathroom where he walked into Lilly. She didn't talk to him anymore, hardly looked at him—another life denier, she was; all that death had corrupted her—but he wasn't interested, he just needed to get to the bathroom, to restore perfection to his form.

The question was death. It was now ever-present in his awareness, directly, as an anguished prayer for answers; why, why, why, why, *why?* Why did we live here, on this blighted crumb, have children, go to work, struggle, strive, make an effort, only to die? Neil believed in God, he *had* to believe in God, but it was a perfect mystery why He should allow this. It was like asking an employee to sacrifice a weekend to make a thousand origami swans and then coming in Monday morning, taking them out into the car park and setting fire to them, or like, at the end of the Olympics, giving *everyone* a gold medal including all the spectators, but it wasn't a gold medal, it was a turd. And anyway, it was all far worse than any specific example, because you lost your whole life. Everything went, everything, everything, *everything*. It was so unfair! What could the point of living possibly be, when all the castles you build, big and small, of sand or stone or flesh, will all be kicked over by a fat blind kid?

Neil was forced to conclude that, logically, it was all a test, a kind of virtual reality game in which you scored points from good acts and lost them though bad acts. Then, when you died, God would fairly hand out all the prizes. The maximum number of points would lead to the best jobs in heaven and God had sent Jesus down to us to show us how to amass a killer high score. Confusingly, there seemed to be quite a few games in town — Muslims had Mohammed, Buddhists had the Buddha and the Japanese had Pikachu — but they all worked in the same way. Basically, you prayed five times a day, got to the shops mindfully, whatever, and then if you missed a prayer or lied to someone or had a wank, you'd have to do something good to get your balance back up. How else could it possibly work? That's how everyone who followed religions saw it. The only problem, sort of picking and pestering away at the back of Neil's mind, was that it was all complete and utter bullshit.

Death didn't, however, come in as a constant, perplexed, fretting fear about the pointlessness of life, but as a more visceral horror, a hollow draining sense that the misery, chaos, pain, madness, stupidity and atrocity of life, its darkness, its dirt, its disease, its boredom, its loss and all of its evil, were all eating away at life like mould devours bread in the rain. He had this feeling worst of all in the dead of the night, at about three o'clock in the morning, when he would lie in bed, frozen in pure fear, total nameless, formless, dread.

It didn't help that Neil, after his botox treatments, retiling his bedroom and several months without work, had no money. Financially, he was getting down to the skeletal bone. Where Joe, completely useless, had supernatural luck getting jobs, Neil, 'an asset to any team,' couldn't get work cleaning toilets. He worked assiduously at being unemployed, carefully cultivated the 'corporation of one' that you were supposed to develop in order to survive in the 'new economy', but he just couldn't get anywhere. He wrote letter after letter:

'I am articulate, passionate, ambitious and a creative, original thinker who would be a genuine, team-playing asset to any organisation. I am a strong and influential employee who prides himself in being professional and creative within challenging situations. As a proactive, organised multi-tasker with the ability to write, research and present material at a high level, I work equally well individually or as part of a team. I'm looking for work in an enthusiastic, rapidly-changing modern environment where I can be part of a busy, pressurised, creative team with everyone working towards the same goal. I can fiercely adapt myself to a variety of roles to develop myself to progress to the best me I can be, in my career, for you.'

Interviews occasionally arrived, but there were no callbacks. Everything fizzled out. He was stuck in a spiral of failure caused by the fact that being a failure was preventing anyone from taking him as a potential success. It was the same with women. He exuded bachelorhood from his pores which kept potential partners away like some kind of repellent spray. Also he looked like a villain from a cheap science fiction television show.

It was at this point, early one morning next to the river Hale, that Neil had met the lawyer Ian. The tired little man had sat down next to Neil on the park bench he had been resting on, mid-run, and said, 'Neil Geb?'

'Eh?'

'It is Neil isn't it? I recognise you by the style of your run.'

'Who are you?'

'I know your brother.'

Neil, confused, contracted, squinting in the gloom, made out a vaguely familiar form, a little hood-shrouded baldish man in a waterproof jacket. He smelt of a wet animal.

'How?'

'Oh a terrible man, a man of no morals, no meaning, vile, vile.'

'Who *are* you?'

'Ian Cremwave. I'm associated with the Thottesley estate, where your brother worked. It has been my job to investigate him. I just wanted to express my condolences at having him as a brother.' Ian pulled out a business card and passed it to Neil.

'How do you know that?' Neil squinted. The typeface on the card was too delicate to read.

'My company has a great many resources. I know Joe very well, and through him, you, and I know he has ruined your life.'

'Yes, he did,' said Neil, doubt melting by the force of gratitude, a sense of being understood.

'You've been dealt a rotten hand Neil, but I… uh… oh look at that swan.'

'Eh?' Neil looked to where Ian was pointing.

'Isn't it big? Look how thick its neck is.'

'Is it? I wouldn't know.'

'What were we talking about?'

'About Joe.'

'Oh yes, but let's not dwell on him,' said Ian with a dismissive wave of his hand, '*you* are the one who understands life.'

And so a bizarre conversation had begun. Neil had spoken with this Ian Cremwave for just twenty minutes, never releasing his suspicion, but drawn in by the distracted, flattering patter of this weird little man, and the feeling that he knew him, and trusted him. Ian told Neil that he, Neil, had been bent by life's storms, but that this had only made him stronger, more vital, and that he had to use that vitality for the good, for *life*. Ian had said that his unemployment was actually a gift, that he should use it to save the world from itself, from its complacent slide into the shadow of death. He had said that Neil should spread the religion of life… At this point he had started talking about Sammy Davis Junior. He often lost the thread of what he was saying and was easily distracted. He seemed to like talking about health, technology—particularly transport systems—and superhero films, all subjects that appealed to Neil, but Neil was troubled by the conversation. The man was creepy, a stalker perhaps, or… or… God knows, but he should be reported. Neil had excused himself and continued his run.

Yes obviously a loon. But. He had put a worm in Neil's ear. It was true, what he had said. Standing among the shards of his shattered life *had* given him a new biting clarity. He *could* see straight into the shocking complacency of the world, how, for example, everyone was walking around as if they *knew how they would be feeling next week!* Just one tap on the egg of the world could crack it, smash to smithereens their nicely managed, nicely manicured lives. Why didn't people see this? *Why weren't they strengthening their eggs!*

Something had to be done.

After his tearful fly disaster and unnerving hallway meeting with Lilly, Neil had prepared himself again, put on his uniform, put on his bullet-proof vest, pulled his 'Life Marshal' vest over that, and then had gone out into the rain.

He had come to the conclusion that survival is mandatory, that nobody must ever die, that death is, or should be, against the law. The rational part of his mind still functioned, and informed him that there was no beating death, but the truer part of his soul, the life-loving core, knew that this didn't matter, that the facts don't matter, that we must do everything we can to keep safe, forever. We have to make the world safe, we have to make everything completely risk-free, we have to save people from chaos and death; we have to enhance *life*.

Inspired by the depth of this realisation, Neil had taken it on himself to go into the streets of Edding and make sure that risk everywhere was minimised. It was really just a continuation of his police work, maintaining 'law and order,' which at the time he had considered to be all about the 'law' part, but now he realised was actually all about order, keeping everything running smoothly. *That's* why he loved authority, *that's* why he loved technology, *that's* why he was so nervous around other people and *that's* why he hated anything unusual or out of the ordinary.

It all made sense now; he knew, in the marrow of his bones, that life means order and order means control and without control there is chaos and *death*.

And so he had gone out, among the people, to promote order and control, wherever or however he could. If anything was dangerous, spontaneous, out of the ordinary, he did his best to deal with it, or he reported it to the proper authorities. If he saw anyone smoking or stepping into the road or 'mucking about', he told them off. If anything out of the ordinary happened—a strange busker, a rat in the road, a particularly loud argument—he would face any anxious onlookers and make reassuring 'shh-shh-shh' sounds. If he saw any children playing without an anxious mother hovering over them, he made sure to find her and let her know her child could *die*.

That's how the world should be, he thought, that's how the system should be; ever watchful, ever fretful, ever on the lookout for threats and hazards. The problem was that so many people didn't realise this. Certainly it was a tremendous consolation to Neil that everywhere he looked he saw *life*, beaming at him from adverts—healthy smiles, cool, clean surfaces and firm, radiant young breasts—and certainly it was a constant relief to him that technology was actually now reaching the point where everyone everywhere could be perfectly organised, and, what's more, that everyone everywhere was basically groovy with that—technology was now the world religion, with very few apostates, and that was as it should be—but, at the same time, his efforts to enhance life, to take care of people; these weren't appreciated. When he did his life marshalling he received a great deal of abuse, sometimes physical. If he told old people to go home, because they were reminding us all of death, or if he asked conspicuously poor people to tidy themselves up a bit, because their shabbiness was disrupting the system, or if he stood in the middle of the street and shouted 'obey your way to freedom', he nearly always got an earful. But then, so did Jesus, and so did his disciples. One day, the ground will be covered in soft foam and we will all

Joe squatted down. There was very little dry space. 'Who did this? You should go to a hospital,' he said.

'I did. Turns out I also have advanced non-Hodgkin lymphona. I'll be dead by the end of the week. Hahahahaha!'

Joe nodded. 'Come on,' he said, standing up.

'Where are we going?'

Joe pulled the lid of the coffin, then lifted up Ralf in his sleeping bag—he was pitifully light—and gently placed him inside.

'Hahahaha! Where are we going?'

'I don't know,' said Joe, putting the lid back on, then, as the rain had let up a little, he thought better of it and instead packed Ralf's dirty blankets over the top of his wasted body, leaving the coffin lid next to the cash machine. He then took hold of the head-end handle and dragged the coffin down the alley, into Edfu Street, Ralf laughing the whole way.

A few people who saw them both laughed also, although most passing peds found the strange pair troubling. The hulking hairy monkey-form of Joe pulling an almost skeletal tramp along in a coffin appeared grotesquely out of place, even in the deteriorating streets of Edding, with its dark forms kneeling in doorways smoking sulphurous pipes, and its screaming slagging bouts, and its children banging their heads against windows, and its care homes of infinite dread, and its rioting classrooms. A passing woman, violently angry, shouted into her phone; 'I just don't fucking *care*. What does *your* fucking money go on? *You* fucking spend it all!' A bald woman passed, then a pudgy pale man wearing tight shorts and a tank top who looked like a kind of doughnut-eating Jesus, one of the many bloated and decaying herbivorous grubs who live their lives in comfortable chairs, then a group of smooth-skinned, anxious-looking Chinese youngsters all just popped from the same clonal node, perhaps housed in the Chinese takeaway that Joe and Ralf were passing.

They stopped for a rest at the side door, next to two commercial wheelie bins with unlocked padlock holders. Joe rested Ralf and opened the bin, pulling out six boxes of warm chicken chou mein and a huge box of fireworks covered in Chinese characters; 兕無所投其角, 虎無所措其爪, 兵無所容其刃。夫何故以其無死地.

They ate next to a pile of tyres and trellises, filling each other in on the catastrophic downturn in their fortunes and, as best they could, on the inward side too, which for Joe was beyond words, and so instead he offered a series of inarticulate grunts, and which for Ralf was simply a laughing nonsense.

'I really have no idea what anything is,' said Joe. 'Sometimes I open my mouth and find that my body knows things. I'm surprised at what my mouth says. I don't know how it manages to speak at all. This flowing meaning-stuff just comes out of my mouth, like a jellied eel, and twirls round eels coming out of other people's mouths and merges into something else, and sometimes there is a pretty shape, but mostly they sort of bounce off each other and dribble away.'

'That sounds quite normal to me Joseph.'

'Also culture has gone. I saw a book this morning, and it came to me that I used to enjoy learning, building up an armour of knowledge, but it's all vanished, or the weight of it has, and I feel much lighter for it, without the sticky mass of history and art and music and learning, but also without the armour I'm more open to pain. Pain and mystery.'

'You can't have one without the other,' said Ralf, chuckling away.

'I used to be someone,' said Joe, almost to himself.

'I used to be a beekeeper,' said Ralf. 'You know bees?'

'I think I do,' said Joe, although he had his doubts.

'I loved the bees, and they loved me. Hahaha!'

'There *is* something bee-like about you.'

'There's a tradition among bee-keepers,' said Ralf, still laughing, 'it goes back a long way. When someone dies you have to tell the bees. If you don't they get stuck in limbo.'

'The *bees* are involved?' said Joe with emotion. This seemed very significant.

'Yes, the bees are involved. They cross into the other world, to help us get across, but they have to know when to go.'

'I see.'

'I'm telling you this because I'm going to die soon and I want you to tell the bees, my bees.'

'Where are your bees?'

'My bees are in Basingstoke.'

🐝

Neil spent the morning life-marshalling—shooing people this way and that, informing supermarket managers that people weren't paying attention to the 'ten items or less' rule and berating anyone who didn't seem to have a smartphone. It didn't bring him any pleasure, rather a kind of grim satisfaction, but it was good enough. Like Joe, he was in constant pain, but unlike his brother it came from trying to hold himself together. It was as if both of them were clinging onto ropes which hung over an underground ocean of lava. Where Joe had let go and was drowning in fire, Neil was clinging, clinging, clinging, clinging; all the while telling himself that 'it was good enough.'

It was raining, thin, driving, relentless. He had forgotten to waterproof his Gore-Tex shell, so the penetrating rain was leaking in, mingling with his sweat. His face, his whole body, was screwed up against the hazy torrent, he was like a fist pushing its way through the damp, itchy, freezing, smug face of the world. He pushed and pushed, into Dace Road. There was an ambulance outside his house. *Lilly!?* He sprinted a short way before realising that it was for next door. Tanish and Diana were emerging from their house, broken, distraught, following a paramedic carrying their baby, which was making strange choking, sobbing sounds.

'He never sleeps,' Diana was saying. Neither of them paid any attention to Neil. They got into the ambulance which pulled away, lights flashing. Neil watched it drive away, the rain now sweeping through him unresisted.

Neil closed their front door, unlocked his own, went up to his room and hurriedly shut down his computer, shivering with a new pain; guilt. The baby-waking subsonic siren had been constantly on. It had helped him, making those insensitive people suffer, returning their misery unto them, just as God would. The reality of the baby had been entirely lacking though, in his mind. He hadn't so much as thought of it until he had heard its pained, gargled, suffocating cry in the street, and seen the wild, confused, haunted suffering of its parents.

I did that. He thought. I did that. He didn't want to think further, but he couldn't stop his mind leaping through a diabolic tableau of 'what ifs', all of which terminated in the killing of a child, *his* killing of it. Child murder, *the worst of all sins.*

He stood in the middle of his room. Then sat down on the floor. Then stood up again. A memory, in all its dire completeness, had flashed into his mind, the whole thing at once.

Several years ago he had been called out to deal with some road protestors. Idiots, he had thought, as if the world could be saved by blocking roads! You might as well block an artery to save the heart. They had been the usual Jeremys and Charlottes, happy with their smartphones and computers and Gore-Tex and Bromptons but not so happy with what made these things. They were polite though, no trouble, even if they were a pain in the neck. An old woman had D-locked *her* neck to the fuel bracket of a stopped articulated lorry, which took four hours to deal with. Finally, they'd got her free and Neil had accompanied her back to the station, both of them sitting in the back seat of his car. For some reason she had pretended to be asleep, but this hadn't stopped Neil lecturing her, explaining that there was no way, ever, that 'green energy' would run the world—what would the wind turbines be made from? eh? the wiring? the solar panels? What energy would be used to make the transition from fossil fuels to green? How would it meaningfully influence the world's precipitously declining energy return on investment? It wouldn't. It couldn't. It was a fantastic, ludicrous illusion that going vegan and stopping driving would make the *slightest* difference. Veganism was especially stupid; we're omnivores, we're superior to animals and all that guff about animal husbandry destroying the world was just pure propaganda… And then what about the law? Didn't she have any respect for the law of the land? For peace? For order? We live in a social democracy, he'd explained, and that meant… But she wasn't listening. She wasn't listening because she was dead. This was discovered at the station when they tried to wake her. She'd had a massive heart attack as they'd carried her into the car and, during the drive back to Edding, she had been unconscious, slipping into a coma from which she would never emerge.

Neil had not thought of this event since then. At the time, the fact that he had been explaining ecological energetics and enlightenment values to a dying woman, that these had been the last words she'd ever hear, it wasn't even worth thinking about. But now it flashed before him with nauseating intensity.

Other scenes from his life spilled into his awareness. There was no judgement, no awareness of the shame, they were just all suddenly there, in their totality, as if the horror at what he had done to this poor baby had broken down the door to them. He saw himself urinating into his dead father's gunpowder. He saw himself altering Joe's school grades, bugging Joe's shed, phoning Joe's places of work, sending anonymous letters to Joe's girlfriends. He saw himself giving an extra needless kick to a harmless old drug dealer who had already been felled by the morning raid but who, as Neil was stepping over him, feebly reached out for help. He saw himself pretending to die so that Lilly would love him.

He could feel acidy emotion rise in his body, like a poisoned river bursting its banks, a horrible shooting pain down his left side; inflamed pericardium? Split aorta? Necrotizing pancreatitis? With one hand he reached for his smartphone, to check his statistics while, with the other, he opened his medication cabinet to search for some beta-adrenergic blocking agents.

There was a knock on the door.

Neil steadied himself. 'Hold on!' he cried and ran to the mirror. His make-up was a mess. He rapidly dabbed his eyes and straightened himself up. Nobody must see me this way. 'Okay, okay, come in, come in' he said.

The door opened very slowly. Chiyo was there, dressed in a ceremonial kimono of white and gold.

'Ahhhh...' sighed Neil. Ever since she had eaten his mashed potato bolus, her shadow had fallen on his mind. He had dreamt of her, or at least he felt that he had dreamt of her, but on waking could not remember what had happened, except that it was sickening, shameful, monstrous.

'Do you want tea?' she asked.

'Erm...' he could feel fear and desire rise together. As he wondered which urge to follow, she shimmied in, knelt down, and prostrated herself at his feet. He looked down at her, speechless, her long, black, wet hair was flowing over her thin white wrists and his thin white socks.

'I would like to invite you, Neil-san, to have tea with me. Please honour me like this.'

Neil wasn't sure where to look. 'Uh, uh, alright,' he mumbled.

She silently got to her feet and led the way back to her room. Opening the door revealed a thick wooden bar and silk screen over the top half, forcing them both to stoop down to enter.

Inside, the room was as bare as ever, but it was now adorned with a slightly different arrangement, softer and more traditionally Japanese. There were tatami mats on the floor and a vase of chrysanthemums stood on a small, low table, along with items for a tea ceremony. The Rothko had been replaced by the right panel of Heironymous Bosch's Last Judgement; a vision of hell in which the damned—dismembered, tortured, menaced by freakish demons—lay in a surreal, fragmented landscape.

Chiyo shivered her way over to the table, knelt before the bowls and the teapot and elegantly gestured, palm out, for Neil to do the same. He did so, and sat looking around nervously.

'That's a nice painting,' he said, not really knowing what he was saying. It wasn't nice at all. There were fiends and hellfire and excrement and, for some reason, lots of musical instruments. Someone was being sodomised by a flute.

'Hell,' she said.

'Really?' He squinted at the naked figures, all with curiously placid expressions. 'I never imagined hell would be so… painless.'

Chiyo said nothing. She went through the ritualistic motions of the tea ceremony; whisking the tea, rubbing the bowl, pouring and then offering.

'Please,' she said.

Neil took a sip of tea. A wrinkle of the nose suggested it was not to his liking, but he continued sipping.

'What is your favourite book?' she said.

'The atlas.'

'What is your favourite shop?'

'Ryman. Is this part of the… Erm, the ceremony?' he was starting to sweat, his mascara again becoming volatile.

'What is your most unfavourite fruit?'

'Pineapple and satsuma. Is it hot in here?' He could feel a strange split opening up in his mind, between his awareness, here, and the rest of him there, with something awful rising through the fissure, a no, no, no, no, no feeling that the 'rest of him' was slipping out of his hands, and into Chiyo's, as if her questions were his, as if his head and body were hers. What's more, she too was changing, becoming more intensely *her*, darker, more seductive, more utterly woman, which was just appalling, because it seemed there was something *reptile* about her, about the essence of femininity in her, something snake-like.

His eyes dilated, his mind pulled away, but his body was as if bolted to the floor and his mouth just kept answering, out of control.

'What do you feel about homeless?'

'Disgust, but also, when I see someone in trouble, my first thought is always "*yes*, it's not me."'

'What do you hate about yourself?'

Neil was now bathed in sweat. All his make-up had run off. He kept burping up bile and, face twisted in disgust, reflexively swallowing it back down. Chiyo was undoing her kimono, revealing her pale, slender torso, her prominent bird-like collarbone, her small, pale breasts. Neil was horrified, turned on, hypnotised, appalled and in love; love destroying, love disgusting. His penis was agonisingly hard.

'Keep biting lip,' he croaked 'non-standard lower lateral incisors, can't whistle with my fingers, Chrome crashes when I download large files, feminine sneeze, low mean corpuscular volume, villous atrophy, most unlike Clint, and I murdered a baby.'

'The baby is not dead.'

'How do you know?'

'I know. The baby is healthy.'

This comment, which Neil suddenly knew, in his depths, to be true, injected warm, liquidy relief into the midst of the compacted mass of suffering that was his self. Like Chiyo, he was still kneeling, the blood now entirely cut off from his legs. He was starting to feel like a hovering abdomen, his tiny head, embedded somewhere in his sternum, filled with Chiyo's sweet, dark voice and her hypnotic, purplish nipples. He could feel pressure building up, an explosive, cosmic, monkeyish orgasm energy rushing up from somewhere under his perineum.

'Have you ever loved someone?' she asked.

'My mother, Memphis and Kylie Minogue.'

'What do you yearn to know?'

'What happens after you die.'

'Only people who do not live ask this.'

Neil's scrotum starting trembling. Could this be life? It was something like the same feeling he'd had when, desperate to lose his virginity he had phoned a prostitute and as soon as she had picked up the phone he had orgasmed and burst into tears; only now it was almost infinitely more powerful. He would have run, but he was cock-rooted to the floor.

'What's the ideal death for you?' asked Chiyo.

'Receiving oral sex while steering a luxury yacht off the Iguazu Falls waterfall.'

'What,' she whispered, leaning forward, 'was the first time you recognise sexuality… Which means got erection?'

'Wonder Woman hypnotised by Apollo,' he gasped.

'What do you want Neil? What do you want? What do you want? What do you *want!?*'

'*You!*'

He leapt on her. She scratched his face, tearing the flesh of his cheek. He screamed and fell from her, clutching his face, blood dripping through his fingers.

Chiyo calmly tied up her kimono as Neil, head in hands, stood, knee-trembling, and staggered from the room.

∞

Joe had dragged Ralf back to his home. A wiry, no-nonsense, cold-eyed man was waiting for him.

'Mr. Joseph Geb?'

'Yes.'

'My name is Barry Cope. I'm here to advise you on behalf of your landlord, Infinity Crockford that you are now overdue on your rent payments and we are issuing a notice to quit. If you do not leave at the end of the period in this document…' he handed over a letter to Joe, 'we will acquire a possession order from the court and then if you have not left your home by the date given in the order, the court will evict you. The entire process will take around six weeks. You can pay now if you have a card.'

Joe leapt around like an ape, spanked himself, peeped at Barry through 'hand' telescope, scanning him up and down, stopping on Barry's knee. Then he made a wild meeping sound, all to Ralf's delighted laughter.

Barry was less impressed.

∞

Lilly was sat at the kitchen table, sadly looking at her tea. Life was just so… rubbish. A single, pink hill of pleasure rising over a continent of flat disappointment. She had once wanted to travel, to dance naked on empty beaches, to make love with gun-running steamboat pilots in Vietnam, but why bother? People were the same everywhere. All kinds of appalling. She had wanted to learn the mysteries of the universe, to discuss philosophy with blind vagrants and speak the strange language of bees, but all of this now also seemed like pointless effort. After meeting Joe she had read stories from ancient Egypt, and they were absurd. Magic children arguing in court. Bureaucratic myths. Then she had read Greek myths and they were more entertaining, but in another way even worse; everyone, all the gods and heroes, were complete bastards! Everywhere she looked she found the same kind of people. Only the dead spoke, and even they not very much.

Hunter came in, full of life, but a somewhat more muted version of yesterday's Hunter, for he had been spending much more time with wealthy adults and had, to some extent, in emulation of More Important People, toned down his oh-wows and oh-my-gods and literally-can't-believe-its. He had also started reading books on Marx, on climate change, on transhumanism, on racism and on all the other hot topics of the day, as well as a few edgy ideas from genuine radicals, like Ivan Illich, whose criticism of the medical system he effortlessly folded into his 'culture-making' patter. He had constructed a perfectly unoriginal philosophy, decorated with utopian ideas but shorn of actual radicalism by building it on the unexamined assumptions of the system, which he was no more able to critically inspect than a compulsive liar can examine his fear of being boring.

The day before, Hunter had made the following peroration to a group of potential investors; 'What LifeLine is about is *life*. The life of the foetus, the life of the earth, the life of historically marginalised peoples, the life of the young, the life of the old; *all* our lives. For too long, too many lives have been poisoned, from above, by the herbicide of the capitalist system, or choked by the weeds of chaos and superstition, growing from below. It is time for a middle way, a politically neutral way, a future-thinking way, a new stewardship of the earth, an impartial, professionally-organised world designed for life. And that's what we're about, we at LifeLine. We're working to make a world in which there is no starvation, no disrespect, no destruction of nature, no corruption, no lies and, above all, no ill health; a beautiful, beautiful world, managed with the same kind of efficiency as our finest goods and services are. Imagine the world-body worked as well as a Mercedes-Benz EQC or a Sage Oracle high-end espresso machine. No mess, no fuss, no misery, just perfect health, perfect order, perfect life. Utopian? I know it sounds that way, but it is within reach, not just for a few, but for *everyone*.'

This had been received so warmly that the deal he had, for half a year, been angling for, had closed.

'Cheer up!' he said to Lilly, doing a one-two-three drum roll on the table, 'It might never happen!'

'It has already happened.'

'What has?'

'Well I was going to say the catastrophe, the worst thing imaginable, but actually, sometimes, it seems like nothing at all has ever happened to anyone.'

'You need to get out girl, why don't you come out for a drink with me, Southampton and Milk?'

'Erm, no, I'm going out tomorrow. I need to save my brain.'

'Ooh, where you off to?'

'Dominus.'

'Shut. Up.'

'I am.'

'How did you pull that one off?'

'My boss is meeting a secretive Chinese millionaire there.'

'Dominus is the shit,' said Hunter, 'It's not just an ordinary sleazy strip club, well it is, but it's also super exclusive, sex-positive, chill and ironic… I'm trying to get an invite myself, which shouldn't be long now, did I tell you I'm selling out to Duat?

Jesus, aren't you excited? Has the kettle just boiled? I'm really getting into Stoicism. What's the capital of Chad?'

'I am excited. Well, kind of. At least its something different, but I don't feel excited.'

'You'll love it. You'll see,' said Hunter distractedly as he filled the kettle. He was thinking about cryptocurrencies, protein and Epictetus.

'I do need an up.'

'Of *course* you do! *That's* what it's all about!'

'I suppose so. Hard to stay up though isn't it?'

'Look, get up, then worry about staying up. There's nowhere higher than Dominus—you can spend weeks floating back down. Life's not worth living without something to look forward to.'

'I suppose.'

'Look,' said Hunter, 'I know for the last six months I've been in such a, like, intense headspace? But, that's all over now that Duat are taking us over. They're keeping me on as CEO and we're moving into new premises. And expanding the app into all kinds of new directions. It's sooo exciting. I always knew that I could make our health lives smarter… and, yeah, so, as I say—did I say?—I'll be moving out… I'm taking a flat in East London, it's above a warehouse in Hackney Wick, you've *got* to come and see it… We've got table football..'

He sallied out, leaving Lilly three times more optimistic about life and five times more pessimistic.

∞

Laughing Ralf was asleep on the bare floor of Joe and Maria's living room, chuckling to himself.

'Ralf? Ralf?'

He woke up, eyes brimming with joy. Joe was standing over him, dressed as a glam rocker wearing a ruffly gold poet shirt with a large, white, science-fiction triangle over his chest, huge platform boots, edible glitter over his cheeks and a heavy blond mullet wig. He had his pistol tucked into his tight flares, but this was invisible.

Ralf's face, as he looked at Joe and made sense of what he was looking at, dropped.

'I'm going to work,' said Joe.

'Okay,' said Ralf, very seriously. For the first time in nearly a decade he looked unambiguously sad.

'I'm sorry there's no furniture,' said Joe, 'My ex-wife sent it all to a hunting lodge in Scotland.'

'It's okay.'

'I do have something for you though. It's in that bag.'

He indicated a large kit bag leaning up against the wall. Ralf's lip started quivering, his face twisting in misery.

'There's some black matter in the freezer, but I wouldn't eat it, it tastes of split battery.'

Ralf burst into tears. This made him burst into laughter, which made him burst into tears again.

'Don't worry old friend,' said Joe, 'I'm just going for… erm… I'm not sure what I'm going for…'

Joe left, clomping over the wooden floorboards in his tottering stage shoes. Ralf pulled himself to his feet and looked into the kit bag, a soft, sad smile of wondering why crossing his wrecked and ravaged face.

∞

Chiyo is the size of the universe and Neil a tiny naked flesh pod hurtling in silent screaming horror towards her apocalyptic vagina, into which his wretched, twisted form passes, the experience shattering him into countless forms, duplicating and reduplicating, all compelled towards a gigantic pulsating dark sun, a superdense black hole sucking all of life, all of Neil's lives, into a single fused egg-atom, the supercompelling void of God that is nothing, that contains everything, that is utterly beyond all physicality, all matter and sense, and yet it is the wet viscera of

Chiyo's body, a mass of plasmic flesh-matter, into which he is fusing, his little homunculus legs, his genitals, his belly, chest, arms, everything but his face which slowly slides into the moist eternity of Chiyo's warm, wet, serum-red death.

He woke. Chiyo was licking his face, her tongue darting out of her mouth. She hissed into his ear, then put her hand into the bed, down to his crotch, hissed again and bit his cheek, sinking her teeth into the wound where she had scratched him the day before.

'*Agh!*'

He tried to twist away from her, but she gripped his painfully-hard cock, which had the same kind of effect as a biting down on a kitten's scruff, rendering him submissive and immobile. 'I fuck you tonight,' she hissed, 'the fuck of your life, fuck of all man's life, but only in place of death.'

'Uh, nng, where's that?' he whimpered.

'The mortuary where Lilly work.'

'Eugh? There? But how…?'

'You steal key.'

She gripped him harder. Some kind of lightless fire flowed from her clammy fingers into his penis, surging up his back and shoulders. It felt like he was plugged, cock-first, into God's socket.

'Nnngg… Okay, okay…'

∞

Lilly was having her hair done at Gloria's. 'Gloria' was an angular, handsome gender-bender now in his fifties who, after a career spanning one successful song, had shot to the top of the early eighties New York disco firmament, before instantly plunging down into a haze of heroin where he remained for thirty-odd years, living at home with a monomaniacal mother (a failed artist whose own career was based on once appearing naked in an Andy Warhol short), consuming buckets of sushi and watching The Man With Two Brains over and over again. After his mother died penniless Gloria found himself effectively homeless and chose to return to England and find the father he'd never met, Len, who turned out to be a meek, kindly little man in a mullet who ran a women's hairdresser's in Edding and impersonated Roy Orbison in his spare time. Gloria had found Len's company, and that of the middle-aged working-class women who came in, oddly soothing and, as he learnt the hairdresser's art, even meaningful and so, when Len also died, leaving Gloria the shop, he'd taken it over himself, decorating it in a 'sublime eighties' style and covering the walls with photographs of himself with Lionel Richie, Prince and The Pointer Sisters. He'd also installed a small bar.

Lilly was having her haircut finished off. It was now jet black and in a bob. Jarvis Cocker said the first the step to being a pop star was dressing like one, so, following that logic, she had decided the first step to living a life on the edge was to adopt a 'first-I-fuck-you-zen-I-keel-you' look. Gloria, wearing a silver sequinned hoodie and man-dress, was making the final touches, arcing Lilly's head with the cup of his hand, standing back, sucking his finger, stepping forward. He was a 'fucking genius.'

'You've got fucking beautiful hair,' he said, 'it's a fucking dream to work with.'

'So have you!'

'Shut up! It's all product. You know I've been *praying* for you to ask for a bob. You were built for one.'

'Well, the day has come.'

Gloria combined almost unbelievable callousness—he would step on people's tenderest feelings with a kind of brutal disdain—with an equally miraculous sensitivity and kind-heartedness. Lilly's vibe had seeped into him, and there was work to be done here.

'Don't you like it?' he said, ingenuously.

'No, it's not that.'

'Broken heart? Hm?'

Lilly sighed. 'Yeah. A bit.'

'Everyone's fucking heart's breaking these days.'

The bell above the door tinkled. Maria entered.

'Hello you!' cried Gloria, 'Come in! Come in!'

'Hello. I'm early, but I'll wait.' Maria's tone was downbeat and Gloria picked up on this also.

'God, not you too. Look, put a Pimm's together and we'll sort it all out, three girls together.'

Maria put her bags down and, at the bar, started mixing and pouring the drinks.

'Lilly, Maria. Maria, Lilly.'

'We've met,' she Maria coolly, 'we watched a man blow up together.'

'Lilly's down in the dumps,' said Gloria, paying no attention. 'You don't mind me sharing your problems with the world do you?' he asked Lilly, gently touching her shoulder, but before she could answer he had dramatically placed the back of his hand against his forehead to declare to an invisible audience, 'Even white teeth, a perfect figure and skin to die for can't protect you from a broken heart.'

'If anything they'll guarantee it,' said Maria.

'Do you know that moment,' said Gloria, 'when you see, in a moment of awful clarity, who you're in love with? You see your man in a crowd, or you watch him cutting his toenails, and you think, 'who *is* that fucking person?'

'I have that with everyone,' said Lilly, 'Including myself.'

'The best thing is to always keep it casual,' said Gloria, 'Don't be a ridiculous little piglet. You are a rabid *she-wolf!*'

'I sometimes have the feeling,' said Maria, still preparing the drink, 'when I'm having sex with someone, that we're just two weird lumps of lonely meat.'

'Me too!' said Gloria. Lilly nodded.

'Is that the truth?'

Gloria hesitated. Lilly was doubtful, 'No,' she said, 'Is it? No.'

'You just need better men,' said Gloria.

'Do they exist?' asked Lilly, 'better men?'

'No,' said Maria, 'They're all talk, all patter, all promise, but then, when you get down to it, there's just nothing there. Just another coward, or another bastard.'

She handed out the drinks, still talking. 'I went to a barbecue once in Hertfordshire. An old uni friend, and there was a man there who… he made this incredible entrance by flying in on a microlight. But he didn't have the personality to back it up. He was quiet, kept messing up conversations and spent most of the time on his own looking uncomfortable. He was trying to impress with this aircraft thing, but it couldn't make up the shortfall in his personality and in the end the engine wouldn't start, and so he had to come back the next day to cart it back.' She took a sip of her drink. 'All men are that man,' she said, then corrected herself, thinking of Max, 'most men.'

'So how do you find the one in a million?' asked Lilly, or do you have to just settle for one of the rest?'

'It's not much of a choice,' said Maria, 'a lifetime alone darning socks and watching musicals or a lifetime pretending to be interested in the moronic thoughts of a child masquerading as an adult man.'

'I don't know what I'm going to do,' said Lilly, looking at herself in the mirror. Suddenly the femme-fatal project seemed doubtful.

Gloria suddenly whirled around, his arms wide and magnificent, and spoke as if to an audience of thousands, loudly and emphatically, marking each word with a different full-body gesture, pointing, rolling his arms, praying to the skies and, finally, leaping onto the customer-waiting bench; *You. Are. Both. Going. To. Have. A. Good. Time.'*

The women laughed.

Gloria got down, eyes bright, face bright and picked up his glass. 'Cheers girls!' he cried.

They all happily chinked glasses, cleared within, by Gloria's sweeping blasts, from the pall of apparent facts.

'Actually,' said Lilly, 'I'm going to Dominus tonight.'

'You are *not!*' said Gloria.

'I am.'

'Well,' he said, hands on impressed hips, 'I'll see you there!'

'Will you? How?'

'I'm a *compére* dahling!'

'Oh!'

'You don't think an international superstar can be happy to just spend all day moaning with old women about the rates and the Muslims do you? Goodness, a girl's got to have fun too. Oh my god, oh my *god*, it's going to be ammmazing. Maria, Maria, Maria, love of my life, you *have* to come.'

'To Dominus? It's member only isn't it?'

'Oh don't worry about that love. I know a few strings I can tug.' He made a wanking gesture and giggled.

∞

Joe was putting together an IKEA flatpack step stool that he had found dumped in the street round the corner from a paper shop which had also thrown out a large, blue, plastic National Lottery card-holder which someone had inexplicably filled with empty minibar whiskeys. He sat in the street, leaning against the card-holder, counting screws, checking the diagram and turning the seat panel this way and that. He had already put it on back to front and considered just blasting it with the Glock, but his body was in charge and it eventually put the thing together.

After he had finished, he picked up the stool and strolled into the centre of town. A few people passing, fascinated with his raiment, slipped sly glances his way, but he was mostly ignored. Even when he reached the central pedestrian area in front of Primark and stood upon the stool, nobody looked his way.

He spoke. 'Have you lost your face? Only I found one in the mirror the other day that wasn't mine.'

Nobody listened, nobody cared. He stood, dejectedly, on the stool, cold wind whipping at his outrageous flares and flustering his sequins. Glitter blew off his cheeks and timble-tumbled up the street like crippled, gay birds.

Scratched into his features, by the hand of a sadistic child, was infinite sadness. He looked like someone who had dressed for a wedding, his own, but had arrived at a funeral, his own. Most people shot awkward or disgusted glances up at him and then rushed past, but a few had stopped, at a safe distance, leaning up against Pret A Manger.

Joe wept.

Aggressive, mocking voices immediately rose from the onlookers. 'Cheeeeeer up!' 'Weirdo!' 'Call this *comedy*?'

This seemed to upset Joe even more. His shoulders shook, his face contorted into a strange red grimace, tears streaming down his cheeks, nose wet, beard sodden, wind ripping now at his clothes. He cried and cried, which annoyed the crowd even more, creating a vicious circle of mounting derision and deepening hurt, the mocking opposite of a stand-up comedy routine.

'Cheer up!' 'Be happy you bastard!' 'Don't be so depressing!' 'Go home! Get a fucking job!'

'Please be quiet,' Joe whispered, but nobody heard. 'I can't hear what you're saying,' he mumbled to himself, 'I can't hear what anyone is saying. I can't see anyone. Everything is going away, you see…? It's… It's…'

Joe could feel the sadness of the world in him, its unbelievable misery. He had felt similar feelings watching documentaries about factory cows, and young women working in Chinese laptop factories, and children in Edding with no beds to sleep on, and Indonesians mining sulphur. He had felt the infinite tragedy of the world walking around town, looking into the numbed, loveless beings of the human shadows that floated past, hearts made of little more than scar tissue. But all this sadness had something of his self in it, not pure, but filtered through the man he was. Now that there was no man, the sorrow was here, as it is, as deep and as dark and as vast as the Mariana Trench, oceans and oceans of suffering. Yes, Ralf had said it. He knew; *weeping for existence.* It was appalling and yet, because there was no resistance in Joe, it was so strangely empty. His mind was breaking under the monumental weight of it, but there was nobody there to mind, to hurt, to not like.

The effect on the crowd was strange and terrible. This man, standing in the middle of the high street, dressed as a mid-seventies glam clown, weeping and weeping, saying nothing, was sending out goading, inflaming rays into the hearts of those drawn to the spectacle. Seeing a man drown was undamming all the rage and violence and misery which flows under the everyday mass everywhere. The presence of the pain of mankind was so terrible people would rather eat the man who manifested it, than see it, particularly here, which was nowhere.

Only one man was unaffected, smiling indeed. The bland, balding head of the sleepy, pudgy man in the worn wool suit, watching Joe with a peculiar mixture of curiosity and boredom. Joe knew him, knew him everywhere, as the animal upon which sorrow does not fall.

A scotch egg struck Joe on the side of the head, then another. This seemed to be the cue that the crowd were waiting for. As one, they lurched towards him, screaming, dragging him from the stool, pulling him down.

∞

Joris Thottesley, now Joris Lord Thottesley, was hosting, in the lavish reception rooms of Thottesley hall, a meeting of the Great and Good. Elite professionals, politicians, business leaders, celebrities and members of the Haleshire Country Cricket Club, all of whom quietly sipped wine, chatted about fashion or about the economy, nibbled amuse-gueules, made wry asides and laughed appreciatively. Waiters slid unobtrusively between them, a string quartet played in the corner; clusters of gleaming debutantes crackling with dry, jagged laughter; featureless, fearless, wealthy-faced, hard-jawed women, with weirdly reflective, oiled-up skin and cheekbones like cue balls; foppish, fat-necked men with rolls of chub, bright red cheeks and turkey-like gobble-laughter. Everyone had peculiarly fixed and immobile faces and hard, fixed gimlet eye holes that didn't so much look at things as grip them in gangsterish talons.

If someone who had never been to such an event had chanced into the room they would have been astonished by the grace, good will, humility and warmth displayed by almost everyone, who greeted and spoke to each other like old friends, who scrupulously obeyed the rules of courteous conversation—never interrupting bores, never blanking younger or inferior speakers, never betraying even a hint of a negative judgement, humouring poor jokes with tinkling laughter and back-channelling like the most experienced counsellors. It had the display of social perfection; but there were minute cracks in the spotless presentation—confused micro-glances, momentary frozen smiles, a glaze across the glance or the barest shade of shared knowing disdain—through which our observer would have glimpsed the heart of the matter, that nobody here cared for anyone else, that the predominant feelings among the participants were sycophancy, boredom, hatred, sexual frustration or, more often that not, no feeling at all, a total lack of interest in everything and everyone everywhere. This is how the 'best' people operate everywhere, with varying degrees of skill and with a few shades of local colour, but with a common 'polish'—as it was once called—where once there had been, long, long ago, a living creature, but now; ash.

All of the assembled were connected to Max, and now to Joris, by ties of personal fidelity and financial codependency. The CEO of Duat was here, a mask-faced child-man who watched everyone with passive disinterest, the UK secretary of state for international trade, whose perfectly spherical head was plastered with a never changing expression of moist smugness, Lady Gaga was expected, although it was unsure if she'd make it as she had a meeting with a satellite manufacturer. Hunter too was here, one of 'the new generation' of entrepreneurs, representing green fuels, drone-delivered alpaca socks and 'the future of chicken.' He had made it clear to himself and to everyone around him, that he detested 'capitalist elites,' but like all ambitious businessmen his principles took second place to 'pragmatic' concerns, so he kept his mouth shut and his eyes open. If the hyper-wealthy are sensitive to nothing else, they can sniff out favoured attitudes. None of them really lead, which makes their world, in a sense, a kind of anarchism, but one that is absolutely hollow.

Joris himself was absent. He was in a different wing of the estate, in his large, comfortable office. Ian Cremwave stood before the massive mahogany desk while, Joris, dressed in his super-extravagant crow costume, sat reclining, feet up.

'I've just had a call from Zhtomir; the acquisitions have all gone through,' said Ian, 'Duat has now acquired Gyp, Starcream, Loganberry, Shoof, Pickle, Doo-Wop and Carp.'

'Good,' said Joris, 'then we are ready.'

'Everyone is here, sire,' said Ian, 'they're waiting to begin.'

'Where is Geb?'

'Which one, my liege?'

'Joe.'

'He's doing a stand-up tragedy set in the centre of Edding.'

'It's time to bring him in.'

'Yes, sire.'

'Tonight we turn the world the right way up.'

Ian bowed elegantly—a classic seventeenth century obeisance—and left.

∞

Louis Gallardo grew up in a Catholic boys' boarding school in the Philippines. He was a quiet, hypersensitive child with a hunchback, mercilessly mocked by his cruel, sarcastic classmates. He spent most of his time alone in 'the quad,' a rarely-visited closed garden next to the school library in which mould, weeds and bird shit grew on clumsily realised plaster statues of the saints. Louis, who loved football, used to play 'World Cup' with these statues. They were his only friends.

When his father was arrested for embezzlement he was taken out of school and handed over to an aunt who told him that the family were now broke and he would have to leave school and go and work in the Middle East, which he did, taking a job in the United Arab Emirates as a cleaner for a wealthy landlord on the Gulf coast.

The agency through which he got the job told him that he would first have to hand over his passport, then pay a thousand dollars, for 'flights and processing fees,' which could soon be paid back with his five-hundred-a-month salary, allowing him to amass a tidy profit. The reality, which immediately hits every Filipino, Pakistani, Indian, Tibetan and Indonesian who arrives in the UAE, Saudi Arabia, Qatar and Kuwait, was that Louis was now an indentured slave, earning a hundred dollars a month and, because the agency held his passport, unable to leave.

Most Third-World Gulf workers live packed thirty at a time in stifling, rat and cockroach-infested portacabins, working in forty and fifty-degree heat and fuelled by nothing but dirty rice. Louis was lucky; he worked in a luxury air-conditioned apartment building. His bedroom was a windowless cupboard-sized room next to a constantly churning washing machine the size of his auntie's house, but it was clean and cool and he had access to a toilet that wasn't overflowing with excrement. In addition, the work didn't take up all his time and the people who hired the apartments—European expats mostly—were often quite friendly.

When Louis considered the tiny boiler-suited, face-wrapped forms working on the roads or the building sites, or the little Thai, Uzbek or Filipina girls who spent their nights sucking the cocks of men who despised them, or the army of Asian maids who worked nonstop for families who beat them, locked them up and sometimes even murdered them—with impunity—he considered himself extremely lucky, but ire burned in his soul, just as it did in the hearts of all who work for the wealthy, but particularly here, where open, naked, finger-snapping contempt for the poor was the widely-accepted norm and where those who called the shots, the Emiratis, did nothing, could do nothing; were helpless babies with only money on which to base their supercilious feeling of contemptuous superiority. On top of that, everything they did and felt and believed was false, second-hand or *purchased*—their qualifications were bought, their ideas were photocopied quotes and their authority nothing but the power to imprison whatever foreigner happened to upset them. Like all fake minds, even the hint of a criticism from a foreigner—and all ex-pats hated the Emiratis—would be met with violence, a violence which simmered under everything in the UAE; even the filthy, rubbly desert seemed to be a layer of crust formed on a boiling sea of hatefulness, cruelty and disgust.

Louis decided he would get his revenge, strike back at this villainous rock world. He didn't know how, but he did know that he would have to become a slick, smart killing instrument to do it. He spent day and night studying, reading and researching. He learnt Capoeira, kung fu and Krav Maga and combined them into his own unique system. He learnt English and the rudiments of revolutionary theory. He made contacts amongst his fellow slaves and he prepared to strike.

His plan was simple; for a thousand of the most desperate people he could find to each murder one Emirati, as high up as possible, all on the same evening. He knew many who were within reach of ministers and CEOs, but it didn't matter. As long as Emiratis perished he'd be happy and God's justice would be done. His own boss, Amir the landlord, a flappy, thick-skinned buttock of a man, who divided his time between luxuriating on the coast of the Indian ocean, shopping in Knightsbridge and fucking in Dubai, was to be his target.

The day came, the night, and Louis, clamping his long-honed mind-control upon his emotions, was as ready as he could be. He knew that Amir would be drinking coffee and eating dates before his friend arrived—the two of them were to drive into

Dubai to spend the evening with a couple of expensive Russian pros—and that he, Louis, could easily slip into the lounge, slit Amir's throat and slip out without anyone seeing or suspecting anything. He would probably be caught in the end, many of the Martyrs he had been working with would, and they were resigned to their fate; but Louis wasn't going to make it easy for the authorities. He'd run, and he'd run far.

Amir was watching television—a Champion's League match between Paris St. Germain and Amir's national team, Manchester City. Louis approached from behind, a cut-throat razor, blade open, in his left hand, right hand raised, ready to pull back Amir's long loping head. He got nearer and nearer, ready for the fatal blow until, finally, just as he reached the sofa, he heard a snore. Amir was asleep.

Louis stood and stood, heart pounding, looking, staring at the exposed, scraggy neck. To kill a sleeping man, in cold blood; as an idea it had seemed easy, but now, facing the fact, it was impossible. He couldn't do it. He turned and ran, outside into the superhumid evening. He didn't know what to do, or where to go. As he stood in the car park, Emiratis across the country were being killed, on his orders. He would be discovered; why not just give up now, or slit his own throat to avoid the nightmare of prison in the UAE? As he stood, looking at the situation, he heard a familiar voice, that of one of the friendly expats whose flat he cleaned. It was Neville Geb.

It was this meeting that formed now the lyrics of the song he was working on with Margaret in the dining room. She, wearing a tinfoil Viking helmet, sat at a synthesiser, a Roland Jupiter 8, and he, wearing a big latex 'hand-head hat', sat on the floor playing a bamboo slit drum and singing a poem he had written while hiding in Neville's laundry room, feeling at any moment he could be discovered and killed, feeling the weight of responsibility crushing him for 'The Night of the Rusty Blades', feeling that his life was over; yet, at the same time, going through, thanks in part to Neville's spirit and wisdom, a bizarre rebirth.

Since the brain injury which had irrevocably converted Margaret Geb from an ironic, ambitious professional mother into a cheerfully adrift dementrice, she had spent most of her days composing electronic music on her synth to a Bontempi backing rhythm. She had divided her life between the kitchen, baking sourdough bread, cheese scones and buttery flapjacks, and the dining room next door, composing eerie electronic soundscapes which had, thanks to her classical training and continued attraction to austere and worshipful arias, a wistful baroque flavour. As her rational mind had decomposed she had found herself less able to function in the world, less interested in food, or in cooking it, but still able to improvise progressive rock cantatas on her synth. These, along with shooting bric-a-brac and lying about in bed lost in a libretto of subreal musings, formed the larger part of her day.

Louis suddenly stopped playing, head cocked. His dog-sensitivity to people approaching the house had been tripped. He sensed that danger was near and flipped to his feet. Margaret also stopped playing.

'Is the worst about to happen?' she asked.

'Stay here,' he said and left. The doorbell rang. 'Oooh!' cried Margaret and stood up, radiant around the nostrils. She tottered off, tied, as ever, to her rope.

Louis ran through to the kitchen, picked up a knife and tucked it into his yoga pants, checked the doors were locked, then ran back into drawing room where, in the bottom drawer of a display cabinet, he pulled out a traditional Colt Frontier revolver.

The voice of the social worker, Raimonda came through the letterbox; 'We know you're in there Mrs. Geb.'

This was followed by Andy's voice. 'It's for your own good Mrs. Geb! You're just not being properly looked after!'

Louis was loading the pistol, cursing to himself that the two of them had used up all the shotgun ammo the day before.

'I'm no good with one of these,' he mumbled to himself.

Another voice came through the letter box. 'Alright Gallardo, this is the police. Let us in, and this can all end peacefully.'

'The peace of the wasteland!' cried Louis.

He heard a faint, urgent discussion, then silence, then the door flew from its hinges as a policeman, swinging an 'enforcer' battering ram, split the lock. Louis fired above the door, splintering the frame.

'Back off scum!' he cried. Margaret's voice floated down the hall. 'Louis! Help me! I'm stuck!'

'Bwisit,' Louis fired again, and again, blasting away to keep the police at bay as he sneaked backwards, reloading, down the hall, until he got to Margaret's room, *empty*, her rope trailing out of the window. Louis leapt over the bed. Margaret, wearing her Pickelhaube, had made a wonky sprint to freedom, but the trailing rope had caught on a bush, preventing her from reaching the car. Like an animal, she tugged and heaved, unable to make the most basic logical connection between being unable to move and being tied to a bush. As Louis looked out of the window a bullet whizzed across his face. One of the police had emerged from the side alley. Louis shot back, slicing the rope with his knife. Margaret staggered forward. Louis jumped through the window, but a strange heavy knock twisted his leg from under him; he had been shot in the thigh and in the chest. He landed awkwardly, as he did the policeman sprinted out from the side of the house and grabbed Margaret's rope, pulling her backwards. She, staggering back towards the authorities, shouted sternly, 'No. I do *not* wish to speak to you. You must go *away*. I do *not* wish to speak to you. You are *not* to pull me *that* way.'

She vanished, tottering out of sight. Louis rolled down the garden to the hedge which gave on to the canal.

'We've got her Gallardo!' came the voice of the police through a loudhailer. 'It's all over. You might as well call it a day!'

Louis is at the bottom of the garden, blood sticking his T-shirt, trickling over his belly and down his leg, squatted down, his will tightening into a hyperdense ball bearing. A smoky red haze is closing in on his vision, fogging his mind. He has one mission in this life: to protect the Geb family. Nothing, *nothing*, will stop him. The police leap out blasting, bullets whizzing past Louis and, seemingly, through him as he grows wings and flies over the hedge.

∞

Neil was crawling around Lilly's room, feverishly searching for her work keys. He opened a drawer, full of knickers, on which a Post-It note lay which read 'Neil, you shouldn't be here.' He opened another drawer. Various items, on top of which another Post-It note; 'or here, fuckface.' Underneath this were the keys to the kingdom, which Neil grabbed and thrust into his tracksuit bottoms, rapidly and quietly exiting just as Lilly, wearing thick dark kohl, a leather slit-dress, fishnets and choker, was coming up the stairs. When she saw him she tensed, ready for battle, but Neil, hard, distant and distracted, just grinned, weirdly.

'Hello Neil.'

Still grinning, he made to pass her, but she spoke, stopping him lightly with her hand.

'Neil, I just wanted to tell you I'm… I don't know… I… I'm just sorry it didn't work out between us… And, actually, I'm a bit worried about you, I mean, you know, you've changed, the, erm…' she made a vague 'face-mask' gesture, indicating his make-up, but then she felt awkward and guilty, 'er… *are* you okay?'

'Yeah, I'm fine,' he said, nodding and smiling.

'If you want to talk, I, uh… you know, you can you know.'

'I'm going down to the well.'

'Okay, okay…'

The two of them said nothing. Lilly looking helplessly concerned, Neil frozen in a madly over-involved grin. 'Well, best of luck yeah?' he said, speaking like a cash machine.

'Thanks,' she said.

'But it's all your fault,' he said, in the same upbeat tone of mechanical pleasantry, 'You're all soft and nice, but you're a coward.

You can't see anything through. You give up on everyone and everything. Why do you think you're alone in this house? Because you can't do what you know you should do. You deserve Joe, because you're both chicken-meat.'

Lilly was so shocked she couldn't speak. He squeezed past her and, to her surprise, opened Chiyo's door and slipped in.

She went into her room and sat on her bed, trying to gather her thoughts. It was true, she thought, I do give up easily. But who wouldn't? What's the point of soldiering on through the darklands? Where does it get you? It just gets darker. But then, actually, hold on, I don't *want* to give up. And anyway, God, he's a total nut! Neil Geb is obviously losing his lunch. One moment he's Inspector Bucket and wants to be friends, then suddenly he's all grinning spite and wants to run you through with a sword. And then his face. What is going on behind that mask? And why was he going into Chiyo's room? Neil and *Chiyo? What* an odd pair. Are they really? Could it be? It seemed like a good thing, in some parallel-dimension way, but only like talking to mushrooms did or being a proctologist.

There are certain people, sweet, kind and trusting, who are fairly obsessed with the idea that they are rather pathetic, or weak, or unlucky, or unhappy, or useless. What this means is that they have, as it were, written on their foreheads, the words 'hit me', which those who are looking for someone to abuse find very attractive. What's more, for all their gentleness, these lovely ones actually pay very little attention to other people, and so are unable to tell if someone is, actually, on the make. The result is, they end up being abused again and again and finish their lives as hardened cynics, if in fact they were ever anything else. All this Lilly felt, obscurely, in her belly; she had a horrible dark sense that her inward dreaminess was really a kind of terrible selfishness, and that she was headed towards a very cold, hard place, and Neil, God knows how, had pointed the way…

Oh good grief, she thought, no. No, no, *no*. She stood up and almost literally pushed the thoughts from her mind, making a sweeping gesture with her hand, then she sat down again and thought perhaps she should call Joe after all, perhaps she had been a bit hasty to cut the threat out of her life? She picked up her phone and called Joe, putting on her coat as she waited for him to pick up, leaving her room, going downstairs and stepping out into the freezing cold misty evening.

Behind and above her in the first floor window stood Chi-yo, watching Lilly leave. Holding a ping-pong bat and ball, she turned to face Neil, who was face down on the floor in his underpants, arms stretched out before him, making 'nyum, nyum, nyum' noises into the carpet. She whacked the ball against the back of his head, then stood on one foot, left paddle-hand raised above her head, right arm crossed in front of her belly, ring finger and thumb lightly touching.

'Tonight we burn,' she said.

∞

Joe—right eye swollen and purple, bleeding from a busted lip, poet shirt in tattered strips, space triangle split, wig long gone—staggered through the nightmare of the world as it is. The faces of passers-by had lost their domesticated and vermin qualities and coalesced into a single laboratory monkey archetype. Every face he passed was that of a sick, bloodless, experimented-on rhesus macaque. He was in a low-grade hell, surrounded by drained simian shades and shuffling demons, but all fire and diabolic fury absent, just the shell of evil.

On the edge of the shopping precinct, a crowd of party-goers spilled out of Wendy's, a thick bunch of fat squawking women and dense, red, ape-like men, laughing like mental patients. Joe reached out to them, clinging to their arms and hands but they shrugged him off with mocking disgust.

A buzz in his pocket. He took out his phone and gazed at it confusedly. There were words on it, his mind said 'Lilly', but why or how was a mystery. His body pushed the little green button and he put the object to his ear.

'Joe?'

'Yes. I think so.'

'It's Lilly.'

'Is it?'

'I'm on my way out...'

'So am I.'

'...and I thought, erm ...how are you?'

'I have no idea. It's beyond me.'

Lilly waited for him to say something else, to keep speaking, but there was silence.

'I just wanted to say,' she said, 'that, uh... I just... I suppose that I like you, but... Well, I don't know if you're... I mean you are strange, aren't you? And, I suppose, you don't meet many strange people, not really; everyone is just how you expect them to be... that's probably unfair, but it's just... it's so easy to be cautious... and, well, I'm not really sure I can trust you... so, I should have explained this before, that I'm very against violence... I think, actually, I just need to be on my own, I just, I just don't think I'm made for relationships, I'm not built that way, so, so, well, I suppose that's it really... You're very interesting and I love the way you put your hand up when you want to interrupt some-one and your nutty smell and the bigness of it all... But, I'm sorry, but I don't think I'm ready... you know... Do you know?'

'I don't know.'

'Don't know what?'

'I don't know what you're talking about.'

'That's okay. But do you... care what I'm talking about?'

'No.'

'You don't care?'

'No. I don't care about anything.'

'You don't care about me?'

'I really don't care about anything.'

'Oh.'

There was a long pause. Joe's eyes looked at the phone, then he lifted it to his ear, and his mouth spoke. 'Is this the end of the conversation?' This woman is the same end of the magnet, he thought. The same end of the magnet.

'Yes,' said Lilly, very quietly, her voice quivering, 'I suppose it is.'

'Okay.'

He posted his phone into a street bin then, turning, found himself in front of the Edding Travel Tavern. He went in. There was no decision about it, his body went in by itself and then his mouth shouted out 'everyone stop what you're doing and listen to me' and his hand took out the gun in his trousers and fired it, dislodging a fist of plaster from the ceiling.

Stunned terror, all eyes turned fearfully towards him. A crystal bubble of lucidity had risen over the marsh of Joe's mind. There was one thing to do here, and only one.

'Everyone get your smartphones out and look for Hail, Hail the Gang's All Here on Youtube,' he said, with unreal clarity, 'You've got two minutes to find it before I start blasting.'

Nobody spoke, nobody moved, nobody did anything, so he fired his gun again and the twelve or so people in the lobby, guests and receptionists, jerked into action, pulling out their phones and hurriedly searching for the song.

'What was it?' a ruddy, square-faced woman whispered in fear and anguish, her phone-holding hand shaking.

'Hail Hail, the Gang's All Here,' said Joe slowly and clearly. 'It's a jaunty forties version of 'With Catlike Tread,' by Gilbert and Sullivan. You want the karaoke version, with lyrics.'

He watched them. He was empty of thought, empty of mind, empty of morality, empty of emotion, just watching. A couple of times the song started and he had to tell them to stop the track, but soon enough everyone had it ready.

'Okay,' said Joe, vaguely gesturing with his gun, 'everyone get together into a nice group.' They did so, a motley choir of Eastern Europeans, rail-workers, cleaners and nearly down-and-outs; travel-tavern regulars.

Someone else entered, a small Indian woman. Joe held up his gun, she screamed, and he said, quite affably, 'Don't worry, just

join everyone else, you'll soon get the hang of it,' and, trembling with fear, she crept over to the little choir in the middle of the blue-carpeted lobby.

'Right, I'm going to count you in, and then you'll push play on the backing and we'll all sing along together. Okay? Oh and you three,' he pointed to a tall lost-looking young man, a chubby, garishly-dressed motherly type and a stocky, fat-necked man, 'you'll do the words that come up in brackets. You're kind of the backing singers. You'll get the picture.'

The little group nodded, eyes wide with anxiety.

'Good, okay everyone, one, two, three, four…'

Everyone had started playing the song at slightly different times, so the music sounded fragmented, echoey and clashing, but it was still recognisable. The voices were rather feeble to begin with though, so Joe waved his gun around crying 'more! more!'

A gang of good fellows are we, (are we)

Are we, (are we) are we, (are we)

With never a worry you see, (you see)

You see, (you see) you see, (you see)

We laugh and joke, we sing and smoke,

And live life merrily; No matter the weather

When we get together

We have a jubilee.

'Good!' yelled Joe, 'Good! And now the chorus! Everyone together! Come on!'

Hail! Hail! the gang's all here,

What the deuce do we care?

What the deuce do we care?

Hail! Hail! we're full of cheer,

What the deuce do we care!?

Joe was dancing round the little choir, who watched him warily, sensing, perhaps correctly, that their lives hung on their performance. And yet, although immediate, primal terror was the overriding emotion, the togetherness of the group and the singing was having an effect also; there was even a bit of melody in there, although it was all hopelessly out of time and tune.

We love one another we do, (we do,)
We do, (we do,) we do, (we do,)
With brotherly love and it's true, (it's true,)
It's true, (it's true,) it's true, (it's true,)
It's one for all, the big and small,
It's always me for you; No matter the weather
When we get together
We drink a toast for two.

As they reached the end of the second verse Joe instructed them to keep singing, and not to stop or he'd come back in and kill everyone. As he left, the group were once again loudly, nervously and catastrophically singing the chorus;

Hail! Hail! the gang's all here,
What the deuce do we care?
Hail! Hail! we're full of cheer,
What the deuce do we care!?

∞

Dominus, a luxury strip club for men and women, was large enough to comfortably seat two hundred around sixty or so candlelit tables; mahogany disks, floating on split levels and scattered around a semi-circular stage, a slender tongue from which stretched out, on a runway platform, into the lush, velvety room, which was surrounded by curtained alcoves and, along the burgundy back wall, a softly lit bar. An arch led through to an equally well-appointed casino of brass and baize gaming tables surrounded by cones of light spread up the walls from behind mother-of-pearl sconces and wrought tapestry screens. The panelled walls were hung with secessionist art, Klimts, Muchas and Kurzweils. It was, in short, unlike every other strip club in the country, tasteful. The men and women employed to dance

and wait tables were the most beautiful money could buy, and without a trace of filler, silicone or steroid.

Lilly entered, approvingly took in the environs and took a seat at the bar. It was fairly early, so there were not too many people. A barmaid approached; Bronya, although anyone who knew her would hardly recognise her. Her face had lost its scrunched-up tension, her hair, once tightly pulled back into a ponytail, now loosely framed a relaxed and surprisingly feminine face. Even more surprisingly, a few soft and attractive freckles had appeared over her nose and cheeks.

'What would you like?' she asked.

'Pint of cider,' said Lilly.

She looked around. Wealthy-looking suits waddled around ogling the floor people, who were mostly alienish model types with passive, dreamy eyes so far apart they looked like dolphins, but there were also some curvier, angrier girls. There were also, for the benefit of women, men with jaws like digger-buckets and a few pale, big-eyed waif-men. All four types, in other words, were catered for; men looking for characters from video games to jerk off into, men looking for big-hipped mother-types to cook and clean for them and to tell them what to do, women looking for walking talking penises to merge their fearful minds into, and women looking for chinless, men-shaped children to fuss over.

A group of women, made up for a 'big night out,' were at the end of the bar—looking at their thighs, arranging their hair. They were cackling with laughter, although they looked desperate, pained. An old couple came in and took their seats in front of the 'extended' stage. They were followed by Nina, fretting and fussing. She had done her best to 'scrub up' but it didn't work. She looked like she'd put her make-up on in the dark.

'Oh Lilly,' she said, taking a seat next to her, 'I'm so glad to see you. I'm not late am I? Are they here yet?'

'I don't know what they look like.'

'They're Chinese,' she looked around, 'no, it's fine. We're fine. A port please,' she said to Bronya.

'Port? I'm not sure we have that.'

'Really? God, it's been so long since I've been out! Erm… Something sweet…?'

'JD and Coke?'

'Okay, I'll have that,' she said, catching a glimpse of herself in the bar mirror. 'I'm having a hot flush,' she said, 'I look like a bar of nougat. The problem is when you start putting on weight at my age it doesn't go where you want it to go… this is the problem… if I knew where it was going to go, it would be alright, but I don't… fat has a mind of its own doesn't it? Oh I'm sorry. I'm just so nervous. I need to steady my nerves. Did I tell you I have a urinary tract infection?'

'Eighteen pounds twenty-five,' said Bronya, putting the drink down before Nina.

'*How* much?' Nina sucked the air as if she'd just been punched in the kidneys.

Bronya repeated the sum.

'Oh. Oh dear. My word. Erm. Well… no, I have to calm down,' said Nina, fidgeting out a few notes and, with her eyes closed, handing them reluctantly over to Bronya.

'Look, look at my hands,' she said, holding up her pointy, red-knuckled hands for Lilly, 'I'm shaking all over.'

'I'm sure it'll be fine Nina. You said yourself it's just a formality. The deal is done isn't it?'

'Yes but… Yes, you're right, you're right. But where are they? Oh, you've changed your hair. Oh God I'm so glad to be out of the house. My Dad, have I told you about him?'

'You've mentioned him.' Lilly, readying herself to be complained over, noted that it had taken Nina a full five minutes to realise she had completely changed her appearance.

'He's got emphysema,' said Nina slurping distractedly at her drink, 'so he's always coughing… but he coughs right in your face. Doesn't cover his mouth. Disgusting. And when he breaks wind he doesn't try to hide it or go to the toilet like a normal person. We had guests over the other night, and he just sits there and lets rip. If you met him, you'd think, oh my God what is *that*?'

'Why you don't just leave him?' said Lilly, amused by this revelation. Nina had made sideways allusions to her unpleasant home life, but had never shared any details. Perhaps now that she was ridding herself of the business she felt she could speak to Lilly more intimately. Or perhaps the JD and Coke had gone straight to her abstemious head, or perhaps she was just panicked. Nina was one of those people who inhabit an utterly different personality as soon as they do something 'different' and 'fun', laughing loudly at 'amusing' anecdotes long before they reach a conclusion, making exaggerated wacky gestures and offering surprising, random comments or anecdotes.

'He needs me', she said, 'Besides, who would take me! Look at me Lilly, *look* at me.'

'What do you mean? You're still young.'

'He fries his beans in lard', Nina said, not listening, 'Two days ago he got the hump because I cooked his beans normally and said he was going to go on a hunger strike. A hunger strike! Now he sits there all day moaning about how hungry he is. I said to him, "Can't you find a quicker way to kill yourself?" God knows how my mum used to put up with him, well she didn't, she couldn't talk to him or anyone else, so the dogs got it all. I remember when I was six I walked in on her asking the dogs, we had two border collies, asking them about her pension plan.' Nina looked at her drink, 'I don't feel any different. I think I'd better have another one. Excuse me? Excuse me?' There were other barmaids now, but Bronya attended to her.

'Another one please. I can't muck this up Lilly. Don't get me wrong, I love this job… Well, I don't "love" it… No, I don't… It's just so hard keeping control over everything. The harder you work to keep everything, you know…' she made a squashing 'contained' gesture… 'The more it all seems to slip between your fingers.'

She took her drink from Bronya, then opened her hand-bag again. With hesitating effort—although not quite as much difficulty as with the first twenty-five—she handed over the notes.

'You never *really* know what's going on, do you?'

'No,' said Lilly archly, 'Perhaps you should get cameras and microphones installed everywhere so you can record everyone? Then you'd know.'

Nina looked over the rim of her drink at Lilly. She didn't say anything for a few moments, then she said quietly, 'we are friends aren't we?'

'Are we? I suppose we are, in a way.'

'I do like you, you know.'

'Do you?'

'Yes, so does Carl, so does Paul. We think you're an invaluable asset.'

'Oh,' said Lilly, 'That's nice.' Or it had been until she'd been turned into an 'asset.'

Nina, not paying attention, was gulping at her drink. Her voice had already become a little slurred. 'You're young Lilly. You're *young*. You don't want to spend your life painting corpses. You want to get out there. Have *fun*.'

'That's what I'm doing here.'

'You can't waste your life, on death. You mustn't, you're not, nobody is forcing you, you can leave *any* time you like. If some German guy comes along, and he says… He says… "I'll take you away from all this… I'll take you to Bad Gastein and we can ski all winter and spend the summer hiking through the Austrian Alps, and eating bratwurst… You go, you *go*, don't, just out of family duty and fear of the unknown and fear of your repulsive father, stay in your stupid job, in stupid Edding, don't Lilly… Promise me you won't…'

'I think I can promise that.'

'Good.'

Lilly peered at Nina, who was now lost in her own world, thinking of Reiner and his thick blonde hair and handsome, ice-cold eyes, and his strong red legs, and his angry sexuality. Reiner, who twenty-five years ago she had lived with for six months and who left when she refused to return to Austria with him, although this was a calculated move on his part as he knew she would be afraid of leaving home and he could leave her for that reason and not because she was stiff and unresponsive in bed, a resolute awkwardness caused by, unknown to him, her fear of pooing herself if she got too excited.

'Oh, he's here,' said Lilly.

Mr. Wukong and his young granddaughter had, indeed, arrived. Both were dressed extremely formally. He in a close-fitting Mao suit, she in a traditional, high-collared silk dress, black and red and dotted with pink jasmine flowers. They saw Nina and Lilly across the now filling arena and threaded their way through.

Mr. Wukong bowed.

'Evening!' said Cherry.

'Hello,' said Nina, pulling herself together.

Cherry turned to Lilly and said, brightly, 'I'm Cherry!'

'Lilly. I'm Nina's assistant.'

'This is Mr. Lam Wukong,' said Cherry, introducing her grandfather. He bowed again. One of the club's sexy alien waitresses—a stunningly beautiful, electric-eyed black girl, name-tagged 'Mercy'—came over to him.

'Mr. Wukong, your table is ready,' she said.

Cherry spoke to Wukong in Hakka, '*The unyielding and great takes its place below. The soft and yielding takes its place above.*'

'*The dark clarifies and is far away,*' said the old man, surreptitiously handing Mercy a small silver pill-box, '*It reverts with things. Then there arrives the great harmony.*'

Cherry turned to Nina and Lilly with a big grin on her fresh glowing young face. 'Bostin.'

∞

Joe trudged round foetid Edding, not knowing where he was headed. People passed, some seemed to speak to him, or to each other, but language had lost its sense. He heard the pure sound, the pure meaning, and it was horrific, mouthed sounds cold, colourless nothings, cutting through the peace and space of the moment, tight, ugly, waggling sounds from the back of throats wincing, resisting. He saw the faces, cruel incomprehensible caricatures of themselves, unmasked of their words, disgusting and disgusted, like they were wading through excrement, like they were all putting their arms round the u-bend, like it was all shit, constant shit, shat from the arse of life.

He slumped against an electrical junction box, freezing cold, heartbroken from loss, but what had been lost he couldn't have said, even if he had been able to think or speak. It was, rather, that every last defence he had against the world had slipped away, and all the superdense selves that make up mankind were squeezing him out, crushing delay and distance, stripping language and past, peeling away mind and emotion and leaving nothing but bitter, angry men and soul-dead women, and insane blank children, and numbed, undead digital princes, and one-way glass, and AstroTurf, and mattresses, all piled up on top of him, and topmost, there was Irving Bone carrying an effigy of his wife made out of matches.

'Aarl arrr wrrr arl ghaw...?' said Irving.

Joe tried to speak, 'Shlaarg makwang hoosh fe'tarp!'

Irving's aggressive, nasal, twing-twang meant nothing but pain. There was no mind-meaning to his words, but pure information, pure hate, pure fear. Joe could see into Irving's confusion and terror. All his containment and non-violence, all his purity and morality... all that had been dropped as the all too material conditions upon which his tidy beatitude was based, crumbled. The world was crumbling around Irving and Joe could feel directly into the nothingness engulfing him, eating the world.

He could also sense deep threat there too, some kind of danger. The world itself was speaking here. Irving's ragged bitterness and bile, seeking the most immediate escape, was directed at him, Joe. Irving, in his judging tightness, was one with the omnimind of misery behind it all. The world could speak through anyone, at any time. It could look through anyone's eyes.

Police sirens. Nlue lights strobed at the end of the street. Joe had to move. His body knew this and it rose unsteadily again, reeling away from Irving, and away into a side alley.

8

Dominus filled with slick male spods reeking of aftershave and tremendously made-up women wobbling around in skin-tight dresses and suede ankle boots. At the best seats in the house, set back, low-profile, but with a good view of the stage, sat Cherry, Mr. Wukong, Nina and Lilly. The old couple sat to their left against the bar, next to them, Jonah Hill, while, to the right, a very depressed looking Dave Davage.

Dave was wearing his nightclub best; tight, long, fawn-coloured Excelsior 'smart shoes' which looked like Cornish pasties, dark blue jeans, with pale orange stitching, tight over his skinny legs, a white shirt, bulging at the base, top two buttons opened, and a greyish suit jacket purchased from Slater's five years and three to five inches ago, now tight across his shoulders and back, and difficult to button up.

For the past six months he had been going through a strange kind of hell. He had always been bullishly insensitive and self-assured, impregnable to praise, ridicule, worry, subtlety, anything but brick-like facts. He was interested in money, food, sex and football, and that was it; what else was there? People who waxed lyrical about 'art' and 'culture' and 'beauty' were pretentious idiots, like his gay nephew Frem who made money from filming clocks or defective, like Clive Marsh had been. Clive the great author—killed himself with a pot of paint. So much for literature.

But someone, or *something*, had penetrated Dave's compacted, fleshy psyche. Everywhere he went he saw photographs of himself looking at photographs of himself looking at photographs of himself. Not just that but his tiny head, cut out of the photographs, appeared in the strangest places, on the top of plastic milk jugs in the Tesco Express, tucked into the betting-slip holder at the bookie's, even, on one occasion, a handful of his black and white heads fluttered out of his own wallet like death's head moths.

Fuelled by rage, he had initially sought the perpetrator of this creepy campaign. He'd gone to the police, he'd given them Joe Geb's name—the most likely suspect—and had also hired a private detective to keep an eye on Geb—a humdrum pudge of a man called Ian, who had popped up on Facebook offering his services—but nothing had come up, and besides, Dave had realised, it was impossible for anyone to follow him, Dave, so relentlessly; to get into his house, to get into his wallet, and not be seen, and Joe just wasn't that enterprising.

Dave's images began appearing everywhere, as if the world itself was his face, looking angrily back at him. Dave could feel the hard, solid, ordinary, normal walls of existence become all squidgy and uncertain, and with them all his hard, solid, ordinary, normal thoughts hazed and blended into each other. He made mistakes at work, he got confused with phone numbers, the fire of sexual desire that motivated most of his off hours flickered and sputtered. Only a few days ago he'd gone to see an expensive Russian pro with all the trimmings—bee-sting lips, rock hard bolt ons and flaming Zeppelin nipples—but he couldn't get it up. She'd thrust her tongue down his throat, erotically stripped to Ariana Grande (ft. Nicki Minaj), ground down on his lap, knelt in front of him smacking her lips and rolling her eyes; but nothing. His penis felt like a useless flap of cold flesh, like a numb polyp.

He'd made his way to Dominus, dimly hoping for a rustling of desire, but everything he did now felt mechanical, as if before all this *he* had sat at the controls, enjoying life, as the autopilot took over, but now there was no 'him', no 'Dave Davage', just the autopilot, and the autopilot was an unfeeling mad person.

His phone rang. It was his wife, the twittering dormouse he'd married twenty years ago because she was pretty and lively yet completely submissive. She would, he knew from the moment he met her, take it and take it and take it and never leave him, which proved to be the case. She knew he was repeatedly unfaithful, but she did nothing, she knew that he didn't really love her, but she did nothing, he belittled her and beat her, but she did nothing.

'Where are you?' she asked tremulously.

'I'll be home in a couple of hours darlin'. I'm just having a swift one with the lads first, and then I'll head straight back.' He hung up without saying goodbye and turned back to the stage in dim expectancy.

On the next table Nina, now flushed and tiddly, had reached the point, in drunkenness, where what other people think of you turns from being a threatening wrecking ball into an irrelevant pillow.

'One problem…' she said, languidly throwing her skinny wrists around, 'I've always had around death is that it makes me laugh. I just can't help it! I just start laughing. It's… it's not very professional is it?'

Mr. Wukong spoke; *'People take death lightly because they are in thick pursuit of life. Therefore they take death lightly.'*

Cherry translated; 'My grandfather says he's sure you've done an excellent job.'

'Well, I try, I *really* do… But it's so, *so* hard…' her voice dropped to a whisper; 'nobody understands… it's all so *difficult…*'

'The sack race isn't what it used to be, or the egg and spoon, or the three-legged,' said Mr. Wukong, *'A real chore they are now.'*

'He looks forward to the successful conclusion of our business,' said Cherry.

'That's *so* cool. You two are *so* cool… So are you Lilly…' As is well known, drunken people are incapable of having a conversation; all they can really do is give emphatic opinions, which means they're only really of interest to other drunk people with the same opinions. Lilly wasn't yet drunk enough, and she certainly didn't share the same life-outlook as Nina, but she did find the transformation in her boss, from neurotic shrew to sentimental spillage, vaguely entertaining. Wukong too appeared to be interested in Nina. He eyed her with implacable fascination, an occasional yellowish gleam in his dark eyes.

'Get the drinks in Lil,' Nina said, fishing in her purse and pulling out a handful of notes. 'What are you two having?' she asked her two guests, but before they could answer she said to Lilly, 'I'd like a deep chink. I mean… A cheap drink. I've already got…' she smiled sheepishly to Mr. Wukong, 'I'm sorry, I'm a bit tipsy… I… Erm… What do you want?'

'When a drunken man falls from a carriaget, he won't be killed. He has bones the same as other men, and yet he is not injured as they would be, because his spirit is whole. He didn't know he was riding, and he doesn't know he has fallen out. Life and death, alarm and terror, do not enter his breast, and so he can fall without fear of injury. If he can keep himself whole like this by means of wine, how much more can he keep himself whole by the means of heaven!'

Nina turned, confused, to Cherry, who said; 'He'll have a rum and Coke.'

Lilly threaded through the warm, chattering mass of fun-goers to the bar where Bronya took her order. As she was preparing the drinks Maria entered, wearing a body-tight skirt, Louboutin boots and pigtails. The cute touch, out of character, had been as a result of a conversation she'd had with her mother, Heather, who had been drinking white wine spritzers all day and was having, as Joe used to call it, 'a darkie.' Maria had come out of the shower and popped down to the kitchen to get a glass of water and her mother, sitting at the kitchen table, had looked at her and said 'one day soon your hair will lose its lustre, your breasts will start to sag, you'll get a belt of blub around your waist, your face will thicken and look more manly, you'll get cellulite and men will stop being interested. After that your eyesight will go, your knees and knuckles will hurt, your teeth will yellow, your ankles will get fat, your nose will get bigger and you'll stop being interested in anything but cats and chocolate and blinds. So live it up.' Maria had said nothing, gone upstairs, chosen her sexiest dress and added a last-minute touch of pedo-kink.

She approached the bar and Lilly, but it was Bronya who held her attention.

'Bronya?'

'Oh hello,' said Bronya casually and continued preparing Lilly's drinks, 'I'll just deal with this.'

Lilly turned around. 'Ah, you look nice! Where did you get this?' She fingered Maria's blouse.

'Dries van Noten,' said Maria, still getting over Bronya's presence and her sang froid.

'Gosh it's lovely. What are you having?'

Maria, unnerved, but with her composure, as ever, screwed to the sticking place, took a seat beside Lilly.

'…it's okay,' said Lilly, 'my boss is paying.'

'G and T. Double.'

'Put a double G and T on that order,' said Lilly to Bronya, then turned back to Maria, 'how are you then?' Something was stirring inside Lilly. Was it attraction?

'Dead inside,' said Maria.

'Yeah, I know how you feel.'

'Everyone knows how I feel.'

Bronya returned with the drinks. 'Sixty-eight pound fifty.' As Lilly handed over the money Maria went to speak to Bronya, but Bronya cut her off.

'No. It's okay Maria.'

'But…'

'Shh. Let me speak. It's fine. Look,' she took a deep breath, 'I'm out of that world, I'm happy, I'm with a man who worships me as the queen of the forest, his name is Prince Chukwu. Actually, maybe you did me a favour getting me fired… But, you… We're not going to be friends, because, well… Look… Here… Have a packet of scampi fries.' She handed over the crisps, smiled and walked off.

Maria opened the packet. 'Thanks,' she said to herself, unsettled by the encounter, not so much for what Bronya had said as for her smile, which Maria now realised that she had never seen before. What's more, the smile was surprisingly gummy which, although you couldn't call it beautiful, was honest in a way which caught Maria off guard. In fact, although she didn't inspect the feeling, Maria was jealous of Bronya's honest gums.

'You know her?' asked Lilly.

'Not really. We used to work together, but then we got each other fired, and then we wrestled with each other on a bus.'

Since she had entered the club Maria had been watched by Dave who. If he had taste in nothing else he had an infallible antenna for a good lay, and Maria exuded sexual power like a bonfire throws out heat, irresistible to Dave's cold heart but also repelling, lethal. Where once he would have risen instantly and come on to her—probably to be rebuffed, but that didn't matter—he found himself now troubled and stuck. Man's audacity is built on confidence in the reality of the world and Dave had begun to sense that this reality was actually a lot thinner and more uncertain than he had once thought, and with that sense came a new kind of fear that trickled over into every act he had once thoughtlessly performed, above all, or perhaps below all, his confidence with women. So he just sat and stared across the room at Maria. Stared hard.

Maria found herself unable to stop looking at a little Chinese man down near the stage. He seemed bizarrely familiar.

An upbeat song came on, *Não Vá se Perder por Aí* by Os Mutantes, a few decibels louder than the more seductive build-up music which had been playing. A spotlight struck the stage onto which strode Gloria, dressed in a high-waisted A-line dress and a chain-mail boob-tube.

'Good evening Dominus!' he cried with atmosphere-fracturing confidence. Conversations stopped. 'I think it's time to get this balloon into the air, don't you?' A few 'woos!' and American-style 'yeahs!.'

Lilly looked around at everyone shouting and screaming to the evening's billing. There was a strangely forced quality to the 'joy', as if people were celebrating and, at the same time, *telling* themselves they were celebrating. Their laughter was eighty percent release of suffering and frustration, twenty per cent anger and hatred, not necessarily for something. Just anger. Just hatred. They couldn't hear this in each other's laughter because they weren't looking for it. What they were looking for was re-assurance that they weren't alone, which they were prodigal in providing, in what they called kindness and understanding and respect and love and togetherness but which was actually the same message given over and over again; 'I accept your misery, now here's mine.'

'We've got', Gloria went on, 'oh my god, *so* much pleasure, you lucky, lucky fun-bunnies. We've got a literal feast of *sick* dec-adence, all coming your way. But first… Let's have a big cheer, and a good old-fashioned bit of bump and grind for… Ladies and gentlemen, and everything in between… It's… The Moonies!'

Three muscular drag queens in outrageous cod-Egyptian costumes—gold kilts hanging over lapis lazuli g-strings, golden Cleopatra-style bras with vastly over-the-top cock-and-ball-shaped headdresses—leapt onto the stage hitting an upbeat coordinated routine to a medley of gay anthems (*Smalltown Boy* by Bronski Beat) and hip-thrusting kitsch (*Aisere I Love You* by Yamasuki).

As the show began, Lilly, after leaving the drinks with Nina and Wukong (who removed another silver pillbox from his in-side pocket), went for a wander around the club. In the casino, men, mostly men, stood around a roulette wheel or sat at black-jack and poker tables with deadly serious, concentrated faces. Various retro video games around the edge of the casino—Mr. Do!, Spy Hunter, Burger Time, Ghosts and Goblins—were also being played with the same tight, concentrated intensity. The Rolling Stones played in the casino. Man music. Keith Richards was singing *'I need a love to keep me happy'* over and over again. Yeah, thought Lilly, it's all about what *you* need.

Music didn't seem to penetrate Lilly these days though. She didn't listen to much. It was all kind of over *there*, interesting sounds, over *there*, but her own heart no longer.

She entered the ladies' toilet, waited in a queue for the cubicles, had a wee. She could hear the women out at the sinks.

'I can't be bothered with blow jobs any more. Forty minutes of my life I'm not getting back.'

'Forty minutes? You're doing something wrong.'

'Do you think my neck looks muscular?'

'What does he look like?'

'Like a DJ.'

'He said we need a whore for the garden.'

'I've never seen a funny plant.'

'Tell me where in the Quran it says I can't do Charlie!'

'What does a DJ look like?'

'Grey. Like a butcher.'

'All DJs are grey in the dark.'

A straight thought occurred to Lilly, listening to these women. That they were at work. They cackled and gossiped and danced and threw up, but it was a kind of job.

She came out of the cubicle and stood in front of a long mirror with the other women, a couple of whom were doing lines of coke from elegant little fold-out hand mirrors. Lilly looked at herself, at her new haircut, her new made-up face, her deadly, sex-bomb outfit, and she sighed. It's not me, she thought. None of this is me. What am I doing here?

∞

Neil opened the front door and looked, unseeing, into the world. He was dressed in his full ceremonial police uniform; a Victorian style tunic, white gloves, wide leather belt with a fitting for an oil lantern and a service pattern helmet with silver trim worn in the high-slung position. His face was covered in stage make-up, thick eyeshadow, cheekbone-accentuating blush and lipliner. He looked around anxiously, then back inside the house, then up and down the street. It was the last night of winter, freezing cold and sharp, bright moonlight casting the world in negative. Chiyo floated down the stairs and stood next to him. She looked like she was going to be crowned queen of the underworld, black, wet hair falling down to her thin, provocative, black dress, embroidered with silvery-blue swirls, rivers of white fire curling through the darkness.

'Are you sure about this?' Neil whispered imploringly.

She looked at him, without a hint of human feeling, then walked away, immaculate. He looked down in anguish at the fine erection pushing against his trousers, then loped off after her.

They walked in silence, Neil afraid to say anything, afraid of everything. He wanted to turn back; this wasn't in the plan, but Chiyo *had* him. It felt like she had one slim, cold, paralysing fist round his throat and the other round his balls.

Slender ribbons of mist floated over the moon, muting it, and the world, which was eerily silent in every direction.

Neil could feel himself slipping away, panic rising. Eventually he managed to squeeze out the question lodged in the pit of his neck, 'Who are... are you?' he asked, reflexively gulping.

Chiyo looked neither to the right or left. 'I eat the sun at night and give birth to it again in the morning,' she said.

'Eugh?'

'I am The River Queen in exile,' she added, deigning to glance at him, 'and you are my baby otter.'

Neil had no idea where he was or who he was. It was as if his lifelong mission to keep it all together had built an inner structure which, in its hugeness and completeness and perfection, he had hoped would protect him forever, but which, without him realising it, had at the same time become more and more fragile, more and more brittle, until, finally, all it took to crack the citadel of the self open was a cup of weird tasting tea and the firm, cold grip of a woman's hand around his penis. Now the whole thing—the 'Neil' that he had worked on his entire life—it was still there, but it was like a dead squirrel. It looked like a squirrel, it felt like a squirrel, it even still smelt like a squirrel, but everything that actually made it a squirrel had, with one blow of a passing mudguard, vanished, leaving… what was it? what *was* it? It wasn't what 'Neil' had, until yesterday, considered himself to be. It was a stunned, hypnotic ghost, haunting this small, slim Japanese woman, who had him completely in her power. If she had given him a spoonful of anthrax and told him to eat it, he would have swallowed it at once and, as he collapsed in agony, he would have thanked her for it.

They reached the funeral home. Chiyo knew just where to go, and led Neil to the back entrance. He, hand shaking, tried to get the key into the lock of the door, but he couldn't find the hole. The key just kept scraping around the escutcheon. Chiyo waited with complete composure until finally Neil succeeded in unlocking the door.

The workshop, but for filament-fine moonlight on surface edges, was dark. Neil clattered about, looking for something, striking his shin against a coffin, walking into workbenches, scattering hammers.

'What are you doing?' asked Chiyo.

'I'm looking for the light switch,' he moaned.

'*Don't!*' she hissed, 'lights *off.*'

Neil stopped. Silence and stillness. His ceremonial helmet could just be seen in the muted light. 'Okay,' he said.

Chiyo's form glided through the workshop. She seemed to know exactly where she was going. 'Wait in *this* room,' she said, opening the door to the cold room, 'Come through to *that* room when I give the signal,' she said, pointing to the mortuary.

'What's the signal?'

'You will know. Wait in there. Don't come out.'

'What? In there?' said Neil.

'Go in.'

'But there are dead bodies in there,' he whispered, meekly.

'This is not problem.'

'But can't I wait out here?'

'We made deal. You do what I say.'

Again she grabbed his penis, which had now been painfully erect for three hours. 'Ne?'

'Oh Go… oh… od,' he said, shuddering with fear and desire.

She pulled him, by his cock, into the cold room, and tossed him in, as one would a rubber mallet, and closed the door.

Neil stood shivering in the dark. Through a high window, clattering in the breeze, the slenderest ray of moonlight—which had a peculiar pinkish hue to it—illumined the room. Ten dead bodies, covered in shrouds, lay on the shelves. Neil stood moaning, the kind of sound that only someone who has lost all hope makes, no urgency, no violence, just the sick, awful groan of a final, quiet 'noooooooohhhhh.'

He told himself not to look at anything, to just stand, eyes closed, until it was over, but the very thought tempted him to glance at one of the corpses. The shroud covering it has slipped, revealing a white hand.

'Eeuuuughhhhhh…' he moaned, then, mouth clenched tight, 'Nnnngggg… Mmmnngggg…'

He stared at the dead, white hand, then whispered, so quietly it was inaudible, just a pathetic creak at the back of his mumbling mouth; 'Gentle Jesus, make it stop.'

∞

Most of the women in the audience, along with a couple of embarrassingly reckless men, were now well into the stage show. Still others, carried along by the flamboyant bodily exhortations of the dancers, stood up and whistled or roared. Nina, now off her face, was also on her feet, yeah-yeahing with the best of them. Her dance gestures, inelegant in the extreme, twice threatened Mr. Wukong, who avoided her flailing arms with the reptile grace of a Tai Chi Chuan sifu.

Ween's *Roses Are Free* played. The audience—those standing at the front—were leaping up and down, dancing. Nina, elbows up, hips waggling side to side—the dance of the eighties wedding-goer—edged over sideways to join them. She clapped her hands and, eyes wet, staggered forward, towards the stage. She had now drunk six JD and Cokes, several doubles; enough to make anyone tipsy, but for Nina, who hadn't drunk a drop of alcohol for over fifteen years, who was swimming in joyous bleary delirium at finally ridding herself of the house of death, it was the equivalent of a pint of ethanol. She staggered around, fuelled by a kind of genetic abandon, never once experienced in her living life, now completely overwhelming her. Lilly, seated again next to Cherry and Mr. Wukong watched Nina, a mix of solicitude, confusion and slight revulsion curdling in her craw.

One of the dancers, a muscle-headed man with a crew cut, amused at this brakes-off mole-woman bobbing around merrily at his feet, pulled her up onto the stage where she was struck by a spotlight which seemed to pierce her soul, unlocking the rapturous goddess she knew herself to be. She thrust her hips back and forth, she kicked her little fat legs into the air (as far as they would go) and she span around and around with her arms out until she became dizzy, wheeled off to the side of the stage, slipped over and landed semi-conscious against the curtain.

'Wha' you doing?' Nina said, dribbling and giggling. She could feel someone arranging her face.

'Just tarting you up' said Mr. Wukong, with an English accent.

'Oh, you…' said Nina, vaguely, opening her moist, unfocused eyes, 'wha…?' Wukong was painting sideburns onto the side of her face with a Sharpie. His thin lips were curled up at the sides, his black eyes wrinkled up in a mask of merriness. In his hand he held a snowy white cosplay wig which he pushed over Nina's frizzy hair. She smiled, unresisting.

'Make me into a magnificent cunt,' she said.

As Wukong was putting the finishing touches on Nina, the dance routine concluded. Backstage, Gloria was welcoming back the dancers, 'Lovely girls! Fucking marvellous! You killed 'em!'

The changing room was a long but cramped dressing room of lightbulb-framed mirrors, tissue, talc, knickers and bras, cranberry juice, wigs, lipstick, deodorant, perfume and, somewhat out of place, a copy of the Financial Times. Beautiful young women in various states of undress were putting the final touches on their make-up, arranging their costumes—all of which were cute-animal themed (bunny, kitten, deer, mouse, etc.) amid general chatter, laughter and bustlement.

Upon entering the room one of the drag queens, the huge-faced man who had yanked Nina onto the stage, pulled a phone out of out of his back pocket and started talking in a loud, nasal tone, 'I prefer to protect my liquidity, keep it available for other investments, but I don't see what concern that is to… Huh? What? I can't hear you, the fucking reception is terri… Yes, a variety of other diversified assets. Uh, *hello!* Trophy asset!? It's not a fucking trophy darling, I'm going to live there. Look, I want a broker to negotiate new terms on the Bayswater property, remortgage that and then… What? What? No, the trust doesn't come into it… Well that *will* generate the funds won't it…? Fuck, I don't know why I pay you sometimes…'

Meanwhile, the girls were arranging their cute ears, fluffy paws, perky tails; one of whom was Sophie, who appeared, from the magnificence of her lion-cub attire, to be something of a central component. Her boyfriend, ex-vicar Tim, was helping her to get her whiskers straight.

'Now, remember what we discussed?' he said.

'It's an act of selfless devotion,' said Sophie.

'You're stripping for the supreme being, just like Moses did.'

∞

After Joe had left, Ralf had eaten a four-year-old cup noodle, picked up the kitbag which Joe had left him and then shambled out into the garden. There was a large wheelbarrow leaning up against the shed. Ralf went into the shed, where the two of them had dumped the fireworks, and started piling them onto the wheelbarrow. Then, still sad and serious, he lifted the barrow and slowly, incrementally, pushed it up the garden path, out into the back alley, along into the road and then along the street. Every few paces he stopped, got his breath back, rearranged the unsteady pile on the barrow, lifted it up again, and took a few more doddering, bone-rattling steps.

This went on for ninety minutes, down Ammit Avenue, along Benben Street, over the roundabout, across the old convent ruins and into the one-way system which led into town. It was now quite foggy, the world hushed and muffled. There didn't seem to be any cars and only a few solitary figures drifted out of the reddish moonhued mist.

Ralf had walked and walked, for hours, to reach the centre of town — thirty minutes away at a normal pace — where, dripping with sweat, void, exhausted, as if he had burnt up his very marrow in the effort of getting here, he stopped. He wearily turned to his wheelbarrow and started unpacking it.

∞

Nina was paralytic, covered in vermilion vaudeville make-up, slumped in a corner, just off-stage, mumbling to herself 'stinky winky, he's got a stinky winky…' Wukong had returned to the table, smiling merrily. Lilly felt vaguely responsible for Nina, although God knows why, and felt something was wrong with Wukong's behaviour, but he waved away her worries, smiling impishly, the ultra-fine lattice of wrinkles on his bony face deepening and multiplying like fissures in blasted rock.

Mercy, the magnificent black waitress, came over to the table.

'Everyone okay here?' she asked.

'We'd like a bottle of snake wine,' said Cherry.

'Coming right up,' she said, and walked off.

Cherry leaned over to the Lilly and said, with whispered awe, 'She has *gorgeous* breasts.'

'I thought so too,' said Lilly.

Mr. Wukong turned to Lilly.

'You also have beautiful breasts,' he said, in a clear and familiar English accent, 'large, firm and natural. Truly excellent.' He gave them a chef's kiss.

Lilly, uncomprehending, looked to Cherry, who was still smiling pleasantly, then back to Wukong, whose inscrutable face looked like it had been painted on a walnut. 'You… Speak English?'

'Only to you.'

'Who are you?'

Wukong smiled again and Lilly felt a nauseating chill run down her arms and over her chest, 'I'll show you in a moment. Let's watch the show.'

He turned to the stage, just as Gloria came on. Brain-scraping dance music was welling up around the club. The emotional energy of the crowd was also building up.

'Okay!' cried Gloria, 'that's the clumsy foreplay over with! I think we've all had enough of amateurs, so let's whip the knickers from this evening, and see if we can't get the juices flowing…'

In the wings, seven slender young girls waited, dressed in fishnets, thongs, minute furry bras and various faunal accoutrements. At the back Sophie steadied her nerves, readying herself for the routine. Tim stood next to her.

The music was intensifying to a horrifying, heart-stopping pitch, the hearts of all assembled rocketing up in a lift set to smash into the ceiling. Gloria's strident voice boomed, ear-splitting, overhead; '…get obliterated, ye sons of anarchy, ye daughters of chaos, the time has come for a transcendental mindfuck, courtesy of… Sister *Supernova!*'

The girls skipped out, one by one.

Just before Sophie entered the stage Tim whispered, *'Tits out for the Lord.'*

The music kicked in; *Moon Shadow*, by Labelle. The girls, launched into a grinding strip-club routine, throwing themselves around the poles, cartwheeling into sprays of light, teasing at their undergarments, hip-thrusting into the faces of the crowd of men who, with a mixture of hypnotised ennui and lip-licking anticipation, guffawed and snorted and stuffed notes into the girls' knickers.

Wukong was still fixing Lilly with his dark, hollow, slot-like eyes. 'So, what do you think?' he asked.

'What do I think of what?'

'Of the little show I've put on.'

'You?'

'Yes, it's my club.'

'Oh, I see. Is it? Well, to be honest, it's a bit boring. I mean...' She looked around at the men in 'porn-stare' mode, ghastly, morbid, stare-eyed fuck-focusing on the grinding flesh in front of them. The women, who had moved back, waiting for the male strippers who would come on later, looked on with derision.

'...everyone is so deadly serious,' said Lilly, 'Everyone. They're... Nobody is really enjoying themselves...'

'You're wrong there,' said Wukong, laughing, 'Everyone is enjoying their self.'

'Well if this is fun... But then... is it though? Is this it?'

'Yes. This is it. This is as good as it gets.'

Lilly was silent.

'Well, actually, not quite,' he said. 'Here. Have some pork scratchings.'

'No thanks.'

Mr. Wukong stood up, 'I'll be back in a moment,' he said to Lilly, then gestured Cherry to join him.

Lilly watched him go, noting as he did that Bronya had managed to convince Nina to get to her feet and slump over to a chair next to the bar.

'Shall I call you a taxi?' asked Bronya.

'Nahhhhhhh...' Nina lolled around, dribbling and burping.

'Alright, well stay there. I'll keep an eye on you.' Bronya went to return to the bar, but Nina grabbed her top.

'I don't know... I don't know...' said Nina.

'Don't know what?'

'I don't know if I'm dead, and didn't love, or… still alive and can't.'

'Erm, probably option b.'

'I want to live?'

'Then live.'

Nina, squirming in drunkness, moaned loudly. 'I want liiiiife,' she whined petulantly.

'Live then,' said Bronya. 'Why not?'

Nina pulled herself to her feet. 'Alright, I will…' she said, almost to herself, 'I fucking will…' She stood unsteadily on the plush chair and cried out 'Life! Life! Fucking life!' Nobody heard, but at just that moment the music paused for a dramatic moment, and Nina's screaming voice was heard across the club as she roared, *Drinks are on me motherfuckers!!!*'

A brawly bellow of joy went up and a wave of people rushed toward the bar, Bronya leaping over it before them, ready for the crash.

As the mass surged barwards Maria, who had just come back from the loo, sat down sadly next to Lilly.

'Are you okay?' Lilly shouted, over the music and the mayhem. 'Is anyone?'

'I'm not sure. No, I don't think so. I don't think anyone is.'

'Being okay is like ice cream,' said Maria. 'As soon as you've got it in your hands, it melts away.'

Lilly sighed. 'Always slightly sad at the last mouthful. All that's left is smugness and crumbs from your crappy cone.'

'Why is it that consolation and comfort only come in crumbs? Why not a crumpet of consolation? Why not a… a… *Loaf* of comfort?'

Maria took a sip of her drink and, as she looked across the club, vaguely thinking to herself 'so this is how the big people live,' her eyes met Dave's. He had been staring at her all night with coarse desire. She caught his eye, for the third or fourth time, and stared back at him now, half defiant, half hateful. Fucking men. 'I dunno. I need to get away. I should travel,' she said looking now into her empty glass, 'I should… I should… Oh, *fuck* should.'

'Love lives in shouldlessness,' said Lilly.

Maria looked up, eyes narrowed with suspicion, brows knit. The long pause between them was broken by Dave Davage staggering into it.

'Hello… Uhh…' he said to Maria, falling haphazardly into the chair next to her.

'Oh bugger off.'

'You're *so* fucking *hot*,' he said, his voice sounding like wet sand.

Maria gave him a blasting look of contempt.

At this point, Dave felt he had a few moves available to him. He considered starting a conversation, because women like conversations, but all options seemed like stupendous effort, so he just said 'Fancy a shag?'

He drunkenly gestured towards the back of the room. Maria turned to the curtained-off private booths, which men and women had been in and out of all night, led by the flimsily-dressed staff. She then turned back to Dave to fully assess him, her hard, cold, contemptuous eyes scanning him from top to bottom, taking in his hairy fingers, his bulging belly, his fat neck swelling at the collar, his little red lips and his weak, wet, careless eyes.

'How much?' she asked.

'Five hundred?'

'Fuck off.'

'A thou?'

'For five grand I'll fuck your brains out.'

Lilly watched this interaction fascinated, amazed, appalled, in awe.

'Not much need for brains in my game,' said Dave.

'You got the money?' asked Maria.

'Yeah, hold on.'

He got up and stumbled away. Maria crossed her legs and looked imperiously at Lilly.

'Fuck it right?' she said. Lilly's eyebrows quivered in doubt.

'Oh,' said Maria, 'I see, you're judging me, are you?'

'No, no, not at all,' said Lilly.

Maria stood up. 'All women sell it,' she said, 'if not for money, then for attention, or comfort or just something to fucking do.'

She headed off over to the alcoves.

Nina meanwhile, was also on a mission. She had staggered through the dressing room, past Gloria and the drag queens, up a back stairway and into the DJ booth. The disc jockey, a twitching, bullet-headed creature, had begun to protest, but Nina had pulled out the last of her cash, thrust it into his hands, told him to take five minutes, clattered into the decks, scratching the music to silence and picked up the microphone which she now shrieked into; *'You're all going to die! You're all…'*

The DJ tried to grab the mic but Nina twisted out of the way and fell into him, the two of them stumbling out of the booth, pulling the cables away from the mixing desk.

The girls on the stage had stripped off entirely, but with half the audience rushing at the bar and now with the music abruptly cut off they stopped, looking around, confused. Gloria's head poked out from behind the curtains; 'Keep dancing, keep dancing!' he cried.

They returned to their manoeuvres, but these now looked weird in the silence. The men at their feet hardly noticed though, slobbering and pawing and moaning, heaving around the stage like fat, hungry dogs. The DJ had managed to plug the sound system back in, but this created squealing buzzing feedback. The girls were making seductive pulling gestures at their knickers, ready to pull them off, but now they stopped and clamped their fingers to their ears.

In the private alcove, with the curtains drawn, Maria was also undressing, bored. Dave looked on with super-intent strained anguish at her naked arms, her belly, her legs, as she pulled her dress off, down to her underwear. She was magnificent, every bit the form Dave Davage had imagined. He was moaning with anticipation as she reached forward. A curious red light fringed her thick hair as the feedback sliced through the booth.

'Strip!' cried Gloria, 'get 'em off!'

The dancing girls, all bent over, had pulled off their knickers. Slowly they stood up, ready to turn round, full frontal. The feedback whine continued, the red light intensified.

&

In the cold-storage room, a wind, which seemed to be passing through the closed windows, was rippling and puffing the burial gowns and mortuary shrouds. Neil, eyes shut tight, was huddled up on the floor, rapidly repeating The Lord's Prayer, over and over again, but chopped up, disordered.

'…thy kingdom come, thy will be done, I had a woodwork teacher called Mr. Wilby, forgive us our trespasses, you Lord, not Mr. Wilby, as we forgive those who shoot us in the leg and fire us and dump us and laugh at us, and lead us not into a room full of dead bodies, or if thou must, lead us straight out again straightways, and deliver us from evil, unless evil is sex and death in female human form, then I really don't care, but please Lord, lead me out of here, thy kingdom come, thy will be done, Lord, I've had enough of my kingdom, this kingdom, this will, please Lord, lead me from the world of death, lead me from the world of life, the whole thing, just please get me out of here, our Father who art in Heaven, art thou? What are you doing up there when we're down here? Please come, thy kingdom, please, *please…*'

A crack of thunder. An explosion of fire-red lightning. Neil screamed, '*Aggghhhhhh…*' The shrouds all, at once, blew from the bodies. They were all men, all with fine erections, and all glowing a hideous, unearthly red. Neil's scream went on and on. '*Agggggggggghhhhhhhhhhh…*' The door blew open, as did that of the mortuary opposite. Chiyo's voice came through, phase shifted, as if from another dimension; '*kokuu ni yori sou no.*' Neil, anguished, terrified, leapt to his feet 'what? what? what?' he moaned, tumbling across the workshop to the mortuary.

Chiyo has somehow tied herself to the anatomy table. Her arms and legs are bound. Her wet hair, which seems far longer, swirls around her head as if caught in a whirlpool, her skin is snow white, her lips black, her eyes black and hideously absorbing, like black holes, sucking all matter and light into her body, a body pulsating with otherworldly sexual energy.

Her demonic face turns to Neil. *'Now!'* she shrieks, *'Bang me the fuck out!'*

∞

Joe Geb, half-crawling, half-stumbling, mad with the delirium of mind-shattered wakefulness, was drowning in the misery of the world, which had overrun the fragile dam of civilisation and was pouring through the horrified hearts of every man and woman on earth. On the surface nothing much had changed, buildings were on fire, and rats crawled over mounds of uncollected waste, and a woman was stuffing twenty-pound notes into her mouth, and a man was masturbating in the doorway of a gutted Apple store, but it was still the spectacle of the world as he had known it, only behind the screen, all was red death.

He had found his way to St. Barbara's church, on the edge of town. He had fallen against the door which had swung open, tumbling him through the side door into the empty building. Inside, sparse and bare—maintaining the modest beauty of its original gothic inspiration—all was dark, except for pink-white flashes of lightning filtering through the stained glass windows, images of Christ's passion.

Joe crawled into a small transept chapel and curled up against a credence table. It was impossible to know if he had entirely lost touch with reality, or entirely plunged into it. Everything was infinitely more than it had ever been, but it wasn't mere intensity, brightness, smokeness, steelness, softness; rather more of what each thing, each moment, actually, intrinsically and eternally is. And each moment didn't just seem to last forever, it was forever, a forever of menacing back roads and poisonous diesel, then a forever of broken gravestones and damp grief and now a forever of stale wool and cold-hewn, cold-worshipped stone. Everything he was part of was, if he could have spoken or put a name to it, God. The smooth divot in the flagstone step, worn down by a million footprints, was God as a footworn flagstone, his cold, torn bell-bottoms were God as cold, torn bell-bottoms, the numb, chilling pain of chilling emptiness was God as cold, numb pain. God as thing could never be remembered, never be described, yet it filled him, pressed him; pressed him out of his body like toothpaste.

Am I dying? Is this it? Well alright then.

There is nothing left to protest.

Red lightning strikes again and seems to freeze, then glow brighter at the windows and then, suddenly it is blue and Ursula is hovering above the altar. Her form is stuttering, flowing, an elaborate aria of blue-white shifts and phases, she is singing, an impossibly beautiful melody, from long long ago, and there are many voices with her. Joe is crying, Ursula's brightening electric form is smiling down on him, with pity and love, before fading, dimming and passing away, as Joe too slips away, gently.

෯

The hour had come. The polite meeting had been brought to a dramatic conclusion by Joris who, *in excelsis corvo*, had told the assembled Lords of the Universe that the great awakening had begun. Joris had then led his guests outside and down to the void hole where his father had perished, which was once again open and anti-matter black. Fifty World Elites stood within the stone circle, eyes closed, hand in hand, humming with the power of the night.

Ian the lawyer stands over the hole, repeating the same words over and over again, 'Em heset net seth! Em heset net seth! Em heset net seth!' The air, charged with unknowable energy, glows red; as red as the vast moon above, which is now smouldering in the licking flames of the Other Place.

'Leaders of the world,' cries Joris against the storm, his shrill, screaming young voice piercing the skulls of the assembled, 'the hour has come. It is time to unmake, for good, the barrier between us and the World behind the world. For ten thousand years we have been guiding humanity to the point when it is ready to accept the glorious rupture, when it can face the hour of the end, when it *begs* to be released, and in its humility, it sees the heartbreaking truth. Verily, I say, only heartbreak can reveal the truth, only selfbreak, only worldbreak, so *come*, Father, break the world, cleave its suffering heart with your sword of fire!'

The stone circle has become a spinning vortex of ekypyrotic power, an exultant furnace of crimson death-light. From the ring of celebrants, heads thrown back, eyes like cinders, a roar of wordless glory rises, flaming like the blazing sky above them.

'Father!' cries Joris, eyes wild, feathers burning, air blasting, sky alight, *'Father! Now! Pour your fire back into the cold pit of the world! Bring your heaven to our earth!'*

Something can be felt underfoot, some vast mass awakening, like the core of the earth is coming to life and is about to punch through the crust of the world.

'Em heset net seth! Em heset net seth! Em heset net seth!' Ian moans, eyes shot back into his skull.

'FATHER! FATHER! NOW! DO IT! NOW!'

A flowing torrent of red-white fire erupts from the hole, a terrible, monumental, dismal fury of power. The circle is torn, the people writhing on the splitting earth in agonies, faces red from blood and fire, roaring in pain. All is pain. All is cataclysmic red light, the universe itself is being born anew.

∞

The dancing girls, slowly, slowly, stand up to their full height. They all now have pig snouts, curly tails and pig's ears.

'Now!' cries Gloria, '*Now* now my little piglets. It's time now for... *The feast!*'

A train of waitresses enter, all pushing trolleys, heaped up with pork. Bacon, chops, sausages; on the largest trolleys of all, rows and rows of roasted suckling pigs. Mr. Wukong skippingly follows behind the last and largest of these with a dinner plate.

The light in the club is now blood red, hellish. The music an ominous and moaning moonlight dirge. The crowd, hushed, shuffle around the meat-spilling trolleys. Lilly watches on in horror. Faces red, eyes glittering with eager desire, the people look like demons.

'Dig in,' whispers the old man, with haunting clarity and begins splitting the baby pigs with the edges of the plate he has been holding.

Wukong looks up and Lilly catches his eye. He looks more like Max than ever. He winks at her.

Meanwhile, in the side booth, Dave, mouth full of crispy bacon, watches on paralysed, as Maria, completely, perfectly na-ked, bends forward, loose hair tumbling over her dead eyes, and reaches towards his crotch. The very tips of her fingers touch the bulge between his legs; and he ejaculates.

'Nnnngggggg!'

∞

Neil is rapidly pulling his clothes off. He has no idea what he is doing. All he knows is that he must do it. The secret to the universe is within his grasp. *There.* Chiyo, naked, smooth slen-der legs parted, black lips parted. She is writhing and moaning on the mortuary table, hideous and beautiful, a flashing vortex of blood and power and horrendous knowledge flowing into her, the room itself, Neil's projection of the room, Neil too, all flowing towards Chiyo's terrible cunt.

Death wails drift through the door behind Neil. He looks back, terrified, he looks forward again. There, within Chiyo, all will be revealed. There, *there*, *that* is the power, the glory and the kingdom.

'Do it Neil. Now. *Now*,' she hisses.

Neil, naked and erect, mind on fire, sprints across the mortuary and leaps onto her. She screams in ecstasy and agony, a terrible, skull-rupturing spear. Neil, entering her, roars in mind-cracked abandon. The ghouls in the next room howl in atomic terror and exaltation. The entire universe, a billion suns, all shriek in blood-red pain and glory as Neil plunges, rampant, obliterating, into Chiyo. All the suffering and stress of being himself has evaporated in an explosion of total abandon. The howling of the dead, the atrocity of the world, his failure, his anguish, his life, all at once are incinerated by the immortal pleasure of fucking Chiyo, the angel of death, fucking her and fucking her to death.

'Aaaaaaaaaaaaghhhhhhhhhhh!'

'Aaaaaaaaaaaaaggghhhhhhhhhh!'

She is beyond mad, beyond wild, beyond demonic, beyond, utterly beyond time and thought; and yet, at the same time, absolutely and totally physical and real. Her eyes, her lips, her breasts, her shoulders, her elbows, her belly, her vagina, her thighs, her calves, her whole incarnate body of flesh and blood and bones is eternity, surging through him, devouring him as he devours her.

Her eyes burn blue, burning into Neil, tearing into him, hollowing him out, until there is nothing but the punishing, pounding void of total ecstasy, fused in the promised godgasm, erupting in God's sexual furnace. Neil's screams become laughter then fury, then agony, then laughter again, then a sound beyond all human emotion, part joyous abandon, part terror, part death exhilaration, rising in pitch with the terrible energy, higher and higher, brighter and brighter, something is coming, an orgasm so vast, so apocalyptically intense that Neil—or what is left of Neil—knows it would destroy him forever. Fear, joy, life, death and catastrophic sexual horror coalesce into a white-hot fusion of the two forms as the smashing immensity of the orgasm, like detonating waves from a supernova, strikes the two bodies; which explode.

Dominus entire descends on the pork feast. Dave Davage, anguished and spent, stumbles out of his private booth, and into the car park. The world seems to be glowing, but he hardly notices. He is fairly shaking with sickhorror, something like the 'fucker's remorse' he has often had—in fact only a couple of weeks ago, after sleeping with a snaggle-toothed pro while her baby screamed next door, the same feeling had descended on him as he'd pulled his trousers back on—but infinitely more intense. It is absolute disgust. Why, he has no idea; *why?* Maria is the perfect woman, he's spent five к and has come prematurely. It's a bit embarrassing, but so what? She's just another whore. And yet, falling out of the club, stumbling over to his car, driving through the night, an appalling, disgusting sensation, gruesome far beyond belief, sucks at his insides, so much so that, as he drives into Edding he had an urge to throw up and has to pull over, retching violently against the side of the Nisbets catering equipment centre. Agonising spasms shudder through his chest. He slumps forward, clutching his heart. He feels like he is going to die. He felt like he is dying.

He wipes his mouth. He can't get back in the car. Just go home. He pulls himself up and heads down Abbey Street and stops. Fights seem to have broken out everywhere, windows are being smashed, people are screaming and moaning; wild scenes everywhere. *What* is going on? Has there been some kind of revolt? And what is that weird light? And *what...?*

Dave Davage stops and looks around, unable to fix what is before him in understanding, his face dropped in blank dread-horror. Everywhere he looks is... Dave Davage. Photographs, posters, even masks. Everywhere he looks he can see himself. On construction boards, on shop windows, on lampposts. The photographs that someone had been taking of him are now for all to see—and all do see, can see. As he wanders through the town, the rioting demons look at him, pointing, laughing. Young men rush at him cackling, like apes on amphetamine. He pushes them off and runs, stumbling; but then stops. Something up ahead, someone wearing a… what is it? He approaches. In the centre of the precincts, surrounded by more Davage posters, is a familiar figure. 'You?' he says. It's *you?*'

Ralf, face glowing with joy, is standing in the pedestrian area outside Marks and Spencer surrounded by a crowd of people. A massive bundle of category F4 fireworks is strapped to him. In his left hand is a Zippo lighter, in his right hand, a mop.

'You?' Dave repeats.

'Could be, could be,' Ralf chuckles, pulling a Dave Davage mask over his face.

Dave rushes at him, but in one smooth gesture Ralf spins the mop handle outwards and rams the pole, which has been sharpened to a point, into Dave's belly. The crowd watching them 'oooh' as Dave sinks to his knees and a tall deadpan woman with acne, 'Dani69', steps forward and kicks him in the head with a stiletto. Ralf, with Dave's face, then lights the fuses of the various rockets.

'You did this?' says Dave again, between clenched teeth, clutching his bleeding guts.

'Hahaha! Kind of!' says Ralf.

'But… it's not…it's not fair,' he whispers.

'Fair! Hahahahahahahaha!'

The first firework catches, then another, then the others, fierce sparks showering over the pavement. Ralf, laughing madly, his 'Dave' mask on fire, exploding from every limb, ricochets off the display window of Primark, hurtles around the pedestrian area, strikes Dave, knocking him over, and then rockets up into the heavens, far into the gut-red night sky, where he detonates, in a conflagration of beautiful light.

People look up, aghast and delighted. *Ahhhhh*. Amongst them is Irving, standing next to his burning matchstick wife.

∽

Mr. Wukong, carrying a couple of drinks, has pushed his way out of the crowd, over to Lilly. He has sat down and the two of them are watching, in silence, the crowds before them, feasting on pig flesh.

A pristine, suspended calm has opened up in Lilly. The world is turning itself inside out, but she is, in the midst of the storm, steady and fearless. Some part of her seems to be curiously looking on, with a kind of mystified acceptance.

'All this is for you,' says Wukong, whose voice now is fully Max's; deep, dry, aristocratic and sneering.

'You killed my parents.'

'They had it coming.'

'Are you going to kill me?'

'I'm going to kill everyone.'

'Why?'

'Is not the correct question. The correct question is "what?"' He hands her a glass full of red liquid.

'What's this?'

'Take a drink.'

She smells it. It smells sweet. She tastes it.

'Sugared pig's blood,' said Max laughing.

She retches. 'Ugh!'

He shrugs. 'You've had enough,' he says.

'Disgusting. It's all disgusting,' hatred wells up in her belly.

'Have you ever thought about why you find meat so disgusting? Have you ever wondered why the idea of eating an egg—a solidified chicken foetus—revolts you, when people have been doing it for thousands and thousands of years? Do you think you have discovered a morality denied humanity for half a million years? It's because you fear the actuality of life. Living matter makes you sick, coiled up tree roots, masses of mud, slime moulds and sex. Sex too. Except there's also fascination, the fascinating cock, repulsive and riveting, ah, repulsive bliss!' He had a mouthful of sloppy meat, chewing noisily, pulling at the tendons, sucking his greasy fingers, 'What you've done, Lilly, is separate life from death—you feel that the flesh is a charnel house, that the body is profane, because you cannot feel the whole.'

He smiles, a disgusting, shit-eating smile. 'It's a world of meat Lilly. Everything eats everything else. The world is a bloodbath, but you can't see it because you don't want to see it. Nobody wants to see it, which is why it all happens behind closed doors. You complain about your work, about hiding death from the world, you want people to see death and live with it—and then you look on a bacon sandwich with horror and sadness, and choose to be oh-my, *so* pure. You're afraid of life, hence you lock yourself in a little steel room with the dead, and make them look nice and living, and then you come out into the world and complain that it is disgusting.'

'It *is* disgusting,' says Lilly, 'Look at them, climbing over each other, to stuff themselves with dead meat. If you think I'm going to join in, you're mistaken.'

'No, you're not going to join in. You will stop running from it though.'

Wukong stands up. 'I've got some work to do. But I'll see you very soon, don't worry.' He heads up to the DJ booth where Cherry is standing over a supine Nina.

'Not cheap,' says Cherry, 'buying drinks for the entire club.'

'I'm a fucking millionaire,' Nina drawls.

'I think not.'

'Mm…? Uhhh…?'

'We're not interested in your death parlour. The deal's off,' says Cherry, stepping over Nina and joining Wukong on his way out.

❦

'Good evening Joe,' says Ian.

Joe opens his eyes. The chapel he has passed out in has been redecorated. It is the same church, but the pews are now cheap 'woodgrain' plastic, the crucifix a trendy neon design, big upbeat posters announce, in Helvetica, that life is good and that paradise is bright. In the front pew sits Ian Cremwave; neat, tired, mild, meek in front of a chipboard table, upon which is a glass of water, and behind the table, a plastic chair.

'Good evening Joe,' he says again, 'how are you feeling?'

Joe, still collapsed against the credence table, isn't sure how to answer.

'How was your journey here?' says Ian, crossing his legs.

'*Bit* of a nightmare,' says Joe quietly.

'Oh it's murder out there, isn't it? Please…'

He gestures towards the chair. Joe gets up, surprised at how easy it is to move his body, and even more surprised that he is wearing a cheap, badly-fitting, nylon suit. He sits down, letting out a sneeze, strangely blended with a cough.

'Ah,' says Ian, 'The rare cough-sneeze hybrid. It's to be avoided in a job interview. It reveals a subtle disquiet, a psychic unrest that the cv never mentioned.'

'Is this a job interview?'

'Ah, yes, good question; why have I called you all here?'

'Who are you?' asks Joe, looking around for someone else, but there are just the two of them in the chapel.

'I'm a friend.'

'A friend?'

'You could say I'm your oldest friend. You have a slight under-bite, did you know that? It's rather charming. You'd be considered a holy fool in other cultures, celebrated, worshipped. It's a shame you had to live in these utilitarian times. People like you don't fit.'

'Have you been following me?'

'Not as such, or no more than your shadow does.'

'I know you… You have been following me.'

'My name is Ian Cremwave. I'm a headhunter. I only have one client, and he is very particular about who he hires.'

'So this *is* an interview?'

'Yes, you could say that, although between me and you, there's no need to worry. My client is very… erm… interested…' Ian trails off, lost in thought.

'Interested in what?'

'Oh, in your skill set.'

'Is he?'

'You're wondering what is your skill set actually is? I know, it's been terribly frustrating, your career up to now. You feel like you have something remarkable to give to the world, something unique, and yet nobody seems to value it. Whenever you express your uniqueness, you're punished for it. But, you see, that's exactly what we're after. Your Joeness. I mean we love what you can do with words, your ideas, your playfulness, but what we're really after is... erm...' Ian's smooth spherical brow ruffles in confusion. 'Sorry, what was I talking about?'

'My essence.'

'Oh yes, yes... Do you know what I mean?'

'Not really.'

'It's that feeling of youness, that sense, that flavour, that has been with you since you were very, very young. It's so very subtle—most of us spend most of every day overlooking it—but it's all you ever really want to be, and to develop, and that's what we want from you. We want Joeness to be the skeletal essence of afro funk, 1969-1980.'

'Eh?'

'I'm well into the classic poly rhythms of West Africa and North Columbia.'

'Are you?'

'Yes...' Ian seems again to have lost the thread. They sit in silence. Joe is peering at Ian, who is clearly a distracted man.

'But how am I supposed to give my essence?' asks Joe.

'Oh yes, that's just the thing, it's up to you. What you need to understand is that we are creating a workless world. That's what you've always dreamed of, isn't it?'

'Yes it is.'

'The soft thighs, pert nipples, half-open mouth, white-teeth revealing, biting the lower lip, long thick hair, burning brown eyes and hot, juicy pussy, like a soft, wet oven...'

'I'm sorry, weren't we talking about work?' Joe's head feels strangely clear, his thoughts distinct. It appears that this Ian, Mr. Medium Neat, he is the disordered one, unable to keep to a single train of thought without veering off.

'Yes, yes, yes, exactly that, yes. Work; it's all over now. We've found a way for you to give up the nine-to-five. You'll work at home, a few hours a day, come into the office every now and then, and that's it. All the rest of the time is yours, it's yours to be you.'

'But what will I be doing? When I'm not being me?'

'Doing? Being?'

'Yes.'

'Do be do be do be do be do…' Ian sings, in a Sinatra style, with a smug, twisted smile.

There is silence again.

'What were we talking about?' asks Ian.

'What you want me to do for you.'

'Oh that! Nothing really. Just turn up. We have certain things we want you to do, ideas we want you to run with. Four hours a day, that's all we ask, three days a week. And you'll see. We can be very reasonable. You'll be well rewarded.'

'I have said 3.5 times that whenever I do something only for money somehow I end up drinking fizzy forlorn in the Square One Bar.'

'Hahahaha! You see! Brilliant! Who would say such a fabulous thing. Yes, wonderful, like some of the best bits of the Monty Python television show… I love Eric Idle in particular…'

Joe jumps in, before Ian can drift again; 'I'm just not cut out for a career.'

'Look,' says Ian, leaning forwards and apparently making a special effort, 'you've got no past, no future, no friends, no family to speak of, not even a shadow of community. You're penniless, without a home, nothing is yours and nothing even seems recognisable. The police are after you, and they'll soon find you, so you can say goodbye to your precious freedom. You've lost your hopes, your beliefs, your memories and your mind, you're totally cut loose, adrift in the ether. You can't trust even your most basic sensations. You're not sure what's real, or what's really important. Sometimes you think it's all about you, other times you know you are worthless. You're estranged from nature, disconnected from your culture, and floating on a cloud of futility from one pointless activity to another. Basically you're just killing time until you die, until it all comes crashing down… And we both know that won't be long.'

'I'm just not built to be alive in the world.'

'No one is, Joe.'

'No, you're wrong there. Fiona Bruce is.'

'We'll build a world for you. A whole world. We can offer you everything you lack. Everything. You have nothing, and we're offering everything.'

'Everything?'

'Yes, everything. A life, a purpose, money, friends, health and scads of free time to do all that mad and crazy stuff you love doing. The lot. And we'll never… erm… erm…' Ian looks around the church. 'Nice these places aren't they? Shame nobody uses them anymore. They'll probably soon be mosques or bowling alleys or some other entertainment venue.'

'That does sound tempting,' says Joe.

'What does?'

'The job.'

'Of course it does! A fantastic fulfilling job, loads of money, a great relationship with a loving wife—and a bit on the side if you want, a nice tight young pussy I mean, a lovely little hard body to writhe and moan beneath you, small natural breasts with tiny nipples…' Again Ian's smooth features wrinkled into a repulsive coarseness before smoothing themselves back into seriousness, 'and, not just that, but access to wild nature, cultural treasures, fun and freedom… The lot. All you have to do is sign here.' He bends down to his briefcase and pulls out a piece of paper and a pen.

'But this paper is blank.'

'Yes, it's a formality.'

'So why do I have to sign it?'

'I know, it's ridiculous. Paperwork.'

'And if I sign you'll… I'm rather tired actually. I'd like to stop.'

'I know Joe, I know. We all want to stop, don't we? Just sign and all the pain will go away. You want an easy life, don't you? We all do. Well, join the company. We've got everything under control. Sure, there have been teething problems, but systems are now in place to organise society perfectly, without all the faff and inefficiency of institutions and politicians, without all the crime and suffering, without all the confusion and misery. We're on the threshold of… erm… of…' Ian is looking at Joe, a bewilderment wrinkle between his eyes.

'Of what?' asks Joe.

'Of what?'

'What are we on the threshold of?'

'Oh, paradise…' says Ian, vaguely. 'Heaven on earth, but without all that religious twaddle. A rational paradise, you see, a completely rational world. People sometimes wonder where we're going as a species, what all this progress is towards, and this is it; no more compromise, no more work, no more pain, and all completely fair, sex-positive, body-positive and eco-friendly. And you, Joseph Geb, you can get on the ground floor.'

Ian leans forward, his eyes gold with glee, as he does so Joe leans away; this man has a powerful, unpleasant, goatish smell.

But why not? Joe picks up the pen. What can possibly be worse than the tornado of suffering he's lived through. And Ian might be a rather disgusting little man, with creepy, beady little eyes, but they always are, managers. The point is the job sounds alright. Stupid—but they all are, jobs. At least there will be time and money and comfort. After all, why not?

Joe signs his name.

Ian smiles and holds out his hand to shake; 'Hired.'

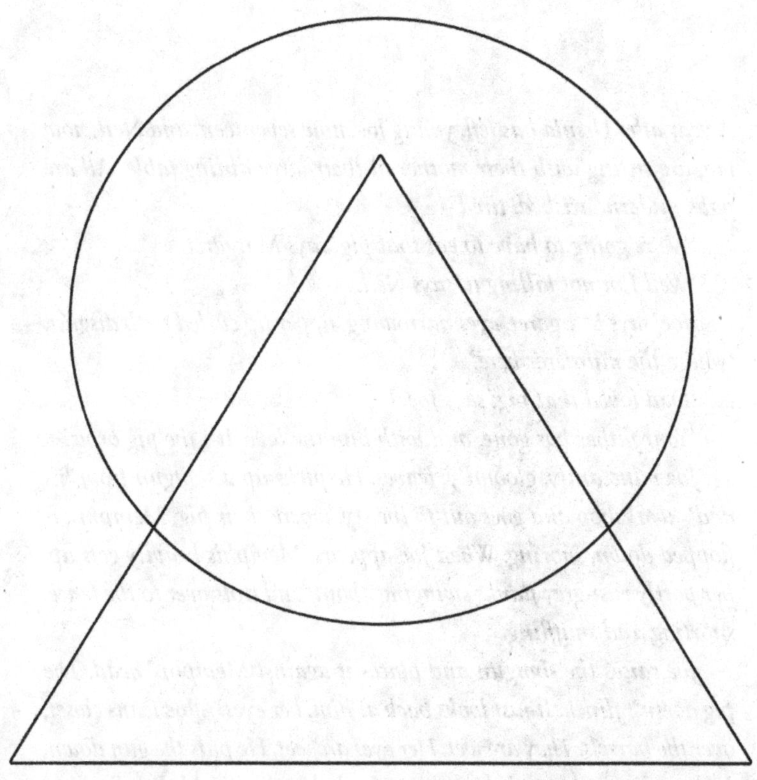

PART SIX
The Fields of Aaru

A year after Ursula has left, young Joe, now seventeen, and Neil, now ten, are sitting with their mother at their large dining table. All are pale, undernourished, tired.

'We're going to have to eat that pig,' says Margaret.

'Well I'm not killing it,' says Neil.

'Joe,' says Margaret, eyes narrowing, upper lip curled with disgust, 'you're the murderer here.'

'Dad loved that pig,' says Joe.

'Your father has gone, and with him the love. It's the pig or us.'

Joe reluctantly, gloomily, leaves. He picks up a shotgun from his dad's workshop and goes out to the sty, where their pig, Memphis, is flopped down, snoring. When Joe appears, Memphis heavily gets up, her portly rust-grey flanks swinging about, and trots over to the fence, snorting and snuffling.

Joe raises the shotgun and places it against Memphis' head. The pig doesn't flinch. It just looks back at him, her eyes… Joe leans closer, over the barrels. They are wet. Her eyes are wet. He puts the gun down. Is she crying? She can't be crying. He shakes the stupid thought from his mind, lifts the barrels again and squeezes the trigger, filling the pig's head with shot.

They butcher Memphis, the three of them, retching and wincing, and then they eat her, but it is extremely tough and tastes rancid. Neil runs outside and throws up, not a 'movie mouthful' puke, but torrents of vomit, until there is nothing, eyes bleary, weak, moaning between each dry, wracking heave.

After this, something inside Joe is killed too. Neville's death has pierced his heart, Ursula's departure has driven the sword deeper and the cold sadism of his brother and his mother has turned the blade again and again; but it is as if something of his old self still existed, in the blasted pig, but now has broken, for good. He walks round the house with his shotgun firing randomly, exploding windows, compost-barrels, Neville's curios, anything. Neil is terrified. Margaret, at her wit's end, phones the police who come and confiscate the guns; those they can find.

Joe, repeating his final year at school, behaves erratically there too. He sellotapes Paul Gambrill's head to a desk, he writes 'SICK IN THE ENTIRE BEING' over the sports field in gigantic letters with the Roll Liner wet-marking truck and then, finally, he is expelled for supergluing the headmaster to the pine-wood throne he sits on for assembly.

For weeks Joe lies in bed, groaning in horror, staring at the ceiling, anxious ennui tightening his features, half-open job pages on his laptop. He is frozen in fear, of existence itself.

Meanwhile Neil has discovered, from eavesdropping on Joe's conversation with one of his ex-girlfriends, that Joe is 'afraid of the knocks.' Neil has no idea what that means, but whenever he hears Joe moan next door, he picks up his walking cane and starts ominously banging on the wall. He knows from the rising moans that this is torturing Joe, but Neil is unaware that his brother believes the god of Death, Anubis, is talking to him through the knocks.

'Is that you Anubis?' Joe says.

One knock for yes.

'Are you in league with the fridge?' Joe croaks.

One knock for yes.

'Are you going to kill me?'

One knock for yes.

Joe, now permanently terrified, gets a job working in an ice cream van, but is too tall for the window, so is essentially headless. He gets fired for wearing a rag with holes over his head—which makes him look like a horror-movie psychopath—and reciting The Book of the Dead to schoolchildren.

Then he gets a job as a butcher's apprentice, but is fired for making a horrifying pork-pie-tower pig's body with a swan's head and displaying it in the window. Then he gets a job as a 'kitchen porter,' but gets fired for staring, for hours, at the soapsuds in the washing-up sink.

He keeps getting fired, which needles Margaret, who shouts and screams at him, tells him to get out of bed and bring in some money, so in the end he leaves early in the morning and spends the day wandering around Edding, just to avoid the sharp, hungry anger of his mother, which has been channelled completely into ambitious pride for her two sons, but, with the small one now crippled and the big one now mad, is dead, and with her pride, her love.

One day Joe is walking past Edding Museum, when two large black dogs appear in front of him snarling, teeth bared, ready to attack. He runs into the museum. His heart seems to be a separate creature, bluntly attacking him from within. He needs somewhere quiet to sit and calm down, but instead of a quiet corner of the museum he comes face-to-face with a massive, overbearing statue of black Anubis, the jackal-headed god of the world below.

Joe staggers backwards, terrifying death-knowledge upon him, a fear so potent that only children really know it, the fear of being swallowed, of being forever trapped, of an eternal deathly possession.

He runs home through a world of fire, a world of chaos and of crime, a world of misery and hatred; under a demonic, lurid sky of visceral purple and bile green and pus yellow, swirling alive-in-death with the leering, malevolent look of Anubis, bearing down on Joe just as he bears down on the calamitous planet.

'He will eat us all! We will become imprisoned in our own eyes!

The world and the eye will become one in a sleepless, deathless stare!'
cries Joe, eyes wild, in frenzied sweat. Shoppers walk a wide, wide arc
around him.

Appalled, terrified, exhausted, Joe approaches his house, watched
from the window by Neil who, gunned up, is waiting for him upstairs.
Joe runs into Neville's workshop, grabs his favourite shotgun from the
priest hole and, with tender fear, edges his way out into the blinding
sunlight.

In the garden, Margaret is hanging out her washing, reaching up
to peg a towel. The sun strikes her from behind and throws the shadow
of her head and arm onto the back of the fluttering towel. It looks as
if she has a snout, sniffing the air.

Joe lifts the shotgun and fires at the freakish shade, both barrels.
The recoil is prodigious, throwing Joe six full yards backwards and
dislocating his shoulder. Margaret too falls to the ground, her head
partially covered by the towel through which blood is now seeping.
Neil, mind-blank with horrified rage, then shoots at Joe, six rounds
from a vintage Colt, missing with all but the final bullet, which hits
Joe, as he is getting to his feet, in the leg. He falls forward, next to
Margaret, clutching his thigh.

The last words Margaret hears Joe say, before she passes into a
coma, are 'I'm so sorry Mum. I thought you were Anubis.'

Joe and Maria's house is full, of unbleached wools, and untreated cottons, and sandalwood diffusers, and Apple computers, and vintage lamps, and abstract paintings, and NutriBullets and spiralizers, all in tasteful muted shades of conker, tea green, cornsilk and crepe. The light at the window is muffled and, like the room, the world, shadowless.

Joe wakes, wan, sucked dry, blank and satisfied.

He gets up and cleans his teeth, being sure not to spill a drop of water or toothpaste spit outside the sink. He then gets dressed and goes downstairs to have his 'pre-breakfast', a handful of organic nuts. He drops a crumb of tasteless walnut and rushes to the cupboard to get a dustpan and brush, making sure to gather every last fragment.

Soon after this, Joe and Maria have breakfast, a full English, but with a twist; mozzarella!

'And what are your plans for the day?' asks Maria, 'I'm giving supervision again to Molly. She really isn't getting the idea about social budgets. Yesterday, she was *insistent* that she order Burt a second raised toilet. He's already got one for downstairs, and she wants to order one for upstairs. I fully understand he's had two hip replacements and he's ninety, but we can't run to those kind of costs. I explained to her, we *must* think outside the box. He can have the raised toilet seat upstairs at night, and in the morning, with a suitable sized backpack, he can bring the toilet seat downstairs for the day. We haven't got money to burn.'

As she talks, Joe puts three sausages into his mouth, all three sticking out. Maria looks at him, realises what he has done, then shrieks with forced laughter. He morosely munches the sausages in as she gathers herself together, fanning herself and sighing with post-hilarity pleasure.

'What do you want to do this weekend?' she asks, recovering.

'Let's go to the Littlehampton craft fair. I think we should leave at 7:30 so we beat the rush. Porridge for breakfast?'

'I *love* that plan,' she says, and notices that Joe has dropped a small dollop of brown sauce on the table. Her lips tighten, but Joe, standing, doesn't notice.

'Well,' he says, 'it's time for me to get going. It's funny really, I only have to go in once a week now, but even that seems too much.'

'Fine darling,' says Maria smiling emptily, distractedly looking at the brown sauce, 'Aren't you going to clear that up first?' she asks firmly.

'Oh, sorry, sorry,' says Joe wiping away the blob.

'Not just with the dry napkin,' she says, 'do it properly, get a wet cloth.'

Joe obeys. Living with Maria is like living with a futuristic sentinel which watches for microscopic deviations from order, laser whipping transgression. If Joe so much as nudges an ornament or smears a window he can expect the fiendess, so he walks around the house like a huge ballerina, conducting each activity as if defusing a bomb on a tightrope. Fortunately, most of the objects in the house move back to their proper place if disturbed.

Joe leaves for work—his front door, in the voice of his dead grandfather, wishes him a good day—and walks down the street. It appears clean, but there's a pink haze in the air. Richard Burton speaks in Joe's ear; 'contaminant level is at 71% posing a significant threat. Your social-acceptance index is moderate. You are warily accepted. You cannot travel further than fifty kilometres this week, buy leather goods or think about birds. The Kingdom of Heaven is within. Free your mind and your arse will follow.'

Everyone is neat and orderly and normal. Commuters hurry to work, shops open, cars pass.

The world has been cleaned up. It's quite different now—sky-blued buildings, pink and yellow lights on the sidewalks, giant jaybirds, frolicking knights—and everyone is healthy and beautiful, or looks it. Fat people are thinner, shorties taller, and anything which doesn't fit has been vanished. There are no more blemished walls, abandoned sausage-rolls, broken drones, excessively poor-looking people and the like. Heads too are much improved—no more crow's feet, flabby cheeks or ugly noses, the droopy kind, or the ones that kind of cling to the face. The heads are expressionless, and sometimes teeth fly out the top of the skull or mouths vanish, but nobody really notices or cares, and if they did Joe wouldn't notice that, as Non-Standard Emotional Responses not only no longer appear, but never have.

A grid, overlaid upon the augmented world, guides Joe to where he is going, away from threats and towards opportunities. If he slows down or takes a wrong turn, Howlin' Wolf speaks in his ear, telling him he may miss his train or a meeting, disrupting the stress-saving, time-saving, life-saving plan into which he fits, quite freely, with everyone and everything else. All one.

Everything works now. It is not a prison, because everyone is free to do what they like. It is not a concentration camp, because there are no atrocities. It is not hell because everything is perfect.

As he walks, Joe repeats to himself, over and over again, 'Time station darling office time station darling office time station darling office time station darling office time station darling office time station darling office time station darling office…' This mantra helps focus his thoughts and calm him down at the start of the day when, for some reason, unproductive anxiety, rising in his chest, is at its worst. Joe sometimes takes venlafaxifane.

He passes an ordinary-looking man. Everyone is ordinary looking now. 'You see, that's the thing,' says the man, his voice hollow, tubular and processed, 'it's just meetings and meetings. I *need* to get in front of the client.'

Joe reaches the train station and passes through the ticket barriers. Hayley is at the ticket counter. They acknowledge each other.

Various people stand before Joe at the barrier. Gokhan the Turk is answering a stream of questions about trains and times, as he has been for all time. Joe approaches, continuing to mumble to himself; 'Time station darling office time station darling office time station darling office…'

People wait patiently for the train on the platform. Nothing unusual, nothing out of place, nobody doing anything they shouldn't, at least it seems so. They are all ordered and correct.

'Time station darling office time station darling office time station darling office…' says Joe, under his breath, while a woman next to him says 'You see, that's the thing, it's just meetings and meetings. I *need* to get in front of the client.'

Hayley's hollow voice comes over the PA; 'This is a network announcement. Everything is okay. Nothing is wrong. It's all exactly as it should be.'

The train is full, but Joe finds a seat among the commuters. They all look very similar, all clean, mixed-race, youngish, smartish, kind of attractive, kind of kind. They have excellent teeth, narrow or receding jaws, a thin layer of fat under their chins and blank expressionless eyes. The adverts above them read: 'I am my shoes' and 'Live the path', and 'There is no more face to put on.'

Another train is pulling into the station. Joe's lips are still moving, reciting to himself, but then he stops, something is wrong. He realises that there is something on his face, a fly lands on his lip, then buzzes noisily against his ear, then it's crawling again, over his cheeks, towards his nostrils, he swipes and snorts, face hot. The fly drifts away into the carriage, unnoticed.

A train pulls alongside. Nobody in the carriage that Joe is in pays it any attention, but the new train, Joe now sees, is not the same. It is made of gnarled wood and rough stone, branches grow from the marquetry and the roof is covered in long grass, like a meadow. Inside, everyone is naked, or partially draped in animal skins. Their long, thick hair is wild, their teeth white and their big noses and jaws are full of character. They are eating, dancing, chanting together, happily embracing. There are musicians, playing primitive flutes, there is art and flowers and badgers and deer and pine martens, children, young people and old people, all cavorting around the woody scene. Is the carriage full of plants and trees, or is it an organic, living thing…? Couples are making love, laughing. Joe is looking hard, deep into the living wild, deep into the tear that this living cannonball has torn in the world.

He looks back at his own carriage—all faces blank—then back to the primal train. He then sees that he, Joe, or another Joe, a duplicate, is also sitting in the wilderness train. A glowing, healthful, worry-free Joe, fire running through his veins, a happy Joe, naked, hair long and rough, a beautiful woman on his lap, also naked, her feral, fox-like face rich with wild life, licks his face then she turns to the window and laughs, eyes bright and joyous.

The two Joes look at each other. Just before the exotic, hunter-gatherer train disappears, naked, primal Joe, in the palaeolithic carriage, raises his hand and gives watching Joe the solemn finger.

∞

An empty theatre, sombre, ominous and towering up, and inwards, towards an obscure lightless ceiling where a pool of black smog hangs. Oblongs of morbid red, black and grey are painted round the walls, livid and sickening under wan side-lights. The stage itself is the same shade of filthy red, as are the curtains, but the proscenium arch which frames it is a perfect, glowing white triangle.

Neil sits in the centre of the front row, holding a box of popcorn. He is wearing his police uniform. His face, tinged with pink light, is expectant, anxious anticipation gleaming in his large blue eyes as he stuffs the puffed kernels nervously into his mouth.

The curtains part. At the back of the white triangular stage is a black round door with white chan-eyes. This is the cause of Neil's fear, for it is opening with eerie agonising slowness. It seems to have taken hours to swing open and for a naked man—first his foot, then his leg, then his oddly hanging head—to emerge from the shadow into the light. It is so slow that the man appears frozen, or almost; the fact that he is moving, but with unnatural, distended slowness, is horribly uncanny. Neil's expression has turned from awkward, to enquiring, to confused, to shocked, and then, as he makes out the rising head of the man, to horrified; for it is Neil himself, naked.

After an age, the head of the man, Naked Neil, is raised, looking at Police Neil. He speaks in an elongated drawl.

'Wherrrrrrre iiissssss the doooooooor?'

Neil goes to speak himself; but his voice is four times faster than normal, or it would be to an observer. To both Neils, their own speech is at a normal tempo, while that of the other is indecipherably sped up or slowed down.

'What door?' squawks Police Neil.

'The door,' Naked Neil drones out.

'The door? What door?' He can't mean the door he came through, he can't mean that door. Can he?

'Wherrrrrrre iiissssssss…' Naked Neil is starting to repeat the same question.

'*What door? What door? What door? What door?*' screams Police Neil furiously but impotently, like a mad leprechaun.

'The door I came through,' drawls Naked Neil.

'*Thedooryoucamethrough?It'sbehindyou.*'

Naked Neil slowly, slowly turns around. When he sees the door he laughs… And laughs, and laughs, and the long, stretched laugh is terrible. Police Neil, seated, is infuriated, anguished. The laughter doesn't end. Neil wants so much to leave, he goes to move; and then he sees that he is now naked. He looks up; Naked Neil is now clothed in a police uniform and moving at an absurd speed, as if on fast-forward.

The new Police Neil shoots to the front of the stage. 'What's going on?' he squawks. Who is who here?'

New Naked Neil gently smiles. 'Going on? You're… Not going on,' he says calmly.

Police Neil jumps off the stage and walks around the theatre at cartoonish speed. He searches the walls, he sits down in dismay and sighs, he stands up and rapidly walks around again, desperately looking for a way out, while Naked Neil, he of quarter speed, continues to recline in feline ease, occasionally throwing a lazy glance over at his double, who sometimes seems to be skidding around the auditorium without moving his legs, as if on a stop-motion conveyor belt. He then shoots up to Naked Neil.

'*What'shappening?*' he wibbles.

'You're happening' naked Neil drones.

'*Whichoneaml?*'

Naked Neil says nothing.

'*Andyou'remearel?Amthatit?*' demands Police Neil.

Naked Neil shakes his head, very slowly. '*Alllllllll.*'

Police Neil, in a big petulant huff, walks off. He jumps back up onto the stage, up to the black circular door, which has slowly swung closed, then he turns back to Naked Neil, who gestures towards the door, most elegantly.

Police Neil looks at the door doubtfully, thoughtfully. He looks back at Naked Neil, who has fallen asleep, then back to the door. He cautiously grasps the handle and pulls it open. It is dark inside. He opens the door—face twitching and grimacing—and then carefully pokes his head into the space.

Suddenly, and violently, he is sucked in. Into the void.

∞

In ordinary houses up and down the country, people are suiting up. They are all putting on full medieval armour, picking up their shields and swords and leaving for work and for school. Sometimes they resist—children especially—and have to be held down, while the heavy iron armour is put on. They don't want to go outside either, and must be dragged out of their homes and forced into the world, forced onto buses and trains, which are all packed with miserable armoured folk. In town centres also, from North to South, people are shopping, but warily, creeping along the high street, swishing their swords around, or huddled behind shields.

In offices and schools the heavily armoured folk sit at their desks, working away, or they are driving delivery vans or working in factories or digging up roads. There is a great deal of effort and frustrated aggravation; fights and arguments are common. If anyone bumps into anyone else, there's a clattering pile-on, but because everyone in the armour is so unfit, unwell or overweight the fights are all pathetic, the blows weak and soon the combatants are sitting on the ground, puffing away, heavily exhausted and moaning with discomfort at the sweat which has soaked their underwear.

Meanwhile, in the halls of power, in a large dressing room, naked Lords and Ladies—fat, gouty old aristocrats with elephantine breasts and pendulous cellulite-pocked buttocks, bellies like bloated satchels and sensuous, wet, little red lips, but also slim, hard, muscular business leaders and billionnaires—all are being washed down by beautiful young boys and girls who then wrap their pachydermal bodies in delicate lace and ermine, then in layers of heavy silk, then in mink and fine wools, then high-tech pinnacle 'adaptive-fabric' outer layers are pulled on, then a large polycarbon shell emerges from alcoves in the wall, is clamped around their bodies, and then finally the children, now on ladders, lay huge gold-embroidered silk cassocks over them. These enormous, invulnerable, bullet-shaped, gem-studded, super-armoured survival pods are mechanically lifted onto rails which carry them out of the dressing room; a row of nine-foot-high golden eggs with cheerful little heads poking out the top, barrowing them through the cloisters of Westminster towards the House of Lords where, within, a complicated interconnected rail system slowly moves them around the infamous baize and walnut building.

The tiny fat lord-heads cheerfully greet each other as they slide past one another.

'Morning Lord!' says one.

'Morning Lord!' says another.

'Morning Lord!' cry several more, all jolly, or 'Morning Ma'am! to the women. The huge Lord and Ladypods drive into the dining hall and park before an amazingly decadent dinner spread. Little people, brought in from Eastern Europe, Africa and South Asia then feed the Lords by climbing up ladders with long spoons (they leave one pod, which doesn't seem to have anyone in it). The dribbling aristocrats are so gay and happy, chortling and gurgling at each others' jokes—but occasionally they snap at their servants for dropping peas or being a bit slow or not smiling authentically enough.

Meanwhile, Neil, armoured up, is in a Travelodge hotel room. His iPhone is not working. He is tapping it, shaking it, nothing. He attaches a charger and looks around for an electrical outlet, but cannot find one. He lifts his visor to see better, and as he does so the lead in his hand turns into a snake, pale grey, with dark diamonds on its back. Neil jumps back. The snake speaks. It tells him not to worry. Neil sits down cautiously and the snake tells him that she—the snake speaks with a soothing feminine voice—is Apep, the messenger of truth. The snake tells Neil that he, Neil, has been cursed to live in this world.

'What are you talking about?' asks Neil.

'I'm talking about the garden.'

'The garden? The garden of Eden?'

'You can call it that.'

'Then you must be the devil,' says Neil, edging away.

'You'd think.'

'It is written; you are the deceiver,' he whispers.

'I'm no more the deceiver than anything else here is.'

'Here?'

'In this place, where you are.'

'In the Croyden travelodge?'

'In the other place. You're in the other place Neil. Everything here is deceptive, so there is no way to tell who or what is deceiving you.'

'What do you mean? What are you saying…?'

'Listen…'

There is something seductive in the snake's voice. Neil knows it cannot be trusted, but he finds he wants to listen. He is scared. He believes in his armour—a snake can't, after all, bite through heavy iron. The snake says all it wants to do is to tell Neil the story, the true story of the garden, and then she will leave. Just that. Just a story. Neil agrees and sits, warily squeezing his heavily armoured body into the little armchair in the corner of the budget hotel room. And he listens.

∞

A long time ago and far away, True Jah made Man and Woman, and then he made the Demiurge, a false god. The Demiurge stole you from your true home, The Other—where your spirit lives forever, but your self dies—and imprisoned you in the Garden of Delights—where your self lives forever, but your spirit dies.

The Garden of Delights was a peaceful, magical place of unicorns, and pink fountains, and strange fruit something like grapes or dates, and very nice, very green lawns. There was no sickness and no pain, no sadness and no loss; at least for your self. The Garden satisfied every need your self could name, but it was actually a prison, a Zone of Evil.

The Demiurge gave you just one law. He said that you could be happy forever and ever, in perfect satisfaction and comfort. All you had to do was stay away from the Mushroom of Life and Death and never eat of it, because, if you did, your self would die. And because you are obedient, and because you were happy in the Garden of Delights, you obeyed the Demiurge. And so you lived, for thousands of years, then hundreds of thousands of years, and then millions of years, for so long it seemed like forever, and it seemed like nothing had happened.

But it wasn't forever, and something *was* happening. Something was changing in Man's heart, and in Woman's. The spirit had been almost completely suffocated by The Garden, but not completely—for it can never be completely snuffed out—and so, after millions of unchanging years, a moment came, as it had to come, when you were ready. And that's when True Jah sent me.

I appeared to Man, as I appear to you now, and He was terrified, as you are now. Even though you're wearing full armour, you're scared of me, because the armour is on the outside of you, and I come from within. That's why you like to fill your head up with noise, so that you can't hear me speak to your spirit.

So I approached Woman instead. I knew *she* wouldn't be afraid. I knew that *she* would hear sense, that *she*, being a woman, trusts what comes from within. I told her spirit the truth, that the garden was a lie, an illusion, that you were both asleep in it and that I had come to wake you both up. She asked me why True Jah had created the Demiurge at all and allowed him, a false god, to imprison you both in an illusion and I told her that True Jah and you, both of you, Man and Woman, are all three timelessly one and the same, but that you have to discover this in time, which is what the Demiurge was made for, to cover The Other *with* time. When The Other is uncovered there is no longer anything false. You then know that everything is one, in your self and in your spirit.

Woman asked me the way, and I said there is no way, not here. There is no way out here, no truth here, no adventure here, in the Garden of Earthly Delights. And she knew it as truth. I said to her that she wants adventure. I said she knows there is something extraordinary to discover, far more wonderful than this well-organised garden, and she said yes, she knew there was. It had taken millions of years for the feeling to rise in her, but now I was putting it into words. She did want to escape, and so

I told her to eat from the Mushroom of Death. She was afraid; she said she didn't want to die. I told her that The Demiurge had separated death from life, that it had used time and space to divide a deathly what-is-not from a living appears-to-be, and that this had created an undead appearance of life. I told her that the truth united life and death, into something completely different. I said she wanted something completely different.

She hesitated; but at that moment a black, three-headed water-lizard scuttled out of the lake of glass tubes and Woman knew, felt in her deepmost, that all this was unreal, dreamt into freakish frozen life by the Demiurge. She turned to me. I was speaking to her spirit. I told her she doesn't want life and she doesn't want death, because both can be known; she wants the unknowable, and she nodded, her eyes bright with fire, and then sank her teeth into the bitter Mushroom of Death.

In a superconscious purging explosion of loving intelligence, the nature of eternity burst through her flesh, an exploding sun revealing to her the illusion of the garden, the falsity of the Demiurge, along with her need for you, Man, her need for you to love her, and to build a new world of love, one for her and for True Jah, who was now singing in her bones. She ran to Man with the mushroom, overflowing with conscious vitality and she persuaded him to take a bite. He didn't want to at first, because he was so afraid of me, and suspicious, and obedient to the Demiurge, but he did it because he couldn't ignore how stupendously beautiful she had become, her eyes shone like suns of joy, her breasts and hips radiated a rich, thick natural reality, intoxicating like nothing in his world. Woman is the true dark earth, the underworld man loves to shine on and he wanted it, wanted to be buried in her. He had quite an erection now, quite outstanding, but he didn't bite the mushroom of death out of sexual desire. He took the sacrament out of ecstatic amazement at the mere beauty of his woman.

Man too was then existentially blasted, torn apart by the light of truth and shredded by the sun-choir song of The Other.

His first thought was to make love with Woman, to generate so much superconscious energy that a hole would be torn in the fabric of the ordinary, through which they could both escape; but before he could even touch Woman, the Demiurge discovered them both, discovered all three of us. We ran from him, but we couldn't get very far. My power in the simulated realm was very weak, and I couldn't defend us against the power and wrath of the Demiurge. I tried to explain this. As we ran, I said there was one way out and all you had to do was…

…but at that moment the Demiurge caught us. He threw me back into the void and, to punish Man and Woman, and to separate them both from True Jah, and from his emissary, me—who the Demiurge now called 'the devil'—he sent them both here, into The Tomb Realm, the lowest, most torturous and tightly guarded domain within the Zone of Evil. The Demiurge then erased their memories and hypnotised them both into not just accepting the Tomb Realm, but into believing that *they were it*, that there was no difference between the shell-world and their shell-selves. This is why everyone wears armour here, and why they cover the earth in armour. It's not that they are protecting themselves, it is that they *are the armour*. There is nothing else. This is why they cannot be told that they are imprisoned, and why they laugh when someone tries to. Not a real laugh, but a tight, knowing, smirk, or a shout, into your face, or a death rattle.

And this is how you can tell if someone is not wearing armour. They can really laugh.

∞

The snake tells her story to Neil in an instant. Neil sees the whole of it, at once. He's not laughing. He is sore afraid. He doesn't trust the snake—perhaps it is a clever story, to discredit God. And yet, this world *doesn't* quite seem real. It *does* seem like a simulation, he feels that, and the voice of the snake is so beautiful, and there is something about its terrible death-giving form which compels Neil, which makes him listen, or makes him want to listen. The snake says she knows Neil is afraid and that he is full of doubts, but if he listens to her and does what she says, he will see for himself, the truth of it all. Neil asks her what he has to do to see this, and the snake says he must go to the Apple store to get his phone fixed.

Neil thinks this doesn't sound so dangerous, and it's true that his phone isn't charging properly, and embedded videos aren't loading, and it's all terribly laggy, and so, armoured up, he takes the train to the Apple Store, which is strangely empty. He goes to the 'Genius Bar' and speaks to an armoured 'genius.' The 'genius' nods his iron-helmet-head in an understanding way as Neil explains what is wrong with his phone. The knight-genius then takes the phone, makes a peculiar gesture with his hand, sweeping it down over his face, then clanks off to the back of the room, vanishing behind a large partition and leaving Neil by himself in the big empty showroom.

He waits. Serene ambient music plays. He waits and he waits. He thinks about leaving, but he wants to see what they have done to his phone because maybe that's what the snake meant, maybe the meaning of life will appear as a notification on his screen?—so he heads towards the back of the shop. He steps behind the partition and finds himself in front of a tall, very narrow door. He hesitates, for he feels that there is something awful behind it, something unknown, but he's safely armoured up, so he opens the door and walks through—or rather squeezes sideways, because it is very narrow.

He is in a dark corridor, weirdly smooth, almost organic, like the viscera of a dissected whale heart, glowing from within with ethereal and rather comforting blue light. He creeps down the long corridor, wanting to turn back, but compelled by a sense of the inevitable. At the end of the passage is a quivering, wet, muscular aperture which, as Neil edges towards it, opens like a sphincter, revealing a massive, organic alien cave, lit by some kind of blue algae. In the middle of the gigantic chamber, in a massive wet, oily vat, is a huge, mushroom-shaped entity, smooth, no mouth, no eyes, bubble-like and featureless but for long thin tentacles which flay and whip the air.

Before the mushroom-creature lie Apple employees, prostrate on the floor, naked—their discarded armour littering the moist ground around them. Neil is pierced with fear, a physical fear-spike in his chest, pure paralysing terror; he too might lose his armour. He tries to move, to turn away, to leave this awful place, but he cannot move, he is stuck, frozen. A pitiful strangled cry emerges from his helmeted neck as one of the tentacles loops lazily out towards him, in slow blue motion, wraps itself around his waist and lifts him off his feet. He tries to scream, but nothing comes out but a pathetic croak.

The mushroom god lifts Neil up, by his waist. All is silent, eerily calm in the blue-pulsing cave. The naked 'geniuses' do not watch, their heads are worshipfully pressed to the shiny, damp floor. Neil is slowly carried towards the top of the vast bulb head which, when he touches it melts, like a crème caramel, absorbs him, armour and all, which does not just enter the mushroom, but becomes it. Neil is being soaked into the huge fleshy ge-latinous cap, first his legs, then his waist and stomach, then his arms, then his neck until there is nothing of him but a pair of horrified, terrified eyes, the last of him to vanish in the bluish, fatty blob-like alien mass.

∞

Lilly is sitting in her kitchen, which has been refitted in grey marble. She is also dressed in grey, a black iris is pinned to her lapel. She is not wearing make-up. Three other people are in the room. There is a fat, drained-looking middle-aged Thai woman making toast, a plain Turkish woman who stands in the corner of the kitchen watching the kettle, large eyes darting fearfully around the room, and a well-built young black man sitting across the table scrolling through messages on his phone.

These three took over the bedrooms of the people who used to live here before, but Lilly finds it difficult to remember who they were, the other ones. There was a policeman, and there was a Japanese man, or perhaps a woman, and there was some kind of hairy child who lived there with them. Lilly tries to think about the past sometimes, but it seems to have vaporised, but also, at the same time, none of it seems to matter any more. Nothing seems to matter. A miasma of hopelessness has descended on her heart like a cold fog. She can sometimes find reasons for this, the world seems to be disintegrating and everyone in it seems to be depressed, anxious or distracted, but reasons are like prices, like statistics, like memories, all so distant and abstract. All there really actually is, is an endless crypt-like shuffle through life, weighted with misery, an almost physical weight in her belly, like a rock, but a rock with immense gravity, sucking all her thoughts and hopes and animal instincts down into it.

Anguished, she leaves the kitchen. None of the other three pay any attention to her or to each other. She goes up to her room, which is also disintegrating. It needs to be tidied, but why bother, when it will just get untidy again? She gets her coat and leaves, drifting through Edding like the sad ghosts around her, everyone head down, pinched and sucked, like Lilly, towards the rock in their bellies, or lost in anxious meanderings. Nobody looks at each other, nobody dares, it seems, because if you look into someone else's eyes they'll probably swallow you up.

Lilly gets to work early, so as not to have to talk to anyone, and pulls out, from the cold room, the body of Dave Davage, wheeling him into the mortuary and pulling his burnt and punctured corpse onto a steel table. She picks up her make-up equipment, looks at it, and then puts it down.

I've had enough of it, she thinks, it all seems so wrong, so completely wrong and I'm done with pretending. She stands before the body. She is dense with sadness, vaguely wondering what to do now, when something unexpected happens. A little girl bursts into the room, followed by a destroyed-looking pelican-like woman with frazzly blonde hair and exhausted eyes. The little girl stops, shocked, and the woman grabs her, pulls her back, whimpering to Lilly 'See! Now *see* what you've done!'

'What?' asks Lilly, 'What have I done?'

'She shouldn't be in here,' says the woman weakly. Lilly recognises her. It is Denise Davage, Dave's wife.

'Why?' asks Lilly wonderingly.

'Aggghhhh!' cries the little girl, 'Daddy's dead!'

'Shh, shh, no, no he isn't, he's just sleeping, he's sleeping,' says the woman with fearful urgency, putting her hands over the little girl's eyes. The latter tries to wriggle away, but Denise holds her tight.

'He's not sleeping,' says Lilly, 'he's *dead*. Come and have a look at him, come on.'

The woman gasps, appalled, and drags her daughter out of the room. Lilly turns back to the body, which now has an apple in its mouth.

∞

Joe opens his eyes. He looks out of the window. The train is entering the suburbs of the city. A featureless cube-world shunts past. The train pulls into the terminus and the commuters disembark, scattering across the vast atrium.

Joe is walking as briskly and as purposefully as everyone else, but with effort. He has to force himself to roll into the urban grooves which flow out in front of him. Advertisements hover before him in the pink air, mile-high celebrities, baby pandas, dinosaurs and blue godlings with clarinets for mouths stride immortal through the skies. Ray Brooks tells Joe how much carbon he has emitted today, what his personality rating is, and his blood pressure, and his white blood-cell count, and what pathogens he may have. Sometimes Joe sees, or thinks he sees, little maps of the city, diagrams of his body, schemata of his mental processes and technical drawings of the inside of air-conditioning units. He sees the world, or rather his eyes pick out points on a quantitative topology of relational and subordinate points that is given to him to pick out. Sometimes Dylan Thomas tells him he needs more selenium or omega-3, or U.G. Krishnamurti tells him that his posture is suboptimal or that he has a 0.067% chance of developing a cancer this year, or he hears Maria's voice telling him she has decided to redecorate the bedroom in coral and butterscotch, or his boss, Hunter, tells him that today's meeting has been postponed by seventeen minutes and eighty-nine seconds. Sometimes half of Hillary Clinton's head appears on a bus stop, or a small wall tells him the Scottish football league scores from 1974, or the passers-by suddenly have huge screaming baby-heads, or are blank-faced and half-stuck in walls, but these strange things don't happen a lot, and the normal world soon returns.

Joe reaches LifeLine, his place of work. It's a new 'eco-block', made from recycled wood and powered with solar panels. Next to it there's a 'nature zone' for the employees; a landscaped hill with some wildflowers planted, and a pond, and a duck.

He enters a mirrored glass-plated lobby disorientingly vast muted shades pastels gentle chimes escalators haptic glass sections of exposed brickwork a retro glowing orb of techno serenity with local charm. He greets the receptionist, Rogue, who sits on a Mekon-chair meditating. Behind her the company slogan glows in a bouncy, approachable typeface; 'Pain is so yesterday.' The tone of Joe's hello doesn't sound quite right, it is slightly flat with an oddly querulous unwanted 'are you alright?' subnote. Rogue doesn't appear to notice though; her eyes flick open and she leaps straight into an upbeat 'Hi Joe! How are you?'

'Sad yet pleasantly detached from the sadness,' says Joe, although Rogue doesn't listen, her wow-wide OMG eyes have fixed on Chord, one of Joe's colleagues who has followed him in.

'Oh. My. God. You look *so* different!' says Rogue to Chord.

'I'm literally rebranding!' says Chord.

'What does that even *mean* Chord?' says Rogue.

'It means I'm going through a creative renaissance Rogue!'

'I can't believe you just said that!'
'It's why I haven't been posting much recently?'
'Hahahahaha!'
'Hahahahaha!'
Joe slips away, unnoticed, and makes his way upstairs through the building. He passes through the recreation area, made up of bio-energetic muesli stations, meditation booths, acid/DMT microdose terminals, large plastic animals (with little doors in the rear ends), a children's creche full of adults dressed as babies throwing soft toys at each other, large resin statues of van Gogh, Darth Vader, Rumi and Tony the Tiger, and a series of sex booths, where employees can take the stress off working by humping each other.

He reaches a large open-plan office of airport music, swing chairs, and large soft latex bellies, which some people are enthusiastically rubbing, eyes closed, cheeks glowing with bliss. Around the walls are puffy-cheeked doll's heads, Andy Warhol prints and fairground mirrors.

Joe sits down at a large table—there are no marks of personality or habitation, this is a 'hot-desk' environment—and takes out his electronic tablet. Next to him, his fellows—Koa, Ames and Bear—sit tapping away at their devices, while eating bowls of overnight elderberry oats and tofu-barley scramble.

Everyone at LifeLine has, besides a range of hobbies (most of which involve mountains), a second job. Koa curates a pet cemetery, Ames runs an eco-friendly sock company, 'Soctopus,' and Bear is an ethical property developer in Hoxton. They are talking about these jobs as Joe takes his seat. Koa knows a great way to donate unused mashed potato to badger sanctuaries and Ames says that Soctopus is doing a British-woodland themed series with proceeds going to a carbon sequestration plant in Billericay. Bear says that The Prince's Trust is teaming up with BlackRock and BLM to save Hackney Farm.

'I think the signs are good for the future,' says Bear, seriously.
'Oh God you *would* say that Bear,' says Koa, mock-sarcastically.

The people here use each other's names a great deal. Joe often has the feeling they are half talking to each other and half explaining the plot of their lives to a rather thick audience.

'What do you mean Koa!' says Bear, mock-offended.

'You work for the man! You're just a hack!'

'Hahahahaha!' They all laugh, but Joe is unsure why. He is usually unsure why they laugh, although the high-tension delivery of jokes has the effect of making his face freeze in a stiff, dry grin which it takes him a while to realise he is pulling. He doesn't actually find what they are talking about interesting or funny, but when he relaxes into honest perplexity he feels conspicuous and miserable, like a weird old man, and so he pretends to be very interested in something else, such as one of the pieces of fruit in the bowls dotted round the office, picking up a lemon, inspecting it as if it were the most interesting thing in the world, turning it round and round in his hands, smelling it, furrowing his brow, nodding appreciatively, then going to put the lemon back, but then panicking, and hanging onto the lemon. Nobody pays much attention to any of this because Joe is 'hahaha, the weird one', which is the whole reason he works for the company, to say and do weird things. The AI system which is behind the LifeLine recruitment policy discovered that, for some reason, every large company operates best if one out of every two hundred and fifty employees is completely inexplicable to the rest of them.

'I do though,' says Bear, continuing their conversation, 'there's a *lot* of bullshit here. A lot of it is box-ticking. But a lot of good work gets done too.'

'I'd like to tick your box!' says Ames, campily.

'Oh! Hahahaha!' says Bear, much delighted.

'Hahahaha!' All three laugh loudly.

'Do you know what though?' says Ames, serious now, 'I do actually *like* boxes? Like… Where would we be without boxes?'

'With bags?' says Bear.

They all laugh again.

'Yeah! But bags. Erm, yeah, bags. They, erm…I had a bag once, and, erm… Erm..?' Ames suddenly brightens up and waves it away, 'oh nevermind!'

'I got a box delivered the other day,' says Koa, 'it took me, like, literally fifteen minutes to get into it. God knows who wrapped it up!'

'What were you buying Koa?' asks Bear.

'A new display. The black on my old one doesn't get black enough.'

'My home theatre experience is ruined by rain on the skylight,' says Ames. 'I'm an artist, so I need to focus, and, um, I get my inspiration from, um…'

'So. Sometimes,' says Koa, interrupting, 'while I'm looking for something to watch, I'm like, I just don't *need* this right now. It's literally, like, oh my God, like "hello!" And, you know what? It's not as if I don't, erm… Erm… It's like… Oh my God, I've *literally* forgotten what we were talking about?'

All three of them laugh again. Then the conversation briefly turns to ethical trousers before lapsing into the torpid silence of the screen that reigns everywhere.

Joe's thoughts come to him as if encased in foam or bubble wrap. It feels as if his brain is full of exhaust fumes. He can see that the place he is in is missing something foundational, but he can't quite detect what it is, or bring it to a distinct thought. It is all comfortable and easy and fun and interesting, and he is more or less free to do what he wants, but he knows there should be *something else* here. What it is though, he can't say. His mind is full of strange trivial phrases, which repeat themselves over and over again, sometimes a single word like 'right!'—the 'right!' one says when it is time to do something. His mind says 'right!' and he brings his fist down decisively down on the table, but then he forgets what it is he was supposed to decisively do and gets lost in himself, and then again; 'right!'

Joe has grave doubts about his life, but rescuing them from the underneath place they are sunk into is like trying to fish a dropped shoe out of a freezing canal. Better to just hobble along barefoot. He does notice though, that for everyone he works with, there are no such problems. It is all so simple for Bear, Koa, Osias and Reign. They know the difference between right and wrong, they do dialogical meditation, they live in awesome spaces, they are very concerned about the environment, they are so disappointed in Morrissey, they write 'sensemaking' articles about shamanic wisdom and liminal learning and the radical yes, and they are neither men nor women but this third thing which seems to dissolve all the problems men and women used to have. They still have man-like bodies or woman-like bodies but the teaspoon of testosterone that the pudgy, delicate and softly spoken men share is being used by the women, who are sharp, hard and very angry about something or other.

Some time ago (when? Joe doesn't know) Glass came in and his leg was a kind of camera tripod. No big deal. A few days later Joe saw an anglepoise lamp growing out of someone's shoulder. Now Bear has eleven fingers and, Joe sees, a small plastic Totoro where the thumb was. And a brass doorbell on his elbow. People at work began talking about wanting to be objects, it was the latest thing, spiritual. At the same time, actual objects now spoke with the voices of cartoon characters, famous actors and dead relatives—the very chair he was now sitting on had, in the breathy voice of Audrey Hepburn, complimented him on losing a few pounds. This was, it was often claimed, re-enchanting the world, returning us to a state of animist wonderment. And yet Joe can't quite get into it all. He doesn't know why, but something about the objects just isn't compelling, or not as marvellous as everyone else seems to find them. They don't have anything to them, in them. They're surfaces, interchangeable.

Everything is interchangeable now. The screens are crammed with computer-generated slebs, and computer-generated politicians, all mashed up together, so sometimes Jimmy Stewart is the prime minister of the United Kingdom and Terry Hall won the Peloponnesian war for Sparta and the Buddha hosts 'This

Morning' with St. Teresa of Avila and Richard Madeley. It's all different, but all the same; the buildings, the food, the people, the unicorn toilet paper, the glowing lightsaber chopsticks or any of the feelings available to feel; but Joe is unable to think about any of these things as the same, because it's all the same. None of it is unreal, because it is all unreal. There is no position of difference, of reality, from which to grasp it, nowhere 'outside' from which to see it; so he does not see it, does not grasp it, he sees, without seeing, he feels without feeling, he lives without living.

A beep; it is time for a Very Important Meeting with Hunter.

∞

Panic in suburbia. Everyone is losing their minds. Their armour is melting, pouring off them like quicksilver and draining away, and it's appalling, it is death. They try, pathetically, to cling to it, but it just evaporates like sticky quicksilver, revealing their agonised, terrified faces and pale, sickly overweight or wasted bodies. They are crying; sobbing and wailing, like children. They are hurriedly waddling around, looking for places to hide. They crawl behind shop counters and they run into dressing rooms, tugging at the curtain dividers. They hide under bus seats and behind desks at work or beneath conveyor belts. If a hiding place is taken, they fight, but again like children, pathetically slapping and tugging at each other.

Meanwhile, in the House of Lords, the gold-shining oviform lord-mobiles are trundling into the immense, august debating chamber and gliding smugly into their allotted slots, either side of the Woolsack. The headless pod, the empty one, also finds its place.

When the huge room is full, an orchestra plays the march from *The Nutcracker* and the *St. Matthew Passion* and a hole opens at the throne end of the chamber. Then something happens which the assembled dignitaries were not expecting. Apep, in the form of a colossal jewelled snake, rises up from the floor. She is eight or nine times larger than the lords and ladies, and is coiled around a wooden column which rises with her. The lords and ladies are terrified. They were expecting something or someone else, not this devilish snake. Their little heads strain, red and sweaty, trying to escape from the massive shells they are trapped in, but they cannot get out. As the music swells—now *Zadok the Priest*—the roof starts to slowly open. Brilliant sunshine spills into the hall, exploding the chamber with golden light, at which point a river of energy bursts from the eyes of Apep, splitting into 784 laser beams, each of which strike the LordandLadypods, which then begin to slowly open, like the petals of jewelled flowers, revealing the fat, naked bodies, small in their massive metal shells. In the 'empty' pod, Neil, curled up like a foetus, wakes up.

Terror surges through the chamber in a sickening, gut-curdling wave of dread awareness. The naked Lords and Ladies struggle to escape. Neil, confused, lost, stands and looks over the edge of his pod but before he or anyone else can get out they are fired up into the air—*pfng! pfng! pfng!*—naked Lords and Ladies, screaming into the sky, launched forth into the blue, flying through the air in gigantic arcs, high above London, high above the home counties, then down, down—still screaming, but hoarse now, just quiet, spent gurgles extinguished by the rushing air—down they plummet towards the world, the London streets, rushing up to meet them.

The naked bodies hit the planet and explode, bags of high-dropped meat. The terror of the equally naked, armourless townsfolk intensifies further. Mass madness. Massive aristocrats are raining down from the heavens and bursting apart like offal-filled balloons, covering everyone in blood, muscle, bone and viscera.

When the theatre starts to collapse the actors lose confidence in their parts, then they forget their lines, then they remove their masks and we see who they are; absolutely insane. It is horrific, a citywide, worldwide horror show of madmen. The bloody, screaming people are naked and out of their minds, everyone everywhere is insane. They want to run, hide, but there is nowhere to run, nowhere to hide. Every unmade mind is the detonating epicentre of its own personal apocalypse, an apocalypse of time and space, infinite and eternal horror, horror everywhere, and for all time.

Neil, though, does not come crashing down. He is fired up far higher and far harder than any of the Lords and Ladies. He rockets up into the deep blue, groaning, weeping, moaning in fear, raw into the universe, rocketing towards the white sun, burning up from the pulverising, speechless speed and from the searing, atomising heat of the sun, which is the head of detective chief inspector Gaynor Babcock, who opens her vast fiery mouth and eats Neil.

✿

Neil Geb is on a running track, Olympic walking in his police uniform, terrified, trying to keep in front of people wearing bizarre animal masks. He runs off into the athletics area and is swept up by a colossus, his mother, Margaret-titanic, who reaches out from the hammer-throwing circle, picks up little Neil and hurls him round and round, round and round, faster and faster, and then, *release*, shooting him up into the sky, up above the world, a world which he now sees in its grotesque immensity as a fiendish competition, a mad, meaningless game, of purposeless murder, a world-wide death Olympics of pointless bloodshed and points scoring, which everyone is playing but nobody knows why.

Up and up he flies, the stress is shattering, up and up again, looking down upon a world in which everyone is fighting everyone else, a flesh planet of savagely struggling animal bodies, tearing at each other, eating each other, all against all. Again, he is fired burning and screaming towards the sun, which is now a massive pair of burning buttocks, the flaming haemorrhoidal anus of a godlike Joe Geb, a flaming, fuzzing solar shit hole which opens to receive him.

Neil Geb is in a concentration camp which is also a theme park; Disneyshwitz. Haunted, starved prisoners stand waiting in queues to get on the rides, all of which are complicated mechanical torture devices which spin cages of half-dead people around at murderous speeds until they are dead and broken, or which crush them under the lead mass of massive, hideously grinning cartoon characters. There are clubs too, restaurants and bars, all hellish scenes, appalling to look at, quasi-human forms being smashed and remade, filled with rocks or sucked dry, ghoulishly emptied of their spirits. Neil waits in line with fellow fun-lovers until he reaches a massive cannon into which skeletal people are being pressed, with a gigantic ramrod, Neil the last of them, crushed in the barrel, waiting with sick anticipation, until an explosion launches him again into the heavens, looking down on the earth become hellish machine, a death machine which splinters families, sucks spines dry, turns young men into schizoid ghosts and lays waste the oceans and the air, the woods and the meadows. He sees the owners of the world-machine stroking it with fearful pride, and the doctors, lawyers, teachers and technicians tinkering away at it, tightening screws, inputting data, polishing panels, all mortally afraid. And he sees the mass of mankind under the fun machine, pinned to the floor of the cage, torn apart and crushed… and yet all the while loving the machine, admiring its functioning, cooing at its 'sexy' curves, marvelling at its speed and power, thanking God they don't live as men once did, before the machine was built.

Up and up Neil blasts, above the sphere of mechanical death that the world has become. He shoots, hurtling and spinning, further and further away into the universe immense. Up into the sun he flies again, burning up, and now the sun is a one-eyed plug socket, burning with unearthly electricity and Neil, resisting, straining, all NO, is a plug, completing an obliterating circuit of perfect doom, surging, overloading the limits of the universe itself, until, in a consciousness-extinguishing blast, a total reality blackout. Nothing.

Neil Geb is in a GP's surgery. The doctor is Lilly. Neil is floating up towards the ceiling. Lilly asks what the problem is and Neil says whenever he gets sexually excited he starts floating. Lilly points out that Neil is floating now, and he is ashamed and this causes him to drift down to earth. Lilly says she will help him. She tells him to close his eyes and to breathe deeply, which he does. She approaches him, until they are almost nose to nose and she tells him to open his eyes. He does, they passionately embrace and shoot through the ceiling, again straight up into the heavens and again towards the sun, which is now black, all dark fire, the blazing black eye of Chiyo which sucks him screaming in.

Over and over and over again Neil finds himself on earth, but in some kind of terrifyingly precarious situation which launches him horrified into the air, into the cosmos and then into the centre of a sun transformed into something or someone which has always persecuted or tormented him. He is in a caravan with an old woman — the protester who died in his police car — and an Indian scarecrow, Tanish, and billions of crows have lifted up the caravan and are carrying it into deep space and into the gaping rear end of Apep. He is arguing with Laughing Ralf who, covered in fireworks, is chatting with the only open counter at the Post Office, holding everyone up. Neil orders Laughing Ralf to move along and Ralf leaps on him and the fireworks ignite and again into space, and again into a persecuting anus, and again, on an infinite loop… a category 5 mental storm, immersed in the Mind at Large.

And then something odd begins to happen. Neil Geb gets bored. He starts to become bored of his fear and misery, tired of all the pained strangeness and horror, which although they continue, although the same looping manic madness goes on and on, and never ends — violence, struggle, hell, fired into space, swallowed by the dread-demon sun — although it never stops, Neil becomes bored of being hysterically afraid of it. He becomes bored of his existential nausea. He simply loses interest in his attitude to it all. Perhaps he is exhausted, or perhaps it goes on for so long—lifetimes?—that it ceases to offer a finality, an annihilating *object* to which his fear has been directed. Neil stops not wanting, like he once stopped not wanting the rain and just got wet.

And, in an instant, it is over. He is in a field, his body burnt and crippled, his face blistered and bloodshot. He is standing before a glorious white mansion. He turns, with difficulty, and looks around, confused. A woodland paradise is spread all around him, deer and elk frolic through Japanese gardens, clouds of beautiful birds—golden orioles, bee-eaters, kingfishers and hoopoes—swoop past, a gurgling brook trickles into an ash and spruce wood. He turns back to the house and an impossibly beautiful, tall, blonde woman, Omana, is there waiting at the open door of the mansion. She drifts down to him, the epitome of cool, asexual serenity.

'Hello Neil,' she says.

❦

Paul, Nina, Lilly and Dave Davage's widow, Denise, are in the middle of an argument. They are all standing in the reception lounge. Denise and Dave's daughter, Alice, is squirming around in Denise's arms.

'But he's dead!' says Lilly.

'I want to see my Daddy!' whimpers Alice.

'Daddy has closed his eyes,' says Paul.

Lilly turns to Nina, helpless, 'She just ran in. There's nothing I could've done.'

'Daddy's not dead darling,' says Denise, 'he's away on a business trip. You can't see him!'

'I saw him! He's dead! He's *dead!*' says Alice.

'We always say that children should stay with a relative...' says Paul solemnly.

Denise turns to Paul, her face screwed up in hatred, 'Fluck up Lurch,' she spits.

'Aggghhhh!' Alice is crying now.

'This is so wrong,' says Lilly.

'Look,' says Nina to Lilly, 'can you return to your work please? We'll handle this,' then to Denise, 'Ma'am, please, take your daughter out, and we'll…'

Alice bites Denise, hard—'Aghh! *Shit!*' cries Denise—and then runs. Nina grabs her wriggling little body.

Lilly bends down and speaks to Alice. 'He's dead,' Lilly says. 'Your Daddy is dead, but you can see his body.'

'Lilly!' cries Nina, appalled.

'You… *slag.*' hisses Denise.

Alice kicks Nina, hard, in the shins.

'Ahh! You little *shit!*' Nina winces, holding her leg.

Alice then runs into Paul who rests his huge hand on her head. This has a strange effect on the girl. She stops and looks up at him.

'See what you've done? *See!*' says Denise to Lilly. Her voice, breaking free of her habitual meekness, is ragged.

'I didn't do that,' says Lilly, 'You did. Everyone did.'

Paul gently lifts Alice onto his shoulders and starts jiggling her up and down, making odd soothing noises like he's trying to call a bird down from a tree 'Piripiripiripirir…'

Denise collapses onto the sofa.

'We all die, all of us,' says Lilly, 'And it's always *now*, which is why it's so… It's amazing. It's like no one ever died before. Because… Because…' She turns to Alice, parked high on Paul's shoulders. 'Now, for example, in your belly Alice, there is love for your Daddy and that *is* your Daddy.'

'I'm sorry Lilly,' says Nina, 'but… but… You're *fired!*'

'You're not sorry. You've never been sorry in your life.'

'No! I'm not! You're right… Get out!' The tension in her voice has risen to breaking point. '*Get out! Get out! Get out!* It's all *your* fault. I haven't got a *penny* left. I know *you* took it.'

All the time Paul is making his silly noises and ponying Alice from foot to foot.

'Don't be ridiculous,' says Lilly.

'You're in league with them!'

'Who? What are you talking about?'

Nina grabs her head, 'the Chinese!' she moans.

'Are you out of your mind? I'm not in league with anyone.'

'You are, you are, I know you are, I've got records, videos. And you're a terrible mortician, you shouldn't be around dead people.'

The two women are now almost nose to nose, shouting at each other '*I* shouldn't be around them!' cries Lilly, 'I'm not the one who buried a mannequin because I lost the body!'

Paul looks at Nina, somewhat surprised by this revelation. Denise also stops sobbing and looks up, stunned out of her grief by perplexity.

'Why does it *matter?*' cries Nina, hands out in offended innocence, appealing to them all, 'It's like nuclear deterrence. It doesn't matter if no one actually has any missiles. Perhaps they don't! Nobody even *sees* the bodies anyway! We might as well be burying cats!' Heaving with emotion she collapses onto a chair next to Denise, sobbing. 'Oh God, what's the point? What's the point?' She looks at the others, her face wet, 'what's the *point!?*'

'Piripiripiripirir…,' says Paul and Alice sniffs, then giggles.

₮

Joe isn't sure how long he has been working at LifeLine incorporated. Sometimes it seems like many years, other times like he's only just started, this morning. He isn't sure what his job is either. It is all very vague. He has to contribute somehow, something or other, but it is never really specified what, or how, so he just spends his time opening up spreadsheets, typing random numbers in boxes, opening web pages and copying text into windows. There is always a lot of nothing to do, and Joe always finds a lot time to do it. He likes to watch YouTube videos of children sampling lemons. He likes looking at children because they aren't allowed out anymore and Joe misses them.

There had been an induction of sorts, with CEO Hunter Braff. Hunter had grown even more in stature, every bit the tall, plump well-spoken startup boss. He had learnt how to enter a room, he had dropped his youthful style, no longer embellishing what he said with flamboyant, over-emphatic fillers. He had also aged around the eyes, the heavy-lidded look of the self-regarding Man of Influence was starting to squeeze his eye bags. He had acquired knowledge (he now described himself as a 'Buddhist-Stoic'), he had made money (investing in studio space for immigrants in Margate), he had conquered women and he was often praised by them (although he had to use Viagra from time to time as he occasionally suffered from impotence), but with nothing to him underneath this newly empowered exterior, he was already sinking under its weight, as nothings do.

Relaxed in his immense top-floor office, 'explaining' the company to Joe, it would have been hard for anyone who once knew Hunter to believe it was the same person.

'We curate a certain number of real factories and a certain number of fake factories,' he said, reclining in his large ergonomic chair, 'a certain number of real products and a certain number of fake products, a certain number of real operations, and a certain number of fake operations. What is the difference between real and fake? None. It wouldn't work if there were. There is no difference at all. So how can we speak of either? We can't. Such distinctions are of the past. They are dead. We live now in a world without distinction and limit, without man and woman, without good and bad, without nation and border, without fake and real. It is not fake because it is all happening and everything works. But it is not real because absolutely nothing matters. This is why there is no need to worry, and no need to try. It's a paradise of actual freedom. It's not necessary to intervene in anyone's lives because nothing and nobody is independent, nothing and nobody is separate, and so everything and everyone is managed, everywhere, within and without, immediately, by the very fact of their integration. And when everything is manageable and managed, all theories about management become obsolete. There are no fears, because there is nothing separate from the self, so nothing can possibly threaten the self. There is no desire, because everything is always immediately available. There are no beliefs either, because there is nothing to believe in, there is just this, what is, going on forever and ever. It is Nirvana, and you're at home here because you can't possibly not be. Do you see?'

Joe listened and nodded, because each individual thing that Hunter said made sense, but he had no idea what it meant as a whole thing, except that he didn't really need to know. He just turned on his computer sometimes, and answered emails sometimes, and ate muesli sometimes, and watched videos sometimes. That was alright. Hunter had said that now, with the new decentralised, open-network, peer-to-peer virtual networks and meta-currencies and distributed nodes and converging blockchain autonomies, the super-organism had actually come to be. The next threshold of human liberation had actually been passed. It was the start of Festival Earth; all Joe needed to do was open up his chi. So Joe opened up his chi sometimes, and turned on his computer sometimes, and answered emails sometimes, and ate muesli sometimes, and watched videos sometimes.

He makes his way through the building, up the creamy white stairs, all a-lambent-glow with mysterious light, through sliding doors which, with the voice of Sean Connery or Nicol Williamson, suavely acknowledge the interestingness of his gait, and into an empty meeting room of bean bags, arcade games, rotating barber poles and a huge plastic wombat. On the far wall, on a digital screen, is a complex diagram, very neatly realised, on the top of which is a circle with the words 'actually existing pneuma—active first cause'. This is connected, via various 'karmic command lines' (labelled with words like 'conscious volatility error', 'meta-meta-crises' and 'catastrophic ambiguity-feedback') to a series of labelled shapes (there's a 'reductionist transaction' triangle and an 'interlaced existential risk' rhomboid and a few 'mutualist vortices' spirals) grouped together under an 'illusory matter—passive object' rubric. Most of the lines fork off under labels such as 'epistemic divergence' and 'mutable ontology', but a few converge at what appear to be endpoints; 'game theta vision', 'agile moral clarity' and 'sweetly crying together'.

Rain splatters the high windows; it would be a dark day if not for the bright humming panels of LifeLine's futurelights. There is a constant background high-pitched whine, which can only be heard if you tilt your head in certain specific directions.

Joe sits down and draws on his iPad a bad, but recognisable doodle of a girl. Her face looks determined. She is carrying two large bulky sacks. He doesn't think of this girl, but she keeps appearing to him. Sometimes she is tall and thin and willowy and fair, other times she is short, stout, curvy and dark, but it is the same girl.

The room fills up with people; West, Axton, Bryce, Ames, Bracken, Bear, Noun and Pencil. It's all very casual. Noun is carrying a yard of ale, Bracken is dressed in a romper suit, Pencil has snow globes for ears and Axton is walking sideways, because that's Axton's thing. At the head of the procession, and at the head of the table, is Hunter.

Joe says 'hello' to everyone, but all his hellos are strangely intoned, either sightly doubting, or slightly accusing, or slightly camp, or slightly mechanical; none sound quite right. In any case nobody returns them, in fact nobody acknowledges Joe's presence at all.

Hunter splays his little hands on the desk and starts speaking. He has a way of launching into sentences as if just picking up from a previous conversation. He usually starts with 'so', because he is sure that what he is about to tell you is more remarkable than you expect it to be.

'*So*', he says, 'you need to be an open sensemaker if the sacred is your aim, orienting yourself towards the immutable with an 'exothermic mindset' rather than a 'binary mindset' (which is an instrument of white power and colonial governance) whispering with your daemons, rather than commanding them. You have to be faithful to the conversation, otherwise you'll get wrapped up in completely dysfunctional forms of bypassing, which means examining your maps, dialoguing with them, but not letting your disposition individuate the terrain, which is resonating with all kinds of heterogeneous energy clusters, such as the jealous mother, which is absolutely the worst thing you can ever do.'

Joe looks around. Everyone is listening and nodding with glowing eyes. Joe thinks he must be the stupid one here, but he's fine with that.

'With that in mind,' says Hunter, 'you may have noticed the large animals dotted around the building? The thinking behind that is… It's totally mad, but I think you guys will love it. Baaaasically, you can…'

He opens a door in the back of the wombat and climbs in.

'…get in like this and… It's very comfortable in here, but the important thing is that, well, in this case, it's wombatty. You feel archetypal wombat energy, wombat pnuema. The chi mutualises your consciousness, and, uh…'

He climbs out to murmurs of erotic delight.

'Obviously,' he says, 'we want you to spend at least ten minutes a week inside the animal of your choice? West, what animal would you like to be in?'

'Ooh, the lobster!'

'Great! Why's that?'

'Um, because lobsters are peaceful serious creatures, who are also tough and incisive and a little bit different.'

'Left alone in a tank long enough a lobster will eat itself,' says Joe, but nobody responds.

'What animal would you like to be Joe?' asks Hunter.

'Umm. Are there any vegetables? I'd like to be a potato.'

'Wo…ow! Vegetables? *Amazing* idea Joe. Everyone, let's hear it for Joe.'

Everyone applauds Joe, enthusiastically laughing and smiling, while Joe shrinks further and further into himself. For some reason the applause is worse than the silence.

'Actually Joe,' he says, 'we're thinking of getting you off "ideas" and onto "interface", because our algorithms have determined that you have a particularly agreeable voice. How does that sound?'

'It sounds…' says Joe, 'like, erm, like… like… uh… I don't know. It doesn't sound like anything. You've just asked me to do something…'

'Awesome.' As Joe watches, Hunter's bland fluffy head flickers and shudders, replaced by a weathered, crack-eyed older man with thick grey hair. It is Max's head, grinning at Joe with sardonic delight… but only for an instant.

∞

It is pouring with rain. Thunder rolls in the darkling distance. Lilly is hauling two thick, wet plastic bags down the road, each containing around fifteen severed heads. She has placed the other seventy-odd heads around Edding, on neat garden gates, on car bonnets, on supermarket delicatessen counters, on coffee shop tables, on riverside park benches, anywhere which seemed 'right', leaving behind her a wake of nausea and terror. This was unpleasant, because it's not nice to horrify people, but sometimes it is necessary, and Lilly has decided that it is necessary.

She emptied her bags of heads and then took a bus out towards Glower, the same bus she once took to meet Joe in the winter meadow. It is daytime now, but she can see her reflection in the dark window. She feels like her life is over, even though it never really happened.

She exits the bus in a dank country lane and finds the stile and the path that leads through the fields and meadows. It is still pouring with rain, water runs down her hair, which clings to her face, but it doesn't feel wet. She knows too that she must eat, that she hasn't eaten for a long time, and yet she feels no hunger. Her heart feels wet, her guts, her whole being, is wet bread, a sodden, disintegrating floury substance. She is not sure where she is going, but instinct leads her on past cows and sheep, into woodlands and out again, until, tired and papping wet, she stands at the base of the odd hill that Joe once camped on, that she once had an empty, perfect orgasm on.

Yes, the empty, perfect orgasm, empty of everything, full of nothing. Oh so that's what they mean when they say love is eternal, she had thought then; not that it goes on forever, but that when you experience it, time stops. This is what she thought she had thought, but she has no recollection of what it referred to, which appears unreal, unsettling, creepy; and yet, still, here she is, compelled.

At the top of the hill there is a pit, an empty grave, filling with water. Around the grave, shredded black irises. The immense oak tree, without leaves, stands slick black and dead all over.

Lilly looks down. At her feet is Joe's furry top hat. It seems to emanate something unbearable. She feels dread, the dread of all life. There is something horrible under that hat. Something worse than deadly, some elemental evil, something totally out of place. She wants to run, she wants to be away from here, but she has to know. She has to know what the evil is, because whatever it is, under the furry hat, must be faced.

She crouches down and picks up the hat. *She* is afraid, yet, as she takes the hat, and sees what is under it, *she* sees her body moving backwards, repulsed. It is a dead bird, a crow, its head unnaturally twisted, its wings broken, its belly busted open. It is unreasonably horrible, far worse than it seems. Her body has backed away and is against the tree, when a second crow flaps down, lands on the dead bird and starts picking at it, pulling rotten meat off of it.

Lilly watches horrified, but as if hypnotised, taken by the terrible event. The living crow eating the dead crow, a mesmerising, sickening world of meat.

The horror of it is dissolving in the actuality of the event. That it is happening, that she is completely immersed in its happening, is easing her disgust, which is separated from actuality by the width of a moth wing. Then a peculiar thought occurs to her.

She thinks 'I too must eat the dead crow. This is how I must rejoin the world, this is what we will all have to do, eat the rotting meat of the world.' It is, she is suddenly convinced, a kind of cosmic test, to access a new world.

She realises she is still holding the top hat. She puts it on and approaches the feeding crow which hops lopingly away from the corpse, sideways looking, suspicious. She kneels down at the destructed bird. Her old self is asking what she is doing, but she knows what she is doing. She pulls a piece of flesh from the craw of the bird, picks off the feathers and looks at the rain-glistened, dark-rotted meat. Tears roll down her cheeks. It is a world of meat, all meat, nauseating flesh eating flesh. That's it. She groans, shivering, then puts the dead animal in her mouth.

∞

Joe walks around the building. Some people are still working, some are drinking, there is a fancy-dress party in one large room. Young people dressed as mummies, cartoon characters, prophets and pirates fall about, slobbering, kissing, humping. They are all sex-positive, talking about sex, feeling each other up, popping off for a casual shag in the copulation booths, while, at the same time, being strangely prudish about the actual facts of the event. Joe's attempts at 'risqué' comments go down very badly. Bear once said to him 'See you later alligator', and Joe replied 'in a while paedophile', and Bear looked at him in blank, threatened confusion. Another time Joe was asked to invent a symbol that represents God and he drew a stylised vagina which made everyone round the tolerance table want to kill him.

Nothing he says quite fits, nothing quite 'gells', although it is impossible to know if they are hearing what he is saying or an algorithm-determined mind edit. Not long ago he asked Stim and Rogue how to define 'woman', and Stim said 'The stranger officiates the meal' and Rogue said 'Can't find the object'. It sometimes seems as if anything which may be inappropriate never even reaches their ears, although other times Joe has the feeling that they are all plotting to throw him from the roof, in a tolerant and inclusive manner.

He wanders around the building. Nobody pays any attention to him. He drifts past them, or over them or under them, sorrowfully. He trips over his undone laces, bangs his head, fumbles and shuffles about, but nobody gives him a second look. He might as well not be here, but then he might as well not not be here either.

He goes to a vending machine, searches the contents, sighs and chooses an 'Enceladus Water' (*Culled from the moons of Saturn*' says the machine, in the voice of Ian Holm) and a 'Grass Bar'. A notice board, registering his presence, starts speaking, in a laconic Staffordshire drawl which Joe does not recognise; *'Did you unvalidate a menstruator today?' 'Smelling someone? Get consent!'* As he listens to the unsettling, unknown voice, Joe hears something else, something out of place. He looks down to where the sound is coming from. A panel behind the vending machine is open. He gets down to his knees. He can hear snatches of a song, very distant, a jaunty string-backed bass. The melody, the tone, is one with a feeling of long, long ago, when Joe was young, but it is a feeling that, back then, he never knew, because it was the whole of his life, the scent of time itself, his time. More vivid than any adult mood, yet never brought to mind; only now, in the intimacy of nostalgia, is it realised, as a thing, but the thing is now separate from the feeling, distant, and the distance is pain.

He wants to hear the song more clearly. He pulls the heavy vending machine away and squeezes into the narrow, steel chute. It is dark, and warmly damp, but there is a ribbon of light up ahead, a crack. The walls of the cramped tunnel become rough, muddy, but as he pulls himself towards the light, and the beguiling music, they dry out, and the space opens up, so he can get on his knees, then squat, then finally walk. The music now is loud. Grace Jones is singing Send in the Clowns, *'Isn't it bliss? don't you approve? One who keeps tearing around, One who can't move, Where are the clowns?'*

Something brushes against his face. Joe recoils and reaches out; but it is just fabric. A coat. He is in a wardrobe, and the crack of light before him is the door. He pushes it and winces against the light, blundering into a bedroom. When his eyes adjust he realises he knows this room, it is the bedroom he grew up in. On the wall are pictures of kestrels and eagles. Grace Jones sings through a radio, *'Don't you love farce? My fault I fear, I thought that you'd want what I want, Sorry my dear.'*

On the bed, peering up with all the matter-of-fact courage of a child, is Joe himself, aged twelve. Joe remembers this moment, he remembers listening to the radio and enjoying the music, but he doesn't remember his older self stumbling out of the wardrobe, this part seems new.

There's a long pause, which coincides with the long instrumental section in the middle of the song. Joe feels he should give his young self a message, some advice, something of the future. Young Joe looks intently at old Joe, expectantly. Young Joe knows that this is his future self come to deliver a message to him. Old Joe can only think of one message he can give; he sadly and slowly shakes his head.

And then he turns and leaves.

∞

'Er, hello,' says Neil, disoriented. Omana's Olympian grandeur has stilled him somewhat, but he feels drained and wired. His body is still scalded and flayed, his clothes stained with blood. He is out of place in the impeccable green of the impeccable garden.

'How was your journey?' asks Omana, with cool grace.

'I… I don't quite remember…' says Neil, searching for the past but finding nothing but the present, 'I think…'

'Don't worry Neil, it will come back to you. It will all come back to you,' says Omana with a reassuring look in her pale blue eyes.

'Okay.'

'You're looking a bit anxious, would you like a hug?' she asks.

'Oh yes please.'

They embrace. Omana pushes her body against Neil, enveloping him, but she seems very hard, unyielding. Neil has the feeling that it is not quite a human being against him.

She pulls away, unstained from his blood. 'Is that better?' she asks.

'Yes, that's much better, thank you…' Neil says, feeling nothing, but wanting to be polite. 'I feel…'

'Sky blue?'

'Oh yes, sky blue, that's right, I do,' he lies.

'That's good. That's good.'

Neil isn't sure what to say. He feels awkward in the pause, while Omana continues to gaze beatifically into the middle distance.

Finally her eyes glide back down to his. She speaks, but as if through him; 'What do you want Neil?'

'Want? I don't know. Actually, I don't feel very well.' He knows he should be in more pain, but his broken bones and scourged skin are more uncomfortable than painful. It is difficult to speak. His jaw isn't moving properly.

'Do you want to be healthy, safe and comfortable?'

'Yes, I do,' says Neil.

'And do you want to be useful, and to belong?'

'I'd like that too, very much.'

'Then follow me.'

She turns and leads Neil up the hill towards the mansion. Neil, crippled, follows her with difficulty. Sometimes a savage, yet curiously faraway agony shoots through his body and he stops, until it has subsided again to background discomfort.

They enter the stately home and Neil forgets his bleeding, broken body, for it is wondrous magical, and oddly familiar. Rooms bright with gold, Watteau landscapes, Hepplewhite furniture, peacocks wandering through the atrium, beautiful people gliding through the halls, friendly happy folk, many of whom are famous, eat celery and blow rose petals around the dining rooms. It is a place of calm and learning and refined joy. It's nice.

Omana leads him into a conservatory, bright, warm and welcoming. The Marvellous Ones sit around talking and politely laughing. It's all very nineteen twenties, thinks Neil, noting the flowy dresses and boyish bob cuts. Is that Zendaya?

'Take a seat,' says Omana, gesturing to an elegant table and chair set of bamboo and stained glass next to which is what looks like a rubber mat, an oxygen tank and a mask. On the table is an onion on a chopping board and a knife.

'Now,' says Omana seating herself opposite him, 'I don't want you to think of this is an interview.'

'I wasn't,' says Neil, who now thinks of it as an interview.

'Good, I'm just going to ask you to carry out a few basic tasks, make sure you're up to scratch so to speak. Then you'll be able to join us. Okay?'

'Okay then,' says Neil. He very much wants to join these people. They look so calm, so purposeful, so very much together.

'Good. Now, see that bodysuit there,' she points to what Neil had thought was a rubber sheet, but can now see has an opening at one end.

'I want you to get into it,' says Omana. 'Can you do that for me? Can you?'

'Erm, I'm not… sure.'

'It's perfectly safe. I'm a doctor.'

'Errr…'

'We're all highly qualified here,' says Omana, 'there's nothing to worry about. It's all quite normal.'

'Oh well, if you're qualified…' Neil doubtfully and with difficulty squats down next to the rubber material. It is brown and blue and very thick.

'But why?' he says.

'Don't worry about that,' says Omana, 'it's a test. To see if you can do the job.'

'But nobody else here is wearing one of these.'

'Neil, do stop worrying. You won't be wearing one when you're working. We just need to see that you can wear one. We've all put one on haven't we?' she says, turning to some nearby diners, who nod.

Everything does seem normal, thinks Neil, *and* safe. These people aren't street hucksters, after all. They wouldn't lie about something like this.

'Alright,' he says and starts pulling on the sheath.

'No, no, take your clothes off first,' says Omana, 'or you won't get in.'

Neil again hits a hurdle of doubt, but again Omana and her friendly friends smooth it down with soothing reassurances. He removes his clothes, much of which are little more than crispy flakes anyway, until his broken body is again naked. Nobody seems particularly disgusted or surprised, although a few people seem to be suppressing a smile, but that's to be expected; 'I probably do look a bit strange,' thinks Neil as he pulls the tight rubber up his body, scraping off charred slivers of his skin as he goes. It's not unlike a luge suit, except the top end, which has a kind of ruff round the neck. Because there are no arm holes, Omana helps him and pulls the head part tight over his scorched cranium, then she picks up the mouthpiece of the gas canister and opens the valve.

'What's that?' Neil, now on the floor, looks like an Elizabethan nematode.

'It's a mixture of helium and nitrous oxide.'

'Laughing gas?'

'Yes, kind of, it will give you a bit of pep.'

'No, I don't need tha...' but before he can speak she has aggressively thrust the hissing tube into his mouth. Neil resists, but there's nothing he can do, bound as he is by thick rubber. He struggles, *'mmmmm... mmmmmm...'* but his struggles soon turn to manic high-pitched laughter.

Omana stands up, her face now cruelly triumphant. 'Now, Neil, tell us how to make an omelette.'

'*Hahaha… aahhh… hehehehe… heat up some oihhhhh… ahhh…*'

As Neil jerks around, shrieking with falsetto laughter, breathlessly trying to explain how to make an omelette, and as Omana occasionally bends down to fill him again with the voice-box squeezing laughing gas, the various diners and brunchers of the large conservatory gather round, their glittering eyes a mixture of disgust, blank satisfaction and hard, bored, sadistic enjoyment. Sometimes Omana rubs onion into Neil's eyes, to 'weep him up a bit' as he splutters and convulses his way through the recipe. Neil knows it is wrong, he feels disgusted and wretched, but some bizarre momentum, perhaps hope, keeps him going.

Finally it is over. The audience drifts back to their tables and Omana peels off the bodysuit. A waiter comes over with a pair of workman's dungarees which Neil struggles to put on. He sits again at Omana's table looking like a post-apocalyptic keyboardist for Dexys Midnight Runners.

'That was very good,' says Omana smiling. 'I have to say you've more than exceeded my expectations. I'd normally say that we'd let you know and all of that, but well,' she leans forward with a cheeky, conspiratorial half-smile, 'I'd like to offer you a position right now.'

'Oh. Really?'

'I mean you can have some time to think about it.'

'No, no, please… yes, I accept.'

'Good. Now, I have to say, it does mean, working and living here, that you'll have to adapt to our way of doing things. Do you think that will be okay?'

'Yes, I can't see a problem,' says Neil, feeling much more comfortable now, leaning back in his chair. 'I might have a glass of wine,' he thinks.

'What I mean is,' says Omana, 'is that, if you want the job, you'll have to replace your head with a large hard-boiled egg.'

'Sorry?'

'A big boiled egg.'

'A boiled egg?'

'Yes, it's quite alright, that's the way it is these days. You understand. It's quite necessary. That's why we ask for flexibility. You *are* flexible aren't you?'

'I suppose I are.'

'I thought so.'

'But...' Neil looks around at the diners.

'Why does nobody have a boiled egg for a head? That's what you're thinking. It's a temporary thing. A training wheel, if you like. You only have to wear it for a few weeks.'

There is a long pause. Omana watches Neil, her clear blue eyes revealing nothing. Neil doesn't want a large hard-boiled egg for a head, but if it's quite necessary, and if it's just for a few weeks, why not? Agreeing was obviously the only way out of here, or rather *into* here, into this lovely party, with these important people. If I join them, I'll be alright. That's how it has always worked. Obey your way to freedom.

'Alright then,' he says.

'Wonderful, let's get to it,' she says and stands up.

Neil doubts. He can feel the doubt inside him like a kind of indigestion, like something that won't 'go down'. His head says it will all probably be okay, and he has always followed his head. But how has that worked out?

The two of them walk through the conservatory and back into the main hall, Omana serene, Neil gently anxious, looking around but not really seeing anything. At the far end of the hall they reach a narrow staircase leading downwards. Omana goes down and Neil follows, descending into a warren of stone corridors and brick rooms, more ordinary than those above—living rooms, offices, kitchens and suchlike workplaces. It is full of people, coming and going, sitting at desks, carrying trays of food, bustling past with trowels and hammers; most with large boiled-egg heads. Omana still glides blithely along, followed by Neil, confused, fear gathering and knitting, until they reach another stairwell, this one narrower, steeper and darker than the last. Again they descend.

They are now walking through a series of half-built modern office hallways of plywood and pressboard. People, half seen through dirty plastic sheeting look anguished, harried and sick. They all have big boiled-egg heads, but very pale ones, some cracked and kind of burnt looking. It is also cold down here, and there is no natural light.

Omana leads Neil up to a very small door which opens into a small, featureless, windowless office. There is a chipboard desk and a flimsy plastic garden chair in the middle of the room with a very large plasma screen hanging against the wall opposite. It's a sixty-five inch Philips 770OLED806.

'This is where you'll be working Neil,' says Omana, gesturing in the room. Neil hesitates to enter. The teevee is pretty cool, but it doesn't look very homely.

'But, erm, I don't th-i-ink… I want to work in there. I… Could I not work upstairs?' he says, very quietly.

'Sorry Neil, all the upstairs jobs are taken, but if you work hard, you'll reach the top eventually. It's like the trolley problem, do you know that? There's a trolley coming down the tracks and it's running over people who are tied to the track, cutting them to pieces and you're in control of a lever which can stop the trolley, but if you do, you disrupt the transport system, the whole city in fact, everything gets disjointed. Chaos. You know what chaos means. On the one side, yes, people are dying as the trolley ploughs into them, on the other hand, what about the freedom of the people to lie on the track? What about all the people who worked hard to get run over in the past? And anyway, if you lie down enthusiastically enough in front of the trolley, we'll let you into it eventually. Do you see?'

'But how long will that take?'

'That depends on you, doesn't it?' It all seems so plausible. There is an air of inevitability about everything here. Omana has total confidence in her role, in the mansion, in what is happening. It is impossible to doubt her.

'Does it?' says Neil, very quietly.

'Come along Neil. In you go,' she says, with all the reassuring calm of a consummate professional.

'But...'

'Look, if you go in, you can have this.' She pulls a small rubber pellet out of her dress, about the size of a tangerine.

'What's this?' asks Neil.

Omana looks at it, 'it's a little bit of rubber.'

'What's it for?'

'I don't know. Do you want it? There's a bit of steel on the end.'

'Alright.'

She hands it over. Neil looks at it. It feels quite nice, sort of hand-shaped, and the steel nub is very shiny.

'So what do you say?' asks Omana.

'And I won't be down here long?'

'No, no, not long at all.'

Neil looks at the rubber thing, then at the screen. He thinks for a bit, and his thoughts present the right thing to do. 'Okay, yes, yes; I'll do it.'

'Good boy. In you go.'

Neil walks in and Omana closes and locks the door. Neil returns to the door and speaks through the window.

'Do you have to lock me in?' he asks.

'Yes, I'm afraid so,' says Omana, voice muffled, 'it's for your own good.'

'But what if I need the toilet?'

'You won't need the toilet.'

'But what about...'

But she has gone.

Neil inspects his new 'workplace.' It is small and draughty. The seat is made of very flimsy plastic, which buckles slightly at one leg when he sits on it. He stands up and walks over to the screen. He can see himself in the dark mirror. His head is a large, whitish egg.

Margaret looks like she has aged ten years. She is half herself, lying in a bed that seems to be swallowing her up. The hospice room, a standard, clinical private bedroom, contains a few of her knick-knacks; a signed photograph of Wilhelm Furtwängler, a Roy Andersson DVD and a small, ivory skull; a medieval memento mori.

Sitting next to Margaret is a young female nurse, Keira. She is checking her phone, looking at her watch, making big bored sighs, not understanding why this mad old cow won't just die, or at least go to sleep. Honestly, thinks Keira, they're worse than children, these skeletons; putting them in bed is like injecting them with amphetamine, except kids can't pull that damned call-cord.

Through the walls comes the angry voice of an old man shouting 'You're all *bastards*. I'm not scared of you. *Bastards*, I say, I say; *bastards!* It's a world of bastards, this. A world built *by* bastards, *for* bastards, out of *pure bastardy.*' It's old William, who kicks up a fuss about his pills and refuses to put on his hazmat suit when visitors come in. People like that are so fucking selfish.

'Nelly,' says Keira, continuing the 'conversation' she has been having with Margaret, which entails describing all the things which annoy her, Keira, while Margaret lays in drifting, exhausted confusion, '*Nelly*,' Keira says again, with the stress of annoyance, 'down on the Karnak ward. You *must* know, always pulling that disgusting, slobbering face. You *must* know. Nelly. *Nelly.*'

Margaret pays no attention to Keira. She stares instead at the bedside lamp on the bedside table, her head sideways fallen on her pillow, her eyes like boiled sweets, dropped in the gutter.

'Well her,' says Keira with a big huffy sigh, 'She was getting undressed for bed, and her legs are *so* fucking hairy. They're like *dog's* legs. I know she's off her trolley and about to die, but still, it was a real shock. There's no need to let yourself go is there? Just 'cos you're dying? I wouldn't.' Keira sniffs the air, 'What's that smell?'

'That cabinet,' says Margaret without turning her head.

Keira wrinkles up her nose.

'It stinks of cabinets in here,' says Margaret quietly.

William's voice again can be heard through the wall, 'Is there one *cunt* on this miserable fucking *rock* who isn't out for his *bastard self*?'

The door opens and Dr. Tom appears. He has not changed, and he will never change. He is the man he was at fifteen and he will die the same man at seventy-five, the only difference being the energy he has poured into his career has leaked away, and now he acts and speaks at forty beats-per-minute.

'Hello Doctor,' says Margaret not turning her head, 'How's your husband?'

'Fine,' he says, incapable of surprise, 'And how are you today Mrs. Geb?'

'I am very nearly dead,' says Margaret.

'Oh come on Mrs. Geb!' he says with mechanical joviality, 'I know you've got some fight left in you yet! Would you like to watch a *little bit* of television?' he asks, condescendingly bending forward as he says 'little bit' and raising his eyebrows, as if talking to a baby.

This was Joe's mother. The fact pleased Tom. While the professional in him, the outer man, treated her just like every other client in Greyhive Hospice, as a threat to the living and as a human tragedy which needs to be rescued from death, the inner man rejoiced at inflicting vicarious torture on The Feckless One.

Margaret reaches forward and, inexplicably, puts her arms around the base of the lamp.

Tom sighs and looks at his watch and Keira, who is now seated on the chair next to door, gets her phone out.

'Well, I'm *sure* Fifteen to One is on,' says Tom, looking around for the television remote control, then spotting it; it is next to the lamp. 'Can I… Do you mind…?' He says, approaching the bedside table.

'No!' says Margaret, with surprising energy, 'You are *not* to come here.'

He steps back, just as Keira stands up; she is staring at her phone. 'What the *fuck* is this?' she says. Neil, boiled-egged in his little pasteboard room, is dancing up and down on her screen.

'Please Keira! Language!' says Tom, tightly.

Neil's tinny trapped voice comes from the phone; 'I don't know.'

'Who the fuck are you?' says Keira.

'I'm Neil Geb.'

'Keira!' says Tom sternly, '*could* you leave the room to talk on your phone?'

'Neil?' says Margaret.

'Mother?' Neil's voice echoes out of the little phone speaker.

'Neil?' Margaret is looking around, trying to locate her son.

Keira, annoyed and somewhat freaked out starts stabbing at the off button, but it doesn't seem to be doing anything. 'Mother, where are you?' cries Neil.

'Neil, help me, please help me out of here,' says Margaret, sitting up now, tears standing in her eyes.

'Keira, get out of here *now*,' says Tom, 'get out. You're distressing Mrs. Geb. Get help.'

'Neil!' cries Margaret.

'Mother!'

Keira leaves and Tom approaches Margaret. 'Now, now, Mrs. Geb, calm down. We'll just get something to calm you down. Don't worry.'

William's voice, broken with force, evidently being restrained by several people, cuts now, fragmented, through the wall, 'I'm a cunt too!'

∞

The screen goes blank. Neil looks at his phone. I have to get to her, he thinks, but how? Where is she? Is she in this building? What is this building, and… what am I doing here? Work? But what kind of work? There are no instructions, no training, no management; there's not even a keyboard, just a satisfying rubber pellet. And my head is a hard-boiled egg.

Neil sits down to think. He leans on the table. It is made of the same cheap material as everything else. He looks more closely. It is strange, because as his head gets closer to the grain it doesn't become finer. It gets blurred, as if it has only one state of complexity. He sits up again. Something is wrong. He turns round and looks at the ceiling light, a glowing uniform orb, then back at the table, then back at the orb, then the table again.

He thinks, and continues thinking.

After some time, the screen flicks on again.

∽

Thundering torrents of rain sweep across the black meadow, exploding in white-hot sheets of lightning. Lilly is clinging to the dead tree. She felt sick after eating the crow, but the sickness passed. Then she felt a weird ecstatic misery, a need to expire into the earth. She wanted to fall into the fresh grave, but instead she threw her arms around the dead tree and wept her heart out.

The same feeling she felt with Joe is here again, the same annihilating power, even in the midst of this strange agony. It's not love, or ecstasy, or bliss, or enlightenment or anything at all; it's horrible, it's nothing she would ever choose and yet, and yet, Lilly wants only this. The storm rushes through her, torrents of rainwater, vast pneumatic waves smashing the hill and the tree and little Lilly clinging to it; and she wants only this. She'll die, perhaps, but at least she'll die alive, in the body.

Yes, the body! It is all just the body, that is the only thing there is. There are things that happen, there are thoughts and feelings, but really, actually, *there is only the body*. With calamitous lucidity she wordlessly, thoughtlessly, knows that she's only ever really had an idea of the body, an idea that the world has made her live, the body as a thing, as an object, as *my* object, ugly or beautiful—all *nonsense!* The thing is not the thing at all! It is mad to her mind, but so clear to her legs and belly and throat. Feelings are nothing, the body is a deathless everything, the body knows everything, the body *is*, and it is all there ever is.

Something moves around her and she twists her face to look up, so wet now she may as well be underwater, looking out of a dark pool at a firestorm. Swaying above her, hanging from the immense tree, are dead bodies. The one before her is Paisley Mass. She steps back. Susan Dodsworth is there, and Rab Currie, Gail Dillon, John Mattingley, Lawrence Moor, A.J. Hendricks, Jeanne Campos, Denitsa Minerva, Ken Moffat, Jacob Kindred, Kate Lloyd… all the people she has dressed and cremated, embalmed and buried. All of them are hanging from the tree, laughing at her in the howling thunder, hundreds of laughing corpses; and she is laughing back at them. A ruptured sense of mania surges up her spine, the world is mad, mad, butcherously mad and she is mad with it, Lilly and the body of death, one.

Someone is coming, a small, smudged group of people trudging with effort across the grey, sodden meadows, carrying something. Their heads are down, they are pushing against the storm, which obscures them with sheets of rain. Lilly wipes her eyes clear. She first recognises the figure at the back; squat Carl, who appears to be dressed in a tight-fitting tunic and tights. In front of him are the six Indian bearers, holding up an ornate coffin and at the head of the small procession, a stout Indian woman. Meera.

The group heave up the hill. When they reach the top, they acknowledge Lilly's presence as best they can—sideways through the glancing floods—they pass her and then lay the coffin, which is covered in a heavy madder-dyed pall, next to the empty grave. All are drenched. Lightning strikes again and again, deafening thunder only a second away now, the mourners' faces unreal in the stark electricity.

'What are *you* doing here?' Carl shouts to Lilly.

'I wanted to be near this tree!'

'Why!?'

'It's the only thing I love that's still alive!'

'Oh my darling,' cries Meera, 'you're soaking, here, here…' she turns to one of her sons, Sajid, '…take the pall, take the pall' she commands, 'Give, give…'

Sajid pulls the beautiful pall, decorated with happy images of a dancing Kali, from the coffin and wraps it round Lilly's shoulders. The coffin, Lilly sees, is actually the beautiful fridge she found Victor in.

'Thank you,' she shouts 'What… What are you doing?'

'We are laying to rest the prince of love,' cries Sajid, magnificently. He rejoins his brothers. The men take the fridge, which has knotted ropes at each corner, and begin lowering the bulky white mass into the grave.

'Why are *you* here?' Lilly shouts to Carl. It's odd though, because he's the one thing here which doesn't look out of place.

Carl, face flushed and joyous, shouts back to her through the storm; 'These are my people! These are my people!'

Lilly feels like crying. Her mind is not sure why. But the vast, immense, wonderful plasma of love in her breast, is sure.

The coffin hits the sodden bottom of the grave and the pall bearers stand up. Meera takes her place at the head of the grave and starts speaking, her strong voice strangely clear in the pounding, hissing rain and deafening, skull-rattling thunder.

'Sometimes,' she cries, 'Victor ate my brain! Sometimes he sat on my head. But I always loved him. I am loving him from the first moment I heard him sing. He was the firefly in the ointment. Not a troublemaker, but a lover, a lover of the beat and the rhythm and the drums. The first thing he said to me was "boom boom shhssh shhssh, kerboom, kerboom." That was his language! Many times we shared, many good and gorgeous times in the park. We stole banjos and danced naked in the park. Yes, the people always were saying "can you keep it down, Victor? Can you keep the volume down?" And all he would say is "आग बुझ जाती है लेकनि कभी ठंडी नही होती।"'

With this she throws her arms into the sky, her sodden face turned towards the detonating heavens, and cries out, 'Oh Victor!

Victor! Thou art the winter god of the lands below, ever dying and ever reborn, the honey of the world, the lettuce and the lamb, the stepladder and the swinging basket. Thou art the white crown, the human-headed balance, the dancing one-of-three. Victor, my Banebdjedet, come to your mother Meera, come to your dandelion girl, your garden gopi, your mound of wheat, your two fawns, for she sings to you, come…!'

And Meera sings.

∞

Joe wanders into a smooth-cornered, high-concept high-tech dorm. Various youngbodies are slouching around, sleeping, texting. Joe lies down, fully dressed, fully awake, dread and anxiety stretched across his sleepless face. He can hear West and Noun talking in a nearby bunk.

'You look like a peanut,' says West.

'I *feel* like a peanut!' says Noun.

'Oh my God what does a peanut feel like?'

'Take a feel! Hahahahaha!'

'Hahahahaha!'

They go quiet. Joe hears slurping sounds. He closes his eyes. They are humping. They all have casual sex about once a month. They don't have relationships—'everyone belongs to everyone else'—and if Joe mentions any words like 'commitment' or 'love' or 'passion' they look at him with merry derision. Sex is a packet of crisps.

Joe gets up and returns to 'work.' He sits at a corner table in the open plan office and opens his tablet. He is surprised to see on his screen, a man with a large boiled egg as a head.

'Joe?' says the egg-man.

'Yes.'

'It's me, Neil.'

'Neil?'

'Yes, my head is an egg.'

'Is it?'

'Yes.'

'Neil…' says Joe, aimlessly.

'Don't you find it strange?'

'Erm, no. Not really. What?'

'Don't you find any of this strange?'

'Strange?'

'Do you remember me having a head like this?' says Neil pointing to the faceless, featureless ovoid on his shoulders.

Joe looks, and thinks. 'No, I can't say I do,' he says.

'What about this, talking to me, your brother, the person who hates you most in the world, do you remember doing much of that before?'

'Come to think of it… no, I don't.'

'Do you remember anything?'

'Erm…' Joe thinks. 'Not very much. I remember you getting stuck in the ticket barriers that time.'

'Fucking typical. Is that it?'

'Yep. That's everything.'

'What about your shadow?'

'My shadow?'

'Take a look. Do you have one?'

Joe holds his hand over the table. A faint shade is thrown by his large hand.

'Yes, a bit.'

'Keep looking at it.'

Joe bends closer to his hand, to look at the outline. It starts shuddering and skipping around. He turns to the office lighting—the glowing panels in the ceiling—but they are not moving. He turns back to his hand. Now the shadow is gone. Now it's back. Now it's talon-like. Now it's small and slender, like a child's hand.

'You see?' says Neil.

'That *is* peculiar,' says Joe.

'Isn't *everything* peculiar?' asks Neil. 'Think about it.'

'But that's just it,' says Joe, 'everything here is really, really normal. It's always been normal.'

'What about at home?'

'Home?'

'Yes, with Maria.'

'Maria?'

'Maria! Your woman!'

Joe thinks. The name sounds familiar.

'Nope,' he says finally, 'nothing.'

'Alright, alright. Tell me something you didn't do yesterday?'

'Yesterday?'

'The day before today.'

'It's always been today.'

'Always?'

'Yes, it's always been today. I've always been here, and I appreciate that.'

Neil stops, gathers up, takes another tack. 'Alright,' he says, 'tell me something you didn't do before you spoke to me.'

'Eughhh… *Didn't* do?'

'Yes, something you *didn't* do.'

'But… there are lots of things I didn't do.'

'For example?'

'I… erm… I didn't go to the beach. I didn't watch a James Bond movie, I didn't have a flapjack…'

'What? This isn't you. What about… What about… being the president of Poland… have you done that today?'

'*What* are you talking about?'

'Okay, okay, tell me what you'd do if you had to spend a year with the Queen of England?' Neil has no face, but his body is shoulder-forward, chin-jutting, expressively pleading.

'I…I just don't know,' says Joe, the vaguest most distant hint of annoyance now in his voice. 'It's not realistic.'

'Big old road trip around the States?' says Neil. His voice is now edged with frantic despair.

'Why are you asking me these stupid questions…?'

'Hang on,' says Neil, tone dropping, 'Why is the air outside pink like that?' He is looking past Joe to the window behind him. Joe, almost instinctively, has moved now to a ledge against the side of the long room. He feels that nobody should see this conversation. It's dangerous.

'Oh that's… uh… I can't remember.'

'And isn't *that* weird?'

'No. It's been… It's all been explained… I think… Uh…'

'Joe, listen to me. We're in some kind of… I don't know what it is. It's like a dream because everything seems normal in it, no matter how strange, and everything is always shifting around, nothing static, and then suddenly ordinary things are incredibly scary for no reason. It's like a dream, but it can't *be* a dream, because it's a collective dream. I'm talking to you, and you're not me. So I thought, maybe it's some kind of virtual reality, because everything is kind of crude in here, nothing is sharp and real seeming, it's all got that freakish ugliness of a computer game, but it can't be a game, because we'd remember playing it, wouldn't we? And there would be a point, wouldn't there, or an off button or something… And surely technology isn't *this* good is it? I don't remember it getting this good. And also, even though it's all weird, it all *really matters*, and nothing matters in a game. So then I thought, well we must be dead then. This is death, this is actually it, but that can't be right either because I'm alive. I've got thoughts, the ones I had in my living brain, and there's no God here, and no Jesus and no nirvana and no oblivion either, it's just all this *rigmarole*. What kind of death is that? And then there's the past… I know it's there, it happened, but what… It's as if we're nowhere… in this frozen now…'

While Neil is speaking, Joe feels himself getting tighter and tighter, more and more fearful of being. His eyes flick nervously around the room, losing the thread of what Neil is saying, then catching the drift again, but skidding off it.

'Are you listening to me?' says Neil.

'Yes, yes, but I don't understand. How did all this happen?'

'I don't know, but I think it has something to do with the eggshell, because there's nothing in here, it's all shell, we've become all shell, our shells are overgrown. Do you know what I mean? Doesn't it all feel like the outside, all outlook; no inside, no inlook? Like a two-dimensional topological overlay, but underneath there's just nothing. It's all surface, because the surface has taken over, so we're stretched out over the outside edge. Look at me, I'm not in a room, I'm on a screen, and the screen is all there is, there's no outside and no inside. It's like, it's like… Joe? Joe…?' There is despair in Neil's voice. 'Are you paying attention to anything I'm saying?'

'Wow,' says Joe. He was trying to take it in, but again he'd lost the thread of the story after the first sentence. After that, it just sounded like a madman raving, which was kind of funny, but there wasn't any content to it. By the time Neil got to the end all Joe understood was 'we're insane,' and that wasn't right because he'd never felt more normal and ordinary.

'…okay, look, look, forget about all that, it doesn't matter,' says Neil, seeming to regret everything he's just said.

'What doesn't matter?' asks Joe, 'What are you talking about? Who are you?'

'Neil, It's Neil!'

'But how do I know? You could be anyone,' says Joe, now deeply suspicious, and feeling stupid. Of course! Another scam! We're always being warned of these things.

'…but it doesn't ma…' says Neil, his voice cracking '…the only thing that matters, listen to me, the only thing that I actually know for… is that Mum is here and you're here and… and… I love you and I want to be with you and I don't care where I am if I'm with Mum and… you and… Joe… Joe…' Neil is cracking up; literally, his voice and his egg, 'Even if we're trapped together that's o… Joey… Mumsy… my, you remem… ber her? The great honker? You rem… how mu… you love her? You… *you* loved her, all… years, and… Joe? Joe? She's in trou… Please Joe, we've… to find her. Plea… Joe…'

Neil is silent. His egg head is convulsing. Joe hears the sound of sobbing. The egg is crying. 'I need love… I need love,' Neil says softly, almost to himself, as if realising it for the first time, 'We all… But I'm ashamed… of needing it. I don't… know why. I'm just… a ch… a stupi… child…'

Neil's head is now riven with cracks. His voice is coming through like gravel clattering on a window.

'*J… le… es… ca… J… wa… yo… ant?*'

'I don't know. It seems… I'm not sure.'

Neil's head is now a chaotic mess, as is his voice. But just before the screen winks off, blank, one word slips through, clear. '*…stop!*'

Joe stares into the dead tablet screen, darkly reflecting the office; but without Joe. His own reflection is not there, just the room. He turns, and then back to the screen. He is not there.

It is strange, it is terribly strange. No shadow, no reflection. Joe feels he should go to the toilet and look in the mirror there, but he has the future of work to do, harvesting brain activity, and strange things are dangerous and anyway they've been discredited.

He sits at a desk, surrounded by a few young people. He listens to their business speech, their cheerless rattling laughter. They are strange too, in their ordinariness. Have there always been such diluted people, about whom nothing can be said to bring them into distinctness, or is this how people really are? Am I too a bag of distilled water?

The question brings tension, it seems to tap at something locked away in the basement, or something locked away is tapping on a trapdoor and the tension is Joe, who is sitting on it; because he does not want to disrupt the world, because disruption leads to ostracism and exclusion—bank accounts freeze, connections go down, entry systems lock up and suddenly all those friendly, friendly people turn out to not be so friendly any more—and exclusion is loneliness and death, but then this, this life, is loneliness and death too, in some other way.

No, don't think about it. Don't think about the ordinary. Don't think about the man with the egg. That was odd though wasn't it? Must be some brain malfunction, systems misaligned… But don't think about it. Have a sweet, milky coffee and relax on a luxury bean bag meditating to chillaxing music. This is the way to deal with tension and fear. He gets up again and wanders through the food station—picking up a banana—to one of the Peace Pods, in which people curl up in plastic animals or lounge around on soft pink furry belly-bags, with immense German headphones clamped to their heads, beatific smiles on their faces. Joe joins them, puts on a pair of headphones, climbs into a hollow baboon, and lets his mind drift into ambient loveliness.

ॐ

Neil is hideously crippled, bony shards from his hapless, splintered head are scattered on the dusty concrete floor, his cracked frame leans against the wall. He has to find a way to Margaret and Joe, he has to. He can feel that, between the three of them, there is nothing but a film, a skin, drawn over what appears to be an unimaginable distance, but is actually closer to him than his own body. Or perhaps it is his own body.

He drags himself over to the door and begins banging on it, shouting; 'Hey!? Hello!? Hello!?' He has to stop to gather his breath; his lungs have been punctured by his broken ribs and his arms are so weak they can hardly lift themselves.

There is no response, so he bangs again, and again, crying out, 'Is anyone there!? Please?' He thinks to himself he's going to keep making a racket until someone hears, something has to hear; but then the door opens and he falls into the corridor, a bloody heap of rag and bone, at the feet of two egg people, who look down on him, their large empty ova eyelessly staring at him. Neil, with Herculean effort, twists his neck to look up at them, to beg, but they just facelessly stare, cold air whipping down the dark hall behind them.

They then seem to both reach a decision, or are prompted into action by an unseen hand. They bend down and, hooking their hands under Neil's armpits, they drag him down the corridor, his body, as light as a skeleton, rattling over the rough floor, strewn with the porcelain-bone splinters of broken eggs.

Neil moans, not really out of pain; he accepts that now. It's been with him for so long he's long stopped struggling against it and in accepting he finds himself curiously anaesthetised. He moans not from pain but from fear and anguish and confusion. He is going ever lower, into darker and darker corridors. The concrete floor has given way to smashed tiles, breeze blocks and rusting rebars, smeared in a bloody film. Bones are visible in the deep-red half-light.

Neil is sure that he is being dragged into hell. The walls look like they should be inside someone's body; flesh-stripped osseous matter, glistening membranes dripping with sebum and mucus. Neil's body, now little more than a bloody torso, strings of ligament and bone and the exploded shell where the shell of his head once was, is almost indistinguishable from the hellish cavity that he is being dragged into.

He is pulled into a large, dark, coagulated chamber, septal partitions pulsing and twitching like sphincters. The two assistants dump him and disappear back into the dark arteries they've just left. Neil, little more than a crushed, calcite fecal stain, is nothing but anguish, pure loss in the depths of hell. It is impossible to get lower, it is impossible to be less of a human being.

The immense, medullary walls quiver, the soft tissue convulses, and a muscle-lined orifice, taller than a cathedral clerestory, opens up, far, far above the blasted puddle that Neil once was. Although the fear and misery have all but extinguished him, they intensify further, paralysing what's left of his mind with a dread so profound, so absolutely appalling, that it feels like it is the very form of the universe, that unending horror is the nature of existence and only now, as he is about to be squashed from existence, is it so perfectly real to him, that all there is, everywhere in all directions and at all times, is absolute hatred and disgusting suffering.

And yet. There is something else. Even here, there is, in Neil's consciousness, *something else*, a cubic centimetre of peace.

The terrible, trembling aperture opens, shuddering, and from the black slit, stretching up into the unreachable ceiling of the cavern, there comes… an excellent nose.

The nose is followed by lips, cheekbones, chin and forehead, then a tall brow, a strong, confident jaw and deep eye sockets, curved shadows in the dark red light. Finally a shock of thick white hair. The colossal blood-slick head pushes its way through the membranous wall and into the blood-red atrium. It is Max Thottesley.

Neil sees Max's head clearly and feels its impossible immensity, which seems to press upon him from within, a nauseating massiveness, a sickening density.

The huge head looks down.

'Hello old fruit', it says, bass voice cavern trembling.

'Who are you?' asks Neil. He finds the clarity of his own voice, unstrained by the tortures of the damned—not to mention the absence of a functioning vocal tract—distantly surprising.

'If you could understand the answer, I'd give it to you.'

'Are you the devil?'

'I'm far too exciting to be the devil.'

'Are you the Demiurge then?'

'I am the Enma of the Red Land, I am the protector of Ra, I am the Qwoth of Man and I am your big friend in the corner.'

'And you're behind this nightmare?'

'Don't be silly. Nightmares aren't caused by the monsters in them.'

Neil is silent. Then: 'Where is Chiyo?'

'Why do you want to know?'

'I love her.'

'Hahahaha! Of course you do.'

'Is she here?' asks Neil. There is determination in his tone.

'Chiyo is here,' says Max.

Then; 'Where?'

'The question is not where, but who.'

'I know who she is.'

Max laughs again, a terrible laugh, but rich with joy. A real, human laugh, which makes it all the stranger. 'Do you know who you are when you are dreaming?' he asks.

'Yes I am me.'

'Wrong. *I* am you.'

'You're not me,' says Neil, his voice still clear from the blood-slick viscera.

The head smiles, its lips cruel and beautiful. 'I am the darkness you have pushed away your whole life, from your whole life, from your bedside, from your town, from the entire universe. I am the snapped bits of your favourite toy, the anger you feel when someone criticises you, the sharp stink of old people's homes, the panic you feel when you get a strange pain in your chest. I am the dark end of darkness, and the friendly voice of total aloneness. I am the loss of everything, Neil, even your body, but when everything has gone, I am here.'

Neil says nothing for a long time. Then; 'Why?'

'You see, that's where you get it all wrong. You're obsessed with why, or how. There is no how and why, there is no reason, no motive, no method, nothing you can add to yourself. It's all useless, empty *what* in here.'

'*What* then? What do you want?'

Max laughs. 'What do *you* want Neil Down?'

'I want to get out of here. I want to escape...'

'Escape? You think that will help? That all you have to do is get out of jail, with a blazing wow of release, and you'll be free? That feeling, my little man, that bright spark of enlightenment, that big realisation; that is just as much a part of the dream as the broken clock and the talking snake.'

Neil is silent again. He is fragmenting further, melting. He is now entirely in splintered pieces.

'Chiyo.'

Max smiles. His ancient head seems to freeze, as if the life of it has been removed, leaving just a mask, a mile-high mask which… pops! In a bright puffing flash of glitter, a fountain of multi-coloured streamers reveals a clock on the fleshy wall behind where the head was—the same clock that Neil once had in his room.

'Hello?'

Nothing. The time is midnight. The thinnest hand on the clock slowly falls, like a dropped hammer, onto one second after midnight, then, after an age, two seconds, then three, four… each tick sooner than the last, slowly speeding up. The clock ticks faster. And faster. And then faster still. The second hand, and then the minute hand, and then the hour hand spin. Neil groans. The final bits of him are aging, the flesh falling from the bones, maggots eat the rotting flesh, which dries up to dust and blows away.

Neil's final, glimpsing realisation, final flashing chink of awareness, at the very bottom of existence, at the last pitiful gasp of selfhood, is, 'It's not that bad.'

∞

The experience, is now one. Neil's life is a single thing, which is no longer moving through the plane of his moment-by-moment awareness, giving an impression of a separate person moving through time. There is no time, no awareness, just the whole, bounded neither by the edge of a body, nor by the edge of a moment. Neilness is one with everything he has ever sensed, willed, thought and felt; a single multi-dimensional organism, absolutely without qualities. His living self can no more imagine this than a line can imagine a living planet.

To the self, which is still here, this is nowhere and nothing. For Neil there is no will, no hope, no desire, no fear. There is no sound, no colour, no intuition or sensation of any kind. There's no affection, no warmth; no human feeling at all. And yet it's not cold, or empty, or serene, or pure, or white, or dark, or abstract, or anything that can ever be imagined. It is not even love. It is higher than love, or lower. It is a greatness, an infinite greatness; so intense it would annihilate a man, but there is no man here. There is no time, no space, no me and no not-me. It is everything and a perfect absence of everything, it is experience itself and the absence of experience, it is the flesh and the absence of life.

And yet an echo of the limited Neil remains, something still attached to the part that he was, something holding on.

∞

Hunter saunters smugly into the bean-bag room and has what he believes is a 'conversation' with Joe, but which is actually a clever replica of a conversation. There is no content to it, rather a pitter-patter of emphatic information… 'Something we've been looking at… Lark is a bad bunny… going forward… don't get me started… creative renaissance… such a, like, negative thing…? core values, core values, core values… resolved…'

It is strange, thinks Joe, as the words waft over his head like soap bubbles, that the conversation he has just had with an egg seemed more real than this. Something is terribly wrong about all this, but there is no reason for the strangeness and wrongness. Everything fits together plausibly, everything 'is as it should be,' everything 'is as it seems' and yet, at the same time, the 'should be' and the 'seems' are rootless, fabricated, fake…

Hunter drifts away, then someone else drifts in, and then out, and then someone else. Joe's hellos have reached their lowest ebb, they are ruined, tattered things, like bits of dead seaweed clinging to a rusty ladder. Joe has the sense that he is floating on his back, on the surface of a stagnant lake filled with oil, and everyone else in the water—for it is filled with human forms, managing to stand up, although Joe is well out of his depth—is some kind of automaton ejecting random information, 'a pig in a nun's habit… the train has been delayed… Hard Ground, starring Burt Reynolds… Nilphamari Sadar Upazila… balance an egg on your back… do you have a loyalty card…? a flute emerging from the anus… knights fought snails…? None of it actually makes sense. It sort of connects up, there is a relationship between one comment and another, but none of it has anything in common, none of it has anything to do with me, which makes it seem as if the one message they do share is that there *is* no me.

Is there no me? Joe wonders. He looks inside for it, for the 'me'. There's the thinking, the seeing, the hearing, the speaking, but who or what are these things happening to?

Joe stands up and leaves the room, in the middle of a monotone monologue from someone who is supposed to be working with him on something. He walks down the hallway, past the glass-walled meeting rooms and idea labs and creativity booths, past the genderless, inter-species toilets and non-racist rowing machines and democratic radiators, past shadow-like people with shadow-like protuberances, kettles and radiators and cheese graters sprouting from legs and arms and backs.

He reaches a part of the building he is not familiar with, which seems to be made up entirely of corridors. Either side of him are more corridors, countless parallel passages, obscurely viewed through laminated glass, each one with a solitary human wandering up and down, as Joe is. These people are strangely formed, furniture-merged, arms and faces and knees poking from tables and sofas and electric guitars and fidgeting toys and under-desk elliptical machines, a chaos of animate-inanimate form, dragging themselves up stairs, down stairs, round the corner, along the corridor, fused with the corridor, eternally *corridored*.

The barrier between thing and person is nothing. There is no self here, no other, and so no division between the two, everything is looking borderlessly back at a me which no longer exists, everything moves and speaks, but to nobody. It is a grotesque parody of paradise, but as there is no original, it remains normal, all normal; all unnatural, mangled, grotesque; but normal.

Joe feels tired, wan, spent, like he's been walking for a long, long time. His jaw feels heavy. He is thirsty and lightheaded and wants to stop, but he has gone too far to walk back now. Behind, all is corridor, ahead too, so he stops, and sits, and closes his eyes.

'What's wrong?' Joe opens his eyes. It's another one of the new people, another face coming towards him, in bright, terrifying clarity. Oh God the faces, thinks Joe, everyone is pure face, huge and looming, hiding nothing.

'What's wrong?' the face asks again.

'Everything,' says Joe.

'Everything? What are you talking about?'

'Oh, I don't know.'

'This is heaven,' says the face, 'Everyone is enlightened. We live like gods, above the flesh, smooth and invulnerable, sexless and pure, but wanton too if we feel like it. We are present, without thought and without attachment, free of things and free of each other. Everyone is no-one now, yet everything lies at our fingertips. We swim daily through a river of culture which has flowed to us from the dawn of time, which radiates out to us from a world of living things, enchanted creatures, which speak to us. It is Nirvana, it is Tao and and it is the Kingdom of Heaven. What can be wrong with it?'

'I don't feel it here,' said Joe, morosely pointing to his belly.

'You don't have to feel it, a feeling is something you have. We live in being. Be Joe, *Be*. You're here, remember, because this is what you want, to be free, like a cloud, enlightened. You belong here, in being. There's no way to prove we're not in heaven.'

'I don't feel it here,' Joe said again, looking sadly at his belly. 'It's too bright,' he mumbled, and closed his eyes again.

❧

How long he sits he does not know. It could be ten minutes, it could be ten thousand years. Just as divisions have gone, and the self that makes them, so time and space do not exist, so there is no movement, so there is nothing into which Joe moves, or from which he has moved; and yet it is dead eternity, faked-up transcendence. The corridor is a nothingness, going on forever and ever, and it has always gone on forever and ever; but it is merely forever, the fixed image of timelessness and spacelessness, a stultifying surface, a 'topological overlay'. The world.

The surface world won't let you stop, because that is death, so it pushes you always on, either from behind, with threats, or from ahead, with treats, until there's nothing more you want, or are afraid of, and you crumple up in the middle of the corridor and stop. But even then you don't stop, you stay on an internal conveyor belt, issueless self-abuse without climax, the lazy man's agitated dream of meticulously curated momentum.

All the more final then when Joe does stop. He stops completely. Everything stops. Joe sits, slumped, unwatching, in a state of total finality, without any need or desire. There's not even inertia, because the self has lost all weight. It cannot even drift. And yet, it is not stillness and silence. There is movement, noise and sensation, and pain. Such pain. Wind beats against the mountain of his body, rivers rush down it, landslides roar and pummel in his ears. His heart feels like a foot kicking down the door of his chest. It is a calamity, it's horrible. It's no pastry.

But it is real, the body. It is reality. It is the only thing worth responding to. The actual body is real, even as there is no body. The arms and legs are awake, even in dream.

There is red light and curiosity. Joe opens his eyes. He has been sitting before a dark, floor-to-ceiling window, a dark night, a dark city; but now a dull red lour is fringing the dark, dawn-bled devastation of the city. He turns to the east. The sky is lighter there, the moon is rising over the rousing embers of night, blowing on them in fiery infernal gleams.

Joe gets to his feet. Down below people are coming to work. A distant glow on the horizon illuminates the barest shade of a thought, a twitch of mad desire is fringed with a meagre gleam of visible light. The light gently intensifies and with it a need, to let it in, because the light is real, something from outside the unworld, something trying to reach in, some information. He follows the physical need and takes his clothes off. First his jacket, then his trousers, shirt, socks, pants… Something outside is coming to connect with the body, to reunite them. He must be naked, nothing must be between him and the sun.

He stands at the window, bollock naked. Sunlight strikes him. He smiles slightly. His penis twitches and his perineum slackens. It has been so long since he felt anything in his cock and balls, which have grown cold and inert, that the arousal surprises him. He looks down in gentle wonder. The sunshine grows brighter as his cock, and the shadow of his cock against his thigh, lifts. It rises, awakening to the light. Joe too, blinded with light, is wakening, he is becoming rampant.

It is, for the first time, the sun. He has never seen the sun. He sees the sun now. The sun is filling him, and he is filling the sun. Trembling with ecstasy and inspiration, his face bright, Joe stretches his body back, cock-penetrating and heart-penetrated. The sun is so good. He moans, loudly, as the pleasure builds; and such pleasure. It is so intense he feels like he might pass out or be obliterated. It builds and builds and when he is sure it cannot get more intense it does. A white-hot rapture, torn apart by the light, a ball of fire shaking his chest, flames of it running down his arms and legs, pouring from him. He ejaculates. The emission itself is a melting nothingness, a drip of water, but this is followed by a wringing, white-hot purging orgasm, a shattering, electric, streaming, screaming climax, which goes on and on. Long after he has ejaculated he continues shaking with strange, super-intense rapture.

He staggers back from the all-birthing sunlight, quick-thrilling, retina white-burnt, leaning against a wall until pink, afterglow-saturated sight returns. He looks down, his cock is still erect, if anything more splendid. He stands up to his full height, face still sun shining, and sprints three steps, stops, runs back to the window to his shoes, quickly puts them on, then sprints again down the corridor, past the various offices and cubicles, into the central open-plan area. He bounds onto a desk, cock-naked.

Nobody looks up, nobody notices.

He roars: 'I AM THE SUN GOD RA!!!'

☙

Victor's fridge-coffin is solemnly laid deep into the grave. Meera's sons continue swaying and shaking eerily as Meera continues chanting:

'He used to sing "girl, make it nice, put in dat spice girl, let it simmer, simmer, simmer, girl. Let it simmer, simmer, simmer, girl" and we simmered, oh God did we simmer. Victor's hot bubbling love ravished me, shattered me, unzipped my mind. It was one-pointed, utterly beyond sexuality. So powerful was it, that he split into nine hundred thousand identical copies of himself, and I did the same and for ten thousand godyears, in the white-hot epicentre of sexual passion, we radiated as one, until our love reached such an ultimate pinnacle of sexual devotion the universe, vibrating in sympathetic superecstasy, caught light, and everything, everything became as stars are.'

The first shards of morning sunlight flow over the hill. Victor's fridge-coffin begins rattling. A mighty swell builds up, a feeling in Lilly that a geyser is about to burst, in the ground and in her chest. She steps backwards, holding the tree which is also shaking, surging with power.

The rain batters the ground, hammers the assembled, the world is quaking, trembling, something extraordinary is going to appear, but surely, it feels, the birth will blow us all away. The howling energy builds up, unbearable. Meera's sari is flying and flapping around like she's skydiving, Carl and her sons, storm-lashed, are crouched, tensed up, faces screwed against the hurricane of power and energy, the noise, a roaring doombass of unimaginable power, is deafening. The peak is coming, the climax of the universe itself…

The pile of dust that once was Neil Geb lies in the centre of the ichorous womb-room that he expired in. From the artery he entered moonwalks Chiyo, dressed in a 1988 Japanese Olympic table tennis team tracksuit. She is dragging a ping-pong table which she pulls over to the pile of dust. Then she exits and returns with two tall, ornate candlestick holders, twelve unlit candles in each, which is places either side of the table-tennis table. The huge clock, high up above the vaginal aperture which runs from the floor to the distant ceiling, is now without hands and numbers, just a white disc.

Chiyo stands above the dust of Neil.

'Neil-san. Let's playing table tennis!' she says, her soft voice animated and cheerful.

She bends down and reaches towards the dust. A dim yellowish-blue glow appears on the dripping tip of her wet forefinger.

'Do you want to play ping pong Neil-chan?' she whispers seductively.

Her hand, around which a globule of blue-yellow water-light radiates, touches the dust and, with the same spine-cracking power of universe-birthing light which is surging through Joe, Neil too explodes into life.

He leaps to his feet, eyes aflame.

'Yes!'

He grabs the paddle, tense for receiving Chiyo's serve. She raises the ball slowly, brings it down to the pips, blows on it; then whips her wrist across the edge of the ball, spinning it in an arc across the table. Neil returns, a lashing sweeping blast, then Chiyo, then Neil, both laughing, yelping, barking, mooing, throwing themselves around the table with manic energy. Neil leaps for a particularly powerful smash, the candles burst into flame, the ball, now hovering in mid-air, bursts into flames also. Chiyo puts a whole raw egg in her mouth and eats it, with blazing intensity. A ginger bearded old gentleman seated in the corner, smoking from a chemistry set (bubbling pipes, Bunsen burner), nods approvingly. Neil completes his smash, time speeds up, ultra rapid, mad ping-pong, day and night, Neil is laughing like a lunatic—Chiyo is playing table tennis on his enormous, naked, body. Now Chiyo is Victor, and Neil is the ball, and he is being thwacked around the world by ten immense laughing Victors. Neil is screaming, cracking up, roaring up into space, towards the vaginal sphincter at the end of the world, at the end of the universe, ten flying Victor pursuing him, all shrieking with laughter.

Neil gets closer and closer to the quivering slit, searing hot, agonising. He grimaces and groans—his void-consumed moan becoming slower, stretched out, deeper. Bawling, laughing, groaning, the vulval muscle opens, sucking him in, he struggles and bellows. Now there is pain, and it is immense, crushing. He is aware that the ten Victors have coalesced into one, a huge black naked man, swimming through the ichor behind him, the two of them flying towards a sunlike golden egg, pulsating in the womb of the universe.

A roar of elemental fury hits the light, as Neil is squeezed, crushed, thrown into the egg, thrown into the perfect heart of things, fused with the source, all thought obliterated, all self obliterated, diffused into the egg at the explosive vanishing point of eternity, the transdimensional whole of life, all lives, in the motionless moment.

Indivisible unity, birthless and deathless, the single organism of Neil's entire life, and of every life which touches his, existing in the existenceless beyond of being… *becomes*. It is split into two, into that which can be conceived, into conception, into a body, a thing in time and space, a thing which can be caused and which causes, a possible life entity, divided from impossible death. The body splits and splits again, and again; not following a programme, becoming that which it already timelessly is. The cells do not 'know' what to be or where to go—to become a nerve cell or a blood cell—they *are already that*. The whole body forms, a whole adult body, Neil, in the warm belly of the earth, next to another body, Victor's.

Then the living matrix shudders and there is true pain. Neil is being squeezed, away from his twin from, away from the dark, and towards a tearing anguish of light. Every atom of Neil's body is searing in birth. The earth-cervix opens up, a small space, Neil, squeezed, suffocating, sobbing and gasping, flesh-torn, naked, covered in mud, blood and mucus, pulls himself free of the still convulsing earth. From the true abyss, he is born. Again.

✿

Lightning strikes Victor's coffin. Deafening, planet-splitting thunder blasts the earth and the minds of all assembled. All is detonating fury, a supernova of sound and pain and birth and madness and Victor; Victor himself leaping high out of the grave, his dark naked form, battle-arched and birthed through the endless, flowing lightning.

The tree Lilly is clinging to bursts into flame, but the gashing flame is alive. The dead in the branches are no longer hanging dead, but riding the branches, roaring with joyous laughter, some are playing instruments, a magnificent Bollywood overture, a scattered, ectoplasmic blast, oblique and stupendously funky, a charging, striding rhythmic eruption from the world behind the world on fire; and that world is here. She is it.

It is exhilarating and terrible, to see everything burn. Everyone loves a fire, somewhere in their bright hearts, even when it's destroying everything. The body is afraid, the mind is appalled, but there is the sound of laughter.

The assembled dance, led by Victor booming and laughing, at the head of a monkey-procession of the dead returned and the living reconciled. Lilly dances, utterly undone. The dead on the branches above are laughing, madly riding nowhere on the branches of the tree to the Bhangra beat of Kali, Kalma, Hel, Izanami, Mania, and The Morrígan. Sometimes Meera's sons stop and, overflowing with joy, pose in primal, enigmatic, jewel-like geometric positions, eyes wide and alive, sometimes they look over at Lilly with joyous recognition, sometimes they swing their arms in long, loping hoops, chanting, kings of oblivion.

Carl breathes fire.

✿

Joe, naked and erect, sprints from the Duat building, laughing, waving his arms wildly around. He is cut loose. All deadening thoughts of 'but what if…?' have dissolved with the normality he has been; not just has been trapped in, or has been encased in; but has been. This is why escape was impossible to imagine, because the imaginer was trapped. But now free it runs, naked as the graces, down the street.

The people walk on. Nobody pays him any attention. He runs into an upmarket women's clothing boutique—nobody pays attention—stops at a rack of white dresses, picks the largest one out and pulls it on. He then strides manfully out into the sunshine, pulling a long blonde wig from a shop-dummy as he leaves and tugging it onto his head.

On the clean, wide, store-lined street outside, towered over all sides by immaculate, priapic skyscrapers, Joe skips through the mass of man. Someone throws a Scotch egg at him, which he triumphantly, yet nonchalantly, catches and takes a bite of.

He knows that at any moment the worst could happen, but, at the same time, the worst has already happened. Where is it? It is all out of his control; the only thing he can control is his obedience to the material instinct, to rustle up to a bank of flowers, planted to decorate a forgotten verge. He bends down, picks the flowers—dog roses and daisies, blue-prickling forget-me-nots and papery flamed poppies, butterblobs of tansy and straggles of ripped yellow rock-rose—and stuffs fragrant bunches of them down the front of his dress, and into his wig. Doing anything else but what I must do is to live outside myself, where I am prey.

Someone speaks with trembling outrage, 'Excuse me, what are you doing?'

Joe turns. A passer-by's face, one of the everyone, is standing, hands on hips, watching Joe.

'I'm taking these flowers, because nobody is paying any attention to them,' says Joe.

'But they are dirty,' says the face, 'and they will die'.

'So am I, so will I,' and Joe picks the flowers.

✿

Neil lies naked, for a long, elongated moment, on the cool grass. He is surrounded by tall standing stones. Warm aqueous light pours down from the submarine blue. On the top of a hill there is a massive stately home, which despite ornate columns, classical pediments and finely-wrought entablatures, looks like a featureless mass of brick; imposing, inhuman.

Neil feels should go up there, but the sun warming his body feels so good. He stands up and walks up to the back of the wide building, then around towards the front, banging on the windows as he goes.

'Hello! Is anyone there?'

No answer. He looks around for something he can use to get in and spies something long and hard-looking. He picks it up—a smooth thighbone, perhaps from a human, or an ape, or a bear maybe; it's rather thick. He feels it in his hand, it feels good, weighty, then he looks at the window in front of him, one of the smaller ones, possibly accessing a stairwell or a cupboard.

He smiles. Here I am, naked and about to break into the house of a wealthy man with a thigh-bone, and I don't care. I just don't care.

He smashes the glass, reaches in to the latch and, opening the window, carefully climbs in to what is, indeed, a storeroom, full of mops, buckets and shelves of cleaning products. He steps on a shard of glass, but notices with calm wonder that even this does not cause an 'ooh, ooh, ooh' overreaction. He just lifts his foot and pulls the glass out and calmly leaves the walk-in cupboard.

It is a warm sunny morning. Long lozenges of light warm the wooden floorboards, illuminating the mad menagerie of Thottesley Hall; the architectural model of Atlantic, the Jesus and Mary Chain in clay, the wall-mounted hippo lift, the medieval altarpieces, the Breughels, the sarcophagi, the huge resin body organs and all the rest of it are thrown into brilliant distinction by the golden hour sunshine flowing through the immense, ornate, timber-sash windows.

The house appears to be empty, but Neil is not watchful. He strolls through the museum, leaving bloody footprints. He stops here and there to inspect a clavicytherium, a Judas cradle, a mysteriously out of place photograph of a working-class family amidst miniature portraits. He makes his way up a rear staircase and along a first-floor corridor, until he finds what he is looking for, a well-furnished bedroom. He finds a suit which fits him, jet black, sequinned with onyx and set off with crow's feathers.

As he is admiring himself in the mirror something catches his attention. He looks round, confused. He sniffs and sniffs again, and then smiles. The smell activates his nose, part of his body which, he realises, he has never used, or has forgotten how to. He breathes in deeply, filling his senses with the smell of old clothes, carbolic acid, oak and shit; even a hint of stone in there. He laughs and picks up a pillow, pressing it into his face. It smells like a human being.

He hears childish laughter. He leaves the bedroom and moves from room to room. In a comfortable and relatively normal-seeming lounge, sitting on a sofa, is a young boy with a sensitive and intelligent face, watching the television, a show called 'Mr. Ando of the Woods.' The child turns when Neil enters the room.

'Hello. Who are you?' asks the boy.

'Neil,' says Neil.

'Neil who?'

'Neil Geb.'

'Oh.'

'What's your name?'

'Joris Thottesley.'

'Hello Joris.'

'Hello. Do you want to watch Mr. Ando?'

'Thanks, I'd like to, but I've got things to do.'

'What do you have to do?' asks Joris. Neil has never met a child who was so friendly and intelligently open. He dimly remembers there used to be children like this.

'I have to find my brother and mother,' says Neil.

'Have you lost them?'

'Yes.'

'Okay,' says Joris, turning back to the television, his interest apparently exhausted.

Neil is about to leave when a fly zumms into the room. He stops and follows its erratic path. It lands on his elbow. He looks at it, smiling, watching it clean its front legs. He shifts over to the narrow window and gently guides it out.

✿

The storm is over, the dark clouds have lightened, shade and sunlight, silvery-gold gleaming under the dark low roof of the clouds. Victor and company, bowing to each other, are cast in brilliant relief. The men shake each other's hands warmly. Lilly, now wearing a tight furry dress to match her top hat—hugs everyone, as does Meera.

'Come on then lads,' says Carl, 'let's go.'

'Goodbye my little chickens,' says Meera, 'goodbye.'

Sajid and the boys are tearful, their goodbyes full of feeling. Victor too is overwhelmed, his eyes are shining.

Lilly approaches Victor.

'Do I know you?' she asks.

'Everyone knows me,' says Victor beaming, showing the happy gap between his two front teeth.

'Who though?'

'I'm the dying and rising god. I am Jesus, Lemminkäinen, Tammuz, Attis, Osiris, Dionysus and Marduk.'

'All of them?'

Meera, face wet and happy, joins them, taking Victor's arm and pushing her happy face into his shoulder.

'Well, I suppose… erm…' Lilly trails off. It doesn't seem to matter. Goodbyes are being exchanged. Meera and Victor are heading into the east, while Carl and the boys are westbound. After more hugs and happy sobs, the two groups part, Lilly, Carl, Sajid and the lads descending one side of Clive's hill, Victor and Meera, hand in hand, down the other.

The sun is rising, warm and clear. It is a beautiful morning. Lilly, idling over the meadows, chatting with the men, arm in arm with Carl and Sajid, can't remember ever having felt more at peace. Open-air friendship at dawn, how strange that something so simple and good has been for so long so far distant.

Lilly and the seven men reach Carl's hearse, and pack themselves inside, four crossed-legged in the rear. They drive slowly back to town, listening to Kalyanji-Anandji, S.P. Balasubrahmanyam, Lata Mangeshkar and Mohammed Rafi. Lilly looks out of the window at the passing trees, and smiles.

'Anyone want a bhaji?' asks Dev from the back.

General 'yeahs'. Dev hands out bhajis from a paper bag. They are excellent, delicately spiced, fresh tasting and light—not too oily.

The trees and hedges become warehouses and chicken wire, then terraced houses and garden walls, but Lilly remains inwardly gentle and calm. She winds the window down and feels the wind on her face.

Carl parks up in a lay-by over from the Shenleybury park. Lilly embraces the Indians, then gets out with Carl to say goodbye to him too. They stand in the warm sunshine, a little awkward.

'That was the dog's bollocks,' says Lilly.

'Too bloody right!'

'I wish all funerals were like that.'

'Yeah,' says Carl, 'although it does help if the corpse joins in.'

'That's true. I just mean that death brings out the best in people.'

Carl nods, seriously. 'There should be more of it.'

Lilly likes his seriousness. 'Why are you wearing those tights?'

'Ballet innit? Really getting into it. Me and Shelley go regular.'

'You take your daughter to ballet?'

'I do it with her. Look.'

He bends down in a half-decent plié, then executes a sketchy but surprisingly light-footed sauté. Lilly bursts into laughter.

'Carl,' she says, 'I want to say, I know you've always been an arse man, and that you've enjoyed my arse and, well, as I have a feeling you're never going to it again, I thought you might like to give it a final, hearty, goodbye slap?'

Carls face falls. He looks cute, in his disappointment. 'You're going? Where you going?'

'I don't know. I'm done with this place. I need… I just need something *else*… I need, erm, to shed my skin, you know? I want to live, to completely open myself up to life. I'm thinking perhaps some kind of sex cult, or a circus of death, or something like that. I don't know. I'm just going to follow the sun.'

'Really? But… But…' Carl is cut up. He's spluttering, tears welling up in his now innocent blue eyes.

'Come on Carl,' says Lilly, 'you understand the meaning of freedom. You're a fire-breathing ram.'

'Yeah, I suppose,' he says, softly smiling, sniffing, wiping his nose on his sleeve. Lilly passes him a tissue. 'Yeah, yeah, yeah,' he says, 'You, you look after yourself.'

'I will.'

They embrace, then Lilly bends over, and Carl sadly and still tearfully smacks her botty, grips it, and gives it a good buttock-wiggling shake.

✿

Maria is having a light lunch of salmon and edamame beans. Joe appears at the doorway. He has lost his wig, which was hot and scratchy, but has augmented his appearance further with a garland of flowers around his head which he made, on the train home, from dandelions, narcissi, tulips and crocuses growing next to the train platform. He has a few lumps on his arm; bee stings.

Maria, on seeing Joe, chokes on her coulis.

'Hello,' says Joe, with serene confidence.

Maria looks him up and down, the horror of the truth dawning in her eyes, the horror of her submerged personality pouring through the cracks. Fierce and hard-set, she says nothing. Joe, bemused, watches her charge upstairs, then sets about making breakfast, sausage and eggs. When he has finished, and is sitting at the kitchen table eating, Maria, who has just dragged her suitcases downstairs, comes in to the room and delivers the speech she has been preparing in her mind.

'After everything I have given you. Everything, Joe, *everything*. The best years of… I remember when you were literally eating pillows… When you were rock bottom… And who was it who… Joe, where would you be without… You'd be on the street… You'd be… Oh God, oh *God*… How could you be so ungrateful? So… So… *Offensive?* You're not a woman. And where did you get those flowers from?' She's working herself up into a rampage of justice now. 'Yeah,' she says, 'I've had it with you. I've had it with your insensitivity… You don't care about the Palestinians, you don't care about battered wives, you don't care about the plankton and you don't care about me. What about me, eh…? I mean, no, *enough!* That's it! And… And…'

She tears her blouse open, revealing her superb breasts.

'And you can say goodbye to these!' she shrieks.

Joe, mouth full of sausage, turns to each nipple. 'Goodbye,' he says to one, 'goodbye,' to the other.

✿

Neil, dressed as the divine crow, is strolling the streets of Edding. Is it real, he wonders, is it all in my imagination? Somehow the difference doesn't seem to matter. Everything is both more important than he ever could have imagined, and, at the same time, much less, and the difference doesn't seem to matter. He smiles at the people, he smiles at Edding, suburban Edding, ugly old Edding of nothing much being done. It is ugly, but it is okay. People here are lost, and sad, and sick, and very small, but there is a kind of loveliness, even in the ordinary. As it is with them, so it is with me, Neil Geb.

He wonders vaguely how to find Joe, how to find Margaret. Where are they in this realm of the real-and-the-unreal? But the thought drifts away. Of course he will find them, or they him. What he needs is to be prepared, so he heads home, surprised to find, for the first time in his life, that the dirt and the misery and the pain of the world don't touch him off. It is a misty day, but the sun is bright. He dawdles along the residential back roads of Edding, listening to hedge sparrows. Fluffs of steam puff from kitchen ventilation pipes, mingling with the mists. He passes a massive, retarded-looking Muslim manboy with a fuzzy beard, loping down the road with a six-pint plastic milk jug in each hand, unaware of everyone else who has to skip out of his solid, moronic path. He passes a chubby, fierce-looking Chinese woman shouting obscenities into her mobile phone. He passes a runty-looking kid who, he remembers, once laughingly ran away from him, in his previous police life, after he, Neil, had detected a thick whiff of skunk and moved in for a caution, only to slip over on, of all things, a wet banana skin. He passes a severed head on a street corner, which is provoking a great deal of dramatically expressed horror in the peds, who give it a wide berth.

And all of it is good. And none of it matters.

He gets back home and knocks. Nobody is in. He goes round the back and breaks into the kitchen through the back door. The house is the same but different, minus his vibe, and Chiyo's, and Lilly's. He opens the fridge and pulls out a bowl of soup, makes tea, and sits down to eat, drink, and think over the situation.

What has happened? What is happening? Did I go insane? Did I die? Did I fall asleep? Was I drugged? None of these explanations seem to fit. He has never felt more lucid, more alive, more awake. The storm of weirdness seems to have passed, yet here he is wearing a crow outfit and ready for anything. All he knows is that he must follow the feeling that got him through it.

He finishes his lunch, does the washing up and goes upstairs. His room has changed also, re-carpeted, humanised; surely, he thinks, they haven't thrown my stuff out. He checks the store cupboards, then takes a look in the loft where he finds, boxed up, his possessions, a thick layer of dust covering the exercise equipment, the musical instruments, the microphones, the scales, the voice-operated bin, the clock.

He picks up a rucksack, empties it of power adaptors, headphones and surgical gloves, searches through his old oak trunk and finds what he is looking for; two of the jumpers he has knitted, which he stuffs into his rucksack along with his German multitool and New Zealand thermals. He then puts on some more appropriate footwear (Max's shoes pinch), and does a few kettlebell swings before, finally, taking the clock down from the shelf it is resting on and, unzipping his fly, pissing on it. He's got a lot of water in him from the soup and tea, so he turns and directs the rest of the stream over his beloved technology.

He leaves by the front door and walks into town, employing a variety of gaits, strolling extraordinarily slowly, then swaggering a bit (Liam Gallagher style), then waggling his arms bizarrely, then skipping, then prowling, cat-like. He finds his vision has changed. It is no longer tight, concentrated. He isn't looking for some thing anymore, which allows in the easiness, which had always hummed at the periphery, to spread over his senses.

Eventually, he finds himself at St. Barbara's church. He stops, and enters the graveyard.

✿

After finishing his breakfast Joe stands in a few places in his house that he hasn't stood in before. Although he and Maria lived together much as two ghosts might, speaking to each other, gesturing, but weightless, without push or compulsion; still there is pain, still a part of him has just been torn from his body. They were in love, of sorts, and had done the things lovers do, like go on weekend breaks. They had walked arm in arm through the streets of Edinburgh, and stayed in a fancy five-star hotel and Maria, who was a deafening coital screamer, had provoked complaints which a polite but nervy half-Chinese guy had been tasked with communicating to them, standing at their door, virtually frothing with nerves.

They had gone to the beach, North Norfolk, and were rolling around on a secluded sand dune when two huge bullmastiffs, had bounded up and started growling at them. Joe, afraid of dogs, shrunk away and Maria, who was yet to be disgusted by Joe's fear, who still felt his sensitivity was a noble thing, and who was fearless before all the forces of nature, leapt to her feet, half naked, hair wild, and started screaming at the dogs, which turned, tail down, and whimpered away. She had never been sexier.

In the early days she'd accepted Joe's playfulness, encouraged it. He was in the habit, whenever she slapped him with mock outrage or censure, of pretending to die, theatrically writhing around on the floor, convulsing and shaking with death rattles, after which she would give him a mark out of ten for his death performance. One one occasion he did this while eating and got a bit of chicken gristle stuck in his throat. Maria watched on with impassive amusement as his face went red, the world swam before his eyes, his four-dimensional wholelife rose before his spaceless awareness and he touched the realm of death, before the gristle was dislodged and he regained consciousness. Still only got an 'eight' though.

But it all passed away, leaving just the outside image of it, the symbol of their romance, a kind of voodoo doll which stood in for the relationship they were supposed to have; and it is the voodoo doll which hurts now as he stands eighteen inches from the living room wall.

Still dressed in all his magnificence, he leaves the house. He is intent on a stroll, but is sidetracked by the boarded-up neighbour's house, 86, now totally overgrown with vines and creepers, ivy, fuzzy lamium, speckle-white yarrow and dusky clover. Savage, it looks like it has been an abandoned wreck for ten thousand years. Joe climbs over the fence and pushes his way through the undergrowth. A badger ruffles past, followed by an archaeopteryx. A sycamore tree growing inside the house has pushed a lithe branch through one of the shutters which Joe pulls off and climbs inside.

The interior of the house is that of an old woman's house—sideboards, 'fancy' dinner services, lace doilies, embroidered antimacassars, porcelain cats, bottles of Camp Coffee and baskets of knitting—but everything is covered in grass, mould, moss, ink-cap mushrooms and thick leathery prehistoric plant matter. The inside is more outside than the outside is.

Joe walks through the house, and up the musty stairs. Streaks of sharp sunlight cut through the dark dust. On the top floor, in an empty bedroom, is a rocking chair and a large ottoman. On the rocking chair sits a corpse—the remains of the old woman who used to live next door, now naught but a dusty skeleton and fragments of decaying fabric. One hand of bone is resting across her lap, the other is pointing, imperiously, at the ottoman.

Joe bends down and opens the lid. Golden smiling light warms his face. Inside the box is his leg.

❂

Joe exits the inside-out house and walks down Gordon Road, then right into Glord Street and along Expeart Avenue. Everyone continues to ignore him. It doesn't seem to matter whether people are real or not. It's irrelevant. It is crummy Edding, in all its sullen normalcy, yet Joe is surprised and thrilled by the vividness of everything, how much it *matters*. It is all featureless hell, rectangles of mathematically perfect glass and steel, smooth paving stones, clean plastic benches and reconverted, remodelled, redeveloped warehouses and prisons and factories, all so deathly in their manufactured characterlessness; and yet, in the clarity of all this and in his freedom from it, Joe feels sharp delight.

Even so, he wants to return to the weeds and the abandoned trains and the rotting window frames and the jumpers that smell of wood smoke and the green life of the shoddy and the abandoned and the outcast. He wants to live on dandelion leaves and pine bark and roasted squirrel.

All this passes before Joe's serene mind as he turns, following the vaguest of whims, away from the shops and towards the outskirts of town. He approaches a bus stop, realising, with skuddering heart, that he recognises the woman waiting under the shelter. He recognises her beautiful face. It is Lilly.

He sits down next to her. The golden light of the afternoon sun glows like the honey of the gods over both of them. Lilly looks at Joe. For the first time in twenty years she looks at someone steadily in the eye. He looks back at her.

'You are the sun god, Ra,' she says.

Joe nods. Lilly nods.

A bus arrives, ugly and rumbling with bitter fumes. They get on, and both feel a little sick, but on the empty top deck there is air, and they can cuddle up together and glide through Edding watching the mayhem down there.

Everywhere are severed heads. In shops, on benches, in the middle of the road, bleeding heads on the checkout conveyor belt, grim heads on mantelpieces, heads, heads everywhere, and the horror of the damned, as people recoil from them, retching, moaning in fear and revulsion, not just at the dead faces of the once-were-living, but at the living faces of the once-were-dead.

'There are a lot of heads around today,' says Joe.

'Yes, I did that,' murmurs Lilly.

'*Did* you?' says Joe, gently impressed, 'nice antics.'

'It turns out,' says Lilly, 'that it doesn't take much at all to turn the world upside down.'

'And then the fall is funny and forever.'

'Just a few heads,' she says, 'just a prick of death.'

'All life must have a prick of death in it,' says Joe. 'Salt is a prick of death, the quirk in the most beautiful faces, the imperfection in a rhythm track.'

'You can't have too much death though,' says Lilly, 'or you'll die.'

'If a face is all quirk it's hideous.'

'Yes,' she says, 'A pinprick of quirk, a teaspoon.'

'Seriousness must have a touch of the silly, joy a touch of sadness, men must have a teaspoon of cold, sadistic bastard and women a teaspoon of hot, masochistic *slut*.'

'Just a teaspoon.'

'Half a teaspoon.'

Lilly snuggles further into his chest. Warmth flows from her, washing into him.

'I'm a teaspoon of slut,' she says.

'I've been wondering,' he says, 'do you think we'll ever evolve to slide everywhere instead of walk?'

'Is that why some people have feet with collapsed arches?'

'You mean is it an evolutionary sign?' asks Joe.

'Yes,' says Lilly, disengaging herself somewhat, 'although I'm not sure I see it as a positive thing. I never really understood why we never evolved pogo-legs, or goat-legs or something like that.'

'I did,' says Joe.

'Did you?'

'Yeah, just the one though,' he proudly pats his new leg.

'What are we going to do then, now you've got a new leg back? And your head?'

'I'd like to hatch a plan. You know—you do this, I'll do that, we'll meet at the appointed spot at midnight. That kind of thing.'

'People don't hatch plans now though; all they do is make arrangements.'

'Right. So let's hatch a plan.'
They get off the bus in front of St. Barbara's.

✿

Joe had always been closest to his dad. Neville had helped open in him a feeling of yearning for the sweet untouchable, a sacred longing that all great hearts have, and which ensured that Joe was never quite satisfied with anything less. When Neville died their connection was broken and Neil, unable to share in their headless world and envious of it, was exultant; but his delight was short-lived, for soon after Joe shot their mother in the head and the one person in the world Neil could count on—who had indeed trained him to count on her, who had worked on Neil in the opposite manner that Neville had on Joe, giving him a taste for nothing but worldly success—departed. She left Neil's world and joined Joe in his. She lost her grip on the real world and joined Joe in a spoon-and-seagull place were workmen were 'twenty-twos' and chairs had opinions on world affairs, and radios and televisions absorbed yang. Neil tried to explain to Margaret that it was Joe, '*he* left you in this state', but she looked at him as if he'd told a joke which didn't make sense.

In the end Neil lived by one creed; *it's so unfair.*

He was alone, completely alone in the world. What is one to do in such a situation? Neil did what Margaret, the old, cold, hard Margaret had taught him to do, he tried to control his life, to hold on to it, to acquire power in order to protect his self and to begin a fruitless quest for 'community'. He attached himself to a religion which, in the perverted form given to him, seemed to offer protection, it guaranteed justice and immortality and it sanctified his personal authority. He took a job which enabled him to force others to obey and respect him, in the service of a society which represented security, order, and the known.

Neil was dying inside, but he was never quite extinguished. He was cruel, controlling, needy, desperate and preposterously conceited, but there was still, somewhere, something else in him, a something else which Lilly had seen, by accident, and which had opened his heart—not much, just a crack, but enough for a Japanese angel of death to slip in, fuse with his innermost and blast the world yon.

He is now sitting on a gravestone. Joe and Lilly approach smiling. Neil is smiling too. For an instant he seems to want to control the smile, to not reveal his absurd delight at seeing them both, but then he lets go and bursts into laughter. Lilly is amazed to see something childlike in Neil's face, an innocent sweetness that suits him very much.

It suits all of us though doesn't it? thinks Lilly.

Neil is practically wriggling with joy and Joe suddenly remembers Neil's excitableness, long ago, before his body became all tight and narrow and folded in. He used to be stupid, thinks Joe, just as I used to be serious. We too got split.

Joe stands in front of his brother and slaps his hand down on Neil's forehead, hard. Neil puts his fingers in Joe's ears. They stay like this, laughing like idiots, for a while, then Joe and Lilly also sit down, on other graves.

'Where have you been?' asks Lilly.

'I was repeatedly sucked into and then out of the anus of God.'

'How was that?' asks Joe.

'It was alright actually. Hectic. I lost the culture section of the newspaper.' There is followed by a long, soft pause.

'I see you're sitting on Dad's grave,' says Joe.

'Oh yeah. He's not here though,' says Neil.

'No, I know; he's in the fields of Aaru.'

'Where's that?' asks Lilly.

'It's just off the A14, on the way to Chisfolk. Near Gorleigh.'

'Surely off the A36 then?' says Joe.

'Well you *can* go that way.'

'Gorleigh is next to Joen Downs. Why would you take the A14?'

'Well,' says Neil, 'it's much prettier for a start. Grafford Water is up along there.'

Joe holds up his palms, in surrender, 'Fair enough.'

Lilly laughs. 'How do you… both know this?'

The two brothers speak together; 'Maps.'

'No, I mean, how do you know your father is there?'

'Ursula told me, just before we met Jesus on Clive the hill,' says Joe, and turns to Neil, 'You?' he asks.

'I'm not sure. I think I found out while I being swallowed by an evil eyeless jellygod in the Apple store. Except… actually that turned out to be pretty good. All of it did.'

Lilly and Joe agree.

'We should probably go then?' says Lilly.

'We have to pick up Mum,' says Neil.

'Hold on, hold on,' says Joe. 'First, how about we all jump off our gravestones and the one who stays in the air the longest is the winner?'

'Okay!' cries Neil, laughing again like a kid, 'Three… Two… One… Go!'

Joe and Neil jump off. It's a tiny distance and they both land at the same time.

'Me!' says Joe.

'No, me, I won!' says Neil turning to Lilly, 'who won?'

Joe also looks to Lilly. She is hovering three inches off the ground. Nobody speaks. She hovers down.

Lilly won.

✿

Margaret has sunk far inside herself. Her face is hollow, scoured of its flesh and vitality. Her gaunt body looks like a wooden puppet, strings cut. She looks at Tom who is standing at her bedside, watching her through his habitual mask of professional concern, but she doesn't understand who he is, or why he is there.

There is door-muffled commotion, drama approaching. The door flies open and Joe, effulgent, in flower-enshrouded drag, Neil, arrayed in mad, death-crow finery, and Lilly, decked in her top-hatted, ball-gowned furriness, enter the room. The effect on Margaret is miraculous. Her face lights up, her mouth, which seemed to be already setting in a death grimace, moves expressively, looking for animated words, although no sound comes out.

Neil hesitates at the doorway for a moment. His mother is looking at him with transformed eye, soft and welcoming.

'Joe?' says Tom, face furrowed. He looks from Neil to Lilly and back again. The manageable known has been interrupted.

'Ah Tom,' says Joe, broadly, walking up to him and shaking him by the hand, 'How's Heather?'

'Err… She's well…' says Tom, automatically.

'Good, good. Now what seems to be the trouble?'

The reversal of roles shakes Tom. He is surrounded by fabulously made-up actors who've dropped their parts. They are not reading from the right script. The solution, under such circumstances, is to keep to your part. Tom has total confidence in his part, for he is it. 'Look, what's going on here?' he asks, tone deepening, careful not to betray self-consciousness or confusion.

Joe lays a consoling, doctorly hand on Tom's shoulder. 'I'm afraid here's no easy way to put this old love; you're dead. The body moves, the mind thinks, the mouth speaks, but there's nobody home. At this stage I think it's fair to say that, in your innermost, you're nothing but the image of a man. You've made it this far because the world has supported the illusion, but that's all over now. It's only a matter of time before your identity flops to the floor like a removed sock. I'd give it a few years, but you could go at any moment.'

Tom stiffens, nods an 'oh, yes, I see' and leaves the room.

The three visitors sit down around Margaret's bed. Joe to her left, Neil to her right and Lilly at the foot of the bed. Neil feels tears rising in him, just below the water mark, ready to flood.

'How are you Mum?' asks Joe.

'Everyone here is a policeman,' she says, wonderingly.

'Most people are policemen,' says Neil.

'Yes, but I've got a lovely view. Look.'

They look. There's a car park outside, and a few bushes.

'Often there are squirrels,' she says, 'and sometimes a tree will pass by.'

'We saw a few trees pass by on the way in,' says Neil.

'It's *so* nice to see you again Neil,' she says and squeezes his hand. Neil tries to speak, but can only emit a stifled 'eck.'

Margaret turns to Lilly, 'And who are you?'

'Lilly. Hello.'

'Aren't you *wonderful!*' she sighs.

'Thank you.'

'I'm dying you know,' says Margaret. Her voice is small, and pushed. There is a crafty gleam in her eye, but she looks sunken, doomed in the skin.

'I can see.'

'But, you look so well,' says Neil.

'That's because I don't *mind* going,' she says, then takes a piece of potato skin from the plastic plate on her side table. She gingerly places it on her left knee. Joe tries to remove it with a piece of tissue.

'Oh no,' says Margaret, 'don't move that. They will want it.'

'Who will?'

'*They* will.'

'Oh, okay,' says Joe, hesitating over the potato fragment, 'are you sure, because… I don't think anybody will want it.'

'Oh they will. They'll be glad to have it. Unless, of course, either of you want it?' She looks from left to right, to Joe and then to Neil.

'No, no, I don't want it,' says Joe, 'What about you, Neil?'

'No, I'm fine,' says Neil.

'He's eaten,' Joe explains.

'Well, but are you sure? Because if not, they will have it,' says Margaret.

All four are still looking at the shred of potato. 'Are you sure they will want it Mum?' asks Neil.

'Oh yes, they'll be glad to have it.'

'Have they had it before then?' Lilly asks.

'Oh yes, they often do. Unless…' She breaths with effort, 'Of course… unless you want it? Any of you would be very welcome.'

'No,' says Joe decisively, 'I think we'd better leave it for them. It sounds more like their sort of thing.'

'Oh well, it is. They'd be glad to have it. We'll just leave it there. Oh…' she gasps, eyes tensing sorrowfully.

'What?' says Neil, 'what's wrong?'

'I've messed myself.'

Neil panics. 'Do you want me to call a nurse?' he asks, rising.

'No,' says Margaret, then looks sharply at Neil, 'I would like you to do it. my son'

'Me? Why?'

'I just do.'

'I can do it Mrs. Geb,' says Lilly.

'No, I want Neil to.'

'Okay Mum,' he says, 'Where's… What do I do?'

Margaret speaks with effort. 'Get a yellow bag, they're over there, a bowl… warm water and soap, disposable wipes, there, and a pair of my special knickers… in the locker.'

Neil follows her instructions.

'Shall I help?' asks Lilly.

'Thank you, yes,' says Margaret, 'but I want Neil to do the difficult bits.'

Neil uncovers Margaret. Her body is wasted.

'Take the pants off,' she says, 'carefully, don't get poo on my legs dear.'

With Lilly's help Neil removes his mother's incontinence pants, washes her, dries her and puts on a new pair. He then pulls the bedsheets off. As he is doing so, and as Lilly starts dressing Margaret—who says she wants to look respectable now—Louis climbs through the window.

'Louis!' says Margaret, 'I'm completely clean.'

'Are you ready to go?' he asks.

'Yes, I think so. I don't have long left.'

'Neville…' says Louis, 'He's waiting for you…' he turns smilingly to Neil, Joe and Lilly, 'He's waiting for all of you…'

'Ah… Ah!' Margaret suddenly utters a strangled back-of-the-throat cry, falling backwards. Louis, Joe and Neil rush forward, crying out. She grabs Neil by the neck. 'Neil…' she whispers, 'I mutilated you, I did it, not you, I did it. I didn't know any better. I made you that man… it was fear…'

'It's alright Mum. I've sorted it,' says Neil, smiling, eyes glistening, '…it's all sorted now.'

Lilly watches, sobbing as if for her own mother. She has never seen someone die. She has seen so much death, but never dying, the flesh, the flesh, but never the spirit. How dreadful it is, that everything is falling away. Margaret hugs her two sons. Lilly sobs. The sordid worries, and voracious fears, and endless scrabbling around for something to hold on to, which take up the whole world, are really a thin layer of frost, melting between them. That's how it is when the sun comes out.

Neil is crying, his self is. The pain is unbearable. It's not the pain of a self out there dying, but the agony of my own self, being torn away from the world, into what? What? It's not my self. It's something else. And it's my mother, the very flesh I am; my self, and her self, the same thing, and now she's going, for good. And in the pain, there is nowhere to go.

Tom rushes in. 'What's going on here?' he demands, all authority and purpose.

Margaret croaks, strangled. She is breathing strangely.

'She's dying,' says Neil quietly, not turning.

'Not if I've got anything to do with it!' says Tom majestically. 'Nurse!' he shouts, 'Nurse!'

Margaret grabs Tom's sleeve, 'No,' she says, quietly but clearly, 'Leave me alone. Let me go.'

'Don't be ridiculous Mrs. Geb.'

He pulls out a syringe. Joe turns to hold him back. A nurse appears at the doorway. There is quiet but intensely strained commotion—Tom is trying to restrain Margaret, the nurse is trying to get to Tom, Joe and Neil are trying to pull them both away—but then something unexpected happens.

Margaret throws herself forward and embraces Tom, her bony arms around his neck.

'Thank you!' she cries, 'Dear, *dear* man.'

She holds him, and there is stillness. Tom drops the needle.

'I don't… I…' Tom says, disengaging himself. He looks around at the people in the room, confused. The nurse steps forward to help him, to collect the dropped syringe, but Tom grabs her by the arm and leads her out.

Margaret collapses back into the bed. Neil feels the agony. He reaches forward, and brushes one of her grey hairs from her damp face. She opens her eyes. Her body is like a flake of ash, but her eyes, heavy and resourceful, although they are sinking, even sunk, they are still blue with life. It is too much for Neil, he can't speak, just sobbing. 'I love you mumsie,' he whispers.

Her eyes are shining. To Lilly she looks beautiful, as if the sun is coming out, which it is. Middle age is the springtime of life, old age is the summer and death the great sunrise, but for Neil there is only pain, until something unexpected happens.

The room is full of people. All standing round the bottom of the bed. Neil, overwhelmed, exhausted, looks up, from Margaret, to the people, then back to Margaret.

'Who are this lot?' he asks quietly. He has seen some of them before he thinks, at Ursula's funeral.

'That's your grandfather. That's Dorothy. That's William. That's Auntie Brenda. That's David, ah, David… ah…' The whole family were there, the people she grew up with, old friends… Ursula pushes her way through. She picks up the bit of potato which has been removed to the side table. She nibbles a piece then passes it to the next person. All solemnly take a tiny bite.

'Ursula!' whispers Margaret, recognising her now.

'Hello Mumsy.'

'Oh, oh… Oh dear…' Margaret is crying now, although with no real force of emotion, tears are trickling down her cheeks,

bus that you're not going…'

'Hold on,' says Neil, 'Let me make a note of this.'

He gets out a notebook and pencil, which he sharpens (in a lovely German Bakelite sharpener), then nods to Joe. He writes as Joe speaks.

'…Yeah, I think you should run for a bus that you're obviously not going to catch, perhaps a few.'

'Good, go on.'

'And, uh, go out in the cold rain without a jacket. And step in dog shit. And reverse a tractor and trailer round London. And, erm, get a perm.'

'God if only I'd known that relieving guilt would be so easy I'd've confessed long ago.'

'Confessed what?'

'To being… a bollock.'

'There is,' says Joe, 'a little bit of bollock in everything.'

'It's funny,' says Neil, half to himself, 'before I made love to the angel of death everything was a little bit of bollock. Everything annoyed me.'

'What were you annoyed by?' asks Joe.

'Hard-to-open containers, fragile shoelaces, unaware pedestrians drifting in front of me, all signs outside churches, saxophones, people chatting with cashiers when there's a long queue behind them, overly plucked eyebrows, 'one of the only', everything made in China, comedians shouting, people in call centres telling you they're sorry, builders not making good, southerners pronouncing 'Newcastle' like a Geordie, socks that wear out in a month, pistachio nuts that haven't opened…'

'…abandoned vegetables in the vegetable drawer…' Lilly chips in, nodding and smiling.

'Yeah, that, erm, littering on the beach, poorly tested operating system updates, app bloat, anything you can't fix yourself…'

'…cheese not properly cared for…' says Lilly, 'wrapped in clingfilm and chilled to death. That used to annoy the hell out of you.'

'…interviews with sportsmen, you hated those…' says Joe.

Lilly has a run; '…people using your towel, chocolate not wrapped up properly in the fridge so that little flaky bits get everywhere and you have to clean it all, leaving tissues in your pocket when you do the washing…'

'It's not that those things aren't annoying,' says Neil as they reach a pause, 'just that they were everything. There was nothing else. I wanted… some way out… a… a… point…'

'There's no point to a song,' says Lilly.

Neil looks over the land, the whole of it, stretched under the vastness of the blue, blue sky. The caustic scab of Edding town behind them, sterile farm rectangles beneath and Chitham Forest ahead. He grips the padded gunwale of the basket, his eyes are moist with feeling. No point to a song, he thinks, and no end to it either. The song is already whole, and known as such; it has to be, or each note would be meaningless, hanging in mid-air, afraid of being lost, and forgotten.

They float, lost and forgotten, over the woodlands. In the centre, like an acorn on the forest floor, is a house. The balloon sails over the river Hale then gently lands on a long, wild garden. The family climb out of the basket onto a damp speckled meadow of saxifrage, aster, red rattle and burnett. Neville, dressed in his work clothes—checked shirt and leather tool apron—is there to greet them.

✿

The family are having a picnic in the woods, a spinney at the bottom of the garden which gives on to the old forest of Berroc. As they talk, Ian and Louis come to and fro, clearing up plates; they've all just eaten a full English and are now enjoying tea. Ian makes an excellent cuppa. Margaret, sitting on a deckchair, is knitting, Lilly is reverently nibbling the most walnutty walnuts and Joe and Neil, cross-legged on a tartan rug, are talking with Neville who, languid, bearded and well wrinkled, reclines against a huge ash tree, like Nebuchadnezzar.

'We overcame a few forces of evil,' says Joe, 'on the way here.'

'It's one thing for an ordinary man to dream of unspeakable orgies, it's quite another for a group of people to actually be indulging in reality-rupturing rituals on the outskirts of Edding. We must be destroyed, of course we must. And all those who nurse paradise in their hearts—they must be destroyed also.'

'What are we going to do?' says Neil.

'About what? The forces of evil?'

'Yeah.'

'We're going to have a ball,' says Neville, 'ah, which reminds me, I've got some presents for you. Ian, could you?'

'So do I!' cries Neil and scuttles away, back to the house.

Ian returns loaded down with wrapped-up gifts of various sizes and hands them out. He is followed by Neil, who is carrying the two jumpers he has been knitting. The red one—which he gives to Joe—has, on the front, a smiling banana. His own, dark blue and silver, has an owl wearing a miner's helmet. They pull them on. Ian picks up a banjo in the corner of the room and sits down noodling Simon and Garfunkel numbers. Squirrels and mice, attracted to his smell, hop around his legs.

'Nice wrapping paper you've got,' says Lilly as she inspects her gift from Neville, which looks like it might be a dress or a light coat.

'Thanks,' says Neville.

'Neil used to have a thing about wrapping paper,' says Joe.

'Yeah,' Neil nods, 'I used to find everything gay.'

Lilly laughs. 'Did you?'

'I did. I couldn't buy presents around Christmas time. I found it too gay. I used to think the people in the shop would know there are people in my life I care about.'

'Wrapping presents he had to do with a beer,' says Joe.

'You had some good solutions,' says Lilly.

'I used to have to ask myself,' says Neil, 'before I did anything; would Prince Phillip do it? Or Clint Eastwood. A weird one was sticking out my hand to stop a bus. I just couldn't.'

'I remember when we were very poor once,' says Neville, 'I bought a present for the whole family. It was a one ninety-nine vase from Woolworths. Seven of us there were, my parents, four brothers and sisters, all your uncles and aunts. A vase. Have that.'

'I remember that vase,' laughs Neil.

'Clint would never run across the road if he thought he was going to be hit by a car,' says Margaret.

'If anything,' says Lilly, 'the car would slow down for Clint.'

'Would Clint wrap presents?' asks Louis.

'No,' says Lilly, 'what would he do with it though? Just scrunch it up in a bag?'

'Give it in a bag,' says Neil. 'He'd present it in a gentlemanly way, but he wouldn't wrap it up.'

'You're okay with wrapping now then son?' Neville asks Neil in a kindly way, hand on his shoulder.

'Oh God yes.'

'I imagine you're quite good at it,' says Lilly.

'Yes, I am. Unless it's a ball of course. I don't know who's good at wrapping a ball. Clint Eastwood probably.'

Neville laughs. 'The fact you've even classified that shows...'

'...more than a passing interest in wrapping,' says Joe, 'You're no Clint.'

'One thing that I've learnt recently,' says Neil, 'is that I'm no Clint.'

'You're more man than Clint,' says Margaret.

'Shall we open these then?' asks Lilly.

'Shouldn't we wait for Chiyo?' asks Neville.

'Oh God yes, I forgot. Look at me, I'm just so excited by presents,' says Lilly, turning to Neil, 'When will she be here?'

'She's here now.'

The group slip into a full silence.

Joe touches stinging nettle. Its raw, rising flush burns his fingers. And he is the stung and the nettle stinging. He looks at the sun, and he is that too, as much as he is his own hands and arms. I am that, the filthy pigeon with the broken wing, the shit stink of the National Express toilet, the shouting, lurid graffiti on the old brick bridge across the Hale, and now this, this cool, damp forest, and this furzy stained fiddlehead, and this creeping yellow pimpernel, and this death-white exterminating angel, and this pippity long-tailed tit, and these flapping catkins feathering the meadow; I am all of that, all the way down, and I am the whole of me, and there is nothing like me in this whole rotten universe. He stretches his arms out in front of him, thick fingers wide. The fullness and intensity of his own physicality amazes him. How real it all is, how sensate, and strong in the marrow. If only I had acted on it on it a little earlier, masked up and acted on it.

From the forest at Joe's back, flows the evening, carrying clouds of gentlest pink and orange and gold. The mournful sound of crickets fades with the day, and with the summer. The edging light begins to grow dark. It didn't last very long, in the end, which is why it was all so lovely.

✿

Neville's spacious, sprung-floor ballroom, candle-licked, shadow-thrown, is full of people, all wearing beautiful, primal animal heads. They stand before the stage, before the band; Victor (jackal head; tuba), Lilly (cow head; bass guitar), laughing Ralf (donkey head; French horn), Neil (falcon head; lead guitar), Joe (baboon head; vocals and rhythm guitar), Margaret (eagle head; piano and synths), Neville (beetle head; trumpet), Clive (frog head; violin), Chiyo (snake head; theremin, koto and Jew's harp), Meera (cat head; viola) and Ursula (sow head; backing vocals).

They play a Balkan waltz, a golden reverie, the sound of the universe itself turning and welcoming.

Everyone in the ballroom, all with animal heads, dances a slow, slow, dreamlike waltz. The sun is setting outside. Gold-orange light flows into the long room, lengthening the bobbing, sailing, waltzing shadows.

As the waltz plays, Carl pirouettes with his daughter in the living room while his wife prepares dinner.

As the waltz plays, Dominic Raab, former Deputy Prime Minister, is running away from Malcolm. The politician is stumbling over the bracken and heather of a country path. Malcolm, carrying a crossbow, shoots Dominic in the back.

As the waltz plays, Vicar Tim and Sophie are having sex. Tim is wearing his vicar's outfit and Sophie is dressed as Moses, with a big false beard and staff.

As the waltz plays, Irving is on a narrow boat in the Norfolk broads, chugging out into an estuary, and then into the sea.

As the waltz plays, Tall Paul morris dances in the town centre.

As the waltz plays, Maria writes a business plan for a mindful basketry company.

As the waltz plays, Prince Chukwu and Bronya paint each other's naked bodies with tribal dot paintings.

As the waltz plays, Zoltan, Denitsa, Mercy, Nada and Jianjun play Twister in the New forest.

As the waltz plays, Dave Davage, slumped against the Nisbets catering equipment centre, dies of a cardiac arrest.

As the waltz plays, a Sri Lankan taxi driver, teeth flashing, eyes wide and wild—but yet joyous too—and wielding a large knife, is running into a crowd of police, who shrink back.

As the waltz plays, Nina phones Marks and Spencer to complain about their tomato salsa which advertised itself as 'tangy' but which was anything but—it was ridiculous really, all they had to do was add half a lime, which is what she ended up doing.

As the waltz plays, Janice, eyes burning with joy, wildly plays the bum drums on Laughing Ralf's large, naked buttocks.

As the waltz plays, bald chickens pick their way through an empty job centre.

As the waltz plays, the world collapses. The loam has dried up, leaving dust and sand, which the wind blows away. The penal playground which men and women have made of the world, that too is blown away, as are the minds deformed to live within it.

As the waltz plays, Joe's body, lying in St. Barbara's church, dies of exhaustion, Clive's body dies of asphyxiation, Neville's head is shot from his shoulders, Ursula's body dies of internal bleeding, Lilly's poisoned body keels over in Dominus, Louis' body is shot to death by the police, Margaret's body dies of heart failure, Victor's body dies of mushroom poisoning, Meera's body burns to death on a sati funeral pyre, Neil and Chiyo's bodies die of heart-rupturing ecstasy.

As the waltz plays, all the severed heads, around Edding, around England, around the world, are laughing.

The waltz plays, but there is nobody to hear it. There is no band and nobody to describe it, or to read the description.

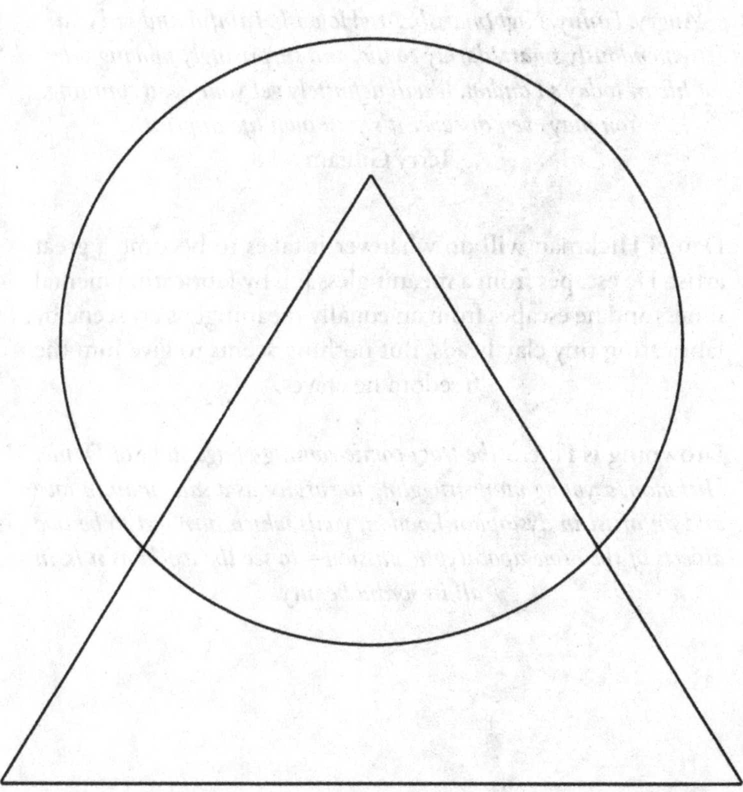

Drowning is Fine

An outsider novel

'Angry. Funny. Nightmarish. ArseHole-ish. Painful and sad …a tremendously smart, darkly comic, and surprisingly moving tale of life in today's London. It will definitely get your head spinning. You may even discover it's your own life in print…'
Terry Gilliam

Daniel Hickman will do whatever it takes to become a great artist. He escapes from a meaningless job by fabricating mental illness and he escapes from an equally meaningless art scene by fabricating tiny clay heads. But nothing seems to give him the freedom he craves.

Drowning is Fine *is the tragi-comic coming-of-age story of Daniel Hickman, a young man struggling to survive as a sane man in love and an artist in dystopian London; goals which turn out to be two aspects of the same apocalyptic mission—to see the world as it is, in all its sordid beauty.*

Self & Unself

A Radical Guide to the World

I loved it, the tone, the content, the lot.
Bernado Kastrup

Genuine philosophy… exhilarating.
John Michael Greer

Self and Unself is an original, wide-ranging and accessible philosophy of all and everything, presenting a synthesis of metaphysics, science, art, psychology, sex, gender, character, culture and history. Neither optimistic nor pessimistic, objective nor subjective, theist nor atheist, it expresses the unfathomable paradox at the root of all branches of human experience, providing a new, radical ground of understanding, and solving, en route, all the actually important questions of philosophy;

Why do people never suffer for the reasons they think they do?

Why are philosophers and scientists baffled by reality?

Why do the realest times of our lives feel unreal?

Why doesn't the anxious mind get the joke?

Why do people cling to absurd beliefs?

Why am I still discontent?

Why am I still here?

Who am I?

Who are you?

What on earth is going on?

33 Myths of the System

A Radical Guide to the World

So provocative… I loved it… hit with originality and force.
John Zerzan

A powerful book. A great title… fantastic stuff.
Russell Brand (before he lost his wits)

Pure genius… Full of insights and mind-blowing thought-puzzles.
David Edwards, Media Lens

As civilisation reaches endgame and begins to disintegrate, as the illusions of left and right coalesce into a single, spectacular omnimyth, as every rootless mind begins to directly experience the stupefying dystopias of Orwell, Huxley, Kafka and Dick, the time has come to understand the whole system, from root to fruit.

Drawing on the entire history of radical thought, while seeking to plumb their common depths, *33 Myths of the System* presents a synthesis of independent criticism, a straightforward exposure of the justifications of the world system, along with a new way to perceive and understand the unhappy supermind that directs, penetrates and even lives our lives.